I0760330

COLORS OF ENVY

A Paranormal Romance Mystery

J. K. Grueber

Mystic Ridge Publishing, LLC

Mystic Ridge Publishing, LLC

Mysticridgepublishing.com

ISBN: 978-1-965796-05-4 (Hardback)

ISBN: 979-8-9878673-1-0 (Paperback)

ISBN: 979-8-9878673-0-3 (Ebook)

Cover design by: Anne Graff, Andrew Grueber, and William Grueber.

Contributing cover photo editor: Sanderson-Decello Design, LLC

Printed in the United States of America.

Previously published as COLOR OF ENVY: A Paranormal Mystery by J. K. Grueber.

ALSO BY J. K. GRUEBER

The Envy Series:

COLORS OF ENVY: A Paranormal Romance Mystery
FACES OF ENVY: A Paranormal Romance Mystery
ECHOES OF ENVY: A Paranormal Romance Mystery

The MacDade Brothers Mysteries:

EXPOSED IN THE SHADOWS: He Who Plays.
A Paranormal Mystery Rekindling Lost Love
The MacDade Brother's Mysteries (Book One)

EXPOSED IN THE CROSSHAIRS: He Who Rides
The MacDade Brothers Mysteries (Book Two)

EXPOSED BY THE RIVERSIDE: He Who Lives
The MacDade Brothers Mysteries (Book Three)

The Vampire Tales:

CURSED AT CONCEPTION:
The Vampire's Henchman

DEDICATION

To Marie and Charles Graff who overcame their many trials and inspired me to forge ahead, and to my many family members who never stopped believing.

Thank you!

PROLOGUE

'The game . . . Papa wants to play the game,' the words floated, ethereal. At the edges of his mind, a soft gentle rhythm began. He heard the humming and recognized the notes of a lullaby, recalled the song though he'd never heard it sung, not to him. Mom`ma had never sung to him, never promised him a 'mockingbird' or a 'diamond ring' . . . but that was the song. The melody sent a shiver through him. No lyrics, not yet, but he would hear the soft fluting sounds, the words, and on another plane, he moaned in protest. He wanted not to hear this song, wanted not to be in this place . . . but he was here, now. A spectator.

A noxious blend of smells assaulted his nostrils, waking him more to the world around him. Bitter tangy odors of cow manure mixed with sweeter tastes of hay and wheat, corn, and molasses . . . he wanted out of here! Wanted not to hear that soft sound that worried rather than soothed! To the whispery tune, his mind riveted, locking onto the notes, ignoring the cows munching and grinding cud, the iron stanchions clattering and clinking as thick necks shifted in iron nooses. He could see them now, immense worrisome beasts with bloated udders, brown and white patches of smooth short hair, huge brown eyes following him with warm dull wit. Gnats, swarms of the wretched little bugs, touched around his ankles and legs, landing on his bare flesh, making his skin crawl, and troubling him as badly as the soft lyrics spilling off his lips.

"Nnnooo," he moaned but the sound filtered away, flowing into a tunnel where all sound became distant. Far more clearly, the soft rolling syllables and gentle rhythm flowed. In a paradox, dread and black rage built inside of him. He wanted not to be here! Wanted away from here! Wanted not to smell these familiar-unfamiliar scents or to hear these soft sounds issuing more threat than comfort off his lips. Heartbeat quickening, his muscles jolted at the grunt of a sow, a soft squeal, but the song continued, soothing and threatening in its persistence. Around him, sights and sounds firmed, from the muted silver moonlight penetrating a filthy windowpane to the rutting of pigs and clatter of iron harnesses, but other images began a slow assault on his troubled mind. In a paradox, his tension and anger ascended on equal planes.

Dirty . . . he felt dirty . . . and small . . . and a rancid scent of human sweat crept beneath the sweet odors of hay and molasses. Child's sweat and fear . . . fear carried a scent.

At the sight of a hulking figure moving deliberately through the shadows, the watcher's muscles gripped. Himself and not himself, he caught a glint of light reflecting from the intruder's hand, something in his hand. The shadowed image glanced toward that shiny object and with a flick of the stout wrist, the pocket-watch face glowed. Hatred and fear battled inside of him. His muscles coiling, tensing, he distracted to an unnatural shift of cloth or a footfall and peered through shadows, searching. Not alone, here. A witness, a spectator, and for a few silent ticks, hesitation.

'. . . *A game . . . a game . . . papa wants to play the game,*' the odd words twittered in his mind. A near giggle slipped off his lips, worrying and frightening him. Paradox.

He wanted out of here! Away from this place! Wanted out of these smells and sounds, away from this voice, humming and uttering soft soothing sounds despite the growing frenzy inside. He wanted out of here!

"Goddamn it, quit your singing and come help me milk these damn cows," a deep angry voice called from a distance away.

Silence, then. Heartbeat hammering, attention riveted through the gaping cracks of weathered wood, eyes glowing feral from the darkness. *The games . . . want to play, Papa? Play the game* . . . and he could hear children's voices, anxious and worried . . . but other images tangled inside his mind. Human figures mixed and muddled in walls of stone and forest scents. A cadence not as soft as children's voices, low and lyrical in a steady rhythm, silver moonlight spilling and glowing on naked human forms. Like piles of maggots, they writhed and heaved. A game . . . the games. Red hot rage rose within him, his six senses coiling and uncoiling as if flexing a muscle, clenching and unclenching a fist . . .

No! He wanted out of here! Away from here! This was the wicked place! The place he'd been before, although no clear memory surfaced . . . and the soft humming notes of yet another lullaby slipped off his lips. His senses swam with a weird delight, images of children's faces going around and around on a carousel, and one of those faces lingered nearby . . . one cast in shadows, worried and waiting, watching.

"Git your ass out here and help with the chores!" the low angry voice demanded.

Familiar, so familiar that deep voice. On a dual plane, he lurched in fear, separate and apart from the fury holding him within the shadows. Soft and soothing, troubling, the whispery notes hissed off his lips, the melody lost within the wide shadowed walls of the barn . . . always a barn . . . *play the game*. His hand gripped around a stout, age-worn spindle, its shape reflective of the top of an hourglass. An hourglass. Time. Almost time. Sand through an hourglass. A gnarled smile crept over his lips. Cold and clammy, his hand gripped the crossbar handle. His focus slid down the shaft to the four flat prongs jabbing the filthy cement. Hazy white, his bare feet poised to propel him from the shadows.

Metal clinked; the suction of nozzles squelched, affixed to one teat after the other, deflating the udders one after another . . . and the melody continued off his lips, paused only as the hulking image passed through the dim light with immense milk canisters swinging from his calloused hands.

Grumbling, the farmer emerged from the final stall, cursing, and mumbling as if to override the soft fluting melody of yet another song. Lugging the last two canisters, his dirty coveralls sagging off drooping shoulders, he ambled through the dull light, the glow muted by fly droppings that coated the single bulbs to dangle in a neat row from wide cobweb-covered beams overhead. Lulled and relieved of their burden, content, the cows munched and clattered their iron stanchions, tails swishing to swat away the gnats swarming from the trench at their hind legs.

Skin crawling, insides trembling, the watcher listened to the clatter inside the milk house in its separate barn and imagined those silver cuffs dangling from cords from the heavy canisters . . . and the twisted memories of those suction cups slid the melody louder off his lips. The sound haunted the very edges of the barn and stirred even the hounds outside in their pens.

Silence . . . as the farmer appeared, the melody silenced and every nerve in the watcher's body keened. His senses rising in anticipation and fear, he watched the image amble past the dark crevice where he remained poised. He wanted not to be here! Wanted to be away from here! Night-chill tingled his bare flesh. The silver glow of s full moon tugged him toward the far door, but his body remained poised, frozen in place. With the lullaby ended, a distant cadence of voices touched him, stroked him, called to him in the moonlight. He'd heard those sounds before, too, recognized the incantations.

"I don't like the damned game you're playing, gal," the man growled as he ambled down the aisle toward the small door, the moonlight. More to himself, he grumbled, "Still playing damned kids' games. Ain't no wonder you can't land no husband . . . damn fool—"

Sprung from a catapult, the naked body lunged from the shadows as if propelled, the four wicked prongs cutting a deadly path. With the speed and precision of an arrow shot from a bow, the silvery prongs sliced through the dim light, advancing on the hulking figure with a mere whisper of sound. In a raging thrust, the prongs sank through the worn denim cloth at the base of the stiffening spine. A short, gasped cry . . .

With the started grunt, gasp, the watcher's mad, maddening cry suffused into a raging tunnel of splashing crimson visions . . . and the black wings flew up in front of him. Dull blue eyes and ashen face, a spider web of red veins, a gaping black circle in a smooth alabaster forehead . . . *'Maaammmma!'*

And another song began as the naked body danced around the sprawled, mewling hulk. "... Ring around the rosy ... pocket full of posies ... ashes, ashes, we all fall down...."

CHAPTER 1

Farmland stretched in every direction, one hill rolling into another in variegated shades of gold and green, a vision of the sublime to counter the looming darkness in Ronnie Bryson's mind. With iron resolve, she refrained from pulling her rental to the shoulder of the interstate though she might justify that delay. A few panoramic shots could serve as ambiance when submitting an article to any one of a half dozen magazines, providing her intuition paid off.

As if to taunt her, a tractor crept from a wooded grove onto a field, almost close enough to read the logo on a red baseball cap gleaming under the morning light. On first impression, the possibility of murder in this neck of the woods seemed as far afield as the golden ball of fire plunging headlong from its pale blue perch.

Unlikely as hell, but a tingle at the nape of her neck lent creed to her course. Too clearly, she recalled awakening to Pete Saunders' hesitant voice proclaiming, 'There's been another one.' By the time he mentioned Bentwood, PA, and another 'farming accident,' Ronnie had been wide-awake. If someone had died, it was the second fatal farming accident in a single month in the same no-name town that piqued her interest a month earlier. By no blasted coincidence, she'd asked Saunders to contact her if he heard Bentwood mentioned again, and judging by his hesitation, he wasn't pleased to abandon his doubts or accept her uncanny nose for news.

Cresting a hill and anticipating the off-ramp, Ronnie braked and drew breath as she swerved onto the sloping exit lane. Like green arms stretched to embrace and cradle the small metropolis, glossy emerald hills and thick forests hugged every edge of scattered rooftops, stone walls, silos, and steeples, and judging by the surrounding hills, acclimating in Bentwood could kill about an hour. Still, the town or City of Bentwood appeared larger than she'd expected. Not a tiny little farming village by any stretch.

Automatically reaching for a handheld recorder on the seat beside her, Ronnie stabbed the record button while starting, "Arriving in Bentwood . . ." She tipped her wrist, fleeting a glance of an upcoming stop sign while continuing,

"It's 7:33 a.m. Saturday. First impressions . . . the town's nestled in a basin of rolling hills where heifers roam, and deer undoubtedly frolic."

A smile flickering on her full lips, Ronnie continued, "And since I'm feeling *trite,* I'll add *quaint* to my list of faux pas this morning and mention an abundance of church steeples scattered among slate roofs and a few three-story structures which I'm sure these folks consider high rises."

Decidedly, she wouldn't apologize aloud for journalistic stagnancy after only three hours of sleep; one of those strapped to an airplane seat while a deranged pilot hit cruise control and formed a halo around the landing strip. If she ever tired of chasing homicidal maniacs, she might investigate the sadistic streak of airline officials who scheduled thirty or forty flights at the same time. Twice in just over a month, she'd arrived on a flight that the attendants had the brass cojones to consider 'on time,' only to suffer vertigo as the plane sailed around and around, just out of reach of the landing strip.

"Big surprise," Ronnie commented into the recorder as she braked. "No major hotel chain in sight, but have faith, I see an immense greenhouse. Note to self: stop and find a new plant for my windowsill. The last one lasted a record-breaking six weeks."

Hitting the off button, she rolled to the end of the ramp. Directly ahead, a surprisingly modern road sign boasted, 'Bentwood to the left, 1 mile; Hazelwood to the right, 4 miles.' Muttered aloud, the words sounded like a knee-slapping, foot-stomping song lyric. A wry smile started and stopped on her lips. If she intended to unravel the mystery behind her intuition, she needed to restrain her city mentality for the next few days. Doubtful the locals would appreciate her sense of humor if any of those witticisms slipped off her tongue.

Without a single car in sight, she pulled onto the deserted two-lane. Perhaps, the town had packed a few wagons and headed west. Even for a Saturday morning, the streets seemed unnaturally deserted.

"Okay, where is everybody?" she muttered aloud before spotting the first in a series of two-story houses recessed behind neat shrubs and trees. Almost suddenly, the highway widened on a slight grade.

On-street parking accommodated the houses that compared nicely to the Victorian styles in older sections of DC. Wrap-around porches with spindle rails and stout pillars rose above manicured hedges. Ornate headers on windows and high-pitched eaves towered above flower islands already bursting with early summer blooms. All in all, the stately elegance defied the farming community atmosphere and sorely grated Ronnie's nerves.

Someday, she vowed to buy a book on gardening and learn whatever secrets 99% of the population seemed to know about sustaining plant life. Killing the cactus that her brother, Bobby, had brought her from Vegas certainly hadn't fared well on her ego, and his comment about her 'brown thumb' still stung despite his musing tone.

Who would've guessed that even desert *flowers needed to be watered more than once a year?*

Distracted by the speckling sunlight on her sunglasses, she shoved the shades headband-style into her thick black curls and muttered a curse as tangled locks cascaded over her brow. Her hair was another travesty for which she lacked patience. Shoving the waves aside, she glimpsed a car turning toward her a short distance ahead and spotted the red light through overhanging branches in time to stop.

Judging by the sight of parking meters and storefronts to her left, she'd arrived on Maine St. at the edge of town. To the right, the lane wove beneath thick sugar maples and oaks, and Ronnie glimpsed at the modern bridge transitioning into a four-lane highway. The main artery to somewhere. This town had probably thrived before the addition of an interstate sent visitors winking by at fifty-five.

By habit, Ronnie touched the record button as she turned onto Maine, reading the street sign, not surprised. "Definitely, Maine St., Bentwood, PA," she spoke aloud and continued a running dialogue for the recorder. "Trapped in time, Bentwood's preserved its country charm. Specialty shops and canvas-topped awnings line both sides of the street. Original cast-iron lampposts—undoubtedly, converted from gas at the turn of the century—stand evenly spaced along the sidewalks. Black stone, red brick, and several ancient trees provide a picture-perfect ambiance for an afternoon stroll. Not the kind of place one might expect—" She refrained from mentioning 'murder.' Too soon for that. "—frequent fatal accidents."

Silently, Ronnie counted two gas stations, a modern minimarket that seemed sorely out of place, two diners, four red lights, and a town square with a bronze war memorial. "Civil War if the horse and uniform are any indications." A white gazebo stood in its center, catching her eye as she drove slowly past, recording the sights. "Perhaps, the town still thrives. We have a hardware store, several boutiques, and two pizza parlors thus far . . . One barbershop and three hair salons, two of which stand side-by-side and probably make for interesting gossip as well as competition. A shoe repair shop, a . . . of all things, a haberdashery and none other than a Leather and Tack Shop. Cool . . . At least two bookstores, a bakery, and two antique and collectible shops compete admirably for fine taste.

"Ah, the piece d' resistance . . . The Bentwood House Inn. No doubt my home for the next few days. It appears to bear a turn-of-the-century motif and right next door . . . no way!"

Ronnie tapped her brakes for a closer look. "An honest-to-God theater with a V-shaped marquee and glass ticket booth within the indented — outdoor — entrance."

If not for the slight increase in traffic, the sight of two police cars, and one unmarked sedan bearing government plates, she might have reached for her recorder if only to verify she hadn't slid fifty or sixty years into the past. "Mm-hm. What have we here? Three official cars parked in front of a firehouse complete with three tremendous red doors . . ."

After a brief tour of side streets, Ronnie reversed course and perused Maine once again. "Traffic's increased, but I wouldn't consider this rush hour. We have a few people meandering on the sidewalks outside of shops and storefronts . . . Uh huh, we're back at the firehouse. A collection of pedestrians suggests a bit of excitement."

Her thoughts halted as she pivoted her head in a doubletake. The words slipped off her lips in a huffed breath.

"Mark Jarvins!"

Stifling an impulse to slam her brakes, Ronnie sped the length of the block, donning her sunglasses at the red light. Three years . . . she hadn't seen Mark Jarvins in at least three years, but she'd know his long, lean physique in any crowd. On him, the standard dark jacket, slacks, white shirt, and tie always seemed more like a fashion statement than a stereotypical Federal Agent. With his blond hair, worn slightly longer than his associates, and his flashy blue eyes, he carried himself with a certain panache that had nearly driven her to the ultimate blunder.

Aware of the light changing, her pulse racing and her hands damp upon the steering wheel, Ronnie turned the corner and pulled to the curb alongside a line of checkered curtains.

Jarvins. Just the name created a flood of tumultuous memories, none of which revolved around the maniac who had begun stalking her on the streets of Chicago. Mark had been one of the funniest, most sincere snakes she'd ever had the brief pleasure of dating.

And his presence verified that her sixth sense had hit paydirt.

Not a wild-goose-chase as her editor, Tom Fielding, had professed when she'd mentioned her interest only four hours earlier. Something was amiss in Bentwood, PA. A farmer dying in a pitchfork accident didn't warrant the attention of the FBI, but here was special agent Mark Jarvins, a member of the Federal Bureau's violent crime taskforce. A graduate of Princeton and a leading authority on serial killers, he wasn't the type one expected to find hanging out alongside a firehouse door. Especially not one that could serve as a prop in a Hollywood production of *Mayberry, R.F.D.*

Her heartbeat winding down to a normal beat, Ronnie barely considered her first order of business, chiefly, how best to use Jarvins' presence, when she glimpsed motion in the corner of her eye. Narrower than Maine, the side street could accommodate two cars, but even with its sidewalks on either side, it was a little wider than an alley. The short distance offered ample view of a man stepping from the single doorway of a long redbrick wall. Mid to late twenties if his style was any indication. Form-fitting, faded jeans, blue-flannel shirt, and trendy, long dark hair.

Like Jarvins, this fellow boasted a lean physique and proportionately square shoulders oddly enhanced by the flannel. Outside the solid gray door, he posed and tucked a brown paper bag, like a school lunch bag, under one arm and fumbled with a ring of keys.

"Olden Time Antiques and Collectibles," Ronnie muttered aloud. Written in Old English script, she recalled seeing the words etched on the glass display windows and scrolled across the classy gray awning covering the sidewalk on Maine. Considering that scalloped canopy, the building had probably housed a 5 & 10 or a J.C. Penny's store in the 40s and 50s. Two-stories . . . the upper floor might still hold apartments. She barely glanced to the string of dirty windows above when the fellow started to turn. Secure behind dark glasses, feigning preoccupation, Ronnie spied him, prepared to be disappointed.

Not disappointed, not by a long shot. Sharp angled features, a dark mustache already curved . . . if his eyes. His gaze locked on her. Thick black lashes, pale eyes . . . not merely looking toward her, at her. He stood poised, frozen in time, looking into her, through her tinted glasses, directly into her eyes. Into her head!

Suddenly, the street narrowed even more, and short hairs lifted at her neck, sending tingles down her spine. Deja vu! Or something similar. She knew him! He looked like . . . like someone . . .

Like someone she'd probably seen on the silver screen! Color rising, flooding her cheeks, Ronnie held her natural pose with an iron will. The twitch of a smile notched one corner of the dark mustache . . . soft full lips. A smirk? Impossible! No way could he see her looking at him! No way! Not through mirror sunglasses!

Time shifted inside or outside the rental. As if he hadn't paused or smirked, he strode in her direction on the parallel sidewalk. Opposite her open window, he veered into the street. Angling a path toward Maine, he stepped onto the sidewalk past the rental's rear bumper.

Unconsciously, Ronnie followed his progress, finding him in the side view mirror, glimpsing at him in her rearview mirror. Waking to her racing pulse, she drew an unsteady breath and muttered, "What the hell is this?" *Some sort of latent neurological defect, like a stress syndrome, to verge on an anxiety attack at the sight of every good-looking man?*

"Definitely a good-looking man." From his thick wavy dark hair barely brushing his shirt collar to his boots gliding across the pavement, to the hint of humor in that half-smile . . . "Damn it."

He was probably married to a Cover-Girl-style wife and lived over that store with a dozen children crammed into a two-room apartment. Behind dirty panes of glass, a half dozen windows on the upper floor wore drawn yellowed blinds. On three curtained windows, neither frilly lace nor knickknacks appeared to suggest a female touch. Not a single round young face bobbed behind the glass or peered between parted dark drapes. As impersonal as a doctor's office, those shaded windows.

"What the hell am I doing, for god's sake," Ronnie muttered, shaking herself from the momentary lapse. Belatedly, she registered the whir of her recorder and the vibration of the rental's engine. Muttering a curse, she jabbed the stop button.

She'd come to this throwback dirt-water town to investigate and report the eventual apprehension of a killer. If she intended to collect any useful information, likely in the form of gossip, she needed to get busy. Pulling herself together, she glanced toward the red-checked curtains through her passenger door window.

The diner was a good place to start and subconsciously, might have accounted for making the turn.

Shoving her recorder into her oversized purse alongside her notebook, she rolled up the window and shut off the engine. A lone woman in dark glasses, sitting in a vehicle with her engine running? No wonder the guy had looked at her. But that smirk . . .? Maybe she'd imagined that smirk. After all, the street wasn't *that* narrow.

Climbing from the car, dropping her keys in her slacks pocket, and digging for spare change, she passed in front of the Escort, muttering, "Big jerk." Probably had an ego the size of Mt. Everest! As if he thought she might be looking at him! With the cant of her head, she might have been reading the stop sign at the end of the block. Annoyed, she shoved a dime in the meter and stared, dumbfounded, when the needle flipped to the two-hour limit. Shaking her head, she continued toward Maine, following the length of red-checkered curtains to the corner.

Upon a time, Miss Veronica Bryson wouldn't have been caught dead entering a restaurant with red-checked curtains, much less Formica-topped tables, and vinyl-covered seats belly up to a long bar-style counter. However, even before the influence of college, Jesse Hagen had introduced her to the more natural world. Doubtful Ronnie could ever repay her best friend for those early lessons. With a nonchalance to betray her Pierre Cardin slacks and Persian silk blouse, she entered the diner and nearly tripped over her Gucci flats.

The object of her latest fascination rested on a stool with his back to the door, apparently, chatting with a blond woman behind the register. In a stopped instant, Ronnie noticed how his mahogany waves curled ever-so-slightly against the blue flannel collar, then nearly cursed aloud for taking an interest. No accounting for it. Only a blind woman wouldn't notice those shimmering dark waves. No greasy tonics for this character. Nu-uh. A good wind would send those waves into a thicket of wild curls, and for just a second, Ronnie wished she'd dragged a comb through her own wind-tangled locks. Blast it anyway! Next, she'd be tugging the visor down at every red light and checking her lipstick like her mother. Stumbling into clothes and packing a bag at four a.m. wasn't conducive to making a fashion statement. If the flight and drive had taken a toll, so be it. She'd neither dressed for a soiree nor expected one.

At the deep end of the counter, three older gentlemen huddled, and a dozen other patrons occupied booths chatting in near hushed voices. A matched set of servers meandered behind the counter wearing dark blue skirts, blue-checked blouses, and white aprons. With their uniforms, the likeness began and ended. One appeared young and perky, probably fresh out of high school; the other dour and grim as she waddled from behind the counter carrying a pot of coffee. Catching a whiff of that brew, Ronnie started toward the counter, considering an ulterior motive for stopping at the diner.

A cup of strong coffee, a light breakfast, a large helping of gossip . . . in that order.

Striding to the counter, Ronnie sized up the woman behind the register. The loose blond hair was deceiving. Wisps of gray reflected in the curls; laugh-lines webbed her temples and smiling pink lips. With a touch of cosmetics to dust her slender cheeks and lengthen her lashes, the woman could pass for an aging thirty or a young sixty.

Slipping onto the stool, with three empty seats between her and Casanova, Ronnie glanced at him.

The brown paper bag from under his arm now rested crumpled on the counter near his hands, both folded possessively around a mug of coffee. Apparently, the bag had carried a gift. Carefully, the woman had begun unwrapping yards of tissue from a rapidly shrinking wad.

With the implication, Ronnie stole another glance at the dark-haired man, wondering if she'd misjudged his age. For the second time in ten minutes, their gazes locked without the benefit of dark glasses or distance. No mistaking his age. Mid to late twenties. His eyes held her rapt. Hazel eyes, very pale hazel eyes nearly the color of jade glittered beneath a shag of thick black lashes . . . and there was something about those eyes. *Familiar.* She should remember him. His head tipped at a curious angle; his brow furrowed to affect curiosity. A peculiar smile haunted his mustached lips, again effecting a smirk. In a half second or less, his smile flashed away into annoyance and his gaze pivoted to the older woman.

Arrogant creep, Ronnie nearly uttered aloud and turned her attention to the perky waitress who arrived to take her order. No doubt the stout young lady was fresh out of high school and susceptible to the tall, dark, handsome types. Even as she jotted 'coffee' on her order pad, she favored the hunk with a wistful glance.

Mr. Personality seemed not to notice, evidently rapt on the older woman. His mother, perhaps?

Annoyed with her own interest, Ronnie considered offering the smitten young lady some free advice. In Ronnie's experience, men who could fell a woman with a look were either too stuck on themselves to appreciate their falling damsels . . . or they were gay.

Three seats away, the coffee cup clattered on the counter, and the handsome jerk started choking on a swallow.

In natural curiosity, Ronnie glanced toward the raucous and caught a searing glance of his hazel eyes. *What?* Did he blame her for his mishap? Not certain whether to be concerned or amused, Ronnie watched as the blond woman clasped his wrist and the stout waitress hustled behind him, clouting him on the back.

"Isaac!" they snapped in unison.

Her gift forgotten; the older woman glimpsed at the third waitress arriving. "A glass of water, Karen," she spoke in a calm, matronly tone, laced with concern.

All this fuss over a swallow down the wrong pipe? *Poor baby*, Ronnie silently cooed as she watched him accept the glass of water. Perhaps, she'd made him nervous enough to swallow down the wrong pipe, but she doubted it. By his casual acceptance of the attention, he was accustomed to women pampering him and catering to him . . . perhaps, with justification. He wore the charming, good looks of a boy with the build and arrogance of a man. *Probably, the mentality of a nitwit!*

Turning her attention to her coffee and the laminated menu Karen had nearly thrown at her before dashing for the water, Ronnie halfheartedly listened to him recover. A bit raspy, that muttering voice. Under normal circumstances, that voice was probably deep. Nearly cursing her interest, Ronnie barely dismissed her concern when she overheard one of the elder gents on her opposite side.

"Think if I start choking on an egg, those gals'd notice before I croak?"

"Wouldn't hold my breath," his pal growled.

Forcing a cough to stifle a laugh, Ronnie dipped her attention to rifle through her purse for her cigarettes.

"Oh, Isaac . . . it's stunning," the woman said with a near breathless note.

"I thought you might like it, Meg," he strained softly.

God! Deep but soft. He certainly had a deep voice and knew precisely how to regulate the smooth deep pitch to send tiny little shivers down a woman's spine. He probably harbored an ego the size of Mohammed's Mountain! Forget Everest!

Annoyed without any good reason, Ronnie glanced toward him, but her attention lowered and locked on the object of the woman's awe. The color, the style, the butterfly pattern of the sculpt turning within the slender fingers . . . Ronnie recalled seeing a similar style in a museum. A Dresden. A Dresden statue? Before she could be certain, both other servers descended in tandem to view the treasure. Luckily, Ronnie wasn't sipping her coffee. To see a piece of fine porcelain passed from one pair of calloused hands to the next, regardless of how carefully, behind a Formica counter, might have started her choking.

"I'm almost afraid to ask how much you'll want for it," the elder woman, Meg, commented.

"Porkchops."

"What?"

"Unless you've changed your menu in my absence, that's your special this evening." Without the strain, his deep voice carried a hint of English accent and a somewhat lofty arrogance. "And that's my price . . . a stuffed pork chop."

Ronnie flashed her gaze down the menu to the weekly specials. *Definitely, a stuffed pork chop dinner on the menu . . . 4.95.*

"Isaac, I couldn't—"

"One stuffed pork chop and all the trimmings, a cup of coffee, and a slice of apple pie to go," he said smugly. "That's as low as I'll go."

A joke, surely! Ronnie looked over and stared yet again. His head tipped at an angle to spark rainbows off his dark hair, his lips curved in a half-smile and enhanced a dimple at the corner of his mustache. The arrogance had vanished. He looked like a little boy, all smug and happy with himself for striking such a grand deal; the mug of coffee might as well be a cup of hot cocoa for as strange as it appeared in his hands.

"That's your lowest, huh?" Meg said as she recovered the statue. Her long delicate fingers handled the fine porcelain with a proper amount of grace and care. Canting her head, laughter lines crinkled at her eyes and pursed lips betraying her sober tone. "The pie, too? No ice cream?"

"It'll melt too fast. No ice cream," he agreed.

"Suppose you have yourself a deal, but I need to tell you, sweetie, you won't make a nickel if you don't learn to haggle. I might have gone as high as spaghetti tomorrow evening or ham and eggs in the morning."

"I knew I should have held out for your offer," he said with a near crestfallen tone. "I can't seem to master this haggling business one wit."

"Honey," Ronnie started and caught his laughing eyes. Her heart slammed a mean beat under his liquid-green gaze. He was neither nitwit nor child. Behind his sparkling hazel eyes, he retained his full faculties and a working knowledge of the valuable piece of porcelain he'd just traded for a pork chop dinner. In split seconds, Ronnie sensed his tension and nearly heard him swearing her to silence. Abandoning the cutting jibe lingering on the tip of her tongue, Ronnie donned a faint smile and continued smoothly, "I'd be willing to spring for your breakfast and dinner tomorrow if you have another of those."

"Hmm, collector of butterflies, are you?" he asked with a faintly puzzled smile.

"Actually, flowers," she said off the top of her head. "Is it possible you own that little shop across the street?"

From the sideline, Karen said defensively, "It's the biggest shop in Bentwood. It only looks small on the outside."

Flashing Karen an appreciative smile guaranteed to snatch the young girl's breath, if not her heart, his gaze returned to Ronnie. "Dealer by any chance?" he asked.

"Collector," she answered with a fleeting thought of dealers needing a license or some such. Safer to adhere to certain parameters, though she walked a fine line between a lie and stretched truth. Antique collecting could be a decent cover, and she was a collector of sorts, although her tastes ran toward pottery. "What time do you open?"

"Noon, today," he said offhandedly and moved his cup, accepting a heaping plate of eggs and sausage. Flashing another smile to the waitress, he appeared oblivious of the young woman's swoon as she delivered the meal like a medieval serf serving her master. His gaze returned, intent. "If you don't mind waiting until we've finished breakfast though, I could let you in early."

Considering her reason for visiting Bentwood, Ronnie commented, "There's no hurry. I'll be staying in town for a few days."

The stately woman who'd watched them somewhat curiously, turned her attention to Ronnie and asked lightly, "Would you like breakfast, dear?"

Looking toward the young server who'd apparently not forgiven her for criticizing the man's shop, Ronnie placed her order for bacon, egg, and cheese on a bagel. She rejected the suggestion for home fries, although when she saw the mounded plate of diced potatoes and onions joining Isaac's collection, she nearly succumbed. Like most country diners, this one neither relied on frozen foods and prefab hamburgers nor skimped on the portions. A wonder this guy stayed trim if he was a regular.

By the time Ronnie received her bagel—twice as large as she'd expected—Isaac had nearly finished his meal, and more customers had filed into the diner. Intent on the conversations, she heard the first whispers about last night's alleged accident. When another elder gentleman joined the trio down the counter, the words began to ring like music to her ears.

"I'm telling you what I know," the new arrival commented gruffly. "They had the coroner's wagon out there along with the Feds... Ole Doc Blackwell had to go out an' give Alice something! Was her that found him, but Erin was there, too! Halfwit or not, had to been a shock to her, too."

"I heard he was found just like Vic. Sliced-up like a butchered hog!"

"Hush yourself! Can't you see they's people trying to eat in here!"

"Yea, well, I want to know what them Feds are doing about this here!"

"Probably be calling a town meetin'," another commented.

Despite his preoccupation with the black-haired woman two stools away, Isaac heard the husky voices at the end of the counter, and the heaviness lingering in his mind increased tenfold.

Fred Engler? Like Victor Farnsworth? Murdered?

Abstracted, his focus slid down the counter, halting, locking abruptly on the black-haired stranger between him and the elders. Without the dark glasses, her eyes were blue . . . incredibly blue, piercing and penetrating from a bisque complexion cut from a cameo portrait. Delicate nose, long slender neckline, soft full lips curved in a whisper of a smile. Under the crosscurrent of fluorescent and natural sunlight, her hair tumbled in shimmering black curls, spilling over her brow, tumbling in perfect contrast to her pale blue cashmere sweater.

Carelessly, she scissored her fingers, sailing long black silk over her shoulder, and his heart skipped a beat. If she'd practiced that move for maximum effect, she'd succeeded to perfection. That was the sexiest move he'd seen in a while.

Unconsciously, his head tipped as a prickle lifted under his collar, and he dropped his attention to his plate, annoyed with his interest.

He had more than enough trouble with women in Bentwood without drawing the interest of an outsider, but he couldn't deny, the lady stirred something not entirely intellectual inside of him. A collector? Flowers? She might be on a personal junket. Perhaps, she needed to furnish a lavish apartment or mansion. Her style leaned toward New York chic . . . the kind of woman to walk into the Ritz-Carlton and receive the red-carpet treatment.

His muscles gripped an instant before the fingers slid under his collar, and a curtain of neon blond hair dropped over his opposite shoulder. *Sax Fifth Ave vs. K-Mart. Silk curtains vs. cotton drapes.*

Forcing a smile, Isaac tipped his head and collided with the magnified face of a Barbie doll. With an elaborate wink of lashes thick enough to be horsehair, Jen Andover—the girl next door—brushed a bright red kiss on his lips.

Seductively, she slid her body against his arm and settled on the stool at his side. Her hand skimmed down his back and circled his arm, hugging. "I thought I'd find my favorite guy in here! How was your trip, darling? I didn't think you'd be home until Monday."

"Change in plans," he managed. Cheap perfume assaulted his nostrils and threatened to spoil the lingering flavors of bacon and eggs on his tongue. "How've you been, Jen?"

A sly smile tightened her lips, and laughter sparked in her heavily shaded eyes as if he need ask. In physical proportions, she could pass for her role model, an anatomically correct version. Tight jeans, ample hips, tiny waist. Bright red—her color of fancy—the tank top clung to her ample bosom, falling lower at the top than the fringe at the bottom and offering a view of her navel from either direction. On both shoulders, black lacy bra straps escaped from beneath the red shoulder harness, more tacky than suggestive, and undoubtedly, she'd exercised her tasteless finesse to wear spike-heeled sandals.

In a split second or less, Isaac drew from his inspection, uncertain of his interest until his gaze slid past Jen, and he glimpsed the bemused blue eyes. *His type?* Before he could react too noticeably, the long fire-red fingernails glinted at his arm; the subtle pressure drew him to the pixie face and pouting red lips.

Nuzzling against him, Jen purred a sound as if eating warm soup and batted her lashes. "It's been so *boring* without you here," she almost whined. "I'm just dying to see everything you brought back with you. If you're finished, why don't we go over to your place, and you can give me a private viewing?"

Viewing? The word sounded funereal. A shiver slid down his spine. "As much as I'd like to, Jen, I'm afraid I can't this morning," he lamented, striving for heartfelt sincerity, belatedly recalling his offer to the newcomer. Hopefully, the lady hadn't heard or misinterpreted his lie though why the blasted hell it would matter, he dared not contemplate. "Prior commitment, I'm afraid," Isaac added, halfheartedly hoping to appease both females and not entirely lying. A mound of paperwork awaited him in his office, but he could've justified postponing that ordeal to accommodate a new customer. Only good business, after all.

Already shifting to reach his wallet in his back pocket, detaching Jen by gesture, Isaac glimpsed the flash of temper under her lashes, not masked by her pout.

"You just got back," Jen whined with an edge. "How can you possibly have a prior *anything*?"

Annoyance flashed through his mind, lifted briefly in his eyes. On the scant three occasions when he'd buckled to a whim and accepted Jen's favors, he hadn't implied or promised anything more than he'd delivered—a few rapacious hours of mutual bliss and physical release. He probably should have refrained in Andover's case despite her limber physique. Garden-variety sex wasn't worth the irritation she was threatening to become.

"I'll see you later, Jen," he said offhandedly and passed Meg a ten, catching her amused eye. Neighbor, friend, and confidant, Meg Price was one of a select few women in Bentwood who found his rakish nature entirely entertaining. She was old enough to be his mother, and by the spark in her eyes, he could imagine the lecture he would receive over dinner. "Porkchops," he stated and almost at the same time, heard another sorrowful low whisper.

"Poor Cora . . . now, Alice. . . ."

Cora Farnsworth, recently widowed . . . now, Alice Engler, apparently more recently widowed.

Stifling a mental sway, nearly uttering a curse, Isaac started to turn, but his gaze snagged on the young woman entirely engrossed in her bagel sandwich, or so it seemed. Without a first or second thought, he passed Jen and touched the cashmere sweater, brushing against the black silk draped over the shoulder. Sparks snapped at his fingertips, jolting him—jolting her. Her fiery eyes lifted sharply, intently, and for a half second or less, Isaac regretted shocking her. A smile quivered on her full lips; mischief danced in her blue eyes. Numb fingertips were worth the price of touching that black silk. Turning his hand offering a handshake, he managed a faint smile, only more curious. "I'm afraid I didn't get your name, miss," he said smoothly.

"Veronica Bryson," she offered formally and touched his hand.

A whirlwind of sensations tingled through his palm. From the heat of her fingertips to the strength of her grip, a no-nonsense grip. "Isaac Bently," he said as he retracted his hand, recovering on the instant. "I'm open until six this evening. I do have some lovely floral centerpieces and several pieces of floral pattern china, from demitasse cups to vases. I'll look forward to your visit."

"Thank you, Mr. Bently," she said simply and fleeted a glance past him. Oh, and there was a dark side to this lady. With a mere flicker in her quick, intelligent eyes, she betrayed her wry sense of humor belying the surface of her soft smile. "I should be in around one," she added, leaving no doubt, that she baited Jen.

"See you, then," he said lightly and canted his head, holding her eyes an instant longer and enjoying the sparkle to linger there.

With an effort, Isaac withdrew, tossing a parting amenity to Meg as well as Jen, and started for the door, catching other familiar faces, acknowledging greetings with a wave or word. Too many grim voices and faces, too many worried eyes. For the number of regulars on any given Saturday, the atmosphere remained far too subdued. Isaac needed only a glance at the two dark-suited gentlemen pushing through the glass door to recognize the sudden drop in tempo. The larger, dark-haired chap carried himself like a Mafia thug from his brawny shoulders to his nearly black eyes, but Isaac judged both as Federal Agents. Tall and wiry, the blond-haired man moved with arrogance and intensity to betray his waxed friendly smile. His pale blue eyes sprinted at Isaac as they passed, dismissing him as if judging him as a farmhand and labeling him somewhere in the category of a garbage collector. The dark eyes were far more perceptive, and in a fleeting instant of contact, Isaac sensed the man's antenna lifting, his own short hairs prickling under his flannel collar.

With an almost imperceptible nod, Isaac passed and reached the door. With a backward glance, he realized the agents were descending on the lovely stranger, and heat flashed through his mind. Stifling an impulse to return to the counter, he forced himself through the door, silently cursing in several languages as he passed the front windows.

Not a collector . . . probably a blasted federal agent . . . but even that seemed wrong.

CHAPTER 2

Ruffling the blond bimbo's feathers had offered an amusing interlude, but Ronnie dismissed any thought of the jealous young lady even before Casanova departed. In a glance, she'd spotted Mark and his partner, Len Devinio, entering the diner. Doubtfully, she could avoid an encounter with Jarvins inside a brightly lit, not-exactly-crowded diner. If only to keep her profession quiet for a short time, she would've preferred to postpone this reunion.

Futile. Futile to even try. The dark suit sliding onto the stool at her side confirmed her thought. Surprisingly calm, she met Mark's startled blue eyes, appreciating the past hour to prepare mentally for this confrontation. Three years was ample time to forget how he'd stormed out of her apartment, her life. She settled on indifference and held his gaze.

In a maelstrom, surprise ebbed toward anger, then dread, then the old standby . . . amusement. With his arrogance, he appeared only lofty and superior with his feigned delight. "My only surprise is that I am surprised." As an afterthought, he added, "Nice to see you, Ron."

Nice eyes, deep voice . . . he hadn't lost his looks or his talent to be suave.

Accepting his handshake, Ronnie mirrored his lofty air, offering dryly. "Charmed."

He stifled a laugh, but his sober blue eyes betrayed his trademark good humor. In appearance, he hadn't changed drastically, although five o'clock shadows haunted his sculpted features, and tension lingered on his lips. Perhaps his blond waves were shorter, more in Bureau regulation, and a few sharp edges hardened his cheeks and jaw. If she needed further evidence to confirm her intuition, the chilly intensity in his eyes ended the debate. He was a man on a case.

Soberly, in conflict with his lingering smile, he commented, "I missed you."

"Flattery will get you nowhere, darling," she said honestly. Three years without a phone call or letter was far more indicative of his emotional investment in their relationship. Maintaining a tense smile, she held his gaze, ignoring the sense of too many spectators taking an interest.

"I don't suppose I could just ask you to leave, and you'd agree, would you?" he asked soberly.

"Don't suppose I would," she answered as forgotten memories surfaced. The musk scent of his cologne . . . his hands flying from darkness, pulling her into a safe warm embrace . . . the taste of his lips. She shoved the unbidden thoughts aside, judging the alarm in his eyes, considering the possibility of danger. "But I appreciate your concern," she said sincerely.

"Ron, this is a nice little town," he started quietly.

Len leaned forward at that moment and spied past his partner's shoulder. His dark Sicilian eyes flashed as much surprise as annoyance far more swiftly than Mark's.

"Hi ya, Len," Ronnie offered with a smile.

"Hey, hey, the gang's all here," he sang in a low, growling timbre reflective of a chain gang ditty. "Hi ya, Ron. Meaning no offense, but I hope you were just leaving."

"Fat chance," she said in reflection of his favorite line. His dark brows drew together into a more pronounced scowl. On his ruggedly handsome face, his expression could be menacing to anyone who knew him less. If not much else, Ronnie remembered and respected his dedication to the Bureau . . . or more precisely, to the apprehension of criminals. If not for Mark, she and Len might have been friends or companionable acquaintances. Such hadn't come to pass, and she'd wasted enough time. In the past hour, she'd heard enough gossip to set her priorities in order. "Unless you were simply referring to this establishment, in which case, you're exactly right," Ronnie decided and dragged her purse from the floor between her shoes.

"Still lugging your suitcase, I see, and it's still worse than my closet," Mark commented.

"I never leave home without it," she answered offhandedly, finding her wallet, and looking into his faintly amused eyes. "Never know when I might need to slam a noggin with a kitchen sink."

Laughter flashed in his baby blues as he lifted a hand, stifling an urge to rub his temple and combing his fingers through his hair instead. "Touché."

Smiling, she slipped off the stool, touching his shoulder as she passed. "See you around, buster."

"Undoubtedly, soon, darling," he tossed over his opposite shoulder with a light laugh.

If her father, the illustrious Robert Bryson Sr. had taught her nothing else, he'd taught her never to burn bridges. On impulse, Ronnie paused behind Len and leaned over his shoulder, brushing a kiss on his sandpaper cheek. "Love you, too, Len," she said and withdrew, glimpsing the searing glance from the blond bimbo. Mark's low deep chuckle followed Ronnie toward the glass doors, but a niggling sense of the spectators prickled under her collar, stifling her smile. She hadn't won any favor by flirting with Mr. Isaac Bently or baiting that young woman, and in a town this size, people noticed.

Passing through the door, she eyed the gray awning on the next block, and a furrow slid across her brow. She wouldn't mind a closer look through those storefront windows. Isaac Bently . . . something about him rang false and yet familiar, but if she'd ever heard that name, the memory was lost. Still, a thought of seeing him somewhere before lingered at the edges of her mind. A foolish thought. If she'd met him, she'd remember. Between his voice, his eyes, and that half-hitched smile filled with promise, he bore a charismatic handsomeness that no sensible woman would likely forget, even if that woman boasted an abundance of handsome men in her social circle. Attractive men, including Mark Jarvins, were not her type. Arrogant, egotistical, lascivious, conniving . . .

She continued filling in adjectives, recalling a time when she'd listed more than a hundred of those pleasantries from a Thesaurus. Mark hadn't received that list. She'd handed it to a high school flame, and even in reflection, the young man's reaction was worth the time spent.

Fumbling for her keys, she panned her gaze up the alley toward the stop sign, barely visible through a tunnel of thick hedges and low-hanging tree branches. A single street of merchants. By the mere impression of houses tucked within the bushes further down the block, the town supported a vast majority of residential homes; undoubtedly, the original townhouse without the modern glamour of condominiums.

'A nice little town,' Mark had started and probably intended to contradict any hint of murder.

Sliding into the driver's seat, Ronnie scanned the span of redbrick to her left. Halfheartedly, she wished she'd accepted Bently's offer, then muttered a curse at her interest. This wasn't a manhunt. Well, not in the sense that every thought of Isaac Bently conjured. She might want to speak to him again . . . on a strictly professional basis.

Presently, however, she needed to return to Maine and check into the Bentwood House Inn.

Jet lag, Isaac attested silently and slumped in his thick cushioned chair, rubbing the heels of both hands in his eyes. Trains, planes, and automobiles flashed behind his closed eyes, confirming his thought of exhaustion, and another night of insomnia hadn't relieved the traveler's lapse. If he thought it would help, he might try stretching out on the overstuffed couch cramped across from his desk, but sleep had become a wrathful mistress, torturing him whether he took her to bed or on the couch . . . and the last damn thing he needed was another woman in his life.

Unbidden, the image popped into his mind's eye. Tumbling black amethyst curls tussled and windblown into a riot of glittering waves, like black bubbles foaming over her slender shoulders. A complexion as smooth as any Dresden doll on a face equally well-sculpted. Full soft lips with a natural curve to hint at a pleasant disposition. Somewhere he'd heard or read that lips curved upward, even in repose, alluded to the inner nature of the beast. Miss Veronica Bryson possessed those pleasant lips no matter how aloof and piercing her blue gaze.

Cobalt . . . *too dark.* Tourmaline . . . *nope.* Blue sapphire . . . *close.* Blue diamonds. *Without a doubt!* Blue diamonds! As deep and piercing as any blue diamond! Turned one way as pale as aquamarines, turned another, as rich as cobalt . . . *Good God, she was something to write home about!*

"Dumbass," he said to no other than himself, belatedly remembering Elaine Connelly, his part-time assistant, standing outside the office door. At least she'd lingered outside the office a moment ago.

Rousted by his own curse, Isaac opened his eyes to find Elaine halted in the doorway just left of the couch where he should be sleeping. Lifting his gaze to her startled brown eyes, he suffered a faintly embarrassed smirk. "Don't suppose you'll doubt I was talking to myself, will you?"

Nearing fifty with a country-girl charm and a matronly demeanor enhanced by premature gray in her puffy-permed auburn hair, Elaine donned one of her infamous blank gazes. If she believed he'd cursed her, nothing showed in her expression. After nearly five years, she still called him 'Mr. Bently' most often. Strictly business, she had the good sense never to ask his opinion about anything other than antiques or the shop, which suited him just fine. Well-rounded, from her flushed cheeks to her sensible brown shoes, she boasted one truly redeeming quality that befuddled and entertained Isaac even on his worst day. She was a dyed-in-the-wool swindler, capable of spotting an easy mark at twenty paces.

'My daddy was a junk dealer back during the war,' she'd confided five years ago when filling out the standard employment application. 'And he always said I could sell refrigerators to Eskimos . . .'

With only a second's lapse, she continued hesitantly into his office, worrying her bottom lip and attempting to smile. Her gaze darted to the open ledger in front of him. Her brow wrinkled before she met his gaze. "Is everything alright with the books, Mr. Bently?"

She probably had heard his curse and taken offense. Sitting up and panning his gaze over the stack of sales receipts, he softened his tone. "I haven't gone through all the receipts, but I'm sure everything's fine." Despite her atrocious spelling, which sometimes demanded verbal interpretation, her printing was far more meticulous than his own, each letter as neat as block-set type on the lines, and her talent with an adding machine had improved considerably. Usually, she even trusted her ability to punch the appropriate numbers without a corresponding printout; however, every sales receipt written throughout his absence carried a strip of adding machine tape stapled to the righthand corner.

Aware of her watching him, Isaac lifted his attention, reading the tension in her eyes. "Something troubling you, Elaine?"

"Well, sort of, there is," she said uncomfortably and bolstered her nerve to meet his gaze. "I was just wondering if you'll be needing me this afternoon?"

He'd hoped to spend the day in his office catching up on paperwork, but she rarely, if ever, called in sick or requested time off. Studying the fine lines about her eyes and lips, noting her pale complexion, he commented, "If you aren't feeling well, Elaine, you could have called in."

She seemed only more nervous and uncomfortable, and a film of tears swam over her brown eyes. "Well," she strained softly, darting her gaze as if she could hide the rising shine. "I'm not sick, exactly. Not with the flu or . . ." Her gaze trailed momentarily, then returned. Her bottom lip quivered as she uttered, "Alice . . . Alice Engler is my cousin, Mr. Bently. I made up a casserole as soon's I heard this morning, but she . . . I think she's needing . . ."

Comfort, company . . . dinner. All of the above; any of the above. Only a damn fool would require further explanation . . . and he'd never quite known how to handle a weeping woman. His personal misgivings annoyed him nearly as badly as Elaine's rising tears disturbed him. "You could have called in," he said quietly, masking his distress behind indifference. "Will you be alright to drive home?"

"I-I can manage alright if . . . if you're sure it's alright for me to go."

"Of course, it is," he said and pushed from his chair, wanting her gone before the dam broke behind her eyes. Stepping around his desk, he reached her side. He should say something, offer a condolence or sympathy, some false amenity; he should feel something, anything, other than a compulsive desire to boot her out the door. Touching her shoulder, turning her toward the doorway, he forced a grim smile. "You have my sympathies, Elaine," he managed, overcoming the insecurities threatening to rise. What was there to say? Words never salved grief. "Take as long as you need to help your cousin," he offered as they passed into the showroom. "If I'd known, I wouldn't have expected you to come in. If there's anything I can do . . ."

"It's horrible," she strained. "It's just so horrible. Why would anyone want to hurt Fred? He was just a good decent family ma—" The dam broke on her words.

Under his hand, Elaine trembled in a convulsive, silent sob, and Isaac shuddered. With her shoulders quaking, tears streaming, she was in no condition to find her car, much less drive home. Sighing resignation, he directed her to the barstool behind the glass cases that extended the length of the interior wall. Patting her back, he rifled under the counter until finding a stack of napkins.

"I-I'm a-all righ-ight now," she blubbered while wiping her eyes. Her graying head bobbed, bowed. She hiccupped. "It's jus-ust that it's so . . ."

Horrible, Isaac finished silently and shivered as he patted the woman's heaving back in a helpless gesture. If even half of the gossip in Meg's could be true, Fred's demise was probably more horrible than Elaine believed, but that made her tears no easier to bear. Death, even violent death, could be considered a natural part of life. Forces existed—

An accident! Until he heard otherwise, he refused to believe anything else.

He shook the thought from his mind, concentrating on the sobbing woman. The sooner she calmed down, the sooner she could leave and seek sympathy elsewhere. This sort of thing was beyond his area of expertise. Leaving her to sob hunched over on the stool, Isaac passed behind the counter and into the small circle of comfortable lounge chairs. Filling a conical paper cup from the bottled water dispenser, he returned, offering it into her trembling hand.

Slowly, steadily, she recovered enough to collect her purse, and Isaac walked her to the front door, receiving her assurance she'd be fine to drive. Embarrassed, she apologized, patted his hand, and thanked him for being so 'understanding,' promising she'd call if she couldn't come tomorrow.

Engaging the deadbolt, his stomach churning, Isaac watched her hurrying around the corner, then turned and started toward his office. Noting several missing pieces, he paused a half dozen times, rearranging glass or china to fill the gaps, unconsciously planning where he might display some of his newest acquisitions.

With an eye for detail and an aversion to clutter, Isaac had modeled his shop after an elegant home. Wide aisles trailed between small inlets where a parlor settee might be featured with an assortment of Tiffany lamps and antique silks, or an entire set of Coalport dinnerware might draw attention decorating a Duncan Phyfe table. Candlewick and Fry glass, Dresden and Occupied Japan statues, and brass and silver accents complemented one display after another.

He loved antiques, loved the longevity, and thrilled each time anew when he held a magnificent piece of history in his hands. Financial gain meant far less than the simple pleasure of owning such treasures, whether he gazed upon an Icart etching or held a genuine Heubach in his palm. Permanence and longevity, a direct cord to the past that could be traced to names and faces through the annals of history to other eras, to other places.

However, as much as he loved his flashy treasures, books were his first true love. First editions, second editions, he could care less so long as the edition predated his own brief term upon the earth. A copy of Dante's *Divine Come*dy printed in the thirties, with all the integrity of Gustave Dore's original etchings on the pages, could offer as much pleasure as the first edition of Sir Arthur Conan Doyle's *Sherlock Holmes.* History, whether coming alive in the written documentation or experienced through the fictitious writing of Shakespeare, history was his mainstay, and those documented treasures, he hoarded for himself.

Breathing in the scents of age, Isaac drew from his idling and scanned the shadows of his shop, delighting in the quiet ambiance. He hadn't bothered with the chandeliers or the fluorescent lights overhead spotlighting his favorite pieces during store hours. Day-glow filtered through the front windows beneath the awnings, which he'd installed to prohibit fading or heating window display items. An occasional flash of sunlight reflected off a passing bumper or windshield, brightened the white tile ceiling, and arced downward to lance silver or crystal.

It felt good to be home, Isaac realized in quiet reflection, and this was his home.

Sighing contentment, he continued past the showcases along the back wall, skimming a glance over the jewelry displays and mentally listing the manual labor ahead. He had little more than a month to prepare the shop for his newest treasures that would arrive in New York on a freighter and in Bentwood via tractor-trailer. Most of his new treasures would be jammed into the warehouse behind the shop, but a few would reach his showroom floor. One, a genuine Bentwood rocker, would need a place of its own near the front of the store, although, in tribute to the townspeople, he might donate the rocker to the tiny museum on the outskirts of town. Doubtful any founding father of this farming community descended from Michael Thonet who'd first crafted the style, but Isaac might need to research that tidbit of trivia before parting with the rocker.

Settling behind his desk, Isaac scanned the mound of receipts grimly. After five years, sales had increased, doubtless, due to the flyers he'd sent to dealers across the country. Whether his success pleased or disgusted him, he couldn't decide, and scanning the sales receipt on top of the stack only enhanced his quandary. Some of his favorite treasures left far too swiftly to suit him, and that Shaker rocker hadn't been the exception.

Shrugging off a moment of despair, Isaac flipped through his ledger to the proper page, jotted the sales amount at the end of the column then checked the small box in front of the rocker's catalog number.

Perhaps, he should change his tactics and focus on reproductions rather than genuine artifacts. The good people of Bentwood would probably be satisfied with copies of fine antiques which would fit more smoothly in their budgets. Keeping an ample supply of pretty trinkets on display and designating the reproduction status had gained Olden Time a respectable number of regular customers. And dedicating an entire showcase to baseball cards, movie memorabilia, and comic books had certainly gained favor from the local youngsters.

Movie memorabilia.

Isaac's thought dimmed momentarily with a fleeting thought of Jen Andover and another flash of blue-diamond eyes.

Muttering a curse, he continued flipping through ledger pages, crossing off more of his treasures. What had possessed him to send those damn flyers and pretend to be a businessman? But that answer was all too blasted simple. Fear had driven him. Fear and restlessness. He'd needed something, needed something to fill the endless void of time stretched in front of him. Primal self-survival instincts had driven him to action.

If left entirely to his own devices, he would go stark raving mad . . . and it was entirely possible, he was more than halfway there already. Muttering a curse, he yanked himself from yet another absent daze.

Paperwork!

If he had any hope of seeing daylight again in the next few weeks, he needed to get this busy work out of the way.

With iron resolve, he picked up where he'd left off and determined to finish at least the first week of receipts before the clock struck noon.

CHAPTER 3

To Ronnie's surprise, the Bentwood House Inn not only offered rooms to let, but the atmosphere compared nicely to any of the finest hotels she'd ever patronized. Within minutes, Ronnie acclimated, unpacked her toiletries and clothes, then concentrated on the necessary components of her profession. Tugging the antique-style table and chairs nearer the wall to access an electric outlet, she arranged her Smith-Corona typewriter, although she doubted she'd use it in this room. She wasn't on a deadline or budget, thank God. Those early days of meeting deadlines had gone by the wayside after her first success in a major publication. Mental conditioning. Eventually, she'd return to her apartment in Arlington, notes in hand, and write a few features to justify her research. The local reporters could bask in the limelight of the initial sensationalism. Her intentions ran deeper. With any luck, she could collect the main ingredients of her article in a day or two . . . and Mark Jarvins' face on the scene might ensure that time frame.

Settling onto the quilted bedspread where she'd placed her camera equipment, she checked lenses for smudges, tallied her film supply, and gauged the light outside before checking the number of shots in her trusty Minolta. The time spent in a photography course was well worth the effort. Without the aid or expense of a professional photographer, she managed to include publication-worthy photos with several past articles, and this one wouldn't be the exception.

With the mechanics complete, Ronnie returned to the table and flipped open her leather-bound notebook. On the plane, before dozing off, she'd outlined her approach; however, she needed to change her game plan. With Mark Jarvins' presence and gauging the speed of gossip to spread in Bentwood which could probably break the sound barrier, she wouldn't remain anonymous for long. If not at this moment, soon, the entire population of Bentwood would believe she was affiliated with the FBI. That circumstance could tip the scales one way or another in her favor. Depending on the local attitudes, she'd decide how best to use that gossip.

Popping a fresh cassette into her recorder, Ronnie rotated between jotting notes and voicing comments, listing an outline of attack in short bursts.

Pausing, she found the local phone book in the nightstand drawer and began searching for local entries.

"Not a single hospital listed in Bentwood," she commented aloud, then recited the names and addresses of the three facilities in Bender Falls. Likely, one would house the county morgue. For accuracy, she wrote each facility, taking care to spell each one correctly, then turned to government listings. Grateful for the dependability of Ma Bell, she discovered a great deal more about Bentwood than she might have learned if she'd visited the county courthouse in Bender Falls.

"The mayor's office stands next door to Bentwood's firehouse, which likewise consists of the municipal building for tax collectors and police headquarters . . . The sheriff's office resides in Bender Falls with most other county government facilities. Ditto for the local quarters of the Federal Bureau and state offices."

Flipping pages, she found a map of the area, suitably impressed with the size of Bentwood.

"As the exit-ramp sign indicated, Bentwood rests between two smaller towns of lesser space. Most of the area consists of farmland, and depending on my success with the locals, I might jaunt over to the courthouse and check the plat maps to locate the Engler and Farnsworth farms . . ."

Without a doubt, she'd make the trip to Bender Falls on Monday morning. Doubtful Engler's body had traveled much further than the coroner's office, located at one of the hospital addresses.

Turning to the yellow pages, consisting of fewer pages than the average Rand McNally, she skimmed down the columns. Becoming familiar with the local atmosphere, she jotted notes when she came across an address for either Bentwood or Hazelwood. Depending on her progress this afternoon, she might drive over to Hazelwood and gain an impression of that small town, too. By proximity, she couldn't afford to overlook its potential until she learned the precise locations of those farms.

Ronnie's attention snagged on one of the larger block ads on the page. The old English script had caught her eye as surely as the name. "Olden Time Antiques and Collectibles, Specializing in American and European Antiques. Period Furniture, glassware, china, etc.," she read aloud for her recorder. "Appraiser on-premises. Browsers welcome. Open seven days a week," the ad boasted and listed. "10: am — 5: pm weekdays. Saturday and Sunday, noon — 6: pm. Evenings by appointment." Unconsciously, she jotted the phone number with a fleeting thought of green eyes and a half-hitched smile. Good God, he was a handsome devil, and that dimple flashing in his mustache could melt butter.

"Jerk," she said flatly and scowled. That Dresden had probably cost him close to five hundred dollars, and he'd traded it for a lousy pork chop. Be damned if she'd ask him to appraise anything . . . But what kind of man, knowing the value, tosses a statue worth five Franklins to a waitress like a piece of cheap glass? Ronnie focused on her hand and gritted her teeth at the name she'd just scrolled alongside the number. "Isaac Bently."

If he had money to burn, what the hell was he doing in Bentwood?

She halted her hand before jotting the question but underscored the name and added a question mark. That he even piqued her interest annoyed her only until she remembered why she'd arrived in Bentwood. She was here to investigate and write about a possible serial killer.

"Pitchfork Slayer," she uttered and scrolled the words at the top of the page. A prickle sailed down her spine. If her hunch was correct, as evidenced by the local gossip, Frederick Engler hadn't died in a simple farm accident as the wire service had indicated.

From the back of her notebook, she drew the few clippings that Pete had handed her, then leafed through her notes to the page where she'd jotted pertinent data lifted from the articles. Scant few details appeared in those local tidbits. Victor Farnsworth, age 53, had been found in his dairy barn, stabbed several times with a pitchfork... The local police chief, Sam Hayward, chose to believe his death was the result of a quarrel turned deadly. Victor was survived by his wife Cora, two sons, Cal and Victor, twenty-five and twenty-three respectively, and a daughter, Valerie, twenty. No suspects in custody. Ergo, the quarrel theory bit the dust, and Mr. Fred Engler's untimely demise at the age of 59, confirmed her suspicion of a serial killer.

A month ago, Ronnie might have enlightened these local fellows that their theory wouldn't hold water. A woman's intuition carried only so far. Whatever the tingle at the nape of her neck when she read the blip on the wire service, she dared not ponder nor mention it too loud in the wrong circles. Bad enough Jarvins knew but enlightening him had saved her life. The ability to sense, to feel the work of a maniac, and to know when the crime would be repeated had become second nature.

She shivered and drew herself from a precarious edge. Her fingertips prickled as notebook pages fluttered in her hand, and for an instant, she remembered Bently's fingers lighting on her shoulder, sparking.

Out of the past, the words erupted, predating Bently, as well as Mark Jarvins by a half-dozen years.

'Maybe you ought to skip reporting,' Max Hagen had professed, and Ronnie remembered Max's smile, neither condescending nor lighthearted. Soberly, he'd continued, 'If you're going to hang around murder scenes and try solving cases, baby doll, you might consider applying to a police academy. You'd make a hell of a homicide detective, and I'd be a lot happier if you had the training.'

Their relationship had come a long way from the early years when she and Jesse Hagan had whiled away many a dull Saturday afternoon in Max's precinct. He'd often joked about the consequences if an unscrupulous reporter took exception to the daughter of revered Robert Bryson haunting a police precinct regularly. When Max had mentioned the Academy years later, he hadn't been joking, and lending thought to his advice, Ronnie had.

A fond smile lingering, she gazed through the sheer curtains. Max and Jesse had both laughed like fools when Ronnie had belatedly confided her ritualistic visits to a Karate instructor . . . Right up until she'd dumped Max flat on his ass in the center of his modest living room. If she never used that talent again, it would be worth every dime she'd spent. The dazed expression on his rugged face had been priceless before he'd flopped backward on his carpet and bellowed like an idiot.

More like a father than her own, Max had often looked at her with the same paternal fondness that he'd shined on Jesse. Max had never needed to be told that he'd influenced Ronnie's career choice. He was a homicide detective, a brand-new gold shield bearer when Jesse had transferred into Ronnie's private school, and they'd become fast friends. Despite his profession and a nasty divorce, Max remained one of the kindest, most noble, and honest men Ronnie knew, and she'd adopted him as a father from the moment they'd first met.

Maybe she'd give him a call this evening. Absently, her gaze landed on the telephone. Intuition or premonition? She hadn't spoken to him since Easter when she'd phoned him from California. Another Hollywood stalker case—one, to her relief, which hadn't ended in murder though the potential had run high. *Sleazeballs*, she nearly spoke aloud before again thinking of Max.

Insanity, he would tell her patiently. Whether through pathology or physiology, no one with a penchant for extreme violence and a disposition toward murder could be sane. Nuts, every one of them, and she refused to believe the theory that every infant carried the ingredients to become a serial killer. If she ever fully accepted that premise, Ronnie might incline to condemn the entire human race. What a lonely state of affairs that would be . . . even if it were true.

Glancing at the digital, she pushed from her chair, collected her notebook and recorder, and tucked both into her camera case. She wouldn't need either before this evening. The smaller notebook in her purse was far easier to manage and far less intimidating to potential interviewees.

As an afterthought, Ronnie pulled her hairbrush from her oversized purse that resembled a knapsack. Absently, she yanked at her curls and nearly cursed aloud when she found her lipstick tube already in her hand. Eyes too large, her nose too long, she wore her father's pointed chin and her mother's high cheekbones, a combination that had never impressed her even when potential lovers had showered her with praise. Her brothers were handsome. All three of those wretches had inherited her mother's eyes and soft walnut locks. She wore her father's eye color, black hair, and his disposition. Softening her scowl, Ronnie dabbed a pastel pink gloss on her fat lips. In a pinch, she might apply enough cosmetics to be pretty, but she'd certainly never land on the front of a fashion magazine. Her lips twisted in a wry smile. She'd gladly settle for Newsweek or Time if her writing ever reached such acclaim.

Like every damn journalist in the world, she would love to wrap her grubby little fingers around a Pulitzer Prize, but that goal paled compared to the thrill of seeing another maniac behind bars. If something in her investigations stopped this maniac, she'd be more than satisfied with her success.

Armed and dangerous, Ronnie mused as she headed for the door, checking her slacks pocket for her room key before passing into the carpeted hall.

The Bentwood House truly was lovely, every bit as austere as a Bed and Breakfast in Switzerland where she and her parents had stayed on one of their rare family holidays. The scents of old carpet, beeswax, and lemon vied for prominence against the aroma from an overflowing vase of lilacs that followed her toward the main staircase. An ancient elevator existed, but the wide staircase offered the quickest, if not safest, route to the first floor. A hum of voices flowed from a wide doorway below, and Ronnie recalled her brief glimpse of the elegant dining room when checking in earlier. Linen tablecloths, crystal centerpieces, and silver flatware provided fine dining, and by the steady drone of voices, the restaurant catered to the public rather than hotel guests.

Barely glimpsing at the spindly woman who poised behind the tall registration counter, Ronnie continued across the parlor and through the front doors where leaded glass swans created colorful prisms on the shined wood floor.

This wasn't DC with its blasting horns, raging engines, and rancid exhaust fumes. Disorienting, the fresh floral scents off a scattering of trees and flowerboxes countered any thought of a city and accounted for her decision to leave her car in the Inn's rear parking lot. Walking the two blocks to the municipal building served a dual purpose, anyway, saving her from finding a parking space and offering her an opportunity to grasp the ambiance of Bentwood.

If the murder had upset the natural harmony of the town, the signs remained invisible to the casual observer. Cars parked along both sides of Maine. Adults meandered with purpose into one shop or another. Children swept past on bicycles. One golden-haired child nearly collided with a parking meter when he looked over his shoulder, lancing Ronnie with his bright brown eyes. A smile playing on her lips, she adopted a sauntering pace and nearly tripped when reading the alleged new release on the theater marquee.

Halted momentarily, she read the painted ticket price on the glass booth within the shadowy entrance. A buck seventy-five? One fifty for the matinee showing at 1: pm? Suffering a mild case of vertigo, she continued her stride. A misprint or a joke, surely. She hadn't seen an indoor theater charge under three dollars in ten years. Progress.

Shaking her head, Ronnie cast her interests ahead, tempted to photograph two older fellows loitering on a park bench on the corner. One sported a fetching fishing hat reflective of Cain's coat of many colors, complete with a license dangling alongside a lure from the back; the other held a newspaper open on his lap and might be reading the stock exchange on a quiet bench in Central Park. A retired doctor or dentist if his suit and tie were any indications.

Her attention spun in time to watch the two kamikaze bicyclists dash across Maine against the red light. Both boys skidded under the elegant gray awning and dismounted in front of the shaded windows of Olden Time Antiques and Collectibles. Leaning their bikes on a strip of corner brick, they engaged the window with cupped hands, their noses pressed to the glass. Isaac Bently garnered a strange following if those youngsters were awaiting his doors to open.

She might need to pay homage to Olden Time Antiques and Collectibles, after all, and a wry grin slid into her lips as she spotted the neon blond hair behind the glass of a hardware store on the next corner.

'Andover's Hardware and Sporting Goods,' Ronnie read as she crossed the side street, deliberately angling her head to scan the display windows. Handmade posters cluttered the glass, boasting sales on everything from nails to bailing twine, nearly obliterating the interior displays of name-brand paint and shiny garden tools. Through narrow slots, Ronnie glimpsed spades and picks, as well as pitchforks, standing in a neat row on a pegboard wall.

Had the same weapon been used in both 'accidents?' Was it old or new? Could a pitchfork be traced or differentiated by the manufacturer's style? Were different grades of metals used, and could those be processed to identify the murder weapon? Depending on who was overseeing the forensics, those questions could be answered soon.

Several ahead, a silver-haired woman stepped from the entrance of a beauty salon, her hair impressively coifed to enhance her slender cheeks, adding depth and cushioning some of the brassy tones of her powdered complexion. The woman started a smile meant for a familiar face. Her rouged lips froze, and her gaze intensified as she nodded curtly and veered sharply toward the street.

Small town courtesy?

In a huddle at the far corner of the counter, the two boys perused the pages of their latest Baseball Card Collectors Guide. Systematically, they rummaged through the two shoeboxes that Isaac had lifted from the glass case. By the Grace of the Almighty, Isaac had remembered to restock at least one of the boxes before igniting the overhead lights and unlocking the front doors. An occasional pop of bubble gum issued from the youngest of the pair, Denny Claymore; short hoots of excitement erupted from the elder, Wade Kreider, a lanky twelve-year-old with a mop of nearly golden waves.

Neither sound offered a distraction as Isaac continued the perusal of his ledgers. Originating in the stereo in his office, the sounds of his latest symphony cassette tape echoed from the wall speakers at every corner of the shop. The renaissance notes muffled the brief arguments to arise over one card or another before the boys settled debates with their books.

For propriety's sake, Isaac had moved his ledger and a partial stack of the daily tickets from his office to the glass counter near the register. One boot hooked on the open shelf under the counter, he sent an occasional glance toward the youngsters. Stifling a smile, he heard Denny break his generally reserved countenance and nearly howl his delight with the card he'd just discovered.

Maintaining his feigned preoccupation, Isaac heard them attempting to temper their excitement. He sensed them watching him and understood their discreet whispers. Between them, they schemed how best to buy the card for their joint assets of ten dollars and eighty-five cents. The son of Rev. Claymore from First Holy Trinity was as honest as time on all matters except baseball card trading; he was a natural-born swindler, which only amused Isaac more.

Eavesdropping, Isaac halfheartedly crossed off more sale items, more content than he cared to consider with this wily pair plotting how best to skin him. He wouldn't trade this Saturday afternoon ritual for the world, he mused while recalling his own bit part in this enterprise.

Like every other divorced, single, separated, or widowed woman in Bentwood, Lynn Kreider had visited his shop two years earlier with her young son in tow. And like every other local female, the lovely lady had more on her mind than buying knickknacks. With a little help from Wade, Isaac had long ago forgiven her. Any woman who could raise a kid like Wade solo deserved an award as well as respect.

Even before the bells jingled, announcing an arrival, a prickle lifted at the nape of Isaac's neck. He lost the comfort of the atmosphere the instant he glimpsed the neon hair. Jen Andover was neither a welcome sight nor distraction, advancing breezily down the center aisle.

From the corner, Wade uttered, "Shit."

Sharing the sentiment, Isaac turned his attention to the ledger, not entirely faking his smile as Denny snapped, "You and your danged cussing." Apparently, they'd settled on the Topps card that Isaac had planted along with their best course of action to fleece him. Neither welcomed the interruption or delay.

"Hi ya, handsome," Jen said as she slowed her advance, sashaying the last few paces.

As much as he'd enjoyed the quiet ambiance of his shop a moment ago, Isaac suddenly wished a flood of customers would pour through the front door. A dozen impatient antique dealers would be easier to manage than one lascivious blond who never seemed to catch the drift of his indifference. And he had only himself to blame for her blasted persistence. Forcing a smile, Isaac collected receipts glimpsing at her breasts, somehow mounded higher than in the diner as if deliberately enhanced and presented as a banquet feast. At the same time, Jen flashed an annoyed glance toward the boys huddled and hissing in the corner.

Thank you, lads, he nearly muttered aloud as he tucked the receipts into the ledger. "Thought you were working this afternoon," he commented while judging the time near one. 'Around one,' Veronica Bryson had suggested, but he'd sensed her lie. Should he thank her for this distraction?

Flippantly, Jen shrugged, her bright red lips smiling, her blue eyes fixed with an enticing shine. "Not too many people shopping today, what with poor Mr. Engler dying last night."

Mr. Engler hadn't just died, as in drifted off in his sleep or keeled over into his plate of roast beef and potatoes. Between the gossip overheard in the diner, and his two young guests adding insight, Isaac had verified his suspicion. Fred Engler had been murdered; however, watching Jen slink in front of his register, Isaac decided not to correct her mistake.

In a slinky move, she draped her forearm over the brass scrolled top of the antique register and rested her chin on her wrist. Her pixie face looming between neon waves, she smiled. "Thought I'd come and pay a neighborly visit, and since we didn't have time over breakfast, I want to hear all about your trip."

"Not a great deal to tell," he commented, lifting his cigarettes from his shirt pocket. "The weather was hot, humid, and it rained more days than not."

"Oh, come on, darling," she said with an enticing curve in her lips, a shine in her eyes. "It couldn't have been as boring as all that. Now tell me the truth," she pouted, pursing her lips. "I bet you have a dozen women tucked away over in those villages."

Undeterred by her pout grating his nerves, Isaac kept his smile while canting his head to catch a flame to the butt.

Still pouting, she continued, "I can just imagine all the little peasant maidens traipsing after you wherever you go."

Far from peasants, he corrected silently, recalling several pleasant moments on more than one terrace. Doubtful enlightening Jen Andover would win him any favor. Shaking his head, Isaac sensed the young ears perking up at the end of the counter and stifled a laugh, speaking in a wistful tone. "If only," he sighed elaborately, shading his gaze from Jen's accusing glare. "What a pleasure it might have been to hole up in a quiet little Inn with the rain hammering the hell out of a thatch roof." Amused, he glimpsed her livid eyes, deciding against fueling fires. "Unfortunately, there's little romance when one happens to get stuck in a foot of mud and ruins a perfectly good pair of boots while wading through a torrential downpour. Not exactly what I'd consider a romantic interlude."

Her expression softened; her lashes dipped more dreamily. Her eyes misted as she reached and touched his arm. "I just love to hear you talk," she said in a quieter tone. "Especially after one of your trips. You always come back with a little more of an English accent."

He'd spent nearly a third of his life on the far side of the Atlantic. Picking up the accent came naturally. Shrugging, Isaac commented, "It'll wear off."

"I hope not," she said while brushing her hand over his forearm. "Why don't we plan on dinner this evening, darling? My house, around seven? We'll consider it a welcome home celebration."

"Sorry," he said with a thought of Meg's pork chops. A fleeting strangeness dashed the humor from his mind. Absently, he added, "Prior engagement."

Unconsciously, he glanced toward the front of his shop, spotting an elder couple veering toward his doors. The gentleman held the door for the woman. Out-of-towners . . . posing as antique dealers? The man wore a white sailing cap with a thin brim cocked rakishly over silver-streaked hair. The woman, all summer-tanned and dressed in a stylish beige-shorts ensemble, carried herself with natural elegance. Genuine articles . . . or frauds? And what was this sudden suspicion of strangers in town?

CHAPTER 4

Behind closed doors, the Bentwood phone lines were humming and voices railing. Only on the surface, the town evoked a lazy veneer for the unsuspecting visitor. Even in a larger community, however, Ronnie knew the mention of a murder could have a dramatic effect. Windows would be locked tight; doors bolted for the first time on rusted hinges; televisions and radios would be turned up, not off when the evening news came on. Newspaper sales would increase one hundredfold.

Strolling through the historical atmosphere, Ronnie half-expected to see a youngster pop from an entrance sporting a golfer-style cap and suspenders. Flagging a newspaper in the air, he'd likely be shouting, 'Extra! Extra! Read all about it!' The cast-iron light posts and park benches lent themselves to the imagination and created visions from another era. She wouldn't be surprised to see a horse and buggy hitched to one of the parking meters ahead.

Instead, she spotted a small crowd on the next block. As she drew nearer the conclave, she recognized enough of the signs to suspect these were her local colleagues. Three men, one wearing a brimmed hat in reflection of Dick Tracy, clustered around a burly young man who stood shaking his head as the trio scratched notes on pocket-sized books.

Three other men stood off to one side. One of those, a mid-aged gentleman wearing casual slacks and a wrinkled shirt, leaned against the fire-red brick, scowling as he watched and apparently listened to the rebounding questions. A woman, probably in her late thirties, or early forties, stood idly aside, silently taking notes.

Advancing, Ronnie heard enough questions to realize this was either Vic or Calvin Farnsworth, a son of the first victim. She might have guessed as much without hearing the words. The poor kid looked like a zombie, with his pale complexion drawn over rugged cheeks and dark patches under his eyes. He stood with his hands shoved in the pockets of his faded jeans, his pale blue eyes drifting listlessly from one man to the other. His shaggy light brown hair hung in a loose wave across his knitted brows.

"... How's your mother holding up? ... Have the police told you how Mr. Engler died? ... Do they have any new suspects? ... Is your sister still in the hospital? ..."

Undoubtedly, Farnsworth had come here to ask the same questions, and seeing the lost look in his eyes, Ronnie's heart went out to him.

"Come on, Cal," the stoutest of the trio nearly pleaded. He wore a wrinkled jacket and a loose tie if only for aesthetic effect. "Just answer a few questions. We're all friends here. What did your mom say when she heard about Fred Engler—"

"If you gentlemen are his friends, I'd certainly hate to encounter his enemies," Ronnie intruded quietly.

All three gentlemen pivoted their focus toward her, but only the slovenly fellow scowled and scoffed.

Piercing each with a chilly gaze, Ronnie lost her edge while looking into the distressed blue eyes. Donning a faint smile, she offered her hand, forcing the Farnsworth to move if only to break through his trauma.

He appeared shell-shocked and uncertain, but he extracted one callused hand. Not a child or slight of build. He stood at least 6' and probably weighed closes to 250 lbs. in contrast to his gaunt features under a shade of beard stubble.

As Ronnie clasped his hand, she spied scrapes on his knuckles and identified a pungent odor of cow manure wafting from his weathered jeans and shirt. "I'm Veronica Bryson. My friends call me Ronnie. I'd imagine your name's Cal Farnsworth?"

"Yes, ma'am," he answered hesitantly, his eyes animating slowly, curiosity raising his knitted brow.

Working undercover in a town this size would be counterproductive, if not impossible. "I'm a journalist," she admitted bluntly. "I know how difficult this must be for you and your family. You have my deepest sympathies," she said quietly and squeezed the hand she still held, feeling the delayed response.

"Thank you, ma'am," he said listlessly.

"Please, Mr. Farnsworth, call me Ronnie," she said lightly.

"A-Alright. I uh ... just Cal," he stammered in confusion. "My uh ... my pap. He was *mister*."

"I understand," she said and clasped her free hand over their grip, feeling the chafed knuckles under her palm as grating as the hurt in his eyes. Victims. Always there were victims, and the list spiraled outward to the living. "As much as I understand why you're here," she continued quietly, keeping her voice gentle. "There's probably not a great deal the police could tell you at the moment."

"They uh ... they said it could take time," he admitted. "Sam ... I mean Chief Hayward said they don't have all the facts in yet."

"I'm sure he's being honest with you, Cal," she said carefully. "There's really no reason for you to subject yourself to this. When Chief Hayward has his facts in order, if this incident is connected to your own tragedy, you and your family will be among the first notified."

Nodding, Cal grumbled, "That's what he said, too."

"I'd imagine your mother asked you to come here this morning," she said on a hunch.

Pain, as well as confirmation, flickered in his eyes as he nodded.

"Unfortunately, there's not much you can accomplish," Ronnie stated firmly, already scanning the nearest street. Undoubtedly, the dented pickup belonged to him, but Ronnie refrained from a possible offense, asking instead, "Is your vehicle nearby?"

He glanced at the pickup and nodded. "That's mine."

Still holding his hand, Ronnie started him toward the street.

"Hey!" the stout fellow intruded, nearly stepping into Ronnie's path. "What do you think you're—"

"What you should have done, sir," Ronnie snapped, lancing the saggy jowled reporter in a fiery glance. "There's no reason for this young man to be badgered by the press regardless of your motives. Now, if you will excuse us?" Without awaiting a response, she nudged Cal forward, not releasing his hand until they halted in front of his pickup. Looking into his more curious, more confused eyes, she managed a weak smile. "I'm a journalist. Not a sensationalist reporter," she clarified quietly and reached in her pocket, finding her leather business card holder. Subterfuge had never served her well and keeping her cards handy simplified matters in an interview. Slipping a card from the case, she handed him one and waited as he read her credentials. "If you wouldn't mind, Cal, I'd like the opportunity to speak to you and your mother at your earliest convenience."

"M-My ma doesn't want to speak to anyone," he grumbled, spying her reluctantly.

Again, her heart reached out to him, and she softened her tone, refraining from the hard sell she'd enlisted in other circumstances. "I can understand that, hon, but sometimes it helps to talk to someone. I can promise you I wouldn't push her. I do know what she's going through, and I can promise you, I wouldn't write anything contrary to what she'd agree to share." Pausing, having said enough, she touched his arm. "Give your mother my condolences, Cal, and if she agrees to speak to me, you can reach me at the Bentwood House. Whenever is convenient for you would be fine. In the meantime, if I hear anything you should know, I'd be happy to keep you informed."

"Would you . . . I mean, you'd call us?"

"Yes, I would," she said honestly.

"It's not right," he said as his pale blue eyes shifted and his hip sank against the grill of the pickup. Not in focus, he gazed down Maine St. "My pa . . . He didn't deserve this . . . Now, Mr. Engler." His gaze returned, hurt, and laced with anger. "Who . . . who would do this? Why? Why would someone do this?"

She could think of a hundred reasons, only beginning with the neurological screws of the human psyche, but none would answer this man's questions. "I wish I knew, Cal," she admitted quietly.

"If Mr. Engler w-was found the same way, then they were wrong," he said unexpectedly. Again, he scanned Maine as if seeking answers. "And I kn-knew they were wrong," he continued. "My pa . . . he never hardly picked a fight in his life. Me . . . Vic . . . we're hotheads, but pa always said that was our Stanley genes. Said we got it from Ma's family. He w-was a lover." A tense smile crooked his rugged lips, and a subtle shine lifted in his eyes. "N-not a fighter," he added as his focus slid to Ronnie. "That's what he always said. So . . . so it just don't make sense, ya know? Why—why the he-eck would someone want to—to stab him? And not just once. They said it was close to twenty times." Even with his stammering, he spoke with an edge and his listless veneer cracked under a shine of tears.

"Twenty fu-freaking times . . . and oh, Jesus . . . the . . . the blood," he whispered as his head pivoted. Blinking, swallowing, he forced back tears, straining. "I—I was raised on a farm . . . all my life," he heaved softly. "Butchered hogs . . . steers . . . and I'm never gonna get this outa my head. Not ever."

Feeling his horror, his pain, Ronnie reached instinctively to clasp his hand, holding tight as she blinked against a sting in her eyes. "Were you the one to find him, Cal?" she asked softly.

After a tense second, he nodded slightly, and a near-desperate shine lifted in his pale blue eyes. "I—I think they—they thought I did it," he admitted with a strain. "J-just 'til mamma could t-talk to them, ya know? I uh . . . I was working late that night. Ma . . . when I come in . . . she was dozing in front of the set and that—that was weird enough, ya know? Cause most nights, by the time I come in . . . they—they were asleep."

Interviewing the family member of a victim on a busy street wasn't Ronnie's general routine or style, but this young man needed to talk. Despite the unfavorable conditions, she could only stand and listen, heart in hand, afraid to interrupt the outpour although she'd love to engage her tape recorder. Ethics, damn it. Unless she asked his permission . . .

". . . It was after midnight. Don't remember just how much . . . And there was ma, joltin' awake on the couch, scaring the he-ell outa me . . ." Worrying instantly that his father hadn't come in from the evening chores. "I 'member telling her the barn lights were all off, and pa's pickup was still in the driveway. Thought maybe he was already upstairs. Maybe in the tub or something. . . ."

For a long time, Cal stood gazing down Maine St., his pale blue eyes glazed with the memory. Before a month ago, he'd probably been a cocky and confident man. At this moment, he just appeared lost and haunted.

"Hon," Ronnie interrupted gently and squeezed his hand, drawing his attention. "Why don't we talk about this after you've spoken to your mother? I'm sure she's waiting for news—"

"I—I wouldn't let her go in," he continued quietly, his gaze losing the cobweb haze. "I c-couldn't let her g-go in there . . . not the—the way I found him," he said and focused on Ronnie, his gaze direct, determined, as if he'd just reached an important decision. "I—I couldn't m-move until I heard her c-calling us, ya know? I—I just s-stood there, l-like my boots were stuck in m-mud. There's my pa . . . h-he was s-sprawled out r-right inside the door. I—I can remember opening the door . . . and hitting the light switch then . . . then it's like I was stuck. I—I couldn't e-even scream . . . j-just in my head, ya know?"

She did know. She knew exactly how he'd felt opening that door, hitting the switch, turning. First, the prickling skin with senses keening to the feral scent of blood, a primal sense quickening . . . and suddenly, too paralyzed, too shocked, too horrified even to scream.

Squeezing his cold, damp hand, Ronnie nodded slightly while suffering the tremors from his memories. "It's okay," she said softly, needing to end this interview. Now. This wasn't how she began an investigation. Facts, clinical facts came first. Clinical facts served to distance her from the events. She would rather see a black and white 8"x10" of the victim than feel the pain and horror of the living victims this early. Once she built the distance, then she could listen and empathize. She could sympathize . . . at a distance.

"I—I n-never been able to tell anybody," he said quietly, his gaze steady now. "I couldn't e-even tell Vic or Val, ya know?" he strained, truly struggling against a well of tears. "I-I'm the oldest . . . the-they always looked up t-to me, ya know?" On safer ground, he collected a breath and managed a weak smile. "They're both in college, ya know? I mean they're doing okay. Val—Val's gonna be a secretary," he huffed. "And Vic . . . he's really something—always has his head in a book. Me—I'm the only screw-up," he said with his false bravado crumbling, eyes glazing. "H-how could I t-tell them wh-what it's like t-to see . . . to see their pa . . . w-with a p-pitchfork s-sticking—"

As much as Ronnie would need those details sooner or later, this wasn't the time or place. Not the way she preferred to receive them. With his halt, she nearly sighed relief.

Head bowed, Cal fingered her card in one hand. His other hand had turned and clasped her fingers in a firm but gentle hold. Tremors coursed through his muscles. How lost he appeared, how desperately lost.

"I can't g-get it out of my head," he heaved softly and closed his eyes tight. "I just keep seeing him there . . . like that . . . over and over again."

"Hon," Ronnie started and stopped, swallowing a tightness in her throat. "It's okay."

He shook his bowed head slowly. "N-not okay," he uttered. "I can't s-sleep . . . ca-can't eat. Can't even go to work without seeing h-him." Slowly, his head lifted, his wet eyes strained. "H-how do you live with s-something like this? H-how do you just carry on when—when some-somebody l-leaves a p-pitchfork in y-your pa's throat after . . . after s-stabbing him twenty-something fu-freaking times?"

Damn it! More details! She didn't want to hear this! Not right now. Firming her resolve, her tone, she spoke quietly. "You get help, Cal. If not here . . . if there's no help available for victims of violent crime and their families in Bentwood, then you go to Pittsburgh or Cleveland." Recovering her footing, she continued, "This . . . It's not something you need to handle on your own. Not something you should even try to handle on your own."

"You . . . you've been through this?" he asked as his swimming eyes lifted, more intent even through the shine. "You've s-seen things like this."

She nodded slightly. "Enough to understand what you're feeling. What you're seeing," Ronnie admitted gently. "If you want, I'll find out who you should speak to."

"I'd appreciate that," he said with a slightly firmer voice. "I don't know what t-to say to people, ya know? I me-ean when they ask me h-how I'm doing. . .? I don't know what the hel—eck to say."

The first time he'd checked his curse words, Ronnie had wondered. Now, she knew. A testament to his parents, perhaps, that he wouldn't swear in front of a woman. Wholesome family values. Bentwood wasn't the Bronx. Smiling slightly, she squeezed his palm. "You'll be fine, Cal," she said lightly. "It'll take time, but you'll get through this, and you'll be alright. You don't have to say anything to anyone right now. When they ask, just tell them 'One day at a time.'"

He studied her for a long moment before a shadow of a smile haunted his beard-stubbled lips. Even that slight effect offered a glimmer of the young man beneath the grief. Not the most handsome man, but charming in a country style. "Thank you," he managed. "I think maybe I needed to hear somebody say that, ya know? M-maybe somebody who—who's been where I am."

"You're welcome," she said quietly.

"Are . . . are you really a journalist?"

She smiled slightly. "Really."

"Who uh . . . what paper d-do you write for?"

"I'm a freelance writer," she answered. "I've had articles in several major publications."

"You uh . . . you're g-gonna write about . . . about my pa?" he asked hesitantly.

"Exclusively, no," Ronnie admitted. "But with your and your family's permission, I may include whatever you'd be willing to share with me."

He considered her words momentarily, then nodded. "I'll talk to my ma," he decided and glanced toward the municipal building for the first time. Almost wearily, as if drained, his gaze listed, returning, attempting to focus. "If uh . . . if you hear something, you'll let me know? I mean, just me, ya know? I uh . . . I want to know before you talk to ma, or my brother and sister."

"Do you have a number where I could reach you?" Ronnie asked and awaited his nod before fishing her notebook from her purse. When she looked up, a slightly more tense smile quivered Cal's lips, and her spirits rose with her curiosity. Flipping open the notepad to a fresh sheet, she commented, "Don't tell me. You glimpsed the state of my purse and just decided I'm a wretched housekeeper."

"I uh . . ." His lips twitched, not fully smiling, but his eyes had lost a little of the listless glaze. "I was just thinking how you didn't look much like a reporter." He glanced down at her leather book. "But I guess you are."

Stifling a laugh, she jotted the home phone number he offered, along with his work number.

"Got to admit," he said offhandedly. "That's a lot nicer notebook than Ted's carrying." As he looked into her eyes, his manner changed subtly, somehow firming. "Guess I best be going, Ronnie," he spoke her nickname as if testing it on his tongue for future use, and if he wore a hat, he might have tipped it. "It was uh . . . it was good talking to you."

"Likewise, Cal," she said lightly. "I'll call you as soon as I hear anything substantial."

Providing the information wouldn't jeopardize the official investigation.

*Turning, she stepped onto t*he sidewalk and gleaned the sneers and snickers as she strode toward the municipal building. Only the fellow leaning near the door drew her interest. Instinct or intuition prickled her neck as she continued toward him.

If not for his black gaze, he would be easily lost in a crowd of three. His facial features rounded and squared without definition. Frosted gray, his brown hair receded and fell into a businessman's cut; sunlight shimmered, glistening on his balding crown and sweated forehead. Arms crossed and folded across his sagging midriff, he glowered, following Ronnie's progress through eyes as shiny and black as hot tar.

Maintaining her focus on the smoke-glass door, Ronnie sensed the man's hostility, ignoring the prickly glare until he spoke.

"You think you're pretty slick, huh, bitch?"

Hackles raised on the nape of her neck. Ronnie froze with her hand on the door handle and turned only her curious gaze to collide with the black shine. He was addressing her; his thin lips twitched in a snarl which might have lent him distinction in a crowd of two hundred. Withdrawing her hand, she veered, extending her palm and donning her most serene smile. "Do I know you, sir?"

"Yea," he growled, his black eyes flashing down and up in a scathing leer.

Skin crawling, Ronnie held her pose, unflinching as his lips twisted in a lewd, chiding smile.

"You think you're pretty slick, fucking with the kid, turning him all soft and chummy just so you can get out there and harass his ma. Let me tell you, bitch, you come sniffing around anywhere near my farm, if I even catch you breathing too close to any of my kin, I'll have you behind bars so fast, it'll make your head spin."

Engler, Ronnie realized and lost a little of her anger. Within arm's reach, she withdrew her hand and maintained a faint smile even with the chill frosting her tone. "Mr. Engler, under different circumstances, I might be inclined to consider you an asshole. Under these circumstances, you have my deepest sympathy, and if it relieves your pain to insult and prejudge me? By all means, continue to vent your hostility. You will excuse me, however, if I don't hang about for an encore." As she spoke, she judged the level of his distress by his black gaze and taut lips. Never burn bridges. "If you change your mind and feel a need to speak with me on more sociable terms, you may reach me at the Bentwood House Inn. I can assure you, I don't camp on a victim's doorstep or sneak around on their premises in search of tabloid-worthy sensationalism. Now, if you'll excuse me?" She turned without awaiting a response and returned to the door, trying the handle before lifting her knuckles and landing three solid blows.

"You don't really think you're gonna get in there, do you?" Engler sneered.

As she'd suspected, Mark wasn't too far from the inside door, and he opened it with weary resignation. "Mr. Jarvins, a word with you?"

Glancing past her to the reporters who'd gravitated toward her after giving Engler a wide birth, Mark's gaze returned, mocking disgust. "We're not making statements at this time. Or answering questions, Miss Bryson."

Anticipating the song and dance, mirroring the formal tone, Ronnie spoke with perfect confidence, "I have information that might be of interest to you, Mr. Jarvins. In all fairness to your investigation, I need a few moments of your time."

He studied her for a half-second, questioning her lie, then stepped aside, letting her slip through the crack. As the four reporters lunged, Mark yanked the door neatly closed behind him, and turned. His brows already drawn in the familiar arch that suggested annoyance, he managed a slight smile and commented, "I expected you a half-hour ago."

"It's her, huh?" The short soft hiss issued off brilliant fire-engine red lips. Anger narrowed Jen Andover's eyes, dipping the artificial lashes, threatening to crack her thick layer of careful cosmetics. "That snob you talked to over at Meg's . . . Virginia or Viola something? That's who you're seeing tonight."

Drawn from his silent commiseration, instantly annoyed, Isaac spied Jen's angry gaze. "Even if I were, I wouldn't apologize," he admitted as his attention divided. Near the front doors, the older couple meandered, browsing, apparently. Sooner than later, they'd need assistance.

Like a cat preparing to pounce, Jen uncoiled from her casual pose and snickered, "In case you're interested, babe, you should know, she was pawing all over those two Federal agents after you left this morning. It wouldn't surprise me one bit if she's one of them. She was sure having a quiet, heated little chat with the blond before she kissed the other one."

"I'm sure that's her business," Isaac said, halfheartedly wondering why Jen believed otherwise. On the elder couple, his attention keened as the woman lifted a delicate piece of Fry glass from the front window display. "Excuse me, Jen," he said lightly and crushed his cigarette butt before moving around the end of the counter. At a leisurely pace, he navigated through the side aisles, sizing up the older man's windbreaker and loafers, and the woman's white leather Gucci purse, before reaching them. judging by the multiple gems on the woman's fingers and a gold nugget wedding band on the gent's left hand, Isaac recognized the couple's affluence. The black Lincoln Continental parked at the curb out front completed the overall picture. "Anything I can help you with today?" Isaac asked while joining them.

The woman had passed the cut-glass serving bowl to her mate, and the gentleman inspected the piece a moment longer before eyeing Isaac over gold wire-rim sunglasses. "Any chance the owner's around today?"

Isaac held out his hand. "Isaac Bently. I'm him."

The man smiled, crooking his thick white mustache, accepting the handshake. "Leland Hunter. My wife, Myra," he offered.

Isaac touched the woman's hand, appreciating her smile, offering, "A pleasure, Mrs. Hunter."

"Likewise, Mr. Bently," she said lightly.

"We own a little shop over in New York," Hunter commented. "Hunter's Cabin. It's over near the Poconos. What's your dealer's discount?"

"Ten percent generally," Isaac answered smoothly.

Hunter nodded, inspected the intricately cut bowl for flaws or nicks then handed it to Isaac. "Nice piece of glass. Any chance you'll go lower than 10 percent?"

Extremely nice piece of glass, Isaac considered and glanced over the cut crystal, shaking his head, smiling. "I'd rather not. I'm fond of it, too."

Chuckling, Hunter commented, "Can't blame me for trying."

"No, sir, I can't," Isaac mused, relaxing for the first time since he'd driven into Bentwood last evening. "If you're interested in Fry, I have a few other unique pieces in the front case. I'll be glad to pull them out for you."

"If you don't mind, we'll just browse for a bit," Hunter commented.

"Take your time," Isaac said and barely leaned to return the glass to the front ledge.

Myra touched his arm, smiling. "If you'll take that to the counter, Mr. Bently? We'll take it."

"Be happy to," he said and withdrew with the bowl in hand, not entirely happy. "If you need anything, just give a shout, and if you need a break, I have a lounge in the back. The coffee's hot and fresh. Feel free to help yourself." Accepting the brief thanks, Isaac turned in time to see Jen slam through the front door. If he hadn't added a decent recoil spring, he might have needed to replace the glass, if not the entire door in her wake.

Offsetting a tingle under his collar, he carried the server to the counter, glimpsing at the boys swaggering in his direction. Wade, as usual, accepted the forward position to begin negotiations. Lifting a brow, Isaac sidled around the end of the counter, spying the card in the boy's grip and the determined knit of his golden brows. "Find something interesting?"

"Na, not too," Wade said nonchalantly and slid the Topps card on the counter. "But we might consider this guy here if you want to price him."

Lifting the unmarred card carefully, Isaac studied the name as if he'd never heard of the player before now, then flipped it over and pretended to read the stats. "Hmm, rookie card," he commented idly. "Old," he pondered and glanced between the two boys.

Wade appeared more hopeful; Denny wore thick glasses to mask the shrewd shine in his hazel eyes. Between his red-orange hair and freckles, Denny could pass for an innocent.

"What say, fifteen?" Isaac commented, starting the bid at less than half the card's current value. "It's in good shape and vintage."

"Pretty steep," Wade said idly, though he couldn't douse the fire of hope rising in his eyes as he glimpsed his scowling partner.

"Fifteen's just plain nuts," Denny scoffed. "It's just an old piece a cardboard with a face on it."

"It's a pristine piece of cardboard with a fairly famous face on it," Isaac countered. "I mean, gees, lads, I may not be current on stats and teams, but I seem to recall hearing this name a time or two."

Wade barely started an enthusiastic attempt to educate Isaac on the player's stats, but Denny elbow-jabbed him hard enough to drive the wind from his sails, if not the air from his lungs. Eyebrows furrowed and mouth clamped, Wade glared at his smaller comrade.

Scowling, Denny said, "More like three bucks, you ask me, Mr. Bently. What do you say?"

"I'm being snookered," Isaac lamented. "Three bucks? That's less than you paid for that Donruss three weeks ago, and I did some checking on that, lads. Skinned me clean, I've come to know."

Wade barely started to apologize when Denny jabbed him again. With Denny's spindly arms and his pointed elbow, the larger boy grimaced while stepping aside. "If you don't—"

"Come on, Mr. Bently," Denny persisted. His magnified eyes expressed pure innocence behind the lenses while his lips pursed in feigned indignation. "That was a good sale, and you know it. The card was all dog-eared and stuff. Can't expect to get top money out of these old beat-up cards. Five bucks. That's as good as you'll get for that card there."

From Denny Claymore and Wade Kreider, Isaac agreed while considering the twenty he'd spent to buy the card six months earlier . . . and the card dealer had been generous. "Five, huh?" Isaac considered while holding the unblemished card. If he hurried, he might return the card to its plastic holder and spare its pristine sharp edges. Looking to Denny with consternation, Isaac decided, "Six dollars, and I'll throw in a plastic holder."

"Not one of those cheap ones I could buy for ten cents," Denny decided. "It's gotta be one of the solid kinds."

"You are one tough character, Mr. Claymore," Isaac sighed as if beaten and slid the card carefully onto the glass in front of their folded forearms. "Should I take this to mean you two have settled on this one card? Or should I prepare to be skinned out of a few more?"

Denny always held the trump cards. He brought his hand up and handed over the half dozen others they'd uncovered in their digs.

This pair was worse than typical card sharks, Isaac wagered as he scanned each card, setting them down like a poker hand one at a time. Taking a moment, he lighted a cigarette, tucking one hand into his back pocket to appear concentrated and tense. Denny had relaxed now. The battle half-won, he rested with his forearms crossed on the metal edge of the glass top. Wade had recoiled. He stood aside, his cheeks burning red with shame over the scam. An odd pair, Isaac considered. Knowing a little about Wade's past, one would expect him to be callous and sneaky, if not outright mean. Lynn Kreider was one tough lady.

When Isaac blew his first exhale of smoke, Denny accepted his cue to comment, "We'll give you ten bucks for the whole lot."

"Thieves," Isaac huffed and glanced between them. Wade's eyes darted away, more embarrassed. "But I suppose, since you're two of my regulars, I'll have to cut you some slack this time." As if resigning, Isaac offered his hand across the counter to Denny, "You have a deal."

"Na, you're getting the deal," Denny said confidently, but he shook on the venture.

"Wade?" Isaac said and offered his hand.

Not happily, the boy lifted his hand, fleeting a glance. "Thanks, Mr. Bently." Quite a bit of the delight had ebbed from Wade's mind. The boy had apparently read and understood the books well enough to estimate they were purchasing fifty dollars' worth of cards.

Isaac squeezed the hand in a quick, firm clasp, deciding, "I'll make you two another deal if you're interested?"

Both sets of ears perked up; Wade anxious to make amends.

"I'm a little shorthanded around here this afternoon. If you two don't have any plans and you'd stick around for a little while—maybe carry things for those customers over there—I'll give you those cards."

"Gees, you serious?" Wade asked before Denny, the more practical and pragmatic where the cards were concerned, could jab him.

"How long would you want us to stay?" Denny asked.

"Hmm, maybe about a half-hour," Isaac decided. "That should give me time to finish my paperwork here, and it will more than cover those cards."

"You got a deal!" Wade said before Denny could find breath to interrupt. "Want me to go ask if they need some help yet?"

"Let's wait a few moments," Isaac decided and glanced at the couple, presently critiquing the Coalport set on the dining room table across the showroom. Isaac suddenly hoped they didn't purchase it but knew his hope was in vain. He should have asked a blasted outlandish price for that set. Wrapping and boxing over eighty pieces of dinnerware could take the better part of the afternoon, and he'd need most of the evening to locate the Haviland set in his warehouse, not to mention washing and arranging the entire collection on the Duncan Phyfe table.

Not only would he be busy packing eighty pieces of fine china . . . he glanced to the door as the bells jangled. He was about to be inundated with customers who'd probably spent the morning canvassing flea markets and yard sales.

Glancing between the boys, Isaac commented, "Mind the store for a moment, will you, lads? I believe I have a plastic holder in my office." The holder from which he'd removed the card a few hours earlier rested on the corner of his desk, and he paused en route to turn up the air conditioner. It was about to become an awfully long hot afternoon.

As he stepped from his office, Isaac spied the golden hair near the front of the store.

Echoing beneath a symphony of classical music, the young voice piped up, "Hello, welcome to Olden Time. Anything I can help you with today?"

God, that's my line! Isaac stifled a smirk and glimpsed at Denny's smug smile from where he now posed behind the counter, arms crossed on the inside ledge. "Swindlers," Isaac tossed down at the boy, who grinned while holding up the cherished card to receive the plastic case.

"You charge two hundred and fifty bucks for a chunk of glass," Denny said while glancing at the crystal bowl. Lifting a toothy grin to show two missing incisors, he finished, "You sure can't call us swindlers, meaning no disrespect, Mr. Bently."

In spite of himself, Isaac chuckled, "Right." He handed the boy the card along with a half dozen heavy plastic jackets for the others.

Maybe the afternoon wouldn't be too bad, after all.

CHAPTER 5

Only a soft static hum of distant voices penetrated the walls of the municipal building, none elevated to offer a clear word, but Ronnie could imagine the tension behind those locked doors. The headquarters of a manhunt. She and Mark stood in a small alcove, a receiving room with a sliding glass window connecting a second room. Behind the glass, the office was dark. A few computer-printed signs were taped to the glass, designating bounced-check procedures, boasting the latest tax bills, and offering updates on payment procedures and billing schedules. No chairs or potted plants. A single black and white photo of an old firehouse, boasting a firetruck and three-man crew centered on an interior wall—1930s vintage at first glance.

Looking at Mark, Ronnie commented, "Suppose leaving we humble members of the press on the sidewalk is your idea of mercy if this is the waiting lobby for the precinct."

"You still sore at me?" he asked.

"Don't flatter yourself," she said in a lofty tone, then forfeited the game and sobered entirely, looking into his deceptively calm gaze. "Make me happy and tell me you have a very small but serious list of suspects on this one, Mark."

"I'd be lying," Jarvins said lightly and glanced about, looking for a place where he might suggest they sit. "Was that smoke, or do you have something for me?"

"When did you get here?"

"Around midnight," he answered, letting her evade the question.

"The MO's the same."

"You know I can't verify that," he said with a slight edge that didn't wear well on him. The job had taken a toll over the past few years.

"You already have," Ronnie said quietly. "New weapon or old?"

"Old," he answered, irritated.

"Prints or partials?"

"None so far," he answered.

"Don't make me work for this, Mark," she said carefully. "You know damn full well I won't interfere in your investigation, and nothing goes in print before you give the go-ahead."

"Don't make me kick your butt out of here," he said with a twitch of a smile. "I'd feel bad about kicking such a pretty little toosh."

"I can see you're crying already," Ronnie mused. "But you do know I had to try, don't you? So . . . local coroner doing the autopsy or one of your own?"

"Joint venture," he answered. "It's being handled through the county coroner's office."

"Be a sport and give me his name," she smiled.

"Mike Harvey," he supplied with a twitch. "Have dinner with me tonight and swap war stories? I believe we're staying at the same Inn, and there's a decent dining room."

"I'll let you know," she said without missing a beat. "Who's doing the forensic work?"

"One of ours," Jarvins answered.

If Ronnie had known him less, she never would've seen or recognized the subtle flash of dread in his pale blue eyes. "Roberta's here?" she guessed and hoped.

"Smart alack," he said bluntly, but his smile returned to twitch. "Next question, and make it snappy, I have an investigation to conduct."

"You're doing the profile," she said lightly without needing verification. "Any chance you can draw a picture yet?"

"Next question."

Reading his bland expression, Ronnie received enough of an answer not to press. "Full moon last night," she commented. "Twenty-nine days ago, full."

"Please don't tell me that was your big lead," he sighed.

"Did the killer strike from the front or back?"

"Ronnie, you're toeing over the line just a nail's length."

"Is Sam Hayward heading the investigation or Sheriff Grant?"

"Joint venture," Jarvins answered.

"I'd like to see the pictures, Mark," she said quietly, ignoring his flash of anger and dread. Unwavering, she watched his silent battle. "You know, the only difference between you and me is that while you carry a badge, I carry a press card."

"That's one helluva difference, dear, and I can name several others which could probably land me in deep shit up to my ears."

His smile was cute but as fake as a three-dollar bill. "Why don't we skip all the fancy talk, *dear*?" she mocked lightly. "We both know I can add something to this investigation if given a chance, or I wouldn't be standing here."

"You haven't changed much, honey," he commented. "When are you going to flush that press card and come to work where you can really do some good?"

"When I decide to change my wardrobe," she said smoothly. "I look horrible in black flats and blazers."

"Tell you what," he said while breezing a glance at his watch. "I have a meeting starting in a few minutes." His gaze lifted. "Why don't you try to stay out of trouble for a few hours, and I'll meet you back at the Inn around five?"

"Sorry," Ronnie decided on the instant. "I have a prior engagement and a great deal of ground to cover if I intend to catch up with you. If I get back early enough, maybe we'll share a glass of wine on the terrace." *That didn't exist.* With her words, she started around him, then paused with a thought. "Any chance you could locate a recent local map for an old pal?"

He stifled a laugh and shook his head, starting toward the door alongside the sliding window. "Give me a second. I'll see what I can do." He passed through the smoke-glass door and returned before Ronnie could read the framed faded newspaper story below the old firehouse photograph. Handing her a map, Mark dipped in a slick move and brushed a quick kiss on her lips. Amused by her surprise, his eyes conveyed a deeper shine to assure her that the flame hadn't entirely doused.

"I meant what I said, Ron," he said quietly. "I have missed you, and the invitation's open for dinner."

"Mm-hmm," Ronnie muttered, uncertain whether to be annoyed or flattered by this latent show of affection. "Thanks for the map, Mark," she said and retreated rather hastily, almost certain if she turned, she would see him smirk. Preoccupied, she stepped onto the sidewalk, startled when three angry reporters descended, hurling as many questions as accusations. Shaking her head, Ronnie passed between them, commenting, "Forget it, gentlemen. They're playing this close to the cuff."

With disgusted harrumphs and grumbles, they retreated to linger outside the doors. If they truly sought information, they'd probably have more luck sitting in a back alley or standing guard at one of the side-street entrances. Undoubtedly, the collection of authorities behind those closed doors would make a few of those ace reporters swoon.

Joint endeavor. Local, county, state, and federal agents.

First stop, the public library, Ronnie plotted while setting a course toward the north end of town. Back issues of the local paper would supply the visuals on Sam Hayward and Sheriff Grant. She wanted to recognize those fellows when she approached them, and if she stumbled across the faces of a few local officers in the process that would be just fine. Mark apparently intended for her to work and wait before entrusting her with any useful information. In the meantime, a little exercise never hurt.

Glancing at the beauty salon windows, Ronnie glimpsed women in various stages of hair treatment and decided a visit might be in order. On impulse, however, she veered into the alcove entrance of Andover's Hardware Store, deciding not to postpone that bit of research.

Hand-crafted signs covered the glass door, an 'Open' sign centered the collage, and the handle gave way under a push. Six wide aisles extended the length of the store; well-worn hardwood floors creaked underfoot. Everything from gardening supplies to plywood sheets stacked against the outside walls and crowded the shelves. In an oddly cluttered organization, plumbing fixtures in bins or on pegboards occupied one side of an aisle while car supplies from oil to floor mats occupied the other.

The neon blond was nowhere in sight, and Ronnie glanced at her wristwatch with a wry smile. A little past one o'clock. Without a need for imagination, she knew why the young woman had stood inside the hardware store window with a clear view of the antique shop on the next corner.

"Looking for anything in particular, miss?"

An ancient, cluttered counter stood to the left of the entrance. A slight, thinning-haired fellow with a round, flushed face stood behind the battered top, contemplating Ronnie with a crook in his thin gray brows. He wore an apron more befitting a chef than a carpenter over a crisp white shirt.

Ronnie strode toward the counter, glimpsing the selection of farm and garden tools that hung and stood in the front window. She'd wanted a closer look at those tools, had hoped for a few seconds alone to check manufacture stamps and construction. One long-handled fork sported five round iron spikes; another shorter, grip-handled pitchfork carried only four flattened prongs, and yet another appeared plastic with the prongs fashioned close together to look like a grass rake. Reaching the counter, she scanned the back pegboard. Car care items from air fresheners to key rings mixed with an abundance of household items from feather dusters to toilet bowl cleaners. Meeting the curious gaze, she asked, "Do you have batteries?"

"Sure do, miss," he said politely and gestured to a small display toward the end of the counter while ambling in that direction. "What size will you be needing, then?"

If only to prompt a conversation, Ronnie lifted her camera from her purse, and the ploy worked beautifully. In mere minutes, she learned the man's name was Carl Andover. The blond bimbo was his daughter. He was a widower and a former mayor . . . and what had happened to Vic and Fred was beyond conceivable. Without shame, the older man—probably near the victims' ages—lifted a blue and white handkerchief from his hip pocket and wiped his eyes.

"Knew both those boys most a their lives," he spoke with a tremor, by no means reflective of frailty. "Fred, he was some few years older than me. Vic, too . . . but we're a small town. Everybody knows everybody . . . Our kids grew up together. My Jen went to school with Vic's boys. His daughter was a might younger. . . . Can't be nobody in this town who'd want to hurt neither of those ole boys . . ."

Whether the killer was someone from Bentwood with a grudge or a drifter who had fixated on the town, Ronnie doubted the madness would end as spontaneously as it had begun. She paid for her batteries, thanked Andover for speaking with her, and wondered as she left, why the man truly had confided in her. The operative word was his 'we' when referring to the town. Undoubtedly, this former mayor's protective instincts would reflect the general attitude.

Old newspapers could be far more enlightening. Ronnie set a course for the library. If the reporters, who'd attempted badgering Cal Farnsworth, were any indication, she'd need to be wary of bias and prejudice in any articles. But she certainly knew how to read between the lines to the meat and bones of a story. Something felt wrong here, and her neck prickled with a sense of someone watching, someone following.

Whether a library or a beauty salon carried more information, Ronnie hadn't decided until she walked out of Curls and Cuts, the proud benefactor of Amy Sue Bradway's latest creation. In forty-five minutes, Ronnie had learned more about Bentwood than she'd learned in three hours of pouring through microfiche editions of the Bender Falls Tribune. The young beautician, with the help of her mid-aged counterpart, Luanne Cartweiler, owner and operator, wearing a pair of leopard-spot tights below a black tunic, had gladly parted with a warehouse of local gossip.

No wonder Frank Engler was testy. In his family alone, a gossip columnist could make a fortune only beginning with his penchant for visiting the Light Tower Pub every evening and 'twice on Sundays, if you know what I mean.' Then came Allister Engler-Hall, who harbored an affinity for younger men despite her marital status to the 'much older' owner and operator of the largest supermarket in Bentwood. Erin Engler, Fred's youngest daughter, Frank's little sister, was considered slightly . . . 'Well, ya know—*slow.*'

Gossip overload. Ronnie rubbed her temple against a headache. Either overload or Amy Sue's enthusiasm had bruised her scalp . . . Especially when talking about Isaac Bently. Ronnie smirked as she glanced down the sidewalk toward the gray awning.

Her attention caught and fastened on the object of her current fascination striding from beneath the awning.

Isaac Bently, in the flesh, carried a large box to the rear of a Lincoln Continental, where an older man wearing a white sailing cap stood guarding the open trunk. Whatever existed in the box wasn't light. The car sagged a fraction when Bently deposited his cargo, but he certainly hadn't appeared to strain.

Nice pair of jeans, Ronnie noticed as he bent over to arrange the box in the trunk. Very nice pair of jeans hugging those lean hips and long legs . . . and the rest of him looked pretty good, too. No wonder Amy Sue had sounded breathless and nearly swooned when admitting half the town ladies secreted a crush on this character. So why was he still single? Why had he arrived in Bentwood five years ago, the proud owner of that corner building, which he'd allegedly bought 'sight unseen' through the local realtor? Why did he allegedly spend his nights cloistered in his rooms above the shop, alone, with few exceptions? One of those was a local police officer, and another the neon blond Jen Andover, daughter of the former mayor and hardware store owner, Carl Andover.

One of the two boys she'd seen earlier, the golden-haired child who'd nearly run into the parking meter, emerged from the shop carrying a smaller box, and Bently hurried a few steps to reach him. One-handed, Bently hoisted the cargo from the straining child. His free hand scuffed the blond head before he turned to the car. That simple gesture toward the boy struck a chord . . . or a nerve. Ronnie was just a wee bit too interested in this far too handsome man. The last thing she wanted or needed was to become the latest addition to his list of smitten admirers. He was probably the type to consider it a grand joke on the female population to flaunt his butt in a pair of tight jeans and keep his zipper padlocked. Probably so damned conceited that he hung mirrors on his bedroom ceiling. Just the kind of creep who would stop to comb his hair in a storefront window, hoping half the world was watching and not giving a damn how vain he appeared.

As if on cue, Bently combed his fingers through his thick hair while nudging the trunk lid closed. His sleeves were rolled to his elbows, maybe to make a fashion statement, succeeding admirably. He looked every bit like a good-ole-boy who'd just spent a long hard day digging ditches. Ronnie wasn't close enough to see if he'd gotten dirty, but somehow, she doubted it. He probably enlisted that boy to do his dirty work.

Well, perhaps, it was time someone gave this fellow a little taste of his own medicine . . . and if that interlude at Curls and Cuts served a greater purpose, so be it. Amy Sue was talented. Even on her best day, Ronnie couldn't have styled her hair with the sweeping waves and elegance that this beauty-school grad had pulled out of a hat. Combined with the khaki green slacks and beige blouse Ronnie had donned after a quick shower at the Inn, she could pass for attractive. Sometimes, she truly questioned her deviousness, if not her motives. This wasn't one of those moments, however.

Down the block, the elegant couple bid Bently adieu with handshakes and waves from their open windows as they drove away.

Changing clothes, donning makeup, and stopping at a beauty salon would have distracted Mark Jarvins, but distracting the fellow striding confidently into his shop could prove far more entertaining and enlightening. Something about this gentleman remained out of kilter, and as much as the signs leaned toward a preference for male companionship, Ronnie had her doubts.

Reaching the corner, Ronnie awaited the light to change, watched cars pass, then crossed to the diner, continuing across the side street. Only one bicycle leaned at the wall, a battered trail bike with a banana seat and rubber grips worn at the edges with the bars poking through dried rubber. A single step from the entrance, Ronnie froze as bells jangled and the door swung toward her.

Barely missing a step, the blond boy rushed out, skidded, and veered to avoid plowing into her. His pale brown eyes flashed shock an instant before a smile lighted his handsome face, and he heaved, "Hi ya! 'Scuse me!"

Before she could return a greeting, the boy sailed around her and shot past his bike. He loped across the side street, with the reckless abandon of his age. Shaking her head, wearing a smile, Ronnie caught the door before it closed and passed through the entrance into the noticeably cooler climate of Olden Time.

What struck first? The simple elegance? Or the open spaces that defied the visual sense of an antique shop? She'd expected clutter, if not crammed shelves laden with tacky art deco and flea market pottery. Instead, she faced a showroom entrance with shined hardwood floors, oriental carpets separating bedroom suites, dining room suites, and parlor suites, each tastefully adorned with the proper paraphernalia to appear lived in. Oh, there were variations—too many vases on an end table or a dresser top laden with more perfume bottles or cosmetic cases than necessary—but the ambiance remained comfortable. Ronnie had visited shops, elegant shops in various cities that couldn't compare with the simple flair of this little nook in the middle of nowhere. A museum, she imagined, or a historical home, preserved and opened to the public for tours. Perhaps, Bently had designed the rooms by historic period to explain the harmony of each alcove. Stunning as well as disorienting. She meandered deeper, scanning an exquisite selection of cut glass and crystal.

Under the soft lyrics of a symphony, she heard the rustle of paper before rounding a tall armoire and halting in time to see the stooped back stiffen. One hand resting on the edge of a ragged box, his head and shoulders remained under the ends of a linen tablecloth. He posed on one knee, apparently collecting a wad of paper under the nearly empty table. Watching the head and shoulders emerge in slow motion, Ronnie tipped her head, a smile playing on her lips as she conjured the image of a little boy caught collecting the peas he'd tossed under the dinner table. He appeared genuinely startled before his hazel eyes flashed to the color of jade, and his mustache curved into a tense half-hitched grin.

Recovering smoothly, he tossed the wad of paper in the box and rose, the box in hand, then turned to tower over her by a good six or seven inches. "Hello, Miss Bryson," he offered in a quiet deep rhythm that carried the faint trace of an accent. He barely proffered his hand, glanced down at his ink-stained fingers, and lifted his gaze. Donning a more crooked grin as he retracted his palm, he spoke smoothly. "Welcome to Olden Time."

"You have a lovely store, Mr. Bently," she said while trying to remain immune to that smile. The slightest flash of straight white teeth winked under the dark mustache, nearly distracting her worse than the spark of amusement in his eyes.

"Thank you," he said simply. "Feel free to browse," he continued with an errant glance. Dread passed through his eyes as he scanned the empty table, but his gaze returned intently. "If you should have any questions or need assistance, don't hesitate to call," he said. "At the moment, I need to wash my hands. If you'll excuse me?"

"Of course," she said, and he tipped his head in a courtly gesture before he turned. So much for dressing up and trying out new hairstyles. Ronnie watched him carry his box of crinkled paper and disappear behind a china closet. Catching another glimpse of him passing through furniture on a collision course with the back wall, she drew herself up and scanned the empty table. Just what sort of dinnerware had the sailor taken away in his Lincoln? Spotting a small tag lying loose on the tablecloth, she stepped closer and lifted it. In a meticulously printed script, it read, "Coalport, 80+ pcs." Bently hadn't listed the price, but she could take a wild guess, influenced by dozens of social bashes throughout her youth.

Perhaps his dreaded glance at the table reflected a financial loss. Obviously, he wasn't having a good day. A few hundred lost on a Dresden? Now a Coalport dinnerware set? With a shop this size and stylish, he could probably make a fortune in her neck of the woods.

So, what was he doing in Bentwood?

CHAPTER 6

Browsing, as Bently had suggested, Ronnie paused to read the string tags, surprised by the reasonable prices and the jotted notations documenting the period of his better wares. Stopped alongside a breakfront dresser, she read, "C 1880." Circa 1880. Thanks to her mother's obsession with museums throughout her childhood, Ronnie appreciated the dark patina and flawless brass handles, and judging by the tongue-and-groove wood and the absence of nails, Bently's date was accurate. A pity this delightful dresser wouldn't fit through her apartment door, much less complement her tiger maple bedroom suit.

At the tinkling of bells, she glimpsed the blond head bobbing through the center aisle and heard the tennis shoes squealing on the varnished floor.

"Miss Megan said to tell you, dinner's ready when you get hungry," the young voice carried, but if Bently answered, his voice meshed with the symphony. His voice not easily muffled, although he tried, the boy asked, "Want me to give this to that lady?"

"You might enquire as to whether she's thirsty," the deep voice echoed in a musing tone.

Seconds later, the boy appeared around the corner of a cabinet at Ronnie's side. Cheeks flushed, he cleared his throat, bolstering his confidence as he lifted a tall Styrofoam cup to her. "You thirsty, ma'am?"

Parched, Ronnie might have admitted but glanced toward the rear wall, not seeing her way clear to find Bently through the furniture. "Thank you, no," she said quietly, deciding against infringing on what could be Bently's drink, or worse, the boy's.

Crestfallen, the boy turned and ducked around the nearest corner, his voice faltering as he commented, "She wasn't thirsty."

"Perhaps, she'll change her mind after she's browsed," the deep voice idled, carrying a preoccupied note.

"Want me to do anything else?" the youngster asked. "I could go clean up around that table or sweep floors or something?"

"You've more than compensated for the cards, lad," Bently commented. "Enjoy your shake and consider it a job well done."

"It was fun," the boy said. "Think . . . you think maybe you'd need help some other time?"

"Quite possible."

"Tomorrow?"

"Perhaps."

"Would it be okay if I stop by again tomorrow then?"

"If it's alright with your mother, it's fine with me, Wade," Bently answered.

"Ma won't care. She thinks you're the greatest," the boy said enthusiastically. "You need me any more today?"

"I think I can manage things from here but thank you. You were a big help today . . . Don't forget your cards."

There was a pause then, and Ronnie had meandered nearer the rear of the store, hearing the boy's less enthusiastic voice. "Can I ask you something, Mr. Bently?"

"Within reason, certainly," the deep voice offered.

"Did you uh . . . did you know . . . I mean, did you collect baseball cards when you were a kid?"

"No," Bently answered distractedly.

"Then you uh . . . you really don't know about the players and stuff, and like, how much the cards are worth?"

"What's one man's trash is another man's treasure, lad," the low lyrical voice mused. "I'm satisfied with our transaction, as well as you should be. You repaid my investment. Let's leave it at that, shall we?"

"Okay," the boy decided bluntly, his spirits lifted. "See ya tomorrow."

"I'll look forward to it," Bently answered smoothly.

Ronnie browsed a few more moments, hearing the bells jangle and feeling slightly uncomfortable for eavesdropping though she wasn't sorry she had. Whatever she might have thought about Bently's treatment of women, she couldn't fault his apparent attitude toward children. Rounding a bend, she came upon the showcases . . . and Bently.

The fellow leaned alongside an ancient cash register, smoke trailing from a cigarette between clean fingers, resting on a stack of apparent sales receipts. His other hand held a ballpoint pen scratching in a leather-bound ledger. Head bowed, his hair falling across his brow, he appeared intent upon his enterprise, which might have accounted for his preoccupation when speaking. A half-second passed before his head tipped as if he sensed Ronnie's presence and his hazel gaze lifted, locking.

Feeling like a deer caught in a headlight beam, Ronnie considered ducking behind the tall armoire, then nearly cursed aloud for her foolishness, and continued forward.

Straightening, setting his pen aside, he flashed another ready smile. With his free hand, he combed the unruly locks off his brow as he had on the sidewalk, a natural habit born of irritation rather than practiced arrogance. "Find anything of interest, Miss Bryson?"

If she were totally honest, she might admit she found one thing of particular interest—something about 6'2" with incredibly unique green eyes. "Several things, actually," she commented. "You certainly have some truly exquisite items on hand." Reaching the counter, she spotted the two Styrofoam cups. Only one carried a straw sticking from the plastic lid. "I was tempted to believe the Dresden a fluke," she admitted, almost distracted by the flash of his handsome eyes darting at random off her face to the cup he lifted off the counter. "It was Dresden, wasn't it?"

"You apparently know your antiques," he said before taking a long pull off the straw. Lowering the cup, he inclined the straw to indicate the other drink. "I seem to have an extra soda if you're interested," he commented idly.

Careful not to slam her purse on the glass top, she set it aside, skimming her gaze over the thick ledger and respectable stack of receipts. Bookkeeping. Glancing to the antique register, she picked up the straw, accepting the soda by action. Oddly, she sensed him watching her even as he shifted to lean his elbow on the wide ornate drawer of the register; his other hand now held both the cup and cigarette. If he'd tried, he couldn't have adopted a more casual pose—something akin to the Jimmy Dean look, with the same rebellious intensity in his eyes.

Taking a long sip of the soda, trying not to be drawn into his gaze, Ronnie scanned the showcase shelves. No fool, this fellow.

Multiple trays of fine jewelry sparkled under lock and key, along with a sizable collection of pocket watches and fobs, quill pens, crystal salts, and sundry items, which could be easily slipped into purses or pockets. Well-traveled, and well-stocked. Intrigued, she lifted her gaze and nearly lost her thought with his curiously tilted head and twitching smile. "You must do a great deal of traveling with the variety of merchandise you carry."

"Obviously not as much as you travel, Miss Bryson, if you are, as I've heard, a reporter."

"I do love the grapevines in a small town," she idled, smiling. "It eliminates the need for repeated introductions."

"Something of a lark, that bit of gossip." A slight trace of the dimple emerged as he spoke; his eyes flashed tiny sparks under thick black lashes. "I don't generally attempt to keep up with rumors, but that one was delivered. So, what publication has found Bentwood of interest or intrigue if you don't mind me asking?"

"I'm freelance," Ronnie answered simply. "I've had articles in the New York Times, the Washington Post, Newsweek."

On the surface, he appeared indifferent to her answer, neither impressed nor interested, but something flashed through his eyes like a ripple on a calm green lake. If only to mask his subtle reaction, his attention dipped to his soda.

On a hunch, Ronnie continued, "I'd imagine, if what I believe is happening in Bentwood holds true, several publications may deem to run this story. I wouldn't be surprised if a swarm of reporters descends on this little town in the next day or two."

Though his reaction was slight, her prognosis disturbed him. Distractedly, he glanced to set his cola aside.

A man with something to hide? Perhaps she'd speak to Mark tonight.

His hazel eyes found her, and for an instant, he appeared desperate before the jade darkened and a curtain descended. "I hope you're wrong, Miss Bryson," he said quietly. "I seriously hope that whatever you're implying isn't happening."

"Two men have been murdered within the past month, Mr. Bently, and there are enough similarities to rule out coincidence," she said while watching his lips tense, his eyes shade deeper. "I wouldn't mind considering this part of a feud, but if what I've heard bears any truth, it's beyond the scope of a land dispute. I'd be interested in hearing any theories you might have concerning motive or whatnot."

He appeared only angry, and that wasn't what Ronnie expected or intended, not to anger him or feel the heat of his anger. By a thread, he appeared to hold himself steady, his gaze locked. "If I did have any theories, miss—"

"Please," Ronnie said smoothly, hoping to tamp the heat in his eyes. "Call me Ronnie."

He stopped. His words halted. His mustached lips froze in a curve more sinister than friendly. For a few seconds, he glared, then turned his attention to mash his cigarette butt in a crystal ashtray. By the time his gaze lifted, the glare had softened. "Isaac," he offered simply.

Strange, very strange, that wild flair of anger to dim as a lantern wick turned low. "For the record, Isaac," Ronnie said quietly. "I hope, I'm wrong, too. I'd very much like to learn that my intuition is off the mark. I'd like to discover that Mr. Farnsworth and Mr. Engler died under accidental circumstances; however, I don't believe in coincidence."

His head angled, he looked at her with a more curious shine in his eyes. "Obviously, you have a few theories about what's happening here."

"Did you know either Mr. Farnsworth or Mr. Engler?" she asked while watching him.

"To see them, yes. To consider them more than acquaintances, no," he answered, and his gaze shifted with thoughts turning behind his opaque eyes. His gaze returned; his attention concentrated. "Just how certain are you that these gentlemen were murdered?"

To her sudden amazement, she realized he doubted. In fact, he appeared to doubt the possibility entirely, and that struck her even odder. "Are you implying you don't believe these men were murdered?"

"As I mentioned a few moments ago, miss . . . Ronnie," he spoke carefully as if he found her nickname offensive. "I am not a firm believer in gossip. I find it in terribly bad taste and generally in rotten form to heed any of the local nonsense. As I understand, Mr. Farnsworth died in an accident, and after overhearing the chatter this morning, I assumed Mr. Engler suffered a similar fate. It's not exactly unusual for accidents to happen or uncommon for facts to be blown out of proportion in a town this size."

Something was wrong, here. Something in his eyes. In his voice. Far too dry and indifferent. More curious, she studied him thoughtfully, recalling several details, that she'd collected from Amy Sue, including the mention of twenty-year-old Valerie Farnsworth as well as Allister Engler-Hall and Erin Engler. "As I recall overhearing, you were away for a time. If you don't mind me asking, how long were you gone?"

"Two weeks," he answered offhandedly and glanced at his watch. Lifting off his elbow, he gathered the stack of sales receipts with a soft sigh of disgust. Closing the ledger, he stacked the two piles atop the book and met her gaze. "You mentioned finding a few items of interest. Did you have any questions I could answer concerning antiques?"

She glanced at her watch. Almost six o'clock? "Perhaps, I can stop in tomorrow."

"Have you had dinner?" he asked directly.

More curious over his confidence, she commented, "No. Not yet."

"If you'd care to join me, Meg's Diner happens to be the finest restaurant in the area."

He was probably just being polite. Nothing in his manner suggested a serious interest, and that alone annoyed and intrigued her. "I'd be happy to join you."

"Fine," he said somewhat indifferently. "If you'd care to browse a few moments, I need to close." Not awaiting a response, he pressed one of the keys on the register, and the cash drawer flew out to greet him.

Not quite sure how to take his invitation or his immediate change in subject, Ronnie gathered her purse, and carrying the soda, took his advice to browse along the showcase. Fleetingly, she glimpsed him pocketing an impressive stack of bills before she turned her attention to the showcase. Stooping, she gained a better view of porcelain figurines and ivory sculpts. On another shelf displayed on black velvet, crystals and uncut gems glittered under a neon light, along with a collection of strange jewelry from brooches to pendants. An iron cross, a dragon, tiny interwoven daggers . . . the theme of the shelf bordered on mystical. Even the rings on another swatch of velvet seemed to radiate an esoteric motif, with the heavy weave of leaves and patterns suggesting the type of ring where a hidden compartment might conceal a powder or poison capsule.

Caught up in her kibitzing, she barely heard him moving about. She had no idea when he'd stopped. Stooped, she glanced to find him leaning at the end of the counter, watching her. Arms crossed leisurely at his chest, his head crooked, and a smile haunted his lips. The pose might have shouted arrogance if not for a childlike mischief dancing in his eyes. Pushing to her feet, Ronnie glanced off the shelf. "Interesting collection."

"Suppose it is," he said and straightened, darting a glance to the case before he motioned toward the door. "Dinner?"

Taking the lead, Ronnie passed through the entrance, stepping onto the sidewalk as he doused lights and engaged an alarm before joining her. Doubtful, this was a date. More than likely, the invitation was a simple diversion to close his shop on time.

Most stores, including the hardware store across the street, had closed. A cluster of teenagers loitered down the block in front of a pizza parlor; a few others stood at the far end of the block, apparently awaiting the movie theater to open its window. Traffic had trickled to a handful of passing vehicles, and for an instant, Ronnie drew a breath of country air and enjoyed the soft orange glow of evening shadows cast across Maine. As they crossed the side street, someone called a greeting from an open car window, and Isaac raised a hand in salute.

"Did you grow up around here?" Ronnie asked lightly, thinking of the quiet suburban atmosphere rather than a story.

"No," he answered and stepped ahead, holding the door for her to enter.

Rather than the counter, Bently motioned toward an empty booth at the front window. A half dozen patrons occupied the counter and booths, one of whom glared openly as Ronnie passed. She'd certainly not made many friends today. Ignoring the slovenly reporter, she slipped into the designated booth, and in proper form, Bently waited until she stopped before sliding onto the opposite bench.

Relaxing, he lifted a plastic menu from between the metal napkin holder and sugar dispenser and handed it to her. "I'd recommend tonight's special, but I do love stuffed pork chops. Meg's a wizard with nearly any meal."

Rather than Meg or one of the morning servers, a petite redhead meandered to the bench, eyeing Ronnie with a leer while turning a smile to Isaac. "Coffee, Isaac?"

He nodded absently, looking toward Ronnie. "What would you like?"

"Coffee's fine," she said while glancing down the menu, detecting an audible sniff from the waitress who turned, scribbling on her notepad. Faintly amused, Ronnie glanced after the redhead, then glimpsed an expression of disgust crossing Bently's face before he turned his attention to light a cigarette. "Another of your admirers?"

For an instant, he appeared slightly startled and angry before a different, nearly curious shine lighted in his eyes.

Uncontrollably, a smile slipped onto her lips in tune with his slow donning grin.

"Suppose you might say that," he said in a dry, disgusted tone.

"Must be difficult for you," she mocked sympathy, enjoying the play of light in his eyes,

"Dreadful," he feigned misery.

Stifling a laugh, Ronnie reached into her purse, routing for her cigarettes, and jolted slightly when the stout body halted outside her side of the booth.

Scowling, the pudgy reporter from the municipal building adopted an aggressive pose. Leaning, looming toward her, his arms laced across a faded dress shirt pulled taut across his sagging girth. Above ruddy round cheeks, his brown eyes glared nearly black.

Instantly annoyed, Ronnie wondered, "Can I help you with something?"

"Yea, you can tell me what all that Fed told you," the man snapped. "Unless you're working with him, Miss Bryson."

"Grimes," Bently spoke before Ronnie could more than draw a breath. For all his boyish charm, his emerald eyes appeared feral as he addressed the reporter. "The lady and I are dining," he commented in a descended tone. "It's in fine poor taste to intrude."

"Don't piss with me today, Bently," the man sneered. "There's a story here, and this *lady* knows a helluva lot more than she's telling."

"Even if that were true, Grimes," Bently said in biting sarcasm. "She'd be a fool to part with information to your benefit, and she doesn't strike me as a fool. While you, on the other hand, are an incompetent ass."

As the reporter listed toward Bently, Ronnie snapped, "Mr. Grimes."

He jerked back, leveling his glare on her.

"Do you have any idea how incredibly ridiculous your demand sounds or how accurate Mr. Bently's statement?" she asked with an edge. "Simply, sir, I have no desire to share information with you, and I'm under no obligation to cooperate with your asinine misconception of camaraderie. Now, if you'll excuse us, we do intend to share a meal without indigestion."

"Listen, lady—"

"A problem here, Isaac?" another deep voice intruded.

Vaguely, Ronnie recognized the Bentwood officer, although he wasn't in uniform. Black hair, dark blue eyes, haunted and somehow haggard, he stood nearly as tall as Bently and towered over Grimes. By his mere presence, he forced the reporter to step back.

"Not that I'm aware, Spence," Bently said with a faintly bemused note. A spark of mischief danced in his clear green eyes as he spied the officer.

"Grimes," Tim commented while insinuating himself to lean sideways against the back of the booth, either shielding or blocking Bently's escape. "I suggest you go on about your business, and if I see you harassing anybody else in town, I'm just liable to toss you in a cell for a couple days."

"Like hell, Spencer," the reporter growled smugly. "You never heard of the Constitution? Freedom of the Press? The public has a right to know what's going on."

"Within reason," Ronnie added and caught the man's scowl. "You can be held liable for harassment, especially if your actions lean toward physical assault. Now, I suggest you back off, Mr. Grimes, or I may be the one who files civil suit against you."

Grimes started a word, but Spencer cleared his throat, and the man hissed a curse. Turning, Grimes stalked toward the counter, bumping the redheaded waitress out of his path. Coffee plopped over the two mugs, and the redhead hissed a curse after him.

"Thanks, Spence," Bently smirked.

"Don't mention it," Spencer said with a hint of amusement despite the tension in his eyes. His attention glinted off Bently to Ronnie as he pushed almost lazily off the edge of the bench, taking a step to offer his hand, "Officer Tim Spencer."

Clasping his large, rugged palm, Ronnie judged him a little older than Bently with more rough edges. "Veronica Bryson," she supplied though she doubted the necessity. "Just 'Ronnie' if you prefer. Your timing was excellent, Officer Spencer. Thank you."

"Just Tim," he said with a casual smile. "Just doing a public service," he added.

Across the table, Bently shifted and stifled a soft disgusted, "Humph."

Flattered and amused, Ronnie retracted her hand and decided, "I appreciate it just the same."

"Just don't judge Ted too harshly," Spencer said while fleeting a reproachful glance toward Bently. "He's not generally such an aggressive son of a gun."

"He's an ass," Bently huffed in disgust.

Spencer lifted his brow while eyeing Bently with a peculiar amusement. "Why don't you just challenge him to a boxing match and get it over with, Sax?"

"I don't box," he said dryly, but his eyes glinted that feral green shine. "I might learn, however, if we can sanction the event within legal parameters."

"Forget it," Spencer stated. "You'd kick the shit out of him, and I'd still end up booking you for assault."

"Ah well," he sighed and favored Ronnie with a wistful smile. "Possibly, I'll just settle for watching you make him squirm. Truly, a delight to be savored."

"I'd love to hear the story behind this apparent vendetta," Ronnie commented and pivoted her gaze to the officer. "Would you care to join us, Tim?"

With a sly glance toward Bently, Spencer accepted the invitation, and Ronnie slipped sideways to lend him space on her bench. Compared to the males she'd encountered throughout the day, Spencer was, at once charming and relaxed, even sending her a conspiratorial wink when the redhead scowled at her while delivering their coffee. Her tension easing, Ronnie managed to order without taking offense.

Rather like visiting the beauty salon, Ronnie settled into the conversation more as an avid listener than a participant, almost grateful for the easy exchange between the two men. Bently did most of the talking though Spencer nudged him on, prodding him for details about his trip, which hadn't been a two-week excursion of junketing in the U.S. of A. Only once, the conversation hitched when Spencer interjected a casual question to wonder what time Bently had arrived in town the evening past. A pregnant pause, a curious tip of the dark hair, a flash of intensity, and Bently grasped the casual interrogation.

Unguarded and not offended, he answered simply, "Around ten, Spence."

Silence lingered for a few seconds as they suppressed questions they'd have preferred to air. She was the reason for their silence, and that revelation only heightened Ronnie's curiosity about the man sitting across from her.

To her surprise, Spencer broke the silence and changed the subject. His arm across the back of the bench behind her, he tipped his head, offering a charming smile, not disguising the quick intelligence behind his dark blue eyes. "You'll have to forgive me, Ronnie," he said smoothly. "Sax, here, is the only guy I know who trots off across the Atlantic regularly, and if I don't set him back on track, he runs around with that flipping English accent for weeks afterward."

Sax? Amused, Ronnie looked to Bently. "You visit Europe regularly then?"

"Annually . . . semi-annually, is probably more accurate," he answered offhandedly, still brooding beneath his attempt at amusement.

The arrival of dinner interrupted then, and Ronnie was pleasantly stunned by the size of the meal to begin crowding the table between them. From the salad heaping in a serving bowl to the stuffed porkchop standing nearly four inches high to the softball-sized baked potato, the meal was a study in overindulgence. To Ronnie's amazement, both men dug into the mounds as if they'd never eaten in their lives, although Bently ate with the manners of English gentry while Spencer engaged his plate with murderous intent. Watching them might have stuffed her, but either their gluttony rubbed off, or the cuisine was exceptional. Concentrating on her stuffed chop, the morning bagel a fond distant memory, Ronnie barely heard Spencer's reference to Mark Jarvins and the question of her past acquaintance.

"We crossed paths a few years ago," she admitted, and Spencer hooked his brow, smiling even as he chewed.

"He strikes me as a professional, Ron," he said with the easy familiarity of an old friend.

Perhaps her years of association with Max Hagen had influenced her natural rapport with officers of the law. Shoptalk came naturally. "He is."

"If I read the signs right, he's mighty impressed with how you handle yourself in a dicey business."

Silently thanking Mark for the open door, she returned the favor. "Truthfully, Tim, as much as I know how some officers feel threatened by Federal intervention, I hope you'll give him your full support. He's extremely good at what he does."

Spencer eyed her in speculation as he chewed and pondered, swallowing. "I'd like to ask you something, Ron, at the risk of offending you."

"I don't offend easily," she said honestly.

"What brought you to Bentwood on a 4: a.m. flight from DC?"

"You certainly dive right in," she mused but held his gaze steadily. He probably believed that Mark had contacted her. "I'm also very good at what I do, Tim. I have a certain knack for connecting tiny details to flash across the syndicated wire service. Hearing Bentwood mentioned twice in one month regarding questionable deaths . . .?" She shrugged. "I've been accused of having a nose for news."

"Meaning no disrespect," he said casually. "But this isn't exactly the kind of atmosphere I'd expect to find a classy lady walking into if you know what I mean."

"Perfectly," she said smoothly. "And thank you for the compliment, even if it came through a side door."

Amused, he commented, "Any chance your old man was a cop?"

"My biological father, no," she answered without either shame or regret, a fond smile playing into her eyes. "But I'm no stranger to the shoptalk of a busy precinct or the perils of a surrogate father's profession."

He winked, and the gesture reminded her so much of Max Hagen, Ronnie started to smile more fondly. Across the table, the cup clattered and drew her attention sharply.

Head bowed at an angle, Bently stared at the mug of coffee held on the table in a white-knuckle grip. The color had drained from his face. His eyes carried a misty shine. His brow furrowed, and mustached lips crooked in a haunted smirk in sharp contrast to his pale complexion.

"Sax?" Spencer asked in a low tone.

"Huh?" he uttered and lifted his head a notch. He appeared blind before he blinked and shuddered visibly. Confusion flashed neon within his opaque eyes, and his smirk gripped with tension as his attention riveted.

"You feeling alright, pal?" Tim asked with an attempted playful note.

"Jet lag," Bently said hesitantly and nodded in an almost childlike gesture as if he sought confirmation. With the dark wave falling over his brow and confusion lingering under his thick lashes, his eyes evoked a strange innocence and vulnerability that seemed entirely out of character. "Think the flight's catching up to me."

"I dunno, Bently," Spencer said in a mocked tough-guy tone. "You don't look so hot. You sure you didn't pick up a bug over there? Maybe you need quarantined or something? I could haul your ass over to County Medical and put you under a plastic bubble."

"Then you'd take time off to keep my shop open, too, right?" Bently asked, his voice firming although his eyes still carried a haunted quality out of sync with his expression. "I can just see Sam giving you the time off."

"Hell, maybe I'll get you quarantined for a couple weeks. I'd have a blast unloading some of that junk you have hanging around."

"Speaking of which, I found something I thought Donna might like. If you have time, stop by later and have a look."

"Not another God-blessed music box. I'll strangle you, Sax, if you brought another—"

"Naaa, just a nice set of tiny little earrings," Bently spoke more naturally. His smirk returned with a spark of mischief. "I promised. No music boxes this trip."

Spencer eyed him suspiciously, then turned his gaze to Ronnie. "He makes that damned promise every trip, and every trip, for a month afterward, I'm listening to Swan Lake or Moon-blasted-River." He winked out of sight of Bently while scowling, "I have to wonder who my wife's thinking about all the time I'm not there—"

"You ought to wonder more about when you are there," Bently tossed over snidely, and Tim scowled in good humor.

Meg arriving and sliding into the booth alongside Bently spared him from Spencer's reprisal. With a lively spark in her eyes, she glanced over the plates and faces, her attention lifting to Isaac, who'd slid sideways to offer her scant space while draping his arm across the back of the bench. "Don't tell me! You lost the taste for my chops!" she sounded mortified.

"Not on your life," Bently said with a quick smile.

"Then you're not finished," she said in relief.

"Stuffed, Meg," he said in elaborate regret. "I may need a to-go box."

Not positive when Bently had stopped eating, Ronnie scanned the sizable portion remaining on his plate. Tim Spencer continued attacking the remains on his platter, sopping up gravy and stuffing with another of the biscuits from a large basket.

"You don't eat enough," Megan said in matronly reproach, her attention held fast on Bently. In her youth, she would've been beautiful with her slender features, blue eyes, and natural blond hair, and the years had only enhanced her attraction. In the proper attire with her fluff of silver-laced hair, her smooth complexion lightly dusted, and lips rouged, she would be stunning. Presently, her brow wrinkled beneath soft bangs, her warm blue eyes intent. "And you're looking peaked."

"Quarantined," Spencer grunted in smug satisfaction.

Bently tossed him an annoyed glance, and Ronnie stifled a laugh.

Meg riveted her more tense eyes on Spencer, flashed Ronnie a peculiar glance then looked to Bently. "Quarantined?"

"He's fantasizing again," Bently said with feigned dismay. "Nothing to be done about it."

If he failed as an antique dealer, this guy would make a mint on the silver screen. Even his expression changed to solemn resignation and concern. Ronnie covered her laugh behind a cough while catching Meg's laughing blue eyes.

"Worse than schoolboys, these two," Meg chastened, confiding in Ronnie while trying to hide the affection under her lashes. "But I suppose I have to put up with them."

Bently softened his gaze, dropping his hand to her opposite shoulder, hugging her toward his side. "You still love us right, mum?"

"Brat!" she said and slapped his thigh.

He masked a jolt under a quick idling laugh and brushed a chaste kiss on the older woman's forehead. Why that smooth innocent affection stepped up Ronnie's pulse and drew her attention to those mustached lips, she couldn't have said. The word *dangerous* flashed neon in her mind. Too smooth, and far too many contradictions existed in this character. From his lyrical voice to his reserved deep chuckles to the split-second changes in his mood, he was fascinating.

Intent, without fully paying attention, Ronnie heard the conversation sober as Meg began. "I've been hearing a lot of rumors flying around in here, today, Tim. Now, I want the truth. How bad's this business with Fred Engler?"

"Without jeopardizing the investigation, Meg, I can say it's pretty bad," Spencer admitted, and his voice lost the lighthearted tone that had carried throughout the conversation thus far. His rugged features lent creed to that simple generalized statement, and for the first time, he unmasked the raw pain and stress of seeing that crime scene.

Ronnie remembered Cal Farnsworth speaking this afternoon, struggling as he admitted to growing up on a farm, no stranger to blood and gore. She could have told him then and could tell this officer now, nothing prepared one for a murder scene. In snapshot flashes, she remembered striding into a shadowed alley, glimpsing the corpse . . . she'd beaten the Chicago Police to the scene by a minute and a half.

"I been thinking on this all day," Meg said thoughtfully, gravely. Her attention fixed on Tim; her eyes deeply shadowed. "And it doesn't make a lick a sense, Timmy," she said quietly, apparently, oblivious of his flinch under the childish address. "I've known Vic and Fred both since they were knee-high. Vic was a good ten years younger than me, but we were a smaller town back then and Fred . . . Freddie and I went to the same schoolhouse," she said with a strain in her eyes, tension drawing the nerves in her neck.

Attuned to the older woman's distress, Bently moved his thumb at her collarbone, hugging her a little tighter, although his shaded gaze shifted from her to Spencer. He spared a cursory glance to Ronnie, countering her glimmer of affection for his show of natural compassion.

She was the outsider, and Bently resented her presence at this table as if she were stealing a privilege to witness this woman's pain. Was he accusing her of something behind that heated flash? In an instant of unreasonable temper, Ronnie barely restrained an urge to remind the jerk that he'd invited her to this table. Perhaps, she'd accepted with a few ulterior motives, but she hadn't twisted his arm or seduced him, any more than she'd anticipated sharing his company.

"Meg, about all I can tell you, is that we're doing our damnedest to find out who's responsible for this," Spencer said grimly. "We have a helluva lot of people working on it from every angle."

"Alice found him," she strained.

Spencer nodded, apparently unable to lie no matter how desperately this older woman sought to negate that rumor.

"Erin," Meg hissed softly, then looked as if she might bite her tongue.

With a mere glimpse of Meg's darting damp eyes, Ronnie knew her presence belied this halted exchange, and a sharp pang of resentment sped through her system. Small-town quirks. Small-town mentality. Small-town murder. A ready-made scenario for a Movie-of-the-Week drama. She was the outsider, a journalist who the townsfolk believed had arrived for the sensationalism. Did they think she wrote for the National Enquirer? No doubt. She carried two strikes against her. First and foremost, male chauvinism was alive and well in this little town, and she was a woman. Automatically, that detail disqualified her credibility as a serious journalist. Second, she was the first reporter outside their jurisdiction to arrive. If not a tart as a few of the females in this diner seemed to believe, Ronnie would probably be considered a busybody . . . and suddenly, she was too damned tired even to attempt proving otherwise.

With the conversation faltered, Spencer tried to lighten the mood with an offhanded comment that Ronnie missed entirely. She was tired. She was angry. And the green-eyed man across from her, leering at her, only confirmed her decision. She wanted out of this booth, this restaurant, if not this whole blasted town.

Rather than interrupt the casual exchange, Ronnie began rifling through her purse for her wallet in a universal signal which not even these country bumpkins could miss.

"I'm picking up the tab, miss," Bently said.

Whether his formal address or his smooth lyrical voice annoyed her, Ronnie lifted a ten from her wallet and favored him with a chilly glance, not exactly receiving any satisfaction from his slight start. "That's not necessary, Mr. Bently," she said with the same easy formality. "But I do thank you for the invitation," she finished and flashed a glance off the intent woman to Spencer, who appeared somewhat startled. "If you'll excuse me, Tim? It's been a long day, and I still have some work to do this evening."

Spencer slid from the booth and started to say something when Ronnie dropped the ten on the table. He retracted his words as she slipped from the booth.

At an angle, Ronnie caught the officer's quick blue eyes. "If you can spare a few moments of your time tomorrow, I'd appreciate it. I'm staying over at the Bentwood House, but I'm sure that's public knowledge by now." His lip twitched, verifying her words, his eyes smiled, and she liked him even more, softening part of her brassy glare. "Leave a message at the desk if you will."

"I'll give it a try," he said with a country boy charm.

Turning to find Meg likewise standing and Bently on the slide to rise, Ronnie offered the older woman her hand. "We haven't been formally introduced, ma'am, I'm Ronnie Bryson."

"Megan Price," she said lightly in contrast to her firm handclasp. "But most everyone just calls me Meg."

"Obviously, Mr. Bently knows his cuisine," Ronnie said with a faintly haughty note. "Dinner was excellent."

As the woman flashed a curious but delighted smile, Ronnie turned, deliberately, trapping Bently on the bench, preventing his attempt at chivalry. Offering her hand, she enlisted the simple formality reserved for strangers, "A pleasure meeting you, Mr. Bently." The heat of his palm sent a prickle through her fingers, but she kept a moderate tone by sheer force of will as she withdrew from his iron grip. "I don't know if I'll get back to your shop tomorrow, but there's a lovely Wedgwood bowl, the serving bowl on that spindle stand near your counter. If you could set that aside along with that aquamarine brooch under your checkout counter, I'll try to pick them up before I leave." Barely pausing as his lips parted for a response, Ronnie finished, "If I can't, I'll send a check to cover shipping and handling. Thank you for a pleasant evening."

He clamped his jaw, then flashed a strange amusement to grate on Ronnie's nerves. "The pleasure was mine, I assure you, Miss Bryson."

Arrogant idiot, she threw at him and flashed another glance to the standing pair. "See you again," she said lightly and picked up her pace to the glass door, passing through and veering smoothly in the direction of the hotel. Without missing a step, she stepped off the sidewalk to cross Maine, avoiding the need to pass Bently's shop. The last thing she needed was either the approval or acceptance of an arrogant jerk who harbored an aversion to the female race, with the exception of silver-haired older women. He was probably one of those little boys who'd never quite grown up, always looking for his mother or grandmother to pamper him. Well, to hell with him! Let him play house with his little antique shop and play hell on the girls in Bentwood. Ronnie Bryson wanted no part of it.

CHAPTER 7

Isaac could feel the muscle in his cheek pulsing as he watched Bryson glide across Maine, and for the second time in a single day, he caught himself appreciating that confident, sleek gait. All too swiftly, he recalled those moments before noon when he'd stood in the shadow of his shop watching her walk the length of his front window. He cursed himself now, as he had then while following her with his gaze as he'd turned off the security alarm, hit the light switches, and unlocked his front door. No one should walk like that unless adorned in an exquisite silk gown. White silk and lace, he imagined, and the vision jumped into his mind's eye, jolting him from his daze.

Across from him, Tim Spencer rested with one meaty arm stretched across the back of the bench, a smile quivering on his lips and his blue eyes sparkling with amusement. "There's a first," Spencer said in a low tone.

Beside him, Meg rested silently, and Isaac needed only a glance to recognize her bemused smile and her eyes likewise twinkling. Shaking his head, he refused to acknowledge what either one found amusing and turned his attention to lighting a cigarette instead. That black-haired witch was swiftly becoming a thorn in his side, and Tim was right. That, if nothing else, was a first.

"I'd love to know what you did to piss that lady off, seeing as how I know she hasn't even been in town for a full day," Spencer prodded, enjoying himself. "Or is it possible you're losing a little of your charm, Sax?"

He could admit, he had no clue what he'd done to offend her. The fact that he might like to know annoyed him more. Offhandedly, Isaac commented, "Typical female."

"I'll take exception to that," Meg interjected, mocking offense and haughty indignation.

Not entirely amused, Isaac passed her a faint smile, admitting, "You *are* the exception to that, Meg."

Her eyes softened considerably, and a smile played at the corner of her lips. As usual, curiosity lingered in her gaze. She'd never breached his trust by asking what grudge he held against the female sex, but she wondered often. Had she asked, doubtful, he could answer, which only made him appreciate her more.

"You know, I wasn't kidding when I mentioned that Federal agent tooting her horn," Spencer said in a lazy tone. "I figure there's more to their association than they're willing to admit just by what wasn't said, but it's fairly clear they have a mutual respect."

"This is all very fascinating," Isaac said as he looked toward one of the few people he considered a friend. "Thanks so much for sharing."

Spencer's lips twitched; his eyes darkened with a deeper shine. "I love it when you get all flippant and lofty, Sax. Reminds me you weren't born in Bentwood."

Tim hadn't meant to slice or insult, but the words reflected his thoughts as clearly as his presence in the diner defied coincidence. Short hairs lifting at the nape of his neck, Isaac turned his gaze through the glass, and his focus trailed across the opposite storefronts.

Andover's Hardware had closed. With evening sunlight spilling across the street and glinting off the occasional passing bumper, the lack of lights behind the glass could be an illusion. Aside from the theater, the mini-mart, gas stations, the diner, and sandwich shops, Maine St. had shut down. Routine. Quiet, dependable routines had offered him as much comfort as his occupation. No illusions. If he crossed the street, he could confirm the store had closed. He could cup his palms against the glass and verify the lights were off. No illusions. He lived in a concrete world connected to the past through tangible, traceable material objects. The words from a book might conjure images and impressions, but he could still clasp a ceramic bowl, run his fingertips over a seventeenth-century vase, and know those things had existed, those artisans had lived. No illusions.

"You do look tired, Isaac," Meg said, touching his arm, drawing him from contemplation to find her worried eyes, her soft smile. "I hope you're not planning to stay up all night trying to catch up on everything over there. Elaine did a bang-up job holding down the fort while you were gone."

"I think she tries selling out while I'm away just to be certain I leave again soon."

Meg laughed lightly, "I wouldn't be a bit surprised. You tend to make people nervous."

"The hell you say," he said simply. "I've never been anything other than proper and polite with Elaine," he said in mild reproach, considering his employee's anxiety just another peccadillo of the female gender. "I never even snapped at the woman when she sold a meerschaum pipe for five bucks because she thought the damn thing was plastic."

"The boy do take offense," Tim chuckled. "This little tirade wouldn't have something to do with a certain blue-eyed vixen sticking in your craw, now, would it?"

"You, sir, are an annoyance I can do without," Isaac decided and looked down at Meg while touching her shoulder. "As much as I love your company, I do have a great deal of work I'd like to finish this evening. If you'll excuse me?"

"Chicken," Tim tossed at him while sliding off the opposite bench. "And you have the nerve to call what you do work to boot," he continued gustily, shaking his head. "More like traipsing around in my granddaddy's attic hunting for hidden treasure the way I used to do as a kid."

"Each to his own," Isaac said dryly, refusing to be baited into that old argument.

Opening a fine quality antique shop in a town where the Used Furniture store had been the largest antique outlet in a thirty-mile radius, certainly had its drawbacks. Spencer, however, wasn't the typical country boy, and for all his razzing, he damn well knew the difference between carnival glass and Haviland china. In fact, Spence had proven to be something of a quick study with a ready grasp for period antiques which he claimed he inherited from his grandmother.

Digging for his wallet to leave a tip, Tim waved Isaac aside. "I'm paying," he said and winked at Meg, handing her another ten to add to Bryson's. "It was worth the price of admission just to see that lovely lady shut down Mr. Personality."

Meg tucked his ten back into his hand. "You may thank Miss Bryson for dinner when you see her tomorrow, Timmy," Meg commented. "Mr. Personality has another dinner or two coming in a trade we made."

"Tonight only," Isaac corrected. "But you still owe me a slice of pie."

She lifted his dinner plate, patting his arm. "I'll send this over, along with the pie in a little while, and I do think you better knock off early tonight. You look tired."

He felt tired. Brushing a kiss on her cheek, ignoring the leers he received from various directions, Isaac winked. "Thanks for the advice and dinner. It was worth the wait."

Not fool enough to believe Tim would leave him alone, Isaac restrained a curse as he strode outside with Tim on his heels.

"Think I'll just have a look at those little earrings," Tim said offhandedly. "Might need them by the time Donna hears I had my arm around a knockout raven-haired lady."

Annoyed with himself for providing Tim with an excuse to follow, Isaac commented, "Keep it up, I may need to engage in a bit of friendly gossip after all."

"Ahh, come on, Sax," Tim taunted. "This isn't like you at all. Bad trip or what?"

"Excellent trip," he said dryly and continued his steady pace around the corner, crossing the street toward his side entrance. Tense and annoyed, he fumbled with his keys deciding on one last-ditch effort and looking at Tim as the locks tumbled free. "Why don't we put this off until tomorrow? I really am swamped, and I'm not even sure I'll find those earrings tonight. I haven't unpacked my suitcases yet."

The veil of camaraderie wavered; the light smile and forced humor faded. "You always have a bottle of good brandy in your medicine cabinet, and I'm not due back on duty for four hours."

Damn him. Isaac shook his head and pushed open the door, hitting the light switch on the wall while continuing inside. A narrow spindle-railed stairway ascended the right side of the wall; the left wall held two doorways with a third door beneath the stairs that led into his warehouse. Three separate offices existed within the matrix of rooms and walls that had become his haven and home.

Without further hesitation, he led Tim up the steps to his more private realm, striking another switch at the top of the stairs to bathe the brief landing in light. To the right, another door opened to the warehouse's second floor. A single door to the left opened into a narrow hallway accessing four former efficiency apartments. One of the apartments supplied space where he kept his more expensive merchandise under double lock and key. Two others he'd converted into libraries. The fourth carried the essentials of life, and he never bothered locking the door. He shared his home with no one.

Inviting Tim into the apartment, Isaac ignited one of several slag lamps, then continued through his living room into his private office.

His 'medicine cabinet,' as Tim called it, was an eighteenth-century armoire that stood against the outside wall between vintage blue-swag curtains. Behind the ornately carved double doors, a variety of antique decanters held a surplus of fine liquors, and crystal goblets glittered in the lamplight.

Bringing one of the fancier decanters off a shelf, Isaac barely glimpsed Tim settling into one of three high-backed chairs in front of his King-Edwardian desk. The heavy furniture dwarfed the room even without the addition of a daybed. With drapes drawn over every window, no outside light penetrated his rooms. Not in his den, not in his kitchen where red velvet hung over the filthy glass, not in his bedroom where no windows existed.

Day or night, the rooms remained in thick evening shade which, Isaac knew, had always disturbed rather than comforted his old friend. Spencer had visited often enough, however, to appear relaxed. Ankle resting casually over his opposite knee, he accepted the filled brandy snifter silently and balanced the crystal on his shin.

Not nearly as relaxed, Isaac moved behind his desk and settled into the upholstered cushion. He might know why Tim wanted to talk to him—*did know*—but he had no intention of offering an opening. Even now, Isaac cursed whatever madness had left him vulnerable to this encounter. Silently, he cursed the day he'd accepted Tim Spencer's offer of friendship and opened the door for too many questions and conclusions.

Sipping his brandy, Isaac trailed his gaze toward the stands where the gold inset titles of his favorite books stood in neat rows between polished brass, bronze, and silver bookends. Every muscle and nerve in his body tensed, and a mild tremor slid through his hand. Setting the glass aside, Isaac fumbled to find and light a cigarette, feeling Spencer watching him.

No illusions remained.

"Ya know, Sax," Tim said in a low, careful voice. "I'm not here just to piss you off or to uh . . . to rattle you."

"Didn't stop you from coming though, did it?" Isaac asked shortly.

Uncomfortably, Tim studied him a moment, then dropped his attention, lifting the brandy. His sculpted, rugged features strained.

Feeling neither sympathy nor satisfaction, Isaac read the fellow's torment. As much as he always enjoyed the camaraderie they'd shared nearly from the onset, he truly despised the man sitting across from him at this moment.

A palpable silence lingered before Tim lifted his gaze, intent. "I don't know what the hell bothers me more, Sax, thinking you can help, and you don't want to, or thinking if I push for your help, I lose your friendship. That's the fuck of this," he said in a low voice. "And that's when I start to wonder how the hell good our friendship is, or if I'm just another asshole acquaintance like all the rest of the folks in Bentwood are to you."

Cut to the quick, Isaac dragged his angry gaze away, watching the brandy swirl inside the goblet that had begun to swivel on the leather armrest.

"I didn't come talk to you a month ago," Tim continued in a careful tone. "First off, I figured it was a fluke. Second, I didn't think you needed the hassle. Third, I was pretty goddamn sure we'd catch whatever maniac did that to Farnsworth."

"I don't know what happened to Farnsworth," Isaac said in a strained voice. His gaze locked on the dark swirling liquid, his system vibrated like an overwound clock. "I don't want to know, S-Spencer. Not about F-Farnsworth or Engler," he heaved softly, shaking his head against a thump. "I don't—fucking—want to know."

"But you know anyway, huh?" Spencer said far more carefully.

Shuddering uncontrollably, Isaac gripped the glass, shaking his head in a ragged jerk as another thud struck his temple. Heaving a breath, his gaze shot to Tim, and he couldn't control it, not this time. No longer mad, not even angry, his muscles gripped in fear. Shaking his head, as much to ward off that statement as the sudden sympathy leaping into the dark blue eyes, Isaac uttered, "Don't . . . don't . . ." *Don't what?*

"Damnit," Tim uttered. "Sax—"

"N-no," Isaac heaved and shook his head. Yanking the brandy to his lips, he gulped the contents, then leaned forward, closing his hand about the neck of the decanter. Instantly, he suffered the heat as if the tiny inlaid gold strands began to crawl against his palm. Concentrating, watching the gold threads swirling around the green glass as if weaving a spell, he refilled the goblet with an effort. Still shaking his head, he glanced at Spencer. "No."

"In . . . in the diner," Tim started and dropped his boot to the floor. Leaning on his forearms, he poised as if to launch off the chair. "When you uh . . . the jet lag. For the record, I didn't buy it then; I don't, now, Sax. You're white as a ghost and shaking like a leaf . . . and if I caused that, I uh . . . I'm sorry."

"I . . . I can't help you," Isaac heaved. "I can—not—help you, and—and I'm sorry, too. Alright? So, uh . . . so just . . ." He gulped another swallow of brandy and pushed from the chair. Struggling for control, his voice still shook. "I'll get those earrings. M-My uh . . . my room," he stammered and hurried. Nearly running from the room, he ducked into the darkness of his bedroom, slamming the door in his wake.

In the sudden blackness, Isaac gasped and froze. Muscles ripcord taut, he remained frozen, momentarily, his heart hammering a wicked beat. Abruptly, nausea snapped his hysteria as stomach acids rose, gagging him.

Fumbling at the wall, heaving and gasping, he found the light switch and staggered across the room into the small bathroom. On his knees, he retched into the porcelain bowl, and in a vicious cycle, head pounding, every heaved breath created another until every ounce of brandy and dinner swirled in the blue basin. Cursing, still heaving, Isaac climbed to the sink, fumbled the faucet on, and rested on his forearms, splashing cold water over his face, gargling and spitting.

Years! Not in years had he suffered such a wretched reaction to his nerves. *Not in years!* Spencer—Tim Spencer—in his house? In his apartment? He needed to regain control and straighten up. *Adult. Not a little kid. Have to grow up!* But the images flashing in his mind, a whirlwind of images, only wavered his precarious balance.

Grabbing a towel off the rack, he brought it over the basin, burying his face in the cloth and heaving the scent of laundry soap. Not a little kid. Tim Spencer—local police officer, friend, ally—sat or stood somewhere outside the door. The fellow asked him for help . . . came to ask him for help.

NO. Don't. Can't. Respectable citizen. Normal citizen. Sorry.

As effective as a paper bag, the towel stifled his hyperventilating, and he fumbled, flushing the commode and wiping his face. A glimpse in the vanity mirror told him more than he wanted to know.

Overlapping, his reflections hovered in the glass. One a wide-eyed man; another, a wild-eyed child. Dark waves shrouded the scattered dark curls. A mustache overlaid the full soft lips.

Swaying, Isaac stepped back from the sink, staring at the funhouse image in the mirror as his skull continued to thump. Sobering, that image. And disturbing on every level.

His past. His present. His future. Merging?

Shaking his head, drawing a thin breath, he forced the images away and keened to the sense of Spencer still inside his apartment.

Lifting his hands, running his trembling fingers through his hair as if he might smooth the riot in his head, he reached the bathroom door and started into his bedroom.

Spencer sat on one of the tapestry chairs at the end of the bed. If Isaac hadn't emptied his stomach a few moments ago, he might need to now. Worried and tense, Spencer feigned to mask his distress behind a weak smile.

With every ounce of poise he could muster, Isaac moved to one of his leather bags spread open on the floor near his closet door. Stooped, he began rummaging in the silk lining for the small parcel he'd packed before leaving his flat in England. His back to Spencer, he commented, "You're cute, Tim, but you're not my type. Wrong equipment, ya know?" Turning, rising with the parcel in hand, he tossed it to Spencer as he asked, "So what the fuck are you doing in my bedroom?"

Tim snatched the bag from the air, straining to grin as he glanced about the room. "Reminds me of a French whorehouse I saw once," he commented, shrugging as he raised a brow, feigning innocence. "I always imagined you'd be more into the King Willie design or some shit. Donna would get a bang out of this setup."

"Keep it up, I may be inclined to show her," Isaac said with cold indifference.

With a humph, Spencer began opening the bag as he pushed off the chair. "Don't think you're her type, pal," he said as he walked to the door, continuing through the arch and into the living room.

Glancing over his shadowed room with its swag curtains, tassel tapestries, and heavy poster bed where more curtains hung, Isaac found no comparison to a French whorehouse and decided to educate his associate. Finding Tim once again sitting in the high-backed chair in the office, already fingering the delicately painted porcelain earrings, Isaac commented, "French bordellos have far more pizzazz and color, providing you visit one with proper ambiance."

Spencer tipped his head, brow raised. He let out a laugh, "Offended you, huh?"

"Not possible," Isaac said dryly but glanced to the earrings to offset his discomfort. "Are those what you had in mind?"

"She'll love 'em," he said as he began wrapping them in the tissue. "So, how many barbecues is it gonna cost me this time?"

Isaac shrugged and moved around his desk, lifting the brandy if only to wash the sour taste from his mouth. "You decide. I've been accused of not haggling well twice today, I couldn't bear it a third time, especially when one of my critics was only twelve."

Tim chuckled, but the notes were off, forced, the tension not lifted. "Alright. Tomorrow evening. I'll do the ribs, you bring the wine, and I'll con Donna into making the fixings."

"Terrific," Isaac said dryly. "You'd make her work for her own gift."

"You want my potato salad instead?"

"Point taken. Tomorrow night," Isaac said and met Spencer's gaze. "I probably won't arrive until after seven, if that's alright."

"You need to hire a few more employees, Sax," Tim said as he rose off his chair. "I swear you put in more hours than I do, and my profession's considered demanding."

Isaac started the usual comment about Tim's career as a 'dog catcher and cattle-herder,' but the words died before reaching his tongue. Too clearly, Vic Farnsworth and Fred Engler came to mind. His voice vibrated slightly, "See you tomorrow, then."

Spencer started to the door, reached for the knob, and paused in indecision before he turned and locked his gaze. "Are you alright?"

"Fine," Isaac managed smoothly.

"For what it's worth," Tim said carefully. "If I caused that, I'm sorry, and uh . . . if you want to talk, you know how to reach me."

"Thanks," Isaac answered.

Spencer hesitated another few seconds, then nodded and let himself out.

Long after he heard Spencer's footsteps creaking down the steps and the door clanking shut downstairs, Isaac stood staring into the glass of swirling black liquid. The tremors came, quick and wicked, flashing through his system and weakening his knees. Stumbling, he settled into his chair and leaned his head back, closing his eyes tight against a sting. Too swiftly, the image of a black-winged angel flew from the depths of his mind. A gasp lodged in his throat. Prisms of color dashed from the flowing black veils; black hair spilled as if tossed in the wind, pale glazed eyes and bloody crimson trails—

Bolting upright, Isaac rested gripping the arms of the chair, heart racing, breath halted, then gasped and ragged. Shaking his head, he pushed from the chair . . . work. He had work to do. The shop. His books . . . he had work to do.

Still fuming, Ronnie passed through the leaded glass doors and managed to reach her room on the second floor without interruption. How that green-eyed monster had managed to crawl under her skin, she suffered no desire to investigate. She'd come to Bentwood with a single goal in mind, a single goal that could offer a twofold benefit. She didn't intend to be put off by a bunch of close-lipped, tight-assed country bumpkins. By God, if they intended to accuse her of being a bitch and meant to treat like one, maybe she'd just need to show them what a *bitch* she could be . . . and that included Mark Jarvins, who thought he could dangle a few lousy carrots and expect her to crawl into a hole.

Anger helped. Anger always diffused the hurt, and she knew at this moment, if nothing else, the cutting edge of those chilly green eyes had hurt. The accusation in that single scathing glance had confirmed her status as an outsider, and even if it were true . . . somehow, that had hurt.

Well, by God, if glances could kill, she would've been dead the moment she'd popped from the womb, and she'd learned to cope, to live with indifference and scorn. If that jerk thought he could get her goat and send her packing with his gaze, he had another thought coming.

Grabbing her notebooks—the small one from her purse and the larger one from her satchel—Ronnie slapped them on the table and settled onto the tapestry chair.

Within a half-hour, she'd scribbled on more than a dozen legal-sized pages. From offhanded notes and impressions to names and family ties where applicable, she'd listed any wayward thought to cross her mind.

The information from Amy Sue alone had filled two entire pages, and every time she initialed I.B. alongside another female name, her anger rose anew. This character hit by storm . . . and that false note clamored.

Turning to a clean sheet, Ronnie began listing what she knew about Bently, beginning with the physical description over which she struggled. "Tall, dark, handsome, mysterious . . . *trite!* Slippery. As phony as a three-dollar bill. Green-eyed snake . . . *a bit melodramatic.*"

'Facts . . . Just the facts, kid . . .' Those were Max Hagen's words spoken in his best Humphrey Bogart voice.

Ronnie settled for, ". . . 6'2". Green-eyed. Walnut-haired. Approx. 185 lbs. Between 25 and 30 yrs. old . . ." The rest came more easily as she began listing what she'd heard or collected in the past several hours. "Regular travel abroad. Antique dealer. Throws money around. In good with a local officer . . ." *Bribery??? Front operation for drugs or contraband???*

For a long moment, she stared at the words she'd written, her mind turning over the past several hours, recalling those first seconds when he'd stepped through the side door and seemed to stare at her. Had he, in those seconds, thought someone could be watching his door? Could he have been expecting a faceless stranger? Arms or drugs? Fenced stolen goods? In the diner this morning, he'd fairly ignored her until she'd spoken, then he'd reacted somewhat strangely to halt her from mentioning the value of that Dresden in front of Megan Price. Casual introduction before departure, an invitation, and the mention of his wares . . .? Had Ronnie, unwittingly, stumbled upon a neat little operation tucked into the middle of nowhere?

Could he have intentionally left her an opening, setting the stage for her to visit his shop for something more than an antique buying spree? If she'd spoken the right words, would he have invited her to a back office and offered her anything from stolen jewels to heroin? She hadn't followed the script. She'd missed the one o'clock appointment and apparently missed her cue. Instead of a trip to a private powwow, he'd appeased her over dinner. Either to throw her off track or to learn what she might have already discovered.

She remembered his outrage over the mention of reporters descending on Bentwood, but he'd covered that reaction and dismissed his concern in a few heartbeat ticks.

He was definitely a man with a very dark secret, a man with a past. As well as a present, she considered as she read her words again.

A front operation for a black-market enterprise? That was more than possible. It was also plausible if he considered these local folks a bunch of brainless backward nits. That could even explain his indifference to women. No ties. No commitments. If the need arose, he could leave in a hurry with nothing and no one to hold him.

Ronnie could almost admire him for that particular logic. Whether he intended to spare himself complications or spare a woman's tender heart, the result was the same.

Green-eyed devil. He was handsome, and apparently, vain enough to know he could snare any blasted woman he wanted. Ronnie could even admit, he had a certain dangerous charm recalling those few fleeting smiles that showed just a teasing flash of straight white teeth.

'Bently' certainly didn't sound Italian, but somehow, she could fit him easily into Len Devinio's Sicilian mold. She wouldn't expect him to wear his given name anyway if he were a soldier in some underworld smuggling operation. He had the kind of features to wear as well on an Irishman as on French, English . . . Sax. Saxon? English? If she recalled her history, the Saxons were of German descent, but they invaded England in early AD. Anglo-Saxon. English. Did that provide some basis for that nickname, or was it far simpler . . . Like Tim Spencer shortening the name Isaac in good ole country boy style? Did it matter one way or the other?

Who the hell was Isaac Bently? What was this fellow hiding? And what was his connection to two gruesome homicides? Somehow all those questions fit together . . . and a crawling sensation slid down her spine, starting her thinking. The possibilities only began with a drug cartel. Maybe—just maybe, the green-eyed monster did a little supplying on the side. PCP could certainly create excessive violence to account for twenty stabs with a pitchfork . . .

If drugs were involved, Mark Jarvins would already know. No way could someone on PCP do that extent of damage without leaving traces of evidence and more clues than Mark would ever need. With the blind Jarvins held over the salient facts, it would serve him right to bumble around in the dark looking for a drug supplier while the local kingpin shared English shopping spree tips with a local lawman over pork chops.

Leaning back in her chair, scanning the list of notes she'd written on Isaac Bently, doubt niggled the nape of her neck. The words were there, enough to form a solid picture, and yet something felt wrong . . . and only seconds passed before Ronnie realized why the entire image remained out of focus.

Stupid—a stupid—sentimental—purely female weakness. Yet once the vision appeared, it held fast. Over and over, she replayed the scene in her head—Bently hurrying two strides, relieving the boy of the box, and reaching reflexively to scuff the blond shaggy head. Once that image firmed, Ronnie remembered loitering in his store, listening to the quiet exchange between man and boy, casual, friendly despite the preoccupation.

'. . . Did you ever collect baseball cards when you were a kid?'

'No,' simple and direct.

Slightly off-key, Ronnie remembered and in retrospect, wondered about his preoccupation. If she'd caught the gist of the conversation, the boy questioned Bently's baseball card savvy. Bently had offered subtle assurance to boost the boy's morale before sending him on his way.

And why the hell had the guy purchased an extra soda so close to closing time? He couldn't have expected her, but he'd expected someone. If she'd waited, would she have seen a sedan parked at the curb?

"Damnit," Ronnie snapped and reached forward, slamming her notebook closed. This was going nowhere. What she needed was a little more than local information could provide, and she wouldn't risk incriminating Isaac Bently without a damn good reason. That had never been her style. If she found hard evidence, something other than her overzealous imagination to warrant Mark's interest, she'd hand that evidence to Jarvins gladly, but not before.

With her thought, she pushed off the chair and strode to the bed; Settling onto the mattress, she lifted the phone.

On the fifth ring, the robust voice answered with a simple, "Yes?"

"Hi ya, Max. How's tricks?"

"Looking up," Max Hagen laughed. "How's my favorite lady sleuth?"

"You are a mean man, Max Hagen," she played, feeling better with every passing second.

"I could say my favorite female journalist, but then I'd get myself into trouble. If Barb Winters ever got wind of this, she'd think I was a snake two-timing her like that. Honey, you have to settle for sleuth," he said as if running out of air. "I've been romancing Barb too long."

Ronnie huffed the first honest laugh of the day. "Max, I missed you."

"Missed you too, baby doll," he said with a paternal catch in his voice. "So, what's up? You didn't just call to hear me rattle on about my love life."

Flopping back on the bed, Ronnie conjured a mental image of Max Hagen. Even all these years later, she blushed with the memory of how horribly in love she'd been at eight years old. At forty-six, he was still one of the most gorgeous men she knew with his slick black hair and fire-Irish blue eyes. He'd been a cop for nearly twenty-five years, more than eighteen of them with a gold shield. He sat behind a desk, now, in one of the finest precincts in Arlington because that's where he wanted to be. "I need a favor, Max."

"You know the drill," Max said, adopting the sober tone of his profession. "But I'm listening."

"I need to run a check on someone, quietly and discreetly, Max. I don't know if this fellow has a record. I know he has a passport, and he travels abroad once or twice a year. I'd like to know what all you can find out, and I don't want it flying across the FBI hotwire if something turns up."

"You want to tell me what this is about, Ron?" Unmasked, his concern transcended the line.

"Maybe if you promise not to laugh all the way to your office," she said, letting her voice and mind relax.

"Uhhh, alright. Boy Scout's Honor," Max played, not quite accepting her ruse.

"It's personal," she said simply. "This fellow's becoming an itch in my . . . neck," she said politely and heard Max stifle a genuine laugh. "Max! You're already laughing."

"Na-aa," he heaved, fighting for control. She could almost see his eyes squinting, his lips strained to clamp shut an iron jaw. "Not me, baby doll. I'd never laugh when a woman's heart starts to pound."

That sat her upright in a hurry. "That's not exactly the kind of *pain-in-the-ass* he's become, Max. This is not Mark Jarvins; although, if you'd care to know, I've seen him recently. Poor guy looks like the job's taking a toll. He's getting old and decrepit already. A little like somebody else I know."

On the other end of the line, Max Hagen struggled against more muffled guffaws though he fought it off gallantly. He managed to snort in her ear only once before recovering enough to ask, "So, you want to give me his name or uh . . . is that the part I have to find out?"

"You're all devils," she said in disgust, but the instant the word escaped, her antenna shot up. Devils. Pitchforks? "I'll be damned," she said softly, distractedly. Devil. Pitchfork. Full moon. *Devil worship?* Had she missed something? Was there a helluva lot more to these murders than the usual psychotic? Symbolism . . . and again she thought about Isaac Bently. The black velvet cloth in his showcase. Most of those trinkets had carried something of a cultist flair with mystical and possibly black magic connotations. Even that heavy silver ring on his right hand bore an oddly mystical flair.

"I'll be damned," she uttered again. 'Interesting collection,' she'd said, and Bently had eyed the case with a bemused glance. 'Suppose it is,' he'd said and flagged her toward the front door, away from the case.

"Ron?" Max asked. "Want to tell me why you're going to be damned, or is it just on general principles?"

"That's not funny," she laughed a little nervously with her train of thought. "Not one bit.

"I'm no longer laughing, baby doll," Max said, and he was certainly not laughing. "Where are you at the moment, and what are you working on?"

"You have enough of your own cases to worry about, Max," Ronnie decided, sobering too. "Why don't I just call you at your office on Monday? And if you feel like telling me anything—"

"Ronnie, you haven't given me a name to check out, and I'd not enjoy running a personal check on your credit cards just to figure out where the hell to reach you. So, where are you?"

"You are not only mean, you're a shit," she said simply, but she parted with Isaac Bently's name and current address, surprised at the difficulty in that simple undertaking. Offering Max the Inn address and her room number was far simpler. They chatted for a few more moments, and Max made her promise to call Jesse soon.

In the lingering silence after the warmth of Max's voice, Ronnie suffered a pang of homesickness. If the big dumb jerk had waited another ten years, she would've married Max Hagen, but he'd dared to remarry nearly nine years ago, breaking her tender teenage heart. Despising Karen, the new Mrs. Maxwell Hagen, might have made life simpler, but Jesse had won hands down in that score. Jess had despised her stepmother with all the vigilance of an only daughter, although she was the youngest of two. Someday Ronnie vowed to enlighten her best friend and to hell with the consequences. Jesse had no right to be jealous of Karen or her two little half-brothers. Max hadn't filed for divorce. Darcy, X-Mrs. Hagen had managed that on her own, stomping Max into the ground and nearly ripping out his heart when taking his girls from him.

Ronnie remembered all the times she'd seen Max's unmarked sedan in front of the school. If only to spend that extra half hour with his daughters, Max had faithfully carted them from their new private school to one lesson or another. Karen was no Darcy Hagen. Karen was the kind of wife and mother Ronnie hoped to be someday. One who wouldn't mind staying home for her husband and children. She would probably need to hire a cook and housekeeper, but no nannies, no sitters every day, no TV dinners left in the frig for her old man . . .

CHAPTER 8

Launching off the bed, Ronnie snapped from her insane idling with that latest hit. *Old man! God!* The last thing she ever intended was to be strapped down to some sagging middle-aged jerk who would fit the visage of 'old man' and make her wear a mantel like 'old lady.' She would be a horrible parent, a wretched wife. In a word, she would be a *bitch*, and the thought of all these folks labeling her so accurately offered no consolation whatsoever.

Ronnie barely reached the table intending to work on her notes, but the knock intruded.

From the table, she called, "Who is it?"

"Room service," Mark Jarvins announced.

Fanning her gaze over the clutter, she slipped her large notebook under the mattress before striding to the door.

Mark had removed his jacket and tie. He wore his white shirt sleeves rolled to his forearms and carried a bottle by the neck in one hand, two stemware glasses in the other. A somewhat weary smirk touched his lips and eyes. "May I come in?"

"This is not a terrace, dear," she said as his gaze swept over her hairstyle, her face, warming in a rapid descent.

"And that's not the same get-up you wore this afternoon." His attention lifted, more interested. "If you went to this trouble to have dinner with me and I missed it, I truly don't deserve you."

"You grovel nicely, but I think that's enough," she decided. "I wouldn't want to burst your bubble or prick your ego by telling you—I did have another dinner engagement with a couple of very handsome men."

His blue eyes clouded, and he nearly sneered. "I heard. Can I come in anyway?"

He heard? Oh, this was rich. How much did he have on Bently? And how fast would the warnings erupt? "Suppose since you brought the wine, I'll have to accept the entire package," she said and pulled the door open.

Closing, bolting the door by habit, she caught Mark's gaze returning from the open bathroom door. Apparently, he'd expected to find one of those handsome men in this room. Undecided between flattery or offense, Ronnie ignored both for the moment. She'd need to check her emotions if she intended to pry a little more information from Mark's locked jaw. Clearing the table, she commented, "This is just so romantic, Mark. I particularly like the ice bucket."

He grinned with a near boyish embarrassment as he produced a corkscrew from his breast pocket. "Desperate measures, Ron. I'm lucky I found a bottle of wine at this hour."

"Oh, come on, can't be that difficult with an elegant dining room downstairs."

"These people do not like their government," he said, annoyed. "I swear to God, they thought I intended to dust the bottle and glasses for prints." He held up one of the shiny crystal glasses, grinning, mocking, "Look, dear. No spots."

She suddenly remembered why she'd nearly fallen in love with the jerk. He could always make her laugh, even in the worst conditions. Relaxing, she decided she must be living right to have Mark follow so closely after talking to Max, especially after the roller coaster day.

His blue eyes caught and held, lighting with a hint of amusement and fondness. "I have missed hearing you laugh," he said in a moment of sobriety.

"Better hurry and open that wine, hon, or we really will need some ice."

He laughed then and popped the cork, filling both goblets before handing her one, lifting his for a toast. "To old and dear friends?"

"We'd have to name names," she said lightly and caught his mocked flash of hurt. "How about just . . . to friends?"

"Good friends," he agreed with a half-smile and touched her glass.

She tasted the wine before looking into the red mix, then tipped her head to read the label. "Very nice," she said and met his intent gaze. "If you used your government discount, it's no wonder they were mad."

"I think they jacked the price up another 50 percent," he grumbled. "Too many stories about twenty-five-thousand-dollar toilet seats."

She laughed, "Sad but true." Motioning for him to sit, she slid into the chair furthest from the bed. "You should have mentioned you earn a modest salary as well as the next guy."

"Good thing you didn't say honest dollar," he smirked. "They'd have really been suspicious."

"Come on," she said, sobering. "Can't be that tough around here."

"I have a county sheriff who believes he's Judge Roy Bean, dead set on hanging the next guy he sees lift a pitchfork, despite a population of over two hundred farmers in the nearest vicinity. I have a local police chief who fully believes my entire reason for existing is to tramp on his toes. And I have an entire battalion of vigilante citizens who will have my head on a platter if they don't get the right head in place first. No, I suppose it's not that bad," he paused, almost managing a genuine smile. "My partner might have carried out his threat to castrate me if I ever saw you again."

"Lenny was always such a dear," she said wistfully and stifled a laugh as Mark's eyes darkened and he huffed a sound. "Alright, count your blessings, Jarvins," she said with an echo of laughter. "Your jewels are still intact."

"That's what I really found charming about you, Ron," he said with his jaw relaxing. "Your sunny disposition."

"You're tempting fate," she said with a mocked threat and decided the foreplay was about over. "So, let's talk about something nice. Like your list of suspects."

"And there's another," he pointed out. "You always go for the gusto."

"Please, no psychoanalysis this evening," she smiled. "I didn't bring my wading boots. But, I'll admit, I'd love to hear your profile. I'm guessing, by the size and weight of the victims, you're judging between 180 and 210 lbs. Any larger, the assault could be slow. Less, the power suffers. Reasonably tall, Caucasian male, age between twenty-five and thirty-five based on the few loose words I've accumulated." She paused to read Mark's blank gaze. "So, how am I doing so far?"

"The weight could be wrong," he offered and shrugged. "We have a few controversial opinions."

"I'd side with Roberta over a county coroner any day of the week," Ronnie confirmed. "What's her take? Or will you make me pester her?"

"You would, and she'd bite hook, nail, and sinker."

"Because she knows I wouldn't jeopardize your operation with a loose lip or a turn of the pen," Ronnie said quietly, watching Mark gauge her words as he studied his glass. Leaned back in the spindle-backed chair, an ankle crossed at his knee, he appeared as young and handsome as ever despite his profession. At first glance, no one would guess that he was a federal agent. They hailed from the same unlikely backgrounds, and to hear him tell it, his parents were no more approving of his profession than her parents were consenting of hers. After meeting his parents, however, she'd questioned that proclamation. They'd seemed only pleased . . . but therein lay the proof. Politically and socially connected, the Jarvins were as adept at subterfuge as her own family. Through that shared understanding, she and Mark had become friends and very nearly lovers. Looking at him, Ronnie knew the friendship had held, the affection lingered, but the flames of passion had doused.

Turning her attention to the case, she commented, "You do know I don't write these stories for the jazz or thrill, Mark." When she drew his thoughtful gaze, she continued, "When, or if this story goes into print, it will be like all the rest—an even blend of fact and fiction to borderline fairytale. I never came into this business to victimize anyone, and you should damn well know it."

"Ronnie," he said quietly, drawing her name to affect sobriety. "It's not a matter of trust here, not with you or your article," he continued. "I know how you write. I know whatever I tell you would be held in confidence. I know you're too smart even to write the damned details down or put them on tape."

"Then why the hell are you holding out on me?" she asked with a subtle edge.

"Because I want you to get the hell out of here," he said simply, his gaze direct. "That's as plain and simple as I can put it. I don't want you anywhere near Bentwood."

And she understood explicitly, softening her voice with the power of his affection. "Mark, I'm not asking for your protection. Or for your permission to be here. Likewise, I'm not leaving until whatever's started here is stopped. I haven't run from anything yet, and I'm not about to start now."

"You are one stubborn young woman, Miss Bryson."

That 'Miss Bryson' piqued her with a flash of Bently speaking that 'miss' in the diner. The arrogant bastard had called her 'Ronnie' only once and had made it sound like he tasted sour grapes on his tongue. She barely started to consider him a green-eyed devil when the thought of black magic flashed in her mind. Cult leader? Helluva front, that classy little antique shop of his. Europe . . . very big on medieval rituals in England and all over Europe. High Priest? Warlock? God knows, he had enough Bentwood women falling over him to start his own coven back in these hills, or were they *harems?* Did he keep them all at a distance, maybe only satisfying them once a month over a stone slab? Black candles, incantations—

"I'd love to know where you just went," Mark commented, snapping the spell of her thoughts.

"Doubtful you'd want to follow," she said offhandedly and remembered where she'd left off. "You can either offer me the inside track to help this investigation in my own subtle way or take your wine with you on the way out, Mark. I don't have time for cat and mouse any more than you do. This won't blow over. And if you're sitting here twiddling your thumbs, then you're hoping something comes in from forensics to lend you direction. I don't have that luxury."

Sighing, he shook his head. "Wherever did I go wrong?"

"You got assigned to a stalker case when you should have been overseeing homicide," she supplied helpfully.

His eyes darkened as he looked at her. "That's one misstep I don't regret, Ronnie. No matter what you might think or feel, I loved being in love with you, and I wouldn't trade knowing you for the world."

"I take back all the nasty things I've ever thought about you," she decided. "You're not a snobby, pigheaded jerk. Arrogant, possibly, but in a charming sort of way. And a very nice man."

"Alright, smartass," he said and reached, collecting the bottle, refilling her glass and his own. Setting the bottle in the center of the table, effecting a challenge, Mark settled onto his chair and met her gaze. "What we have, is a bona fide psycho. Smart, vicious, and quick, which is where the weight theory becomes twisted. The speed of the jabs may have been more powerful than the force behind them. This person—and I'm using the term loosely—picks his victims carefully, watches them, and knows their routine. When you see the locations, you'll understand how easy that bit of stalking could be. The barns are large enough to hide a world of sins along with one patient psychopath. We believe the killer was inside the barn before the victims arrived.

In neither case were the tools stored near the doors, and both bodies were found near the door. Both men were struck from behind when leaving the barn. With deadly accuracy, this son of a bitch severed the spinal column in both first strikes, and I don't believe that was coincidence or luck.

"First strike, the back stiffens, shoulders jerk. Before these gentlemen knew what hit them, the spikes were out. They were flat on their backs. Then the fun really started," Mark said with a flat, leaden tone. An orator to a macabre play, his eyes listed to the wine glass. "Next strike, straight through the larynx. Exit screams. The first victim, Farnsworth, might have gotten lucky. His cause of death was listed as massive cardiac arrest. By the scant traces of blood in the lungs, he checked out early and missed the main event. Engler wasn't so lucky."

Making a mental note, Ronnie listened silently as Mark described the jabs with the clinical precision of a coroner. In chronological order, he listed which major organs were systematically destroyed as Engler lay helpless.

"The guy didn't have a prayer," Mark said woodenly. "There's evidence he might have tried crawling, but that only suggests this psycho toyed with him, probably talked to him, and tormented him between jabs. We estimate the killer spent between twenty and thirty minutes with Engler. We're also reasonably sure the killer knew that Farnsworth departed the party prematurely. The pattern was there but with no delay. By the trajectory, we're estimating 5'8" to 6' but coming in low and fast. The weight's probably between 165 and 180. We're not talking size or bulk, just fast and pumped." His gaze landed on Ronnie with a powerful intensity. "And that's what sucks here, Ronnie, because I'll tell you what the fuck this feels like to me, and it bugs the hell out of me."

She waited, already sensing what he was about to say.

"I think you have the age right, twenty-five to thirty-five. We're dealing with a helluva lot of suppressed hostility. We have some scrawny little asshole with a grudge that might have been building some ten or twenty years. Maybe his daddy beat the shit out of him or abused him. Now, all of a sudden, his cork blows, and he's out for blood. No more drowning kittens or strangling chickens out behind the barn. We have this little asshole making haystacks out of these guys, and what sucks is, I don't think he'll wait for a full moon to strike again. I think he fucked up with Farnsworth, but he enjoyed Engler. He's got a taste for the kill, and he's not about to hold back. Meanwhile, we're scratching our asses because there's no trace of this little bastard. No footprints on the floors with hay all over the damn place. No footprints to say where or how he entered or exited the barn with a hundred cows milling about. No getaway car parked anywhere that anyone noticed. No prints on the fork handle, and it was worn smooth enough to pick up prints. If this character left his mark in that barn, it's literally like trying to find a needle in a haystack, and he was smart. He never got close enough to leave a physical sample."

"You're not ruling out sex crime," Ronnie said quietly.

"Total annihilation of human functions, Ron. But this character didn't leave anything of himself lying around."

"Then sexual mutilation was evident."

"Without a doubt," he said wearily.

"What was taken," Ronnie asked and held Mark's tense gaze. She was asking for his complete trust, and she understood the battle behind his hesitation.

"You won't let me get away with a partial analysis, huh, Ron?"

"You use your forensics and formulas, Mark," she said patiently. "I'm not knocking those. I know you read those signs like an open book, and you're the best. I work differently, and my methods may not have a yardstick to gauge for accuracy, but with enough pieces, you know I'm effective."

"Too damned accurate, Ron," he said with a troubled frown. "That's what scares the hell out of me. You put this together at the wrong time in the wrong place, and I have a loose cannon ready to detonate. I don't want you in the blast. You understand? I don't want you suddenly face to face with this maniac pushing the wrong buttons."

And he would suffer tremendously if that scenario ever came to pass. They might not have become lovers in the technical sense, but they'd been in love, and he did know how she worked. He would blame himself if he supplied the rope to hang herself. "Alright," she conceded. "Keep the brass ring."

"That was too easy," he said suspiciously, eyeing her with his wine glass poised near his lips. "What's the catch?"

"You might consider me mellowing with age," Ronnie commented. "I've decided to go easy on you for the same reason."

"Oh, good, now I know I'm had," he said more suspiciously as he lowered the glass without taking a sip. "A concession and a dig all in one breath?"

"See what happens when I try to be nice," she said with mocked irritation. "Screw you, Jarvins. Don't tell me another thing if it will make you feel better."

"I stopped feeling good three years ago," he said in a pensive tone, his gaze softer. "I still feel like a heel."

She smiled, realizing perhaps for the first time that she'd truly survived the pain, the shame of their parting. After all, they'd reconciled for a time before she'd finally walked away. "It's in the past, Mark. Let's let sleeping dogs lie, shall we?"

"If I'd have known you were serious—"

"Mark, drop it," she said without malice or regret.

Several seconds passed before he finally seemed to grasp her words. His brow smoothed as a smile crept into his mustached lips.

"About that first autopsy," Ronnie continued quietly. "I had a chat with someone who saw that crime scene. As I understand it, there were massive amounts of blood, and the fork was left protruding from the neck. Are you positive Farnsworth died of cardiac arrest?"

The smile had vanished instantly. "Who the hell have you been talking to?"

"Come on, dear, let's not squabble over details. Just tell me how a man manages to bleed like a butchered pig after a major heart attack stops the beat?"

Irritated, Mark answered, "According to the coroner, Farnsworth might have hung in for about five minutes, and there's where we have speed again. Twenty-four strikes in vital organs within five minutes or less. I saw enough of the photos to judge your witness's accuracy."

"The fork. Was it left in Engler?"

"You want in on this in the worst way, don't you?"

"That's the worst way to put it, Mark, but I don't like timebombs any more than you do."

"Alright," he said bluntly, his gaze steady. "Here's the deal. I'm bringing you in as an official consultant to the Federal Bureau of Investigation. I'll have your goddamn badge here in the morning. I've already cleared it with my superiors, and you can tell your daddy 'Thank you' when you get around to it. One thing I'm going to make very clear, Veronica."

Stunned, she waited, disbelieving the words.

With a slow cocky smile, he commented, "I'm in charge."

"Excuse me?"

He laughed then, a low good sounding rumble. "God, it felt good to say that."

"You're insane," she decided and reached for her wine glass, studying him suspiciously over the rim of her glass.

Still smiling, he commented, "Don't look at me like that. I don't bite. Although I sort of feel akin to the cat that swallowed the canary."

"You've been in Bentwood too long, pal," she said lightly and lowered her glass. "You're slipping."

Leaning, plucking the bottle off the table, he reached to fill her glass, but she slashed her hand forward to cover the rim. Amused, he leaned back and filled his goblet with a generous amount. After he took another sip, he adopted a more sober expression and rested contemplating. "It's like this, Ronnie. The minute I saw you this morning, I knew the chances of getting you out of here were slim to none. You won't apply to Quantico and get the damned credentials to follow proper procedure, so I didn't have a helluva lot of choice. Enlist you as a consultant or arrest you in the interest of national security. You're a tough lady, but I didn't think you'd like the food behind bars. Ergo, consultant."

"Then what the hell was all that song and dance? You could have taken me into that damned station—"

"Slow down, slugger," he said haltingly. "First of all, I don't want you flashing your consultant badge. Keep it on you but consider this undercover work." He smirked. "Pretend you're a freelance writer working for the Post."

"You are a shit," she said, smiling slightly.

"Next, and this is important, Ron, no leeway on it," he said soberly. "I am in charge. I'm calling the shots. If I tell you to back off, you back off. This is not turning into another case like three years ago. I don't want to run down a damn alley and find my gun pointed at your head, you understand? If you breach my trust with this, if you go off on one of your hair-raising sidetracks, you're out of here. I want to know where you go, who you're with, and when you're getting back. And I want you to hear me when I say, 'no way.' Or 'not yet.' Get it?"

"You were testing me," she said absently. "Should I question the details you gave me?"

"All legit, Ron," he said with enough dismay to prove himself. "But yes. Part of the reason I told you was a test. Three years can change a person, and can change a person's perspective," he admitted quietly. "So, maybe I was testing me, too. I had to know you weren't some overblown figment of my imagination. I remembered you as bold, brassy, and tough as nails. I had to be sure. This is one vicious mother, and his handiwork's already turned a few sturdy gentlemen green."

She understood entirely, and she could fault neither his need for a test nor his method. "I passed."

"Like a trooper, but I still don't know why you let me slide on the souvenir."

Smiling faintly, she commented, "I knew you'd be miserable if I forced that out of you and something happened to me."

He studied her for two seconds before his face turned the fancy shade of curdled milk, and he huffed a quiet disgusted laugh that sounded more like a punch in the gut. "So, I toss you the whole fucking enchilada." He shook his head, smiling weakly, "Len's right. That damned arrogant dago's right. I'm so nuts about you, I can't see my ass from a hole in the ground."

"Len always had such a way with words," Ronnie said breezily and decided he looked far too genuinely hurt to hurt alone. Slipping off her chair, she rounded the table and leaned, wrapping her arms about him, realizing she'd wanted just to hug him since he'd come through the door. With his arms closing about her shoulder and waist, she remembered how easily they had fit together, how comfortably the slow idle moments had passed. "Thank you, Mark," she said smoothly against his ear, breathing in the soft musky scent of his cologne.

Against her neck, he brushed a kiss as he uttered, "I am nuts about you, Ron."

With a sense of how swiftly this could become something more than she was willing to finish, she slipped from his arm, clasping his hand. Touching his cheek, she leaned and brushed a quick kiss on his furry lips. Looking into his warm eyes, she remembered how she'd once believed she could drown in those pale blue depths. The flames had doused. "Partners shouldn't become romantically involved."

"Yea, that's what Len says," he said and flashed a quick annoyed smile. "Probably why he jumped on this consultant idea. Little prig knew I'd get tangled in my own rope."

Ronnie laughed lightly, "I can't understand why he finds me so offensive."

"Hell," he said while letting her ease away a few more inches, probably for his benefit. "That's easy, slugger. He's about 99 percent in love with you the same as me, and he can't convince his Godfather to let him marry outside the church. If you converted, he'd be on his knees.

"Converted? To Catholicism?" She *was* Catholic.

A sly smile crept into Mark's mustache; mischief danced over his tired eyes. "He uh . . . he has the impression you're Jewish."

"I'm . . . Jewish," she said slowly, sensing an odd cynicism belying his musing shine. "Why would he think that?"

"Hey, I had to do *something*," he feigned innocently, sounding like a ten-year-old. "You wouldn't believe the hassle it is to fudge one of those goddamn forms that we pop out of those damned computers. Took the best hacker this side of Kansas, but it was the only goddamn way to convince Len. Son of a bitch thought he'd do a Don Juan on you or play Marco Polo and blast me out the gate—"

Not entirely certain that he was joking, Ronnie stifled a laugh, but with the mischief returning in his eyes, she lost rein. Laughing, After the roller coaster day, it felt good to laugh, and she couldn't stop. She was becoming hysterical, and Mark was unmerciful when he was on a roll.

"Just don't tell him, alright? When your badge comes in tomorrow, just say 'Tannenbaum' or 'bar mitzvah,' or say 'chutzpah.' As long as it sounds Jewish or German. Hell, he won't know the difference. Just be careful with chutzpah, he might think you're trying to cuss him in Italian, and he's fluent in his native tongue. Probably take offense, too, him being the big sensitive type . . ."

By the time Ronnie drew a clear breath, she rested on the floor, accepting the tissue Mark handed her and still huffing soft laughs. All kidding aside, however, they had work to do. And the floor seemed as good of a place as any with thick carpet and bed as a backrest. Without needing to consult her notes, Ronnie began simply. "Suppose I'll need to tell you a few things I've discovered."

"Officially, you're on the payroll," he said while flopping to rest beside her, donning another infamous smirk. "A hundred bucks a day, which uh . . . probably won't touch the publishing fees, but from here on, Ron, you go fiction on this one."

"You better up my wages, buster," she commented but let him off the hook. Methodically, she contemplated the salient points reflective of his scenario. Now that she'd drawn a partial profile, she could investigate the proper age groups. High school yearbooks should be easy enough to find, and those gems could hold a warehouse of information in a town this size. "We're looking for someone born and raised in Bentwood," she said and watched Mark for the verification, not entirely relieved by his hesitation.

"Not necessarily, but I'm banking on it," he said in guarded consideration. "Someone with a grudge against farmers. Rough guess, born and raised on a farm. If not in Bentwood, someplace like it."

Skin prickling, Ronnie sensed Mark's reluctance, and she knew abruptly—Isaac Bently was the cause. Something about Bently triggered Jarvins interest, over and above her sharing dinner with him. "Any suspects you'd care to mention?" she asked carefully.

"None we've come close to narrowing down," he answered somewhat evasively. "What do you have?"

"A lot of gossip," she said honestly and turned her attention to the facts. "Or, I should say, a little gossip. These people are as tight-lipped as a crooked politician. I had a good run while having my hair done," she admitted and lifted a hand, fluffing her ruined do. Just walking had probably sent it into a torrent of frizz and laying on it had probably mashed the hairspray to a flat mat against her scalp. "You know how I hate to gossip, Mark," she said with far more seriousness in her eyes. "What people tell me in earnest, I must weigh in earnest. If during someone's outpour, I find something I know you need, you'll hear about it."

"That's not how this works, Ron," he said carefully. "I need to know what you have to get where you're going."

"Take a hike, then, Mark," she said soberly. "I'm not a gossip columnist. That's not how I work or write. I can tell you generalities. Quite a few wives are not happy with their husbands and vice-versa. There are a few shoplifters under the age of eighteen . . ." And a thought sprang to life in her mind. Her gaze misting, she looked away, remembering an article on the microfiche. She'd skipped through several reels of film, scoring the Bender Falls Tribune in search of the political history of Bentwood, in search of Sheriff Taylor Grant's rise to a county office. "Twenty-five to thirty," she said absently and found Mark studying her. "That's the age parameter," she said absently. "And I think our psycho's homespun."

"Want to fill me in?" he asked quietly.

"Fifteen years ago, Bentwood had a little piece of dirty laundry they tucked under the rug but not before warranting a few clips in the Bender Falls Trib." Her gaze misty, she stared across the carpet, remembering. "Dogs . . . a dozen dogs disappeared . . . the carcasses were found in the woods over several months. Family pets," she said absently. "Eventually, someone got pissed and decided to notify the paper when Bentwood P.D. couldn't find the 'pack of wild dogs' responsible. No one mentioned kids or a kid, but I sensed the pack of wild dogs was never found, and I doubt a mountain lion was running around town. Fifteen years ago," she said absently. "Suppose a ten-year-old could pull that off, but not much younger, and I'm betting anyone over fifteen would've been more careful. I'm having a hard time believing whatever started then waited this long to continue." Her gaze shifted to Mark, seeing his wheels spinning as well. "I think we're looking for someone who didn't quit but got careful when it went public. It's possible, that this character went away for a while and returned. But I don't think the killing stopped. Are you sure there's nothing in your files resembling this MO?"

"I'll run it again," he said idly. "But I don't think I'll find anything. I'll buy your theory that we'll find acts of violence. Missing cats, dogs, hell, even sheep, but that could've been covered up. I'm inclined to believe the homicidal acts were repressed, possibly fantasized. I'll need the police reports from fifteen years ago. After seeing Farnsworth . . . I think he was the first."

What she'd not said, what still nettled the nape of her neck, was another single premise. Devil worship. Black mass. The use of animals. "I'd like to see the photos if there are any, Mark," she said simply.

"You just earned your first hundred bucks, partner," he said lightly, smiling crookedly with the tip of his head. "Nice catch. One that'll probably have me facing off with a certain crotchety police chief at the crack of dawn. The son of a bitch was on the force fifteen years ago."

"Don't be too hard on him, Mark," she said lightly. "We're talking about people he's known and lived with all his life."

"I profiled a goddamn serial killer in his office this afternoon, told him and his band of country cronies what the fuck we were looking for, what signs could lead to other signs, and that son of a bitch sat there tongue-in-cheek like King-fucking-Tut."

"You truly haven't had a good day," Ronnie said while thinking of her own roller coaster. Tipping her wrist, she stared momentarily, doubting the hands could be correct. The evening light had long ago faded, leaving only a soft glow of streetlamps on the sheer curtains and darkness between the cracks. Almost eleven o'clock, and she hadn't slept more than four hours in the past thirty. Just the thought forced her to suppress a yawn as she glimpsed at Mark's softened gaze. "It's late. How about we pick this up over eggs and coffee? My treat since I'm earning my keep."

Lazily, he shifted his hand, running the back of his fingers over her arm propped on her knee. Smiling just a little, he touched her cheek. "Don't suppose you'd consider letting me stay, would you?"

"It's going to be very difficult working with you, partner," she said and clasped his hand, halting the tingles down her neck. Using his strength, she started off the floor, counting on him to help and not disappointed when he lent her a boost. Standing, she tugged his hand. "Let's go, Marco Polo. Up and out with you."

"I'm dead on my feet," Mark commented as his legs sagged on the floor, and his head flopped backward on the mattress. "Have pity?" he heaved and snapped his eyes shut.

Huffing a laugh, Ronnie dropped his hand and commented, "Fine. But you get the floor, and I'm not sharing my pillows."

Breaking from an elaborate snore, he lifted one eyelid with a genuine effort and sighed, pushing smoothly off the carpet. "Alright, already. A guy knows when he's not wanted."

She did want him or thought she might like to have him, which was a good reason to keep her mouth shut, walk him to the door and nudge him into the hall. Even accounting for a few bad scenes, life with Mark Jarvins had been sort of nice. He would make love the way he did all else, smoothly, efficiently, gently with a rush of raw fierce energy . . . and that should be enough. That should be more than enough to satisfy a woman.

Jerking herself off the door where she'd sagged, Ronnie jolted at the motion in the corner of her eye. Belatedly, she recognized her own reflection in the dresser mirror.

Why the hell did she look like a scared rabbit? *For God's sake!* Eyes as round as silver dollars, lips parted, face pale . . .

Exhaustion!

"Go to hell," she snapped at the apparition in the mirror and turned her attention to collect her nightclothes from her single garment bag. Debating between a laugh or a curse, she held up the teddy bear nightie with the blasted 'teddy bears' printed all over it. These weren't the silk pajamas she'd intended to grab from her dresser last evening . . . and what the hell was this sudden fascination with pajamas? She just slept in the stupid things anyway!

Half asleep before hitting the pillow, a pair of green eyes lingered in Ronnie's mind long after the lights vanished.

CHAPTER 9

Stumbling, cursing, Isaac bumped the wall and trotted down several steps before catching his balance. Halted, heaving breaths, he studied the dozen glittering gold edges of Haviland dinner plates in his arms, the last load of the entire set that he'd just spent the past few hours unwrapping and washing. With a fleeting glimpse of painted glass exploding, he gasped a thin breath and clutched the plates more securely against his waist and chest.

Very slowly, carefully, he descended the last several steps and carried the plates through his office door, setting them gently on the desk to complete the sparkling collection. Only after he backed away, distancing himself from the glittering stacks of china, could he draw breath and relax. At roughly eight hundred dollars a setting, his misstep might have cost him more than five grand, but the money wasn't what niggled the edges of his ragged mind, never the money.

The money was a curse . . . or was cursed. No matter how much of his wealth he threw away, lost, or gave away, he acquired more. Stock dividends, bonds . . . "Fucking lottery," he muttered and turned from the sparkling surfaces. The magnificence of those dainty gold-edged plates glistening under neon was too bright to bear without aching.

Snapping the office light off, he locked the door for the first time since beginning his evening vigil and dragged himself up the steps, hitting the light switches in his wake by habit alone. In the morning, he would set the empty table in his shop . . . in the morning.

Peeling off his filthy clothes as he passed through his private suite, Isaac arrived in his bathroom, finished stripping, and turned the brass knobs full blast. Stepping into the claw-foot tub, he sank to rest in a cradle of old porcelain. If for no other reason, he would've bought this building for its ancient deep bathtub. Not like those modern washtubs with the sharp blunted edges to wrench necks and bruise heads. Good solid porcelain covered the cast iron basin with a nice long slope where a fellow could drop off into never-never land under warm suds and water.

The only drawback struck him belatedly. He hadn't bothered to engage the brass drain plug to raise the water around him.

Cursing, he dragged the plastic curtain into the tub, slammed his heel on the only modern contraption in the tub, and heaved a more contented breath as the water pounded him from the overhead shower nozzle. Better, that was better. He'd never minded the rain. He could sleep under a steady rain . . .

How long he dozed before the cold water rousted him to grope clumsily for the knobs, he had no idea, nor did he give it much thought. When he rousted for the second or third time, he clawed his way through a plastic curtain, waking as his knees slammed the tile floor. Only in his mind's eye, he saw the gray slashing rain, watched blood-red trails pouring over black stone . . .

Breath caught, muscles shivering from the cold, shaking from the tension of whatever torment had tossed him from the tub, Isaac dragged himself afoot and hung onto the sink to collect his balance and muddled thoughts. The images receded at a dizzying speed but still not fast enough. Images flashed neon with a kaleidoscope effect.

"No," the word dropped off his lips. His hanging head shook. "No."

A dozen more times, he spoke the word before finding sense to test the hot water, not entirely relieved by the heat. It was an old ritual, a familiar ritual. He stepped into the tub, remaining afoot and enlisting enough soap and shampoo to employ the warm water. Drying, collecting a silk robe from his bed, he belted it as he passed through the lighted rooms to his living room. The decanter of brandy remained on the desk in his office. He didn't bother with a glass. Flopping into his leather chair, he chugged several long swallows from the green and gold vessel while scanning his desk, finding his book.

Between glimpses of renaissance England and gulps of fine imported brandy, he managed to doze and sleep, waking and reading, drinking and dozing, waking and reading . . .

Somewhere between Queen Elizabeth and five a.m., Isaac set the bottle aside and read until his mind awakened to the feel of dawn outside the glass.

Checking the contents of his refrigerator, he stared in vacant wonder that he even bothered to leave the appliance plugged in. He should have turned it off two weeks ago before leaving for England. The baking soda and saltbox occupying the top shelf probably would've survived just fine, and eventually, he could've rechilled the two six-packs. Obviously, he'd need to find time to grocery shop. Then too, maybe he'd just send someone on an errand. Luckily, Tim had eaten before his visit last evening. Spencer would've had a field day with a glimpse of all those empty shelves.

In his room, Isaac gathered his scattered dirty clothes, disgusted with himself as he tossed the bundle into the laundry basket in the closet. As he collided with his reflection in the vanity mirror, he paused to consider what kind of night he'd endured, but the signs had vanished. He looked as he looked every morning—awake, rested, ready for another day—but looks were deceiving.

In a lousy mood, Isaac dressed in his usual ensemble, blue jeans, a plaid shirt, boots. Checking for his wallet, which had become an obsessive-compulsive habit to need to be repeated several times before reaching the first floor, he descended the steps.

The sunlight hurt after the dim watt of the hallway—especially glinting off the chrome dome and windshield of the Bentwood patrol car. With the wheels barely missing his boots, Isaac stood his ground and donned a faintly annoyed smirk as Tim beamed at him through the driver's window. At such an ungodly early hour, that smile shouldn't be nearly so pleasant. "You should scowl, Spence," Isaac commented idly. "At this hour, you should be scowling."

"I always smile when I annoy you. Or haven't you noticed?" Tim commented. "You still coming out tonight?"

"I agreed to come," he remembered.

"Yea, well, how about bringing your Jag? Tee's been dogging me for the past month to ask you to take him for a ride."

"Don't suppose he'll settle for the Vette, huh?" Isaac asked with his spirits lifting slightly.

"What's wrong with the Jag?"

"It's in front of the Vette, and old lady Handler will call your office again if I'm playing musical cars."

Spencer huffed a laugh. "Blow her a kiss. She'll faint," he suggested. "But either's okay. You got the kid spoiled rotten. See ya at seven."

He would take the Jag. If Tim Jr. was pestering his father, the boy would have no trouble manipulating his honorary Uncle Sax. The kid was a con artist. "Seven," Isaac agreed and held his breath as Spencer hit the gas. Thank God for good suspension on police cars.

"Maniac," Isaac threw after the receding rear bumper, then continued across the street.

Belatedly, he realized how early it must be for Spencer to be behind the wheel of his cruiser rather than his pickup.

On a hunch, Isaac veered toward the rear of the diner, not disappointed when he found the kitchen door open and glimpsed Meg through the screen. Already elbow-deep in flour, she stood at the cluttered counter, humming a soft rock tune until his rap of knuckles drew her quick gaze. "Any chance a neighbor can make an egg on your griddle?"

"You bring the egg?"

"No, that was part of my problem over home," Isaac admitted.

Wiping her hands on a towel, Meg came to the door, flipping the eyehook latch, smiling. "Okay, handsome, I'll bite. What was the other part of the problem?"

"I didn't have the toast or bacon to go with the egg," he mused as he stepped into the narrow workspace. Amazing, how much cooking could be done inside this compact area.

Smiling more, looking as fresh and delightful as ever with a smudge of flour on her cheek, Meg commented, "Let me get this straight, then. You want me to give you an egg, bacon, toast . . . and I suppose you'll want coffee, too?. . And you want to make it on my griddle."

"That's about the extent of it. Unless of course, *you* want to make it on your griddle, then I'll just saunter out to the dining room and become a paying customer."

She nearly giggled as she patted his arm. "Honey, if you could peddle those antiques as well as you haggle for breakfast, you'd make a mint."

"Ah-hah! My first compliment of the day. Life is certainly looking brighter," Isaac said delightedly and donned a sheepish smile. "Does that mean we have a deal on the first? Or second offer?"

"I've never known a man yet who didn't think you had to burn a griddle to make an egg," Meg sighed. "I'll take the second deal, and you keep your money in your pocket. I figure it'll cost me less to make your breakfast than clean up after you."

"Well, you certainly stuck a pin in my bubble in a hurry," he commented. "But I won't complain, especially if that coffee's nearly finished."

"That, you can help yourself to," she said.

"You're a gentlewoman and a scholar," he decided and crossed the narrow space, lifting a thick ceramic mug from the plastic holder. "And a good sport," he threw over his shoulder with a wink.

"Honey, you keep heaping on the bull, I'm gonna need to start checking your eyes to see if they're turning brown." She spoke while bringing the eggs and bacon from one of four immense refrigerators occupying half the rear wall.

Life was good. Life was just fine. Adding a dollop of cream to his coffee, he replaced the carton and meandered into the shadowed dining room, cup in hand. Settling onto the stool at the corner, Isaac lifted the Sunday morning edition of the Bender Falls Tribune from alongside the register. In the hazy gray light, he read no further than the headlines.

"Farmyard Slayer Claims Second Victim"

Hot coffee spilled over his fingers. The cup clattered and toppled. In slow motion, he lowered his gaze, watching the hot dark liquid spiral across the counter, barely missing his thighs when it poured over the edge and sailed between his legs . . . *Today wasn't going to be a good day.*

The need to speak to Officer Tim Spencer had become a moot point, but he stood at the bottom of the staircase like a uniformed suitor paying court in a fancy parlor. As Ronnie descended the steps, his cobalt blue eyes flashed over her, sweeping down and up with a quick appraisal but whatever he was thinking remained masked behind a friendly smile.

Where Cal Farnsworth had alluded to tipping his hat, Tim Spencer touched his shiny police visor smooth as silk and sounded like a schoolboy addressing his favorite teacher at the start of class while offering, "G' morning, Miss Bryson."

Smiling, Ronnie sized up his dark blue uniform with all the silver and black accouterments pinned to his broad chest and lean hips. Wrinkles in his knee and elbow joints suggested he might be coming off duty, but Ronnie had no idea what standards the Bentwood chief enforced. "Just going on or getting off, Tim?"

"Coming off," he answered and darted his glance through the arch toward the dining room past her shoulder. "You asked me to stop by. Hope you don't mind I ordered coffee." He smiled as he added, "And a couple donuts to go."

To go? Where?

"I don't know about the donuts, but the coffee will be greatly appreciated." Ronnie barely finished when a perky little brunette with a bright smile bounced through the arch, rustling two bags.

How the coffee stayed under the plastic lid with the girl's flounce was a mystery, but neither bag leaked when she handed them to Spencer with a bright, "Here ya go, Spence."

"Thanks, Ginny," he answered in a friendly tone. Accepting and dunking his change in his hip pocket, he flashed Ronnie a glance and motioned toward the door. "Care for a stroll?"

With Ginny's speculating glance and less-than-friendly grin, Ronnie wondered if Tim Spencer could be the town's second-greatest heartthrob. Likewise, she understood Tim's subterfuge. "I'd love a stroll as long as you don't Bogart the coffee."

With a comfortable chuckle, he rearranged the bags as he started toward the ornate front doors. Handing her one cup, removing the other for himself, he wadded the bag. Not missing a stride, he sent the ball sailing across the width of the parlor and landed a splendid two-pointer in a corner wastebasket. With the quick wit reflective of the past evening, he winked and smiled while holding the door for Ronnie. "I never miss."

"Let me guess. College basketball?"

"Four years," he answered easily.

One didn't need four years of college to become a policeman.

Ronnie lost the thought as she drew a breath of clean morning air. Somewhere in town, church bells heralded a morning service but not a single car moved on Maine, not in either direction. With glorious morning sunlight and blue skies stretched between the peaked roofs and scattered trees, the deserted street wore the ambiance of a ghost town, eerily quiet with the mooring echo of bells and a dog yapping in the distance. Sipping her coffee, welcoming that first smooth swallow, Ronnie accepted Tim's lead to the closest corner, somehow not surprised when he turned down the side street. As she'd noticed on her first perusal, the business district began and ended with the first buildings along Maine. Just past the hedges that decorated the side walls of the Inn and wrapped around the immense back porch, a brief lawn and small pavilion separated the private parking cove for the guests. Tall hedges concealed the wooden fence to separate the lot from the parallel alley. Crossing the mouth of the red brick alley, Ronnie stepped onto a narrow strip of sidewalk, and the illusion of town vanished. Stately houses, decked with porches and porch swings, ducked back from the street behind hedges, flowering rhododendrons, and lilacs. Immense trees relieved the stark sunlight that had poured down on Maine. Not a single car engine intruded. The scrape of their shoes and rustle of paper amplified in the silence.

After her second or third sip of coffee, Ronnie tipped her head and found Spencer glancing at her, a smile fleeting on his lips, in his eyes. Belatedly, she realized her silence created that curious smile, and apparently patient, he awaited her choice of topics. "Lovely morning," she said lightly.

"Sure is," he answered. "You'd have thought the fields were painted gold the way that sun burst over the hills this morning."

An aspiring poet? "What did you take in college?" she asked with a smile.

His eyes sparked mischief. "The usual, but I guess you'd say my mainstay was business. I have a bachelor's that says so."

With his smug smirk, she had to laugh. *Too cute.* "So, how does a business major end up on a police force in Bentwood?"

His lips still quirked with an easy smile, he fell into a dramatic country boy drawl, "Well, now, I come home with that degree tucked in my hip pocket, and I took a look at how this ole town fell into the great scheme of economics, took a look at how things got done, and decided, hell, why mess with a good thing? All those fancy big business techniques I just learned didn't mean diddly squat to folks who'd been running their own businesses for fifty or sixty years." If he was bitter, nothing showed; he appeared only amused. "So, I took another look around and decided what the town could really use was another cocky young cop to push a few wild youngsters in line." He shrugged, "The shoes fit."

Without a doubt, Ronnie had just received the edited version of an honest story. Early thirties, bright, not overly ambitious, but comfortable in his shoes. A thought struck. "Seems to me you could've put your degree to good use in one of the industrial mills I spotted in town."

"Let you in on a little secret," he said as he ducked his head closer. His eyes sparked with a conspiring shine. "Those mills are one of the reasons I went for my degree."

"Oh . . .?"

"Yeas, ma'am," he said with a charming drawl. "Ya see, my daddy, he owns one of those mills, and he was real sure all four of his sons should follow in his footsteps."

A rebel and a rogue! Ronnie laughed with him, enjoying the low idling rumble of his chuckle. Somehow, she believed every word and wondered how the hell she'd missed the connection when surveying those papers yesterday . . . and then, she knew. The black and white picture she'd seen of Allen Spencer, the current CEO of Bentrel Steel, depicted him as a trim, thinning-haired man wearing a sharp-cut business suit, the stereotypical industrialist and entrepreneur. They might have looked alike once. "Allen Spencer's your older brother," she commented.

"We all have our crosses to bear," he said in feigned sorrow. "That one's mine."

God, he never let up! Again laughing, she realized he reminded her just a little of Mark Jarvins, and it was no wonder she hadn't fallen entirely for that country boy charm. Her thoughts adrift, she followed his cue to cross another street, and they continued strolling beneath an overhang of shaggy maples. All too easily, he'd permitted her to set the tempo of the interview, keeping it light, but no illusions existed in his relaxed posture. Underlying his easy stride and friendly overtures, he was coiled and ready for whatever she meant to ask him.

Recalling the underlying stress of last evening, she read the signs, still obvious though masked behind his smiles. Keeping her tone light, friendly, she asked, "Do you always work the night shift?"

His eyes flashed sober, changed in the instant. "We only have seven guys on the force counting Chief Hayward, and I'm the second youngest." He tried the smile, not quite smooth. Shrugging, his gaze slid forward. "I swing-shift with Rick Handel."

"You were on Friday night," Ronnie nudged.

Tension hiked in his rugged face before his focus returned, his eyes carefully masked. "We're not a big city force," he said in a guarded tone. "Unless we're in the office, our calls go through County dispatch, and none of us are in the office too often. I was on my way to the station when the call came across the radio. The dispatcher over at County put it across as an accident. Officially, I wasn't on duty yet, but I was the closest to the Engler homestead. I was the first officer on the scene."

The leaden note in his voice spoke volumes of details about that scene and the depth of his shock. Even the most hardened officers, homicide detectives included, could be tripped by the violence of humankind.

"Even if I wanted to, Ronnie," he said with a tight rein on his voice, a genuine apology in his words. "I wouldn't tell you what I encountered at the Engler homestead, and I'd be grateful if you didn't ask."

Gauging his dark, pensive eyes as they stopped at the corner, Ronnie understood. Police ethics and policy aside, he would never discuss what he'd seen, not with her, not with any woman. The violence and horror remained his private cross to bear. "I understand, Tim," she said quietly. "And I won't ask, not about what you saw or anything about your investigation."

Wariness flickered in his eyes, but the curiosity flamed higher. "Could I ask you something without offending you, Ronnie?"

"I truly don't offend easily," she said, recalling him speaking those same words in the diner last evening. "Ask."

"What are you doing here?"

A shortened version of his questions asked last evening, but part of her reason had changed with her new status. Mark hadn't mentioned if her alleged 'undercover status' should extend to the local law agencies. She should've spoken to him, and should've asked for closer guidelines. If she lied to Spencer and he learned she was now consulting with the Bureau, her credibility would be a wash. He was waiting for her answer, however, and though she'd never been a particularly good liar, she'd learned the evasive techniques that every good journalist needs.

The truth. "I'm here to help, Tim," she said quietly and held his gaze, sensing the deeper curiosity in his dark blue eyes. "I am a journalist, but if you've ever read any of my articles—published under Ron Bryson if you're interested—you'd realize that I'm not here to either slander your town or its people. I'm not a gossip columnist. I don't sensationalize the violence for public consumption. Frankly, I don't give a damn about what sells newspapers or magazines. When I write an article, it's generally to help the surviving victims heal." She paused, feeling the speculation behind his gaze, gauging her words. "I write about violent crime, Tim. Generally, murder." And if she admitted that much, she needed to finish. "During my investigations for a story, I've been known to uncover a few leads which helped solve several crimes in the past half dozen years."

"You're acquainted with Agent Jarvins," he said with his interrogation technique apparently polished.

"I worked with him once before," she admitted. "He was working on a case that I happened to be working on as well—not unlike this one. And please don't mistake that, Tim, I'm an investigative reporter. I will eventually write a story about your town. In the meantime, however, if during my investigation, I come across some tidbit of information that could lead to a suspect, I'm neither brave enough nor hard up enough for a story, to conceal it. That doesn't mean I'll run to you or Mark with harebrained notions of Betty Sue jumping in the sack with Bobby Joe and Engler or Farnsworth ending up deceased because of it. If there's enough evidence and I can document that Betty Sue and Bobby Joe's affair led to a crime, I'll be on your doorstep. Not a moment sooner."

For a long moment, Tim studied her with a pensive half-hitched grin, his thoughts turning. "Investigative reporter or uh . . . Nancy Drew?"

Amused, Ronnie laughed, "Miss Maple."

Spencer chuckled, shaking his head and glancing about as if, only now, realizing how far they'd walked. He still held the bag of donuts. He lifted it toward her, his eyes sparkling. "Want a donut?"

Accepting the bag, she was both surprised and delighted with the breakfast rolls she spied in the bag. "Lucky you didn't tell me what you had in here sooner," she said as she brought one of the cinnamon rolls from the bag, handing him the first only after making sure there was another. "These just happen to be what I consider the main ingredient of the basic food group."

"Something like a cinnamon roll and coffee for breakfast, lunch, and supper?" he asked before taking a bite.

Rolling her eyes, she favored him with mocked disgust. "The man's determined to know my every secret before we return to the Inn." And with a thought, she met his gaze, "Any chance you've already been investigating me?"

"Nope," he said with a smug smile. "Lucky guess."

"You're a very lucky guy," she decided and bit into the roll. Savoring the flavors, she was delighted with the taste of melted maple. Flaky dough melted on her tongue. A hint of nutmeg and a heavy dose of sugar and cinnamon swirled with the layers. Interview over, she decided, content to walk back to the Inn, enjoying every bite.

Spencer finished his cinnamon roll in record time, but he continually flashed her glances as she picked the leaves apart, biting one layer at a time in a spiral. "Ronnie?"

"Mmmm?"

"Bentwood," he began idly, glancing forward. "Usually, it's a pretty decent town. You coming here, into all this . . . I feel pretty bad about how you're getting treated around here. People are understandably scared and edgy."

She could only nod with a mouthful of gooey dough and cinnamon. "Mm-hmm."

He looked at her with a spark of concentration within his smile. "How about coming out to my place this evening for dinner? My wife and I would love to have you, and we're planning to barbecue. Just family. Give you a chance to relax and get a feel for how things usually are around here. The only thing is, I'd rather we not talk about what's going on in town too much. Donna knows most of the local gossip, and I bet you two would hit it off great, but uh, I don't talk about work. We have two little ones, six and four, and they're a little too quick sometimes if you get my drift."

Married, two kids . . . she would love to meet this Donna who could latch onto this character and hang onto him for six or seven years. "Be delighted," she decided after swallowing.

"Great," he said with a quick, anxious smile. "Say about six? I'll give you directions . . . ahhh," he flashed a sheepish grin and darted his eyes as if to make sure no one stood within twenty feet which, considering the nature of their earlier discussion, struck her funny. "Just uh . . . don't mention this to anybody, okay?" he said in a conspiratorial tone. "You mention barbecue around here, and we'll have to butcher a hog or two, and I already have one lined up for next weekend."

Too cute, Ronnie agreed with a smile. "Mum's the word."

Amusement lanced his blue eyes. "Great!"

Outside the Inn, she scribbled directions in her notebook, then watched Tim Spencer saunter to his pickup truck—an oversized emerald Ford with monster tires, a great deal of chrome, running lights, and several antennas rising above the hood. Somehow, the truck matched the driver. Wearing a smile, she strode up the steps to the Inn. She needed at least one more cup of coffee to kick off the morning.

CHAPTER 10

Meg came partway, hesitantly, then hurried, grabbing a towel from under the counter.

Paper trembling, the ends dangling and sopping up water, Isaac could only watch as the elder woman snatched the soggy newspaper away. Motion slowing, she collected the cup and began mopping the spill. His hands fisted now, one to either side of the mess. He could only watch as she clasped his wrist, moving his leaden arm from the puddle, and could only listen as her anxious words filtered to him. The sounds echoed as if through a long narrow tunnel. He'd been here before.

Meg stood beside him, gripping his arm, tugging at his dripping sleeves, "Thank God . . . God almighty. Isaac! Come on, sweetie . . . Isaac . . ."

Not Isaac. His name wasn't Isaac, but not even those words would come. He watched his sleeves slide up his arm, chafing his forearm. Tanned flesh turned red like a sunburn . . . a burn. "H-hot," he said absently and looked up into the watery image of a strained face, a face from the past. "H-hot, Nanna—"

"Oh, God, Isaac," the soft voice heaved, shaken. Her hands shook, too, tugging his head to rest against her warm, cushioned shoulder. "Oh, Isaac, come on . . . Come on, baby. Don't . . . don't do this. . . You're alright, honey . . . Come on, talk to this old woman . . . You have to talk, Isaac . . ."

'Read . . . read for me, you wre'shed shild . . .'

The words, the voice, and the scent of incense echoed from the past, but the hand stroking his head drew him forward. Hard, though. Heavy. His muscles were heavy as if filled with lead. With an effort, he animated, but a wicked pain flashed from his stomach . . . stabbed. Stifling a groan, he dragged himself away from the protective fold and caught himself against the counter, nearly landing his head on the Formica as he cradled his waist against the sharp pains. He needed to move, to rise, to leave . . . the aroma of coffee and sizzling eggs mixed badly with the tangy incense smell dwindling from his mind. Meg . . . Meg Price was here. He caught the freshly laundered scent of her apron and felt the clasp of her delicate hands on his shoulder, his arm. Shame and embarrassment flamed in his mind. He'd been here before.

"I-Isaac, n-no," Meg stammered, her voice on the brink of a sob. "J-Just sit. You're—you're alright."

"Home," he said softly, his throat constricted. He couldn't look at her. Could not. Would not. He knew. Knew what he'd see, what she'd think. "God . . . a mess," he heaved as he stared at the bleary, shadowed puddle of coffee between his boots. "M-made a-a fucking mess."

"It's all r-right, honey. It's all—"

"Not . . . not alright," he whispered, shaking his hanging head. Finding sense and strength to lift his arm from his waist, he uncurled his fist with an iron will and cleared the fuzz from his eyes. No hiding the tears. He palmed the water away and combed his fingers through his hair. Still trembling, he couldn't bear to look at this woman who'd always been a friend, only a kind friend. "Never all right," he heaved softly. "Never."

"Wh-what's not alright, Isaac?"

"I'm sorry," he strained and drew breath, swallowing, recovering. "I . . . I better go," he said as he started pushing to his feet. At a glance, he identified the woman's distress, her gentle concern, her fear. Fear for him or of him? He couldn't decide. "I'm sorry for the mess, Meg," he said as he rose, looking down at the puddle. Lifting his gaze, he started an offer to find the mop, but the intensity of her gaze halted him. The words died on his tongue. Not afraid of him, this gentle woman wasn't afraid of him like another so long ago. Afraid *for* him, he understood and tried a smile that fell short. "I uh . . . I haven't been feeling very well, Meg. I probably should have tried sleeping—" And she wasn't buying it, not one word of it.

"Isaac," she said gently, clasping his arm in a firm, comforting grip. "You don't have to explain. Not to me, honey," she said in soft concern. "When you're ready . . . when you want to talk to me, I'll be here, okay?"

Never. He could never explain, never talk about it, not to her, not to anyone. "Thank you," Isaac said quietly, and when she moved against him, wrapping her arms around his shoulder and hugging him, he leaned deep enough to return the embrace. "Thank you, twice," he uttered against her soft silver-blond curls. She wanted nothing, expected nothing. Like so many other simple gestures over the last five years, she offered honest affection and expected nothing in return while giving him the world. Through her, he found sanity and strength to recover more firmly on his feet.

Stroking his hair, she held him a few seconds longer, uttering, "You're welcome, boy. You're very welcome." Slipping free as if she knew by instinct how long to hold him, she wiped unashamedly at her eyes and forced a smile. "You owe this old woman," she said softly. "You're—you're going to sit down and eat the breakfast I make for you for giving this old woman a scare, you hear?"

"I uh—"

"No ifs, ands, or buts, Isaac," she said quietly. "You're eating breakfast. My daddy always said it was the most important meal of the day, and by God, if he didn't live to be almost a hundred. Now," she pointed to the second stool.

"You sit down while I get you another cup of coffee and get those eggs on the griddle."

"On one condition," he managed, and she eyed him with a warning that all decent mothers and grandmothers perfected. "You let me get the mop."

"That, you can do," she agreed readily and turned. "It's in the kitchen."

Not going to be a good day, Isaac considered as he followed Meg into the kitchen.

If Elaine called off, what the hell would he do? If he closed, he would draw too damn much attention. He advertised 'open seven days a week,' . . . and the increase in customer traffic off the Interstate, had no bearing on his quandary. The last time he'd shut down for an afternoon, nearly half of Bentwood's citizenry had banged on his front door or delivered chicken soup. If he offered a sign reading 'by appointment only,' it would be just as bad. The phone would ring off the hook.

As Meg handed him the mop, Isaac asked offhandedly, "Know anyone who'd like to buy an antique shop cheap?" Barely finishing the words, he considered what he'd said and found her frozen, worried gaze. Feeling repentant, he offered a sheepish grin. "Sorry. It just seemed easier than taking a day off, and it was foolish anyway. I wouldn't know what to do with a day off."

"You might try resting and relaxing, Isaac," she said carefully. "That might be a first."

More than she knew. "Na, I'd get bored. Guess I'll just have to open and muddle through."

Not happily, he carried the mop to the dining room and cleaned the spill. Scrubbing floors would be a pleasant, harmless way to spend the day, but he could well imagine dropping the mop handle and destroying an entire shelf of Haviland or Wedgwood. In a single flashing instant, the image sprang lifelike . . . glass shards scattered and blasted as if a bomb had detonated. Slivers shot sparks from under tables, on oriental carpets . . .

Shuddering, he drew a breath and nearly spoke the word aloud. *Paperwork!* He would spend the entire day cataloging and reviewing more of the ledgers! He hadn't even tallied the weekly receipts or entered the deposit slips in his bankbook.

If Elaine called off and Wade Kreider showed up, Isaac decided he would hire the youngster to carry whatever needed to be carried. Not again would he lift a piece of glassware, not one piece until this . . . this, whatever it was, passed.

Feeling better, Isaac returned the mop to the kitchen cupboard and paused to look over Meg's shoulder, admitting, "Those smell fantastic, and I'd love to know how you always manage to make them perfect."

"Lots of practice. Now, go sit," Meg chastened lightly. "Men in my kitchen always made me nervous."

"Bet it was hard beating them off to make an egg," Isaac said, and she eyed him with a bemused sparkle.

"Don't you be worried about this old woman's love life, handsome."

"I'd ask you to marry me if I thought you'd accept," he said offhandedly and ducked the towel she whipped at him. Stifling a laugh, he reached the opening of the dining room and looked over at her. "I'd marry you in an eyeblink, Meg."

"Then I'd have to beat off all the gals in Bentwood just to keep you safe, and I'm not up to all that aggravation," she said in a surly tone. "You better set your sights on someone young enough to put up the good fight."

"Doomed to remain a bachelor through all eternity," he said wistfully, winked at her, and passed into the dining room. He'd wait for his coffee to be delivered . . . but on impulse, he returned to the kitchen, collected a Styrofoam cup, and helped himself to more coffee.

Not one more piece of glassware—not china, not porcelain, not even a damned chunk of ceramic! Not one damned hunk of breakable anything! Good God, there were a lot of breakables in his shop.

Not one goddamn piece of it would he touch!

Mark Jarvins sat in the dining room, alone at a small table near the outside wall where he might have seen Ronnie stroll past chatting with Spencer. One look at his tight-lipped smirk and intent eyes, her attention riveted, sobered considerably. Had he learned something of significance since last evening? The lab results shouldn't have come back yet. Her smile faded as she slid into the chair across from Jarvins. An empty cup rested in the space in front of her alongside a slightly battered napkin. With two corners twisted into stiff spikes like horns, the napkin stood as a trademark and a testament to Len's frame of mind. "Len didn't sleep well?"

Mark huffed a laugh, flashing his gaze over the telltale signs. "He has it bad," he admitted.

Looking over into Mark's tense eyes, she suffered an inkling, an intuition, and in an odd moment of crystal clarity, Ronnie knew this arrangement would never work out between them. As much as she still cared for and about Mark, the spark had died. "What's on today's agenda?"

"What did you and Officer Spencer talk about?"

"This and that," she said idly and held his gaze firmly. "Not about the case. He's too good a cop for that."

"He was the first officer on the scene," Jarvins said with a hint of sarcasm. "It would be natural if he wanted to get some things off his chest and if he happened to get a few bylines—"

"You can stop there," she said as she looked into his angry eyes. No, this arrangement wouldn't last. Too clearly, she recalled the fatal flaw that had ultimately destroyed their relationship and now threatened their friendship. Jealousy. And possessiveness. His sense of entitlement. If anything, his authority in the Bureau had increased his arrogance. And her thought lent her pause.

Was she, like Mark, a byproduct of her social class? A prisoner to the status and the inherent traits of her ambitious father? Would she readily sensationalize this crime at the first opportunity to further her career as if she was entitled to air their grief for her gain?

Shifting her gaze through the window, she stared absently at the side of a building across the street. Jealousy . . . for Mark it was jealousy and his need to possess and control.

For her . . . fame? Had she lied a short time ago when talking to Tim Spencer, offering him her motives? Who was she trying to fool? Or deceive? Perhaps she'd come here not so much on a hunch, an intuition, to see justice done, but to weed out the crime and become famous with its telling.

"Ronnie, if we have any hope of solving this crime," Mark said carefully. "We have to be objective. Right now," he said in a quieter voice but stopped short when the bouncy brunette approached.

"Do you need a menu, ma'am?" Ginny asked with a hint of disdain.

Looking up into the accusing blue eyes, Ronnie suddenly felt like belting her. "Coffee's fine, and another cinnamon roll," she said aloofly, lifting Len's cup and napkin to the edge of the table. Whatever relaxed comfort she'd gained while strolling with Spencer had vanished. Tension coiled through her under Mark's curious tense gaze. How dare he force her to question her motives through his arrogance! Outside influence. She was still too damned receptive and susceptible to outside interference, especially while on a case.

Too clearly, Mark believed himself superior to these simple country folks. In a few short strokes, he'd elevated himself above Tim Spencer, and the natural rivalry between local authorities and the FBI was the furthest thought from Mark's mind. Spencer was little more than a country bumpkin and considered a great deal less.

"What are you thinking?" Mark asked carefully, leaning forward on his forearms in an intimate pose.

"That you're an ass, but I'll keep that to myself," she said simply.

Mark's lashes snapped in quick surprise. His brow lowered as he studied her more closely. "You're already falling for this character."

"Oh, that's rich," she said while flipping her hair off her shoulder, shoving it aside in genuine irritation.

"Ronnie, we're conducting a murder investigation," he said darkly. "This town may look like it popped out of a Mark Twain novel, but for God's sake, behind one of those smiling faces lies the mind of a monster."

At least he held that much in perspective. "And Spencer's on your list of suspects?" she asked and watched his wheels spin behind his intense gaze.

"At this point, everyone's a suspect," he said darkly.

"Then let me help you with this one, Mark," she said and leaned forward, resting on her elbows, locking her fingers in a fist under her chin. "You can cross him off your list. He's not our bad guy."

"Oh, dinner and a morning stroll, and you've cleared him? You're amazing, Ron. Sometimes it takes a jury a month to decide after hearing all the evidence."

"Let me guess," she said quietly. "He was in the vicinity. Claims he was on his way to work . . . Of course, he could have snuck into that barn, minus his police uniform, did the deed, returned to his truck, then conveniently answered the call to an 'accident.' But let's see . . .? He lives with his wife and kids, and considering the ages, I'd guess Donna was home . . . And you haven't spoken to her yet, have you?"

"We have a statement," he growled intemperately.

"Hmm, but the wife could lie for her husband. And she'd never be forced to testify in court. So, let's see . . .? Right! Donna and Tim fight. He stalks off mad . . . but he stops off to collect his uniform . . . And after Donna hears what happened to Engler, she welcomes Tim back with a kiss and hug and covers his ass with an alibi."

"Stranger things have happened," Mark growled.

Ronnie smiled without humor. "Do you know what your problem is, Mark?" Not awaiting his answer, she continued sweetly, "You don't know when to quit while you're still ahead. You and I both know Tim Spencer's a good cop. If you spoke to him for ten seconds—which you did because he knew you and I were acquainted—you know he's as torn up by what he saw in that barn as any man I've ever seen. The last thing he expected when he answered that accident call was to find, what he found, and the last thing he wants is to remember it, much less talk about it and gain publicity for talking about it. Aside from this, he doesn't fit the profile in one main area."

"I'm listening."

"Liste. n very carefully, Mark, because you'll understand, immediately, why I know Tim Spencer's no longer on your list," she started but paused as Ginny came from the kitchen entrance across the empty room. Easing from her dreamy posture, Ronnie offered Ginny a pleasant smile and watched the young woman struggle to return the amenity. By the time this town finished with her, Ronnie might end up in the National Enquirer. What were the odds that she'd be accused of having an intimate affair with a married policeman and a Federal Agent by mid-morning?

Stirring cream into her coffee, recalling the cream already in the cup Spencer had handed her, Ronnie awaited the girl to leave, but Mark commented, "Thought you were having eggs this morning."

"That was before I tasted these rolls," she said offhandedly and leaned forward again, landing her attention on Mark's strained smile and softer gaze. "Tim Spencer is the youngest brother of Allen Spencer, who is CEO of the largest industrial mill in the county. Somehow, I doubt Tim grew up with a serious grudge against farmers. If someone were here shooting industrialists, I'd peg him number one; the same as I'd wonder about you if politicians started dropping. Now, are you finished with your petty jealousies and macho shit? Or should I resign from my post?"

For a moment, Mark stared at her, betraying the absence of prior knowledge of Spencer's connection. In an annoyed tone, he said, "Shit."

"There you have it in a nutshell," she said bluntly.

His gaze darted to his coffee; he leaned back and cast his focus through the glass while taking a few sips. A distracted haze curtained his eyes as he lowered his cup and looked over. "Allen Spencer's on the Town Council," he said in annoyance. "He was one of a dozen men I spoke to yesterday afternoon, and I never made the connection. Nor did anyone bother to mention it."

"Probably some family conflicts," she said lightly and shrugged. What kind of older brother wouldn't mention a younger one, especially when the younger one happened to carry a badge and had walked in on a grizzly crime scene? "What's Allen like?" she asked offhandedly and pulled off a piece of the roll before looking at Mark.

"Intense," Mark said evenly, contemplating. "Mid-forties, 5'10" at the most, nearly bald, and probably the next candidate for the State Senate or House. He has a politician's grace and sophistication."

Which explained the difference between the brothers and Mark's inability to connect the pair. Country boy charm and an honest smile, vs. slippery grin, and an outraged politician. If not still annoyed, she might be flattered by Mark's jealousy.

Dismissing the thought, Ronnie chewed and swallowed, catching Mark's keen gaze and faint smile. "So, back to my first question," she barely started when she spotted Len striding from the front entry.

A newspaper dangled in his hand; a scowl darkened his clean-shaven, sharp-cut features. With the fanfare of an angry child, he dropped the paper in the center of the table and yanked out a chair. "One or both of you better have a look at that."

Ronnie glimpsed only the headline before Mark snatched the paper. In slow degrees, Mark's expression transformed from annoyance to shock to anger and finally to dread. By the time he looked toward Len, every emotion had vanished, but his eyes had turned crystal blue. "Well, we certainly have a lid on this, don't we?"

"Right," Len stated dryly and sent a black, scathing glance at the paper before looking at Ronnie. "You better read it, too. You made the news."

Not sure she liked that tone or his gaze, she reached and sat back with the paper in hand, controlling her tension with an iron will. First and foremost were the pictures of both victims, side-by-side, one nearly bald, the other wiry and shaggy-headed, but Ted Grimes had certainly milked the page for all it was worth.

Between half-assed facts and innuendoes, Grimes managed to shout 'serial killer' without ever using the term . . . and apparently, Frank Engler decided to see his name in print with a gruesome depiction of finding his murdered father.

Grimes, in one fell swoop, managed to botch what should have remained a quiet, careful investigation. Without scruples, he'd mentioned both victims and families, law enforcement officials including the names of both Federal agents and called Ronnie the equivalent of an ambulance-chasing bimbo who'd arrived in Bentwood to profit on the pain of the poor grieving families.

"Christ, that asshole should submit this to the Enquirer," Ronnie uttered as she finished reading the last few lines, which alluded to the incompetence of the Bentwood PD and the Federal Bureau. As an aside, the crackpot condemned those same officials and the *system* for allowing Fred Engler to become the next victim. The most damaging tidbit of print revolved around the single mention of Frank noticing his 'daddy's wedding ring missing.' The souvenir. The telltale sign of the deed to earmark this case as the definitive work of a serial killer. Always a souvenir.

Lowering the paper slowly, Ronnie glanced between Mark and Len, who studied her with similarly concerned gazes. Like bookends, these two, or chess pieces. One blond and blue-eyed, tall and sleek, the other dark-haired and black-eyed, built like a ball buster for the Mafia . . . And they were, at this moment, worried about how she would react to this media. If she wasn't annoyed again, she might be flattered. "Your whole case just went down the toilet, gentlemen," she pointed out quietly. "My reputation as a journalist doesn't quite compare."

"Ron," Len surprisingly spoke first, his husky voice dark with emotion. "That's some pretty lousy shit in that paper. If it'll help, I'll go find this asshole and stick my .38 up his schnozzola, make him do a second take."

"Sweet sentiment, Len," she said with a twitch of a smile, understanding him far better than she had before. "Unfortunately, he'd just find a way to slander your fine character, and I wouldn't want that on my conscience."

"How about I just break his knuckles, then?" Len suggested with a thin smile that promised pain. "He won't be writing for a long time, huh?"

"He'd hire a stenographer," she said. "Why don't we forget this asshole? The pen, my boys, is always mightier than the sword, and I might have a letter or two to write to the editor in the days to come."

"Ronnie," Mark said quietly. "A story like this, even one this badly written, will syndicate very quickly. We'll have a helluva lot of company in a short time, and a whole lot of people will be hunting for Veronica Bryson."

"A fine excuse for you to keep me locked nice and tidy in the local police station with a cup of coffee and a few more of these cinnamon rolls." Considering how best to repair this damage, she looked at Mark. "We need to write an extremely coherent statement for the press, and I think you have the camera presence for the TV station."

"I was thinking the same thing. I mean about using the media coverage," Mark said with a hint of embarrassment. "Actually, I think you'd make a good spokesperson, but I don't suppose you'll take the job."

"Not on your life, bub," she said. "My face is better off-camera, and that's not saying much."

"Why don't we pick up this conversation down the block," Mark decided. "If this is already on the wire, we'll probably get swamped soon."

Lifting the last half of her roll in a napkin, Ronnie collected her purse and rose. She glanced over as Mark tossed a ten on the table, smiling when he reminded her that she was supposed to pick up the breakfast tab. "Hands are full, sorry. I'll get the next one."

"Right," Len said dryly. "Heard that shit before."

CHAPTER 11

Understanding how a president's daughter must feel with Secret Service escorts, Ronnie kept a steady pace between the two dark suits. On the flip side, for any interested party, it might look as if she was under arrest, and Ted Grimes would have a field day with that mistake. At her thought, she smiled only until she glimpsed the motion ahead.

If she hadn't seen him first, she wouldn't have noticed the slight pause in Bently's stride when he stepped from the diner entrance. A half-block, more than a half-city block between them, and she could almost feel the heat of his eyes lancing her, positive she saw a fleeting grin quiver his dark mustache. Without more than a slight glitch in his stride, he continued as if he hadn't seen her and rounded the corner. By the time she and her escorts reached the end of the block, she barely glimpsed blue denim before he disappeared through the side door.

Mark missed nothing, and his glance offered no comfort as they stepped onto the next curb. "For the record," he said quietly. "I'd like you to keep your distance from that character."

Why was she not surprised? "Another suspect?" she wondered idly.

Mark flashed a wan dread, undoubtedly thinking about his reaction to Spencer, but he stiffened and sobered on the instant, far too clever to repeat that mistake. "Let's say a potential, okay? And I'm serious. I know you had dinner with him last night, and for the record, I know you omitted a few details when we spoke."

What she knew about Isaac Bently wasn't enough to place him on a suspect list for murder, and that was reason enough to avoid putting him on Mark's radar. After she talked to Max . . .

"Damnit," she said quietly and stopped. Her bookends halted a step ahead. Glancing between them, noting Mark's sudden intensity and concern, she almost lost her thought. "Messages," she said with a faintly embarrassed flush. "I forgot to check at the desk for messages, and I'm expecting a call."

Mark studied her, doubting, and glanced past her shoulder toward the gray-canopied corner to betray his thought. His gaze returned and held fast. "Ronnie, I'm not kidding. I want you to leave this guy alone until I—"

"Do you know how hard it is to offend me?" she asked in a chilly, dry tone and saw him flinch just a little before digging in his heels. "You just managed it—hands down."

"Ronnie, I just don't want you—"

"I am returning to the Inn. I am picking up my messages if I have any. And then—if I don't have a lingering urge to kick you square in the knee—I'll join you. In the meantime, Mr. Jarvins, I suggest you get a tight rein on your libido and ego because if either rears its ugly head again, I'll cut it off clean. Got it?"

"Good time to just say 'got it,' Amico," Len helped with a thin grin.

Flashing blue fire, Mark glared at Devinio. "You're just having a grand morning, aren't you?"

Lenny shrugged both of his broad shoulders, holding out his hands in an innocent gesture. "What the hell'd I do? Huh? Just minding my own business walking along. I'm not the one pulling the Napoleon routine on a big girl."

Despite her irritation, Ronnie lost part of her mad and smiled at Lenny. "You're a real pal, Len. Want to walk me back to the Inn? I'd love some decent company."

Lenny flashed Mark a glance and decided, "Why the hell not? I've been walking this damn street so often, I already feel like a damn beat cop." Turning, he offered her his forearm, passing Mark a snicker over Ronnie's head as she laced her arm about his. "Always told you this lady has too much class for you, flatfoot. Now, beat it. The lady and I need to catch up on old times."

"Old times, my ass," Mark snapped and probably would have said more if Lenny hadn't already started them walking toward the corner.

God, if Grimes thought she was a bimbo yesterday, the man would be drooling this morning. Three different men in just over an hour. Shaking her head, she glimpsed Mark stalking up the street in the opposite direction, caught a fleeting glimpse of Lenny's wicked smile, and smothered a soft laugh, "You're rotten."

"My mamma didn't raise no fool," he smirked and continued his casual stride.

They were past the gray canopy when Len broke the silence in a quiet, careful tone. "About that guy back there, Ron." He hesitated, sober without the added pressure of jealousy. "Might be a good idea to steer clear just until we get a make on him."

The words, rather than the tone, sent a prickle of alarm down her spine. When the FBI wanted a make on someone, they didn't need twenty-four hours to accomplish it. A name in their computer could spit out a litany of intriguing details. Looking up at Len, she knew whatever they'd already learned belied Mark's reaction. "Want to tell me why you're red-flagging him, Len?"

He considered how much to divulge before starting. "Mark told me about that article you read in the local paper. Hell of a find," he said with an unusual hint of approval. "Yesterday, we were looking for someone new to town. Possibly someone just passing through or visiting for the summer. There are quite a few summer camps and cabins back in these hills. Guess the fishing and hunting brings them in. Anyway, Bently's name came up." He slid easily back on track. "What we know so far — he has a fat bank account, carries a passport that he uses about twice or thrice a year, could have been in the neighborhood Friday night in time to do Engler, and he doesn't have a past."

Those last words were dropped like pebbles but resounded like boulders. *No past?* As in 'no rap sheet?' Studying Len sideways, Ronnie said, "No past?"

Appearing uncomfortable, Len shook his head. "Nothing beyond six years ago when he applied for the passport and started negotiations on that building in absentia. But keep this under your hat, alright? Could be something simple and better left unsaid."

Anything from a black-market smuggler to a candidate for the government witness program. With the thought of involving Max Hagen, her stomach gripped. She should've known yesterday. She should've guessed neither Mark nor Len would miss that call.

New residents. Visitors. Serial killers might stalk their own neighborhoods, but they were mobile beasts. More believably, the killer lived somewhere other than Bentwood and had chosen this town as an easy mark . . . except that strangers in a town this size would be noticed. A strange car parked somewhere near one of those farms would be questioned.

And there was still the ritualistic aspect to consider. She wouldn't breathe that thought to Mark or Lenny, but something niggled at the nape of her neck. Something . . . something here. Something not quite right in this quiet little town, and that alone kept her focused on the town, on the town's background, rather than searching beyond the perimeter for a visiting wacko.

The similarities between victims lent more credence to that thought. Nothing random here. The victims were chosen. Whether this wacko posed as a bible salesman and made his rounds of the farms, or saw them on a street corner, or knew them personally, something about these two men had singled them out . . . And the ages and occupations seemed the most obvious.

At the entrance to the Inn, Ronnie broke her hold on Len and continued silently to the alcove opposite the dining room. When she'd checked in yesterday morning, she'd compared the spindly woman to an aging librarian, and the image remained firm. Rail thin, wearing a paisley print dress and a sweater despite the summer heat, the receptionist wore her short kinky hair in a stiff set. Lifting her interest from the front page of the Sunday paper in front of her, she peered at Ronnie and her faded blue eyes magnified behind her thick glasses, eclipsed by the small bifocal squares at the bottom.

Sensing the woman's instant recognition and disdain, Ronnie decided that Lenny could stick his .38 up Grimes' snout any ole time.

The woman all but stuck her pointed nose to the ceiling and sniffed, and the sight of Lenny leaning casually—about as casually as a Bull Mastiff in the arch behind Ronnie—only widened the old bird's eyes by a fraction.

"Could you check and see if I have any messages?" Ronnie asked lightly.

The woman never flinched; she just turned from the counter to a stack of pigeonholes and lifted a folded sheet of stationery from one of the slots.

Annoyed, Ronnie accepted the note, restraining the urge to touch the rope-like fingers and spread a contagion. Instead, she backed a pace and flipped the sheet. The words were simple enough, "Please call ASAP. C.F." Cal Farnsworth. Ronnie checked her watch, looking again at the note, searching for the time which should be provided. No time listed. Looking over to the woman, Ronnie asked, "How long ago did this call come in?" *Would he be at home or work?*

"IIII," she drawled. "Have nooo idea."

Halted, studying the cant of the head, the indignant posture, Ronnie's hackles rose. "Well, honey," she said sweetly. "You have about thirty seconds to get some idea. Was it ten minutes, twenty minutes—a half-hour? Was it in this *century?*"

"As I said," she sniffed. "I have nooo idea."

Ronnie drew a soft breath, in no mood to play foolish games with a spindle-limbed old dame, whose finer senses—what was left of them—were offended by occupying the same air space. Her temper on hold by a fraction, Ronnie spoke quietly, "Did you take this call?"

"Nooo, I diiid not," the woman drawled snippily.

No? "Do you know who did take this call?" Ronnie asked carefully.

"III have—"

Leaning on the shiny mahogany counter, crossing her forearms on the high ledge, Ronnie commented, "If you say you have no idea to me, in that tone again, Miss—" She read the nametag. "Dunner, I will likely broadcast the incompetence of this hotel across a nationally syndicated network, and I will be sure to mention the hospitality toward paying guests. Whatever fame and fortune this establishment has seen in its fifty-odd years will go to hell in a handbasket. Now, do you want to pretend you know how to run a hotel and make sure my messages, hereafter, have a specific time etched onto the corner and are delivered to me promptly? Or do you want me to become an extremely irate guest very shortly?"

"We know what you're doing here!" the woman snapped.

"That's rich," Ronnie said quietly. "You don't even know what *you're* doing here. Now, have we reached an understanding? Or do I find the owner of this Inn and voice a very loud complaint?"

"You may complain to *whomever* you like—" The woman's gaze darted past Ronnie. Her lined lips froze open, and her focus dropped, following the federal badge as it landed on the counter alongside Ronnie's elbow.

"Ma'am," Lenny said in a low deep growl. "I suggest you write a large note and tape it alongside your telephone to have all of our notes, hereafter, date and time stamped. If, for any reason, something happens to a phone message that comes through that switchboard . . .? Whether it's to me, my partner, or Miss Bryson for the duration of our stay, you and every member of your staff will be under federal indictment for the obstruction of justice during a criminal investigation. Do I make myself clear?"

For a few seconds, Ronnie feared the woman might lapse into cardiac arrest, but Dunner heaved a breath and sputtered, bobbing her head like a crane.

"Good," Len said in a short stroke. "I'll expect all of us to receive our messages promptly, even if you need to post a sentry to watch for us coming or going." He looked down at Ronnie. "Do you need to know when that call came in?"

"It would help, but I suppose I can try a few numbers to reach the appropriate party," she admitted and looked at Dunner. "For the record, Miss Dunner, your Mr. Grimes, there," she said while skimming a scathing glance at the newspaper. Meeting the woman's magnified eyes directly, she continued, "He should be writing for tabloids, and if you believe half of the crap he's written in that article, you're not half as bright as you appear. It's horrific sensationalism, and it turns my stomach to think of the effect it will have on your town. Now, if you'll excuse me?" Without awaiting a reply, Ronnie slid her arms off the counter and motioned to Len. "Unfortunately," she continued in a voice to be heard. "It's people like Grimes who give journalism a bad name."

When they were outside, Ronnie looked at Len and commented, "I thought you killed her."

"I had a few bad seconds there, myself," he admitted with a thin smile. "Talk about bad publicity. Christ, could you have seen what Grimes would've done with that?"

"FBI Slays Little Old Lady," Ronnie supplied. She regretted her honesty when she saw Lenny's scowl only until she spotted the crowd at the far end of the street. "The circus just hit town."

"Looks that way," he growled.

Touching his arm, she halted him. "Let's take my car," she decided. "I'm guessing there's a backdoor we might manage to slip through if we hurry."

"There is," he commented and turned with her.

She would need her car anyway. First a look at whatever Mark would show her, and then she intended to see these farms at least from a distance. By the time she reached her car, however, she reversed that order. Unless she made use of the map and visited the farms first, she'd be fighting traffic even for a bird's eye view if the cars collecting in front of the municipal building were any indication. By noon, Bentwood would be flooded with reporters, camera crews, and sightseers.

When they were both sitting inside her car, Ronnie looked over. "You think Mark could hold down the fort a little while longer?"

"What's on your mind?"

"I haven't driven by either of the crime scenes," she said quietly. "It could speed up the process if you want to point them out to me."

"You just want to drive by?"

“I’d like to get a feel for the locations,” she admitted. “Something Mark said last night keeps playing in my head.”

“Take a left on Maine,” Devinio commented.

“Thanks,” she said and twisted about to back from the parking space. How does the killer stalk without being spotted? That was the question of the hour, and an eyeball on the locations could offer the answer.

Fifteen minutes later, she reached two conclusions. She was glad Len had agreed to go with her, and the killer might have stalked the victims for days, if not weeks, without interference or notice.

With the Farnsworth house, dairy barn, and several outbuildings scattered within a cluster of trees in a small basin, anyone could have watched the entire farm from any number of hills. Undoubtedly, a few tractor paths or dirt roads trailed through the trees and hills connecting fields and valleys.

Ronnie’s heart ached with the sheer beauty of the peaceful setting and the horror of what had happened there. For the first time, her eyes stung with tears as she scanned the well-tended hills.

A herd of black and white dairy cows, Holsteins milled near a few barns, and others grazed on a hillside in a backdrop of green fields. Spotting a tractor ambling across another emerald field, perhaps, mowing hay, she knew this would be either Cal or his brother, the younger brother who’d been away.

Her heart wrenched with pain for them, for all of them.

Even knowing she couldn’t possibly capture the serenity devastated by this monster, Ronnie brought her trusty Minolta from her oversized bag and snapped off several shots. Using wide-angle and telephoto lenses, she captured the essence of the farm before turning away.

“You okay, Ron?” Len asked as they walked to the car through a shag of gravel and grass. He’d directed her to park in a stand of trees, offering her the perspective he and Jarvins had discovered only yesterday morning.

From this vantage point, a stalker could’ve rested for hours, but something . . . something felt wrong. Or twisted.

“It’s not just a murder, Len,” she uttered as she slipped into the car. “It’s a sacrilege . . .”

The Engler farm was just as lovely . . . just as remote and magnificent, and just as accessible to a psychopath. The hills stood closer with thicker forests and deep valleys, but all the main buildings stood in a cluster. A killer could watch from a dozen vantage points, armed with a pair of high-quality binoculars or telephoto lens. Again, the farm could’ve been under surveillance for days or weeks . . . But again, something niggled at the edges of her mind.

Doubt.

“Routine,” she said as she scanned the red-painted structures. “That’s where the theory of an outsider falls apart, Len. This maniac knew the routine. Might have known these gentlemen tended their cattle alone at night. That suggests night scopes, serious lenses, or close-quarter surveillance unless it was someone they knew. To get down into those barns is a hike. That takes time, and planning . . .

"And you can rule out Isaac Bently," she realized as she continued scanning the barns. "He was gone for two weeks. Unless you find out that he never went to England, he's out of the running. Whoever did this knew . . .

"First, it was a full moon coming. Second, no other Englers were present in that barn. Third, how to get down there and back with time to spare. We're talking a lot of time, a lot of sitting and waiting, watching, and a whole lot of knowing. It's not random. I'd bet my life, it's not random. Someone knew these men, knew them, and chose them for reasons we have yet to learn."

She paused, her mind drifting over the details she'd accumulated as she continued scanning the farm, feeling . . . she could feel the presence of this crime. A shroud of darkness hung over the valley; an essence of death flowed over the hills as if the land, itself, cried out for justice.

"Whoever did this couldn't see the beauty," she said softly. "They couldn't feel it . . . And maybe in their dementia, that's all the reason they needed. They knew it was here, knew the beauty was here, but they couldn't feel it, couldn't taste it or touch it anymore. Demons . . ." she uttered. "Hatred and bitterness . . . like biting into a green apple . . . That's what our killer felt when looking on this farm, on Farnsworth's farm. Those men paid . . . paid because our killer couldn't feel the beauty of this land . . . saw them as evil . . . demons . . . hatred . . . retribution," she uttered as a strange euphoria washed over her, through her. "Retribution . . ."

Len gripped her arm, his fingers nearly bruising, catching her from a sway and tugging her with his sharp, "Ronnie."

Shaking her head, shivering suddenly, Ronnie collected her balance and found Len's dark, intent gaze.

"Do you know what you've been saying?" he asked carefully.

"I . . . I'd imagine I do, Len," she said with an all too familiar heaviness pouring through her veins. Absently, her gaze trailed to the cluster of buildings. "It's all connected. The beauty, the hatred, the land, and the victims . . . and it's someone who grew up in Bentwood," she said without another doubt in her mind. Looking to Len, reading the trust as well as the speculation, she nodded, "This wacko was born and raised around here . . . and these men were not random choices."

CHAPTER 12

With every ounce of his will, Isaac controlled his impulse to demand Elaine's presence when she phoned to beg off another day. Propriety won. He accepted her excuse to console her cousin and managed a few words of sympathy.

Resigning and confining himself to the couch in his office, he refrained from getting too close to his desk. Several stacks of sparkling china remained front and center, awaiting transport to an empty dining room table in his showroom, all of which he ignored. He'd worked steadily through the remainder of the receipts, aching, and cursing when he realized Elaine had sold several of his favorite items. He should never have decided to become a businessman, not in this business. A collector, yes. A merchant, no. He enjoyed too damn many of his acquisitions, and no amount of mental tag could convince him he should part with the damned things. No wonder he was accused of being a lousy haggler. At least if he gave his merchandise away, he could convince himself he retained ownership.

Cursing and laughing at himself silently, he set the books aside and ventured to the display room, judging the time. Perhaps, he'd finally done it, fallen straight off that precarious edge that others referred to as sanity, or perhaps, he'd never been truly sane.

Walking carefully toward the front of the store, he stayed dead center on the hardwood floors. He nearly reached the glass entrance while digging for his keys when several things struck him at once. An awfully lot of cars were passing on Maine, two boys loitered on his stoop outside the doors, and several teenagers clustered on the opposite side of the street. Entirely too much activity for a Sunday afternoon.

For a few seconds, he had the queerest feeling that he might have lost about two weeks, and a shiver spilled from his neck to his heels. The Fourth of July parade? The Firemen's Fair at the end of the block? God! Had he lost almost two weeks? Should he have delivered a few boxes of rummage sale items to the flea market for the Firemen's Fair? He'd lost time in the past but to this extent . . .?

Impossible! For God's sake, he might be slipping slightly, but he'd never lost two weeks of his life! Surely, not entire weeks!

Barely, he considered hurrying when the first of several clocks scattered throughout his shop began to chime the noon hour. Halted, he stood frozen, darting his gaze from one clock face to another as more of the chimes and gongs joined the crescendo. The faces seemed to jump out at him, every pair of hands spiked to the twelve o 'clock, his senses spinning suddenly with the tunnel effect.

'Time's up . . . time's up . . . timmme's uppp . . .' the words rang inside his pounding, pulsing skull, swaying him as he stood in the shadows. "Timmme's uppp," he uttered within the chaos of clamoring clock chimes.

As the last gong faded, he jolted from his halted pose. With a quick shiver and shake, he hastened to the door in an unnatural panic. Late! He was too late! Opening late . . .!

Hitting the light switches first, he drew an unsteady breath, then juggled the key nervously into the alarm board inside the door to defuse the windows and front door security. Outside, Wade and Denny nearly hopped with their excitement to come inside, their familiar young faces offering relief as Isaac unlocked the door.

Again, Isaac slid his gaze through the glass, scanning the activity. The cars were no illusion. A solid stream of cars cramped against the curb, lining either side of the street. People, total strangers, milled and hurried in either direction on both sidewalks. If he didn't know better, he might wonder if his entire store had teleported to the center of a large city. It looked as bad as New York on New Year's Eve, as busy as New Orleans during Mardi Gras, and as dangerous as LA during a racial riot.

Far more carefully than usual, he opened the door and jolted at a burst of people noise and Wade blasting, "Look at all these *folks*, Mr. Bently! You *see* 'em! We're gonna be *hoppin'* today!"

"Ain't it *something*!" Denny said with uncharacteristic exuberance. "My dad's up there with the mayor!"

The reason slammed him before he ever stepped out of the cool shadows of his shop and into the noon heat. Stopped under the awning, Isaac glanced in either direction. Inclemently hot, the June sun steamed the pavement and baked the paint of a coup parked on the yellow line that nearly blocked the side street, but the heat wasn't responsible for his sudden pang of grief. All these people, converging for the grizzly thrill of a manhunt or hanging . . .

He could easily imagine this crowd transported a hundred years into the past, carrying sturdy ropes rather than banners, screaming for blood. Shaking his head, he scanned the horde in either direction. Equally divided, they congregated between the municipal building to his left and the small park three blocks to his right. Faces gnarled, several men stalked past, and Isaac heard some mention of the 'bureaucracy' and 'a maniac' nearly in the same sentence. He was lucky to recognize one of every twenty faces streaming in either direction.

"Ain't it *something*!" Denny said smugly. "This is the biggest thing *ever* to hit Bentwood!"

Dismayed, Isaac looked down at the boy's flushed face, and the expression sickened him. "It's something," he said absently and turned away, walking into his store. He hadn't bothered flipping the plastic sign to read 'open.' He would've preferred to lock the door and shut off the lights. He wanted no part of this madness. No part of this sickness. He could close. Anyone with any good sense and a store filled with precious glass would close in deference to the angry mob gathering outside. What good would that do? If the mob got out of hand, his windows would be smashed, and wouldn't that just be a fantastic irony? After all his care to keep from smashing his merchandise, to have a riot obliterating his wares?

Not even the anger would rise to wipe out the dread filling him.

As he emptied his bank envelope into the slots of his cash register, Isaac glimpsed at Wade sauntering down the aisle, hands shoved in his hip pockets, his blond hair hanging in a clutter over his brow. The boy no longer appeared thrilled or excited with the world outside. Perhaps, that was some shallow consolation. Returning to his office, Isaac collected the bankbooks he'd needed, along with yesterday's used Styrofoam cup that he'd rinsed to reuse as a coffee cup. Almost amused, Isaac glimpsed at the plastic jug he'd enlisted to fill the coffeemaker rather than risk carrying the glass pot across the lounge.

By the time Isaac returned behind his showcase, Wade leaned alongside the counter, watching him with a lifted golden brow. Undoubtedly, wisely, the boy questioned Isaac's sanity as he stood debating whether to place the heavy bankbook on the glass counter or retire to the couch in the small lounge. If he was careful, he could slide the book onto the glass without dropping it or shattering the showcase.

Annoyed, Isaac carried out the ordeal with the precision of a surgeon and smirked at Wade when the boy eyed him a little critically, his golden head tilted in curiosity. Noting the silence and absence, Isaac wondered, "Did Denny desert you?"

"He went up with his ma," he answered. "Guess his dad's gonna lead some kind of vigil for Mr. Engler and Mr. Farnsworth."

Isaac masked his relief, more intent on the boy's gloomy expression. "If you have someplace you'd rather be, lad, you needn't feel obligated to stay here."

"How's come you felt bad looking at all them folks?"

Stopped, Isaac studied the boy, realizing his dour mood had altered the child's attitude toward the festivities. "I've always enjoyed parades," he answered honestly. "But I prefer celebrations, Wade. That—" he said and glanced toward the front window. "That's not a celebration. Those men should be mourned with respect, and the authorities should be left alone to solve the crime. Each to his own, however."

The boy considered the words for a moment as Isaac turned to collect the high stool, but he spoke again as Isaac slid onto it. "Where did you grow up?"

"I don't know that I ever have," Isaac said and winked at the boy before turning his attention to organizing his paperwork.

"Mom says I shouldn't bug you so much," Wade said as he settled his forearm on the case. "She says you probably don't need no little kids hanging around in here and how it ain't polite for me to ask you stuff all the time." He looked up with a faintly desperate shine. "Do I bug you?"

Amused, Isaac shook his head. "No, I can safely say, you don't bug me, Wade. I'd be a little annoyed if you were the type to race through my aisles or play soccer with my wares, but you haven't given me cause to evict you. In fact, if you'd stick around and take care of customers as you did yesterday so I can catch up on my paperwork, I'd make it worth your while."

"Gees! You mean it?" he asked warily.

"Consider yourself hired, at least for today, lad," Isaac decided, genuinely relieved.

"Think uh . . . think I'm dressed okay?" he asked with painfully transparent insecurity.

Isaac made a fair display of leaning over the counter, glancing over the boy's worn-thin jeans and faded T-shirt, and commented, "I don't see any problem. You'll likely be filthy if we have to wrap another hundred pieces of glassware today anyway." And he was almost proud of the fact that he managed not to shudder as he spoke

"You're the *greatest!*" Wade said, then flushed nearly the color of his red stripes. "I mean, well . . . you're cool."

The doorbells jangled, saving either of them from further embarrassment, but a few older women trailing through the door offered no relief. This was likely only the beginning of the day's trade. Before he could recover from that first dreaded thought, two teenage girls trounced in wearing cut-off shorts that barely covered their rumps and cut-off tops hiked to their ribcage.

"Hi ya! Mr. Bently!" Trudy, the shorter, stockier of the pair, called out happily as they strode down the aisle.

Her more reserved, long-legged friend smiled with all the wiles of a woman in contrast to her freckled face and ponytail. "Hi," she offered in a softer tone, honing her skills at seduction.

"Hello, girls," Isaac said and decided he better forget the books and help the elders. Otherwise, he could be trapped behind a counter at the mercy of two young women who could have him arrested for indecent thoughts. That his thoughts ran toward disgust wouldn't matter one wit. Slipping the book off the counter, Isaac tucked it under the register and glimpsed Wade eyeing the sedate blond, wondering if he should point out the more salient talents of females over fifteen.

"Hi ya, Marcy," Wade managed.

"Hi, dork," the girl said in a vapid tone. "What're you doing? Buying more bubblegum cards?"

The boy would learn soon enough, Isaac realized and caught the boy's bold, confident tone as he commented, "Na, I'm working here."

"You?" Trudy snapped and started to laugh.

"No joke. Huh, Mr. Bently?" Wade said boldly.

Coming from behind the counter, Isaac glanced between the doubting, chiding faces, one of which softened like butter into a warm smile. Deciding on the instant, he commented, "No, joke." And perhaps, just for the hell of it, Isaac looked toward Wade, suggesting, "Why don't you assist these ladies with whatever they'd like to see." Picking the keys to his jewelry cases from the counter, he tossed the wad, delighted when the kid snatched it from mid-air. "Those open the jewelry cases. Just bring one tray out at a time, though. Store policy."

Isaac left the boy beaming, the girls gaping and walked up the aisle toward the three older women. Restraining an urge to sink his hands in his jeans, he commented, "Welcome to Olden Time. Anything I can help you with today, ladies?"

Good God, even the little woman with the snow-capped head of kinky curls, blushed like a schoolgirl as she darted a shy glance in his direction. "I'm just looking."

Cursed. He was cursed. Had been all his life, Isaac decided and resigned to be charming despite the scowl that the larger-boned, boxy elder woman tossed toward him.

"I collect carnival glass."

"Then you've come to the right place," Isaac commented and cringed behind his slight smile. "I have quite a bit of carnival scattered about."

The third woman, comfortably dressed in white cotton slacks and a yellow jersey, chimed in with a whiskey voice, "I collect Cambridge and Haviland."

A conspiracy! A God-blessed conspiracy! Isaac kept smiling. "I'm a little more partial to china, but I have a few nice Cambridge bowls and glasses."

"I don't buy anything that's chipped, cracked, or nicked," the boxy woman stated crossly.

"Neither do I, ma'am," he said smoothly. "If I couldn't put it on my own mantel, you won't find it on my shelves." *As if he had a blasted mantel!*

"Pretty bold statement, sonny," she challenged. "You got a lot of nice glass."

"If you find a chip, dent, or ding, ma'am, you have my permission to smash it outside my backdoor," Isaac said sincerely, wondering if he were tempting fate. What was this sudden fixation with glass? First, fearing he would drop it. Second, fearing a riot would smash it. Now, by God, he was asking for someone else to break it? If his shop survived the afternoon, it would be a bloody miracle!

And the day just kept getting better and better. Glancing toward the jangling bells, he watched a few more pedestrians trickle in. A damned curse, no other explanation. How could a mob wanting blood, anybody's blood, everybody's blood, take time out to do a little antiquing?

Before Isaac could slide away to greet the new arrivals, the sturdy-built woman, holding a fluted carnival glass bowl, asked, "Can you do any better on this?"

Famous last words. He barely glanced at the bowl. "I'm a little shorthanded today, ma'am. If you'll carry it up front and wrap it yourself, I'll take ten percent off whatever you buy." He fanned his gaze to include the other two with a smile and wink. "Goes for all of you ladies." *And might become store policy*, he added silently as the three happily agreed with the bargain.

He might need to make a sign,

'10% discount if you carry it and wrap it yourself.' Certainly more attractive than, 'If you break it, you buy it.'

"Hello there, welcome to Olden Time," Isaac said as he approached yet another couple. "If there's anything I can help you with, don't hesitate."

Falling into the rhythm of the afternoon, Isaac batted not an eye when the woman mentioned Candlewick, and he refrained from a grimace when the man asked about a beveled-glass cupboard. Within minutes of engaging the older chap in a discussion about antique cherry wood vs, walnut, Isaac knew he should have counted his blessings. His shop was crowding, and more than a few familiar faces appeared in the growing number of patrons. This wasn't what he intended when opening an antique shop for Chrissake! A nice quiet little store! He felt like he was running a damned department store without the luxury of self-service islands . . . and the conversations added a grim lull as he jotted sales tickets and collected cash or checks.

By midafternoon, Isaac had heard about Mayor Mick Lawson's speech to calm the masses, about the television cameras and anchormen and women from the major networks, about the various eulogies from each of the seven or eight congregations in town. State and county police had arrived to help with crowd control. The Bentwood House Inn was filled to capacity. Reporters flooded the streets, banging on doors, shoving cameras in faces, and leading the pack of wolves hounding the city officials.

"Isn't it a riot?" Jen Andover asked as she draped herself over the top of his cash register a lot like a Siamese cat on a mantel. "You'd think the president had come to town."

"I think it stinks," Trish Freshcorn commented while flashing Jen a sneer. "I don't know why the sheriff doesn't just boot that whole mob out of town."

"Freedom of the press," Jen said, smiling. "The public has a right to know."

"Well, I don't think it's fair," Trish snapped. "I think the Farnsworths and Englers been through enough without having this to contend with."

"Hell, Frank's out there screaming for blood like the rest of them," Milt Freshcorn commented, unintentionally siding with Jen and receiving a scorching glare from his wife. More meekly, he muttered, "That don't make it right."

"You can say that again," Isaac uttered and finished adding the ticket to hand to Milt. "That'll be twenty-three sixty, Milt."

Grumbling, Milt pulled out his wallet.

"It's all that woman's fault," Trish said scornfully. "That Bryson! She's the one who started this! I heard she's been sleeping with every man in town trying to get a story."

"Trish, that's enough, now," Milt said.

"Really, Milt," Jen put in sweetly. "Trisha's just telling it like it is, isn't that right, Isaac?" Jen said while turning her big blue eyes to him. "She tried getting your attention in the worst kind of way."

As much as that black-haired beauty had annoyed him, to hear her name again dragged through the mud when she'd been less annoying than most sent a flash of heat through his mind. "If you call buying a Wedgwood bowl for her mother a 'come on,' then she came on like a tiger."

"Come, now, babe," Jen played. "The whole town knows you two had dinner together. If that's not fast work, I don't know what is."

"I heard she's even having an affair with one of those FBI agents," another party chimed in, and Isaac glanced at Vicky McCuddy bellying up to his counter as if lounging over at Crowley's. "One of the maids over at the Inn said you could hear them carrying on half the night."

"Funny," Isaac said dryly and looked to Milt with a conspiratorial wink. "People used to say they heard me howling at the moon when I first moved to town."

Milt, whose memory wasn't too shabby, started chuckling as he commented, "Seems to me, they got it proved when you and ole Timmy Spencer prowled the Crowley Inn on one a them full moons."

"Worst hangover of my life the next morning," Isaac attested.

"Oh Lord, I remember that night," Vicky flushed.

"Damned near got ole Timmy booted off the force," Milt added.

"Timmy should be booted off the force," Trish put in. "He's worse than some of the boys he hauls in every Saturday night."

"I just hope Donna doesn't hear how that reporter was hanging all over him this morning," Jen said with a nervous whisper. "It'd break her heart."

Christ, the claws were out today. Gratefully, Isaac heard the doorbells jangle again. "If you'll all excuse me," he commented and strode around the register, avoiding Jen's hip by a hair's breadth. The woman did walk a fine line between vamp and viper.

Recognizing the dark-suited men coming toward him, Isaac paused a few steps into the aisle, not fool enough to doubt the nature of their arrival. He'd wondered how long it would take before they paid him a visit. Behind him, voices silenced, and in various locations throughout his aisles, conversations hushed and ebbed, "Good afternoon, gentlemen," Isaac offered. "Something I can do for you?"

In tandem, they held their wallets ready. The blond halted close enough for Isaac to read his badge when he flipped the billfold open. Wearing a chilly gaze and thin smile, Agent Jarvins announced, "Federal agents. Wonder if we could have a word with you, Mr. Bently?"

"Don't suppose I could convince you to come back in about two hours, could I?"

"Suppose not," the man commented in a faintly arrogant tone. "Do you have someplace private we can talk?"

"Privacy's not an issue," Isaac admitted, unconsciously pronouncing the words with his lingering British accent. Glancing around his store, he found Wade loitering a few steps away. *Brave lad*. Isaac looked at the agent. "Would you like to ask my customers to leave, or would your partner care to help Wade man the store for me while we step into my office?"

The agent glanced around the store, counting heads, then looked to his dark-haired partner, who wore a few sharp edges and the hint of a broken nose that added character. His gaze came full circle, landing on Isaac. "Maybe you better pick somebody and put them in charge, huh?"

Shaking his head in mild disgust, Isaac looked at Wade. "Think you can handle this mob for a few minutes, lad?"

"I'll sure try, Mr. Bently," Wade said boldly.

Isaac flashed a faint smile and turned, motioning the agents with him and shrugging indifference to the collection of bodies at his counter. "Covering their bases obviously," he commented as he passed around the counter.

"We'll help li'l Wade for you, Isaac," Milt offered.

"Thanks, this shouldn't take long," he said and led the procession into his office. Glancing at the china on his desk, he forced himself past the stacks of glass before turning, watching the broader, dark-haired fellow nudge the door shut.

The light-haired man stepped closer, his eyes steady. "Any chance you have your passport handy, Mr. Bently?"

"The last I looked, I stood on American soil. I certainly don't have it in my pocket," Isaac answered calmly.

"Maybe you better figure out where you do have it and go get it."

Annoyed, Isaac glanced at the closed door, then the two agents, and decided, "If you intend to poke around in here while I go upstairs, do be careful, will you? A few of these odds and ends are irreplaceable." *And glass*.

A prickle slid down his spine as he turned and walked through his rear door. A minute, two minutes tops, plenty of time for them to nose around in his desk drawers and on the shelves where he kept his price guides and files. If they wanted to read his electric bill, he didn't mind.

He climbed the steps at a natural pace and needed a few moments to find his passport in the jacket he'd worn on the plane. He returned to find the blond holding one of the dinner plates. Far more nervous about the plate than handing over his passport, Isaac watched the glittering platter land on the corner stack and winced with the scrape of glass-on-glass. There was a reason he separated each plate with a thin slice of cardboard as a protective barrier, but that wouldn't prohibit the glass from shattering.

This fear of breaking glass was a new, truly unsettling fixation.

Isaac glanced at the agent flipping through the passport. The dark-haired man remained leaning against the door. Standing in the guard dog position, he appeared more than ready to draw, aim and fire if, for any reason, Isaac decided to bolt. They were doing their job under extremely harsh conditions. If they hadn't come to speak to him, he would've been a little concerned over their competency.

The blond tossed the book to his partner and focused on Isaac. "How was England this time of year?"

"Wet and busy," Isaac answered.

"Pretty general answer."

"Pretty general question," Isaac answered.

"Have a lot of friends over there, huh?"

"A few," he answered.

"Do you stay with friends or opt for Inns?"

"Both, on occasion," Isaac answered honestly. "If you'd like to skip the foreplay and ask what you'd really like to know, I wouldn't mind."

"How does a guy suddenly appear out of nowhere six years ago and end up in Bentwood PA?"

"If you have evidence that I've committed a crime, Mr. . . . Jarvins," he remembered the name from either the glimpse at the badge or some snippet of gossip. "I'll be glad to answer you. Until then, I'm afraid that's none of your business."

"Changed your mind about being cooperative?"

"I'll cooperate as well as the next chap, Mr. Jarvins, but I draw the line at an invasion of my privacy without just cause."

Jarvins studied him a moment, then suggested, "Why don't you make this simple, Mr. Bently? Sooner or later, we'll find out who you are and what you're running from. A guy doesn't just pop up with a tidy sum in the bank and set up shop with a whole store of expensive antiques. I'd put your age around thirty. What were you, about twenty-three when you hatched? So, what is it? Are you running from the mob? Maybe your old man's a Don? Or maybe, you're one of those child prodigies. Maybe started knocking guys off for a living back in grade school. Or maybe, you were born around this little fleabag town and decided to come home to nest. What's the story, friend?"

Annoyed, Isaac listed his gaze. He'd known, had always known nothing lasts forever. Sooner or later, it all comes back to haunt. Looking at Jarvins, he spoke carefully, honestly. "I haven't committed any crime, Mr. Jarvins. What I've done with my life, my past, to which you're obviously referring, is my business. It doesn't affect anyone but me. Believe that as you may or may not, but until you offer me a better reason than idle curiosity or simple harassment, I'm not answering that question. As it wouldn't have any bearing on your investigation, I hope you'll leave it be, but that's your prerogative," he paused, his gaze unwavering. "If you'd like to ask me anything directly relative to the alleged crimes you're here to solve, I'll help however I can. That's the best I can do."

"No, I think you're going to do better than that, Mr. Bently. I think you're about to be very helpful, very soon, or my friend and I may feel a sudden urge to secure a federal warrant and turn your little shop upside down," he paused with a slow smile. "I don't think you'd like the way we search for contraband and the like. Sometimes," he lifted one of the dinner plates, running his fingers over the gold edge. "Things get broken."

"You're right, I wouldn't like that," Isaac admitted quietly, trying not to watch those lily-white fingers caressing the delicate gold scallops,

"How much does a set of dishes like this cost, do you think?" Jarvins asked while glancing over to his partner.

"Got me. Looks pretty old though," the other answered with a hint of disapproval.

Jarvins looked at Isaac. "How much would you say, Bently?"

"More than I'd care to mention before you return it safely to that stack."

"Come on. Be a sport," Jarvins said lightly. "How much would this set soak me?"

"Five K," Isaac answered tensely, his gaze steady on the bemused blue eyes. *That plate was doomed.*

"How much would you pay?"

"Less than five K," he answered honestly.

"Complete set, isn't it? What? About a hundred pieces?"

"Fair estimate," Isaac said as he glimpsed at the fingers still smoothing over the gilt edge. Nervous, tense, he looked into Jarvins' eyes. "If you're attempting to make me nervous, you're succeeding," Isaac said quietly. "I deal in antiques because I enjoy far more than the financial value, and if you're as knowledgeable as I believe, you're aware of my financial freedom to indulge my pleasure. I'd rather not see one of those plates broken when they've survived more than a hundred years in mint condition. If you have the urge to break glass, there's a mug behind you, feel free."

"You seem to think we're playing games here, Mr. Bently," Jarvins sneered.

"Aren't we?" Isaac asked quietly.

Jarvins studied him for several seconds before asking, "What time did you get in Friday night?"

"I went through customs around eight, as I'm sure you know. I got home around ten."

"Stop anywhere between the airport and here?"

"Aside from the ticket booth leaving the airport parking lot and a few stop signs, no."

"Drive the speed limit the whole way?"

"Doubtful, but I wasn't pulled over," Isaac said honestly.

"So, it took you roughly two hours from customs to here, speeding?"

"It took me a half-hour to find my car," he remembered absently and offered a faint smirk as he shrugged.

"A half-hour to find your car in a parking lot?" Jarvins smiled, too, but he wasn't amused.

"I don't sleep well in the air," Isaac admitted. "Not much of an excuse, but I forgot which car I drove," he added. "You might find the airport security guard who helped me track it down. Eventually, he grew tired of watching me wander around and offered his assistance."

"Just out of curiosity, what car did you take? The Jag, the Vette, or the Maserati?"

By the man's snickering tone, this wouldn't sit well, but Isaac answered truthfully. "The Maserati. I was running late when I left. I usually take the Vette, slightly more space for suitcases." He shrugged. "That's what threw me in the parking lot."

"Keep all these cars just hanging around, huh?"

"We all have our weaknesses," he commented.

"All licensed and insured. It must cost you a mint a month," Jarvins idled.

"So?"

"Pretty lopsided with your finances, aren't you? I mean here's this plate, five grand for a hundred pieces, and you probably pay that much in car insurance a month. I don't get it?"

"Yes, you get it just fine," Isaac knew as he watched the plate starting to slip. By reflex, he lunged, ducking and thrusting his hands, and watched, with a chest-wrenching pain, as the plate descended past his fingers, falling the length of the regulation-black slacks. In a split second, the delicate porcelain shattered. Shards blasted outward, lancing the black cuffs, shiny black shoes, and hardwood floor. His knee hitting the wood as the blast resounded, Isaac withdrew his hovering, suddenly trembling hands, hearing the low deep voice offer.

"Oops. It slipped."

Trembling, Isaac gazed down at the scattered fragments, scanning the glittering slivers with his anger sparking. He heard a banging at the door, an anxious voice. Shaking his head, he blinked against a sting in his eyes, aware of the heat rising, racing through his veins. Controlled, he pushed off his knee, combing his hair off his forehead as he turned away.

"You ready to talk to me yet, Bently?" Jarvins asked.

For a long moment, Isaac gazed at the cluttered shelves and file cabinets lining the back wall. Recovering his breath, his balance, he heard the fists pounding at the door, the voices calling to him. With a quiet rage, he turned and met Jarvins' bemused blue eyes, "Come back with a warrant, Mr. Jarvins," he said in a low dark tone. "Bring that, and you can bust every fucking thing in my shop, but until you bring that, sir, I suggest you and your associate get your asses off my premises."

"I don't think so," Jarvins said as he reached for another plate. Again, he began sliding his fingers over the scalloped gold trim.

Through the door, Wade cried with a near desperate note, "Mr. Bennntly! Are you okaaay!"

Flashing a glance at the dark-eyed agent Devinio, then to the door, Isaac raised his low voice enough to be heard, snapping, "Fine. Mind the store, lad."

"Cute kid," Jarvins commented. "He looks a little old to be yours. You banging his old lady?"

Calm dark anger held him steady now. He folded his arms across his chest, his gaze locked on Jarvins. "Is the question germane to your murder investigation?" Isaac asked.

Jarvins offered a careless shrug, letting the plate slip slightly before recovering his hold, feigning a fleeting horror. "That's the trouble with a murder investigation, Mr. Bently, I never know what could be relevant. That's what makes my job so tough. That's why I must be curious about a lot of things. So, are you banging her?"

"Irrelevant," Isaac decided simply. "Next question."

"My partner and I will decide what's relevant, Mr. Bently," Jarvins said with a soft edge. "And from what I hear, who you're banging could be extremely relevant. For all I know, you're doing the old lady and the kid, and whacking decent, hard-working men just for the hell of it. Maybe you got the idea while banging one of the farmer's daughters . . . or sons. So, how about you come clean and tell me how well you know any of the Farnsworths or Englers?"

"I've had business ventures with members of both families, buying, selling, and in one instance, trading antiques with one or another."

"Tell me about this trade," Jarvins stated. "With whom, when, and what."

"Three years ago, Cora Farnsworth. A crystal vase for a stamped piece of ironware," he answered evenly.

"Did you get the crystal?" Jarvins asked with a smile.

"Actually, no," Isaac answered.

"So, you traded crystal for iron. Make any money?"

"It was a signed Griswold skillet, it held its own, but no, I didn't turn a profit on the trade."

"Lose money?"

"It happens," he answered.

"That Val Farnsworth, she's a pretty little thing," Jarvins said evenly. "Three years ago, she'd have been seventeen. Any chance you got a little more than iron in that trade?"

Isaac recalled the brief incident with young Valerie shortly after that deal, but he certainly wouldn't consider a child's crush worth mentioning. More disgusted than annoyed, Isaac held Jarvins' glittering eyes. "No. No chance at all, Mr. Jarvins. I won't deny I've had a few brief affairs with a few women in Bentwood; however, those relationships have always been with single, consenting, adult females. I do not '*bang*' married women, or children, of either gender."

"Name a few of the women, Bently," Jarvins stated.

"Go to hell, Jarvins," Isaac said in a matched low tone.

"You're being uncooperative again, Mr. Bently, and for all I know, maybe I have a jealous boyfriend on the loose. A list of your trysts—or conquests—may break this case wide open."

Considering the words, Isaac hesitated a few seconds before shaking his head. "Doubtful, Mr. Jarvins, but if you can lend evidence to support that scenario, I'd be willing to name names. Until then, I respect the women's privacy."

"Not a kiss-and-tell kind of guy, huh?" Jarvins taunted.

"Personal relationships should remain personal, Mr. Jarvins," he said quietly. "And I've already admitted that I value my privacy. It's a standard I apply to most aspects of my life, including romantic endeavors."

"You're a real prince among men, huh?"

Unwavering, Isaac held Jarvins' angry gaze. "Obviously, it's a lonely position, but some of us need adhere to a higher standard."

The subtle dig wasn't lost on Jarvins. The blue eyes fleeted dark amusement . . . and he lost his grip on the plate.

Isaac's heart lunged. His gaze followed the colorful hand-painted treasure to its doom. Flinching, his heart wrenching, he watched the china shatter as his muscles gripped in reflex. Not the money. Never the money. Colorful slivers of china sparkled on the floor. Some of the larger chunks glittered and reflected the neon light from a single track overhead. Resigning to the loss, he shook his head and lifted his distressed gaze to find Jarvins studying him with unveiled intensity. "You needn't have done that, you know," he said with quiet, restrained anger. "I would have apologized if I'd known you were so sensitive."

"Was an accident," Jarvins said with a more forced amusement, slightly less mockery in his tone. "Suppose I owe you an apology instead."

"More than a hundred years ago, a nameless, faceless artisan sat for hours applying one layer of paint after another to create the masterpiece you just shattered in a split second," Isaac said in quiet conviction. "An apology wouldn't replace the beauty or the tiny piece of history you just destroyed." He paused only an instant. "I'd prefer you arrest me if that's your ultimate goal than to watch you break any more of those plates."

Again, the knock intruded, rapping in quick, anxious thumps, but it was Jen Andover calling, "Isaac, are you alright? What's going on in there, babe? Answer me!"

Dismayed, Isaac glanced toward the door, only faintly surprised to hear genuine concern in Jen's sharp voice.

"Girlfriend, huh?" Jarvins chided. "*Babe.*"

Numb, Isaac listed his gaze over the shattered shards on the floor, and his anger returned on a slow, boiling wave. Lifting his focus to Jarvins at an angle, he spoke carefully, "I think you should leave, Mr. Jarvins. This interview or interrogation is over. Whatever common courtesy I'd have afforded you in the hope of saving a life, ceased the instant that second plate shattered. If you have any further questions, I'll expect a warrant, and I'll have my attorney present."

Jarvins started to speak, but Devinio interrupted, "Mr. Bently, did you have a relationship with Allister Engler?"

Looking toward the dark-eyed man, Isaac commented in a low even tone, "Perhaps, you should have asked that question ten minutes ago, Mr. Devinio. No comment."

"You've been cooperative, Amico. A few more questions and we're gone. We save each other a lot of hassles, and maybe we get closer to catching a real bad guy."

Every nerve taut, Isaac gazed at the darker man. "Bring a warrant, federal, state, or local, and we'll chat, Mr. Devinio. You've both worn out your welcome."

"Ever have any dealings with either of the victims, Bently?" Devinio asked.

"No comment," Isaac said evenly.

"Any idea who might hold a grudge against either of those two fellas?" Devinio asked.

"No comment."

"In a town this size, folks tend to be neighborly," Devinio commented. "You ever go out to either of those homesteads, maybe do a little socializing? A picnic? A cookout?"

"No comment."

"Whether you were born and raised here doesn't make much difference. In a small town, folks tend to get acquainted and friendly. Even if you just knew those two gentlemen in passing, I'd think you'd want to help find whoever murdered them, and they were murdered, Mr. Bently. Seems to me, the cost of human life runs just a little higher than those two fancy plates," Devinio commented. "So, why don't we just start over, and you answer a few simple questions so we can be on our way?"

"Twenty minutes ago, I gave you the benefit of my doubt and determined to cooperate, Mr. Devinio. I've wasted my time, and you're wasting yours," Isaac said quietly. "If you have questions for me, you have two options. Charge me with a crime and arrest me, in which case, I'll get an attorney and won't say a word whether I'm indicted or not. Or, you can send over one of the state, county, or local officers, and I'll be happy to answer any relevant questions."

"Think you're pretty clever, huh, fella?" Jarvins asked.

Isaac looked at him directly, his expression a mask of indifference as he offered, "No comment."

"Here's an easy one, Bently," Devinio said with a forced light tone, his pose relaxed against the door. "Any idea who might be crazy enough to murder a few of your neighbors?"

"No comment," Isaac answered evenly, likewise pinning Devinio with his indifference.

"Did *you*, by any chance, kill a few of your neighbors?" Devinio asked.

"No comment," Isaac repeated indifferently.

"You do realize we could trot you over to the station and hang onto you for the next twenty-four to forty-eight hours, don't you?" Devinio commented. "Even if you're as innocent as a newborn, your neighbors will start asking a lot of questions. Maybe start looking at you a little differently. You have a nice setup, here, Mr. Bently. Quiet small town. No shortage of women. Lots of fine folks treating you just like one of the gang. I'd hate to see all that go to shit when you obviously worked hard to make this tidy little nook for yourself . . . And I'll tell you, Amico, in case you haven't looked outside for a while, this place is crawling with camera crews and photographers. We walk you through that mob outside, and somebody's bound to get the idea we're taking a maniac into custody. Strobes start flashing, cameras snapping . . . your pretty mug gets splashed all over the front page of the major papers and on network TV." He paused as if to let his words sink in. "You see what I'm getting at, Mr. Bently? How your privacy is going to be invaded in a big way, and maybe how somebody you don't particularly want to see again, could be sitting down to the evening news? Hell, buddy, for all we know, you could have an ex-wife out there who'd really like to drive a Maserati. Be a shame if she got that chance just because you couldn't answer a few simple questions in a friendly environment . . .

"Now, what do you say we start over?" he asked in a friendly tone.

"What say, you take your mistaken innuendoes and questions with you when you leave, Mr. Devinio?" Isaac said quietly. "Or carry out your threat and escort me across the street if that's your idea of furthering a murder investigation. Either way, I won't answer any more of your questions without my attorney present," he paused a half-second. "I will mention, however, the punitive damages awarded to private citizens in cases of false arrest by the Federal Bureau is running pretty high these days." His gaze shifting to Jarvins, Isaac continued quietly, "Now, I suggest you get out of my shop, and you make damn sure you have your facts in order before securing a warrant, else a half-assed murder trial will be the least of your legal concerns."

A few silent seconds passed before Jarvins commented, "We'll see you again, Mr. Bently."

"I'd imagine so. Bentwood's a small town," Isaac said and watched the jaw twitch. Something . . . something about this fellow. Familiar?

"Don't leave town," Jarvins said and turned, motioning to his partner.

Beneath a surface calm and indifference, Isaac was furious, and a glance at the shattered china enhanced the flood of rage, amplified by the worried gawking faces filling the doorway in the departing agents' wake. Milt, Trish, Vicky, and Jen had all crowded behind the counter, and several others had gathered on the receiving end of his showcase.

As Isaac started to the door, they backed from his path, each one talking at once, sputtering questions and outrage over the agents pestering decent citizens. Glancing off his watch, Isaac decided, he had remained open as long as he intended to remain open. With a glimpse at the two agents passing through his front door, seeing a few more patrons entering, one holding a camera, he confirmed his thought.

Catching Wade's tense, worried eyes as the others hurried from behind his counter, he commented, "Go flip the sign, then do me a favor and make a pass around the store to tell people we're closing."

"Isaac, don't let them assholes bother you," Milt growled. "They been stirring up folks all over town."

Doubtful, Isaac could've said but let it ride and met Milt's gaze. "If you'd give the lad a hand clearing everyone out, I'd appreciate it, Milt."

"What did they *saaay*, Isaaac?" Jen whined.

A man leaning at the counter several paces away asked, "You sure you wouldn't want to make a statement . . . Isaac, is it?"

Glimpsing the notebook on the man's hip, Isaac met the musing eyes and commented, "I'd imagine you heard, I'm closing in a few moments. I'll expect you to be one of the first to leave, and you may quote me if you like."

"Come on, buddy," the guy said in a congenial voice. "Those two were Feds. If they're running around like their asses are catching, harassing everyone in town, the public's got a right to know. So, what kind of questions did they ask you? They got any suspects . . .? Are *you* a suspect?" he asked with a laugh.

"Perhaps, you didn't hear me, after all," Isaac said in a guarded tone. "I'm closed, and this is private property. You may walk quietly out the door, or I can have you escorted. And again, you may quote me."

At the front of the store, Wade flipped the sign even as another patron tried to enter, and a well of fondness rose as Isaac heard the bold voice saying, "We're closed. Come back tomorrow."

In front of the counter to Isaac's surprise, stocky little Milt Freshcorn squared off with the reporter and commented, "Your hearing not so good, mister? You need some help to find the door?"

Already, the second camera-holding man strode forward, obviously, ignoring the boy who had mentioned the store closing when they had passed in the aisle. "Were those Federal agents I just saw coming out of here?" the photographer asked in a jovial voice.

If ever Isaac regretted delving into business, never more than, now. His home invaded, people milling and crowding around him, at least a half-million dollars in fragile glass and furniture which could be destroyed in the blink of an eye. History shattered. Still angry and becoming more annoyed, Isaac looked at the new arrival and commented, "No, they were insurance salesmen. Now, get the hell out of my store." His gaze sharpening, he glanced over the nearest faces. "That goes for all of you," he decided and walked around the counter.

"Business hours are over," he stated and continued walking passed the stunned man.

At the door, he dug out his keys and turned, leaning against the wall. Most everyone had turned toward him. Without a need to raise his voice, he commented, "This is private property. Anyone still on the premises in five minutes will be arrested for trespassing . . ."

Nervously, little Vera Rinkle, one of his regular Sunday customers approached, holding a cranberry vase in her age-brittle fingers. "I'd like to buy this today, Mr. Bently," she said in a quavering voice.

"Take it, Mrs. Rinkle," he said simply and sidestepped, holding the door for her.

"But Mr.—"

"Go on," he said with a tempered rage. "Maybe you can bring me a slice of that peach cobbler I've heard so much about."

Barely a husk of flesh and bones, her thin lips widened in a smile, and she patted his arm, clutching the bowl against her paisley-print sweater. "You're a dear young man."

CHAPTER 13

"He's hiding something big," Mark Jarvins said for the third or fourth time as he paced inside the small room like a trapped tiger. "The bastard's hiding something so fucking big it'd put this case to shame."

Sitting back in her chair, drumming a pencil on the table where she'd been sorting through the surprisingly large amount of information collected, Ronnie watched Mark. He looked a little more like a cougar than a tiger. Sleek, angry, and dangerous, his blue eyes flashed fire as he gulped another sip of coffee. Len remained slightly more composed, sitting at the end of the cluttered table, hulking more like a brooding ape with his hands clutched around a cup. His dark eyes followed Mark with a kind of black fury that would've sent shivers down her spine if directed at her.

From the instant this pair had invaded her private tiny space, she'd realized that the interview—just a 'casual visit' with Isaac Bently—hadn't gone well. She hadn't known they intended to see Bently, or she might have warned them, might have mentioned, that he didn't strike her as a pushover. Irritating, classy, reserved . . . but no pushover. What they had hoped to gain by visiting him, she had yet to learn, but the phone call Mark had placed before their exodus had probably determined the need. Government Witness Protection Program was out of the running although she dared not wonder just how Mark Jarvins had managed to verify that information.

"You didn't have to bust his fucking plates," Len said in a low growl.

Startled, Ronnie barely glanced off Len before her gaze landed on Mark, and if ever she saw him more angry or dangerous, she couldn't recall the moment.

"Fuck his *plates,*" Jarvins stated. "At least we know the bastard doesn't move like lightning though I'd give him a goddamn A for effort."

"You broke—" Ronnie nearly bit her tongue when Mark's fire-blue eyes lanced her.

"It slipped," Mark snapped, lying gallantly.

"He didn't believe it the first time and he sure the fuck didn't believe it the second," Len growled.

"Jesus H . . ." Mark lanced Len. "It was a fucking plate, not the Holy Grail, Len. The bastard could afford to replace that set ten times over—"

"Had nothing to do with the money," Len growled with a strange note of anger. "You fucked up, Mark. The son of a bitch might not have been giving us a hell of a lot, but he was talking. Now, where the fuck are we?"

"The same damn place we were before we talked to him," Mark said in controlled rage. "We didn't lose a damn thing. We just verified the son of a bitch has something to hide."

"That doesn't make him our business at the moment," Len said carefully. "I'll nail the bastard to the wall if we find something to pin on him, but I gotta tell ya, Amico, my first take on him is . . . he's not our wacko."

"He's involved," Mark said with equal tenacity.

"Yea, the way half this damn town's involved," Len said in mild irritation, lifted his cup, and sat back almost tossing the coffee down his throat. His black eyes remained steady on Mark who stood glowering from a coiled pose against the wall. "What strikes me different about this character is that he didn't start to whimper when we flashed our badges. We could have sat over there chatting to him all night and he wouldn't have flinched."

"Right," Mark said. "And we wouldn't have learned a damn thing for our trouble. The bastard would've stonewalled us every step of the way."

"Remember when you were giving him that scenario about boyfriends?" Len asked but didn't await a reply. "Remember how he paused? Ten seconds or less," Len commented. "I'd almost bet my ass the bastard ran through every name in his little black book and cross-referenced jealous boyfriends. I don't think he was stonewalling us. Squirrelly? Yea, this guy has that perfected to a fine art, but I don't think he was fucking with us over this case . . . and if he knows the wacko, he doesn't know he knows."

"Gentlemen," Ronnie interrupted quietly and glanced between both pairs of angry eyes. "If I could make just an itty-bitty suggestion, here," she said carefully and decided on Len. "Why don't you check out whatever that was you said about the car at the airport, clear him, and move on to someone else? Obviously, our mysterious Mr. Bently is going to remain a mystery for a little while longer, and if I caught the gist of this tantrum, if there is something else to be learned from him, he offered you a reasonable solution. Send, a God—blessed—state policeman to his door, and be sure to tell the officer not to break any plates."

"The only problem with that, Ron," Len said in a more reserved tone. "I happen to agree with Mark about at least one thing. This guy's dangerous. Whether that can work for or against us, I'm not sure, but there's a . . . call it intuition, a feeling you get when you come up against a guy who's been down the road. This guy has a real nice veneer, spit-shined and polished, real personable kind 'a guy, except it doesn't wash. He dumped about a quarter of a century's worth of living down the toilet and holed up in this little town. He takes his little holidays, maybe to catch a thrill, like a junky needs a fix, but he's hiding just the same." Len looked at Mark. "And you know what bugs me the most about that interview?"

"He didn't waiver when you threatened him with exposure," Mark said evenly.

"You got it," Len said carefully. "So, what I'm thinking is, we're not dealing with an American citizen here. That's what I'm thinking."

"I was thinking the same thing when I caught a bit of that English accent," Mark commented. "But that still doesn't make a hell of a lot of sense. We put his face on national TV, it won't make a big splash across the international scene, but it could pick up a few seconds on satellite. The bigger the enemy, the wider the connections, the better chance of those seconds gaining attention."

Mr. Bently was becoming more interesting by the moment, Ronnie considered as she watched two of the brightest men she knew hashing out the same conclusions she'd considered. The man had gotten under their skin, and if she wasn't just as worried about his past as they were, she might find this show somewhat fascinating, if not amusing.

"You know, there's maybe one more possibility we haven't considered," Len said absently.

"He's an alien from outer space? Got it covered," Mark said with an irritated laugh. "I'd have sworn that color of green only comes on contact lenses."

"Naaa, I've seen that color eyes on my TV set," Len said in a low idle tone. "Course, I had to get a new set when the color went out," he barely paused, his gaze intent upon Mark. "I was thinking more along the lines of him telling us the truth."

Mark lost his half-smile, far more concentrated. "The one about having his own personal reasons?"

Len shrugged, "Stranger things have happened."

"Not buying it," Mark said bluntly, hesitated, and decided, "We'll put him on hold." His gaze slid to Ronnie. "Did you come up with anything else in that mess?"

As much as she hated to admit it, she hadn't struck upon a single harebrained idea all afternoon. She'd read over police statements taken from the Englers and Farnsworths, their neighbors, and friends. She'd looked at the single document that Chief Hayward had found concerning animal disappearances fifteen years earlier. She'd scored through seven years' worth of yearbooks that Mark had commandeered from Bentwood High at the edge of town. Names and faces were rolling through her mind as if on a high tide, but nothing connected anything to anything else.

Oh, there were connections. The Englers and Farnsworths had both lived in this town all their lives. They knew the same people, went to the same schools, and attended regular services at two different churches. They shopped at the same supermarket, patronized the same shops, and kicked up their heels at the same socials. Just not the right kind of connections. Nothing to suggest why these two men had become the victim of such a heinous crime. According to a few of the statements, Carl Farnsworth had been a shy, quiet man, always ready to help a friend in need. Vic Engler, slightly more real, had been noted for an occasional row with a neighbor—mostly over his coon dogs getting loose—and tended to 'fly off the handle now and again,' but he, too, was generally a hard-working family man who spent more time tending his fields and livestock than stirring up trouble or giving other folks grief.

Looking down at the list of names she'd accumulated from documents, a sense of futility swam over her. Why had she even bothered? A copy of the latest census would've worked just as well. Even narrowing the possibilities between the ages of twenty-five and thirty, and eliminating those who had left the area, more than two hundred names remained on her list.

Aware of the silence, Ronnie glanced at her watch, surprised to realize most of the afternoon had passed. If she intended to accept a dinner invitation, she needed to get moving. Pushing from her chair, and collecting her notebook and the list, she glanced between the two curious agents, remembering Mark's question. Had she found something? "Not yet," she said simply. "I'm going over to the Inn for a while."

"It's a mad house out there, Ron," Mark said bluntly. "If you want to go over, one of us better—"

"Don't be ridiculous," she stated. At some point during the afternoon, she'd decided not to mention her visit to the Spencers'. Inevitably, Mark would react badly. "You and Len have more important things to do than babysit me," she continued simply. "And I have a few calls to make. If I come up with anything, I'll call you."

The room where Ronnie had spent the afternoon was connected to the mayor's office which doubled as the magistrate's office. By sheer luck, the rooms and offices connected in a maze, enabling her to slip through a backdoor and land nearly at her car door. She was inside the car and pulling from the narrow alley before the first reporter spotted her rear bumper. Traveling by alley, she reached the Inn parking lot and managed to enter through the rear entrance. Barely starting onto the back staircase, she drew up short as a young man wearing an apron and carrying a handful of folded papers flew at her.

"Miss Bryson! Your messages," the boy huffed.

With the memory of Len terrorizing the shrew at the front desk, Ronnie refrained from smiling as she accepted the papers, offering a pleasant, "Thank you, dear." If she'd ever received such prompt delivery in her life, she couldn't recall the event. Climbing the narrow steps, she began leafing through the stack. Over a dozen reporters had either phoned the Inn or stopped at the desk asking for her room number. A few had handwritten messages, leaving their hotel and room numbers. More than a dozen men had phoned to leave fan mail messages, and an equal number of women had left hate-o-grams. Ronnie could just imagine that bird-nosed Miss Dunner writing a few of these ditties with glee.

In her room, Ronnie continued scanning the messages, tossing them aside one after the other, finding only a half dozen she needed to answer. The others, she started to dispose of in the trashcan, considered how hard up some reporters might be, and tucked the entire wad into her purse for safer disposal. Moving to the bed, she lifted the receiver to her ear and reached for the dial.

"Hello! Miss Bryson!" a male voice jolted in her ear.

With a half-second to decide, she touched the dial tone button, counted to ten, and lifted her finger cautiously, relieved to hear a dial tone. Priorities. She dialed the long-distance number. At the gruff hello, she smiled, "Hi ya, Max."

"About blasted time you call," he said with a natural irritation. "Where the hell have you been all day?"

Getting chewed out wasn't unusual. It was the quick concern she heard that sent a tiny little prickle of alarm down her spine. "Sort of busy, Max." Isaac Bently, she realized abruptly. "Any chance you found out something for me?"

Hesitation, then, "About?"

Tense suddenly, she gripped the receiver. "No games, Max. Did you find out something for me?"

"I've caught some pretty strange news clips today, baby doll. Want to tell me what's going on in that town?"

Evasive tactics from Max? "The usual, Max. Small town, homicidal maniac on the loose, fame-starved reporters going for the gold . . . what did you find out, Max?"

"You're like a dog with a bone," Max commented but he sounded more annoyed than taunting.

"I'm returning your call, remember?" she said with a start of annoyance. "If you didn't want to talk to me—"

"Damnit, slow down," Max said in a more natural voice, undoubtedly, cursing himself. "I did find out something about that uh . . . name you gave me," he said with a strange note of tension. "This guy . . . he's in that town? You've talked to him?"

Something extremely peculiar here. She'd told Max she wanted the background check for personal reasons, but after everything she'd learned from Mark and Len, she remembered wishing she'd not involved Max. Max was involved, and whatever he'd learned . . . the absence of knowledge? Was that why Max was behaving strangely? Stupid question. Max was too good a cop not to get the willies worse than Mark and Len. "Yes, as a matter of fact, I have spoken to him," she said carefully.

"You said this was personal, Ron," Max said carefully. "Now, tell me the truth, is he connected with that murder investigation?"

Whatever Max knew wasn't good. She could feel the short hairs rising at her hairline. "He's not a suspect as far as I know," she said quietly, sounding buoyant, knowing the futility. "Should he be?"

"You wanted the background check run quietly," Max said in her ear. "Why?"

"He wasn't a suspect, Max," Ronnie said tensely. "And I'll ask again, should he be?"

"What's the chance of me getting you to drop this one?"

"Jesus, Max! Who is this guy? International hitman? Mafia? Terrorist?"

"Slow down, damn it, I just . . ." Max's voice drifted with a more unnatural distraction and Ronnie realized he'd truly not sounded good from the first instant of this call. "As far as I know, he shouldn't be a suspect," he said firmly. "If he's not connected with the investigation, leave it that way."

"Max . . . I said he's not a murder suspect, and he's not as far as I'm concerned, but he's caught the attention of a few Federal agents. I felt bad for getting you involved in this at all after I caught wind of their interest. So, what I'm saying is . . . if you're trying to steer me clear of someone you believe is bad news, thanks."

There was a long silent pause before Max, sounding worse, spoke again, "This is a tough call, baby doll. Maybe one of the toughest I've ever had to make," he said with a leaden voice. "But uh . . . it's not a question of him being bad news, Ronnie. He's . . . just leave him alone, alright?"

The words were right; the tone was way off-key. She'd known Max Hagen too long not to know when something bothered him deeply, and something about this guy bothered Max very deeply. "You know who he is," she realized in a stopped instant and heard the hesitation, the silence as it dangled between them.

"I know . . . who he was," Max said with a low, weary sigh. "I know who he was, Ronnie. Leave him be."

The words, the voice . . . dismayed? *Sad?* "Max . . .? Who was he?" she asked carefully and listened to more dead air as Max struggled in a silent battle.

"If uh . . . if he wants you to know, he'll tell you," Max said with a tone she knew too well, his mind made up, the line drawn. "Just don't hound him, Ron."

"Max," Ronnie said carefully. "I told you Mark Jarvins is here, and uh . . . he's going nuts trying to figure out who this guy is or was before six years ago. If you can help . . .?" If he could help, he would. If Max Hagen thought for one damned minute that Isaac Bently should be a suspect in this murder investigation, he wouldn't be talking to her. He would've phoned Mark Jarvins or one of the Bureau chiefs the moment he made the connection.

"Max, tell me this," she said carefully. "Do you think he's dangerous?"

"No," he said evenly.

"You won't talk to Mark, will you?" she guessed,

"You'll have to trust me on this one, baby doll," he said in a low voice. "I'll do what I can."

For whom? That was the question rolling around in Ronnie's mind long after she disconnected the call and sat gripping the receiver if only to keep the phone from ringing. Who would Max help? And that answer sounded all too simple . . . Isaac Bently.

Twenty years of police work . . . closer to twenty-four or twenty-five. Eighteen years on Homicide . . . and Max Hagen knew Isaac Bently. Bently would be close to thirty . . . could have been as young as four or five when Max had known who he was . . . and it would have involved a crime . . . in or around Arlington where Max had lived and worked his entire life.

"Damnit," she uttered and breezed a glance at her watch. Less than an hour to be at a 'barbecue' . . . and she still needed to make a few calls. Looking down at the sheets, she hesitated then threw caution to the wind. If Mark or Len wanted to throw a fit, more power to them. She'd opened the door for Cal Farnsworth, and somehow—call it intuition, she snickered silently—she didn't think he was their wacko. Both of the phone numbers Cal had left when he called again around noon were busy. Ronnie cursed her foolishness for even thinking she would get through. The Farnsworth phones were probably off the hook to keep reporters from calling. Hopefully, he would catch up to her later.

Turning her attention to the next message, smiling just a little knowing what to expect, she dialed the number and within seconds after a hello . . .

"Don't suppose you intend to speak to Mother any time soon, do you, sis?"

"I trust you to fill her in," Ronnie mused.

"You do realize that some wild and industrious reporter managed to make the connection between a certain Veronica Bryson and another certain Robert Bryson, Sr., and the son of a bitch dared to track down the unlisted number to the house . . . You do realize, a certain matriarch and patriarch of the family are fuming beyond all reasonable doubt."

"I feel so much better now that I know, Bobby. I don't know what I'd do without you to keep my spirits up."

The jerk dared to laugh. "Hey, I still love you. As I said, the folks are fuming but they need a good rush every once in a while. I swear I haven't seen Father quite that shade of crimson since Watergate."

"I'm feeling better by the minute," she said dryly.

"Would you feel better if I offer to start a liable suit against this character . . . Grimes, I believe his name is? Theodore Grimes, ah, yes . . . 1230 Prosper Dr., Bender Falls. The fellow truly should have changed his address long ago, but you might like a little house on Prosper Dr. What do you say? Feel better? I have most of the papers drawn up to serve him in the morning."

"Bobby, Jesus, he didn't steal my virginity," she huffed. "He's a sleazeball reporter."

"He questioned your virginity," Bobby said while losing his lighthearted tone. "And I'd like to serve these papers myself for the tabloid shit I've read. Unfortunately, I've had to retain a friend of mine in Pittsburgh, but he assures me, it's in the bag. How's a hundred G's sound to start? We can nail the paper for at least that much."

Good God, he was serious. "Bobby, I don't—"

"Listen to me, sis, over and above what he's done to you as far as your public image, there's a little matter of your career along with our good name getting dragged through the mud. I certainly don't mind a little dirt, but I'll be damned if I'll let some *sleazeball* reporter from Kalamazoo drag my little sister through the shit. Now. Do I get a whack at this guy for you or me? There's the only question remaining."

"Why is it that I'm the only one who doesn't give a damn what this sleazeball wrote?" she asked absently.

"Because you're a stubborn, bullheaded brat who refuses to see the world's truly an ugly place."

"The question was hypothetical, Bobby, but thanks so much for your analysis."

"So . . . for you or for me?" Bobby asked stubbornly.

"Give me twenty-four hours to think it over," she decided.

"Twelve," he said simply. "If I don't hear from you by . . . six a.m., I'm pushing the buttons."

"You're not a nuclear physicist, for Chrissake—"

"Leave Linc out of this," Bobby interrupted. "He's the second line of defense. This doesn't work . . . there's always that little house on Prosper Dr."

"Good God, you're all maniacs."

"Sis, you don't even want to *know* what James wanted to do to this guy," Bobby said with exasperation then softened his sober voice. "Face it, brat, we all love you, and nobody's messing with you, not in this lifetime."

Suffocated, Ronnie considered even as she ached at his honesty. They did love her. Sometimes, just a little too much as if the three of them needed to rally around her and protect her from the world. "Ten o'clock, Bobby," she said quietly. "I'll call you before then and we'll discuss this. Right now, I have an appointment to keep. Love you." She disconnected the call, glanced over a few more notes then left the receiver lying on the bed.

CHAPTER 14

If he hadn't needed to back into the narrow alley behind Mrs. Handler's woolly generic rose bushes, which she inevitably accused him of hitting, Isaac might not have spotted the dark sedan parked down the alley. For the first time in five years, he wasn't annoyed with the thought of scratching a fifty-thousand-dollar car on a scrub hedge that should have been cut down during the Stone Age. By the time he climbed into his Jaguar after returning the Vette to the deep end of the warehouse, Isaac had decided to forgive the widow Handler for being a crotchety old hen.

Less than five minutes after reaching the four-lane highway toward Pittsburgh, Isaac outdistanced the surveillance car enough to enlist evasive maneuvers. Swinging onto a secondary road, he sped through country curves, navigating a circuitous route to Spencer's little hide-a-way.

Tucked back from one of the smoother county roads, the house stood within a backdrop of immense trees and hills. In an outlandish combination of peaked roofs and logs in an A-frame construct, the house might have disappeared into the foliage if not for the spread of tall windows reflecting the descending sun. To hear Tim tell it, he'd hand-selected the logs one by one and might have melted sand for the glass.

If one happened to enjoy a lot of light and bright colors, the house would be considered attractive. In Isaac's opinion, the only sensible room in the entire manse was a small alcove off the living room which Donna called 'Tim's Cove' or 'Den' after which Tim generally added 'of inequity.' Dark-wood paneling, heavy walnut shelves laden with books and whatnots, sensible-sized windows equipped with thick dark curtains, the room offered a welcome respite from all the color.

The outdoors, however, was splendid. Lattice-covered walkways decked in grape and rose vine shaded the tiered path to the backyard. Immense copper pots overflowing with flowers marked the flagstone landings. Behind the house, the lawn spread into a collage of flowerbeds, sandlots, and mowed grass. A plethora of children's toys, bikes, and balls scattered at random.

Already listening for Deedee and Tee squealing in the backyard, feeling slightly better than he had all day, Isaac climbed from his black Jag.

The Spencer children were not in the backyard. The twosome sprung from the ornate front door as if popped from a jack-in-the-box and sprinted across the raised porch. Shouting delightedly, they dashed down the steps to greet him.

Like her mother, Deedee wore long auburn ringlets of a texture to escape from whatever braid or newfangled hairpiece hit the market. A fact to lend her a Raggedy Ann appearance whether she wore a lacy-collared dress for an Easter Vigil or a pair of denim shorts and a T-shirt. Watching her trot down the steps, her brother hot on her heels, Isaac enjoyed a strange comfort and delight, only amused to see a bright red ribbon sail free of a braid as Dee's sneakers touched gravel. Tim Jr, who preferred to be called Tee, resembled his father with scruffy brown waves and impressive solid shoulders for a child of four years. By his own design, Isaac had become something of a Dutch Uncle over the past five years, and by no surprise, when both finished strangling him in hugs, Tee wondered, "You got us presents?"

"Tee!" Tim snapped as he emerged from the vine-covered tunnel alongside the house. "What the heck did I just get done telling you?"

Ensconced firmly on Isaac's hip, Tee looked at his advancing father and commented, "Uncle Sax always gots presents, Daddy." Boldly, he turned his bright blue eyes to Isaac, favoring him with a grin. "Wight, Uncle Sax?"

"Nothing to be done about it," Isaac said and caught Tim's mocked mortified expression. "When the lad's right, the lad's right."

At his hip, every bit her mother's dignified daughter, Deedee wondered, "In your car, Uncle Sax?"

Looking between the grave blue eyes, Isaac chuckled idly and slid Tee to his feet. "In the car," he resigned. "Help yourselves."

"Oh Jesus," Tim commented as he watched his two youngsters descend on the shiny black beast like birds of prey. This time, his blue eyes carried a genuine hint of concern when he looked at Isaac. "I swear, you got more money than brains, pal, you turn those rug-apes loose in that car."

Shrugging, his smile lingering, Isaac watched Deedee take charge, opening the car with a reverence that would put some adults to shame. His mood soured with a memory flash of Jarvins dropping the plates. His eyes clouded and his tone changed as he commented, "I trust them."

"I didn't expect you for at least another half hour," Tim commented offhandedly. "You must have been cleaning out the carbs on the way over."

He should have begged off entirely, Isaac considered as he watched Deedee dole out the first gift-wrapped box, one as large as a shoebox. The second box, she kept for herself while scooting carefully off the leather seat and tapping the door closed with the care of a princess.

Without preamble, both looked to him for assurance, and with his nod, the colorful paper from one of the finest toy stores in London flew like confetti. If there was anything more enjoyable than a touch of history etched on fine china, it was watching a little girl unveil a hand-painted porcelain doll adorned in handspun silk and genuine jewels. Equally delightful was watching Tee lift a replica of a 1940 Studebaker from the box and recognize his name hand-painted on the running boards. Collector's items, both, but Isaac hoped to see them well-worn before either child realized the value. Money, he supposed, had its advantages, and although he doubted it could buy happiness, he received a healthy dose of enjoyment from spending it on occasion. Both youngsters flew to his arms, hugging and thanking him with ample cheek kisses.

"We gotta show Mommy!" Deedee decided, and Tee took flight on her heels, racing up the steps.

"Let's go out back," Tim decided. "I've already got the ribs on."

Preoccupied, Isaac followed Tim through the covered arch, climbing the tiers between the side of the house and the garage. Already, hickory-scented smoke flavored the warm evening air, and a red-checkered cloth covered one of the two picnic tables on the deck. An abundance of maple trees and oaks offered a welcome reprieve from the heat, providing enough shade to keep the temperatures mild.

"What's your pleasure, Sax? Beer, wine, soda . . .?"

Distracted, Isaac scanned the back lawn, ignoring the words, lighting a cigarette. Could he do it again? That was the question lingering in his mind. The question that had haunted him since he'd locked the front doors of Olden Time. Could he walk away again and not look back? How many times in a lifetime? How many lifetimes could that happen before he ran out of lives? Could he do it again?

"You want to tell me what's on your mind?" Tim asked while handing over an open beer bottle.

Isaac reached for it but withdrew his hand before touching the amber glass. Distracted and annoyed, he tipped his head to find Tim studying him intently. "Pour that in a plastic glass, will you?"

"Come again?" Tim asked.

"I've had to repeat myself so damned often today, I feel like a parrot," Isaac commented. "Doesn't anyone understand the King's English anymore?"

Tim never blinked. He just plopped the bottle down, strode from the table, and disappeared into the house through one of the sliding glass doors.

Irritated with himself by the time Tim returned, Isaac watched the red plastic tumbler slap down in front of him. Beer foamed and frothed to the rim; Isaac looked up with a simple, "Thank you." As he took a few hearty gulps, the door slid open at his back, and he wasn't surprised when Donna's long mane fell over his shoulder.

"Hi, handsome. The gifts are lovely," she said and brushed a kiss on his cheek.

Some people were born lucky, Isaac considered as he glimpsed Donna over his shoulder. "Glad you like them." Tim Spencer was one of those people, and he was smart enough to neither squander his luck nor take it for granted. He had a beautiful wife whose blue eyes could melt butter and whose legs could put a model to shame, two beautiful children, a lovely home for the most part, and a respectable career. Born lucky. Isaac's gaze panned across the lawn. His attention paused on the smoking barrel-shaped grill. Absently, he watched Tim flip the lid and brush another layer of red sauce on the slab of ribs.

As if sensing him watching, Tim looked over, his rugged face masked, pensive. "Things pretty hectic in town today, huh?"

"A zoo," Isaac said dryly.

Tim nodded, finishing his project. Lifting his beer, he crossed the deck, swinging onto the opposite bench, his dark eyes, curious, searching. "I talked to Sam a little while ago. They had enough reinforcements to cover half the county. You have any problems today?"

What kind of question was that? What kind of problems had Tim expected? Looking into the dark blue eyes, Isaac couldn't decide, but too swiftly, he recalled those moments in his apartment last night. His gaze listing away, he lifted his beer as the two youngsters bound from the house with their gifts. Welcoming the interruption as Deedee landed next to him, Isaac managed a smile despite his descended mood. Children had a way of filling space, their busy minds spewing chatter off their lips as swiftly as water over a dam.

Did Spence know about that visit from the feds? Had Tim paused for a few seconds in the house and called the station to report a certain antique dealer's whereabouts? Did Tim now know, proof positive, that Isaac Bently didn't exist? Might never have existed? A phantom. A myth. An apparition. An illusion. His whole life had been an illusion. Believing he had a friend in Tim Spencer wasn't the exception. An illusion.

Isaac had learned that lesson long ago. Had known never to trust, never to believe, never to depend on anyone or anything.

He could walk away from the illusions. Money had bought him the freedom to walk away from illusions like Tim Spencer and his children, from an antique business that was more a masquerade than an illusion, from a town full of neighborly people who could drop their masks and show their true faces. He could walk away and not look back.

Finding the Spencer homestead had proven simpler than finding a way out of town without a half dozen reporters dogging her, and Ronnie was still fuming when she pulled into the driveway. Those jerks called themselves reporters! They were *jackals*. A disgrace to the writing profession . . . and she need only recall that glimpse of Grimes, wrinkled and disheveled, swaggering into the Bentwood House lobby, sucking up to a few of their esteemed colleagues while chewing on an unlit cigar. A disgrace! And that oaf had the nerve to call *her* an *ambulance chaser*? To persecute *her* for capitalizing on a story? If she wasn't so blasted angry, she might appreciate the irony. She was probably the only reporter in town who hadn't quipped a single word for the masses.

The sight of a black Jaguar in the driveway alongside the emerald pickup only heightened her annoyance as she recalled that asinine conversation about a Maserati and a Corvette. Isaac Bently. He was just one more enigma and Max's interest in him, just one more annoyance. She'd known Max for nearly twenty years. If anyone should know she could be trusted with confidential information, it should be Max. For God's sake, she'd grown up with the hood of National Security hanging over her head. She'd probably popped from the womb with a blasted gag in her mouth.

Climbing from the car without truly considering her actions, Ronnie slammed the door shut in her wake before she saw the young woman halt halfway down the steps. Poised, somewhat like a ballerina preparing to dive, the woman stood with uncertainty etched on her slender face. Her soft blue eyes remained direct and clear. A Mona Lisa smile touched her barely blushed lips. With long auburn hair glistening in the sunlight, she looked like a teenager at first glance, her jeans and checkered shirt lending credence to the thought. A teenager who could win the Miss America Pageant hands-down, Ronnie considered as the woman broke from her frozen pose, apparently determined to make the best of this strange situation. Perhaps, accepting this invitation had been a mistake. By now, it was more than possible that this lovely woman had heard several vicious tales about a loose female reporter and local police officer.

Warily, Ronnie stood her ground, assessing the smile and gauging the sincerity running toward high. The woman wore the same laughing spark in her eyes as in her husband's eyes.

"You have to be Ronnie," she said with a soft lilting voice, her blue eyes shining beneath a thick fan of lashes as she offered her hand. "I'm Donna Spencer. It's a pleasure to meet you."

This was different. Ronnie smiled a little warily as she accepted the handshake. "Very nice to meet you," she decided. "I hope I haven't come too late."

"Not at all. Tim's still nursing the ribs," she said pleasantly. "I'd imagine it's a bughouse in town."

"An understatement," Ronnie said and noted the flash of sorrow for the circumstances surrounding that circus. Levelheaded, this Donna Spencer, and Ronnie understood why a man like Tim Spencer would request special items brought from Europe. Scanning the enchanting house set against the backdrop of the forest, Ronnie commented, "You have a lovely home."

"Thank you," Donna said while gesturing, starting them toward the rustic wood steps. "Just don't believe Tim when he tells you he carved the logs by hand," she mused. "Depending on his mood, he might even claim to have melted the sand to make the glass."

Ronnie laughed, liking this woman more with every second. "I bet he loves having you tell all his secrets."

Eyes sparkling, she confided, "Don't tell him I told you, and just watch how carried away he becomes . . . and I better warn you about my other two monsters," she said with a quick smile. "They'll probably be shy for about thirty seconds. After that, you're fair game. They'll be all over you like a long-lost cousin."

If Ronnie harbored any doubts about coming, they were gone by the time she reached the dining room. The short walk had taken nearly five minutes, with the little ones intercepting them halfway across a sunken living room which had taken Ronnie's breath away. This town certainly had its surprises, and to find herself standing inside a house to equate nicely with a resort lodge, was just one among many.

In genuine surprise, Ronnie recognized the collectible baby doll 'Uncle Sax' had given the beautiful little girl, a doll remarkably similar to several Ronnie had displayed on a shelf in her childhood bedroom. Equally impressive, the hand-tooled truck that the handsome little boy proudly presented was of vintage quality. An avid observer, Ronnie recognized the fleeting concern through Donna's eyes as she glanced at the doll. A genuine French Bebe Doll could be worth a small fortune, and the doll appeared to be an original.

"He's spoiled them rotten," Donna confided as she veered into the kitchen. "The man has no concept of the word 'practical,' but I don't have the heart to tell him so," she said with a smile. "I've heard you two have met."

"Interesting fellow," Ronnie admitted cautiously.

Donna mused, "He can be a bit much. What can I get you to drink? Wine, beer, soda, iced tea . . . coffee?"

"Iced tea sounds wonderful," she decided. "I've had enough coffee today to keep me awake for the next week."

"Tim tells me you're a writer," she said as she glided around her kitchen, lifting a glass from a rustic tree designed to hold wine bottles. Without missing a step, she brought a tall glass pitcher from the refrigerator. "I think that's fascinating, but I don't envy you," she said lightly. "All the travel must be difficult."

How much had Tim told her? "It has its moments," Ronnie commented. "For the most part, I love traveling." And this felt strangely like a setup, Ronnie considered absently, watching the woman buzz around the kitchen, collecting ice for the tea. Apparently, this was Donna's subtle way of judging her, maybe getting acquainted, which was about as subtle as a rock. "Do you work outside the home?" Ronnie asked as Donna delivered the tall glass with a wedge of lemon on the rim.

"Part-time," she said with a faint smile. "When I'm not cleaning up spills and being a mom, I work in interior design. Consulting, mostly, since the little ones came along."

That explained all the exquisite furniture, from Persian rugs to signed landscapes scattered throughout the arid spaces. "If your home's any indication, you do lovely work," Ronnie said sincerely. "It's beautiful."

"Joint endeavor," she mused. "But dear God, don't mention that too loud," she said with a glance toward the dining room arch. "Tim prefers to lay the blame entirely on me rather than admit he dared to hang a painting."

"I'd imagine a few of those came from Olden Time," Ronnie mused, recalling the banter between the two men.

"More than a few," she said with a slight spark of mischief. "Sax has extremely good taste."

Sax was an enigma, and this woman's fondness for him only furthered the curiosity.

The little boy chose that moment to trot through the dining room entrance, demanding, "Mommy, how come Uncle Sax is mad cause the lady's here?"

Betrayed. That was the single thought raging through Isaac's mind as he stood, glaring at Tim Spencer, who stood blocking his path. He'd been betrayed, and the last of the illusion had shattered.

"I don't know what the hell's gotten into you, Isaac," Tim said in a low, volatile tone. "But I think you better slow down and sit down."

"I think you need to step aside," Isaac spoke at an equal volume. "I'd rather not create a scene in front of your wife and children."

"Then sit down and finish your beer," Tim said in casual demand. "As far as I've noticed, Miss Bryson hasn't grown fangs or horns, and forgive me for noticing, pal, but you weren't exactly in a hurry to part with her company last night."

"That's supposed to excuse this little fucking charade?" Isaac asked. "It's not bad enough you didn't mention the Feds elevating me to the top of their fucking Most Wanted list. Now, you set me up with a goddamn reporter?"

"Wait one goddamn minute, pal," Tim said with his blue eyes darkening. "What the fuck are you talking about? Who told you the Feds have you on their wanted list?"

At least that much of his theory was wrong. Tim hadn't known about the federal agents' visit before this minute. "That particular tidbit of information doesn't matter one wit, not one way or another."

"Like hell it doesn't," Tim snapped, his gaze level. "What happened in town? And don't snowball me, or I'll drop your ass on this deck. Who said the Feds are after you?"

"It truly doesn't matter," he said with his anger defusing, his attention wavering to the two women coming from the glass doors. Donna appeared worried and anxious; Bryson appeared only curious. Why the mere thought of her presence had set him off, Isaac couldn't decide. Other than her profession, he could find nothing seriously wrong with her.

She was certainly attractive with the whimsical beauty of a wind goddess. Black hair blown in a tumble of loose curls and her slender body tucked into a neat pair of jeans and flowery summer blouse, she appeared closer to eighteen than twenty-something . . . Not the sleek, dark-haired sophisticate who had meandered about his store like a cat on the prowl.

"I like your hair better in that loose style," Isaac said before his brain caught up with his mouth. She appeared as startled as he felt, but that offered shallow consolation against his sudden annoyance.

"So glad I meet with your approval," she said with a flash of temper in her blue eyes. Her gaze slid down him and up as if appraising a side of beef. "Suppose you wouldn't look good in a suit."

"Excuse me?" he asked in mild irritation.

"Well, if we're about to start nitpicking over each other's hairstyles, why not go all the way, Mr. Bently? We get past hair and clothes; we can go straight for carpet."

"I complimented you, for chrissake," he snapped. "At least you could have said, *thank you*."

Her eyes flashed. "That's rich," she said in a chilly tone. "Should I curtsy or give you a big kiss with my humble gratitude?"

At this moment, she would like nothing better than to douse him with the glass of tea hovering in her firm grip. His gaze slid warily to her vibrating hand and back to her eyes. Those eyes snagged him. Hot and cold, those eyes, like blue diamonds, sparking and flashing. Uncontrollably, his senses reacted, tensing . . . and something was happening inside of him. Suddenly, he felt as if he were drawn as if he could drown inside those crystal gems.

Dangerous!

Dangerous!

With every ounce of her will, Ronnie stood her ground. Glaring into his jade-green eyes, she felt as if she stood too near an open flame. She'd felt the same way yesterday when he'd looked across the street and again inside his store when he'd leaned against his counter, appraising her. Those eyes of his were lethal! And pushing him too far could be dangerous.

Whether that thought or the sudden revelation that she stood among strangers startled her, she wondered at her current aggression. "I'd imagine I owe you an apology, Mr. Bently," she said with slightly more edge than intended. "If that was truly your idea of a compliment, perhaps, I should have just thanked you." And she'd stayed long enough to know this wouldn't be the quiet, pleasant evening she'd dearly hoped it would be. As Bently had made clear last evening, she was the outsider. To complicate matters, he'd probably heard and believed the rumors that had, inevitably, circulated concerning her and Mark Jarvins. If that interview had gone as badly as she suspected, it was no wonder he intended to leave rather than suffer her company.

Deciding within fleeting seconds, she glanced to Tim Spencer, who appeared far more tense than any time last evening, then landed her gaze on Donna, likewise distressed. "As much as I appreciate the invitation and enjoyed meeting you, I do think I should go—"

Donna reached and clasped her hand, stopping Ronnie from turning. Her blue eyes flashed anger toward both men, then softened toward Ronnie as she commented. "I'm sure I don't know what this is all about, but I'd like you to stay. Why don't you and I go inside—" She stopped short, and her focus darted.

Likewise, Ronnie pivoted her attention, certain only that she didn't want this fellow advancing another step closer.

He stopped short, his green eyes tense, his mustache cocked in a slight smile. "I don't do apologies very well, Miss Bryson," he said in a smooth, careful tone. "If you'd be willing to forgive me for behaving like an idiot, there's no reason why we can't both enjoy the finest dinner we'll likely find anywhere east of Texas."

He was right about one thing; he certainly didn't do apologies well. In fact, he managed not to do one at all, but if not the words, his deep voice carried sincere remorse. "If it's any consolation, I haven't had a good day either, Mr. Bently."

For the briefest second, a smile touched his eyes. There and gone so fast, Ronnie doubted she'd seen it at all. Even more unnerving, however, the sorrow dimmed his eyes as he commented, "No, I'd imagine not."

He knew. In that single line, he verified his knowledge of every rotten thing written or said about her in the past twenty-four hours . . . and it hurt suddenly. Why his sorrow touched her . . . Why this green-eyed devil's acceptance suddenly mattered, she couldn't begin to fathom. She hadn't been moved by Mark or Len's concern, not even by Bobby's touching reaction to defend her honor and reputation. How could this stranger make her feel the hurt as if he mirrored her pain in his eyes? How could he crumble the wall she'd wrapped around herself to safeguard against the pain?

Cautiously, he took another step, offering his hand, speaking quietly, "Why don't we sit down?"

Strange, very strange, this numb feeling as her hand freed from one grasp and fell into another, to feel as if she might crumble entirely and burst into tears. With the heat of his fingers, she jolted from the momentary daze, cursing herself before ever reaching the table. She'd not wept over the attitudes of others since her childhood. She'd steeled herself against such nonsense long before arriving in this wretched little town. How, in God's name, had this man spoken a few simple words and nearly reduced her to tears? He'd not spoken an apology, not voiced sympathy. He'd merely acknowledged the simple truth.

With the hand touching her shoulder, she jolted slightly, looking up into Tim Spencer's troubled gaze. Regret unmasked in his grim smile.

"Glad you came, Ronnie."

A setup, she considered, certain that Mr. Tim Spencer had deliberately set her up for this little rendezvous. For what purpose remained to be seen. She hadn't accepted a blind date since high school and only once, at Jesse Hagen's insistence. Belatedly, the annoyance surfaced while she considered what Tim Spencer might have had in mind when arranging this encounter. Perhaps, it was some sort of running game between these two good friends. A contest to see how many females Bently could seduce in a lifetime. *New gal in town, a loose woman* . . . she could picture the scenario. Good ole Tim sees things aren't working out so well for his old pal and takes matters into his own hands to lend his friend another shot at the brass ring. For all she knew, they could have set this up in the restaurant last evening, and good ole Sax was one hell of an actor. Maybe he harbored a few genuine second thoughts when she arrived, but what better way to retaliate against a federal agent than to seduce his former girlfriend . . .? And if Sax happened to score—all the better.

Her thoughts racing, she heard the children converging carefully to rally around 'Uncle Sax,' the small boy asking, "How comes you was mad at the lady, Uncle Sax?"

Smooth and low, that voice of his. "I wasn't mad at Miss Bryson, Tee. Sometimes people speak without thinking."

And sometimes they say the first honest thing on their mind, like the fact that her hair met his satisfaction and might be shallow consolation since he was forced to endure this enterprise. She suddenly felt very foolish, very used, and very tired. Pouring over mounds of information, writing a press release to salvage part of the investigation, listening to the details of those murders, and reading the testimonies of the living victims . . .

Very tired. Very alone. And very angry, Ronnie decided as she sipped her iced tea, scanning the scenery of the back lawn. Indifferently, she viewed the mounds of flowers and long stretches of grass between islands of color. Children's toys, from plastic pedal tricycles to swing sets, were scattered in wild abandon. A wide footpath, probably for the little girl's bicycle, cut into the forest to the left. Grape arbors and flower tresses trailed through patches of slanted sunlight.

Somehow, even with its far more rustic setting, this backyard reminded Ronnie of her parent's home, the gardens, where she'd played in those early years. Fanatically, her mother had buzzed about the multitude of rose bushes; her father had brushed her aside, sending her to play in amongst the other thorns. Something Freudian inevitably existed there to explain why Ronnie could never keep a single flower in bloom for more than a couple days or a plant alive for more than a month. An analyst would undoubtedly tell her she harbored a subconscious desire to rebel against her parents, therefore, sabotaging her efforts at gardening.

Who the hell gives a shit anyway? When she wanted flowers, she could stop on a street corner and buy a bouquet!

She had arrived in Bentwood to do a job, an exceedingly difficult job, which had become far more difficult than she could have predicted by the neanderthal mentality of the inhabitants. If they wanted to call her a *bimbo* and treat her like a *slut*, so be it. She had no one to answer to but herself and God, and so far, the Big Guy hadn't condemned her.

Halfheartedly, Ronnie heard Tim send his children inside to help their mother gather plates. She'd been a fool to consider a quick friendship with Donna Spencer. The woman had conspired with these wretches. If anything, Ronnie should hate her from the get-go. All those pleasant smiles, sparkling mischief, the casual mention of Bently . . . Warming Ronnie to the devil before the big surprise?

Apparently, the children were innocent; neither would have kept the secret.

As if her thought had conjured him, the tussle-haired boy appeared alongside the table, delivering napkins and silverware.

This might be a good time to bow out gracefully. Honestly, she could beg off with a headache. If not for a thought of cowardice, Ronnie would route around in her purse for her aspirin, but she refused to afford these nice folks the satisfaction of seeing her distress.

"Are you mad at Uncle Sax, ma'am?" the little girl asked directly while putting plates on the table.

She was such a pretty little thing with her near-golden braids askew and her big worried blue eyes. A pity she would grow up in this town. "No, dear," Ronnie answered quietly. "I'm not."

"You ain't talkin' to him or nothin'," the girl pointed out and darted a glance past Ronnie to where her beloved Uncle Sax sat at arm's length. Leaning, the girl whispered to Ronnie, "Want me to tell him somethin' for you like I do for mommy when she's mad at daddy?"

Cute. "No, dear, but thank you," Ronnie said with a faint sincere smile. This truly wasn't how she intended to spend her evening. If she wanted to relax, she could return to the hotel and call room service. Glancing at her watch, glimpsing Tim skewering the ribs off the grill, Ronnie reached a single conclusion. She wasn't hungry enough to justify becoming the brunt of a practical joke. There were more important things on which to focus.

Lifting her glass, Ronnie drained the iced tea, overhearing Bently asking the little boy to pour his beer and looking over to see the liquid frothing into a red plastic tumbler. For the briefest second, she glimpsed the feral green eyes, not certain why he looked away. She'd definitely been here long enough. Unfortunately, with Donna delivering a bowl to the table, it was already too late to make a graceful retreat. Pride was a wicked vice.'

"Is there anything I can do to help?" Ronnie asked before Donna could escape. With Donna fleeting a curious glance toward Bently, Ronnie's nerves jangled. *Obviously, Mr. Charm wasn't performing up to his usual standards.*

"Please, just sit and relax," Donna said with forced cheer. "We'll be ready to eat in a few moments."

Terrific, more grueling moments of silence. Little more than an arm's reach away, Bently hunched over the table, leaning on his forearms. At a glance, Ronnie read his distraction. He was staring into the shaded forest. His mustache tipped in a grim curve, not to be mistaken for a smile or a smirk. Ronnie had to admit, he was a handsome man. The strong angled cut of his jaw countered the more delicate line of his full lips and long eyelashes. In profile, his eyes were far more innocent, like those of a small boy, and if not for his mustache and the brooding aura of his smile, his mouth could be gentle.

He could be gentle, she decided and tried to imagine the confrontation between him and the agents. Whatever he'd said, whatever he'd done, had gotten the best of Mark and Len. Belatedly, she remembered Len speaking, apparently impressed with this character. Beneath every warning and word, Len's respect had lingered. If evidence pointed to a crime, however, Len would act.

Again, the thought of Max Hagen distracted her as the children began arranging plates, the little girl playing hostess to deliver silverware. The clamor of the mounded platter of sizzling ribs landing in the center of the table jolted Ronnie before Tim ever opened his mouth.

"What the hell's the matter with you, Sax?" Spencer demanded in an angry growl. "I invite the most decent young woman I've met in a while to have dinner with us—with *you*—Fur Brain, and you sit here like a God Blessed bump on a log sulking over your damn beer."

"I don't sulk, over my beer or otherwise," Bently started with apparent surprise.

"Bullshit," Tim snapped. "You're sulking," he stated, sounding a lot like a ten-year-old chiding a peer.

"You've lost your mind," Bently said matter-of-factly.

"Dadddy?" Deedee whined while posing in reflection of her mother. Hands planted on her narrow hips, her head tipped, she glared up at her father from her position at Bently's shoulder. "How come you're yelling at Uncle Sax again?"

"That's my girl," Bently mused and leaned to wrap an arm around the lean shoulders. He drew her protectively against his side and chest, coaching, "You tell your daddy to quit yelling at your Uncle Sax."

"Uncle Sax needs his God-blessed head examined!" Tim snapped with a quick angry glance over their heads toward the sound of sliding doors.

"I'm not the one accusing me of *sulking*, for Chrissake," Bently said in annoyance, his green eyes flashing to their host.

"I'm not the one ruining a perfectly good beer by drinking from a plastic glass," Spencer noted. "If that's not sulking, I don't know what is, and I think you better knock it off."

This conversation was a little too peculiar, Ronnie mused as she watched them glaring at each other. A little like the earth and sky, deep blue eyes and deep green eyes collided at an angle to crash somewhere in the space above the sizzling meat. Both appeared serious, and sincere, which struck her even more funny under the circumstances. She might even forgive Tim this asinine game if she believed the words.

"I happen to have a very good reason for drinking my beer in a plastic container, which I'm not about to discuss with you. Any more than I intend to have this ridiculous conversation—"

"You set yourself up to have this ridiculous conversation when you damn near accused me of setting you up with the Feds, pal," Spencer growled.

"Tim?" Donna interrupted with a warning tone. "Dinner's ready. Why don't we discuss all of this after dinner?"

"Because we need to clear the air before I get a goddamn ulcer," Spencer said and crashed his gaze against Bently again. "If you're pissed off at me, that's fine, but I'll be damned if I'll sit by and let you take out your hostility on a lady whose company might do you some good."

"Good God, it wasn't my imagination," Bently said, with a note of disgust. "You did set this up."

"Damn straight, pal," Spencer said with a smug, angry flash before he looked over, pinning Ronnie. "I probably owe you a ton of apologies, Ronnie, but I can assure you, I didn't mean to offend you. Nor did I intend to hurt you. If I've done either, I truly am sorry."

This wasn't a staged performance. The shocked anger on Bently's face was genuine.

Unwavering, Tim continued, "About now, you probably think we're all a bunch of assholes, and you may be right, hon. But the fact is, my buddy here has no God-blessed idea what it's like to just sit and carry on an intelligent conversation with an attractive young woman."

"Good God, it's getting worse," Bently said with an echo of mortification beneath his disgust. His eyes flashed pure jade fire off Tim to Ronnie and turned entirely to the little girl who appeared horrified by her father's attack. "Don't worry, sweetheart, we can get your daddy help. He'll be fine with the proper—"

"Mr. Bently," Ronnie interrupted shortly and nearly regretted intruding with the fire flashing in his eyes. "I don't think it's quite fair to involve that sweet little girl in this apparent quarrel, and I certainly didn't think you were the type to hide behind a child."

"I don't recall asking for your opinion, Miss Bryson, nor do I particularly care what you think—"

"If you are attempting to offend me, I should mention, you're wasting your time," Ronnie said with her anger stirring. This man, with a word, a glance, could annoy her beyond all reason. How dare he hide behind that lovely little girl to cover his insecurity!

"You certainly do have a talent for intruding on matters which are none of your concern," he said with an echo of arrogance. "It's no wonder you're a reporter. It's the only profession in the world where you can be paid for prying into other people's business."

"You arrogant, sanctimonious—" She halted the string of curses on her tongue with a glimpse at the wide-eyed child nestled against the man's chest. After all the scathing glances in town and narrowly escaping the mob less than a half-hour ago, to hear this man insulting her profession, and her integrity as a journalist was the final straw. "How dare you judge me for what I do when you haven't the foggiest clue what that is," she said in a chilly tone.

"Oh, I'm well aware of what you do, Miss Bryson," he said in a low tone, his long lashes shuttering the jade inferno scorching her. In slow motion, he moved the child away, rounding to face her more fully. "You, and all the rest of your associates," he continued darkly. "You destroy people's lives. You lay them open with the skill of a surgeon until there's nothing left. It doesn't matter to you, who gets hurt, or what's left when you're finished. It doesn't matter where the truth ends, or the lies begin. You did your job. You invaded and destroyed. Then it's on to the next victim . . . you're worse than a fucking parasite—"

Without conscious thought, she swung her palm on a collision course with his arrogant face. Her hand halted in a grip of iron less than an inch from its mark. Her own eyes lancing blue ice, she glared at him, her palm trembling with anger within the vice grip on her wrist. The color . . . jade . . .

Jade! Publicity. Max Hagen. Eighteen years ago . . . eighteen years ago . . . Arlington, VA. A media circus . . . Max Hagen had just begun his career in Homicide. Darcy Hagen leaving him. Jesse Hagen transferring into St. Augustine's, Ronnie's private school . . . Jesse's father working the case . . . murder. His mother . . . Jade . . . the boy's name was Jade. . . Two grades ahead of her . . . her school . . . St. Augustine's.

"Oh my God," she said softly as she looked into his blazing green eyes. Jade . . . his first name was Jade; his last name had been French . . . La . . . La-something. His mother . . . dear God, his mother had been famous . . . a psychic advisor, an astrologist . . . Felicity! The woman had been a psychic advisor to some of the most influential people in Washington . . .

Less than an arm's reach away, his eyes were changing, blazing, and fading. His thoughts spiraled with splashes of hurt and pain flaring like neon behind the murky jade hue. His jaw pulsed, clinging to his anger by a thread, but he knew, at this moment, he knew what she'd just realized. "Damn you," he heaved in a soft breath and released her hand, starting to pivot and slide off the bench.

Scrambling off the bench, Ronnie clasped his arm, halting him as he turned away. The media . . . in neon flashes, she remembered the media circus. She'd been only eight years old, but she remembered, and looking into his scathing glare, she suffered his pain as fiercely as his anger. Years . . . years later she'd written a thesis on that murder, on the media's handling of that case. Dear God . . . that famous murder case had affected her in so many ways, had shaped the course of her life in so many ways . . . and she remembered abruptly, Jade

Laquette. Fifth grade . . . she'd been in third at the time. He'd been the one to find his mother . . . had gone home from school and found her murdered . . . and the media had ripped him apart . . . a psychic . . . his mother's prodigy . . . a seer . . .

He started to pull away again, to turn, Ronnie clamped his arm more firmly, holding him with a piercing gaze, seeing the hurt, the anger . . . understanding. "I'm not like them . . . Mr. Bently," she said while searching his murky eyes, feeling the vibrations through his muscled forearm. "I'm truly—*not*—like them."

CHAPTER 15

He believed her . . . with no good reason, for no reason at all, Isaac believed her and perhaps, that was the most frightening revelation of all. She knew him. It was in her eyes, in her face, but it wasn't the thrill of a woman who'd grab a pen or race home to a typewriter for an exclusive. Instead, he saw himself mirrored in her crystal blue eyes and read the sympathy and understanding unmasked on her lovely face. Tears shimmered on the surface of her eyes. Her soft full lips quivered ever so slightly on the apex of a silent sob. Never . . . not ever in his adult life had a woman drawn him more thoroughly, let alone by the power of her sorrow and understanding. She was beautiful. As beautiful on the inside as on the outside.

He wanted . . . needed to kiss those quivering lips, taste the beauty she held inside. He needed to embrace her and feel the power of whatever spell she'd woven around them to be trapped in the moment.

Hesitantly, he tipped his head, looking into her wet eyes, feeling, sensing her shared attraction. Never had he wanted—needed—to kiss a woman more . . . and she neither pulled away nor pushed forward. As if she possessed a mystical power, a lodestone inside her breasts, she waited for him to come to her, not demanding, not pursuing. Waiting and offering, welcoming with the slightest tip of her lovely face.

Like electric, that first shock against her trembling lips. His heart staggered a quick beat. His senses rushed to the warmth and gentleness within her grip. He willed himself deeper, unable to pull away. Unwittingly, Isaac lifted his hand, sliding his fingers into her wild black silk and tipping her head. Beneath his touch, she quivered. Trembling, her hand clasped his arm with a fierce grip, braced against the forces swirling around them. Through them. Never . . . not once in his life had he been drawn by a woman, never quickened at such a dizzying speed. Good God, she was incredible . . . and he wanted her. Not just the sweet taste of her lips pressed against his, not just the touch of her silk, he wanted more—

"Yuck!" a small angry voice snapped.

A second, faintly irritated young voice demanded, "How come Uncle Sax's kissing her after she was gonna hit him?"

The low deep voice mused, "It's a bright man who knows when he's beaten and surrenders, sweet pea. Why don't you finish setting the table?"

Heart hammering, Ronnie suffered a pang of pain at his parting, no more certain of herself than him. Drawing a slight breath, she gazed into the simmering green depths. She was trembling. Her entire body vibrated. Her nerve endings lifted and tingled as if she stood too near an electric tower. Exciting and frightening in the same instant—and he was the source, the powerhouse generating this strange heat and vibration.

The devil was smiling, too. A whisper of a smile curved one corner of his mouth, and his eyes smoldered nearer to emerald than jade. As if he knew he'd just wiped every clear, rational thought from her head with that one heated kiss, the devil was smiling . . . and what a smile. No big surprise here. The look in his eyes, that whisper of a dimple, could stop any sensible woman in her tracks. Any sensible woman would know enough to back off, to back away from that wicked hungry shine.

Jade Laquette, the boy, the mystery . . . the man, her mind fumbled around as if lost in the dark. She'd known him. She'd glimpsed him a lifetime ago in St. Augustine's playground, and even after all these years, she remembered the aura of darkness shrouding him, the loneliness to touch her. Only after the media circus had begun, St. Augustine's hummed with rumors, and she'd learned the boy's name. And years later, after she'd begun researching for her thesis, she'd fully understood the horror of what he'd endured. He wasn't a child, now. He was a devil with a talent for seduction, and if that was a sample of his skill, he'd taken lessons from a master somewhere along the line.

His head tilted in a slow, lazy motion. His gaze lost part of the feral shine, becoming curious . . . and more amused if that cocky smile was any indication.

Belatedly, Ronnie realized they had witnesses and remembered the children present, Spencer's comment from a few seconds ago.

"I was wrong," Isaac said in a low voice that sent a tingle down her spine. "I won't apologize for my words," he continued quietly. "I still believe them, but I will apologize for including you in the majority. There are exceptions to every rule."

If not for the sincerity in his voice, the arrogance in his words might have sparked another tirade. "I'll try not to stereotype you, Mr. Bently, if you'll give me the same courtesy," Ronnie said softly.

His mustache twitched; his eyes sparked a hint of amusement. "I'll certainly try, Miss Bryson." He hesitated only a heartbeat. "Would you care to join me for dinner?"

The shit! Those were the same words he'd spoken last evening, and that invitation certainly hadn't gone well. At the moment, however, she sensed him attempting, perhaps, gallantly for the sake of their audience, to be playful against the lingering cloud in his eyes. "I'd be delighted," she decided, and a tingle skittered through her elbow as he turned her to the bench which they'd exited so unceremoniously.

If she wasn't extremely amused at the various expressions, Ronnie might be slightly embarrassed, but it was amusing. At a glance, she spied Tim Spencer. He'd settled on the bench across from Isaac, and his black mustache kinked in a smug smile, reflective of the cat that swallowed the canary. Donna tried, impressively, not to grin too openly, but her sparkling blue eyes betrayed her. The little boy—tucked down on the bench between his parents—scowled at Isaac as if betrayed. The little girl, who sat primly in the center of the bench seat, refusing to budge, forced Ronnie to sit at the far end of the table across from Donna.

With the honesty of her age, Deedee wore her hostility in her puckered lips and livid blue eyes. How such a rounded, freckle-dusted face managed to appear offended and indignant remained a mystery as the little girl accepted Ronnie's plate and handed it to her father to receive a portion of ribs. Apparently, Deedee had neither tolerance nor fondness for any woman who'd attempt to strike her favored uncle.

The man certainly had a way with women, Ronnie mused while trying to appear humbled under the little girl's wrath. But God, it was hard when she felt like laughing while catching Isaac's gaze over Deedee's head. The devil had recognized the little girl's attitude and clearly intended to milk it for everything it was worth, adopting a smirk as if to say—at least someone loves me. *The rogue!*

"Can I get you 'nother beer, Uncle Sax?" the little girl asked primly.

"I'm fine for the moment, sweetheart. Thank you."

The few cinnamon rolls Ronnie had eaten at breakfast were a distant memory, and as she began eating, she had to admit, the ribs were about the best she'd ever tasted. In fact, the potato salad and barbecued beans ranked in a class of their own. The warm fresh air, the ambiance of evening shade falling over the lawn, the lingering scent of hickory smoke . . . *the company?*

Complimenting both chefs between bites, Ronnie decided she would forgive both Spencers, somehow not surprised when Donna sensed her attitude and began to relax. The woman had conspired with her husband, but she'd acted on his intuition.

Between idle chitchat which covered the ribs' origin on a neighboring farm, the seasonably mild weather, and a few more anecdotes of Bently's trip abroad, which Donna wheedled him to discuss, Ronnie's thoughts volleyed with the flair of a drunk on a Wimbledon tennis court. A serial killer had brought her to this town. Mark Jarvins here. Jade Laquette here. Evening breeze. Soft music drifted through the screen doors at her back. A little girl flirting avidly with a man who took it all in stride. Sitting at a picnic table with strangers discussing

England. A single kiss wiping out every thought in her head . . . and that one was a hard nut to swallow.

Ronnie had never come that close to losing control of her senses, not even with Mark, the only man she might have loved once. In the six months of that heavy romance, she'd never fully reached that moment of total submission. She'd always hung onto that last thread of dignity, that last ounce of her reserve. In the end, she'd left him to escape the heated quarrels at the apex of every intimate evening.

Whatever else she did, she needed to be careful around Isaac Bently. The man was dangerous in ways she'd rather not consider.

If he even tried to hit the right buttons, he'd succeed, where countless others had failed.

Comfortably full and suffering from too many years of social graces to leave the moment the meal ended, Ronnie accepted the offer of a glass of wine along with Bently's casual escort to an alcove adjacent to the patio. Soft light spilled from the glass doors; globed candles were lit to offset the first shadows of evening, and again the aura resembled some posh mountain resort. The little town of Bentwood, with its gruesome murders and dandy hypocrites, seemed a million miles away, and how easy it would be to forget exactly why she'd come to this place.

The memory remained, though. A taint on the atmosphere and the conversations, starting and stopping too often. When both children accepted their parents' suggestion and ran inside to get ready for bed, the conversation plunged into forbidden territory. Surprisingly, Donna tipped the precarious scale on which they had all hovered.

"Did you know the Englers' farm is just down the road from here?" she asked across the short glass-topped rattan table.

"Yes," Ronnie admitted smoothly. She'd recognized the turnoff that she and Lenny had taken the morning past. The Englers lived less than a mile from the Spencers' driveway.

"It's horrible," Donna said with the first genuine touch of fear in her lilting voice. "I didn't know Mr. Engler very well, but I've known Alice since I first came to Bentwood several years ago."

"You're not originally from Bentwood, then?" Ronnie asked in an attempt to avoid the conversation as Tim had requested.

Donna smiled, glimpsing at Tim as her tone softened with a touch of amusement. "I doubt I'd have married this scallywag if I had been," she commented. "No. I grew up in Chicago, actually. Tim and I met while I was still in college. He was at a police convention where I was bussing tables . . ."

The conversation carried a few moments, Tim boasting over his fine taste catching Donna's eye, which received a scoffed humph from Bently, who hadn't spoken more than a few words. All too naturally, the fateful conversation of the carved, hand-selected logs came to pass, and Ronnie laughed with her secret knowledge, made worse when Donna rolled her eyes.

Casually, Bently leaned over the short glass-topped table between them, offering confidentially, "If you believe this line, Miss Bryson, I have a Rembrandt in my warehouse, I'd be happy to sell you."

God, with a voice like that, she'd probably buy it, and with the way the candlelight glittered in his eyes, she'd hock her soul to have it. The added sweep of his fingers brushing her forearm, tingling her flesh, and lifting goose bumps beneath the soft cotton sleeve only startled her more. With an effort, Ronnie commented, "Don't you feel just slightly silly, calling me Miss Bryson, Mr. Bently?"

Without losing that half-hitched smile, he commented, "I'll admit, I'd prefer a less formal address, but silly? I don't think so."

"By all means, Isaac," she said and managed to slip her arm from under his tingling fingers, offering her hand. "My friends call me Ronnie."

"Your friends are obviously idiots," he decided and clasped her fingers, capturing her eyes before she could take offense or offer recourse. "You don't look like a Ronnie to me, Veronica Bryson."

"If we're about to get nit-picky again, Sax," she said with subtle emphasis. "Perhaps, I should admit, you don't exactly look English to me."

Flashing a quick amusement, he held her hand, commenting, "You'll have to take that up with Deedee, I'm afraid. She was a bit young though to decide on my lineage when she shortened my name."

Sighing, mocking resignation, Ronnie idled, "I'm afraid my brothers suffered the same dire condition of youth when nicknaming their little sister. It's been a burden I've had to bear and one I've become too comfortable to change."

He hesitated, then chuckled and sat back, releasing her fingers, and appraising her across the short distance. His head canted; lips quirked. "Ronnie," he rolled the syllables as if testing the word on his tongue and looked as if he'd bitten a sour grape. "It doesn't do you justice," he decided, apparently attempting to make amends for his expression, but plunged headlong into dangerous water, asking, "Your brothers aren't daft, are they by any chance?"

Studying his quirky, arrogant expression, momentarily, Ronnie spied Tim Spencer currently enjoying this brief exchange from his slump in a thick cushion. "Clearly, we still need to work on your pal's conversational skills," Ronnie commented dryly, then returned her attention to find the smirk slightly more reserved. "You have flirting down to an art, so maybe there's hope for you, dear. And to answer you—no, my brothers aren't daft."

"That is a relief," he said with an off-key note.

Whether she'd seriously offended him or just blown his flirting rhythm, Ronnie couldn't decide. "Bit touchy, are you?"

"Not generally," he commented and slid a heated flash down and up her. He wasn't talking about his emotions when commenting, "But I could make an exception for you, honey."

Two points, that 'honey' had been as condescending as her 'dear.' Flashing amusement, she commented, "I wouldn't want to put you out, Mr. Bently."

"Would you quit with the Mr. Bently shit already?" he said smoothly. "Just Isaac—or Sax, if you prefer—will do."

"My, my . . . you're testy, too," she said with a deeper amusement as his eyes flashed fire.

A half-second of anger, a wicked smile, a softer expression . . . in an eye-blink, the man could transform the beast. "You seem to bring out the best or the worst in people, Ronnie. A perfected talent, I'd imagine. A credit to your profess—"

"You, sir, may halt right there," she said shortly, holding his gaze. The words he intended to speak could very well bring out the worst, and not only in her. He was angry again or trying not to become angry, and the man had more lines of defense than NATO. When he became angry, he would bite, very quick and sharp . . . and she'd certainly not meant to push him toward that end. Nudge him a little . . . *maybe*. A little anger to counter that spark in his eyes when he'd spoken her name was good for both of them.

"I demand a truce," she decided. "I won't slay your ego if you lay off my profession." She saw his lips part to speak and continued sharply, "Under normal circumstances, I'd not give a damn what you said about my esteemed colleagues, as I had a great deal of respect for enough of them to withstand the assault. Currently, however, if you push me toward defending them, I'd likely become extremely angry with you. I'm quite comfortable with my present level of disgust and hostility toward my associates. I certainly don't need any reminders or boosts from you. Thank you very much."

Somewhat warily, he studied her, apparently, uncertain of what to say.

Which was just fine with her. "Unfortunately," she said and tipped her wrist, reading the time and judging the descending shadows across the back lawn. Nearly nine o'clock. "I should be getting back to work."

"This late, Ronnie?" Donna asked while rising with her.

"I probably shouldn't have taken this much time off," she admitted, regret falling over her shoulders like a cloak. She'd truly needed a reprieve from the madness.

"I suppose you have a deadline to meet," Isaac said with just enough contempt to raise Ronnie's ire.

Looking into his eyes, she began simply. "There's something you and I need to work out before I go, Mr. Bently." Barely pausing, she continued in a chilly tone. "Despite what you seem to believe and what your nemesis, Ted Grimes printed about me, I am an investigative journalist, not some brainless twit writing for a tabloid. I do not seduce men into my bed or coddle grieving widows to coerce secrets or twist tales. When I'm working on a story, I spend an average of ten to twelve hours a day inside libraries, courthouses, and various other archives, pouring over records. If I speak to people occasionally, it's to gain perspective, and very rarely do I include quotes, much less divulge confidences shared with me.

"As I understand where you're coming from, I won't take offense to your attitude, but understand, sir, I have no intention of wasting further of my time defending myself or justifying myself for your benefit. And while we're having this little chat . . . if on the outside chance, you're thinking about going to bed with me, you can forget it. That, too, I'm afraid, doesn't fit into my eighteen-hour workdays regardless of the slaughter job your nemesis did on my reputation.

"Now, if you'll excuse me," she stated. "I may not have a deadline, but if my skills as an investigator can prevent any further catastrophe in your little haven . . .? I damn sure don't intend to waste any more of my time sparring with you or tiptoeing around your contempt."

Turning, she snagged Tim's bewildered, tense eyes and flashed a glance to his startled wife, extending her hand, softening her expression slightly. "I apologize for that outburst. It's been an extremely trying day. Thank you tremendously for a pleasant evening and fabulous dinner."

"You're . . . welcome, Ronnie," Donna said hesitantly, then spoke hurriedly. "Why don't I walk you to your car?"

Pausing, offering Tim her hand, Ronnie spoke simply. "Tim, thank you for the invitation and your hospitality. It truly was a lovely evening. Possibly I'll see you in town tomorrow."

"Count on it, hon," he said smoothly.

Glancing at Bently, refusing to be trapped in his gaze, she acknowledged him coolly. "Mr. Bently, a pleasure." Not awaiting his reply, she turned and started across the patio with Donna hurrying to keep pace at her side.

"Isaaac," Tim drawled. "I don't know what the hell you do to that gal."

Genuinely bewildered and annoyed, Isaac tipped his gaze from the arch where Veronica and Donna had disappeared. "I didn't *do* a damn thing that time."

Tim shook his head, glancing to the arch and speaking in mocked dismay. "I don't think there's any hope for you, pal. You may's well just marry her and be done with it."

His heart missed a beat, his lips started to part, and he clamped his jaw shut even before he recognized the wild spark of amusement in Tim's eyes.

Taking a step closer, Tim reached and clasped his shoulder, looking him dead in the eye. "Ssson," he drawled with a heavy country accent. "You got it so bad, I'm taking my life in my hands just standing this close to you."

"You may be right about the latter," Isaac said in a low, angry tone. "The last damn thing I needed to ice the cake on a truly, lovely day was a confrontation with a hotheaded, arrogant, egotistical, self-centered, stubborn—"

"Don't forget beautiful, witty, charming, intelligent, and sensitive," Tim added kindly.

"If that's what you believe, you need your eyes, if not your head examined," Isaac snapped. "The woman's a viper."

Tim stifled a laugh unsuccessfully and shook his head. "I'm telling you, Sax, you may's well throw in the towel. I damned near got scorched standing three feet away from the two of you. And that's not even talking about when you had her in that lip-lock. Jesus, boy, you're so blasted accustomed to gals chasing your rangy ass and falling at your feet, you're too damn dumb to know when it's your knees hitting the ground."

"Thank you for that colorful bit of observation," Isaac said dryly, but he had a queer sense of something hitting a few nerves, if not the ground. Annoyed, as much with Tim as himself, Isaac glanced again to the arch, noting the deepening shade, the darkness descending. "Damnit," he uttered. *She could end up lost on these back roads.* "I suppose I need to be leaving as well."

"Yea, I wouldn't let her get too far ahead of you," Tim said gravely.

More annoyed, Isaac sniped. "I do intend to see that the silly twit returns to town safely."

"Heyyy? Did I say anything?" Tim asked while retracting his hand, holding both up and stepping back. "By all means, escort the little lady home."

"You—are an ass," Isaac decided and started past him, refusing to acknowledge the low deep chuckle following him across the patio. He wouldn't need his headlights just yet, and if he stayed far enough behind, he could avoid worrying her. That he intended to go to the trouble, should even incline to see the *twit* back to town safely, annoyed him more than he cared to consider. He should stay here, say good night to the kids one last time, and have another beer with Tim and Donna. Tomorrow . . . tomorrow, he might need to pack his bag and walk away.

Striding down the steps, slowing to the sound of female voices, he halted in the shadows alongside the house.

". . . I do want to thank you again for having me, Donna. Tim said something this morning about seeing how things normally are around here. God knows, I didn't know how much I'd need a little time off . . . but thank you. You've given me a sense of what Bentwood was like before all this began."

"It's . . . it's been dreadful since Mr. Farnsworth died," Donna said quietly. "Tim never talked about it. Never breathed a word about what happened, but this is a small town. People talk. No one wanted to believe that someone could've been murdered right here in our backyard. It's frightening."

"I know this isn't any consolation, but all of this will pass," the soft voice drifted. "There are dozens of people working on this case. Whatever's going on, whoever's doing this, will be stopped. If there's one thing I've learned over the past several years, it's that this kind of thing can't last forever."

"In the meantime, I'm scared out of my wits," Donna said with a nervous laugh. "Don't tell Tim this. But I've been leaving all the lights on in the house every night for almost a month. He'll probably cry when he sees the electric bill."

A soft laugh. "I don't think so, hon. He seems like the kind of guy who'd understand completely."

"He is," Donna said with a light laugh. "I still feel like an idiot, so if this ever comes up? Please, don't tell him."

"Our secret," the soft voice mused. "Frankly, if I were living out here, just on general principle, I think I'd buy a Doberman or Rottweiler to keep me company."

Donna laughed. "At the risk of furniture, rugs, and shoes, I've already made up my mind. The Kennedys over on Bakely Run have a litter of Irish Setters. I've heard they make a decent family dog and protective . . . Here I am, going on about nothing, and you said you have work to do . . . Will you be staying in Bentwood long, Ronnie?"

"I can't say for sure," she answered lightly.

"You . . . you're staying until this is over, aren't you?" Donna asked with a soft sober note.

Hesitation, then, "Probably. It's how I work."

A pause then. "You have to come back out," Donna decided. "Tonight . . . well, it was a bit strained."

"Just a bit," the soft voice mused. "But that's probably my fault, hon, not yours. I get a little strung out when I'm working."

"I don't know what's gotten into Isaac," Donna said with mild annoyance. "He really is a great guy when you get to know him."

"I'm sure he is," her voice changed, becoming dry.

"I truly think something's troubling him," Donna said with a softer, more sober tone. "I don't know what that was all about, Tim talking about the FBI, but . . . well, I just know he wasn't acting quite right even before you came, so I hope you won't hold it against him."

"Really, Donna. It doesn't concern me," Bryson said with a strange note. "I'm sure Mr. Bently has his reasons for behaving the way he does . . . I really ought to get going before it gets too much darker . . ."

She didn't hate him, Isaac considered from where he hovered in the shadows, listening distractedly to the parting amenities, a car door slamming, engine igniting. He supposed that was something—

Why the blazes did it matter one way or the other, for Chrissake!

The sooner she finished whatever she started here and departed . . . he would be the one leaving.

For whatever reason, he'd seen the recognition in her eyes. She'd known him, what name he'd worn, from where he'd hailed. How . . . how after all these years could she have recognized him? He'd been speaking. He remembered those seconds before the perception had exploded in her blue eyes. How in God's name could she have connected Isaac Bently to something, someone, who'd lived eighteen years ago? How, for that matter, had she even known he'd changed his name?

Investigative reporter or . . . the rumors about her and that Federal agent? Jarvins.

His blood running cold, Isaac watched the car pull out, watched Donna wave and call farewell before she turned and headed toward the main steps. No other way could that young woman have known he wasn't who he claimed to be unless Mark Jarvins had told her.

Damn her, Isaac nearly uttered aloud, breaking from his haven, and striding toward his car. He'd see the twit back to town, but by God, he wouldn't venture within ten feet of her again even if that kiss had—

He wasn't about to think of that either! This little witch was worse than all others. *A lying, conniving little viper!* He could just imagine her racing to town to rendezvous with her lover, and he could imagine the headlines. Psychic—

Nooo!

"No!" he snapped. His fingers trembled as he twisted the key, overrevving the engine and not giving a damn what Tim would make of that. He had to stop her! Jesus! He had to stop her.

Mind-bend her!

No, damnit! Another way!

He just had to convince her to keep her knowledge to herself just until . . . until he could get out of town. He needed to get out of town right now, he realized, as he sprayed gravel, spinning a U-turn in Spencer's driveway. He couldn't afford to stick around and become tomorrow's headlines. Jarvins. That son of a bitch would like nothing better than to smear Jade Laquette's face all over the front page. Why that bastard had come gunning for him in the first place, Isaac couldn't readily imagine, but that asshole had been out for blood . . .

Because one Isaac Bently had shared dinner across the table from his girlfriend? Because the little witch had run back to that Inn and fed him some long line about a certain antique dealer who hadn't afforded her the time of day?

The witch! Worse than all the others! Worse! Or just as bad, at the very least.

This certainly wouldn't be the first time that Isaac had encountered problems with former boyfriends, husbands, current boyfriends, brothers, fathers . . . hell, even the jealous little tarts, themselves. It was a conspiracy . . . one he'd not counted on when finding the pleasant little town this side of nowhere. How was he supposed to know, to predict that he'd become the focus of a few dozen fantasies and obsessions? God knows, he'd never had trouble finding a date in any of the cities he'd traversed, but he'd certainly never felt like a side of beef.

Catching a flash of red lights traveling into a bend ahead, Isaac braked, cursing his speed. If not for that flash of brake lights, he would've run up her damned tailpipe. Figures the wench would be the type to neglect igniting headlamps until the last moments before pitch-black. Everything about the woman was a blasted annoyance! Her—with her big innocent blue eyes and that tumble of black curls. *Witch!* He knew all about witches. Black-haired, blue-eyed witches, soft smiles, bubbly laughter—

He shook his head, uttered a curse, and fumbled in his shirt pocket for his cigarettes. Out of the darkness at the edges of his mind, the black veils flew upward, fanned from outstretched arms, stark black sheer cloth—

Gasping a breath, Isaac blinked the image away and yanked the steering wheel to avoid the tall grass at the edge of the road. "Driving," he heaved softly. "Pay attention . . ."

Driving himself crazy is more like it. Had been for years. Driving himself stark raving mad, and suddenly, he knew why the black witch image was back, haunting him as badly as ever. He understood, without a doubt, the omen of that image every time he thought too deeply about the vixen rolling along in front of him.

The images, the visions which pulsed inside his head every night, the faces and things he refused to see, couldn't allow himself to see . . . all the insanity he'd learned to hide . . .?

This witch marked his end. His doom. She was his catalyst. The catalyst which could shatter his fragile hold on sanity.

Keeping a distance away, Isaac remained near enough to know she turned onto the right connecting roads. He'd never quite understood Spencer's need for the hills. Privacy, Tim professed, but that made little sense. A man's privacy could be invaded. Whether he dwelt in the center of town or on a mountaintop in the middle of a desert, his walls of privacy could be breached. Nowhere was safe. All an illusion. And the illusion was about to shatter, had already begun to shatter.

This witch knew. Soon, Jarvins would know. Soon, the whole quiet little town of Bentwood would know, and history was about to repeat itself. Bentwood, then the world. His face on the blasted television screen wouldn't have meant a damned thing; his name 'Isaac Bently' was just one more asshole in the crowd. It wouldn't be that name splattered across the newspapers, television screens, or tabloids. Not just that face flashing across America to stir every weirdo and fanatic in the country. No one would've connected his face, not with that of a ten-year-old. No one would've connected his name 'Isaac Bently' with the past, not with a few flashes of coverage on the evening news. Those agents could've waltzed him across the street, and he could've smiled into the cameras. Only one person in the world would have made the connection . . . but somehow this witch had made the connection and the safety, his 'haven'—she'd been right about that, Bentwood had become his haven—gone, now. In a few swift strokes, all the safety he'd worked for years to provide for himself would be destroyed.

And maybe it was time. Perhaps, as Tim had said, it was time to 'throw in the towel.' Life was too hard to live in shadows, in darkness, in fear of the night. Cloaking himself in darkness hadn't protected him or made it any easier. Illusions and deceptions . . . he'd once sworn he'd never live with illusions, but he had. He'd become worse than his greatest abomination. He'd topped his mother's achievements, her deceit, her tricks . . . He'd become her prodigy, a charlatan, his father's prodigy . . . No, damnit! He'd never delved that deep into the darkness!

At the turn onto the highway, Isaac hesitated, letting several cars pass before pulling out. It was a straight shot into Brentwood, now. Not likely she'd get lost.

How long before that surveillance team returned to hide behind bushes, headlights off?

A Sunday night in Bentwood shouldn't be so busy. On a normal Sunday evening, he could drive into town without passing a single car. Cars ahead, cars behind. Headlights flashed through Isaac's line of vision. People walked on sidewalks and gathered in the park, currently lighted with several strobes as if the Firemen's Fair had set up early. A circus. A circus to celebrate the advent of a psychopath . . . How could they not know what this would do to that maniac? How this fanfare would fuel the fires?

Isaac turned off Maine a few blocks from the Bentwood House, turned down the first alley, and shot through the shadows. Headlights off, he crossed the connecting streets, advancing on the rear of the Inn. No harm in seeing that she got inside safely.

"Damnit," he snapped and stomped the brake in time to avoid shooting from the alley into the path of the very car he was trying to evade. Stopped, Isaac watched the rental turn into the tree-shrouded tunnel ahead of him. He waited until it reached the end of the block, then drove more cautiously through the side street, creeping in the rental car's wake. Perhaps, he was insane, playing cat and mouse, passing through the only portal of light midway through the darkened tunnel. Loading docks, service entrances, parking inlets, and industrial trash receptacles extended the length of the block to his left. On his right, tall ungainly hedges and overhanging trees from back lawns blocked whatever remained of the silvery-white light of the moon.

Stopped in the mouth of the alley, Isaac watched the glimmer of headlights and taillights extinguish within the private parking corral cater-corner to him. His attention riveted, he watched the pool of light at the rear entrance to the house, and his muscles tensed. A pulse thumped at his temple. He gripped the wheel with a greater intensity against his conscious effort to relax.

Beneath the soft rumble of his engine, his soft moaning breath touched his senses, a denial, a plea. Shaking his head as if to offset the pulsing effects, his heartbeat racing, he struggled to focus on the pool of light at the back entrance, pleading with the last of his will to see the woman passing through the entry. But she wouldn't walk through that light, he knew at this moment. She wouldn't walk through that light and stride gaily through the rear door.

"Nnnooo!" His hand lashed toward the door. "Nooo, Veronnnica!"

CHAPTER 16

A block before the Inn, Ronnie turned down the side street, deciding she would prefer not to show her car or her face at the front of the Inn where a small mob loitered. With any luck, she could park and pass through the rear entrance near the back stairs.

Nothing about the town even remotely resembled the quiet serenity of a single evening past. Where the streets had emptied by eight o'clock last evening—a Saturday night, she remembered—the small downtown currently resembled a city block at the peak of the evening rush. She wouldn't be a damned bit surprised if the movie theater had added another show and the thrift shops had remained open.

Breathing a sigh of relief, Ronnie pulled into the cove of the parking lot. Not a soul in sight. A single light fixture, no brighter than a private residence porchlight, brightened the rear entrance. An ordinary light switch inside the backdoor ignited that single bulb, a detail to catch her eye last evening. An Inn with a back porch had been a surprise and added another layer to Bentwood's pleasant ambiance. Before a month ago, Bentwood had been a lovely little town.

Ronnie only hoped she hadn't lied to Donna Spencer, hoped it would return to normal when this madness ended. Too many small towns in America were swallowed by progress, innovation, and renovation. Too few areas remained where the prime economic growth could be considered farm and dairy produce. Her heart sank to think this maniac had struck here, at the very heart of the American dream, at the very heart of America, and she suffered only bitterness toward those of her colleagues who would capitalize on that event.

Climbing from her car, Ronnie snapped the door shut and started to turn. To the glimpse of motion at the front of her car, she pivoted in a perfect karate arc. Reflexively, she clutched her purse, prepared to swing, but stopped short before letting fly. Breath easing out with the recognition, she huffed, "Lord, you startled me."

Stopped a step away, Cal Farnsworth hovered, his features distorted with the soft glow of light from the porch. He hadn't shaved, not since their last encounter. With his proximity, she smelled the pungent odor of cow manure and sweat . . . and whiskey on his breath. He stood firm, not swaying, but one shiny eye twitched, and an oddly crooked smile gnarled his pinched lips.

By instinct, Ronnie's chest gripped; her heartbeat quickened. For the first time since this morning when she'd read this young man's police record, she fully believed him capable of assault. She didn't need the glimpse of a whiskey bottle hanging from his fist to realize how Cal had spent the past few hours, nor did she need to hear the liquid slosh to sense the rage trembling him.

"You didn' call me back, bitch," he slurred in a low growl. "I called yous like you ast me to." His smile broadened, bitter. "*You* ast *me* to call yous . . . I talked to my Maa like you ast me, too."

Collecting her breath and steeling her nerve, Ronnie willed the calm through her system. "I did try to call you back, Cal. I tried both of your numbers, but the lines were busy. I was hoping you'd—"

"I got my pickup right back in ta alley," he sneered. "You an' me. We gonna go do some talking again, now. Just you an' me an' my special place."

"Cal, I'll be glad to speak with you, but I'd prefer to speak with you over a cup of coffee. Why don't we go inside the Inn, and we can—"

He stepped with surprising speed, blocking her sidestep, and corralling her against the car. Waving the bottle upward to one side, he landed his hand on the hood to catch his balance. Glass smacked glass close to her shoulder; whiskery breath filled the space between them. With his face entirely in silhouette, his shoulders blocked the light and her escape as he growled, "We gonna go in my pickup."

He was large and appeared even broader than yesterday morning, with the darkness swamped around them. He was also very nearly drunk and a mean drunk, according to several police reports.

Unlike his quiet father, Cal Farnsworth was considered a 'hooligan' since his teenage years. On more than a few occasions, he'd been caught sharing a few cases of beer behind the football stadium, and in more recent years, he'd landed in the 'slammer' after knocking back a few too many shots on a Friday night. On the night of his father's murder, he'd stopped for a few beers, a detail he'd conveniently omitted when describing that evening with Ronnie. Perhaps, like most witnesses to a violent crime, the facts had distorted in his mind. But just how distorted had those facts become? A few popular beliefs suggested that Cal Farnsworth could have distorted quite a few details, only beginning with the missing hour between his stop at Crowley's Bar and Grill and his arrival at his home.

"Cal, why don't we go inside?" Ronnie asked carefully. "I could use a cup of coffee."

"You didn' hear me, bitch. You an me's gonna go for a ride. I knows about yous now . . . Knows how you likes to do your talkin' lyin' down . . . Been thinkin' on this all day." He slurred and swayed only slightly as his free hand lashed upward, surprisingly quick to clasp her hair and yank her head back.

Pure fury exploded in Ronnie's mind as his mouth and whiskey breath found her lips. Her knee rose by reflex and conditioning. Her free hand slid up his muscled chest, intending a push, but he slammed forward, laughing into her mouth. In a split second, his shaft rammed against her abdomen before her knee connected with his thy, just shy of soft tissue. The whiskey bottle dropped, clattering against the car, but she drew shallow consolation as she heard it smash. In a greater rage, he pressed against her, growling like a wounded animal as his immense, work-calloused hand groped at her breast, bruising.

"You bastard! Get—" His mouth covered hers, breathing his noxious breath up her nostrils. She lashed her teeth into his lip, seeing stars as the back of her head cracked against the rental's hood.

In slow motion, he reared back, snarling and howling, and in a single second, Ronnie wondered if she held his lip in her teeth. Another instant passed when she saw his hand coming, curling into a fist.

"Youuu, biiitch!"

In the next instant, he whirled away.

His voice drowned under the unmistakable sound of a fist cracking skin. Blinking through spots and unemotional tears, Ronnie gleaned only silhouettes of bleary bodies performing some strange dance. Like a stage show of Punch and Judy, she thought crazily as one body staggered under a wicked thud.

Collecting her balance, her senses swimming with the sparks swirling behind her eyes, Ronnie saw Cal staggering, not certain about the other until Cal wheeled about, snarling, "Bennntly, I'll fuuucking kill you!"

With the grace of a ballet dancer, the phantom image wheeled in the shadows, deflecting Cal's charge, catching, slamming, toppling the beast in smooth graceful motion.

What the hell had just happened! Bently? Isaac Bently? Was Cal dead? Had Bently just killed him?

Swaying, Ronnie saw Farnsworth flat out several paces away, sprawled motionless, spread-eagle on the gravel floor. The fellow hadn't even cried out! Not a groan or gasp—

Bently spun toward her, then closed the distance in two strides. To the hands clasping her shoulders, Ronnie jolted under a spread of electric tingles. His deep voice flowed into her as if through a tunnel. "Veronica! Are you alright—?"

Belatedly, her knees wobbled, her head whirled, and the darkness seemed suddenly darker, like a camera shutter closing in slow motion. Ronnie understood the blackness engulfing her as the arms enveloped her, firming, lifting. Her shoes skimmed off the gravel as her hands groped for purchase, finding a wad of a cotton shirt on a muscled chest. "Good lord," she heaved as the world swam. "Put mmme down!"

"No," the low voice vibrated simply.

Good grief. What was worse? Being mauled by a drunken lecher or held captive by a pair of arms that felt more than capable of holding her indefinitely. . .? *And wasn't that just a stupid question?* "Mmmister BBBently." She couldn't help it; her voice quavered on the brink of a hysterical laugh, an extremely nervous laugh as she blinked spots and tipped her pounding head against his shoulder.

"It's Isaac, dammit. Just Isaac! Or Sax, if you prefer," he snapped, sounding irritated. In silhouette, his head tilted, and his eyes shined, almost feral in the dull light. "If you call me Mr. Bently again, by God, I'll . . . I'll . . . You're hurt," he stated sharply, far more worried than annoyed. "You need a hospital—"

"No, I don't—"

"Yes."

"No!" Ronnie said and lifted a hand to his muscled chest, intending to push from his arms. "Ow!" Her hand flew to her spinning head, and she glared up at his double-exposed silhouette. "Put me *down!* Isaac!"

"No," he said simply.

Damn him for sounding so *smug!* "Listen, you arrogant snob," she strained, collecting her bearings if only by the threat of medical attention. "I do *not* need a hospital, a doctor, or a paramedic. I need my feet on the ground, my purse, and my room key . . . And if you want to be *helpful,* you can find a bag of *ice.* Understand?"

"Perfectly," he said, but he wasn't putting her down. Instead, he stooped, and they were both rising again. Ronnie remained trapped at her knees and across her back, and she suffered only a floating sensation of him releasing her for a split second. "If you'd hold on, this might be easier," he suggested.

"If you'd put me *down,* this might—" Cal Farnsworth lay prostrate, motionless. Ronnie glimpsed at his image as they swept past, her vision swimming with their speed.

"I'm not setting you down only to watch you fall down," the low voice carried without a trace of arrogance.

"Cal . . .? Is he de . . .?"

"No. He's not dead," Bently said in mild irritation. "He's resting."

"Police . . . ambulance. We have to call—"

"Would you just hang on?" he asked simply. "We have a few moments to reach your room and have you lying down . . . Unless you'd like the ambulance for you?"

"No!" Damn it! Apparently, he wasn't putting her down at this moment.

At the steps, he'd be forced to set her down. Annoyed, Ronnie wrapped her arm over his shoulder and clasped his collar. Soft, dark hair brushed against her fingers lighting tiny little sparks through her nerve endings. The strength of his arms, his chest, and shoulders, touched off the strangest sensations through her vibrating limbs, and she wasn't sure it was all from an adrenalin rush. Still holding the back of her head, feeling the pounding at her temple, she sank against his shoulder. A scent of expensive spiced cologne touched her breath;

the memory of his kiss ignited, triggered by the fragrance. Exotic. He smelled exotic. Like something wild and dangerous. Exciting.

"Hit my head," she muttered.

"I'm aware of that," the low voice echoed with a faintly amused tone that helped roust her as they passed through the backdoor. He still held her. He wasn't pausing to put her down. Instead, they rounded the corner to the narrow stairwell.

"Mr. . . . Miss . . . Messages!"

To the strange stammering voice, Ronnie rolled her head enough to recognize the same boy who'd thrust a handful of notes at her earlier.

Another stack swayed in her vision, and Bently caught the wad under his thumb as he spoke, "Call over to the police station, Lyle. Have them send a squad car to pick up Cal Farnsworth. The lad's lying in your parking lot. Next, call Dr. Blackwell, and see if he's available for a house call. Send him up to Miss Bryson's room when he arrives." Already moving onto the steps, he continued, "In the meantime, bring a few large bags of ice and a bottle of brandy up to Miss Bryson's room." Over his shoulder, he asked, "Do you have all that?"

"Yes, sir! Mr. Bently!"

"Get to it, then, lad," he said by way of a nudge.

Not entirely sure whether to be amused or impressed, Ronnie squinted up at his handsome profile, catching a glint of jade under thick lashes, noting a peculiar lift of his brow.

"Still with me, sweetheart?"

Sweetheart? The man was a devil! "You could put me down any time, now, Mr. Muscles."

His mustache twitched. "Suppose that's an improvement over the alternative," he commented dryly. "Do you think you could tear your hand from your dome long enough to collect your purse and find your room key?"

"You could put me down, and I'd be glad to."

"If you like, I can kick the door open," he offered with a crooked smile. "It's no problem, really. These old hinges and nails will just pop right off these old frames."

"You're a *shit!*" she decided and nearly bit her tongue, flinging her hand downward to collect her purse dangling by its strap from his wrist. As she dragged the bag to her waist and began fumbling inside, she was starkly aware of him watching her, waiting patiently.

"I don't know which weighs more, you or that purse," he commented glibly.

"You're just filled with those underhanded compliments, aren't you, Mr. . . . Charm," she decided while wading into the side pocket where she habitually stuck the key.

He huffed a sound, not quite a laugh. "If you carry that gunny sack often, it's a wonder you're not built like an Amazon."

"You're just gushing with flattery," she grumbled and produced the key, thrusting her arm to hit the mark. With a sharp twist and push, she sent the door flying inward. The sooner she escaped his arms, the better! And just when she started not to like him again, he delivered her onto the bed, setting her down with a gentle dip. Carefully, he caught her head and held it aloft as he fluffed the pillow. Only after she rested comfortably, he shifted and ignited the lamp, then pushed off his knee and crossed the room to shut the door. Holding one hand to her head, almost feeling the knot rising under her palm, Ronnie watched him pass through the bathroom door and heard the water running.

Without his hands and body to distract her worse than her thumping skull, she collected enough thought to wonder how he'd reached the Inn in time to save her life. Unfortunately, she had no time to ask. He returned in seconds, carrying two wet cloths, and settling sidesaddle on the mattress beside her. His eyes conveyed his concern, flinching when she flinched, quivering a smile as he eased the chilled wet cloth under her palm against her head. With the second cloth, he wiped her forehead, her cheeks, her lips. His action, his silence, his gaze intent upon her seemed more mesmerizing with every second.

"Don't fall asleep yet, sweetheart," he said in a low gentle voice.

There was that 'sweetheart' again and in a voice to send tingles down her spine. No malice. No contempt. His eyes had softened to a shade of jade, near the color of spring grass as he studied her in peculiar concern. Without fully controlling her limbs, she lifted her hand to cup his face. Her thumb slipped over the tense curve of his lips; his mustache shivered under the pad of her thumb. Looking into his faintly confused eyes, seeing, feeling the strange hurt behind that soft shade, she uttered, "Thank you . . . for being outside, Isaac."

His hand closed over hers. He slid her palm to brush his lips on her fingertips, stirring even those distant nerves with his touch. "You're most assuredly welcome, Veronica."

No one . . . no one had ever spoken her name quite like that. No one else could roll those odd syllables off the tongue to sound beautiful. If she never heard her name spoken like that again, she wouldn't forget that sound or the sensation it swept through her body. Disappointed, she felt her hand lowered to rest on her waist, not sure what to expect when he turned slightly. He moved only one arm, reaching one-handed to slide her shoe off her foot. The warmth of his palm skimmed and heated the ends of her toes. How could he do that? How could he take such a simple thing as removing a shoe and transform it into a need to feel his hand linger?

When both shoes had disappeared, he pushed off the bed and moved to the table, reaching for the bottle of wine. He stopped short, withdrawing his hand and turning, wearing a peculiar intensity. He barely parted his lips to speak when the phone emitted a sharp metallic ring. Returning, he lifted the receiver, eyeing her with amusement as he said, "Yes?" The twinkle extinguished in a split second. His tone descended, he commented, "I believe you have the wrong room. She's down the hall." He snapped the receiver down; his cheek pulsed.

"Let me guess," she said wearily. "Obscene phone call."

Rather than answer, he leaned and lifted the stack of notes, flipping one open. His focus riveted, and his green eyes flashed a fire to send a chill down her spine.

"Those happen to be mine," she said carefully. "That's rather like opening someone's mail."

As if he'd not heard, he opened another.

"Isaac," she said quietly, suddenly not as worried about him reading her messages as about how he might react to them. A man now . . . but he'd been a boy when the media had crucified him. No! She didn't want him reading that mail! Or lifting her phone to hear obscene phone calls! Dear God! What it must have been like for him! A mere child!

"Isaac!" she snapped, and his head jerked, his eyes shined near emerald when he looked at her. The anger, as quick as the pain, haunted his sculpted features. "Don't," she stated and pushed onto her elbow, fighting the sudden sway, reaching and sliding the messages from his trembling grip. Squinting against the physical pain and suffering a rise of tears in empathy for what he was feeling, she stated, "Don't."

Blinking, he looked younger, lost suddenly. Hurt.

Dropping the notes in the trashcan alongside the bed, Ronnie reached again and clasped his palm. His fingers responded in reflex to capture her hand. Holding his abstracted gaze, she tugged, landing him beside her as she clasped her head, not releasing his hand. "Just sit here with me, okay? Just sit here."

"Th—" He drew a breath. For the first time since she'd met him, he suffered a tiny crack in the armor he wore so well. "It's worse than I'd imagined," he managed quietly, his eyes shuttered under thick black lashes "Has . . . has this been going on all day? The phone calls? The messages?"

She smiled, not as lightheartedly as she would've preferred, and even less as she thought of Cal Farnsworth . . . and the rumors that had driven him to assault her. "It doesn't matter, Isaac. It'll pass."

At the sound of footsteps and hammering knuckles, he slipped his hand free and rose.

As she watched him cross the room, she thought again of what he must have suffered at the media, remembering her research. The Arlington papers had started the circus. Like Grimes, an unscrupulous reporter had written the first story, sensationalizing the murder of a moderately-famous celebrity.

Across the room, Isaac opened the door for the bellhop, accepted one of the ice bags, and motioned the young man inside as the boy rushed his words, reporting his progress. "Police are on the way! Doc Blackwell's coming!"

"Pour the wine, will you, Lyle?" Bently commented while bringing the ice bag to her. "There are a few plastic cups on the vanity." Already sitting, he wrapped one of the cloths around the bag and caught her eyes with an apology. "This might hurt just a tad."

How smoothly, how easily he'd taken charge of this entire ordeal. From the moment he'd yanked Cal away, he'd taken command, and Ronnie remained strangely content simply to watch him. Perhaps, she *had* hit her head too hard. She winced just a little as the swollen lump touched that solid wad of ice blocks. She'd never willingly let other people handle her affairs. Lying still and letting him pamper her like a wounded dove wasn't her general style. She should be in the parking lot, waiting for the police to arrive and collect Farnsworth. She should be preparing to offer a statement.

As he handed her a plastic cup of wine, she decided, "I really am feeling better, hon. We probably ought to go down and speak to the police."

"The police can find us," he commented, but a thought creased his brow. "Speaking of whom, I should call Tim." Leaning, plucking the receiver off the hook, he barely held it to his ear when he paused and flashed a peculiar glance toward her before commenting, "Hold on, please." Lowering, covering the mouthpiece in his palm, he commented, "Do you, by any chance, have a brother James?"

"Oh Lord," she uttered, all too aware of how her brer could begin ranting on the instant his call connected. Was she truly up to that battle? "Suppose I better speak to him."

Isaac considered only for a second, lifted the receiver to his ear, and spoke with an arrogant smirk. "James, I'm afraid your sister can't come to the phone right now. If you'd care to leave a message . . .?"

Watching the amusement flash in the hazel eyes, Ronnie suffered a strange hysteria. By now, her younger brother might be threatening bodily harm.

"Lad, you will simply have to wait," Isaac said in a smooth, deep voice. "I'll be certain she calls you at her earliest convenience. Take care, now." He reached and touched the receiver button down, looking at her with a bemused smile. "Afraid you may have some explaining to do soon, sweetheart. The lad did sound distressed." He lifted his finger and began dialing.

"The lad will likely strangle you if he ever gets within ten feet of you," Ronnie mused. "James tends to be the more hotheaded of my three musketeers."

He lent her a cockeyed smile. "Naturally." His eyes sobered as he waited through several rings. "Tim . . . Somehow, I knew you'd have your damned scanner on . . . Yes. No. No, I think she's fine other than a lump on the head, but I sent for Blackwell. . . No, I left her lying in the parking lot, for chrissake. Of course, I'm with her . . . Hmm, I think we're about to get more company. I truly doubt there's anything you can do here . . . I'll call." He hung up and pushed off the mattress, almost to the door, when more knuckles assaulted the wood.

Oh, this was an odd moment. From her slightly elevated position, Ronnie saw Mark start a single step forward. He froze. Isaac poised as solidly as a granite statue blocking the door. They stood nearly equal in height, although Isaac stood a shade taller, and very nearly equal in width, both long and lean. After feeling the strength in Isaac's arms, however, Ronnie decided he was slightly broader. The expression transforming on Mark's face ran the full spectrum from concern to black rage. His jaw pulsed, lips thinned, and his blue eyes darkened, but it was Isaac's low sinister tone to send a prickle down Ronnie's spine.

"I don't believe this is in your jurisdiction, Mr. Jarvins. It's a matter for the local police."

"Get the hell out of my way, Bently," Mark said in a low pitch and started another step forward.

Isaac never flinched, never moved. "I've spared the lady one inconvenience this evening, I don't mind making it two."

"Mr. Bently," Len's low voice cut from the deeper shadows of the hall. "I think you better step aside. The lady happens to be a friend of ours, and I don't mind going through you to see if she's alright."

Mark started in again, apparently intending to push Isaac aside, but he stumbled awkwardly when Isaac stepped back and aside of his own accord.

"Suppose when you put it that way," Bently said smoothly.

Mark sent him a hostile flash while collecting his footing, and Ronnie glimpsed the dark arrogant shine in the green eyes, following and lancing Mark as he swept passed. The man had some killer eyes, Ronnie considered an instant before she realized Mark had caught her admiring Bently.

If anything, Mark's blue eyes emitted a greater rage before he seemed to remember why he'd just breached the capable blockade. His hostility melted on the instant, his stride long and quick. "Ronnie, are you alright?" he asked as he landed on the mattress next to her, clasping her hand in a fierce grip.

"It's nothing, Mark. A bump on the head."

His gaze flashed over her face and darted over her lips. His fingers lifted gently, brushing against her cheek.

And suddenly, she felt like crying. He could be so gentle, so sweet, so patient . . . and his touch ignited none of the electric pulses nor created any of the sensations to engulf her when Jade Laquette just looked at her.

"He did hurt you," Mark said quietly.

"Honestly, Mark, I'm fine," she said as Len arrived above Mark's shoulder. "It was nothing, really."

"I caught the mention of a doctor on the way," Len commented. "Think maybe we'll wait until after he sees you before we pass a vote on that, Ron. Meantime, think you're up to telling us what happened? Nobody downstairs knew a hell of a lot."

"There's not a lot to tell," she said while glancing between the two, noting Isaac in the background, sipping his wine and watching her. "Apparently, Cal had been drinking. He wanted to talk to me. He . . . became a little adamant about wanting me to go somewhere with him. When I refused," she shrugged. "He was drunk. He started becoming difficult, making passes. Isaac—" How smoothly that name had slipped off her lips that time. "—intervened and Cal put up a fight."

Len turned a sidestep, finding Bently. "You leveled the asshole in the lot?"

"No comment," he said with lofty indifference, a benign smirk.

Len's jaw gripped, and Mark pivoted his incensed gaze to Bently. "Buddy, you're playing the wrong game with the wrong people," Mark warned in a dark tone. "If you know what's good for you, you'll answer these questions, or I can promise you, I'll have you behind bars so fast it'll make your head spin."

"Mark," Ronnie said, drawing his heat but glimpsing the jade fire directed at Mark, and suddenly, she was very sure that Mark would lose if they ever came to blows. Lifting her attention to Len's dark angry eyes, she commented, "Incontestably, Isaac leveled Farnsworth in self-defense. Cal was drunk and ugly, and there's a smashed bottle of whiskey alongside my rental if you need further proof."

Again, Len looked toward Isaac. "Want to tell me how you just happened to be in the vicinity?"

"I'm sure you'll read it on an official statement eventually," he answered indifferently.

"You still pissed about the fucking plates?" Len asked with an edge before Mark could breathe a word.

"No comment," Isaac said offhandedly and sipped his wine. Impassively, his gaze volleyed between the agents.

More footsteps, more knuckles. Ronnie watched as Len stalked across the room, and she paused her gaze to catch Bently's flash of amusement in her direction before he wiped the green slate clean. He was playing with fire, and he knew it.

Mark squeezed her hand either to express his disapproval or to draw her attention from Isaac before Len yanked the door open.

The broad-shouldered man sauntering into the room with a deputy on his hip only vaguely resembled the photographs in the local papers. Sheriff Grant carried himself with the suave of a Texas ranger. Hat brim dipped low over gray-black brows, his gray-blue eyes read the room as keenly as any seasoned veteran. Pausing near the foot of the bed, his gaze fleeting over Ronnie, he raised his hand to touch his hat, "Evening, Miss Bryson."

"Hello, Sheriff Grant."

He smiled, his gaze trailing from one agent to the other, pivoting to Bently, to whom he smiled and nodded, "Hi ya, kid."

"Sheriff," Bently said with a note of respect underlying his musing smirk.

"Thought there was something familiar about how that fella was lying out back," Grant commented without losing his smile. "You just might be getting yourself a citizen's award with that talent of yours, son. Lotta folks are gonna wish they'd got a whack at that boy before too long." Grant barely paused as his gaze returned to Ronnie. "The Doc should be here any minute, miss, but if you're feeling up to giving us a brief statement on how all this came about, I'd appreciate it."

Ronnie agreed, but even as she sped through the dialogue again, she sensed something out of kilter. Something about this sheriff's swagger, his almost smug demeanor when glancing off the agents, disturbed her more with each passing moment.

Like Len, Sheriff Grant looked toward Bently and asked, "You want to fill in the missing parts, kid?"

"As the lady said, Cal had been drinking. It certainly wasn't much of a fight," he answered with a shrug. "I think she's oversimplifying the assault but therein lies the lady's prerogative."

"So, you figure ole Cal was pretty serious about his intentions, that right?"

"A bit too serious for my taste, sheriff," Bently said with a glance to Ronnie. "I'd imagine Cal would've hurt her more seriously if given a chance."

"How'd you happen to be on hand?" Len put in.

Isaac barely favored him with a glance. His attention returned to Grant, far more intent as he commented, "Drunk or not, sheriff, Farnsworth belongs behind bars."

Grant might sound like a good ole country boy, but he was quick on the uptake. "I'd be a little interested in knowing how you happened into this, Isaac."

"Actually, I stopped by to make sure the young lady reached the Inn without incident," he answered. "With the madhouse in town, I couldn't justify letting her slip through the back door of this hotel alone."

The Devil! He made it sound as if she'd intended to sneak into the Inn through the back door to avoid sullying her reputation, and the implication had struck at least one mark. Jarvins cast her a cool blue glance, speculating, judging.

"I take it, then, you and the young lady were together this evening?" Grant verified.

"Spence invited us out for a barbecue," Bently said with a casual note. "It was a little after dark, and we were in separate cars." He shrugged. "I intended to follow a little more closely, but I ended up quite a distance behind."

"Thought that was your Jag sitting over in that alley," Grant commented. "Had half a mind to have it towed," he continued, one of his thumbs hooked at his belt. "Kid, you gotta remember to shut and lock the doors when you're leaving those seventy-thousand-dollar cars of yours sitting around. I'd like to keep this a quiet county. You dangling carrots and leaving the keys in the ignition, doors wide open—?" He shook his head. "That's not gonna happen."

Ronnie glimpsed the flash of amusement in Isaac's eyes, the smile on the young deputy who'd been writing profusely on his clipboard throughout the exchange.

"I'll try to bear that in mind, sheriff. Any chance you picked up the keys?"

Grant reached in his pocket, lifting the loop of braided leather, and dangling the dual set of keys. "You mean these ones?"

His dimple cut into the corner of his mustache as he smiled with his comment, "Those would definitely be the ones."

Grant nodded, flicking his wrist and catching the silver keys in his palm. His gaze held intent on Isaac as he again hooked his thumb at his belt. A friendly smile curved the thin bowtie of a gray mustache across his lips. "There's just a little thing we have to discuss, here, about these keys, kid," he spoke with a smile. "I'll tell you, I'm about 99 percent sure, these here keys are the same ones belonging to a little black Jag that one of my boys spotted early this evening doing about 130 heading out toward Canterton. Now, I don't guess you'd want to tell me I'm right, would you, kid?"

"I can safely say, I would definitely not like to tell you, you're right," Isaac said with a faintly more amused smile.

"Naaa, I didn't think so," Grant drawled. His pale blue eyes held fast, his fist remained secure, his lips curved. "That brings us to another little thing I've been meaning to talk to you about, kid," he said with the flair of a southern lawman addressing the local desperado. "Seems another of my boys spotted another little black racer here on Friday night and seeing as how you're partial to those little power packs, I thought maybe you could help me out with this." He paused a heartbeat. "This little black sprinter was doing about 110 when my deputy spotted it coming off Highway 9. Now, you wouldn't want to take a guess what kind of car that was, would you? Just hypothetically speaking, mind you."

Oh, Bently was cute. The son of a gun dared to appear thoughtful, wrinkling his brow, listing his gaze. "Well," he began after a reflective pause. "If I were to guess, I'd say it was probably a Maserati. Handling and suspension and all considered on those bends."

"Eh-hmm," Grant murmured thoughtfully. "Now, mind you, this was Friday night. About what time would you guess that car got spotted? Just a wild shot in the dark, here?"

"Hmm, I'd guess about 9:45—9:50. Somewhere in there, sheriff."

"Kid," Grant said with a mocked appreciation. "If you see a jar full of marbles at the Firemen's Fair next week, I think you better stop and take a wild guess or two at how many marbles are in that jar." His lips twitched; one gray brow arched. "With talent like that, you'll win, hands down."

Good Lord, Grant was a charmer, and Bently's mirrored smile offered a comic relief considering he'd just been cleared in connection to a homicide.

"Now, there's just one more thing we need to discuss," Sheriff Grant continued as he dangled the keys, fingering them and glancing off them to Bently. "I'm only going to say this once, ssson. If I, or any of my boys, happen to see a little black racer doing anything more than ten miles over the speed limit, don't matter whether it's on state, county, or township roads, we're not even going to waste our time chasing it. What I'm going to do, is . . . I'm going to have one of my deputies drive me over to your door. I'm going to knock on that door, and I'm going to do this—" He held out his open empty palm toward Bently and continued as he flopped the keys onto his own palm. "And you're going to do that. Then, I'm going to be driving one of those little black cars for quite a while, seeing as how the county doesn't have money to spend on any hi-pro chase cars. You get my drift here, kid?"

"III . . . definitely get your drift, sheriff," Bently said with his dimple winking at one corner.

"Glad to hear it," Grant said and tossed Isaac the keys. In slow motion, he turned his gaze about, flashing his quick gray eyes between the agents, one of whom appeared furious. Len just stood with his thin smile affecting his scowl, his dark eyes nearly black with amusement. "Now," Grant said while facing off with Mark. "How about you boys coming along with me? We'll have us a little chat about wrapping up this homicide investigation, seeing as how there's a real good chance we have the culprit in custody."

"Sheriff, if you're referring to Cal Farnsworth," Mark started with a thin rein on his temper. "We need a good deal more than an attempted assault to make a murder charge—"

"We have what we need, Mr. Jarvins," Grant spoke without a hint of country charm. "Now, let's we go sort this out. Then, you boys can be on your way." Without awaiting a response, Grant acknowledged Ronnie with a polite tip of his head. "Ma'am, appreciate it if you'd stop over to the station when you're feeling up to it and give Chief Hayward a formal statement and a signature on the complaint forms. We don't want any loose ends on this case."

"I'll stop in the morning if that's alright, sheriff," she agreed.

"That's fine, miss," he said and flashed another glance to Bently as he headed for the door. "I'll be expecting you to stop by tomorrow, too, kid, and hereafter, you keep that size twelve shoe from smashing those tiny pedals. Hear?"

"On both accounts, sheriff," Bently said, but his smile was fixed, his eyes not quite right as he seemed to zoom in on Mark.

Very strange, this position. Deliberately, it seemed, Mark paused from following the sheriff, leaned, and brushed a chaste kiss on her cheek. "I'll be back as soon as I can, dear," he promised, but the preoccupation and anger conflicted in his eyes.

"I'll be fine, Mark," she said a little coolly, deciding nearly at the instant, that she didn't appreciate this position. No matter what rumors had circulated and what Mark seemed to be taking for granted, they hadn't returned to any former status of romantic endeavor. More annoyed than she cared to consider, with her head thumping and a few bruises beginning to surface, she watched both agents walk out. Len acknowledged Bently with a nod; the amenity returned with a slight tip of the head. She and Mark were overdue for a serious discussion at the earliest opportunity.

At the moment, however, Ronnie had something far more important to consider . . . and she couldn't do that lying down. Cal Farnsworth . . . homicidal?

CHAPTER 17

Unconsciously, Isaac pulled the blind down over the window and tugged the string to draw the drapes and block the glow of streetlights off Maine. In a few atomized seconds, what remained of his serenity had vanished. No other thought held more firmly in his mind as he glimpsed at the young woman pushing off the bed. Caught between anger and agitation, he let her rise to the edge of the mattress. His heart tugged as she fingered her head. Her eyes flinched slightly; her lips winced. Already, the lovely curve at the corner of her lips had swollen, and a bruise had begun to form across her porcelain cheek.

"Damn it," he uttered and strode to her, touching her shoulder as she started to stand. "You better lie—"

"Knock it off," she said with an air of preoccupation, her eyes lifting to him with a quiet intensity. "I'm not glass. I don't break that easily," she said with an edge of irritation. "I've had worse lumps falling off a bicycle. If you'd like to be helpful, you could pour me a little more wine."

Glass . . . his fixation with glass. Uncomfortably, he withdrew his hand and glanced down to accept the plastic cup she thrust at him. Breakable . . . glass. 'I'm not glass,' she'd said, but looking at her, into her suddenly intent blue eyes, his heartbeat quickened. Glass. Glass wasn't the only thing that could be broken . . . she could be broken.

Shuddering, he turned away, striding to the table, his mind suddenly racing again, his heart pounding. She could be broken. He needed only a flash of the pain he'd suffered when Farnsworth had started pawing her to know she could be broken.

Trembling, belatedly, he tried reaching for the wine bottle. His hand retracted, fisting. He'd felt it, seen it. He'd suffered her pain and his rage in one blinding flash as he'd bolted across that alley. Too late! Even in hindsight, he recalled believing that he'd be too late . . . positive that he'd again be too late. She could be broken. He could find her lying . . . He shook his head, refusing. Never again! Never again! Almost too late. He had to get out of here, away from her, away from . . . from this place. Shattered.

"Isaac . . .?"

"That's," he heaved softly, his gaze fixed on the emerald bottle, his mind stopped by the force of her voice slicing through his broken thoughts. "That's not my name."

Her hand touched his elbow, sending sparks through his system as her soft voice soothed, "I know, hon."

Tilting his head, he studied her soft blue eyes, seeing the understanding and feeling as he had earlier. She was beautiful. Her electric blue eyes were as warm and calming as a summer sky. Releasing his fist and lifting his hand, he touched her cheek. Cupping her chin in the nook of his thumb and forefinger, he recalled those seconds when she'd touched his face with such tenderness. How . . . How could she have managed this? He'd steeled himself against the wiles of women. He'd wrapped himself tight against the touch of a woman. Yet here she was, this impertinent, aggravating woman, pricking and probing places he'd not even known existed.

His thumb caressed her chin; he scanned her puffy lips and the wicked thumbprint bruise forming in the cleft of her silken cheek. His gaze locking on her, he penetrated her irises. Unwittingly, probed the places where her heart raced in a staccato rhythm to match his own. He heard her . . .

Mind-bending. 'You wre`shed shild . . .'

But he couldn't stop. Like a miller to a flame, he was drawn toward the warmth, the light inside of her. And her to him . . . to the darkness inside of him.

"You . . . are a vexing woman," he said honestly, wishing he could add malice to his words. He wanted, needed only to feel contempt for her, and that, too, she seemed to grasp.

Her warm eyes sparked in soft amusement. Her puffy lip tilted in a slight smile. "I've been told that on occasion."

Impertinent, he considered, but a smile quivered a corner of his mustache as he dipped his head, brushing a kiss on her unmarred cheek. Stepping backward a pace, he pulled out a chair at the table, touched her shoulder, and sat her down, willing her into acquiescence with his gaze. "I do believe I hear Dr. Blackwell. Do try not to be too stubborn with him. He's rather up in years."

Before she could snap one of her comments, Isaac pulled away and strode to the door, reaching it before the elder knuckles could sustain damage.

Dr. Blackwell, if for no other reason than his romance with history, remained one of the only physicians in town who still meandered from his office to conduct an occasional house call. Out of mutual affection for antiques and a more genteel era, Isaac had become rather fond of the old fellow who dressed impeccably from his visor hat to his polished wingtips.

With a stately elegance and a lofty arrogance, the elder ran his gaze over Isaac even as he started into the room. "You need some ice on your knuckles," he said in quiet observation. Beneath a fluff of bushy brows, which matched the white shock of his neatly cut hair, Blackwell's quick brown eyes panned the room, reaching conclusions and looking at Isaac. "I'm sure you have somewhere to be for a few moments, Isaac. Don't hurry back on my account."

Faintly amused, Isaac nodded and glanced at the young woman still scowling at him from her position at the table. By the resignation of her head resting on her palm and her elbow propped on the table, she wouldn't fight Blackwell. "You're in good hands, sweetheart. I'll see you shortly."

"Don't hurry back on my account either," she threw at him.

Glimpsing Blackwell's curious eyes, Isaac shrugged and smiled, sidestepping into the hallway. His smile vanished the instant he closed the door. His tension mounted even before he reached the narrow stairwell. All too clearly, he heard the din of anxious voices muffled through the thick walls echoing from the main stairway. Paused on the first landing, Isaac shivered uncontrollably.

One or another of the authorities had posted a guard in the hotel lobby, apparently blocking passage to the handful of reporters who'd caught wind of Miss Veronica Bryson's involvement in what was sure to be a media frenzy. If not already, then soon someone would add Isaac Bently's name. His serenity had shattered. He need only consider Sheriff Grant's mention of an award to realize his quiet existence had shattered in one blinding instant of violence . . . and Isaac had felt this coming. Braced against the wall in the narrow stairwell, he realized he might have sensed its advance for weeks.

His lips curved in an angry twist as he considered Grant's words. 110 mph off an exit ramp. If that were true, he'd been in one hell of a hurry to reach Bentwood. What he recalled was feeling like an ass wandering around the airport parking lot. His garment bag strung over his shoulder, his suitcase in hand, he'd swung the Spencer children's gifts at his hip as if he were out for a stroll. He hadn't lied to the Federal agents. He hadn't remembered which car he'd taken, but even now, he couldn't recall what he'd been thinking while meandering through that sea of cars. If not for the security guard taking pity on him, he might still be ambling aimlessly like a blind man in a department store. God knows, he lacked the presence of mind to find even one of his cars, much less the right one.

A media circus. Exposure. The hounding calls and shouts, the accusations . . . the *fear*.

Shuddering, Isaac started off the wall but halted. His gaze already fixed on the corner, he watched Tim clear the top step and freeze with a start.

No humor lingered in Spencer's blue eyes or the natural curve of his lips. He released his hitched breath with his question, "How is she?"

"Blackwell's with her," Isaac answered. "She bumped her head, but it's obviously thick enough to withstand a mild earthquake." Damn it! He'd not intended to be annoyed with her, much less to kindle Tim's amusement. His annoyance thickening toward anger, Isaac cast a scathing glance toward the descending stairway and landed on Tim. "Imagine most of the hounds have taken off?"

"There are still a few reporters hanging around in the back lot," he offered. "You want to tell me what happened in longhand?"

"Farnsworth was apparently waiting for her when she arrived," Isaac spoke with the anger returning in force. He would've preferred the foresight to rain a few more blows on that bristled face. If not for what Cal had tried to do, if not for the aggravation and chaos, then certainly for the bruises now marring that lovely face. A few more blows would've been justified.

"From what I gathered outside, you intervened and put a serious hurting on that boy," Tim commented, trailing his gaze over Isaac as Blackwell had. His gaze lifting, his smirk notching, he commented, "Didn't even manage to get your knees dusty. Must've been a pretty short encounter."

"The asshole was drunk," Isaac said irritably. The last thing he needed was for Spencer to consider him a hero. "I did what I had to do."

"Easy, pal," Tim said with a quiet retraction, reining his amusement, sobering. "What are you planning, now?"

'As an encore?' he nearly snapped but swallowed the words. His attention wavered as he considered the implication. His car remained in an alley, and if he was swift, he might manage to reach his warehouse before any reporters learned where Isaac Bently lived. With any luck, he could be inside his castle before anyone decided to camp on his doorstep . . . and then what? Veronica Bryson. She'd be trapped in this Inn, mobbed when she stepped through the doors, inundated with mail, calls . . . messages. A prisoner to a room in Bentwood House until the authorities released her of the obligation . . . and she wasn't leaving soon. Not anytime soon enough.

"Care if I make a suggestion?" Tim interrupted.

Distracted, Isaac looked at him.

"Depending on how soon Ronnie can travel, I think she'd be a little safer and more comfortable out at my place. Donna's already making up a guestroom . . . and we have two of them if you'd be interested in spending some time in the country," he barely paused. "If we work this right, we can slip both of you out of town before anyone knows you're gone. Once you're out of sight, we can let Sam know where to find you. Knowing how much you like reporters," he said with a quick smirk. "I don't think I oughta have to twist your arm."

Lending the proposition a few seconds of thought, Isaac asked, "How do you plan to make the slip?"

"Things aren't too crazy out back. You could probably get to your car and take it to your place. Pack a bag and I'll be around to pick you up—"

"Won't work," Isaac cut in. "Old lady Handler knows your pickup. We'll have the press on your door in thirty seconds or less." He considered another instant. "Where's your pickup? On the street?"

"Down the alley behind Morrisey's," Tim mused. "I wasn't sure how bad this mess would be, so I sorta slipped in through a backdoor. The same one we'll take to slip out once we work out the details. Most of our guys have already taken off—probably over at Bender Falls."

Isaac considered another moment. "Alright, if we can get her safely to your wheels without being spotted, you can take her to your place. If I park far enough from my shop, I should be able to keep the Jag from getting spotted while I . . ." He wouldn't need to go anywhere. He could hole up in his castle for days . . .

The alarms kept going off . . . over and over . . . the fence alarms wailed . . . He tried putting a pillow over his head, tried . . . but the sound pierced the stuffing, pierced his skull. . .. In the closet . . . sleep in the closet! Hide! . . . *Make them go awwwaaay, Nannna . . . make them gooo!*

"Isaac?"

Jolted, Isaac cringed as the hand clasped his arm, reorienting under the intent gaze. Braced against the wall, he stood, both of his fists shoved in his jeans, his muscles knotted, gripped. Releasing his held breath, Isaac read Tim's curiosity as he had countless times before when the man had witnessed his insanity.

"You're coming out to my house," Tim said firmly.

He nodded, dragging a fist from his pocket and combing his vibrating fingers through his hair. Not even his natural smirk countered Spencer's curiosity or concern. They had been friends too long already for the fellow to remain oblivious of the flashbacks. Shaking his head, glancing toward the ascending steps, Isaac nodded again and pushed off the wall, collecting his balance as well as his scattered thoughts. "Blackwell should be about finished. How . . ." He looked back at Tim. "Where's the backdoor?"

Agitated, Ronnie drew the line at having a needle shoved in her arm. "If you want to leave something slightly stronger than aspirin, Dr. Blackwell, I'd appreciate it, but you're not sticking any bayonet in my arm."

Sighing patiently, the man sat back in the chair that he'd pulled alongside the bed. "I was only suggesting, after an extremely harrowing experience, a mild muscle relaxer might do you some good, dear. If you have an aversion to needles, I can assure you, it won't hurt."

"I have an aversion to my brain turning to mush," she said while pulling her blouse sleeve to her wrist. Grimacing against the twinge of pain in her shoulder, she nearly cursed aloud. She would like about ten more seconds with Cal Farnsworth—ten seconds with her purse in hand. It might be worth replacing her trusty Minolta just to see that big oaf holding his head for a while. Victim or no victim . . . psycho?

By the time Dr. Blackwell produced several sample packets of the latest wonder drug for stress-related ailments, Ronnie wanted him out of the room. She needed a few moments to sit down with her notes and review a few details. Cal Farnsworth might be a mean drunk, but somehow, nothing felt right when she tried fitting him into the shoes of a psycho.

Peace, however, wasn't anytime soon coming. She verified her thought with a mere glimpse of the two sentinels outside the door, a pair of matched aggravations even if she was becoming rather fond of them. As she slipped into her shoes, she heard Bently and Spencer covering the basics with Dr. Blackwell, annoyed when the old doctor spoke to Bently as if offering him care instructions. It was her head! Her possible concussion! Her 'bruises' and 'banged up' body these oafs were discussing! How dare this country doctor, who looked a little like an aging professor on an austere college campus, tell Isaac Bently to ". . . keep an eye on her. She may start to feel nauseous and suffer a few dizzy spells . . ."

Deciding to set Bently straight the moment the doctor exited, Ronnie turned her attention to collecting her messages from the trashcan. Before she could breeze through more than the first two, Tim arrived alongside her, brushing a kiss on her forehead as if they had known each other for years.

Looking into her with as much sincere concern as her other defenders, he commented, "Rough day, huh?"

"The spice of life," she said absently.

Bently was far less sedate. Holding one of the packets of wonder drugs, he arrived carrying a plastic cup already filled with water. "Think you better take one of—"

"Listen," she said and favored him with one of her sweeter smiles . . . something in his eyes, something other than arrogance distracted her from another wounding jab to his ego. He appeared almost worse than he had when standing by the bed and reading those nasty messages. How could he appear so blasted smug one moment? And wear the open wounds of a child the next? "Really," she said, far gentler than she'd intended. "I don't need or want one of those just yet. Maybe a little later, alright? I'll pop one before lying down. The doctor was kind enough to give me an aspirin."

"Maybe, hold off, Sax," Tim commented soberly. "She can take one when we get out to the house." Before she could grasp those words, Spencer turned to her and began outlining the course of action that he and his compadre had schemed up while she was being poked, prodded, and annoyed.

"I can't imagine how I got this old without you two," she said with far more annoyance than she cared to consider. "Has it occurred to either of you that I might not mind remaining behind locked doors—"

"Veronica . . ."

He did it again. He spoke her name with that soft symphony of sounds to slip past her ears and into her heart. How could she refuse a voice like that? A gaze like that? Dear God, the man was a hypnotist . . . no other way to account for this. Somewhere between speaking her name and making his demand, she'd gotten lost. She found herself whisked down the narrow hallway, down the steps to the first floor. Spencer cleared the way with a uniformed officer; Bently held her at the waist while carrying her suitcase strap slung over his shoulder. He wasn't carrying her, but by the time they descended into the basement, she held his arm to offset the sway and thumping. Without fanfare, he scooped her off her feet, and she mumbled against his chest, "I feel like an idiot."

"You feel fine to me," he uttered in the shadows.

"Do you think—" She struggled, seeing stone walls passing in a blur, smelling his cologne tainted slightly with the smell of wet brick and basement dust. "—the professor slipped me . . . a mickey?"

"Does your head hurt, sweetheart?" he asked.

"Uh-huh, pounding, spinning a little."

"I do believe you have a concussion," he said in a clinical voice. "And I don't believe you were ready for a hike. How much further, Tim?"

"Right this way . . ."

"You really didn't go to all this trouble just for a date, did you?"

Spencer had a nice easy laugh. "Son, it was worth every hairy minute of it."

Vaguely, Ronnie sensed them passing through a cavern of boxes and shelves, blinking to offset the dizziness in time to realize they followed a flashlight beam. It struck her odd to find their way paved by a public servant paid to protect private property and prohibit vandals, as well as trespassers. "I hope you own this building, Spencer," she muttered.

"Never mentioned my gramma's maiden name, huh?" he asked as they slid through a narrow slot.

"No," Ronnie managed.

"Bentwood," he answered with a chuckle, and Ronnie shook her head, not doubting it for a second.

His family probably owned the Inn . . . *dear God*. "Dunner's not your spinster aunt, is she?"

"Matter-of-fact, think she is," Tim mused. "But I wouldn't swear to it . . ."

"I wouldn't admit to it," Bently put in dryly. "The woman's a shrew."

Ronnie laughed, uncontrollably squeezing her hand against his neck and shoulder just a little tighter. The situation was too strange, this pair was a little too strange, and Isaac Bently felt all too nice.

In mere seconds, Bently settled her onto the front seat of Spencer's emerald chariot, and even with the whirlwind in her skull, Ronnie dreaded the thought of his departure. In an odd moment, she snagged his hand, probing his troubled eyes, and she understood why he wanted her out of town, away from the mad rush of her colleagues. This wasn't the time to tell him, not the place to remind him, she was a member of that fraternity. She would hold her own against public assault. He was the one who needed to be away from the certain madness that would descend on him when this story leaked.

"Be quick, hon," she said gently.

"Half hour at the most," he said and leaned, brushing a kiss on her cheek, sending tiny sparks tingling through her.

"The man's gonna make me nuts," she uttered after he shut the door.

Starting his pickup, Tim mused, "If it's any consolation, I think the feeling's mutual . . ."

Laying her head back, glimpsing the darkness, thinking and remembering the strange events throughout the evening, Ronnie shook her head slowly. This wasn't supposed to be happening . . . not to her. She had a career, a game plan for her life . . . but it was happening. At this moment, she knew without a doubt that it was happening. She was falling in love with the big jerk . . . less than two lousy days . . . and she was falling in love with this green-eyed-devil. "That's not supposed to happen," she uttered, watching the headlights blaze a path into a wooded lane.

"What's that, Ron?"

"Nothing," she said with a glance to find Tim glimpsing at her, his face cast in a glow of gauge lights. He was a handsome man, too. Bright, witty, charming without a doubt . . . why couldn't she fall in love with someone like Spencer? Why did she have to fall for a guy who failed even to wear his own name? A guy who could lance her to the quick with his strange-colored eyes? A guy who hated her profession from the bottom of his battered heart. "Life's so unfair," she decided.

"Ya know, darlin," Tim mused. "You're not relieving my mind with your muttering. Any chance you're falling asleep? Maybe getting delirious?"

"Why . . . why did you do that today, Tim?" she asked, again looking over at him in the shadows. In the glow of gauge lights, she saw him glance her way and read the tension in his smirk and knitted brow. "Why'd you set us up like that?"

For several seconds she doubted he would answer, but he surprised her, speaking in a low sober tone. "He needs you."

Somehow, that wasn't the answer she'd anticipated, but it wrenched her heart to know the accuracy of that simple, honest statement.

Isaac was wasting time. He was wasting time, and unless he managed to escape soon, he wouldn't leave. He knew them, knew how their mind's worked, how they could persevere. They would breach his security. If they thought he was in here, they would break in and suffer the consequences later. He knew how they operated. Voices and cameras and microphones . . . the images flashed like neon inside his head. His insides trembled with the memories.

A half-hour, Isaac had told Veronica, just a half-hour, but a half-hour had passed.

He'd heard the clocks chiming twice since he'd entered his apartment. He felt them ticking around him, through him. A half-hour, more than a half hour had passed since he'd navigated the darkness and entered his bedroom. The room was dark. The entire apartment was dark. His entire cavernous dwelling lay in darkness except for the soft nightlight in the showroom. Those doors were locked. The alarms were set to protect the showroom . . . but windows could be broken. Security could be disabled. They could invade with flashlights, could poke through his things, his mother's closet . . .

"Oh God," he uttered and gripped his head against the whirlwind raging inside his skull. "Not ten . . . I'm not," Isaac strained softly. "Not the same . . ." This wasn't the same. No one knew him. No one could accuse him. He hadn't done anything wrong . . . hadn't done anything.

'Be quick, hon,' the silky voice slid through his mind torturing him for the thousandth time, stirring him for the first time.

He'd told her a half-hour . . . and he wanted to see her, needed to see her again. The things she made him feel . . .

Struggling, Isaac pushed off his bed, wading through the black curtains to drape from the mahogany canopy overhead. Somehow, he must keep her safe. Must protect her. Trembling, he ignited the lamp and concentrated. Details. He needed his satchel—the smaller of his leather bags. He hadn't unpacked. He checked the contents, although why he bothered was a mystery. He'd known better than to empty the bag. A few extra clothes. His travel kit. Hell, even his extra billfold and a few banking essentials remained in the bag.

Slinging the bag over his shoulder, he turned off the light and strode through the darkness, his insides trembling. Nowhere was safe. "Nowhere," Isaac chanted as he descended through his warehouse. "Nowhere." But he needed to keep moving. He needed to pass through the door, the small side door that opened into the alley. Just an alley, the same alley he'd entered hundreds of times . . . nowhere was safe.

At the wall alongside the door, he leaned, braced, heaving breaths. His heart raced; sweat rose and trickled down his spine. Deep breaths. He'd been here before. If he turned on the lights, he would never pass through the door. The walls would close in. His vision would become a tunnel of rocking, rolling images. Somehow, he must push off the wall, pass through the door, and enter the alley. Once he was outside, he could breathe again. Nowhere safe . . . he could be found, his privacy invaded.

"Ssstop it," he heaved softly, hating the sound of his desperate whisper. This had passed! This part had passed! How could it return so swiftly? How could he feel like this again after all these years? Not a child . . . he wasn't a child any longer. He hadn't truly feared anything, anyone, not in years . . . how could the fear be so fresh and alive inside him again?

"Nnnot a chiiild," he heaved. "Grooown mannn, for Goddd's sake . . . Move. Have tooo mooove . . ."

But it was hard, as hard now as sixteen or seventeen years earlier. His hands shook. His feet molded leadenly on the floor. Cold sweat rolled off his temples, pouring under his shirt collar. There were still so many gaps, so many black holes during that sojourn.

Pushing unsteadily off the wall, Isaac clasped the knob, fumbling the lock open. With a held breath, he yanked the door and propelled himself through the opening, heaving night air in gulps as he pulled the door closed behind him. No one here. No one other than himself to fear. Far away, voices fused in a distant hum; engines vibrated. Closer, crickets chirruped; dogs barked. Stumbling a few steps on the gravel, Isaac collected his balance, the effects draining as he loosened and lengthened his stride.

Free. He'd broken free as he had a million times in the past.

His steps faltered, a sense of something, someone, alarming him. Stopped, he fanned his gaze over his octogenarian nemesis's wild rose bushes that stood higher than the hedge of an English maze. At his temples, the pulse quickened, threatening to become a migraine.

Shaking his head, Isaac continued far more slowly, carefully, watching the darkness, listening for footsteps in his wake. At a rustle of branches, he paused, rubbing at his temples. Someone followed . . .

From one insanity to the next, he realized even as he clung to the shadows, retracing his footsteps to his car. He still felt as if someone followed him, watching from a distance, and that detail determined his direction.

Cautiously, Isaac navigated the back streets, breaking from Bentwood on a southern course, hitting the highway, and lending the Jag rein to fly over the pavement. Fleetingly, he considered Grant's warning, knowing the sheriff hadn't been kidding regardless of his lighthearted tone.

With the feeling of someone on his bumper, Isaac continued past the expressway entrance, swept into the next county without a thought, and nearly reached the next county before the pulse began to ebb. Whatever disturbed the beast inside of him existed in Bentwood.

Cursing his insanity, he doubled back, clinging to the country roads, flying through the curves and brief spurts of a straight dark highway. Whatever he'd been thinking was long gone before he pulled into Tim Spencer's driveway and rolled into the open-bay garage.

Mechanically, the garage door began to descend even before Isaac turned off his engine. By the time he climbed from the car, Tim leaned in the connecting door to his basement, soft light spilling around him, casting his image in silhouette.

"That was one long half-hour," Tim commented as Isaac pulled his bag over his shoulder. "You run into trouble?"

"How is she?" Isaac asked as he strode forward, halting when Tim remained frozen.

"She's sleeping."

"She wasn't supposed to sleep," he remembered absently, trying to read Spencer's expression in the pale light. "I'm supposed to wake her periodically—"

"We've been friends for what . . . about five, maybe six years, now? Is that about right?"

Wary, alarmed, Isaac nodded, "I'd imagine so."

"You want a beer?" Tim asked.

Something told him he might need something more potent. "Not particularly."

"Let's have one anyway," Spencer decided and pushed off the arch, turning and motioning Isaac to follow.

Leaving his bag at the base of the open staircase, Isaac followed Tim through the shadowed living room, not surprised to enter Tim's Cove, where they'd spent many an evening dealing poker and sharing a pint. Settling onto a leather couch, becoming more anxious, he nodded when Tim decided on something stronger and offered bourbon.

"Glass okay? Or are you still on a plastic kick?" Spencer asked.

"Plastic, thank you," Isaac said with an edge, automatically glimpsing the time on a brass sunburst clock on the dark wood wall behind the desk. Good god, almost four a.m. No wonder Tim appeared angry and tense. Studying the coiled posture, Isaac accepted the drink, watching as Tim settled into a cater-corner chair disturbed. His tension mounting, Isaac took the initiative. "Want to tell me what's on your mind?"

With his chair tipped back, ankle crossed, Tim studied him pensively. "Six years is long enough, Sax," he began simply. "Who were you before you popped up in Bentwood?"

Tense, angry, suddenly, he snapped, "Obviously, you've been chatting with someone—"

"Don't start with any of your bullshit," Spencer said in a low voice. "I've known for the better part of five years that you weren't born with the name Isaac Thomas Bently. Some guy comes to town with a lot of money, keeps to himself quite a bit . . . gets a speeding ticket about once a month." Tim shrugged. "Makes a guy start to wonder, and when a guy like me starts to wonder, he does some quiet investigating. What I know is that you changed your name about six months before you came to town. Legally, as far as I can tell, but that's not saying much." He paused, his gaze direct. "The way I figure, when a guy goes to that kind of trouble, he has his reasons, and if he wanted trouble, either to make it or find it, he wouldn't pick Bentwood. I also figured, sooner or later, if that fella meant to be trouble, I'd know about it."

"I always wondered," Isaac said idly, his gaze direct.

"Yea, what's that you wondered about?"

"When the illusion of friendship would shatter."

For a long moment, Tim studied him with a faint hurt emerging behind his determination. "I'm not going to shit you and say we were friends from the get-go, but it's a little late in the game to call it an illusion. Like it or not, Sax, I'm a hell of a lot closer to you than I am with my own brothers and sisters . . . which is why you're going to tell me who the hell you were," he said bluntly. "I can't do a damn thing to keep those Feds off your ass, and I can't stop some fucking reporter from harassing you unless I know what the hell kind of shit you're running from. And don't mistake that, I'm in the thick of this whether you like it or not. Now, why don't you tell me why, exactly, an investigative reporter recognized you all of a sudden this evening? And don't sugarcoat it on my account."

Spencer was too smart, too damned smart not to read Veronica's eyes, her face at that picnic table. His gaze drifting, Isaac sipped the bourbon, considering, realizing the futility of maintaining his anonymity. If Tim knew, then others would know as well. Sooner or later.

"My name was . . . Jade Laquette," he said as he gazed into abstracts realizing how hard this would be, how hard just speaking that name had become. "That's uh . . . it's the name I started with," he continued and looked toward Tim, seeing only concentration, not recognition. "I've changed it a few times before," he admitted quietly and shrugged, looking into his bourbon. Unconsciously, he searched his shirt pockets, finding his cigarettes, lighting one despite a mild tremor in his hand. Again, staring into abstracts, blowing an exhale of smoke, he commented, "Didn't help. Never does. This is the longest I've ever been someone else . . . I became too comfortable." He looked over to Spencer, "I uh . . . I enjoyed living here. Enjoyed the illusion of normalcy. The illusions of friendship and neighbors and faces I recognized from day to day. You don't have that when you move from one city to another . . . one country to another."

"Why do I get the distinct impression that you're talking in the past tense? As if maybe you're planning to depart Bentwood in the not-too-distant future . . .? That just maybe, you were about halfway gone already this evening?"

"Because you're perceptive," Isaac answered.

"So, let me ask you this one again. Who were you? Who was Jade La . . . quette?"

Hard. Extremely hard, this discussion. His gaze listed; his muscles tensed uncontrollably. The pain never stayed buried forever. "Some little asshole who . . . who saw his mother murdered," he answered and caught Spencer's suddenly tense, more intent gaze. "Before it happened," he said quietly. "And while it happened," he added, seeing the tension enhance within Tim's blue eyes. "I made a big splash in the headlines," he continued in a leaden tone. "Reporters loved me. I was the hottest thing since apple pie. Boy-fucking-wonder. I saw her murdered through the eyes of a killer . . . night after fucking night," he said as his gaze wandered. His skin crawled with the first flashes of memory surfacing . . .

Up and moving, Isaac paced a few steps, veered to the window, and pulled the drapes closed. His hand froze, gripping the cord; his gaze locked on his trembling fist. "I . . . I can't . . . cannot do this," he said as he withdrew his hand with a concentrated effort. Turning, he shook his head, finding Tim. "I can't, okay? I thought I could . . . thought I could handle telling you. But I can't. Not you. Not anyone. Not, now. Not, ever."

"Sax—"

"I liked that, too," he said absently, his gaze panning the room, taking in the familiar dark woods. He remembered the laughter and comfortable silences over a poker hand. He remembered the first time Tee had climbed afoot and wobbled a few steps in this room. "Loved being called 'Uncle Sax,'" he said absently and read Tim's worried eyes, smiling faintly. "I never had a family. Not genuine family. My name was Laquette . . . my mother's maiden name. I never imagined I could be an uncle. What your children have given me, I could never repay, not with a thousand gifts."

"They love you, and that has nothing to do with gifts," Tim said in a low thick voice. "Kids have a natural instinct about people."

"This is hard," Isaac said quietly. "Maybe too hard. If your curiosity's satisfied . . . that's not fair," he said absently and walked to the couch. Looking over as he settled onto the cushion, he commented, "I'm not a criminal, Spence. Not even a parking ticket left unpaid from one life to the next. In a sense, I suppose you could consider me an escape artist, but I haven't broken any laws in my endeavors."

"Ever think maybe it's time to stop running, Sax?" Tim asked quietly. "Maybe think about making a home, a life?"

He shook his head. "Not in the cards."

"How old were you when uh . . . when you first changed your name?" Tim asked tactfully.

"I didn't change it the first time," he answered honestly. "I was twelve when it was changed."

"Who changed . . . Adoption," Tim said.

Not entirely amused, Isaac shrugged, "In a sense."

"What sense?"

"I was a bastard, Tim, but I did have a father for a time," he answered, refusing to let those wounds open, holding his gaze steady. "Suffice it to say, I had the opportunity to change my name again when I turned eighteen, and I made that decision on my own."

"So, basically, you didn't start running on your own," Tim said simply. "But you can stop on your own," he continued. "If you . . ."

He'd begun shaking his head, his gaze steady.

"What, no?"

"I can't remain here," he said evenly. "I won't be able to remain Isaac Bently."

For another long moment, Tim paused, his thoughts turning as he swirled his bourbon. "Publicity," he said absently. "That's what you're afraid of. What you're running from. You're afraid someone will make you as . . ." The revelations tumbled in his mind; his gaze fixed.

Even watching the revelations dawn, Isaac became tense. Tipping the tumbler to finish his drink, he pushed from his chair. It would come, now. Spencer was too good at his profession, and he knew too many of Isaac Bently's quirks. How long before the uncertainty and fear emerged? How long before Spencer decided this—he—was a freak or insane? A *monster?*

"You've . . ." Tim's voice trailed, searching, then finding the words. "You really have seen these murders."

He'd almost done it, almost clasped the neck of the bottle, but his hand had frozen again. "I'm fucking insane," he uttered and looked at Spencer. His hand shuddered as he retracted it. Foolishly, he stood holding his empty plastic glass, darting glances from the bottle on the sideboard, back to Tim. "I am, you know? And maybe that's why I need to keep moving. What I need to keep escaping. Insanity. It's a curse."

Pushing from his chair, Tim joined him at the sideboard, lifted the uncapped bottle, and filled the tumbler nearly to the brim. Setting the bottle down, he looked over directly. "You are seeing them, aren't you?"

"I can't help you," he said quietly and started to turn, halted with the grip on his forearm. Every muscle cringed; every nerve pricked.

"I didn't ask you to help, Sax," Tim said tensely. "I only asked if you see them."

"I . . ." He shook his head. "I can't see them."

"Don't shit me. I've seen you do some strange things. I've chalked a lot up to coincidence, but not all. Like the time you called me at work to mention you hadn't seen Evan Barker in town for a few days, and if I got a chance, I oughta stop in there real soon. The next thing I know, I'm doing CPR on a guy at four in the morning, and what do I find on his kitchen table after the paramedics arrive . . .? A sales receipt from Olden Time with the same day's date . . ." He paused, his gaze steady. "That's one example, but I could think of about a dozen more off the top of my head. Not even counting how many times people walked into your shop and found some heirloom or keepsake they were looking for. So, don't bullshit me, okay? You have a talent for seeing things, for knowing things, and what I want to know is . . . did you see Farnsworth and Engler murdered."

"I won't . . . cannot let myself see them," he spoke in slow, careful syllables. "Can't you understand that? I cannot let myself see those murders. I can't . . . I can't do it. It's . . . that part of me . . . I had to shut it off. I had to put a lid on it and screw it down tight. I cannot . . . will not let myself see what you're afraid I've seen. I don't . . . don't even let myself see what you're accusing me of seeing. In my fucking head, I didn't see Barker . . . Didn't know why the fuck you needed to see him, check on him . . . Consciously, I can't do it, Tim. Not ever . . ."

"But it's still there, huh, Sax?" Tim asked quietly, glancing down at the tumbler trembling in Isaac's hand, to the bottle. His gaze lifted. "It was there last night when you lost it for a while in your bathroom. It's there every time you reach for a piece of glass and can't bring yourself to touch it. You might have put a lid on it, but that lid's having a hell of a time staying on . . . and that's gotta be real goddamn scary."

"It's gonna shatter," he said absently, looking into Tim's studied gaze, feeling suddenly ten years old. The shudder coursed the length of him, tears leaped into his eyes before he could blink them away. "I'm gonna shatter."

Tim's grip firmed; he shook his head. "I don't think so, Sax. Any guy who—"

He nodded. "If she gets hurt . . . I won't be able to protect her. I won't be able to save her."

"You already did. She's upstairs, and she's fine."

More than anything in the world, he wanted to believe those words but the pulse, the throbbing at his temple, held him from surrendering. "I have to leave," he said and turned from Tim's grasp. Walking a few steps, he braced and wiped his eyes with the heel of his palm. "I have to go," he said more firmly.

"You know, no matter where you go, you'll be taking this with you, pal."

"I made a mistake," Isaac said as he collected more of his equilibrium. "I never should have remained in Bentwood this long." He looked over at Spencer. "I never should have allowed myself to become close to you, to your family, but I won't apologize. The time I've spent here has been too important to trivialize with a mundane apology."

"Why'd you come back tonight, Sax?" Tim asked. "What made you turn around?"

No answer came readily. All the reasons he should've continued down the highway and lost himself in the masses of a city flashed neon in his mind. In answer to Spencer's simple question, however, his temple throbbed. "I'm tired," he said abruptly. "If you don't mind, I'd like to check on . . . Miss Bryson. She's supposed to be rousted every few hours."

"Last door on the right upstairs," Tim answered. "Donna fixed the room across the hall for you if you want to use it."

Taking his bourbon with him, Isaac strode from the room, lifting his bag at the base of the staircase. When he settled onto the mattress alongside Veronica's sleeping form, he realized exactly why he'd returned. A small lamp in one corner of the room emitted a soft glow, no more than a night-light intensity, and yet her fluff of raven curls shimmered in dark contrast to the floral-print linens. How incredibly young she appeared. Her face tipped into the fluff; a spray of curls scattered on her high brows. Even in sleep, her lovely lips curved. His heart ached as he studied the slight swelling, the brush of a bruise across her cheek. No anger would come, now. Only the distress and pain of his failure remained and added greater reason to leave. Far too easily, he could be attracted to her. For her, he'd returned, and for her, he'd depart.

Carefully, he fingered the soft curls, taking in the contour of her shoulder, the spread of her long ivory fingers resting on the pillow in front of her face. She was so incredibly beautiful, this irritating woman, even her name. "Veronica . . .?" he whispered, touching the curls gently off her forehead. "Sweetheart . . .?"

Her brow furrowed as if puzzled; her lips twitched with a soft smile. Her long lashes fluttered and started to lift.

"Shhh, darlin," he uttered. "Nothing to worry about now . . ."

"Mmm-hmm," she murmured, her lashes lifting more. In the subdued light, she tipped her head, her eyes misted and murky. "Hmm . . ."

"Shhh, mon amour," he uttered, wishing he hadn't awakened her, wishing he'd trusted his senses enough to know she slept well. Leaning, he brushed a kiss on her forehead. His hand lighted gently on her shoulder, and even that slight caress affected some part of him. "Go back to sleep, sweetheart . . ."

"I'mmm having a verrry nice dream," she murmured, her eyes already closed when he lifted, her lips smiling. "I like jade . . . lovely color . . . mmm, the man . . ."

Tipping his head, he felt the smile slipping onto his lips. She would hate him in the morning. But for now, he appreciated the haunted smile that seemed to linger on every soft contour of her face. She truly was beautiful, and if he tarried too long, he would surely wake her. The instant he raised his hand, however, her lashes flickered, and she murmured, "Don't go . . ."

His heart gripped; his hand slipped to rest over her warm, soft fingers. Beneath his touch, her fingertips turned, locking over the edges of his palm.

"Better," she muttered.

She was right. It was better. For the first time in his adult life, he held a woman's hand, satisfied with that simple gesture, content just to sit and watch her sleep. He suffered no desire to hurry away like a thief in the night.

CHAPTER 18

Waking in a strange room to strange sounds had never bothered Ronnie. Waking with a thumping headache and stiff muscles was no more natural than finding a man's face on the pillow next to her or feeling his hand clasped loosely over her own. If not for the pounding at the base of her skull, she might believe this a dream . . . a very nice dream.

He slept like a little boy. Head pillowed on a fold of his arm, his hair a wreck of loose dark waves to tumble over his temple and shade his eyes. Even in sleep, the shadows remained. Only an echo of a sad smile lingered on his mustached lips, which could flash from arrogant to sinister in an eye blink. His lashes flickered. She watched his eyelids ripple, remembering the sleeping stages. The REM stage was the dream state, the state where the eyeballs continued to move, seeing pictures and images created inside the mind. Beneath his hair, his brows were drawn slightly, troubled . . . and she ached to reach up, to smooth those soft lines, to touch the frown from his lips.

Tipping her head on the pillow, flinching only slightly, she panned her gaze over his shoulders, down the long, lean length of him, breathing the scent of his cologne and remembering that kiss. If ever she'd encountered a male physique she'd like to explore, this was it. Too clearly, she remembered those moments in his arms. Even dazed, she'd known the strength and comfort of his hold, reveled in the steady beat of his heart against her ear with her head against his muscled shoulder . . . and she better figure out how to slip away from his hand before her thoughts sailed any further astray.

For God's sake, even asleep, he was dangerous!

Very slowly, barely moving, she started slipping her hand from beneath his palm, her eyes on his for the first sign of movement. Somehow, she wasn't prepared for the instant clasp of his hand before his long lashes parted. Lazily, his face tilted, and he leveled his murky gaze on her. With her hand trapped in a careful, encompassing clasp, she could only gaze in stunned surprise as his mustache curved into what could pass for a pleasant smile.

"Bonjour belle."

The devil spoke French*! French* at . . . at whatever the hell time it was in the morning! And his eyes carried a mischievous amusement to make her wary in rising seconds. Apparently, he was accustomed to waking up with strange women in strange beds, ready with a smooth line and quick smile.

He skidded her hand over the pillow to his lips and brushed a kiss on her fingertips . . . and Ronnie had a feeling this fellow knew how that touch tingled through her hand and zinged her brain.

"Are you awake?" she asked him sweetly.

"Mm-hmm. Quite."

"Then you won't mind getting up and finding your own bed, will you, dear? This one's occupied."

"Woman, you do wake up testy," he said with a passive smile. "Or is it—?" He rolled his head backward, affecting a more comfortable pose as he slid his gaze down her length. By the grace of God, her teddy-bear nightie remained covered under a lightweight flowered spread. His gaze returned, misty and amused. "Waking with a man in your bed makes you nervous?"

"Obviously, waking with a strange woman isn't a problem for you, Mr. . . . Casanova. Now, do you mind? I'd like to get up."

His eyes changed; the amusement vanished. Tense in a split second, he asked, "How are you feeling?"

She barely considered claiming a headache when she realized he was seriously concerned. Recalling how he'd tossed her around from one place to another, she decided, "Not too bad. I would like to get up, though, if you wouldn't mind."

"As much as I know I may regret indulging you, sweetheart, I suppose, now is not the time," he said somewhat wistfully and uncoiled, starting to rise. Stopping partway, he leaned and brushed a kiss on her forehead, winking as he retracted and slid smoothly to his feet.

The man was a devil, pure and simple, a devil.

At the door, he paused. "Do you always wake at the crack of dawn?"

"Internal alarm," she shrugged.

"You should try sleeping a little longer, but if that's not possible, you should at least remain in bed. I'll bring you a cup of coffee shortly."

He was gone before she could protest, and only one thought surfaced in his wake. She needed to get up, get dressed, and try to make sense of the evening past.

Only vaguely, she recalled arriving in this room, mildly disorientated to wonder if she were in a resort. Private bath, closet space, and thick rugs underfoot, the room sported a wall of windows with floor-length curtains and drapes drawn to offer only thin strips of light. Donna had hung her clothes and fussed over her, loitering inside the room, and waking Ronnie more than once if her faulty memory served.

Collecting a pair of jeans and a deep yellow, long-sleeved summer blouse, Ronnie navigated to the bathroom to check the damage. A thorough scan in the vanity mirror lent her pause to wonder why Bently had stuck around as long as he had; she looked like crap. It could have been worse, though. It could have been a great deal worse if not for Isaac's arrival. For whatever reason the fellow had followed her, she could only be grateful. A puffy lip, a bruised jaw, and a few thumbprint bruises on her arms and wrists were scant comparisons to what that drunken idiot had intended.

Belatedly, the anger surfaced . . . anger at Cal Farnsworth for what he'd intended, anger at herself for not being able to defend herself when it counted, anger over letting herself land in that predicament. If she'd halted that spontaneous interview as she'd intended and waited for a clear picture of the situation before speaking to family members, that wouldn't have happened. Everything in Cal's case history pointed toward aggression rather than the whipped puppy he'd portrayed on the street. She should've been prepared. She shouldn't have allowed herself to be affected by the man's bereavement. If she'd have researched him before that interview, she'd have maintained a far more cautious distance, a more objective viewpoint.

Making use of the shower and finding a few more bruises on her legs, on her shoulder, and hip, her anger grew. She'd press charges against Farnsworth. Being drunk was no excuse for attempted rape, and maybe the gals around Bentwood found that treatment acceptable or feared repercussions, Veronica Bryson had no such qualms.

As she began applying cosmetics to soften the battle scars, Ronnie realized the problem in her thinking. While she believed Cal Farnsworth dangerous, she still couldn't pigeonhole him into the role of a psychopath. The profile was all wrong. History of violent behavior, yes. But the mind of a serial killer? A genius? Not hardly. More the mind of a bully. She couldn't imagine Cal Farnsworth plotting the murders—not his father's, not Engler's—and those murders were plotted.

What evidence did Sheriff Grant have, and what was Mark Jarvins' take on that evidence?

Questions humming in her mind, her senses already kicking into high gear, Ronnie dug her notebook from her purse. Carrying the bag with her, if only to find aspirin and a cigarette when she wanted one, she made her way from the room. No others in the household stirred. She found Bently by following the scent and sound of perking coffee. He'd taken time for a shower. Like her own, his hair still lay in dark wet strands. He wore socks, no shoes, and his soft cotton shirt hung open as if he'd deliberately strived for a casual, natural seduction. If so, he'd succeeded.

With a soft black mat of curls sliding down his lean muscled chest and tapering under the snap of his jeans, his head tipped with a shag of wet locks on his brow, and a cocky smile curving a corner of his mustached lips . . . he looked like a model for a blue jean commercial. Or a macho cigarette ad with the smoke curling about his hand. The man was walking sex. No other explanation, Ronnie decided and gulped a breath under his shaded green gaze.

"Seems to me, you're supposed to be lying down," he commented, still leaning against the counter, his ankle crossed and foot hitched.

He probably possessed a little black book the size of an Atlas!

"I don't recall agreeing to any such thing," she said while avoiding more than a casual glance in his direction. Nonchalantly, she sidled around the counter toward the coffeemaker over which he seemed to be standing guard. She could use an aspirin or two if only to offset the headache he was giving her. Flopping her purse on the counter, she waded through the contents, finding the bottle with relief. She could still feel him watching her, and she wondered how he managed to make her nervous without even opening his mouth.

This was insane! Sidestepping, Ronnie collected a glass, drawing water from the spigot. Last evening before the chaos, she'd decided never to speak to him again, and since then . . . he'd been her every waking and sleeping thought. This wasn't how Ron Bryson investigated a homicide, not how she intended to continue.

She needed to gather a tight rein on the hormones this devil unleashed. Far too much work remained to solve this case, and she couldn't afford to be sidetracked every blasted time this—

His arm slid about her, his hand slipped under her chin and tipped her head, and her thoughts skidded out a backdoor as his lips touched down. No accounting for it. Soft as silk, his lips brushed against her own. His hands ignited sparks, touching her cheek, her hip, drawing her to become a part of him. Electric current tingled through every fiber of her body. Her hands slid over his muscled chest. Her palm paused of its own volition, recording the drumbeat of his heart before her fingers rose into the damp tangle at his collar. She heard him groan, a soft, pained sound, and she shared the quickening between them. By the hungry pursuit of his tongue twining about her own, she sensed his rising distress equaling her anticipation. For the first time in her life, she recognized a desire to consummate that final act of union. She wanted nothing more than to join her spirit with another and soar beyond the confines of her body. She wanted to become one with him. Sensations she'd never known burned through her as his hands skimmed over her, drawing her through a thin ethereal barrier.

Heaving a breath, he drew from her lips. His soft hazel eyes turned emerald, as stunned, as shocked as she felt while floating on the edge of physical escape. "Good God," he huffed softly, his breath ragged. His hands and body vibrated against her.

"My senti-ments exa-ctly," Ronnie heaved, looking into him, knowing, if not this man . . . none.

A quivering smile touched a corner of his lips; innocent bewilderment touched his eyes. Head canted, he appeared as puzzled and befuddled as a child. "I would love to make love to you," he uttered demurely as if those words were foreign on his tongue. His eyes softened, searching, near pleading with silent hope as bright as the flame of desire.

She wanted nothing more at this moment, not one thing more in the world. A hesitant smile forming, she felt her wariness and bewilderment mixing. On the verge of surrender, on the cusp of a decision that she knew she'd never regret—

"Yuck! Kisssing a-*gain*."

Jolted to the earth, cheeks flushed and flamed, Ronnie spun her gaze as sharply as Isaac.

The little boy stood at the end of the counter. Hair tussled, he wore space-ship-covered PJs wrinkled and askew on his stout frame, dragging a blanket at his barefooted heels. Fists on hips, Tee bounced his big blue eyes from one to the other, scowling critically at his adopted uncle. "Unnncle Sax," he drawled with a tone of indignation. "Whatcha *doing kisssing* her a-*gain*?"

"Lad, shouldn't you be in bed?" Isaac asked with a careful tone.

"Is *mornin'*!" Tee announced with further indignation and Isaac withdrew slowly, resigning to the interruption. The little boy took his cue. A smile broke across his face, spreading to his eyes as he flew across the floor. His sturdy arms flew upward to be caught and lifted. "G' mornin', Unc' Sax!"

Dazed, Ronnie eased back against the counter, needing the edge of the cabinet to collect her balance. Amused, she watched the youngster replace her, strangling Bently in a neck lock, smacking a kiss on his cheek. The laughter in his eyes was worth the price of admission, and Ronnie was only more amused when Uncle Sax sent her a helpless, near apologetic smirk. When she returned his smile, his eyes flashed a strange intensity before warming. Considering what she might have just done and where that kiss had been heading, Ronnie suffered a conflict of gratitude and regret at the little tike's timing. She forgave him wholeheartedly when he turned his charm her way, offering a delightful, "G' mornin'! Miss Bi'son!"

"A very good morning to you, Tee," she mused, thinking this morning was certainly off to a great start.

With the ease of a man who enjoyed children, Isaac kept hold of the boy, pouring the coffee that had just finished perking. His smile lingering, a spark of mischief and something closely resembling determination in his eyes, he handed her a cup.

Killer smile. Killer eyes. The man was a devil.

He was also not quite as composed as he portrayed. She detected the tiniest flinch in his eyes as Tee squirmed to reach an overhead cupboard. Not completely naive, she read the evidence of his predicament to notice where those bare feet were wiggling. Far more amused and strangely elated, she knew herself partly responsible for his current distress. Shallow comfort considering her own heightened sense of awareness and the vibrations still echoing through her system. If that were a sample of what his kisses could do, she dared to wonder what the rest could be like. And as if he sensed her doing exactly that, the devil winked over Tee's rumpled head, sending her a cockeyed, faintly arrogant smirk.

The man was a natural-born nuisance, Ronnie decided and sipped her coffee, trailing her gaze to her notebook. Work. Her work had always provided an effective distraction against the internal kibitzing of intimate relations, and with calm resignation, she realized where her priorities should lie.

Glancing at her watch, Ronnie oriented, suddenly, preoccupied. She'd left word at the Inn for Mark and Len before retiring. She'd placed the obligatory call to her parents to assure them of her safety, promising to call again soon . . . After which, she'd spent countless miserable moments thinking about Isaac Bently. An enigma, this man who plopped Tee on a high stool at the bar counter and freed his hands to fulfill the child's demands for cereal and juice.

Over and above the fact that she was probably falling in love with him, his past remained an intrigue and mystery. Far more clearly than the details of her research while writing her thesis six years earlier, Ronnie remembered the question that had burned in her mind, the question which had become the theme of her paper. 'Fact or Fiction: Where do investigation and fabrication merge in today's journalism?' The media coverage of Madame Laquette's murder had posed as a masterpiece of misrepresentation. Only three facts had run true from one article to another. First, Madame Laquette, a psychic advisor to some of the most influential names in government eighteen years ago, had been murdered assassination-style at point-blank range in her home. Second, her ten-year-old son had discovered her body. Third, the crime remained unsolved. Mismanaged facts were too numerous to list, only beginning with how Jade Laquette had managed to find his mother.

One particularly fascinating article implied astral projection, slamming the concept of psychic phenomena in every cutting word. The entire article had been an editorial sniggering at the believers of astrology and paranormal disturbances . . . and hanging a ten-year-old boy on the cross to be crucified. Not exclusively, that article had implied the boy had conspired with 'guardians' to make a name for himself and secure his importance to his mother's clientele.

'Psychic or Scam Artist?' 'Nostradamus Reincarnate?' 'Murder or Hoax?' God, the list had ranged from ludicrous to wicked, accusing Madame Laquette of everything from staging her death to boost her 'career' to committing 'suicide.' Accusing her son of everything from being a gold digger . . . to a *murderer* in one truly vicious assault.

Even now, Ronnie wondered how those journalists had justified their participation in that scandal. She'd questioned what type of machine had motivated so many *professionals* to write about what should have been an event confined to a small space in The Washington Post. Madame Laquette had privately counseled some of the biggest names in DC, but her fame hadn't extended beyond DC until after her death. At least one reporter had shared Ronnie's curiosity and alluded to a government conspiracy, nearly accusing someone in government of murdering Madame Laquette. The article had triggered a dozen others, arousing yet another faction of weirdoes to rally for or against the government and further persecute the deceased psychic advisor and her son.

With his hands touching her shoulders, Ronnie started from her thoughts, awakening to a tingle down her arms, her back. At some point, she'd turned toward the window. Her focus cleared to the image of forest and flowers. Sun streams spilled like strobes to glisten on dew-dampened leaves and brilliant petals. Jade Laquette. Even his name conveyed an aura of mystery, offering a paradox of thoughts, from exotic oriental lands and ancient mystics to images of moonlight romance on the French Riviera. Tilting her head, her thoughts as murky as her eyes, Ronnie found him looking over her shoulder, smiling ever so slightly, a touch of curiosity in his gaze.

"I'm sorry if I startled you, sweetheart," he said smoothly, his gaze still searching, still flaming. "You truly were a little lost in your thoughts, and I'm vain enough to believe you were thinking about me."

Turning within his grasp, putting her back to the counter, she considered how easily she could be woven into his spell, but alas, too many questions remained unanswered. "At the risk of inflating your sizable ego, hon, you're right," she said while trying not to melt under that spark of delight in his eyes. "Unfortunately, I have work to do," she said carefully.

His focus held steady, but the soft shine had already begun to ebb as he commented, "As I recall, you don't have a deadline, and you truly should be resting."

With him, upstairs . . . and her brain taking a backseat to the flood of adrenaline he sent rushing through her system with the soft massage of his thumbs on her shoulders. She shook her head with an effort, forcing her concentration as she held his gaze. A psychopath . . . serial killer . . . Cal Farnsworth's assault. She needed to resolve those issues and finish what she'd started. Then . . . only then, could she afford the time to investigate what she felt within his arms.

"It isn't right." She struggled with her thoughts, collecting and gathering her wits against a tide of emotions she couldn't afford to feel at this moment. "Cal . . . Cal Farnsworth . . . it's not right," she said and read his flash of anger. How easily she could believe he hated Farnsworth for what he'd attempted to do to her . . . and the quick sympathy on the heels of his outrage only enhanced her belief.

"He won't hurt you again," he said with a strange conflict in his eyes. "If understood Sheriff Grant last evening, Cal won't be harming anyone ever again."

"You don't understand—" She'd almost . . . *almost* called him 'Jade.' Recovering smoothly from that near catastrophe, she knew he'd registered the glitch even as she continued, "Cal Farnsworth . . . he's probably an alcoholic. Aggressive and dangerous, I'll grant you, but . . . but I don't—"

"Veronica, please," he interrupted quietly. "It's too early in the morning to discuss Farnsworth. Why don't I make breakfast? You could take your coffee out on the deck, and I'll join you shortly. For a little while, at least, we can enjoy the tranquility and share a pleasant morning."

His words were music, a lullaby to soothe and comfort, and how easily she could be drawn toward that end with him. "I can't," she said while firming her conviction. She needed suddenly to escape his touch, to gain distance where she might find the rational thoughts that sailed from her mind when he spoke. Stepping aside, she broke the connection of his hands, recovering her coffee cup and moving to the pot. With her back to him, she continued carefully, quietly. "This isn't how I operate, Isaac. I came here for a reason, and I have to finish it."

Turning, coffee cup in hand, she leaned at her hip, glancing off the little boy munching happily and watching them with idle curiosity. Children's minds were such busy little machines. Lifting her gaze to find Isaac studying her far more intently, she continued with an effort. "I don't know what evidence was found to charge Farnsworth with anything other than what we both know he's guilty of, but that's one of the things I need to find out. The man might be an aggressive idiot with a violent streak a mile wide, but I don't believe he's capable of—" She refrained from using any number of colorful clichés with the tender ears present. "Homicide."

"You can't possibly be that naive," Isaac said with an edge that enhanced his clipped English accent. "After last night—especially—I'd think you'd have a better perspective on what that particular *idiot* is capable of. I'd think you'd want justice served."

"At what cost?" she asked shortly, her gaze heating in reflection of his. "At the cost of another life? I don't think so, Isaac, and this conversation is pointless," she realized. "Until I know what evidence Sheriff Grant has, I can't very well dispute it."

"Why, in God's name, would you want—? Never mind," he said irritably and lifted his plastic cup off the counter.

A cute little plastic mug with cartoon characters dancing in a ring, she noted and fought a tug of amusement at the contradictory image. He truly appeared agitated, if not furious, while drinking from a plastic cup that he'd apparently chosen for himself . . . and her cup wasn't much better. Smiling animated figures danced in her hand. A full wooden tree of glass mugs stood alongside the coffeemaker on the counter. Shaking her head, she met his still angry eyes. "I need to make a few phone calls."

"By all means, there's a phone in the living room," he said aridly.

Carrying her cup, she slipped her purse and notebook off the counter and glimpsed Tee as she passed, noting the boy's speculation even as he smiled around a spoonful of cereal. She rounded a corner into the living room just as Donna cleared the bottom step.

By no surprise, Donna appeared as chipper as a schoolgirl, complete with jeans, pony-tale, and a T-shirt. Concern flashing through her eyes, she hurried a step before seeming to realize Ronnie wasn't about to fall on her face. "You shouldn't be up, yet," she said smoothly. "I thought it was Sax down here with Tee."

"He is," she commented. "They're both in the kitchen. I was just about to use the phone if you didn't mind?"

Her brow troubled, she asked, "How are you feeling this morning?"

"Right as rain," Ronnie said offhandedly and smiled. "Really, Donna, it wasn't that big a deal. I'll be fine."

"Do you still have a headache?"

"It's not bad," she admitted. "And I do need to use the phone."

"Of course, hon. Either here in the living room or in Tim's Cove if you'd rather a little privacy," she said and motioned to the arched doorway past the steps.

Accepting the latter, Ronnie offered her thanks and continued to the Cove. A man's domain, clearly, the Cove consisted of heavy furniture, dark wood, carved teak sculptures of wildlife on the stands, and heavy base lamps. With one set of drapes drawn, hazy light spread across half the room. She found the phone on the corner of a masculine mahogany desk. Tim's Cove, she considered while settling into his leather chair, scanning the room, and noticing more than a few expensive knickknacks from mantel clocks to brass spittoons. As she'd suspected after seeing the Spencer home last evening, Tim didn't survive on a policeman's salary alone. He kept his hand in at least one family business or another.

Within seconds after Mark answered, hearing the hostility in his voice, Ronnie strained to rein her temper; after all, Mark had probably not slept. Getting past his outrage over her quiet exodus from the hotel . . . his anger over her leaving a message and not finding him personally to arrange for her safety. Getting past his implication that she was holed up in some sleazy hotel with none other than Isaac Bently, Ronnie asked in controlled aggravation. "Why are they charging Farnsworth with murder?"

Stopped, his breath held, Jarvins hesitated long enough to count to five hundred before speaking in a steady, sober tone. "Let me ask you this, Ronnie. Last night, when he attacked you, did you notice anything . . .? Say, about his hands? I know it was dark, but you might have noticed something peculiar . . ."

Considering, remembering, she gazed into abstracts, recalling the image of Cal backing her against the car. His right arm had swung. The heel of his palm slapped the hood above her shoulder; the bottle had smacked the driver's door window. Tense, she played the scene through her mind, forcing herself to concentrate, to recall details. His fingers had locked on her wrist, his hands groped, bruising. His mouth—

Drawing a breath, she said, "I don't remember anything out of the ordinary, Mark."

"Think, Ron," he said carefully, apparently remembering and depending on her knack for recording details.

At the peak of chaos, she forgot nothing. She'd remembered even a tiny mole on a face in semi-darkness as that face had gnarled into an insane mask, as the hands had clasped her throat, cutting off her oxygen supply. Forcing the image away, she drew upon the evening past, calling Cal's sneering face to the foreground. Fleetingly, she reviewed the memory of him growling and slurring his demands and compared that image to the man who had stood, straining his words through an impromptu interview. Vaguely, she recalled holding his hand in quiet support . . . his hand. She'd held his hand outside the station. Unwittingly, she'd formed the attraction, the connection, which he'd misinterpreted. She'd set herself up to become a fixation in his already tortured mind, but how innocent that creep had seemed. Nearly despondent over the loss of his father . . . and yet, he'd sounded incredulous with the mention of accusations, of being a suspect in his father's murder.

"Damn it," she heaved softly. "He didn't do it, Mark," she said while shaking the thoughts from her mind. "He's ill . . . but it's the wrong sickness. He didn't commit these murders. You know it. I know it. The profile's all wrong. He doesn't have the mind to plot murder. He might have hated his father, might have despised him, but he would've acted on those emotions instantly. He wouldn't have waited." She hesitated, hearing Jarvins' silence, feeling his similar thoughts. "I'm right."

"He had both rings on his fingers," Mark said quietly. "Both missing rings. One on each hand. He uh . . . he's claiming he doesn't know how they landed on his fingers. Claims he never saw Engler's ring before. He was still fairly drunk."

"That's the evidence? The only evidence?"

"We dusted the rings for prints and got a few good partials, Ronnie. Farnsworth's a match on both, but no others."

Listening, Ronnie heard Mark's doubt. "You don't believe it either."

"I need you to think about something else, honey," Mark said carefully, his tension unmasked. "I need you to tell me if there was anyone else . . . If you saw anyone else outside that Inn last night?"

Considering, she shook her head absently. "Cal came out of the dark from the front of my car. I didn't see him until I was closing the door."

"Now, tell me this . . . Did you . . . Is it possible when you bumped your head . . .? Did you pass out for any length of time?"

Oh, God. The implication was there, in that single question. Was there a moment when Isaac Bently could've slipped those rings onto Cal Farnsworth's fingers? And she did remember vaguely . . . a feeling of darkness closing in, of sinking into Isaac's arms but she hadn't passed out or hit the dirt. She remembered the strength of his arms, her shoes skimming the gravel, and she'd awoken fully in his arms.

"No," she said with quiet conviction. "And I don't think I like the implication."

"You're lying," he said quietly into her ear. "And I know I don't like that implication.

Mark believed Isaac Bently was capable of murder. It was in his voice, in his words.

"He has an alibi, Mark," she said in a chilly tone, recalling Sheriff Grant's interrogation.

"Bullshit," Mark snapped. "If you mean that half-assed interview with Grant last evening? It's bullshit, Ronnie, and you're letting your emotions get in the way of this one. You're falling for this son of a bitch, and you've already lost your perspective," he said with bitter determination. "Some half-assed deputy claims to have seen a car . . .? Listen, dear. This guy, Bently? He's smart. Possibly a goddamn genius, and he's as squirrelly as a three-dollar bill. There's something not right about him."

A great deal not right about him, she could admit if only to herself, but being a psychopathic killer . . .? His mother's murder was never solved. *God! Stop it!* Child prodigy . . . his mother's prodigy . . . scam. *Stop it!* All those reporters twisting the facts, fabricating, questioning. For months . . . the articles had spanned six months. Those reporters had relentlessly hounded a ten-year-old boy, pounding on the twisted evidence . . . Max. Max had answered that call, and he knew the child's innocence.

"Ronnie, he had time," Mark said in her ear, careful, persuasive. "He had time. Plenty of time to find his car, drive like a bat out of hell to reach his destination, do the deed, and return to his house. He could have even backtracked on country roads and come off that exit to be spotted by a hapless deputy. I talked to the men I had surveilling him last night . . . He was hitting about 135 mph when they lost him." Mark hesitated. "A hundred and thirty-five, Ronnie. He could have reached Bentwood in under an hour from the airport . . . and I still haven't found anything on him from his alleged trip to England. We have him clearing customs on both sides of the ocean, then nothing. No credit cards. No traveler's checks. No listing on any Isaac Bently staying at any Inns so far . . ."

"He doesn't—fit—the profile, Mark," she said with quiet conviction, refusing to see, not letting herself admit that, in a way, he did. His mother's murder . . . unsolved.

"We don't know that," Mark spoke in her ear. "We don't know that at all yet, and I'll tell you, it scares the hell out of me that you're with him now. This character, he's a loose nut, but he probably is a genius. God knows the morning papers have turned him into the eighth natural wonder. A hero. And I don't care for that scenario either, Ronnie. This guy is too smart, and I can imagine him taking advantage of last night's situation. He frames Cal. He becomes a hero all in one fell swoop. He's probably laughing his ass off this morning."

He wasn't laughing his ass off. Presently, he leaned in the doorway across the room, arms crossed, watching Ronnie with a strange intensity. A glimmer of a disheartened smile touched a corner of his lips.

And God help her, she couldn't disguise the questions spiraling in her eyes. Was it even possible? Could he be capable of cold-blooded murder? Of the torture preceding the final blows on those gentlemen? She didn't truly know him. She knew what she felt when he looked at her. She knew the thrill of his touch. But she didn't know the man. Not what he felt, what he thought, not where he'd lived, or how he'd lived for the past eighteen years. She knew absolutely nothing about this fellow who was winding her into a spell of his captivating eyes. He was capable of violence, that much she did know. He could be dangerous—

"Ronnie?" Mark spoke in her ear. "I'd like to pick you up. Just tell me where you are, and I'll come get you. We'll have you on a plane this morning, and I'll have a car waiting for you in DC. I've already been on the phone with your brother."

"I'm not going anywhere, Mark," she said quietly, her gaze locked on Bently.

"Damn it, Ronnie, listen to me," Jarvins said with an edge. "If I'm right about this guy—"

"You're not," she cut him off shortly. "I have to go, Mark. I'll see you around noon. I told the sheriff I'd be in to make a statement on Farnsworth's assault."

"Damn it, Ronnie, don't make me pull rank—"

"See you then," she said and moved the receiver to land in its cradle.

Across the room, Bently continued to lean idly against the doorjamb, his plastic cartoon cup held at his elbow. His gaze steady, he lifted the cup to his lips.

How could she, even for a moment, believe him capable of murder . . . and how could she not? He was dangerous. Everything about him emanated a kind of primal, primeval peril, from the strength of his lean muscled arms and shoulders to the intensity of his eyes to the sensual essence that seemed nearly ethereal. He was a devil, or very much like one with his mocking arrogance, his natural seduction . . . his aloof, distant charm.

Without a word, he lowered his mug and pushed off the doorjamb, looking at her, tipping his head as he started toward her.

The man walked like a cat, slow and quiet, smooth and sensuous, and every damn thing about him enhanced, heightened by the sheer force of his mesmerizing eyes. She knew suddenly how a bird felt when a cat approached and wondered if what she'd once heard about cats hypnotizing birds could be true. She felt paralyzed.

Rounding the desk, he settled sidesaddle onto the corner, still looking at her, his mustached lips poised in a crooked grin. No amusement lighted his eyes; no hint of a smile lingered as he gazed into her. With his coffee cup in hand, resting on his thigh, he glanced over her notebook.

Leaning back, heart hammering in her chest, Ronnie considered his silence. He'd used silence last evening. Long silences when he'd sprang into action. Long silences during dinner, after dinner. Very few words had passed between them. The longest he'd spoken had slipped off his lips in contempt of her profession. Every other communication had been broken sentences, catty quips, taunting arrogant remarks. Not once had they spoken, person to person. Communication. Tim Spencer had said something along those lines, and she wondered now if that was true. Either Isaac truly had no talent for speaking to women . . . or he simply had no tolerance for women. He used them, that much Ronnie had gathered. He used women for convenience to relieve his sexual appetites, but even that first morning—God, only three mornings ago—when that blond had hung on him, Ronnie had sensed his mere tolerance. She'd witnessed his annoyance when Andover had spoken to him . . . and if the victims in this crime were female, Ronnie might be far less convinced of his innocence.

"That call . . . Jarvins?" he asked with a dry tone. *A note of jealousy? A touch of venom?*

"Yes."

His head tilted a fraction, and his eyes became more intent, more opaque with thought, darkening a shade. "Something I should know?"

"Probably," she said honestly and noted his brow quirk just a hair, his curiosity rising.

"Don't tell me. . ." he said with a droll mocking tone, a smirk. "He's put an APB out on me for kidnapping you."

The shit! He did know that she and Mark had been involved, and the arrogant shit appeared rather smug for pulling one over on Mark. "He's not a man to be played for a fool, Isaac," she said quietly, honestly, braving his flash of annoyance to continue. "He's very good at what he does, and it's an important job."

"Obviously," he said dryly, his contempt not well hidden behind his concentrated gaze. "Convinced you rather swiftly to hold me at arm's length. If not kidnapping, though, I need to wonder what crime I've been accused of committing for you to look at me like a stranger again . . . or need I bother even to wonder?" he asked with his tone descending, his eyes darkening.

Dear God, his eyes changed in split seconds, and he knew or suspected what Mark had just said. Psychopath. Homicidal maniac. Instead of shock or outrage, he appeared only darkly amused, insolent.

"Isaac," she said quietly, not fitting the name well on her tongue. His name was 'Jade.' In her mind. In her heart. He wasn't Isaac Bently. He'd stopped being Isaac Bently the instant she'd remembered his real name.

Head angled, curiosity replacing his near cynical amusement, he studied her, waiting.

"Yesterday," she forced herself to continue, realizing she hadn't once uttered his real name aloud. "I did realize who you were."

His eyes changed yet again; his emotion cloaked as if he'd drawn a curtain over a window. His half-hitched grin remained more animated, more plastic.

"I have no intention of enlightening anyone—"

"Appears a bit late for that profession," he said in a chilly tone.

"Excuse me?"

He glanced at the phone with a contemptuous leer, unveiling some of the anger he'd attempted to conceal. "Obviously, you and your boyfriend share trade secrets, Miss Bryson," he said with black contempt dripping from his tone. "You expect me to believe you haven't given him the answers to his questions? And what now, Miss Investigative Reporter? Should I prepare to have my life ripped open?"

She leaned forward, clasping his hand, halting him, and seeing the fury in his eyes. Her gaze held him with equal intensity. "Your first mistake is to refer to Mark Jarvins as my boyfriend, Mr. Bently. Yes, he and I were romantically involved a few years ago. No, I didn't know he'd be on this case when I arrived in Bentwood. No, I have no intention of rekindling any romantic relationship. Yes, we have salvaged a friendship, and I care about him as a friend. That he may still have feelings toward me? I wouldn't doubt. And I've already determined to discuss that situation in due time. Though I'm sure with your help, he's gotten the message."

"With my help," he said in mocked indignation.

"Knock it off," she snapped, annoyed. "You worked overtime last evening to imply that you and I rendezvoused in this house by mutual consent. I might not have retained my full faculties with my head pounding and spinning, but I wasn't unconscious. You baited him and played on his emotions as if he were a fish on a hook. I didn't particularly care for it. It was underhanded and obnoxious," she said and noted the change in Bently's eyes yet again. *Damn him for appearing slightly amused.* "I still don't like it," she snapped, withdrawing her hand, sitting back, and satisfied with his instant annoyance. "I don't appreciate being used, Mister Bently. Any more than I appreciate having my integrity questioned . . .

"As for the exchange of information between Mr. Jarvins . . ." Time to clear the air. *Damn it!* Looking into his tense gaze, she knew the risks, knew if she was wrong, she might never survive long enough to regret her mistake. Leaning, she dragged her purse from the floor, finding what she sought in record time. Handing him the laminated card, she held his gaze as he accepted her offering and lowered his attention.

CHAPTER 19

The witch. The witch was a special consultant for the Federal Bureau of Investigation.

Unfortunately, that revelation only confirmed his belief. She'd told Jarvins her discovery and probably shared more than a few trade secrets. Why should that matter one way or the other? Sooner or later, the news would break.

Handing her the card, reading the curiosity in her eyes, he commented, "So, you have a legitimate reason for sharing information. I suppose I'm not surprised. In my experience, a journalist, and I use the term loosely, wouldn't have been put off by a slightly fractured skull, and I noted you didn't race down to snap photos of Farnsworth getting carted off."

"I'd imagine your opinion of reporters is justified," she said while sitting back again, slumping. "But I better mention, I am a member of that fraternity. My consultant status is temporary." Her eyes played over him, not quite as angrily as a few moments earlier, still intent and far more curious. "As for the sharing of information," she began again quietly. "I don't relate all of my findings with the Federal Bureau. I retain the right to withhold information not directly relative to this case. You, sir, fall into that category at this moment." Her blue eyes riveted, she continued, "If I'm making a mistake, it's one I'll live with."

The lady certainly had a temper and knew how to use it, Isaac considered absently. That he believed her, again, struck a chord inside of him. At the moment, his past would remain between them, but he knew how swiftly circumstances could change. He'd learned early how a single instant could create irreversible damage.

'You . . . at this moment,' she'd said, and he knew a contingency hinged upon that single phrase.

Distracted, Isaac lifted his coffee, his gaze shifting away from her. If he had any sense, he'd leave—should leave—but he'd tried that once already. Whatever had brought him back, held him still, and looking into Veronica Bryson's eyes, he knew what bound him. Where other females had tried, this impertinent little witch had succeeded. She'd touched him, and he'd be a fool to deny, that she touched him still.

"You and I need to talk—"

That catch in her voice again, the instant hesitation when she'd nearly spoken his name . . . his given name.

"I really don't know you," she continued, with her gaze as steady and piercing as a diamond-tipped drill. "I know who you were. I have no idea who you are."

"Could I ask you . . ." He suffered a similar instant glitch, wanting to call her Veronica or darling or any other number of endearments to slip easily off the tongue when locked in an embrace. Nothing seemed quite right. Not with daylight spilling through the curtains and her eyes pinning him. *Damn it!* "How exactly did you discover what you seem to know about me?"

For the briefest second, her eyes warmed. A relief after the chilly gaze he'd received from the moment she spotted him in the doorway. A smile touched the corner of her mouth, a lovely mouth even with the bruised haze at one corner. Cal would pay for that—

Good God, it was hard to concentrate when her eyes misted with reflection. He wanted very badly to lean forward and taste that smile, to feel the warmth of those eyes that softened even more with concern as she studied him.

"I don't exactly know how to answer you, without either making you angry or bringing back the pain I've seen in your eyes. You're a difficult man to read."

"Read a lot of men, do you?" Damn it! Defensive again, and she'd suffered that direct hit. He felt like a damn fool!

"Actually, I read a lot of people, but not always well, I'm afraid," she said, and distress touched her eyes.

Cal Farnsworth.

"You can't blame yourself for what he attempted."

Her eyes riveted, intent. "Obviously, you have a talent for reading people as well."

"You have very expressive eyes, Miss Bryson," he said sincerely.

"Would you like me to answer your question, Isaac?" she asked with a soft, sweet smile to make him wary. He'd seen that demure smile just often enough to know she could cut to the quick in the wake of that serene expression.

Recovering, sobering, he decided, "Yes, I believe I would."

"Then turn it off," she said flatly.

Good God, the lady bites! And she was clearly accusing him of something. "Excuse me?" he asked, mocking her tone of earlier without meaning to.

"You have flirting and seduction perfected to an art form, but I don't intend to be distracted at every turn," she said with a slightly irritated edge.

"I believe I resent that implication," he said with genuine doubt. "I was merely stating the obvious. You do happen to have expressive eyes.

"Alright, forget it," she huffed in exasperation.

"Love to," he said with a twitch of amusement. The woman was making him crazy!

"Tim's right," she said matter-of-factly, studying him with a bemused smile. "You have no idea how to carry on a serious conversation with a woman."

"Darlin, I'm trying," he said in genuine resignation and dismay. He couldn't, exactly, take offense when she wore such open amusement. "You're making this very difficult."

She stared at him for a second before huffing an unladylike sound and shaking her head in bewilderment.

Good God, she was lovely. "You wouldn't want to pick up where we left off in the kitchen, would you?"

"You win," she said and gazed at him with a faint smile. "We can't have this conversation, but speaking of the kitchen . . . I'd love another cup of coffee."

He supposed he asked for that. Leaning, reaching, and collecting her empty cup, he pushed off the desk and commented, "Donna mentioned something about pancakes. Perhaps, we should attempt conversing on a full stomach."

"If you think that will help," she said and let the sentence dangle as she pushed from Tim's chair.

Possibly he did have a problem conversing verbally with women, but he'd never considered that a serious problem, let alone an insurmountable barrier. No woman had ever complained about it before.

With a mental shrug, Isaac escorted the young lady through the living room, and apparently, something of his bewilderment remained on the surface.

In about thirty seconds or less, a groggy, red-eyed Tim, who hung at the counter worshiping a mug of coffee, growled, "What? Somebody snatched the whistle out of the cereal box before you?"

Following Tim's red-eyed glance at the plastic Disney mugs in his hands, Isaac caught on and mustered a shred of dignity to decide., "It's your fault."

"I don't even eat fucking cereal," Tim growled with a wider, red-eyed gaze.

At the opposite end of the counter, two beautiful women looked in their direction, and Isaac glimpsed the puzzled smiles and bewilderment on both faces before firming his gaze on Spencer. "I'm referring to the fact, that Veronica's convinced I have no social etiquette whatsoever."

"Yea? You're also an arrogant, conceited son of a bitch. So what?" Spencer growled and lifted his coffee to cover his smile, his red eyes filling with laughter.

Isaac parted his lips to fire a reprisal but halted, realizing those words carried a degree of merit, but it wasn't a second thought sending a shudder through his system. No second thought weighted the plastic cup. His gaze descended; he watched the cup clatter on the counter. Hot coffee plopped over the rim, scalding his fingers as his hand withdrew. Shaking his head slowly, shuddering, Isaac skidded his hand to the edge of the counter, holding on. The tunnel. He could see it opening, feel it. Heartbeat slowing, pounding, throbbing—

Tim clasped his arm in a bruising grip. "Isaac."

Jolted, heaving a breath, he snapped his head up and stared, blind for a few seconds. Blinking, he drew Tim's intense gaze, his sleep-lined face into focus. "Huh . . .?"

"Shit," Tim said, loosening his hold, his gaze still steady and searching. "You couldn't have gotten much sleep last night," he said as both women started toward them. "Maybe you better go back to bed for a while before you pass out on your feet."

Collecting, drawing a breath, Isaac looked down at the plastic cup, the puddle. In sharp contrast, coffee spattered and streaked across the white counter for the second time in recent memory. "Shiiit."

"Yea, shit," Spencer reiterated.

"Tim . . . Sax?" Donna asked. "Are you . . .?"

Glancing over the anxious faces, noting the concern lifted in Bryson's eyes, Isaac decided on the instant. Swaying, he pushed off the counter. "I do need to lie down."

Rather than climb the steps to the bedroom, however, Isaac passed through the dining room and sliding glass doors, making his way to the stuffed deck chairs. Elbows on his knees, he combed his fingers into his hair and held his still pulsing head. Not right. This wasn't right. This happened at night. Not in the daylight. Never . . . not since he was little . . . Not since he was ten years old had he suffered the pulsing and tunnels in broad daylight. Like an epileptic's aura that tunnel opened . . . a warning.

"Are you alright?" the soft voice asked.

"Fine," he managed and jolted slightly under the soft stroke on his head before realizing the strange comfort in that touch.

"I think Tim's right," she said quietly. "You probably didn't sleep. You should be lying down."

If she kept touching him, he would be lying down, lying down with her, and he was suddenly positive that wasn't such a good idea. Sliding from under her touch, combing his hair off his forehead, he looked into her troubled eyes as he sat back. "A dizzy spell," he said absently. "It's passed . . ." And they did need to speak. She planned to return to town to brave the chaos and make a statement for the police.

"You said there was something I needed to know," he remembered. "Perhaps, we should discuss that, now."

Concern flashed neon in her eyes, but she reached a decision. Stepping aside, she descended into the chair where she'd rested the evening past. She sat sidesaddle on the end of the cushion as if she might spring afoot at any second. More concentrated, she studied him. "I have to go back into town," she began simply. "As much as I know you and Tim brought me here to protect me, I can't stay here."

"You'll be hounded," he said before he could retract his words or contain the disdain in his voice.

"I can't begin to imagine what it was like for you, honey," she said softly, and he averted his gaze if only to escape her sympathy. "What I started to tell you inside, I have to tell you, now." She hesitated. "There are several reasons why I realized who you were. Doubtful, anyone else could have figured it out."

Drawn by her words, her compelling tone, he found her expressive eyes.

"I attended St. Augustine's Academy," she said quietly.

Halted, his mind stopped, he stared at her, doubts echoing in every corner of his frozen mind. Unconsciously, he shook his head.

"It only begins there, hon," she said quietly, a wavering smile on her lips, her eyes moist. "I was in third grade . . . a little girl moved into our school that semester. Her uh . . . her name was Jessica Hagen."

For a few seconds, he failed to grasp the significance, but his mind flashed neon. Det. Maxwell Hagen! Was it only a few days ago . . . just a few days ago that name had blind-sided him, jolting him? In the diner . . . *Good God*. In the diner . . . Max Hagen. Isaac had not thought of that detective in years. *But Veronica Bryson had thought of him.*

"Jess and I became best friends," she continued quietly, holding him spellbound with her compelling gaze. "Her father became something of my surrogate father and my mentor. Whether I became interested in writing about violent crime because of him or chose him as my mentor because of my strange intuitions, I've never decided. I do know he was instrumental in pointing me toward my career."

She paused as if to let him catch up or catch his breath, continuing quietly, "In my junior year of college, I wrote my thesis paper on the miscarriage of facts by the press. It came natural for me to choose a case that touched me in some way. Whether I chose it because it affected my mind in third grade or because . . . because I remembered the boy who was persecuted by that event, I couldn't say. I . . . I did remember that boy," she said as she looked into him. "I don't think we ever truly met, but I remember seeing you once." Her lips smiled; soft color rose in her cheeks. "In the playground," she said with a hint of amusement. "And don't ask why that memory stayed with me all these years."

"Good God," he uttered as a flash of memory touched his mind's eye . . .

A little girl, long curly black hair bouncing as she skipped across the playground . . . her steps faltering, halting, her eyes turning toward him. He'd felt her there, sensed her watching him, staring at him. The light—her light had drawn him. He'd seen her again . . . and again after that, aglow in the playground, under the spread of oaks, on the swings—

"Anyway," she continued softly. "I do know you, and I understand why you rescued me from the press, why those messages and that phone call affected you. I can understand how you feel . . . and I'd give anything to change last night," she said with a shine of moisture in her eyes. "I can't though. We . . . we'll be hounded, at least for a little while. It won't be the same though, honey. You . . . if what Mark says is true, the media has learned of your involvement, and you're being heralded for your heroism.

"Maybe . . . maybe in some small way, the media will make amends for what they did to you so long ago, honey. I don't know, but I hope. And I'll do my part to see that happens. I just . . . I couldn't let you walk into town without knowing what you'll be walking into. Do you understand?"

He understood . . . he understood far better than she did how the 'media' could turn the tides and destroy a life. He knew too well how reporters could distort reality and twist the facts until the revered became the damned . . . And it was too late to reverse the damage. If she was right, it was too damn late.

Dropping his head back on the cushion, he studied her only a moment more, then turned his gaze toward the lawn. "You're so naive," he uttered. "If you truly believe it will make a difference, you are so damn naive."

"I'm not naive, honey. I know the fallibility of my profession. There are too many men and women like Ted Grimes, but there are a lot of reputable journalists out there, too."

He looked at her, knowing his glare worried her and unable to conceal it. "Don't . . . don't even attempt to convince me that the *press* is a friend or that most of your colleagues are decent upstanding citizens. You, my dear lady, might be the exception to the rule, but that's the extent of my tolerance. I'll go into town, simply because I agreed to offer my official statement to Sheriff Grant, but don't . . . don't even attempt to alter my opinion of the media. And don't expect me to corroborate any statement you feel inclined to make or write. If even one of your colleagues fabricates a statement on my behalf, I swear, by God, I'll . . ."

Nothing. Not one thing could he do. Not one damned thing. Even with more money than he could spend in a lifetime, he couldn't begin to crush the mechanics of mass media. He could escape its claws, could fade again, run again, hide . . . but he could never annihilate the machine that had destroyed his life.

Pushing smoothly to his feet, Isaac looked down into her tear-swamped eyes. "I'm going to lie down for a little while, Miss Bryson—" Bryson . . . *Good God, even the name!* Even that *name* was familiar! Bryson—Arlington, VA. A Bryson a year ahead of him in St. Augustine's. A brother? Named after a president—

He shook his head, focusing on her. "When you're ready to go into town, you may let me know. I'll be happy to drive you."

"Ja—"

Frozen, he looked into her wet eyes, knowing, without a doubt, she would be his end.

"I'm—I'm sorry," she stammered as a tear slipped down her cheek.

As much as he would like to lean down and brush that tear away, he couldn't bring himself to touch her, to be touched by her. Turning, Isaac walked across the deck, passing through the glass doors, and continuing through the dining room.

"Hey, musta smelled these flapjacks—"

Without a glance or word, Isaac continued through the living room and climbed the steps. In the guest bedroom, he slid down the wall to rest on his haunches, knees drawn, hands clasping his pounding skull. She would destroy him.

How long she sat staring into abstracts, feeling the pain, forcing back tears, Ronnie had no idea. She hadn't meant to hurt him, but she had. No other thought remained clear in her mind, no other pain fiercer than the scorch of that green fire in his eyes. He hated her, now. Whatever had started, whatever he might have started to feel for her . . . ended before it could take hold. In one fell swoop, she'd confided her affection, opened her heart to him, for him . . . and opened all the wounds that hadn't healed inside of him. How . . . how couldn't she have known what the awakening of so many memories could do to him? Dear God, she needed only to realize what lengths he'd gone to escape those wounds to know how deeply he'd been cut . . . And here she was, destroying the peace, the harmony he'd found, threatening his serenity, his anonymity.

She needed to escape, needed out of his sight. Just the sight of her would hurt him, now, and he'd hate her for every second of it.

Steeling her nerve, recovering, forcing herself to maintain the dignity that Robert and Fiona Bryson had bred into her, Ronnie strode into the Spencer house.

In a few words, she gained Tim's consent to offer Len directions, assuring Tim that Isaac's whereabouts would remain their secret, although she doubted that detail would remain a mystery for very long. Picking at a pancake smothered in homemade maple syrup, she suffered the half hour before Len pulled into the driveway. As she'd requested, he was alone, which offered shallow consolation.

Hugging, thanking the Spencers, not entirely surprised when both little ones offered their hugs and kisses, telling her to come back soon, Ronnie climbed into the front seat of Len's rental. His black gaze told her everything she needed to know about what he thought of her great escape. Her thoughts drifting, her heart aching, Ronnie could feel no worse if he lit into her. What he did was worse. What he did lifted tears to her eyes.

His immense hand finding her palm across the seat, he squeezed lightly, nearly uttering, "I'm glad you're alright, Ronnie."

How he could even bear to look at her, she dared not wonder. She'd betrayed him, betrayed Mark, betrayed every man she'd ever cared about, every man who'd ever loved her. Love . . . love wasn't in her cards. True love, the kind between a man and a woman, wasn't in the cards. She was better off as Ron Bryson, just one of the guys. Better off doing what she did best . . . investigating and helping to solve homicides . . . and this one wasn't solved. No matter what the media or Sheriff Grant or Jade . . .

"You want to talk about what's bothering you?" Len asked with an unnaturally gentle tone.

For Len to treat her with kid gloves, she must really look lousy. She glanced at him, catching a black glimmer before his focus returned through the windshield. "I want to know what all they have on Cal Farnsworth. The rings. What else?"

In profile, Len's expression darkened. His mood remained pensive for several long seconds. When he spoke, his voice was firm. "Think you better forget about this one, Ronnie. I'll take you to the precinct to give your statement, but after that, I'm taking you to a hotel—"

"Like hell you are," she said in a chilly tone and caught his fleeting glance. She waited for his doubletake. "You're not my keeper. You, nor Mark, and you both better damned sure get that straight. I'm on this case because I chose to be on this case. If I'm no longer listed as a consultant, I'll find what I need by other means, but I'm not going anywhere until this psycho's caught. Get it?"

"That's uh . . . that's part of the problem, here, Ronnie," Len said in a more careful tone. "As far as the locals are concerned, they've got their man thanks to your pal—"

"Don't you start," she snapped and caught his glance. "Mark made it perfectly clear who he thinks our killer is, and I don't agree with him. I believe, if anyone's perspective is fucked up, it's Mr. Jarvins'," she stated in a chilly tone. "He's been investigating this with blinders on since he saw me speaking to Isaac Bently, and you know I'm right. He's attacking Bently because he sees him as a threat over some harebrained idea that he's still in love with me. Now, facts. Bently was in England for two weeks before this second murder. Fact: Bently was seen driving toward Bentwood when he claims to have driven to Bentwood. Fact:—our psycho sat on that hillside long enough to be certain Engler was alone. Granted, Bently could've raced from the airport to Engler's. He could've run the eighth mile to that barn, done the deed, and ran the eighth mile back to his car. He could've driven all over the fucking countryside in hopes of hitting an expressway exit and getting spotted by a county deputy for an alibi. But, Len . . . I can't see Bently wandering around an airport parking lot for a half-hour before starting that asinine marathon. Can you?"

For a long moment, Devinio was silent, but his lips twitched in his natural scowl. "No. Can't say as I can see any of that, Ronnie."

"So, let's knock off the shit about Bently being our number one suspect. The only thing he's guilty of is being a good-looking single guy who likes his privacy. And you might as well know that he and I arrived at the same dinner last evening because his friend, Officer Tim Spencer, who happens to be a great practical joker, knew that Bently and I weren't seeing eye-to-eye. Now. Do you understand?"

"How'd he end up rescuing you, Ronnie?" Len asked quietly.

"My guess is, he was still fuming over a few of my parting shots," she said as she gazed through the side window at a wheatfield, recalling that golden field off the interstate only two days past. "Plausibly," she continued grimly. "He might've intended to have the last word, and it was already dark. Maybe he was afraid I'd get lost out here . . . The guy's an arrogant shit, but he's decent, Len."

"I uh . . . I hate to say this," Len said quietly. "But I think you're right."

Looking over, doubting she'd heard those words, she studied Len's pensive expression. He wasn't just agreeing to appease her. "Come again?"

Len glanced over, his gaze reflective as he returned his attention to the road ahead. "It hit me yesterday . . . something you said about our wacko when we were standing out by the Englers'." He paused, contemplative. "You said something about our psycho not being able to see the beauty . . . not being able to feel it."

"I remember," she said, watching Len's profile.

"This might sound dumb as hell, but it hit me at the time, Bently wasn't our man. It was something he said, and the way he reacted when Mark busted up a couple plates."

Ronnie waited in silence, wishing she knew the whole story behind those broken plates. In the next instant, she suffered only greater heartache.

"He said something about Mark destroying pieces of history," Len continued. "The beauty of what some artist had labored nearly a hundred years ago to create. It wasn't so much what he said as how he said it. The message came in loud and clear. He considered those plates beautiful, and it damn near killed him to watch Mark bust them. Eight hundred bucks for a service setting, I'd have been busting Mark for that bit of slippery-fingered shit."

"Mark . . . Jesus," Ronnie said, feeling worse, feeling ill over the trouble she'd created in Isaac Bently's life. She'd leave him alone . . . but how her heart wrenched with that thought. Nothing had ever felt more right. No one had ever felt more right.

"Anyway, I figure the guy's not our psycho, but I'm still not sure what he is. There's something screwy about him, about these trips to Europe. I'd uh," Len looked over. "I'd like you to keep some distance, Ronnie, and I'm not telling you that for any reason other than I don't want to see you hurt."

"I appreciate that, Len," she said quietly, aching. "But you could save your breath. I uh . . . I won't be seeing him again."

The silence lingered. They were nearing the outskirts of town. Clusters of houses appeared within the trees. A few billboards boasted everything from car dealerships with horse trailers among the economy cars to dentist offices. A thriving metropolis—

"So," Len interrupted the silence. "You got any hot tips on a possible suspect?"

"It wasn't the butler," Ronnie said distractedly.

"Cal Farnsworth?"

"Not unless he's suffering a Multiple Personality Disorder," she said absently. "Too aggressive. Our killer comes from behind. Immobilizes then destroys. Cal would plow in with both fists flying. He might grab a pitchfork if it were handy, but he'd just as soon grab a shovel . . . You want to tell me what else they have on him?"

Lenny hesitated, then offered, "They found Engler's watch under the seat of his pickup."

In slow motion, Ronnie looked over to see Devinio scowling at the highway. Engler's watch? Fred Engler had his watch heisted, and this was the first she heard about it? "What else have I been missing, Len?"

"We didn't know about the watch, Ronnie. Not until last night," Len said carefully. "It's a pocket watch. It hung on a fob from his hip pocket. Apparently, someone forgot to mention it. Turns out, uh . . . turns out Farnsworth had one, too, and the interesting part is—Engler's watch . . .? The face was smashed. We're nearly certain it records the exact TOD."

"Farnsworth's watch is still missing?"

"Wasn't in the truck."

"Len, we're missing something else," she said carefully, her thoughts clicking. "If the rings and watches were missing, then there's still something we're missing. Something we don't know was taken. Souvenirs . . . there's got to be something else missing. Our killer wouldn't have parted with both items unless he still had something . . . and that sheds new light," she realized absently. "What's Mark's take on the watch? What does he think it signifies?"

"Mark's hung up on you," Len said, then scowled more deeply as if he might like to bite his tongue.

"Want to explain?"

"He's connecting it to Bently," Len said in disgust. "Pocket watches, watch fobs, antiques . . . Olden Time. If we didn't have Farnsworth in custody, we'd have been raiding Bently's place within the hour."

"Goddamn it," she breathed softly.

"Don't be too tough on him, Ron. He can't help it if he has damn good taste. Hell, if you weren't Jewish, I'd give him a run for his money."

Even feeling miserable over Mark's deceit, she smiled slightly. "That's the nicest thing I've heard all day." Only more lies. More betrayal. Was she destined to hurt every man she met? Or just the ones she truly cared about?

Her thoughts turning in miserable circles, Ronnie tried to concentrate. Mulling over the details, she paid little heed to the passing scenery until a discrepancy surfaced in her mind. The crowds were gone. Morning traffic reminded her of the streets when she'd first arrived. A few pedestrians strolled the sidewalks; cars parked on either side of the street; a few people loitered around the park. "Where'd everybody go?"

"Disappointed?" Len asked.

She sent him a scathing glance, more genuine than she cared to consider until noting his tension. "Everybody migrated over to Bender Falls, huh?"

"You got it," Devinio said. "Cal's going to be famous."

"Len," she said quietly, her gaze locked on him when he pulled in front of the fire station and parked. "Our wacko won't like Cal getting the glory," she said quietly. "Even if he handed it over, he's not going to like it . . . He won't be satisfied . . . and he has to have something else brewing. To let Cal take the fall and get the attention . . .? Our whacko has something else in mind."

Len studied her for a long moment, his brows drawn as he commented, "You're too good at this, Ronnie."

"Mark's already got that figured out, and he thinks it's Bently. That's why he sounded panicked earlier."

"Touché."

"It's not Bently, Len, and we don't have any goddamn idea who it is," she said, with a prickle down her spine. "We can't even take a wild guess at what this character has in mind for an encore."

"That's what I've been thinking," Len admitted, his dark eyes guarded.

Another prickle skittered down her spine as she realized what else Len was thinking. Not Bently. Even if it weren't Bently, the psycho had stood outside the Bentwood House Inn last night. Had . . . the maniac had watched as Cal had attacked her. Watched as Isaac Bently rescued her. "Oh-mi-God," she uttered, looking at Len, feeling the first serious inkling of fear.

Following Cal? Or waiting for her?

CHAPTER 20

Chief of Police, Sam Hayward appeared larger in photographs than in life only until he clasped Ronnie's hand in his solid grip, leveled his cool gaze, and spoke. "I'm glad we're finally getting a chance to meet, Miss Bryson. I just wish it were under better circumstances."

No false smiles or bravado inflected his rugged voice; no tricks or deceptions lingered behind his eyes. He was a man with a lot on his mind and not inclined to enlist subterfuge. Escorting her into his private office, a cubbyhole affair that made Ronnie ashamed of the walk-in closets she'd enjoyed as a child, Hayward directed her into a metal armchair alongside his desk. He waited until one of the two patrolmen in the small outer office delivered two coffees, then got down to business.

Letting her run through the events at her own pace, he interrupted on occasion, asking a direct question, clarifying a detail, drawing a diagram of the Bentwood House parking lot, and jotting placement. Even being a small-town police chief, Hayward portrayed an air of calm cool efficiency. His short crop of dark hair lent a military precision to his countenance. His steadfast tones and thoughtful expressions chiseled permanently on a face bearing traces of recent wear and tear added to his persona.

Without a need for imagination, Ronnie understood how a man who stood little more than 5'8" could command the respect of a man like Tim Spencer. A cross between tough cop, strict father, and statesman, the chief managed to exact a full and accurate account of the evening past. The longer Ronnie sat alongside the desk, the more she became convinced she had found a kindred spirit. The man didn't believe for an instant that Cal Farnsworth was guilty of murder. Attempted rape and assault, yes, and he wouldn't take that crime lightly, but murder, no. He knew a psycho was still loose in his town and it wasn't sitting well with him.

As Ronnie finished reading over her statement and leaned signing her name to the bottom of the two-page account, Hayward sat back, idly tapping his pen on his desk. The green felt mat muffled the sound to a dull thump, but the sound might have been a drumroll. He was a man with something else on his mind, speculating as Ronnie leaned and delivered the pages to the mat in front of him.

Leaning back, she met his gaze.

"That Isaac, he's something isn't he?" Hayward said offhandedly.

Feeling a quick pang of dread, Ronnie held her gaze steady. "Interesting man."

"Boy's got more moves than a chessboard," Hayward said without effect. "The problem is, miss, when you live in a small town, you get to know people. You see them on the street. You stop off and share a cup of coffee a time or two. You sit across a poker table on occasion. You can learn a lot about most folks over a poker game."

"I'd imagine so," she agreed. *Did Hayward believe Bently could be his man?*

"Isaac has himself quite a reputation around here," Hayward continued with a more pensive gaze. "Course, like most small towns, people do a lot of talking and things have a way of getting blown out of proportion," he paused, watching her with a curious gaze. "Bently's reputation is like that though it's not for lack of merit. He's single. He has a touch of class to him that ain't often found in a town like Bentwood. He's well-educated and pretty well-off financially. All told, if a few gals didn't put the make on him, I'd have to wonder what was wrong with them."

Hayward was certainly headed in a direction, Ronnie just hoped she would still be alive when he reached his destination. This wasn't the conversation she wanted to share with Sam Hayward. "I can see your point, Chief Hayward."

"I'm not sure you can, miss," Hayward said pensively. "The fact is, Bently's a pretty decent kind of guy. He keeps to himself more often than not, sort of quiet that way, but everyone has their own way to get from day to day. I'm not saying he's not sociable, mind you, miss. He'll talk your ear off if you get him started on the history of some of his antiques over there, and I'll tell you, there aren't too many people in this town who haven't come out of his shop with something they've been wanting for quite a while. I can't tell you how many times I've seen something come out of his shop that probably cost him a hell of a lot more than he got out of it. It's sort of a standing joke around here that he's about the worst haggler this side of the Atlantic, but I guess you'd say that's most folks' way of saving face. As long as nobody gets hurt by it, there's no harm in it."

Was this character trying to kill her? Did he have any idea of what he was doing to her? She needed no picture painted. "I'm sure he's a decent man, chief," she conceded with her heart in her hands, her gaze direct. Hayward had something on his mind, but it didn't sound like suspicion of a homicidal maniac. The man would need to be an Oscar winner to hide that motive so well behind this steady, thoughtful dialogue.

"I guess what I'm getting at is this, miss," he said with a steady gaze. "I wouldn't want to see a young man like Isaac Bently getting a raw deal because of circumstances he can't control. I figure a man has a right to his privacy and he shouldn't be held accountable for being in the right place at the right time and doing the right thing . . . if you know what I'm saying?"

God almighty, loud and clear. Hayward knew Isaac Bently hadn't been born 'Isaac Bently.' Hayward either knew or suspected something existed in Bently's past, and he knew Mark Jarvins was trying to pin this crime on Bently because of her. He fully believed or suspected that she, Ronnie Bryson, was a part of that ultimate goal. In his own subtle way, Hayward had just told her to back off, to leave the guy alone. Had he somehow endeavored to soften his accusation if perchance she intended to get even for . . . *for being rejected in romantic pursuits?*

"Yes, I believe I do," Ronnie said in a hollow voice. "And I'd like to assure you, I have no intention of besmirching Mr. Bently's reputation. I am extremely grateful to him for saving my life last evening . . ."

"You look lousy, Ron," Len observed as they were leaving the station. "If I can't convince you to hop on a plane, I happen to know you still have a room at the Bentwood and I think you better use it for a while."

"I think you're right," she said in a vapid voice, gazing absently through the passenger window, letting Len do the driving. At the Inn, Len carried her bags to her room and dawdled for a few moments, something else on his mind. When he handed her the .22 Midnight Special, she just stared at it.

"I know you don't like carrying a peacemaker, but I also know you know how to use it," he said firmly. "At least keep it in that backpack you call a purse. You run across any other assholes like Cal, you feel threatened in any way, you pull that out and use it. You won't likely kill anyone unless you get mighty lucky, but you'll slow them down."

She hated guns, even little guns which appeared as harmless as a squirt gun, but with a thought of someone in the shadows, watching as she'd been brutalized by a drunken bully . . . "Thanks, Len."

By the time, Isaac collected himself and pushed off the floor, he knew Veronica Bryson had left. As if she'd taken something with her, the house that had always struck him as warm and well-occupied felt empty and chilled. An illusion. The ceiling fans in the beamed ceiling hummed to keep a cool breeze moving through the open rooms. From the open screen doors, he heard Tee and Deedee playing on the deck. He found Tim lounging on one of the plush stuffed couches, an architectural magazine lying open on his lap but doubtful holding his interest since he'd been staring off toward the stone fireplace when Isaac started down the steps. In no mood for any more banter, or any criticism, Isaac barely sent him a glance with his comment, "I'm taking off."

Rather than comment directly, Tim followed him to the garage, returning the electric garage door opener to the off position, and forcing Isaac to turn. Locking a steady, angry gaze, he commented, "No lectures."

"I won't ask what went on between you two," Tim decided. "She looked like hell, and you don't look much better. I'm not even going to ask you to stick around and ride this mess out. You're going to do what you're going to do. All I'm going to say is . . . think about it," Spencer said gravely. "Don't leap before you look. You have a hell of a lot of people in this town who'd feel pretty lousy if you pulled up stakes."

"Are you finished?" Isaac asked in a wintry tone.

Spencer gazed at him for a few ticks then turned, slamming his palm on the wall switch to ignite the garage door opener as he passed through the door.

No sense trying to apologize. No sense trying to explain. Nothing to explain.

Tossing his bag on the passenger seat, Isaac climbed behind the steering wheel, his thoughts still humming as he spun out of the garage. The lady had her facts in order. By some freakish coincidence, the lady had put together his past, and if fate could land one nasty blow, it could land another. Sooner or later, the hounds would sniff him out and it would be worse the second time around.

Nanna . . . Maggie. Maggie Duncan, he remembered far too swiftly with all the walls crumbling around the places, the memories, he'd tried to seal away. Their housekeeper, his nanny, his ally when his mother went off on one of her tangents . . . Felicity Laquette was so flighty. Nanna was solid . . . stout of build, steadfast, an anchor. She'd tried. She'd tried to protect him, tried to hold the wolves at bay . . . her and Mr. Vancourt . . . Paul Vancourt . . . their butler . . . up in years . . . There were others though. His mother's secretary, business advisors, clients . . .

Faces, all the faces were returning, flashing through his mind like stone busts caught in a tornado. Face after face . . . the shouting and hailing, the alarms erupting . . .

'They're coming for me, Nanna . . .'

"God, help me," he uttered as his hands gripped the wheel against the rising whirlwind. Everything he'd believed forgotten . . . everything from the moment he'd found her lying in their foyer . . .

"God!" Even his father's face flashed vividly within his mind, taking his breath away with the sudden panic. Not a word of French, not a word of French had he understood when his father had stood above him for the first time . . . a giant. The man had been a giant compared to his own five-foot frame, and not a word of French had he understood. Even English had become a problem, but he'd understood his father's words, understood the thin sniggering smile, the disgust blazing in the emerald eyes . . .

'Re`ceived more than she bargained for, eh, my own bastard . . .?'

Too fast. He was driving too fast, and he sensed the mistake, but it was already too late to worry about mistakes. Too late!

Driving on autopilot, Isaac reached the alley behind his warehouse, climbed out, and waded through his wad of keys en route to the door. By habit alone, he waved to the silver-haired old woman who spied him through a gap in the hedges, a routine he'd adopted not long after meeting every officer on Bentwood's force at least once. She was twice as feisty when he backed his pickup from the warehouse. Inevitably, she shuffled to her kitchen, waited near her telephone, and placed that call the instant he returned.

"You keep that blasted car outa my flowers!" she shouted through the hedge.

Flowers? He waved again while pulling into the warehouse. A person would need a grand imagination to consider her scrub hedges *flower* bushes, which is exactly what he'd told her the first time she'd accused him of trashing her damned hedge. Still, there was comfort in hearing her voice, in seeing her poised on her back porch, stoop-shouldered and supported on a cane, glaring at him.

Locking the doors from the inside, he passed through shadows. The faces continued to rage through his mind. He needed to put the memories away, needed to concentrate, needed to decide if he should even bother opening the shop today.

The decision to open had been taken from his hands. To the sound of cymbals and horns, he froze inside the dividing hallway. He hadn't even thought about calling Elaine but apparently, she'd decided to come in . . . and that struck him odd. Very odd considering her relationship with Alice Engler. With Cal Farnsworth charged with the murders . . .

Not a tornado, a hurricane, Isaac corrected as he caught up to himself entering the police station. A hurricane had broken loose inside his skull and the winds just kept ripping between his ears. Feeling distant and distracted, he accepted Sam Hayward's escort into the private office. With an effort, Isaac collected enough of his thoughts to repeat most of what he'd said to Sheriff Grant. Hayward was more thorough, prodding and pushing, drawing diagrams, demanding Isaac's attention to answer his questions.

Going over the diagram one more time, Sam hesitated between, ". . . You were here . . . Your car was here . . . She was here . . . Now, while you were traveling from here to here, did you happen to see anybody else, maybe over in here?"

With the eraser of a pencil, Hayward touched down on the row of hedges and fence that separated the parking corral from the alley and extended the length of the block behind the Inn.

Staring at the diagram, Isaac felt the pulse at his temple, suffered an internal shudder, and caught himself from swaying. Already shaking his head, he held his balance with an effort. "N-no . . . no one."

For a long moment, Sam studied him then sat back, tapping his eraser on the desk, his gaze fixed as he spoke, "You know, son, if there's something you'd maybe like to talk about, I make a pretty good listener and I don't have to write down or record everything I hear."

"N-o, nothing," he managed while collecting his thoughts, his poise.

"I've never been one to pry into another man's personal life unless I have a damn good reason," Sam continued in a congenial tone. "I figure whatever a man's done, wherever he's been, it's his own business so long as it doesn't become my business. Take you, for example," he said offhandedly. "You keep to yourself. I respect that in a man. You do a lot of good in this town, always ready to do a good turn. I respect that, too . . ."

Confused, only more confused, Isaac walked toward his store trying to make some sense of whatever Sam Hayward had just said to him. Sounded a whole lot like Sam had tried to tell him something. Something a little like what Spencer had said a short time earlier. Something about sticking things out and the Federal agent "barking up the wrong tree."

. . . And something about noticing anyone else behind the Inn. Not behind the Inn. He'd sensed someone in the alley behind his . . .

Raking his fingers through his hair, he stood on the sidewalk cater-corner to his shop, watching several cars pass before breaking through his confusion and starting off the curb.

"Mr. Bently!" a female voice called out and for an instant, his heart lurched with a thought of Veronica Bryson.

Half turned before he could stop himself, Isaac watched the stranger hurrying toward him. Her flat-heeled shoes clicked on the sidewalk. She held a long-strapped purse cleaved to her hip to halt its bounce. He'd never seen her in town before. Large dark sunglasses covered her eyes; platinum blond hair fell in a straight short bob framing her cheeks tapered into a knobby chin. She was too slim for the beige slacks and tunic blouse. The whole ensemble appeared cluttered as if bought for a woman twice her size . . . and she was a reporter.

Turning, he stepped off the curb, barely glimpsed a pause in traffic, and strode across the street destined for his apartment.

Something happened to that decision. He found himself sliding onto a stool at the end of the counter in the diner. The stool next to him was occupied by Cy Trascar, a retired mill worker who divided his time between Meg's Diner and Charlie's Pub at the other end of Maine. Charlie's was an evening haunt. Meg kept the coffee flowing and plenty of old-timers stopped into the diner to keep Cy entertained throughout the day.

"Hell of a fine job, you saving that gal, Bently," Trascar mumbled. "Did the whole town a service catching that Farnsworth boy . . . Hope that som'bitch gets the electric chair for what he done."

He didn't want a damn citation. He wanted to be left alone!

"Coffee, sugar?" Rae Ann Anderson smiled, hitching her fine rounded hip against the counter in front of him.

Nodding absently, Isaac sent a distracted glance over his shoulder . . . a dozen customers lounged in the booths and tables. A few smiled. One or two called a greeting. More intent on the curtained windows, he scanned the open space above the valance rods, shaking his head. Empty. The streets were empty. The circus had moved to the next town. Was it possible? Was it actually possible this wave had passed him by? Had he escaped the media madness? Was it possible he'd been wrong about Bryson blowing his quiet existence into the stratosphere? Farnsworth was behind bars, undoubtedly making the headlines . . .

Valerie Farnsworth. The girl he'd just mistaken for a reporter . . . Valerie Farnsworth! Good God, he hadn't even recognized her behind the black glasses . . . and she'd lost weight, a great deal of weight since he'd last seen her. He'd heard she was away at school, attending some business college in Pittsburgh. Shit. If he'd needed any reason to feel worse, she'd just given him one. No matter what her brother might have done, the girl had just lost her father, for God's sake. She didn't deserve to be snubbed.

Then, too, perhaps it was for the best. What he remembered of Valerie, the girl might be as inclined toward disillusionment as her brother in affairs of the heart. God knows the youngster had attempted to make his life miserable several years ago. If he'd not kept his head, the little viper would've had him arrested on a morals charge.

"Penny for your thoughts, handsome," Meg said cheerily as she slid a stout mug to him.

"Could you put that in a to-go cup?" Isaac asked as he spied her intent gaze.

She slipped the cup away and handed it to Elsa. "You heard the man, sweetie. He's on the go."

"Hmm, and I wouldn't mind going with him," Elsa said and winked at him.

Cy grunted a sound, leaning and jabbing Isaac in the elbow, grumbling, "Son, if I had a nickel for every time one a these gals winked at you, I could throw away my pension. When you gonna settle down to one and give the others a rest?"

"Think that would solve it, do you?" Isaac asked absently.

Trascar chuckled, repositioning more fully on his stool, "Hell, no, boy. The gal who snags you'd wear herself ragged trying to beat them off with a stick."

What in God's name was this? First Spencer, then Hayward alluding to settling down? Now Trascar? Had the whole damn town decided he needed to take root? A conspiracy.

"Isaac," Meg interrupted drawing his attention to her troubled gaze. "How's Ronnie?"

Veronica . . . "I'd imagine she's fine," Isaac said with an edge and cursed his reaction. Meg's brow furrowed, the questions burning in her eyes as livid as her concern. Good God, that wasn't fair! Meg had asked out of genuine concern over the assault. "Banged up," he said absently. His gaze faltered to accept the cup Elsa handed to him. A slight concussion, bruises . . . it could've been worse, and his heart hammered a mean beat with the thought. "But she's fine."

"She strikes me as a pretty tough cookie," Meg said thoughtfully. "It's a damn shame how folks around here were treating her."

"She sure was a pretty little gal," Trascar commented. "Ask me though, she was just asking for trouble. Come snooping around—"

"She didn't *ask* for a damn thing," Isaac snapped and riveted his angry gaze on the startled old man. "She was here to do a job and that didn't include jumping into the bed of some drunken asshole's pick-up truck, any more than it included laying every male in Bentwood as that asshole Grimes claimed."

"I wasn't implyin' nothing," Trascar said humbly. "That Farnsworth boy's been trouble since day one. I just meant how maybe she shoulda been more careful seeing as how we had trouble aplenty—"

"She's an investigative reporter," Isaac snapped, the words bitter on his tongue, his senses spiraling with anger and unable to find a reasonable outlet. "Obviously, a very good one considering how swiftly she ferreted Farnsworth from his hole."

"You saying maybe she knew it was Farnsworth?" another voice asked from somewhere behind him.

How in God's name had he gotten into this discourse and why'd Meg look at him with such a peculiar gaze? *To hell with this!* He needed to get home! Needed to find something to do . . . he had plenty to do. A mile-high stack of paperwork stood on his desk!

"I'll talk to you later, Meg," Isaac said and slipped off the stool, offering a cool glance to Trascar. "Cy."

He wouldn't catch up on his paperwork, he realized within ten minutes after settling into his office chair. Elaine had cleaned the glass off the floor and removed the entire set of Haviland. She ventured into his office, nervous as always, and managed to stammer something about putting Wade to work setting the dining room table.

". . . Dag-gone phone's been ringing off the hook," she confided meekly.

Ten minutes was all the longer people needed to begin wandering into the store, asking to talk to the 'boss.' A few didn't bother to ask, merely meandered behind the glass counter and wrapped knuckles on the door-frame, shoving the door open.

Without so much as a hello, Jen Andover breezed into his office, rounded his desk, and threw her arms about him. Planting her lips on his, she plopped sideways onto his lap, her bare legs in short shorts, draped over the arm of the chair. "My hero," she breathed with a winning smile, then pout. "I almost wish I'd been the damsel in distress."

She would have enjoyed it too much to be distressed, he nearly said aloud and cursed his thought. "That's nothing to joke about, Jen," he said soberly.

Her big blue eyes adopted a hurt shine; the pout softened to a more natural frown. "I say the most horrid things without thinking," she said dolefully but a little smile crept onto her full lips. "A bunch of us are meeting out at Crowley's tonight and you're the guest of honor. Say you'll come . . ."

Her offer was the first, but he received several other invitations within the first hour, including a phone call from the State Representative who wanted to know if Isaac and Miss Bryson would be free for dinner.

Miss Bryson. The name kept blindsiding him. Again and again, 'How's Miss Bryson?' 'We heard she moved back into The Bentwood . . .'

Three different city council members had already visited by the time Allen Spencer strode into Isaac's office. As always, Allen carried himself like a man pressed for time, emphasizing points with hand gyrations which always fascinated Isaac into a smile. nothing amused him on this visit. Even his usual silent debate over heredity failed to cheer him as he listened to Allen's praise, faintly reflective of a campaign speech. The man was sharp, his mind like a steel trap with business, and his plans for the town could well modernize everything from parking meters to public restrooms, but he didn't possess his younger brother's physical assets or easy nature. Cutting-edge, Allen made his adulation sound like gratitude for a personal favor, as if in one fell swoop Isaac had rid the town of a murderer and saved Allen's chances at the House.

". . . You do know Miss Bryson is the daughter of Robert Bryson, a personal friend to at least three presidents that I know of . . . I wouldn't be surprised if you receive a special Letter of Recognition from the president . . ."

Nudging Allen out of the office, barely breezing a hello to Hazel Lawson, the mayor's wife who had stopped by in place of her husband, Isaac closed his office door. Continuing through his second door, he closed and locked it behind him.

Alone in his apartment, he paced, muttered, cursed, and alas, struck upon the only reasonable solution. He was on his fourth can of beer when he realized he was wasting time and tried switching to brandy. At 120 proof, he could find peaceful oblivion, blessed oblivion far more rapidly . . . but the damn bottle was glass.

CHAPTER 21

Back to square one, Ronnie realized as she began flipping through the pages of her notebook. Names, dates, and faces jumped off the page, and for long idle moments, she sat gazing into abstracts. Inevitably, her thoughts distracted, her mind conjuring visions of Jade Laquette. Repeatedly, she replayed those moments in Tim's Cove, recalling the cute little smile to set off his dimple as he'd tried to appear innocent of his evasive tactics. He hadn't truly wanted the answer; he'd asked the question, but he hadn't been prepared for the answer, and she'd been a fool to give it to him.

A man doesn't go to such extremes to conceal his past only to have his past tossed in his face.

The more she tried to concentrate on a murder investigation, the more she found herself standing at the window in the shade of sheer curtains, gazing toward the gray awning. In a steady stream, people entered and departed. Some remained inside for a few moments; others, like the neon blond, had remained a lot longer.

Andover . . . Jen Andover, 26, born and raised in Bentwood, only daughter of former Mayor Carl Andover. Not surprisingly, Jen had often appeared in four of the Bentwood High yearbooks that Ronnie had scanned the previous afternoon. Gazing toward the fancy gray awning, Ronnie recalled seeing Jen in a pleated skirt, standing on the shoulders of other girls, forming the peak of a human pyramid. Clearly, she'd been chosen for her pixie size and face. Cheerleader, homecoming queen, prom queen, class president two years in a row . . . with a campaign slogan concerning new jerseys for the football squad. Plausibly, Andover was just Bently's type—undemanding, willing, available. He wanted just one thing from a woman. If nothing else, Ronnie had discerned that much from Spencer's prank. Subject Bently to a female with a brain and shake him up . . . and Tim had no idea what he'd done when throwing them together. No idea the damage, the pain . . . the rage festering behind his friend's eyes.

Why was she torturing herself? If she had any sense, she'd take Len's advice and board a plane, let the proper authorities handle this one. Sam Hayward offered hope. That man wasn't about to drop his guard or let an innocent man hang for those murders. She could leave, could let Mark and Len . . . Mark wouldn't give up. The man was obsessed with the idea of hanging Isaac Bently, obsessed with the mystery of Bently's past.

And finding out about Jade Laquette wouldn't tamp Mark's tempest. If anything, the unsolved murder of Felicity Laquette would fan the flames. Too easily, Ronnie could picture Mark recasting his profile to fit Jade into the role of the Farmyard Slayer . . . and Isaac Bently wouldn't survive. The darkness she'd seen inside of him would take him. In her heart, Ronnie knew Isaac Bently wouldn't survive a second assault from the media. The pain of losing his mother, the horror of finding her . . .

He'd been the one to find her. Whether he'd raced home early from class, gone into convulsions as one account suggested, or simply walked into his house after regular school hours . . . he'd been the one to find her. He'd phoned the police and remained alone inside the house with his mother's body for over an hour because a police dispatcher had sent the wrong call signal over a radio. Max had confided that information to her, verifying one reported account that had been squelched in the initial flood of exposure. Max . . . Max had been the homicide detective who had responded to the second call after two uniformed officers had arrived on the scene. Max had never confided in her about the boy . . . but she could still remember the look in his eyes when he'd finally agreed to offer a few personal glimpses of his former case.

Max Hagen had never forgotten that case, had never justified its outcome in his mind. He'd never forgotten the child, and something about that case troubled him even now.

It took three tries to track down Max, but she found him in the middle of a conference with several department chiefs. "I need a few minutes, Max," she said soberly. "Call me as soon as you can."

Three minutes later, her phone rang, and she barely started a greeting when something held her tongue. Silence. Dead silence on the line, not even heavy breathing. A prickle trickled down her spine. Ronnie replaced the receiver slowly, unaware of holding her breath, aware of the temperature dropping inside the room. Shivering, she felt her chest tightening, her gaze moving slowly to the curtain that puffed slightly with the breeze through the screen. Bright sunlight poured past the windows, and heated air blew through the lace, but she was freezing.

The phone blasting another ring jolted her, loosening her breath with a short gasp, drawing her focus. On the second ring, she reached with a slightly trembling hand, cursed her foolishness, and grabbed the receiver, yanking it to her ear. Again, her breath held—

"Hello? Ronnie?" Max asked hesitantly.

Heaving a breath of relief, warming suddenly, she huffed, "Hi, Max."

"How are you?" he asked directly.

"God," she uttered. "Good news does travel fast, doesn't it?"

"Depends on the inside track," he said evenly. "Think I need an answer, baby doll. How bad were you hurt?"

"Not too, Max. It could have been worse. A couple bruises and bumps, and it was my own damned fault. I got sloppy and careless—"

"Bull," Max cut in sharply. "Even a veteran cop can get blindsided once in a while. If you're alright, that's the main thing."

"Thanks, Max," she said while trying to collect her muddled thoughts. That silence on that first call had blindsided her, too, and that wasn't Cal Farnsworth. "You uh . . . you know who saved me," she said quietly.

"I heard," he answered in a guarded tone.

"Max . . . I figured out who uh . . . who he is," she said and listened to the silence, a different silence altogether.

"I sort of figured you would," Max said quietly. "You're too good for your own good sometimes."

All the hurt came rolling over her chest, the pressure growing as she strained to keep the pain from her voice. "I'm not enlightening anyone, Max. I told him I'd keep it to myself, and I meant it, but . . . but a few things are bothering me, things about that case. I probably read almost every shred of publicity written . . . but there's no explanation for any of it. Why . . . why did that become such a circus, Max? Why does that case still trouble you?"

"Because it became a circus," he answered evenly, his attention distracted. "It shouldn't have happened. Information that should have been confidential leaked out of our office as if we had a funnel straight into the press . . . and we've discussed this before, Ronnie. Rehashing it won't repair it. If he's . . . if he's forgotten it, let it go. Don't reopen this one, baby doll."

Tears quickened in her eyes, the pain weighting her chest as she uttered, "It's . . . it's too late, Max. I . . . I talked to him this morning . . . and it's too late. It's open and I need to know . . . I need to know how to help him close it again," she realized. "He's . . . he's still so hurt."

Mulling his thoughts, Max remained silent until Ronnie could stand it no more. "Max . . .? What . . . what still bothers you about that case?"

"It was never solved," he said in a leaden voice. "And you didn't need me to tell you that."

"Did . . . was the media responsible for that case not getting solved?" she asked, struggling to make some sense of what she knew.

"Someone arrived at that house in the early afternoon. It was a bright clear, sunshiny day, and we had no witnesses, no evidence aside from the slugs . . . And the lady's clientele read like a Who's Who in Washington. She was assassinated, Ronnie. Executed. The lady knew something she wasn't supposed to know, and someone decided she was a liability. That's what should have been printed, but that was ignored right at the beginning. Instead of attacking the real criminals, the press persecuted a little kid and made him out to be a monster. The whole damned mess made me ill . . ."

She heard the catch in Max's voice, heard the glitch of thought making his voice trail. "Max?"

"Ronnie . . . he saved your life last night, didn't he?"

Considering the third party behind the Inn, she uttered, "Yes, Max, I think he did."

"Then save his, honey, and leave this alone," Max said quietly, no malice intended. "If he's learned to live with it and apparently, he has, then just let him deal with it. He uh . . . he was a pretty tough little guy from what I remember."

"He's . . . he's still pretty tough," Ronnie said absently, thinking of the man who had intervened last evening. He'd tossed Cal around like a rag doll, laying him flat with one blow. Physically, Isaac was tough . . . but Max was wrong. Inside, somewhere inside Isaac Bently, the memories remained raw, and he hadn't resolved that crime of eighteen years ago. The anger, the pain, the horror, and trauma—all of it festered.

"Any chance you'll be getting home soon?" Max asked.

"I'm not sure. Why?"

"Karen's been on my case since I talked to you Saturday. Been a while since you've dropped by. How about planning on dinner as soon as you get back?"

"It's a date, Max. I'll call you when I get in."

"Uh, one more thing, Ronnie," Max said and hesitated. "Is the Federal Bureau still hot to trot on Bently?"

"I haven't talked to Mark Jarvins since this morning," she answered. "At that point, I'd have to say, yes."

"Boy, some guys don't know when to quit," Max said with a sigh of disgust. "Hey, keep your chin up, baby doll. See ya soon . . ."

Feeling a quirked grin tugging at her lips, Ronnie replaced the receiver. Maybe, just maybe everything would be alright. Maybe Max, who had the inside track, could keep Mark from pursuing Bently—

The telephone jolted her yet again, and her attention riveted. She could ask the front desk to hold her calls or screen them, but for the moment, she would rather not arouse any suspicion. Nor cut off any lines of communication, even if one of them led to a psychopath. Lifting the receiver, she decided on the instant, "Yes?"

"Miss Bryson?" a subdued female voice asked.

"Yes?"

"My name's Emily Landslow. We haven't formally met, but I saw you Saturday morning outside the municipal building. Would it be possible for us to meet? I'm right downstairs. If I could come up to your room, I won't take up more than a few moments of your time."

A reporter, Ronnie realized and flashed a thought of the woman who had hovered outside the trio of men assailing Cal Farnsworth on the sidewalk. Ignoring the sour taste of the memory, Ronnie decided, "Why don't we meet in the dining room . . .? About ten minutes?"

"I'll wait, thank you."

Before meeting with Landslow, Ronnie needed to place a few calls, starting with Len. She tracked him down at the police station, beginning simply. "Len, I've been thinking about last night . . . If what we believe is true, I think the killer might try to contact me. Without creating suspicion or setting off any alarms, do you think you might arrange for a trace on this line?"

"Consider it done," he said simply. "And I might as well tell you, I've already arranged for undercover surveillance on you . . . What's one more screwy reporter in that Inn, eh?"

"Just make sure they're not overzealous, Len," she said soberly. "I'm not about to remain holed up in this room twiddling my thumbs, and I don't want everyone I talk to getting body slammed or held at gunpoint."

"Ron, this could be a long haul," Devinio said quietly. "Farnsworth's being held without bail. Depending on how smart this psycho is, he might just be willing to bide his time, and we have the full moon angle to contend with. It's uh . . . it's also possible the guy already skipped town, and he's on his way to a whole new ballgame."

"I hope you're wrong," she said honestly. "And I think you're wrong. The connection's in Bentwood, and if our killer's as methodical as I believe, he won't hold off because he set up Cal. I'm more tempted to believe that was an ego trip. This character's sitting back alright, and I think Mark's right, the guy's pretty pleased with himself. Farnsworth was a red herring, a sideshow to put one over on the authorities and clear the path. It's someone in this town, someone whose face we could've passed on the street. Someone who belongs here."

"Yea, I know," Len said with a hint of agitation. "I've already gotten a few printouts on that list we put together. I've come up with a few possibilities."

"Where's Mark?"

"Still over in Bender Falls."

"Hold on a sec," she said while stretching to slide her leather-bound notebook toward her. Fifteen years wasn't that long ago. "I'm going to read off a small list of names, Len," she said as she flipped through pages, finding the notes she'd made on the animal disappearances. Reading down the list, she asked, "Do any of those names coincide with your possible suspects?"

"Hansmar and Trendle are on the main list, Ron, but I don't have anything back on either one. As far as I know, they're squeaky clean besides a few parking violations. Uhhh . . . Hansmar has a local address. Julie Hansmar."

"Want to give it to me?"

"Not particularly, but I guess if I don't, you'll just open a phone book . . . 138 Banesville Lane."

It struck her as she replaced the receiver . . . they kept referring to this psycho in the masculine tense. Rings, watches . . . no trace of semen to suggest the erotic high the killer should have achieved. No physical evidence whatsoever to suggest this wacko had personally touched the victim at any time throughout the ordeal until the finale when the rings were removed . . .

Shoplifter . . . like a damned shoplifter or two-bit mugger. Rings, watches . . . what else? What else might these men have carried in their hip or shirt pockets to attract the attention of this lunatic?

And that was a seriously troubling thought, if for no other reason than because the killer had parted with those two significant souvenirs. Rings, watches . . . especially the watch, Ronnie realized. That item held enough significance for this lunatic to smash it, then part with it? To part with that kind of trophy . . . something else had been taken, something which meant more to this lunatic than wedding bands or pocket watches.

Shaking her head, Ronnie glimpsed the time on her watch, uttering a curse as she pushed off the bed. Emily Landslow.

Timing was a curse. A wicked rotten curse, Ronnie considered as she descended the steps, recognizing the tall slender executive who breezed through the front door on a collision course. Allen Spencer. Like every eager politician she'd ever met, he'd honed his smile for maximum effect. Not too broad to appear simple, not too small to appear surly. This fellow even managed the concerned-parent crease in his brow. Only his blue eyes, as dark as a summer sky, bore a slight family resemblance to the man whom she'd already begun to consider a friend.

"Miss Bryson," Allen Spencer spoke in a reverent deep voice, conveying an intensity to match his eyes. "I was just on my way to see you," he continued as he offered his hand. "Allen Spencer, Bentrel Steel Co. I'd hoped to meet you sooner, but things have been pretty hectic around here the past few days. After last night . . . I understand you saw Dr. Blackwell, but I'd like to suggest you see my personal physician . . ."

Perhaps, more than the blue eyes had carried from one brother to another. Allen was far more zealous, but her first impression swiftly dissolved. In mere moments, he conveyed a sincere concern for her safety and well-being, apologized for the town's reception toward her, and expressed genuine dread at the circumstances.

"Having been born and raised near Bentwood, I'm appalled by what's happened here . . ."

She nearly did it again, nearly walked straight into an interview at the drop of a hat, eager to ask Allen a few questions about the victims, about the town. When he suggested she join him for dinner, after assuring himself of her physical health, however, Ronnie hesitated.

"Why don't I send someone around to pick you up at five, Miss Bryson? My wife and I would love to have you."

Bently . . . the instant thought of sitting down to dinner with another Spencer and the fear of being set up by another Spencer stifled her acceptance. Almost certainly, she would suffer too many thoughts of Isaac Bently even if he were not present.

"I'm afraid I have to decline, Allen. I would like to speak to you, however. If you could meet me tomorrow morning, possibly, here in the dining room . . .?"

Her thoughts crowded with Isaac, Ronnie entered the dining room, belatedly waking to several heads pivoting before she spotted the lone woman in a corner booth across the room. Cursing her preoccupation, Ronnie composed her thoughts as she wove through the tables. Twice someone stopped her, offering sympathies, glad she was alright.

Rattled, Ronnie slipped into the booth across from the vaguely familiar woman. "Sorry I took so long," she said as she glanced at the slightly older woman.

Emily Landslow wore her coppery-colored hair in a short quick style of stiff curls to press against the nape of her neck where she wore a thin gold chain, probably sporting a religious ornament under the bold purple blouse. A lavender skirt added to her secretarial style. All business, she wore a pair of plastic gold-rimmed glasses with tiny sequined gems along the side of either post. Her pale blue eyes magnified behind the lenses to afford her a perpetual expression of wide-eyed wonder if not shock, but she still managed to look down her skinny nose, a lot like Ms. Dunner.

"I do remember seeing you," Ronnie admitted and offered her hand across the table. "Ronnie Bryson."

Landslow hesitated then seemed to force her hand across the linen. She barely touched Ronnie's fingers in reflection of those obligatory formalities of airy cheek kisses that Ronnie had learned to endure and despise very early in life.

Instantly annoyed, Ronnie adopted a more formal tone. "What was it you wanted to speak to me about, Ms. Landslow?"

"Please, call me Emily," the woman said with a hint of condescension.

"I assume you're a reporter, Ms. Landslow," Ronnie said and detected a trace of Jade's cynicism inflecting her tone. "I'd imagine you have a press card?" To go with the notebook alongside her coffee cup and the recorder undoubtedly humming inside the beige vinyl purse situated at the back of the table. Like Grimes, she probably made her own rules concerning illegal taping devices.

"I'm not currently working for any specific paper," Landslow spoke aloofly. "Although I submit to both of the larger Pittsburgh papers."

The waitress arrived then, smiling at Ronnie with a conflict of emotions on her lined face. "Can I bring you a menu, Miss Bryson?" she asked while reaching for the overturned cup.

Warding off the coffee with a subtle hand gesture, appreciating the timing, Ronnie returned the smile while reading the nametag on her white blouse. "I'll have to pass on the coffee, Shirley." Turning her gaze to Landslow, Ronnie commented, "I'm afraid I really can't stay—"

"Just a few moments of your time, Miss Bryson," the woman said loftily, a hint of condescension in her tone, contempt in her magnified eyes.

"I'm sorry, Ms. Landslow. Something's come up," Ronnie said as she started from the booth.

"I don't imagine you knew you were dealing with a maniac when you agreed to rendezvous with Cal Farnsworth last evening, did you, Miss Bryson?"

Halted, Ronnie turned her cool gaze to Landslow's smug leer. "Miss Landslow, I have no idea where you collected your facts to ask such a ludicrous question, but I suggest you find another, more reputable source. Unless of course, you're simply fabricating details. I might further suggest, if you have a penchant for gossip, you should forget trying to peddle fiction to major newspapers as you may find a more lucrative career in submitting to tabloids." Still angry, Ronnie sidestepped around the waitress, glancing at the startled woman. "If you get a moment, Shirley, perhaps, you could send a cup of coffee and one of those divine cinnamon rolls up to my room?"

"Right away, Miss Bryson," Shirley decided and cast her vote with a slight smile.

The nerve of Landslow for implying that Ronnie had *arranged* to be mauled by Farnsworth! Emily Landslow. Little Miss Emily Landslow might need her wings clipped.

Her first call went to Pete Simons, but even before she replaced the receiver, Ronnie knew she was being petty. Enlisting Simons to contact his pals in Pittsburgh wouldn't likely squelch the story. Still, the woman might think twice before distorting too many facts. The witch was probably in league with Grimes although Ronnie couldn't imagine what she'd done to gain Grimes's disfavor—

"Oh, shit," she uttered as she remembered the call she'd promised to place to Bobby. By now, Grimes could be receiving official papers, and perhaps, her negligence was something of a Freudian slip. If not for Grimes, Cal Farnsworth might not be sitting in jail without bond, and she might not have a golf-ball-sized knot on the back of her head . . .

And she would never have known what it felt like to wrap her arms around a phantom, or to be kissed senseless—

"Stop it," she uttered. "Just stop it." A job to do! She had a job to do here, whether her heart was still in it or not.

Armed with the short list of names from ancient police reports, Ronnie pulled the phonebook toward her, not surprised to find five of the seven names listed at original addresses. Turning to the map Mark had supplied Saturday morning, she began marking the locations with stars. Scattered, the addresses were scattered all over town, and she tried to imagine a child hiking the distances between stars. On the last name, her attention shattered briefly to note the house existed directly behind Olden Time . . .

She would save that stop for last if she even gained the nerve to make that visit.

At all costs, she would avoid Isaac Bently . . . For his sake, she would stay out of his sight.

Somehow, she hadn't anticipated the sudden prickling when she passed through the rear door of the hotel. She hadn't even considered how the image of Cal advancing could sideswipe her as she walked toward her car. Concentrating, she scanned the thick hedges, noting the wood fence barely visible through the soft leaves of the lilac bushes. In the spring, that hedges would be beautiful, she considered in an attempt at distraction, but her focus fell to the telltale signs of broken glass in the gravel outside the rental's driver's door. In a gray haze, evidence of fingerprint dust remained on the silver hood. the door and on the windows. For a long moment, she stood alongside her car remembering that glimpse of Farnsworth lying sprawled on the gravel . . . but more readily her thoughts riveted to those seconds where Jade had caught and lifted her, held her . . .

Damn it! She needed to stop thinking of the man as 'Jade.' She needed to stop thinking of the man altogether!

On route to her first stop, she searched for the tail Len had mentioned, but aside from the nominal flow of traffic, she spotted no one in her wake. Dismissing her search, she pulled into a gravel drive alongside a house that more resembled a cottage with its lacy white curtains on every window and small covered porch. On route to the front door, Ronnie prepared her speech, but after several attempts at the doorbell, she accepted the obvious. No one home.

"Anything I can help you with, Miss Bryson?" a female voice called. Pivoting, Ronnie found the speaker above a squat, neatly trimmed hedge that bordered the driveway.

Wearing a straw hat and gardening gloves, the woman appeared to be in her mid-fifties. With her round ruddy face, brown-streaked hair pulled back in a ponytail, baggy faded jeans, and sleeveless plaid blouse, she conjured images of Tom Sawyer idling down the mighty Mississippi, and in flashing instant, Ronnie knew she'd never met this woman before. And yet, the lady had called her by name. Apparently, the gossip mill was running smoothly, but whether her fame would be a help or hindrance was yet to be determined.

Striding off the porch, passing her car to reach the hedge, Ronnie donned a faint smile. "Possibly, you can help me," she said smoothly. "Would you happen to know if Mrs. Bickerson will be home soon?"

"Sure doubt it," the woman said. "But I might know where you could find her if it's important."

"Not that important," Ronnie conceded as she scanned the slightly larger cottage next door. Overflowing, flowerboxes of Geraniums hung on the front porch railing, and vivid yellow flowers draped from bulging hanging baskets off the eaves. The gloves and hat were not a ruse. The woman had a green thumb. "Your home is lovely," Ronnie managed without an ounce of jealousy. "You must spend hours gardening . . ."

Giving most people an opening to talk, supplying a willing ear, could produce more results than a brutal interrogation. Within five minutes, Ronnie learned that the yellow flowers were Angel Wing Begonias, and she rested in a wicker chair sipping lemonade and listening to Thelma Green relate the town's history. Without much effort, Ronnie managed to slide into the general direction of her investigation as Thelma offered her dread and mortification over the tragedies.

"Even small towns have their problems, Thelma. Bentwood's been lucky," Ronnie offered in a segue. "As I understand, there's not been a serious crime around here since those dognappings several years ago. That's sort of what I wanted to speak with Mrs. Bickerson about," Ronnie continued smoothly. "I'd like to get a little background, possibly slant a human-interest angle about the town's excellent record. I understand the Bickersons lost a pet during that siege . . . I'd imagine children were involved. I thought, perhaps, she might be able to tell me if the culprits were ever caught."

"I remember well enough," Thelma pitched in and continued with a far more thorough account than Ronnie had expected, dropping names of troublesome children like manna from heaven. No one had bought the animal attack or dog pack theory according to Thelma. She was far more apt to believe a few local kids had gotten a hold of some of that 'wacky tobacky' and 'got up to no good.' Her children, close to the same ages as the Bickerson children, ranging from seven to sixteen at the time, had never touched the stuff . . . they were good kids, like most of the children in Bentwood. . . ..

A half-hour later, having spotted the white van in her wake, Ronnie sat with another elder woman who displayed a knack for macramé and sported some beautifully beaded wall hangings in her living room. More names, more suppositions, and more theories on those animal attacks surfaced along with a few tidbits of information that Ronnie stored although she wasn't immediately certain why the words triggered her interest. Several names were repeated, not the least of which was Cal Farnsworth who used to accompany his father to town and hang out with a bad crowd while the elder Farnsworth ran errands. For a town with a low crime rate, the number of children labeled 'trouble' certainly merited curiosity.

On the third house call, Ronnie heard the first hint of something she would rather not know, but she listened, taking mental notes, collecting and hearing similar names, cross-referencing those at light speed.

"I'm telling you, Elvie," the elder man who'd been growling his accusations, continued, "That whole gang was nothing but trouble. Our boy," the man said while snagging Ronnie. "He got mixed up with that crowd. Course, nobody wants to talk about it. Who wants to admit your own kid could be out there consorting with the devil? Hell, even now, nobody wants to talk about it and if you ask me, old Mayor Andover's the one who got the whole thing covered up. His daughter, you probably seen her strutting around town . . . a lot of blond hair and bare legs. Hangs out in her daddy's store . . .? She was mixed up with that band. Wouldn't surprise me if she was one of the ring leaders, the way she used to come sniffing around my boy, Henry . . .."

"Don't mind my husband," the woman said while walking Ronnie to her car. "Ever since he had his heart attack a couple years ago, he's not been the same . . . It was just last week, he claimed the government was bugging our phones and flying missiles over our town . . . Everything's a conspiracy to him . . ."

If it were a delusion, it was one that Elsa Briggs, a widow across town shared. Within minutes of her next stop, Ronnie listened to the sad little woman talk about the 'hellions' in town, and the prickles slid down her spine.

"My own Elsie, she graduated from high school that year. She's my youngest," Elsa said while meandering to her television where elaborately framed photographs crowded the surface. "I had five, three girls, two boys. All good kids. You might know my son Tom? He serves on the Town Council. He's a superintendent over at Bentrel Steel . . . now there's a fella who's going places . . . not my Tom. I mean Allen Spencer. Tom's just happy lending a hand and putting the town in order, but that Allen," she said with a sad little smile on her lined lips. "Wouldn't surprise me if he runs for the Senate. . . He's never been one to let any grass grow under his feet."

"Lovely girl," Ronnie said honestly as she eyed the photo of an attractive brunette.

"She lives in Los Angeles now . . . She was too smart to get mixed up with the shenanigans in this town. She went off to a business school and got a job with an insurance company. She's a branch manager now . . . married with three little ones of her own . . . She doesn't come back home too often . . ."

Smart girl, Ronnie considered and headed to her next stop, her mind turning over the details. Disappointed, she encountered another locked door, shuttered windows, and no neighbors in sight. With the shade slanted across the tended lawn, Ronnie grasped the afternoon sailing toward evening, and with the discomfort lingering at the edge of her mind, she set her course for town.

At the Inn, just the sound of murmured voices altered her intention to have dinner in the dining room. Quite a few reporters had remained at The Bentwood House, and society was just degenerate enough for a few people to patronize the Inn because a murderer had been nabbed in the parking lot.

Alone, Ronnie started up the staircase, barely a few strides when a young woman hurried from the registration desk and thrust another short stack of notes at her. Anticipating the contents, Ronnie refrained from opening them until she stood inside her room, safely ensconced behind a locked door. Fan mail, she sneered as she read the first note that fairly accused her of single-handedly destroying the widow Farnsworth.

Glimpsing the pages, concentrating only to read those with a familiar name, she found a message from Mark asking her to call, leaving his number with a Bender Falls exchange. To blazes with him, too.

Bunching the pillows against the headboard, Ronnie settled against them, propping her notebook against her raised thighs. Within seconds, she stopped thinking about the case, stopped thinking about a cultist group of troublemakers. Her thoughts had turned to Jade Laquette, to the phantom images of him moving about the room only an evening past, to the genuine concern she'd sensed in his every gesture and glance.

CHAPTER 22

The door chime chirruped at a wall speaker, rousting Isaac from a nearly successful attempt to lose himself in the Middle Ages. Drinking hadn't helped. A dozen beer cans stood like a picket fence at the edge of his desk. Still, the instant he looked up from the pages, rather than his office, he saw the black-haired witch looking up at him, tears glistening in her eyes.

Cursing, he meandered from behind his desk, but his footsteps slowed as he reached the dim hallway that separated his store from his warehouse. Reporters? More good-intentioned neighbors? Spencer? The witch herself? Before ever reaching the top step, he pivoted and strode back into his apartment. Flopping into his desk chair, he collected his beer rather than the ancient tome. Why he bothered drinking, he couldn't even decide . . . and the thought of Cal Farnsworth soured him even more. There was no such thing as a good drunk. No such thing as drunken oblivion.

The chirrup continued several more times, a damn irritating sound to have him staring at the wall from which it emanated . . . and he wasn't happy to find himself again rising and walking steadily through the hallways. Not stopping, Isaac continued down the steps and to the side door. His hand trembled as he unlocked the door; his anger spiraled as he pulled the panel open to find Sheriff Taylor Grant poised on his doorstep. In slow motion, Isaac looked from the glowering dark eyes to the open palm hovering in front of him. Two bemused deputies idled alongside the county car at the curb. Several spectators had already gathered at the corner, watching this exchange. Again, Isaac looked into Grant's eyes. No use even asking if the fellow was serious. No sense even trying to talk his way out of this. He'd asked for it.

Silently, Isaac dug his keys from his pocket, separating the leather weave from the wad and tugging two keys from the collection. Angry, he slapped the keys onto the palm and watched the fingers close like an iron trap. Looking again into Grant's faintly bemused eyes, he asked, "For how long do you intend to borrow my car?"

Grant smirked, "D' know, kid. Might decide to start a collection of little black racers for the county. At the rate you're going, we could have a whole fleet before the Fourth of July."

Isaac felt his mustache curve, not amused.

"Seeing as how you did our county a service, I wouldn't want to make this too painful," Grant mused. "Why don't you just lead me to it, and I'll be on my way?"

When it rained, it poured, Isaac considered as he stood moments later watching his Jaguar backing from the warehouse. Why should he even be surprised to lose one of his favorite possessions? It was his own damn fault.

Angrily, he slammed the panels shut before Grant found first gear. *On loan*. If he could convince himself that the car was *on loan*, perhaps, it would ease some of his hostility . . . but he doubted it.

Fuming, Isaac strode between his two remaining black sports cars, sliding his palm over the Maserati from back to front. His irritation compounded as he continued through the row of stacked furniture and boxes, which rose nearly reaching the rafters. He had more than enough projects to keep him occupied for the next twenty or thirty years. More damned boxes to sort, chairs to repair, cabinets to clean than he could finish in a lifetime, but at the moment . . . he wanted another damn beer and a good book. He could swamp his mind in the Middle Ages when the nearest thing to a reporter would be a damned court jester!

"The son of a bitch took my car," Isaac muttered as he climbed the steps, and that witch . . . somehow that witch was to blame for this, too! The woman was a viper!

Relentless! Worse than any female he'd ever met! A witch with her diamond blue eyes, and soft, generous lips . . . and her hands to send tingles through his flesh, heating his blood faster than lightning.

If Tim Spencer thought this Miss Veronica Bryson was different than any other female, ole Tim had a lot to learn. Sweet, intelligent Miss Veronica Bryson . . . with her claws in the government and her hooks sinking to the Oval Office. And she wanted him to believe she was here to solve a murder . . .?

Bullshit! If the witch had known Det. Max Hagen, if she'd truly written some academic *paper* on the slaughter of Jade Laquette, then it was no damned coincidence the witch had arrived in this town. He could almost believe . . . he could almost believe that someone in the government had ordered these killings. A conspiracy. These murders could be part of a government conspiracy . . . and she was here for him.

Pacing again, cursing, he prowled through his crypt-like rooms with his muscles coiled and adrenaline racing. Something! He had to do something! Halted, poised suddenly with a blinding epiphany, he knew what he needed to do . . . knew *exactly* what he needed to do!

Only beginning to collect her thoughts, Ronnie jolted with the first drumbeat rap of knuckles on her door. Staring at the wood, she drew breath and called, "Yes?"

Another blow of knuckles, more insistent than the first.

Already tense, she closed her notebook and stepped off the bed. The surveillance man lingered just down the hallway, prepared to come to her rescue if the need arose. Her confidence firming, she continued across the room, closer when she asked, "Who's knocking?"

"Mr. Bently, Miss Bryson," the low voice slid through the wood with an edge. "Open the damn door before we create yet another scene."

He'd threatened to bust it open last night unless she produced the key.

Heartbeat accelerating, uncertain if she suffered anxiety or anticipation, Ronnie fumbled the deadbolt open and pulled the door inward.

Startled, she froze. The devil certainly owned something other than blue jeans and plaid shirts. He stood as if posing for a shot in a fashion magazine. One panel of his black suit jacket bunched at his wrist; a gold watchband glinted at his hip with his hand tucked in his pants pocket. Tailored, in a double-breasted design to appear elegantly casual, the three-piece ensemble of heavy black silk contrasted beautifully with the soft jade-colored shirt and the fire-lanced hue of his eyes. She'd been wrong . . . extremely wrong with her offhanded critique of an evening past. The man could dress up very well . . . and by the slight angry twitch of his mustache, he read her appraisal. "Mr.—"

"I've come to take you to dinner, Miss Bryson," he said while moving his hand, touching his fingers to the door, and stepping forward. "I see no good reason to break the routine we've established. Do you?"

Stepping back, suddenly, not sure about the angry shine in his eyes or the subtle contempt in his tone, Ronnie wondered if she ought to shout for help . . . or plead forgiveness. For God's sake, the *devil* was still smiling as he touched the door shut in his wake. His focus slid downward and rose in slow seductive speculation. "I—" she started and swallowed.

"*Ma copine*, I know you have something more appropriate than denim to accompany me downstairs." His eyes glittered with dark amusement. "I'd be happy to assist if you need help to change."

He was crazy! The man was stark raving mad! Or drunk! His eyes carried a trace of red, but that could be an illusion of the evening light or the devil's influence. She could deal with the hurt. She could accept that he was hurt . . . but he was furious. Every fiber of her body confirmed that simple detail. He was furious, nearly insane with his rage, and far too ready to act on his hostility. Whether his hatred or intention to seduce her hurt worse, she couldn't decide. Tears leaped over her eyes with the revelation—she'd brought him to this end.

This wasn't natural. Natural . . . natural was his hand reaching to scuff a boy's head or catching a little pajama-clad child in mid-flight or swooping her off her feet before she fainted and carrying her to this room. This, waltzing in here dressed fit to kill, and dead set on seducing her . . .? Not natural.

At his forward step, she backed sharply, avoiding the hand he lifted toward her cheek. Looking into his feral eyes through a blur of tears, she strained softly, "Don't."

"As I seem to recall, Miss Bryson, you were rather receptive to my touch only this morning," he said with a low silky tone, a twitch of a smile. "Should I believe I've suddenly grown horns or warts? Become an offense in your eyes?"

"I didn't mean to hurt you," she strained and saw a near-violent flair in the green depths. "I wanted you to understand what you'd . . ." *Encounter in town with the fame Mark had implied*. She'd meant to promise to keep his secret, to help him remain anonymous if that was his choice. Never had she suspected he could've hidden so much hurt behind those arrogant smiles and intense gazes . . . and she understood his rage. A rage born of pain as she'd experienced in her own past. Weeping never helped. Only anger offset the pain. "I'm sorry," she said as she braved the fire-green embers. "I truly never meant to hurt you so badly."

"You are an annoying witch," he said shortly, and his eyes lanced fury. "Do you wrap a spell around all your admirers, Miss Bryson? Is that why your former lover remains so obsessed with you? The man's possessed! Blinded by your wretched innocence!"

Not a lover! Mark Jarvins had never been her lover! She barely thought to shout the words when Isaac took another step toward her. The heat of his fury rippled off him in waves to prick her.

"Where are your baubles, witch? Where are the amulets and concoctions you use to beguile your other lovers?"

The sneer in his voice, the bitterness of his seductive smile, and the scathing shine in his eyes . . .? He was the same man she'd held. The same man she'd kissed only this morning who'd set her blood to boiling with his touch. But he was changed, and she was the cause. Somehow, she'd unleashed the fury barely contained inside of him. She only wished she were a witch with the power to transform this beast back into the man, to banish the pain belying his fury.

Tears threatening to burst, she parted her lips to voice her sorrow, but in a lightning-swift motion, he clasped her arm. Sparks flew under his touch, singeing the words in her throat before his mouth covered her lips. Only for a second, she thought to push him away. Only for an instant, she meant to break and shout . . .

Even in anger, his kiss sizzled sensations through her, stilling her protest, and her hands betrayed her, rising to clasp his neck, drawing him deeper.

He'd meant only to silence the witch! To break the spell she'd intended to cast with her wretched tears and sorrow! Too late, Isaac knew his mistake. The taste and touch of her lips melding and molding incited a riot in his system. Of its own accord, his free hand lifted snaking into the black, silky bubbles, clasping the back of her head where the small knot stirred yet another conflict. If anyone had cause to hurt this vixen, he did!

But his hand softened, capping the wound as he tilted her head, plunging himself deeper into his doom, as mindlessly as a moth seeking light.

Damn her! Just damn her for tasting like a fountain of spring water! She'd done it again! He felt her weaving her spell about him, drawing him in with the urgent touch of her palm on his neck, her fingers tingling the roots of his hair. Damn her for shaking him to the core with a mere touch! For making him want her! Need her!

He'd come here to break the spell of her soulful tears! To free himself and salvage what remained of his life, which she threatened to destroy! In a conflict of rage and flaming desire, he ran kisses down her neck, tasting the magic of her power as sweet as mountain dew on his parched lips. Against his conscious will, his palms slid to the collar of her blouse. On another plane, he thumbed the buttons free and traced the path of his fingers with his tongue.

He would turn the tides on this witch! Surely! Whatever her motives for enthralling him, she'd succeeded. But he'd turn this tide. That he thirsted for her more than a dying man in a desert needed water, needed her more than he needed fresh air to breathe only enflamed him more. He would turn this tide. When he satisfied his desire, when he drank his fill of her kisses . . . he could walk away. He could walk away as easily as he'd escaped the clutches of every other female who'd tried to trap him with their treacherous smiles and wanton touches.

Just a woman! Surely, she was just another woman! Another of that wretched conclave designed to deceive and betray, to covet and condemn all men! But even as he growled his anger, his palms slid down her silken back and hips, sliding the cloth away, succumbing to his desire to feel her tingling flesh molded against him. Never—not ever in his life, had he wanted something—anything—as badly as he wanted this witch. To have her essence saturating him would be ecstasy.

Damn her! Damn her fumbling fingers at his breast, bumbling like a schoolgirl with his buttons. As if she'd never set herself to this task for which she was surely a master! Only more enraged as her quivering palms resigned to rest against the silk at his chest, he growled as much frustration as desire while skimming his lips to drink again from her urgent lips. Only then, as he held her captive, he allowed her hands to break the connection and cruise along his chest, his body shedding the silk as easily as a snake shedding its skin. Blood racing, the throbbing pulse of his desire heated his loins. His knees weakened with the deceptive innocence of her touch upon his heated flesh.

How dare she try to deceive him even now! To cloak herself in the guise of a pure maiden with her shy touches even as he felt her desire transcending his physical form, striking him at the core of his primal needs.

Good God, she was worse than all others! Manipulating him even now! Portraying the epitome of innocence as her body flamed against him and her every ragged breath drew him deeper toward her center!

He'd known she could bite! Had felt the venom of her tongue and the sting of her piercing blue eyes from the instant she'd lanced him three mornings past. Lifting her, he brought her full against him, holding her silent with a force of his will as he carried her the scant steps to the rumpled bed. No hope for him now. The press of her need, the scent of her womanhood, held him as much a captive to her desire as his own.

He hated her . . . he surely hated her. The sounds muffled against her breast resembled the growl of a tortured beast but his hands . . . his hands felt like sunlight spreading over her body. Inch by wonderful inch, he warmed her from the inside out, and her rational thought spiraled away into a soft thermal cloud.

Ronnie had no clear image of reaching the bed, of lying down under him. Only once, she gasped a protest and thought to stop him. Not love. This wasn't making love . . . It was a tempest of hatred, his every innate talent turned against her, torturing her with a bitter-sweet gentleness . . . and she still wanted him. She wanted all of him, from his glowing green eyes to his shaft throbbing against her. Surely, this wasn't how it was supposed to be! This couldn't possibly be how it was *supposed* to be . . . but she didn't want it to stop, didn't want him to stop.

As she'd sensed, he was a powerhouse. Barely contained, the vibrations rippled out of him into her. The urgency of his need held her rapt; the ecstasy of his touch drove her own need higher. Surely, this wasn't natural, wasn't right, but with every fleeting instant, her body betrayed her, responding to the wonders his magic touch revealed.

Her fingers laced within his waves as his mouth slipped over her breasts. Wild tension spread through her bones and flesh. Her back muscles arched against her will to offer him more, demand more of whatever this devil offered. Gladly, she'd hock her soul at this moment if only to suspend herself within this splendid heat and warmth forever. *The man was a devil! A beast!* A magician, stripping her of her will to leave her uttering pleas and writhing for the fulfillment he promised.

Dear God! He was a master! His hands weren't hands at all. Merely extensions of soft breath and lips, his palms cruised down her thighs and brushed against the frontier that rose to welcome him. Nothing had ever felt like this! She would surely incinerate with the flames igniting at the very core of her existence. Never had she felt so alive! Her blood raced to his command; her mind suspended within an energy field. Only at the fringes of reality, she felt his fingers stroking her, stoking the flames higher. He was killing her! Surely! Only at the brink of death could she feel so alive!

"Veronica," he whispered in a thick angry snarl to send her spiraling further on a thermal tide of abandon. "Veronica . . ."

She was losing control—had lost control if she ever had it. Something wondrous happened inside her, freeing her from whatever bonds had held her in such reserve. With his voice, his hands, his mouth . . . with the electric sparks off his muscled limbs, he'd sent her into another dimension where no boundaries existed. Images bursting through her mind, she found sense only to speak his name, a plead for an island, an anchor in a sea of sensations.

"Jaaade . . ." She wanted it ended, wanted it never to end . . . wanted him!

Long and low, he growled and lifted, looking down into her. His eyes blazed emerald as he glared at her. "You are a witch," he snapped and descended fast, hard, and angry, gliding into her with the precision of a surgeon.

A single short cry of pain escaped, and in the same instant, an explosion rocked the center of her universe then . . . stillness. All motion stopped. The sea of madness halted as if time itself had frozen. At her ear, his breath had ceased, and with her senses enhanced, Ronnie woke to her fingers molded into his frozen back muscles and glimpsed the fringes of his sweated waves at her temples. Time had stopped. The air crackled around them. Sounds filtered through a funnel into her foggy mind.

She rested in a hotel room with a man she loved but hardly knew, and she'd just delivered herself to him. Time stopped. She lay at the apex of a fierce and frenzied storm . . . and she feared the moment time would begin again. Feared the man, who poised over her, waking to the revelation of what he'd just taken.

A shudder spilled through him, and Ronnie suffered the release of time under her fingertips as his breath started in a soft low growl against her ear. When he began to move, her hands splayed, holding him. She wasn't ready, not willing to see the look in his eyes.

If he hadn't hated her when he arrived, he might despise her now . . . and she feared his contempt. Like no man before him, she feared the contempt of this devil who could crush her with a single scathing glance. If she could just hold him against her for a moment, postpone the inevitable for a few moments . . . She wanted only to revel in the vibrations still coursing through her veins. No regrets. Not for a moment would she regret her surrender. Even in that wild rage, she'd grasped the beauty, the ecstasy of joining with him, body and soul.

In her hair, his fingers relaxed, but his sweated limbs remained poised, shivering as he drew soft, shallow breaths. "You . . ." he heaved a whisper, his voice muffled against her hair and the pillow. "You are a witch . . . Veronica."

Tears stung her eyes. She held him tighter, feeling the answering press of his forearms wrapped against her ribs and shoulders on either side. "D-don't ha-ate me," she heaved softly. "Please, don't."

"Hate you?" he uttered with a peculiarly strained note. A huffed sound, almost a sob escaped. "Wish that I could, witch . . . wish that I could."

"Y-you don't?" she breathed her doubt, daring to hope.

He lifted, dragging his head up and tipping his face until their eyes locked.

Through a thin film of tears, she saw the soft shine of moisture in his eyes, saw the doubt and sorrow etched on his handsome face. He appeared, in a word, distraught.

"You . . . do you hate me?" he asked in a soft voice, his eyes evoking a more desperate shine.

Only now, only at this instant, looking into his pained eyes, she realized why he would appear so mortified, why he would fear her hatred . . . He'd seduced her. He'd come into this room to seduce her. And he'd succeeded, getting a little more than he bargained for. "Wish that I could," she uttered with a slow quivering smile. "You're a devil . . . you're a green-eyed devil," she said softly and watched his eyes soften more, relief and something akin to wonder washing through a wave of concern.

"I-I hurt you," he said absently.

"You could have," she said with a thought of the hatred she'd feared, the contempt he could've wielded against her to excuse himself for his cruelty. "But you didn't."

CHAPTER 23

Good God. "You're beautiful," Isaac uttered as he gazed in wonder over Ronnie's delicate face, into her moist blue eyes. *What to do* . . . what to do with a beautiful woman in his arms, a beautiful woman whom he'd come here to hurt? Who he'd succeeded in hurting far worse than he'd ever intended. Had he thought, had he believed even for a second that she'd never been with a man . . .? She'd never let on. Even those fleeting denials had seemed more like the wiles of a woman playing games with him. He'd fully believed she was teasing him, no different than the dozens of loose women he'd engaged since his fourteenth birthday. A whore, he recalled. His father had enlisted a whore to introduce him to the finer pleasures, and she'd toyed with him, physically and emotionally, teasing him to the brink of madness.

He'd believed Veronica to be playing the same game . . . and the wicked beast to dwell inside him had chosen a fine time to forsake him.

Fleetingly, he remembered enhancing his efforts to drive her past her defenses into a frenzy where she had no choice but to surrender.

Never, not once in his entire life, had he regretted his treatment of a woman more than at this moment. Never had he been humbled as she humbled him at this moment. She should hate him. She should be ripping his eyes out or striping his back with her nails . . . But she held him as she'd held him throughout.

He should get up, should gather his clothes, and run like the dog that he proved himself to be. Never had a woman deserved his treatment less, and never had he treated one worse. "I don't know what to say to you," he admitted as he looked into her compelling eyes, wanting to apologize, needing her forgiveness. "I don't know how to apologize—"

"Do you know how long I've waited, wondering if I'd ever find someone I'd want to share this with?"

She could've stopped him; it was in her eyes, in her voice. He'd seen her fighting Farnsworth . . . Cal could've hurt her, might have overpowered her and taken her, but she would've shredded Cal before surrendering. To him, to Jade Laquette, she'd surrendered willingly and matched his fury with the abandon of a seasoned woman . . . and he knew at this moment, he was falling in love with her. He might have been in love with her since he'd seen her sitting inside that rented Escort and felt her watching him through her mirrored glasses. She'd pretended to gaze up the block. All those tumbling black curls had glistened in the morning sunlight; her pensive lips had curved like a porcelain cameo. Even now, her black silk tumbling over his hands, her delicate face tilted in an angle which could be considered impertinent . . . and he could feel himself quickening, his anticipation kindling anew.

Her eyes flickered; a trace of curiosity troubled her brow.

Good God, he was still inside of her! She may be naïve, but she certainly wasn't stupid. With a serious effort, he began slipping away, easing himself down the sweat-slicked silk of her slender body, but her hands firmed again, halting him. For an instant, he doubted the spark of amusement and questioned the implication, but he wasn't stupid, either

Far more slowly, he lowered his hips and sank to rest against her. Far more gently, he touched her . . . and she was touching him. Her hands slid over his damp, quivering muscles, awakening him far more swiftly to his need. The woman was a witch. No other explanation could he fathom as she began to explore him, testing her not-too-inconsiderable power over him. In what could only be seconds, she turned the tables on him with the mastery of her investigative skills and indulging her curiosity with her hands. Illumination brightened her eyes as she watched him quicken with the torment of her quest.

He deserved her wrath. Deserved this torture of her tingling palms gliding down his quivering back, down his hips, skimming like a cool breeze over his heated flesh to shiver his insides in anticipation. He wouldn't move. Couldn't move against her. Not to hasten her nor halt her discoveries, and by God, she was making more than a few, electrifying the whipcord strands of nerves to strain his six senses.

For the first time in forever, he didn't feel like a third party merely watching his body in action. In every instant, she held him rapt, his mind consumed in her wonder as well as his own.

He had no desire to finish swiftly, no urge to finish and escape this shadowy room. If he never left this room again, he would die in ecstasy . . . but his body betrayed him, driving him toward that place from which there could be no turning back.

Uncontrollably, he groaned softly with the agony of desire throbbing and pulsing at his core. No control. He had no control over his body responding to these fluttering touches, drawing him to taste her satin neck, her shoulders. His senses surrendered, buckling willingly to her desire, holding off until he knew her needs matched his. When her name slipped off his tongue, it was a plea as much for release as forgiveness. By the tempo of her vibration and pulse, by the breath of his given name at his neck, he knew . . . it wasn't contempt she felt for him.

As if she'd somehow set him free from the darkness inside of him, he knew himself soaring on a wondrous cloud of light and ecstasy, no longer confined to the physical pleasure his body had stolen in the arms of other women. When his body exploded, it wasn't death, not the 'little death' as another had referred to sexual fulfillment. But life . . . life pouring out of him, into him . . .

In weird wonder, Isaac lay propped on his elbow, looking at her as he collected his breath. Cheeks flushed, eyes filled with strange dancing light, she appeared as bewitching as a wood nymph from some Irish folklore. The smile playing on her lips only confused and bewildered him more. "You cannot possibly be real," he decided as he reached his palm, riding the rise and fall of her breath. By the rapid beat of her heart, he remained enthralled. "It's not possible," he decided matter-of-factly, a quiver starting in his lips. "You're an illusion. Some fairy-princess-illusion come to shatter all other illusions."

Laughter played on her lips and in her eyes. "That, I suppose, makes you a prince?"

"A humble peon," he mused. "No hope for me against your prowess."

"Hmm, in that case," she turned, laying her palm flat against his chest, tipping him back, and rising to her elbow to look down at him with a sober shine. "Guess I better take advantage of you, huh?"

"Good God, woman," he uttered in dumbfound, but she was at least, partly, serious. A shudder swept up his abdomen as her hand skidded on his sweat-slicked chest.

Her gaze fanned the length of him, taking an avid interest on the return trip. Her eyes glimmered when she locked on him. "I knew you were an interesting man, Mr. Bently."

She'd called him 'Jade' as they were making love, and as much as that worried him, he wanted to hear it again. It had been so long . . . so damned long since he'd heard the name he'd worn as a child. "That's not what you called me earlier, sweetheart," he said quietly.

Her eyes flashed quick regret and a touch of worry.

Finding her hand on his chest, he held her with his gaze. "Say it now. My name?"

"I . . . Jade," she said softly. "I'm sorry, but . . . but when I look at you, when I think about you, that's who I see. You're not Isaac Bently in my head. Or in my heart."

She knew what she was saying, and it grieved her. Not deliberately would she betray him, but looking into her eyes, he knew she would slip. That name would slide off her tongue with the ease of an endearment. "I can't bring myself to think of you as Ronnie either," he said after a long pause, clasping her hand and skidding it upward to touch his lips, kissing her fingertips. "In my head, in my heart, you are Veronica. A lovely little witch who's stolen something from me that I'm not certain I want back."

Her eyes brightened with laughter and warmth, and he knew he was doomed. Doomed beyond all rhyme and reason.

"Like witches do you, sir?"

"Love witches," he said with a faintly wicked smile. "Especially, beautiful witches with a stubborn will and silky unruly curls, and big blue eyes . . . with the name Veronica."

"You aaare a devil," she drawled, and mischief danced in her eyes. "But I'm beginning to think I love devils, too. Especially, green-eyed devils with a dimple and long wavy dark hair and . . ." Her eyes skidded down him and back. "Long, very lean capable muscles."

His thoughts had tripped, his attention snagged as before when she'd first called him a devil . . . a green-eyed devil . . . his mother. His mother had been the only one to call him a green-eyed devil. No one else had ever dared.

Her fingertips brushed against his jaw, drawing him from his distraction to find her searching eyes. "What were you just thinking?"

"That you should call me Jade," he answered smoothly.

Stunned, she studied him, searching deeper and sending chills through him. "No . . . no, hon. I'll try harder," she said with stark determination. "I've never broken a promise to keep a secret. I won't start, now. Not with you. Especially not with you."

"I've been a fool," he said quietly. "A fool to think I could remain anonymous forever. To think I could truly hide behind another name. It . . . it wasn't something I planned. It just happened, and once it had begun . . ." His gaze held hers even as his thoughts drifted, remembering. "I became comfortable with my anonymity. Perhaps, too comfortable. I began to think if I wore another name, I could be someone else. I could . . . I could be a cross-country race driver and attend the rally in Monte Carlo. I could be an English noble and wear a title that puts a 'Sir' or 'Lord' before my name. I could be an international spy and travel the world like a phantom. I could be anyone other than what I am, who I am. I could even be Isaac Bently, a connoisseur of fine antiques and collectibles in the little town of Bentwood, Pennsylvania . . ."

"Good heavens," she uttered, looking at him with wonder. "You own your own . . . when you go to England . . . you change . . .?"

"I have a home there," he said absently, watching her bewilderment, wondering if that would change her feelings toward him and realizing the difficulty in sharing these confidences. He'd compartmentalized his life so long ago, had shared nothing of himself with anyone in so very long. "It's not a large home, not a castle by any means, but it does include a Lordship." He shrugged, still uncertain of the look in her eyes. "I once believed if I wore a title, I'd be content. I was wrong."

"A . . . title," she said vacantly.

He held her palm against his chest, afraid she'd draw away from him, afraid the illusion would shatter.

"And you drove a . . . a race car in Monte Carlo."

Jade shrugged, still uncertain at the vacant tone of this woman, propped on her elbow, gazing down at him. "I enjoy driving fast." And that thought reminded him of Grant, kindling his annoyance until he saw her lashes flinch as if he'd stung her.

"You don't have to tell me this, hon. None of it," she said quietly, and her fingers brushed over his chest in comfort. "I want to know you. I'd love to hear every fascinating detail if these are only the highlights of your life, but not . . . not at the risk of hurting you or being hurt by you," she said quietly. "I never want to see the hatred in your eyes again . . . Isaac. I never want to feel like I did today when I knew how badly I'd hurt you. If . . . if or when you want to tell me about yourself, I'll listen. I'll listen and love you all the more for your trust."

"Then listen, now, Veronica," he decided quietly. "I've never spoken to anyone about the things I've just confided in you. I've never felt a need or desire to be known by anyone until now."

"A moment ago, when you spoke of driving, I felt your annoyance or anger. It was in your eyes. I don't want to—"

"It wasn't directed at you," he said with a faint smile. "I lost my Jag today. Grant said he'd take it, and he's a man of his word."

Her eyes widened slightly in disbelief; her lips parted. "But . . .? For God's sake, he can't just *take* a seventy-thousand-dollar car, Jade—damn it! Isaac! This is America! There are laws!"

Amused, as much by her indignation darkening the hue of her irises as by the slip of her tongue, he commented, "I suppose lending him my Jag beats the alternative of losing my license. A fact, I'm sure he'd be glad to point out to me if I attempted to mention the injustice of this arrangement."

Looking at him, she realized, "He's done it before?"

"A few years ago," he said in mild irritation. "I do like to drive fast. A weakness that has drawbacks on busy thoroughfares. One of Grant's new lads tried to give chase and failed to realize a Chrysler doesn't handle as well as a Maserati on curves. He went askew on a bend." He shrugged. "Grant took my wheels for several weeks. The only consolation is that he knows how to handle a sports car, and he returns it clean."

"That's an abuse of his authority," she said shortly.

"Suppose it is," he mused. "But who would benefit from me landing behind bars, my car impounded, my license suspended for several months? If not indefinitely revoked, considering the speeds I reach on occasion? Grant's methods may be slightly unorthodox but effective. Doubtful I'll be so careless for a time."

She studied him, then shook her head, quivering a smile as she leaned, brushing a kiss on his lips, her eyes laughing when she tipped back.

Hmm, and that kiss wasn't enough. Lifting a hand to cradle her head and lay her back as he tasted her lips, he uttered against her breath, "Woman, you are a wonder . . ."

A definite wonder as she rose to meet the challenge, heating him within minutes. She was also a quick study, pushing buttons with the skill of a concert pianist caressing ivories. Nearing the heights of no return, Jade shivered and drew up for a breath, head cocked, senses tuning. Almost in harmony with the rap of knuckles, he uttered, "Oh, shit."

Her eyes lost the glossy shine. Thought surfacing, just awakening, she looked up at him before turning her focus toward the door. "Oh shit."

"Ronnie!" Mark demanded through the wood.

"Coming! Hold on!" she shouted with a hint of panic and riveted her focus on Isaac, whispering. "We have to get up!"

He supposed maybe they did, but that revelation only enhanced his slightly angry smirk as he slid off her.

In a mild panic, she scrambled, and his focus followed her even as he reached to collect his pants off the floor. Black hair askew, face flushed, her lips slightly swollen with the ardent kisses they'd exchanged. . . . Good God, the woman had the body of an athlete, long and limber, curved in all the right places, soft and full where—

Her eyes flashed to him. A rise of color lifted higher on her lovely cheeks as she caught him staring. "Hurry!" she heaved.

"Ronnie! Open this damn door! I know Bently's in there!"

Amusement flashed through him as he stepped into his slacks, standing up and fastening the waistband as he watched Veronica swoop to recover her blouse, searching for her bra. Motioning to where her bra lay halfway across the room, he suffered a greater amusement to see her aggravated flash toward him.

"Ron, come on," the second husky voice urged.

"Hold on!" Ronnie snapped and fumbled with her bra, looking over at Isaac. "Hurry."

"I'm decent," he said with a shrug and noted her sudden dumbfound. "Mon amour, we're two consenting adults. If the lads don't know what we've done, they certainly shouldn't be carrying badges and guns." He shrugged again. "Why don't you collect your things and use the bathroom, though I doubt you'll lose that healthy blush any time soon."

"You are a devil," she said softly, but her eyes darted amusement as amply as dread toward the door. Tilting her gaze to him, she uttered, "I haven't spoken to Mark since this morning . . . He might want to kill you for this."

"Suppose we'll see," Isaac commented and paused en route to the door, collecting parts of his attire and tossing the bundle to the bed. As Veronica resigned and ducked into the bathroom, he opened the door, feeling a slight degree of déjà vu. The fist—currently raised to knock—hovered differently, turning and vibrating in an aggressive pose. "Seem to be making a habit of this, Agent Jarvins," he said lightly and decided to be civil for Veronica's sake.

Stepping back and pulling the door open, he flagged them inside. "Please, do come in. Always a pleasure to entertain such prestigious guests."

Scanning the room, Jarvins sized up the situation, then pivoted, reaching toward him. "If you hurt her—"

Stepping back and aside, Isaac deflected the hand with the heel of his palm, his gaze steady on Jarvins as he put distance between them.

The second fellow stepped inside, shutting the door in his wake. His dark eyes far more intent than outraged, he clasped his partner's biceps, halting his advance. "Think maybe we better wait to see what Ronnie has to say about any of this, Mark."

"Bently," Jarvins said, his blue eyes smoldering. "I don't know who the fuck you are or what kind of game you're playing with Ronnie, but I'll tell you right now if I find out—"

"My name is Jade," he said smoothly and suffered only a momentary panic in the center of his chest. "Jade Laquette, Mr. Jarvins. I was born in Arlington, Va. on October 31, 1962. With that information, sir, I'm sure you can find out whatever the fuck you believe you need to know. As for whatever goes on between Miss Veronica Bryson and me, should you feel inclined to pursue your obsessive jealousy beyond this point, I can assure you, I won't be as tolerant."

"Issa . . ." Veronica halted a step from the bathroom, her eyes level on him, startled.

"Don't even attempt it, sweetheart," he said, warming suddenly. A sense of rightness swelled through him as a smile played on his lips, and she appeared more startled. "I'm not ten years old, ma copine," he continued as he turned and strode to her, clasping her hands, and looking down into her stricken eyes. "I'm relieving you of your promise, Veronica. Know me for whom I am. Call me by the only name you have in your heart." At the tears lifting in her eyes, he shook his head slightly. "You are a wonder, woman. I give you a spark, and you hand me a torch." Tipping his head, he tasted her lips, the salt of her tears, and felt her hands slip from his, wrapping about his neck, returning tenfold what he offered.

With a thought of the men behind him, with a strange sense of pain . . . he withdrew, his gaze misting, senses rising. Mark Jarvins . . . he felt the man's pain. An awakening . . . something inside of him was waking.

"Jade?" she whispered, her eyes searching.

Oh God, the lid . . . the lid he'd screwed on tight. Spencer was right. The lid was coming off, the entire jar shattering. He stepped back from Veronica, spooked suddenly by the prickling and pulsing tingling through his nerve endings. "*Mon Dieu,*" he uttered.

"Jade!" she snapped, stepping to him, clasping his hand, and drawing his misty gaze.

Shuddering, he shook his head and lifted a trembling hand to comb his sweated hair off his brow. "I . . . I better go, sweetheart," he decided and met her gaze more firmly. "You need to speak to these gentlemen . . . one of them at the very least, and I—"

"Dinner," she said shortly. "You invited me to dinner, as I recall, and I haven't eaten since this morning."

Recalling how the evening had begun and considering how her reputation might suffer if he left carrying half his clothes, he drew a more collective breath, deciding, "Suppose I can get a shower while you and these gentlemen chat. If you like, we can order something from the dining room."

"I would like," she said with a soft smile.

With an acknowledging cant of his head, he turned and moved to the bed, collecting his clothes, needing to stoop to gather a few odds and ends. Barely glimpsing at the hostile blue eyes, he nodded toward Devinio before migrating to the bathroom. In the tub, he slid under the shower spray, nearly groaning his dread.

What had he done? What the hell had he just done?

CHAPTER 24

Heart aching, Ronnie glimpsed the pain in Mark's eyes. Looking toward Len for either recrimination or salvation, she saw only a strange conflict of dismay and understanding in his expression. Drawing breath, she crossed her arms over her breasts and met Mark's gaze. "I'm sorry, Mark," she said with soft conviction. "I never meant—"

"How long have you known his real name?" Mark asked in a voice that turned suddenly cold.

"Mark—"

"How long, Ronnie?" he asked firmly.

"He's not the person we're looking for."

"Answer the goddamn question," he snapped unnaturally.

Firming, her temper notching, she met his glare for glare. "I didn't know yesterday afternoon when you stormed over to his store to harass him," she said flatly.

"Last night, him just happening to be at the right place at the right time? No coincidence, huh, Ron? What? Were you two planning to arrive up here separately—"

"You can stop right there," she interrupted, her temper chilling her tone. "What I do with my private life is my own business, but I do resent you implying I've been having some sordid affair behind your back. What you and I had was over three years ago in case you've forgotten. I didn't come to Bentwood with any intention of renewing old acquaintances, any more than I intended to fall in love—"

"You've only known him for three fucking days," Mark snapped. "You . . . Arlington," he halted and looked at her. "Apparently, you have known him longer and that certainly explains the phone call I received this afternoon telling me, in no uncertain terms, to back off Bently. I'm almost relieved to find out you might not have been responsible for that intervention—"

"Mark, he's not the person we're looking for," she said quietly, pleading only with her eyes. "I'm asking you to back off. If not for the sake of his innocence, then do it for me."

For a long moment, he gazed at her with cool blue indifference. "As of now, Ronnie, you're off this case in any official government capacity. For your safety, I'm asking you to leave Bentwood. If you'll excuse me . . ." He turned and started to the door.

She knew better than to try halting him or discussing his decision. Her gaze locking on Len, she asked quietly, "Would you stay a moment, Len?"

Len caught Mark's scathing glance and commented, "I'll catch up to you."

As Mark stalked out, closing the door quietly in his wake, Ronnie moved to the small table, recovering her notebook from the floor, trying not to notice the condition of the bed. They hadn't climbed under the sheets; the quilt was a travesty of folds and twists that brought a slight blush to her cheeks. The situation lent new meaning to making a federal case out of losing one's virginity. Annoyed, faintly embarrassed, she struggled to collect her bearings before looking over and colliding with Len's sober gaze. "We do need to talk, Len. If you're going to condemn me and tell me what a fool I am, get it over with."

Devinio's lips twitched. His eyes lighted a slight spark as he shook his head. "You're a big girl, Ron," he said and glanced at the closed door as he came forward, his gaze returning. "I'd guess you know what you're doing."

"Len," she started, her concern unmasked. "Jade's not guilty but there is something in his past. If Mark pursues this, if the press gets wind of this, we'll have a media circus ten times worse than yesterday's fiasco. You need to convince Mark to back off and avoid opening this can of worms. It won't further this case. If anything, it will hinder it."

"Maybe you better tell me what he's hiding," he said with another glance toward the door. The shower water could still be heard through the walls. Sober, he looked back, "Or what he's running from."

Deciding on the instant, she motioned Len into a chair while settling into another. "It happened eighteen years ago," she began simply. "Jade was ten when he found his mother murdered in their home. His mother . . . you could say she was something of a celebrity around DC. She was a psychic guide to some of the most prestigious names in Washington. The media had a field day with that case, but rather than attack the government officials who might have been responsible, they twisted the story around and persecuted a child. The case was so horrendously distorted, not even the detectives handling the case could sort through enough facts to solve the crime."

"How was she murdered?" Len asked intently.

"She was shot, Len. Twice. Once in the chest, once in the head, and . . . and he doesn't need to be reminded of any of this, much less have it thrown in his face at this late date. I don't want him hurt, especially not over a misconception on Mark's part, and I'm afraid that'll happen as soon as Mark reads that name on a report. Now, more than ever, he'll want to see Jade hung out to dry and it won't be a highlight of his career as far as either good judgment or investigative skills."

"Mark might be a little preoccupied but he's a good investigator, Ron—"

"I'm aware of that, Len, but I'm afraid he truly has lost his perspective. He's already 99% sure Jade's guilty of some horrendous deed. If he finds an unsolved murder in the past, he won't need much convincing to start revamping his profile of our psycho, and the implication in a few of the articles written eighteen years ago won't help his frame of mind." She held Lenny's gaze steady. "I'm putting you on the spot, Len, but I don't expect you to take my word for any of this. I'd like you to call Lt. Max Hagen in Arlington. Talk to him. He was the homicide detective in charge of the investigation eighteen years ago."

Len mulled the words a moment then nodded. "I'll give him a call."

Relieved, she glanced at her closed notebook, turning her thoughts to the information she'd gathered. She'd collected enough details to offer Len a partial picture of what she was beginning to consider a motive. Behind the bathroom door, the water had silenced.

Ronnie returned her gaze to Len. "I spent the afternoon doing a lot of footwork, Len, and a few oddities turned up. I don't know if they're connected but I'm not fully convinced they're not."

"I'm listening."

"Saturday, I started getting a few weird vibes," she admitted. "Today, they got worse." Not entirely sure how to continue, she wondered if she might have lost as much perspective as Mark. Sighing, she ran with her instincts. "It seems about fifteen years ago, about a dozen or so of the town teens were considered . . . bad news," she decided. "They hung out in a pack. Extremely clannish. You might say 'cultish,' which is one of the words I heard used to describe them. What exactly these kids were up to, I couldn't say, but at least a few of the people I spoke with today, were more than half convinced that those kids were responsible for the dognappings and killings . . . and what bothers me, is that most of these kids are still here. All the names I heard mentioned are names on our list."

"What are we talking here . . .? Conspiracy, Ron?"

"Cult . . . witchcraft," she said irritably and met Len's intent gaze. "That's my feeling. I could be way off base but that was one of my first thoughts the other day when reading about those dognappings and talking to Mark. You know as well as I, those bands are noted for animal slaughter. Maybe it was a passing fling. A bunch of bored bright teens in a small town get together; one of them comes up with a brainy idea to start chanting to the devil. The next minute, you have animals disappearing and a small clique of teens walking around like they have the world by the ass . . . and my thought is, if we find out which of these kids hatched this bright idea, we might just find the wacko we're looking for."

"Any chance Cal Farnsworth's name came up?"

"A lot," she admitted quietly, sensing Len's mind working behind his dark eyes. Leaning, she opened her notebook. She had begun jotting a list before

Jade's arrival. She glanced down it, now, recalled another name, and jotted it on the page before handing it to Len.

The door opened across the room and for just a moment, the sight of Jade Laquette distracted her. The devil did know how to dress for effect, and she was glad Mark had already gone. Between the sleek black silk and jade green highlights, he could've stepped off a movie screen.

Even Len did a double-take and watched him move to collect his shoes. Shaking his head, wearing a peculiar arch in his brow, Len glanced off Ronnie and returned his attention to her list.

Settling on the side of the bed, Jade caught Ronnie's gaze and smiled, glancing off Len while pulling his stocking foot to don his shoe. "Have you ordered dinner yet, sweetheart?"

She shook her head, glimpsing Len's dark flash.

"If you need a few more moments, I suppose I could walk downstairs and place our order in person," he commented.

"I think we're almost finished, hon," she said while looking over to find Len's face more pensive. With his gaze intent upon the page, he eased back in his chair, possibly settling in. "Those are the most often to arise but there's a secondary list of possibilities."

Len looked at Jade directly, his gaze intent. "Any chance I could convince you to take that walk downstairs to place your dinner order, Mr. Bently? Ronnie and I could use a few more moments, after all."

Slow and dark, Isaac smiled as he agreed. "Be happy to, Mr. Devinio. Would you like me to order something for you as well? I understand you have a room here where I might have it delivered."

"Na, I already ate down at the diner, but you could bring me a cup of coffee if you feel hospitable."

Not bothering to comment, Isaac pushed to his feet and strode the few paces, dipping and brushing a kiss on Ronnie's lips with a wink and flash of his dimple. "See you shortly, mon amour."

Wistfully, she watched him stride across the room, noting again, that he walked like a cat with a hint of swagger in his easy glide. At the door, he tossed her another wink and smile. The devil! Ronnie wiped the faint smile off her lips as she caught Len watching her. "So . . . what do you think of that list?"

Len quivered a smile before sobering and looking down at the list, all business, once again. "As of about two hours ago, Cal Farnsworth confessed to the murders, Ron," he said quietly.

Her heart missed a beat. "He . . ."

Devinio nodded, more thoughtful as he looked at the paper in his hand. "But if you hit on something here," he continued in a low voice. "It might make sense."

"Protecting someone," she realized.

"Or something," Len said and met her gaze. "You were right a few minutes ago, Ronnie. Every one of these characters lives in or around Bentwood. Some of them left town for a few years but they all returned . . . and I think you're right about something else," he said idly skimming over the list. "One of them is one sick puppy." His gaze snared hers again. "Any chance you've shown this list to your pal?"

Considering how they'd spent the past few hours, she felt a little uncomfortable while shaking her head. "Not yet, but I'd like to," she said soberly. "He's lived in this town for the past five years. He could probably offer some insight into a few of these characters and narrow that list by at least half."

Len considered momentarily then started pushing from his chair. "Hold off on that until I get back," he decided. "I want to check on a couple things. I shouldn't be gone long."

"Len," Ronnie rose with him, catching his dark eyes. "Thank you." For being a friend, for being an anchor, for not judging or letting his emotions cloud his judgment.

"No problem," he said in a low voice and left her standing with a quick sting of tears in her eyes.

Tempted, sorely tempted not to return to that room, Jade stood on the landing, hearing the agent pass in the hallway above. For Veronica's sake, he should walk away but in the same instant, he knew it was way too late to consider that possibility. Just the thought of leaving her, of walking away and not looking back, gripped him with a wild panic. Doomed. He knew he was doomed, might have known it as much as three days ago when he'd told Wade to buy an extra soda expecting her arrival in his store, in his life. Tapping his knuckles on the door, he shook his head, feeling the warmth of her approach as if she were an apparition to reach through the wood.

Good God, just the warmth of her smile as she pulled open the door, just the delight in her eyes to have him return, destroyed whatever annoyance he might feel to be so wrapped in her spell. As if she were the light, and him the simple miller, he felt drawn to kiss her yet again wondering if he would suffer the fate of one of those mindless bugs and end up a carcass at her feet. A curse, a damned curse to suffer such an atrocious thought with the woman of his heart's desire in his arms. With an effort, he pulled from the kiss and looked into her mesmerizing eyes, amazed that she might truly want to return to their earlier enterprise, and only more startled by his quickening with anticipation.

Shaking his head, he commented, "I am doomed."

Laughter lighted in her eyes as she commented, "It can't be that bad."

"Woman, you're not standing in my shoes," he said idly and slipped his hands from her waist fearing where that slight connection could lead all too swiftly. "Dinner will arrive shortly. It occurred to me, I have no idea what you'd enjoy so you have your choice of my two favorite entrees, prime rib or stuffed pork."

She stifled a laugh, "Knowing the price you've paid for pork, I'm glad I love prime rib." Flashing a more amused smile and glancing down his attire, she commented, "If you'll excuse me for a few moments, I do feel slightly underdressed for such dignified company."

Recalling how this evening had begun, his own rude, if not wicked proposal to help her in changing, he withheld an offer of assistance and noted her stifling a laugh as she spun away and strode into the bathroom.

Left to his own devices, he idled momentarily, moving toward the table, his attention drawn to the notebook lying on the bed. The shiver down his spine was enough to divert his interest. His attention riveted on the slight stack of notes lying on the stand. To those, he felt a similar aversion, but a greater urgency moved him. As the shower water ignited in the adjoining room, he lifted the stack, his fingertips tingling, his senses quickening. One after another, he flipped them, reading the brief messages with his tension growing. Several reporters had named themselves and their papers, leaving numbers for her to return their call. A few calls had come from long-distance numbers with an Arlington exchange. Several more ranged from sympathies and well wishes to truly wicked implications concerning her methods to trap an innocent man.

When he came upon the single, simple note, his fingers caught fire. Gasping, he released the sheet of hotel stationery and backed away sharply. His stricken gaze followed the paper to the carpet. It landed slanted against the nightstand. His muscles coiled. The pulse thumped at his temple and his brow furrowed. *In for a penny, in for a pound* . . . and he was in. Like it or not, willing or dragged kicking, he was now involved, irrefutably. Even trying to deny what he felt for the woman in the next room would be foolish.

With an effort, Isaac stepped forward and stooped. Steeling his nerve, he enlisted only his thumb and forefinger, flinching and wincing on contact. Irritated rather than hurt, he dropped it on the end stand, then sidled to the chair where the agent had rested earlier.

He'd wanted to believe this part of his life had ended . . . but he heard her silky voice crossing the void of time, suffered her fingers clasped about his wrist, forcing his fisted hand downward . . .

'*. . . Re'd for me, mon shild . . . Tell me whot you see . . .*'

He shook his head against the memory, pushing off the chair, and raking his fingers through his hair. No. Not again. Not ever again. He wasn't reading . . . not reading cards or objects. Books! Just the flashing memory started his heart hammering a drumroll in his constricted chest. Never again . . . but the black chiffon wings swam in front of his mind's eye, taking his breath away, staggering him. Sinking to rest on the edge of the mattress, he caught his pounding head between his hands, groaning a soft breath as the image continued to materialize.

Whether she materialized to stop him or in ill-omen, he was no longer certain, but he saw her glazed blue eyes staring at him, her alabaster face carved as if from polished ivory. A thin crimson trickle spider-webbed at her temple—

"Nooo," he groaned softly. *Don't haunt me!*

Long black hair flowed around her head, a funeral shroud of black silk fanned and meticulously laid out against the brilliant white tile . . . black wings spread and flowed from outstretched arms—

Up and moving, pacing and shaking his head against the memory, he moved to the bathroom door listening to the movement inside, wanting, needing Veronica to hurry and join him, to hold him. His insides vibrated, quaking as if his vital organs threatened to break loose and crash together inside his flesh. Moving away from the door, he started toward the exit, toward escape, but he halted before taking the last step to twist the knob and run. No running from this one. No running and hiding. He was no more capable of running now than he had been eighteen years earlier. Trapped. Cornered. No escape even in madness . . .

The knock preceded a lofty, "Room service."

Forcing the tremble from his hands, Jade strode to the door, seeing the doubt and surprise on a familiar face. Vaguely he recalled placing the order directly with the chef rather than venturing into that unnaturally crowded dining room. If he wasn't wound tighter than a seven-day clock, he might find the young woman's surprise amusing. Not amused, he suffered the strangeness to feel the woman scanning him from head to heel, appraising him even as he motioned her toward the table. "If you could just set it there, Kim, I'd appreciate it . . ."

He'd received similarly stopped, shocked glances while walking up the street, amused as heads had spun. Rarely, very rarely had he dressed formally in Bentwood, let alone in an Armani suit. He'd learned years ago that decorum in Bentwood could be considered a pair of brushed denim jeans, a cotton shirt, and a sports jacket with a pair of suede shoes or boots to complement the ensemble. To seduce the little witch who'd gotten under his skin, he'd outdone himself, too damn dumb to realize the woman had already stolen his heart.

Without half thinking, he lifted his wallet and tipped the waitress, not realizing until after she'd gone why she'd looked at the money, then him so strangely. He'd just treated the young woman who'd been patronizing his shop regularly since his grand opening as if she were a stranger, tipping her as he'd tip any room service waitress in a strange hotel.

Not good. This wasn't good. He felt suddenly as if the world had tilted on its axis. He had no idea where he was, who he was. This was Bentwood . . . and not Bentwood. He owned an antique shop down the block, He'd been living above that shop for years . . . but he felt displaced as if he'd never heard of Bentwood, as if he'd seen that waitress only in passing through the halls of this Inn.

Who the hell was he if not Isaac Bently? If not the same man who had opened the store down the street daily for six years . . . who the hell was he, now? And all too swiftly, he received his answer. It came to him as the soft lyrical voice broke into his silent hysteria.

"Jade?"

Good God, he was Jade Laquette . . . and the woman who stood looking at him with such a soft curious smile, such warm concerned eyes . . . was stunning. In the space of fifteen minutes or less, she'd showered, dusted her face in powder to cover the bruises and soften the flush, applied a soft green shadow, and lined her eyes to enhance the natural contours. She stood wearing a mid-length summer skirt in dark turquoise, and a pastel blouse of the same hue in perfect contrast. His gaze rising from her sandals to her eyes, he commented, "You do wear that color well, mon amour."

She smiled, mischief dancing in her eyes, "Bet you'll never guess my favorite color."

"The color of envy," he said and started toward her, wanting her in his arms.

She danced a quick step, her eyes laughing as she darted a glance toward the table. "Emerald, but I'm becoming rather fond of jade . . . Dinner, sir? I'm starving."

"I'm rather famished myself, but I doubt what exists under those tin lids will satisfy my appetite."

Almost soberly, she met his gaze while sidestepping past the bed toward the table. "Hungry little devil, are you, then?"

How in God's name could she seduce him with a mere glance? "Getting worse by the minute," he admitted and started toward her. "You've hexed me, witch."

Her smile returned in force as she took a quick step and slipped around the corner of the bed, clasping the chair. He caught her tiny waist before she could slide onto the cushion. She feigned a struggle for a half-second before twisting and answering his need with a taste of spearmint to lance his senses.

Breaking from the kiss, she looked up at him. With her hands playing at his collar, with his hair, her eyes devoured him. "Do you have any idea how right this feels?"

Strangely enough. "Yes, I believe I do."

"Let's eat."

Startled by her blunt statement, he stifled a laugh and shook his head as he glanced at the table. Apparently, the lady needed sustenance, and if the promise in her eyes was any indication, he might need a little extra energy to see the dawn. "By all means," he said and reached past her, sliding the chair out and releasing her to slip into it. What had possessed him to order champagne, an event that demanded he lift the bottle as well as the crystal goblets? Bad enough, the coffee cups were heavy ceramic. Uncomfortable, suddenly, he slid into the chair across from her, managed to lift the silver dome off his plate, and realized yet another dilemma. He had the lady's prime rib . . . on a thick ceramic plate.

Glancing over into her perceptive, curious eyes, he looked at the platter in front of him, the champagne bottle, and delicate stemware glasses. *For her.* "We seem to have a problem here," he commented carefully and caught her gaze, recognizing her more intent, intense curiosity. *For her.* He reached intending to lift the plate, but his hands shook, his muscles locked. Cold sweat lifted on his palms as he withdrew his hands and shook his head in silent protest.

"Glass," she said quietly, her gaze searching. "Why . . . why are you having a problem touching glass, hon?"

Why, indeed? Insanity. He'd been lifting fine crystal, ceramic, porcelain, and china all his life, literally tons of it in the last six years alone. Now he couldn't bring himself to even touch the thick ceramic plate in front of him? Shaking his head, he looked into her intent blue eyes. "I have no idea," he admitted quietly. "It's a fairly new fixation which I can safely say, is putting a definite cramp in my lifestyle. Not to mention, making me feel like a total ass in front of a woman I would very much like to impress."

"Hon," she said with a hint of amusement. "You've outdone yourself in the impression department." With quick and elegant ease, she leaned and clasped the plates, switching them then reached for the bottle of champagne. With a glance at the crystal glasses, she eased back and spied the coffee mug. Her brow troubled, she looked over.

Faintly amused, he found her concern as well as her acceptance, touching.

"This is a problem," she said bluntly and sat back in her chair, her gaze more intent. "Saturday," she said bluntly. "In the diner, you didn't have a problem lifting a coffee cup. Last night . . . beer in a plastic tumbler," she said. "Coffee in a plastic cup this morning." Pausing, she studied him. "What happened between Saturday night and . . .?" Her voice trailed, her thoughts spiraled, and enlightenment dawned in her eyes. "Mark . . . plates. I know he broke two expensive plates. Could that be—"

Rather than a blast of shattering glass, he jolted to a flashing image . . . a sharp, crimson-glistening spear impaling circular glass, a tiny pang of sound, and spider-web cracks shattering the shiny surface. Magnified, the image filled his mind; his breath halted for an instant or an eternity; his body suddenly gripped in a convulsion of agony.

In an instant, he rose with enough force to send the chair slamming to the floor behind him. The image shattered. Staggering, he landed against the wall, his body shuddering and knees buckling. With a quick pained gasp, he dropped, hitting the floor on his shin and knee. His head swung as his hands flew to clasp his reeling skull.

"Jade!" the soft anxious voice reached him through a tunnel. Hands tugged at him, holding him, sending sparks through his spastic muscles. Heaving breaths, he was vaguely aware of his head caught and cushioned, arms wrapped about him, a hand clasped over his fingers. "God . . . Honey, shhh . . . God . . . Jade . . . Honey. Breathe . . . it's okay.."

Panting, panting as if he'd run a marathon with the spasms ebbing into a steady vibration, he collected slowly, finding the grit to release his skull with one hand. Clasping the fingers locked over his own, he dragged the small trembling hand off his head as he sank against the wall.

Holding the fingers firmly, he blinked spots from his eyes, waking to the puddle of dark turquoise around his folded legs . . . and the reality. He knew . . . knew without a doubt what had just happened, what had driven him off that chair, what had blasted through his mind, and the revelation lifted a blur of tears over his eyes. Behind his arm propped on his raised knee, his hand still clasped to his hanging head, he rested drawing slow, calming breaths and straining against a sob. He knew . . . knew what was happening, and it scared the hell out of him for reasons he could only begin to fathom.

"It's okay, honey," Veronica whispered in a quivering voice, her hand trembling slightly as she rubbed his back. "It's okay."

"Not . . . it's not okay," he uttered.

"Just catch your breath, hon. Will you be okay for a second? I have a bottle of wine . . ."

"Won't help," he heaved with a sick, resigning laugh. "Won't help at all." But he released her fingers and let her slip away.

CHAPTER 25

Wine bottle in hand, along with a plastic cup from the bathroom sink, Ronnie stooped alongside him. Her hands trembled as she poured the wine. His panic, the frozen hysteria in his wide eyes, had scared her as badly as the anguish wrenching his face. An epileptic seizure, that thought had blasted through her mind as she'd launched off her chair, a grand mal seizure, but by the time she reached him, she'd negated that thought. Whatever the hell had just happened here, it wasn't an epileptic seizure.

"Here—" she started and collided with his gaze, halted and startled on the instant. At close range, she saw the shine of moisture shimmering beneath his thick, clotted lashes and read the anxiety washed over his face, twitching the corner of his mustache where his dimple should be. With his head leaned against the wall, he appeared weary, if not entirely exhausted.

"He-ere," she uttered, lifting the trembling cup toward him, feeling the quiver of his hand as it closed over her own around the cup. What was he thinking? What was he feeling to appear so sad and far away as he gazed at her?

He barely swallowed a sip before moving her hand, lifting the cup to her lips. "Believe you need this more than I, darling."

Wishing she could deny his observation, she swallowed in gulps, watching his lips form a more natural smile. How the devil could he smile? She was shaking, *still*. Worried, *still*. Afraid for him, *still*. And the devil was already calming down, his hand firming and becoming steady on her own as she lowered the cup. "What . . . what happened here?" she uttered, seeing the hurt unmasked in his eyes.

"Do you think we could save that discussion for another time?" he asked with a hint of desperate hope.

As much as she wanted an answer, she couldn't refuse his request. "Whenever you're ready," she decided.

He nodded, and his gaze listed toward the table as he breathed an audible sigh of relief. His hand still on hers, he rose off his knee and shin and drew her afoot in one smooth motion. Not quite as steady as he appeared, he leaned against the wall, looking down into her with a shallow grin. "Perhaps, we should dine quickly before I test your tolerance any further."

"I can think of a few better reasons to get dinner out of the way," Ronnie said shakily, then nearly bit her tongue until she caught the brief glimmer of amusement in his haunted eyes. Dismissing her embarrassment, she accepted his escort and returned to the table.

Whatever had happened had passed, but the effects lingered between them as they began eating in comfortable silence. Preoccupied with the questions and worry, recalling those seconds in explicit detail, Ronnie shivered internally. She'd been talking about his fixation with glass, trying to work out whatever bothered him. She'd mentioned Mark breaking the plates . . . and he'd stared at her as if blind for a few seconds. In a shattered instant, he blasted off the chair, his eyes flaming with horror, his face a frightening mask of pain.

At the motion across the table, she glanced at him, and her attention halted as his hand froze. Darting her gaze higher, she saw his attention riveted on the ceramic mug hovering in his hand. His surprise mirrored her own as he lifted his gaze to her.

Relief and amusement lighted his eyes; his lips twitched with a smirk. "Appears you've rescued me from my hex, darling," he said as he put the empty cup alongside his plate and reached warily toward the champagne bottle. More relief danced in his eyes as he lifted the bottle smoothly. "Amazing how many of life's small pleasures we take for granted," he mused.

Belying his flippant tone, she sensed his genuine relief and delight, realizing for the first time how deeply he'd been troubled by that 'fairly recent fixation.' The devil did have his quirks. Apparently skilled, he popped the cork with natural ease and reached smoothly to collect a crystal glass. Stifling a laugh, she sensed his few seconds of wonder before he shook his head in bewilderment and poured the bubbly. He looked exactly like a man who had just been relieved of a wicked witch's curse, pleased and relieved with a few errant glimmers of childish wonder.

His eyes sparkling with mischief, he handed her one of the glasses, holding his own. "A toast on this most auspicious evening, milady?"

Lord, but the man did have class. Smiling, she held her glass. "Hmm, what should we drink to, do you think?"

"To an enchanting evening?" he wondered and shook his head, his eyes still dancing. "Doesn't begin to cover the vibrations in this encounter," he decided. "What about . . . to the most stunning woman I've ever had the pleasure of falling in love with?"

"Fall in love often, do you?" she mused.

"Daily," he said with mocked resignation, his eyes betraying his mischief. "But I suppose I should admit, this is the first time with a beautiful enchantress, and I suspect it's my final folly."

"That, I will drink to," she said and touched his glass, holding his gaze and hoping if this were some wondrous dream, she never awoke.

If she hadn't been staring into his eyes, she wouldn't have seen the feral flash or the dread as he darted a troubled glance toward the door, but she did see it. Glancing at the door, wondering for a moment if she'd missed a knock, she barely started to question him before the rap of knuckles intruded.

How many times had she seen him do that, she wondered as he set his glass aside, his gaze sober as he slid from his chair. Without a word, he opened the door and backed a step, motioning Len inside. Strange, this ritual of testosterone to have them circling like wolves prepared for a fight. If not for the sobriety on Len's face or the like shine of wariness in Jade's eyes, Ronnie might find their dance entertaining. For all that Len reminded her of a grumpy teddy bear, his posture reminded her that he was every bit a federal agent, as austere and methodical as any official she'd ever met if not more so.

"Don't let me interrupt your dinner," Len said with a hand gesture. "I seem to recall you were ordering a cup of coffee for me. Thought it'd be rude if I didn't stop back and collect."

"I'd be happy to pour it to-go," Jade commented and came forward, lifting the heating pot and filling the third cup on the table. As an afterthought, he topped off his own, then lifted and handed Len the extra. "You could always leave the mug in your room for the maid service to pick up."

"You could always put down your dukes and call a détente, too," Devinio said and held Jade's gaze, gravely intent. "We have a serious problem in this town, and there's a remote possibility that you can help us correct it. If it's any consolation, I've already cleared the order to reimburse you for the plates."

"The financial loss wasn't an issue, Agent Devinio, as I'm sure you're aware."

"Right," Len said in a surly tone. "But there's not a hell of a lot I can do about the historical value, and I'd think the potential loss of life outweighs whatever differences we may have over the loss. Bluntly, Mr. Laquette-Bently—" He barely paused for effect. "I'd like to ask you a few simple questions, none of which include where you've spent a third of your life, and I'd appreciate a few honest answers. The past five years concern me, and I do think you're in a position to assist in my investigation." Len paused, his gaze unwavering. "Like it or not, Amico, you and I have a mutual friend who can benefit from your cooperation. So, do you want to finish your dinner? Or should we just dive right in?"

Jade held his silence momentarily, then commented, "Suppose I've finished dinner. Ask your questions, Mr. Devinio."

Len glanced over the table and caught Ronnie's gaze. By his sobriety and faint nod, he verified his tentative trust in Jade's innocence. "You want to finish your dinner before we go over that list?"

Glancing over her nearly empty plate, she started lifting dishes, pushing out of her chair. "I'd imagine I'm finished, Len."

In moments, they cleared the table and pulled a chair from across the room, settling into opposing curves as if prepared to deal a poker hand. Instead, Len leaned back and lifted the quarter-folded page, flipping it open, looking toward Jade. "Understand, first of all, we're not accusing anyone on this list of any crime. I'd like your opinions and observations. Any impressions you can give me could be helpful. Not every name on this list is a potential suspect, and you won't be betraying anyone. No matter what you tell me, I won't arrest anyone on your word alone."

Lighting his first cigarette since his arrival, Jade nodded. With his exhale, his posture relaxed. Crossing his ankle over his knee, he leveled his gaze on Len. "An opening statement isn't necessary, Agent Devinio. I'm not under oath and I have every confidence in your investigative talent."

"I'd like you to understand one more thing, Mr. Bently," Len said quietly, his dark eyes intent. "One of the people on this list could be a serial killer regardless of how innocent they may appear. Try to bear that in mind before you hold back anything you believe could be either damaging or mundane." Enough said. Len offered the first name on the list. "Lionel Morten."

"Dull," Jade said simply and continued without persuasion. "I've not had personal contact with him, but I've seen him around. Works at the lumber mill and spends his off-hours in Crowley's or one of the other taverns in town. Doesn't seem to take a major interest in women. Single. A heavy weekend binger. Not much I can tell you about him other than he has a penchant for hitting the wrong nerves."

"Not interested in women . . . homosexual?"

"You're getting the message," Jade said lightly.

"Hit on you?" Len asked.

"Suppose, subtly, but he had a quick change of heart."

"Any close companions?"

"You're in the wrong town for that kind of information to be made public."

"Take a wild guess," Len urged.

Considering, Jade offered three different names, his tone and gaze indifferent.

Two of those names, Ronnie knew, were on Len's list. As Len continued with the next two names out of order, Ronnie suffered a mild tingle down her spine. Connections existed between a few other names on her list. Males and females alike, this same crowd remained casually associated.

"Patricia Hawthorne," Len stated.

"Trish married Milt Freshcorn a few years ago. She toned down quite a bit from when I first arrived. She's still a flirt when Milt's not in tow. He adores her to the point of subservience, and she takes advantage of him."

"Think she's having an affair?"

"Does it snow on Christmas in the Arctic?"

"Care to take a wild guess and name names?" Len asked.

"You already have," Jade answered and leaned, crushing out his second cigarette, looking to Len as he settled back on his chair. "Why don't I take a few more wild guesses and name some of the others on your list?"

"Go for it."

"Jarred Hancock, Jen Andover, Luanne Conners, Billy Skyles, Ralph Peterson . . . how my doing?"

"Your buddy, Sheriff Grant was right," Len mused. "Hell of a batting average for guesswork."

"There's a pattern," Jade commented passively. "Ages ranging from twenty-five to thirty, obvious friends, lovers, and social status."

"How about Tim Spencer?"

"Married, has two small children, devoted to wife and family. He's not having an affair, doesn't spend time at Crowley's, nor hanging out with old acquaintances. And I don't think he's on your list," he said without changing his tempo.

"Na, he was a wild card," Len said bluntly. "How about Elsie Briggs?"

"Met her a few times. Her mother brings her into my shop when she's home for a visit," he answered evenly. "I believe she lives in L.A., and she hasn't been in Bentwood for at least six months that I know of. I'm afraid I haven't seen her often enough to add further insight."

"Let's get back to the names you mentioned," Len commented. "What about Jen Andover?"

"Major flirt, a bit on the wild side, not particularly involved with anyone though she does seem in avid pursuit of yours truly. She works in her father's hardware store when she feels like it, but not with any regularity."

"She's an only child," Len commented.

"It's not unheard of," he said with a slight twitch.

"Any hobbies that you know of?"

"She's an old movie buff," he offered and caught Len slightly off guard. Shrugging, he commented, "If you get her started, she can name more B-rated stars than I believed in existence."

"Ever been to her house?"

"A few times."

"How many of these folks are regular customers?"

"About half."

"Collectors of any particular items?"

Leaning, Jade held out his hand. "Give me the list."

As Len handed him the list, a tremor slid through his hand, and his lashes flinched, shading his eyes, as his attention dipped.

In a peculiar hollow tone, he read the list of names, adding the type of merchandise each had bought. By the time he finished, his hand trembled and his voice strained. Almost angrily, he flung the sheet to skid in front of Len and pushed off his chair, turning and taking a few steps, halting. Both hands fisted, sinking into his hip pockets, bunching his jacket at his wrists. His head bent at an angle as if to spy the window. By his square shoulders and solid footing, he remained tense from head to toe, no longer trembling.

Len brought his gaze from Jade's back to Ronnie with the silent question.

Watching Jade, she barely glanced at Len, far more intent upon this sudden transition, and with a memory flash of that episode before dinner, her tension hiked in milliseconds. "Jade?" she asked quietly.

"Not . . . not on that list," he said with a soft low strain. "What . . . who you're looking for . . . not on that list."

"Mind telling me how you're so sure of that?"

For a long moment, Jade remained coiled and silent, then with a visible effort, he half turned and returned to the table, brushing Ronnie's shoulder as he passed. The same hand trembled, lifting a piece of paper off the nightstand. He held it by a single corner, his eyes darkened nearly to emerald in the lamplight as he sidestepped and dropped the stationery in front of Len, meeting his gaze. "There's who you're killer, Agent Devinio," he strained quietly. "Find who wrote that and you'll have your psychopath."

Len didn't reach for the piece of hotel stationery. When Ronnie tipped her gaze to read the words, Jade touched her shoulder. His emerald eyes pinned her as his head shook. A prickle skittered through her shoulder and down her spine. A sensation of heat emanated from his fingertips, drawing her gaze to his fingers . . . and he wasn't touching her. The pads of his fingertips hovered a half inch from her shoulder. Her gaze lifted to find his eyes studying her, his brow troubled, his mustache quivering with an effort to smile. When she again looked at his hand at her shoulder, the fingertips had landed, warm and comforting, leaving her to wonder if she'd seen that gap at all.

Across the table, Len skidded the list over the note and leaned back, his dark eyes lifted and fixed on Jade. "My question again, Mr. Laquette," he said with a definite change in tone and deliberate use of the name. "How do you know this is our suspect?"

Focused on Len now, he commented, "While you were gone, you looked into that name, into my past. With what's recorded in your archives, do you truly need to ask?"

"For the record, I did do a little research, but I'll be honest, I don't believe everything I hear."

"If I didn't have a sense of seeing is believing applied, here, I'd be inclined toward relief, Mr. Devinio. Unfortunately, I do have a sense of where certain things will lead . . . and I'm not pleased with my foresight."

"Would either of you care to tell me exactly where this word tag's leading?" Ronnie asked.

Jade favored her with a faintly desperate shine. "Your friend's about to ask me to do something I promised myself I'd never consciously do again, mon amour, and I'm about to break my vow because I've found something I cherish more than my sanity."

He. . her love? His love for her? She shook her head, more in tune with the genuine distress haunting his eyes. "No," she decided. "Whatever it is, no."

A sad smile touched his lips in conflict with his misty eyes. "I don't have a choice, Veronica. I've backed myself into a corner where lethargy and inaction will drive me insane faster than action, any action, but you have to make me a promise, mon amour," he said quietly and lowered. Stooped, collecting her hand in his, he clasped her fingers firmly. "You must promise, you will never be afraid of me. Fear what's inside of me. Fear what I can do, what I can tell you. Fear for me, if you must, my love, but please, promise me you will never be afraid of me."

"You're already frightening me," she said softly as she squeezed his hand. But she wasn't afraid *of* him. Not once had she truly feared the man. The force of anger and pain inside of him, the power of his contempt and scorch of a scathing glance, but never had she feared him. Even when he'd come into this room a few hours ago, intent upon hurting her, rapt upon his hatred, she hadn't been afraid of him. She had, instead, trusted him enough to place herself in his hands. Looking into his beseeching gaze, she knew the only way to answer him. "I promise, Jade, I'll never be afraid of you."

For a long moment, he looked at her with nothing short of wonder in his eyes, then bowed his head and brushed a kiss on the back of her hand. His gaze lifted with a shine of tears. "I do love you, Veronica," he said quietly.

Tears stung her eyes as she dipped her head, leaning and tasting his lips, feeling the integrity of his words as powerful as her own as she pulled away to see his eyes. "I think I've always loved you, Jade."

"No matter what you see," he said in a low soft strain. "No matter what you hear in the next few moments, remember your promise, remember your love for me."

She was afraid *for* him, not of him. "You don't have to do this. Not for me. Not because you love me."

A slight smile haunted his lips as he nodded. "Yes, I do," he said simply and rose, pausing partway to brush another kiss on her lips, holding her with his murky green gaze. "Yes, I definitely do."

Rising, releasing her hand, he tipped his gaze to the table, to the list for a long moment then glanced to Len and turned away. In slow animation, he slipped off his jacket and folded it, laying it on the bed. His tie followed in short order. Sidling, he emptied his pockets onto the nightstand, wallet, keys, and loose change. His watch followed his other items along with a thick intricate gold ring off his right hand. An archaic signet ring similar to those in his jewelry case, Ronnie identified at a glance.

Turning toward them, Jade loosened the button at his collar, leveling his now blank gaze on Len. "Before I do this, Mr. Devinio, there's something you'll promise me, as well," he said evenly.

"I'm listening," Len said evenly.

"I haven't consciously done this. Not in nearly eighteen years have I done what I'm about to do, and I have only a sense of meeting with some success. Frankly, I'm infinitely more of a skeptic, as well as a cynic than you, sir. But on the outside chance that my hunch is right, that I do succeed, you need to promise me that you'll weigh your doubt with all the integrity of your analytical mind. I'd rather not wake up in handcuffs behind bars."

Ronnie felt her fear notch another degree as she looked to Len who gazed at Jade with a steady black shine.

"Fair enough," Len said after a reasonable silence.

Jade hesitated, looking into him a moment, then lowering his gaze to the papers. Wariness held in his tense features, but his gaze remained indifferent, glancing at Len as he stepped closer to the table. "Uncover the bottom one," he directed as he continued to look at the pages.

If he needed a drumroll, he wouldn't need to go far to find one. Ronnie's heart ricocheted a rising cadence; her mind swelled with fear that no amount of rational thought countered. *Just paper! Just a piece of paper*! How could a single piece of paper hurt him? Why did she suffer such an overwhelming desire to grab him as he lowered his fisted hand toward that paper, to grab him and push him away, to stop him . . .? She saw his fingers opening, splaying, hovering, descending, and drew breath to shout an alarm.

Darting her gaze to his face, she saw his blank eyes beneath shuttered lashes, his mustache kinked, strained, and she had no idea why she stopped, why she knew she mustn't stop him or interfere. Heart hammering, she watched his hand hover an inch off the surface, noting, as did Len, the stationary rippled as if a breeze sailed across the table.

In one wicked-fast motion, the palm slammed down as if blasting through an invisible shield, and his opaque eyes flashed fire before snapping closed. His lips parted on a caught breath as if were punched in the chest; his head swung into a deeper bow; his shoulders hunched, and a shudder swept visibly from his head to his heels. Collapsing, his other hand landed with a flat, dull thud, catching himself from a fall. The fingers of both hands splayed, the tips overlapped, touching both the stationery and the notebook paper.

'No!' she barely cried the word inside her mind, wanting this stopped, wanting him to stop whatever he was doing or about to do. The sound never reached her tongue.

Hands blasting off the table, he stifled a cry as he stumbled back. Ronnie caught only a glimpse of his blind, fire-lanced eyes. His hands flew upward. The heels of his palms covered the glowing orbs as he staggered and swung himself away.

In one motion, she rose. The seizure! It was happening again! He landed against the wall, his breath already panting, and she needed to reach him!

Len reacted, too. His hand lashed out, clasping her arm, halting her with a sudden fierce grip. She barely glimpsed at his black eyes locked on Jade before her gaze riveted, and she realized he'd stopped. Panting, he braced against the wall at his shoulder, hands pressed against his eyes . . . but something had changed, was changing even as she watched. His fingers moved, skidding into the hair at his temples; his entire body shivered.

Coming out of it! He was coming out of it!

She watched him firming on his feet and heard his panting breaths breaking.

"I-I ca-an't," he heaved in a soft, strained breath. "Ca-an't . . . D-don't ma-ake me d-do this," he stammered in a soft, near childish voice. "Pleeease, Mom`ma," he whined softly, and Ronnie's heart lurched with her revelation.

He wasn't coming out of it.

In slow motion, he lowered against the wall, controlling his descent.

Not coming out of it. Her heartbeat racing, Ronnie could only watch as he folded, stooping, compacting. In the faded lamplight, his jade silk shirt shimmered with the tremors vibrating through him.

"Mom`ma, nooo," he whined in a muffled voice, his dark hair spilling over his knees, over his fingers. His body rocked as a sob broke. "You're g-gon-na die," he hiccupped, rocking from the balls of his feet to his heels against the wall. "G-gon-na dies, Mom`ma . . . don-ohhh GGGod nooo," he whined in a deeper voice, his entire body shuddering.

Before Ronnie even realized he was tipping, and falling, he hit the floor on his haunches. His hands slapped down clumsily, and his heels skidded. Head swinging, a strangled sound escaping, he spider-walked backward until his back jammed against the corner wall.

"Nooo," he seethed, and Ronnie tried yanking free, lurching forward. She wanted him to stop! *Wanted this stopped!* Through a blur of tears, she glimpsed at his squinted eyes as he swung his head.

"Don't . . . don't . . . don't want to . . . oh, GGGod, it's commming . . . ssstop iiit . . . Mom`ma, mmmake it ssstop," he whined in a conflicted, accented young voice of rolling sounds and pitches as he braced himself in the corner.

Breath held, Ronnie dared to hope, dared to believe he was coming out of it, now. Surely, he would rise gracefully and tell her this was a joke, a horrid practical joke. She prayed to see his eyes spark with amusement, to see his dimple wink from the corner of his mustache. She would forgive him! She would forgive him for this horrid joke if only he stopped.

"A barn," he spoke again, his voice changed yet again, leaden and empty, young. "Alwaaays . . . alwaaays happens in the . . . barn. Nobody knows . . . nobody cares . . . hurts . . . hurts. Oooh GGGoddd, donnn't make meee seee," the childish voice whined. "Tiiimmme," he drawled, and a cynical laugh slipped from his buried head.

A wicked shiver slid down Ronnie's spine, alarming on every level.

"Tiiimmme's uuup . . . don't you hit me," he said clearly and shook his head. "Ssstop . . . wrong," he seethed. "Wrrrong . . ." His hand skidded off the floor. His arm folded, pressing over the side of his head as he drew up his knee. "Innnsane . . . am . . . insane. Haaave tooo ssstop . . ." Laughter, low black laughter spilled from the shivering form. "Tiiimmme's uuup, pappa!"

Jade launched from the corner as if shot from a cannon.

Even Len reacted, grabbing Ronnie's arm, yanking her stumbling a backward step as Jade halted a few steps away. For a half-second, he stared at her through wide vacant eyes, blind eyes.

In the next instant, he pivoted into the corner, landing his forearms flat against the wall and catching his head between them. Feet braced, his long, lean form shuddering in place, he stood heaving ragged breaths.

Seconds, seconds ticked by in double-time against the racing beat in Ronnie's chest, but she could hear him breathing, his breaths slowing, his shudders ebbing. He was coming back! No doubts, now! Yanking her arm from Len, Ronne hurried to Jade and barely toward his waist, his back—

Don't," he heaved softly. "N-not yet," he nearly uttered on a breath. "Don't touch me . . ."

Pain and exhaustion haunted the soft deep voice. His words were a soft desperate plead to tear at her heart as she halted her hands.

"Time," he heaved softly. "Shattered . . . the glass . . . a clock . . . time's uuup. A game," he heaved softly. An echo of pain and anger inflected his low voice. "It's ss-some kind of game . . . ohhh, fuck," he said heavily. "Fuck . . . it's hide-n-go seek . . . time . . . time's important. Shattered . . . I've seen the glass-face shatter . . . prong. Time's uuup . . . Those are your psycho's words, D-Devinio . . . a game. Goood Goddd, sooo sick . . . a child's gaaame . . . children. M-more than one," he heaved softly. "More than one . . . children. Playing . . . a game . . . Time . . . have to hide . . . I can't do this," he said, and his head rolled, shaking. His words heaved. "I ca-an't do this. Something's wrong . . . I can feel it. Something's coming at me . . . something's coming. Someone's coming."

Closing the gap between them, Ronnie wrapped her arm about his waist, drawing him off the wall and looking up at him as he turned into her embrace. His wet eyes shuttered, haunted, and his smile lingered like a phantom buried within the deeper worries and fears masked on his handsome face. With an exhausting effort, he drew his arm about her shoulder and held her against him. Enfolding her, he buried his face against her hair. Holding him, burrowing against the nook of his neck and chest, she understood the words he'd spoken before touching that paper, the promise he'd asked from her. She understood in blinding flashes what Jade Laquette had been hiding, and she could never blame him. If what she'd just heard and seen could frighten her so badly, what must he have felt? What must he be feeling even as he held her? Lingering, the vibrations shivered in his arms and chest like the aftershock of an earthquake.

Against her ear, he uttered, "You can't stay in this Inn, Veronica. You . . . you have to come home with me."

On the heels of her revelations, his words startled her, rousting her to look up and find his warm worried eyes looking into her.

"I can't protect you here," he said quietly, his hand lifting, his fingers brushing at the dampness she hadn't felt on her cheeks. With the wonder of a child, he looked over her face, his worry no less intense. "Say you'll come with me, my love. My home's a fortress to lend even the devil pause. Come with me."

How could he doubt even for a second that she would agree? She barely nodded her assent when she heard footsteps, several pairs of footsteps outside the door . . . and whatever he'd seen coming at him had just arrived.

CHAPTER 26

Feeling like a survivor of a natural disaster, numb and stupefied, Ronnie stood at the cast-iron railing, gazing off the balcony outside her childhood room. Listless, she scanned the tall hedges and islands of livid color spread before her. A rose scent wafted from the vines that steepled white-arched tresses with the flowers in bloom from velvet white to deep crimson petals. Neither the sweet scent nor the brilliant petals drew her attention or held her focus. Beneath blazing morning sunlight, the flora glistened from emerald to pastel jade, and everywhere her gaze landed, a reflection of his green eyes looked at her as he'd looked at her only last evening. Anger and dread had simmered on the surface of his stunning eyes before vanishing behind indifference.

The man was psychic. Incontestably, psychic. '. . . Something's coming at me . . . something's coming . . . someone's coming . . .'

Mark Jarvins and three state officers had breached the door, and in retrospect, Ronnie knew she needed to thank Len Devinio for the civility of those moments. Clearly, Mark had prepared to drag Jade away in handcuffs, '. . . For questioning in connection with the murders of Victor Farnsworth and Frederick Engler.'

How exactly had that come to pass?

Ronnie remembered standing in stunned silence as one state trooper had read the Rights Act, and the other had forced Jade against the wall frisking him. Not a word had Jade spoken, and she remembered the color of his eyes, as emerald as the ivy leaves contrasting with the white lattice in front of her. Feral, his lash-shaded gaze had studied Mark with an intensity to send a shiver down her spine despite the heat rising with the morning sun.

'Not taking any chances or playing any more games,' Mark had professed while mentioning the Federal building as their destination . . . 'for questioning.'

Ronnie had only begun hissing unholy oaths at Mark as the cuffs had come out. The second wave of officials had arrived inside the suite then, and reporters had flooded the Victorian hallway, crawling out of the walls like cockroaches.

In near military precision, Bobby had entered the suite with two stony-eyed private security men whom Ronnie had recognized on the instant. 'Dad wants you home. Now, Ronnie.'

And what daddy wanted, daddy got, she considered bitterly, her eyes filling with as much anger as pain.

Kicking, fighting, and screaming had never been her style, any more than crying, but the tears had risen the instant she'd looked into Jade's emerald eyes. In silence, he'd stood between the state police, appearing indifferent to the discourse between Mark and Bobby. Mark's suppositions and innuendos had condemned Jade in Bobby's eyes and convinced him to transport her to the municipal airport without further ado.

Later, within the confines of the private plane chartered by her father to whisk her out of Bentwood, Bobby had unleashed the full weight of his trust and belief in his old college chum. Bitter chords and angry words could never be rescinded. Bobby, her brother, her mentor . . . his words had stunned her into silence, startled her to the core, and she could still hear them, a bitter testament to what he thought of her.

'. . . It was bad enough you chose such an asinine career, Ron, one you knew our parents would find as offensive as if you'd become a prostitute . . . But for God's sake, to wallow with the worst possible criminal elements . . .? Jesus Christ, did you have to sleep with that psychopath to catch him? If you couldn't have kept your dignity for your own sake, at least you could have thought about all of us . . . It's no goddamn wonder you didn't want to fight that asshole reporter! You could have at least warned me that he wasn't fabricating . . .'

Numb, still numb, Ronnie couldn't even hold onto a decent rage. Of her three brothers, Bobby was the last one Ronnie would've expected to turn against her. Until last evening, until he'd shed his mask, she hadn't realized how like their father he'd become. If it had been James, she could have understood, might have excused him his flighty temperament, his assault, but not Bobby.

Shaking her head, Ronnie focused on her mother's garden, but her attention dipped to the gold watch she'd lifted off the nightstand before leaving the hotel room. Was there an omen in those moments? Had Jade emptied his pockets, leaving everything on the nightstand in anticipation of his arrest? Not a word had he uttered before the state police had escorted him from the room—just a slight backward glance with a flash of green fire in his eyes.

If the vintage Rolex was exact, it was only a quarter past nine.

How could a single night last so long? Not for an instant had she slept, not a single wink . . . and she was finished waiting for the inevitable summons from her father. Either Robert Bryson Sr. would take ten minutes out of his busy schedule to see his daughter, or he could kiss his daughter goodbye.

She turned from the railing and swept through the curtains, striding through the frilly room adorned with dolls and teenage paraphernalia without a second glance.

Reflective of a southern plantation, the second floor opened into a balcony overlooking the foyer. A tiered crystal chandelier centered the room, throwing prisms against the walls from skylights flanking the double doors. She'd always loved this house, the austerity emanating from the wide doorways to the stately elegance of genuine antique furniture.

Jade would like this house. Wistfully, she continued down the wide staircase similar to the Bentwood House entry and caught herself admiring her parents' fine taste. Strange, she should see reflections of Jade's shop in her parents' home. The simple elegance and natural style flowed from delicate figurines on lace doilies, painted flower vases, and gilt-framed portraits, adding touches of color to enhance the raised, paisley wallpaper.

What had Jarvins found to call for that official questioning? What had that obsessed agent uncovered to suggest a connection between Jade and those murders? Or had Jarvins fabricated the evidence as he'd once produced a weapon in a stalker's hand?

Those were the questions that would drive her insane if she didn't soon learn the answers, and by God, she wouldn't be held a prisoner in her parent's home while the man she loved was being held for 'questioning.'

Len Devinio. She needed to trust Len to balance Mark's insanity . . . and God help Jarvins when next she saw him. *God help him.*

Across the room near the elegant front door, one of the security men who'd escorted her and Bobby on the plane rose from one of several tapestry parlor chairs. His gaze locked on her, his intentions apparent. If she meant to leave, he would block her escape.

A prickle slipping down her spine, she halted, looking at the former military man as she heard her mother's muffled voice carried through the arches to her left. "What are your orders, Mr. Chandler?"

"You need to speak to your parents about that, Miss Bryson," he answered smoothly. "I think your mother's in the garden—"

Oh, she fully intended to speak to at least one parent, and her mother wasn't the one. Without a second thought, Ronnie pivoted right and picked up her pace. At this time of day, her father would be sitting behind his desk, wielding his power via phone cable. As Chandler started a protest and quick step to catch her, she grasped the brass handle of her father's office door and yanked. The deep voice halted as she stepped inside. No one entered Robert Bryson's domain without his invitation, demand, or voiced approval. That rule had applied forever, but Ronnie ignored the protocol. Her gaze fastened on the blue eyes turning toward her.

On a tapestry chair in front of the wide walnut desk, Bobby turned; his gaze froze.

Refusing to acknowledge her brother, Ronnie continued forward, halting dead center between the high-backed receiving chairs facing her father.

From Robert Bryson Sr, she'd inherited her raven hair and natural curls; from him, like all three of her brothers, she'd inherited her pale-blue eyes as surely as the fire flashing behind them. Midway through his fifties, Robert Sr. could pass for a decade younger. Between his sturdy shoulders, forever enhanced in tailored dark suits, and his jet-black hair barely touched with gray, the man appeared as capable as twenty years earlier. By his presence alone, he might have reached his level of success, but old money carried through a few generations had paved his road. He was, without a doubt, an aristocrat with more connections in the main governing body of the government than any of the three preceding presidents. Quiet, stately, and elegant, her father had always impressed her despite the distance between them.

"I'd imagine you have a very good reason for storming into my office in the middle of a private conference, my dear."

"Oh, there's no doubt about that," Ronnie said as she held her gaze steady If she knew little else about her father, she knew he wasn't a man who would tolerate weakness, a fact which had cast each of his children into a mold of overachievement and hot temper.

"Ronnie," Bobby started in a chilly tone. "I intend to speak to you after father and I—"

Her gaze pivoted, landing on him with icy indifference. "If I never speak to you again, Robert, it may be too soon," she said flatly, seeing his jaw clench, feeling only the bitterness of his betrayal and hostility of his words.

"Ronnie—"

"My name is Veronica," she said smoothly, pinning him in a vicious glare. "And if, as I suspect, this conference concerns a scandal, which you believe I am guilty of creating, then I suggest you pick up your briefcase and withdraw from this room. You are not my attorney or my public relations manager. Not my editor-in-chief, father, or brother as of this moment. Now, get out and, by God, don't you come near me again."

"Ronnie—"

"Bobby," the low voice intervened, and Ronnie looked to see her father glancing off her to her brother. "If you'll excuse us . . .?"

Unmoving, letting her brother vacate his chair on the opposite side, she continued to study her father, noting the tiny lines pinching the corner of his lips. Visibly, the heaviness of his thoughts weighted his drawn brows. The man didn't hold onto a family fortune and cultivate his affluence by being stupid or careless. Both of which Ronnie counted on as she watched him reach and lift a cigar from a crystal tray. His eyes dipped only to direct a flame from his silver lighter, lifting and landing again as the door snapped shut across the room.

How long had it been since she'd stood alone in this man's presence? Since she'd faced him down and held his attention longer than thirty seconds? Ten years or better, she remembered. The day he'd decided that she didn't need a driver's license since they employed a chauffeur. And maybe that memory slid through his mind as well.

"I don't imagine you've come to plead forgiveness for creating a public scandal," he spoke with an exhale of thin smoke.

"If I believed I created a scandal, I'd consider it," she admitted bluntly. "I have no idea what rumors you've heard or what Robert felt obligated to bring to your attention. If, as I suspect, he told you some sordid story as related to him by a certain Federal Agent—"

"A Federal Agent with whom, I understand, you were working in the guise of a Special Consultant via your unique investigative skills," Robert Sr interrupted.

"And I understand, I have you to thank for that post," she fired back, weighing her temper against his indifference, mirroring his calm.

"I assumed you'd enjoy putting your talents to good use, and I believed it would be to your benefit to hold a certain authority." He shrugged, leaning back more comfortably, gauging her and his words in the same instant. "I might have extended a word or two in your favor. A miscalculation on my part, as it certainly didn't spare you from landing in the thick of danger."

His logic struck suddenly, but rather than be touched by his parental concern, her anger flamed a notch higher. "You condescending—" She bit back a string of curses, glaring at him. "You can sit here pretending that you put in a good word for me, in answer to a phone call from one of your old dear friend's sons . . . and you dare to pretend you acted on some paternal instinct to protect me?"

His eyes narrowed with a trace of anger; his cigar pinched slightly between his forefinger and thumb. "Young lady, do not take that tone—"

"I'm a grown woman," she said with a careful rein on her voice, her insides shaking with anger. "And I'm well aware of how you felt about my former relationship with a certain federal agent whose father you've known for decades. What a thrill for you. The ultimate achievement. To exercise a paternal touch of concern as well as pride, putting me on the sidelines of a federal investigation while at the same time throwing me to your old pal's son. What? In the hope of gaining a worthy son-in-law and grandchildren?" She glared at him; her temper barely restrained. "Damn you," she said in a low soft voice.

"I've heard about enough of—" He started to lean forward.

"Like hell you have, Mr. Bryson," she snapped, taking a step closer. "Before you dismiss me from this room or your sight, you will hear what I have to say. What you choose to believe is truly no concern of mine, Father, but you will listen because I have no intention of remaining either a prisoner in this house or a prize to be bartered to a man whom I've come to loath more than sewer slime. And make no mistake, I'm referring to Mr. Mark Jarvins, whose blind obsession may yet cost a few lives.

"Not only has his infatuation with me hampered this investigation but he's also used your influence as a means to his end. And that end, Father, amounts to no more than a quick roll in the sack with your daughter. People are dying in that little town, and Mr. Jarvins is so obsessed with his libido and his jealousy over a man I've fallen in love with that he doesn't give a good damn how many other men land in the morgue in Bentwood, Pa . . .

"Make no mistake, Father, Jade Laquette, a.k.a., Isaac Bently, is not the prime suspect in this case. In fact, he was removed from the suspect list shortly after being placed on it. The man was in England for two weeks before this recent murder and arrived at his home in Bentwood after the incident. Those details, you may verify for yourself, unless in Jarvins' perversity, he managed to destroy official documents as easily as he destroyed the love and trust I had in my brother."

She drew breath, still glaring at her father as she continued, "And frankly, I wouldn't put it past him. Jarvins is so jealous that I truly have fallen in love with a man who makes him look and sound like a two-bit actor in a B-rated movie, I think he'd do just about anything to destroy Jade. The worst part is, I believe Jade may be the only one capable of catching this maniac before he kills again."

She paused, seeing her father's dark, intense gaze, wondering not for the first time how much he knew about Jade Laquette . . . about Felicity Laquette. She had wondered a half dozen years earlier, and she wondered, now . . . And it bothered her immensely that her father's summons had come within a few hours of Jade's admission. "Just how much do you know about his mother's death?" she heard herself asking, and her father's eyes twitched in alarm.

"If you are finished, young lady, there are several details which your brother and I were discussing, which do, in fact, concern you. The first being, you are not, under any circumstances, to return to Bentwood—"

"You can stop right there," she said shortly. "I haven't lived under your roof, much less your thumb, since high school, and I'll be damned if I'll start now. I am returning to Bentwood, and if you've ever cared for me in the slightest, you won't attempt to stop me. If you want to use your influence to accomplish something of significance, then use it to remove Mark Jarvins from that case. He doesn't belong there, and you needn't take my word for it. Speak to his partner, Leonard Devinio, who was in the room last evening with Jade and me when Jarvins burst in with his ridiculous official warrant."

"I am well aware of the official warrant issued against Laquette," Robert Sr said. "I don't happen to consider the signed affidavit of a man who is already being held for murder, ridiculous. As I understand it, Cal Farnsworth not only confessed to this crime, he alluded to coercion by Jade Laquette, naming the man as an accessory—"

"Cal Farnsworth is no more guilty of killing his father than I am," she said shortly. "I don't know why he confessed to that murder but given the mentality of a few of the officials in that county who would rather a quick end to their fame than true justice, I have my suspicions. That's one of the questions I intend to pursue when I return to Bentwood. As for him naming Jade as an accessory, I can easily imagine how Jarvins pulled that off. Considering that Jade saved me from being raped by Farnsworth Sunday evening and left the man lying unconscious in the parking lot, I doubt Mark needed to twist his arm to corroborate the lies. Regardless of what you've heard, you should know that Jade and I were not secretly rendezvousing. If anything, Jade followed me back to town out of a sense of honor, even though I verbally lashed him before leaving his friend's home." She held her father's gaze. "Jade Laquette is no more guilty of accessory to these murders than he was guilty of killing his own mother."

Robert Bryson flinched. He never flinched.

In a heartbeat, she knew—her father knew more than he cared to admit about that ancient crime.

Far more quietly, Ronnie said, "I will want those answers, Father. Not right now, but when this is finished, when the real killer is sitting in that jail, I will want to know what you know about the murder of Felicity Laquette. That event nearly destroyed the man I intend to marry, and I believe he has a right to know why his mother died, why he was made an orphan, why he was persecuted in the wake of that crime."

"I have no idea what you're insinuating, daughter, but I don't appreciate the implication—"

"Don't lie to me," she said quietly. "It's one of my more perfected talents to feel when people are attempting to deceive me or manipulate me. Perhaps, it's inherent. You do know something about Jade Laquette. Otherwise, I wouldn't be in this house.

"Distance. By no coincidence, you demanded my distance from him the moment you learned his name. If . . . if I find out that you had anything to do with what's happening to Jade at this moment. If through any reason other than ignorance, you've assisted in Mark Jarvins' assault on him because of an eighteen-year-old crime . . .? So help me God, I won't rest until I've seen the Bryson name splattered on every newspaper, television, and radio station around the globe. And that promise extends to any interference, on your part, to stop me from returning to Bentwood. If Jade's made to suffer any further pain or persecution via government hands, I won't rest until I've uncovered the conspiracy surrounding his mother's death and exposed every name involved. You, Father, will have to order my assassination to stop me."

"When did your opinion of me stoop so low, daughter?" her father said in a low, strangely sober tone.

"It's called an equal return on your investment, sir," she said in a clipped, angry tone. "Now, I do hope you'll excuse me for not saying it's been a pleasure," she said shortly. "And unless you fully intend to see several blips on the evening news, you'll revoke whatever orders you've given Mr. Chandler concerning my freedom. You, as Bobby likewise inferred, may consider my career choice a step down from prostitution, but I can assure you, I'm damned good at what I do." Without awaiting so much as an utterance, she spun and strode across the room, shoving the door open and leaving it open in her wake.

Bobby rose from a chair outside the door, his lips parting.

Turning on him, her gaze locked, she spoke grimly. "I truly don't think I'll ever forgive you, Robert. As much as I once loved and trusted you, I despise the sight of you, now. Don't call me. Don't attempt to see me. Don't even think about me if you can help it, Robert. Or, by God, you'll learn first-hand what skills I've acquired as an investigative journalist, and I can assure you, I don't crawl between sheets to uncover dirty laundry."

Enough said, she turned and left him standing clench-jawed in the foyer.

Rather than her room on the second floor, she continued past and entered her younger brother's room, hearing him snoring, spotting him in the contours of his summer bedspread. As quietly as possible, she lifted his private phone off his nightstand and dialed the office to reach Pete Simons. "I need a favor, Pete . . . If I don't call you by five o'clock this afternoon, I need you to call the local station . . ."

The second call, she placed to a cab company. As she was securing airline reservations with a third call, James rousted. Bleary-eyed, he started to smile before his brow furrowed and a scowl creased his lined lips.

"What the hell are you doing on my phone?" he demanded and reached toward the base of his phone, intending to disconnect the call.

Deflecting his hand, she confirmed her flight and dropped the receiver in the cradle while meeting his angry bloodshot eyes. "I've disowned one brother, today, James," she said quietly. "If you'd like to join your brother Robert on my list of those I'll never see again, you may say what you're thinking about me at this moment."

"I doubt dad's given his approval for you to return to that town, Ron," James spoke as he struggled to sit up, keeping the sheet and blanket at his bare waist. Already angry, he continued, "I don't know what the blazes happened up there, but I know, you're in way over your head, sis. This Laquette guy, he's bad news from what I've heard—"

"When you phoned my room Sunday," she said as she plopped down sidesaddle on his bed. Reading the outrage in her brother's eyes, she smiled faintly. "Yes, that was Jade you spoke to. No, I wasn't having mad passionate sex with him when you called. I wasn't even thinking about it at the time. I was holding an ice bag to my head and trying to make sense of a spinning room. The man not only saved my life, but he was taking care of me as well as the necessary details which I wasn't capable of handling—"

"The son of a bitch made it sound like a joke," James growled.

"Would you rather he'd panicked and told you your sister, who was a few hundred miles away, had just been assaulted and nearly raped?"

James' slender young face drained of color; his blue eyes evoked genuine concern, suddenly spooked. "Not particularly."

"You'll understand when, or if, you ever meet him, James," she said with a faint smile, a touch of sadness. "You'll understand what kind of man he is, and hopefully, you won't believe everything you've heard or will hear. He's truly not guilty of any crime other than falling in love with me, and I'm just as guilty of that offense."

"Dad won't allow you to return there, Ronnie," he repeated with a touch of worry. "If last night was any indication, he's hotter than I've seen him since I nearly got expelled in junior high."

"I spoke to him, James," she said lightly, but the anger rose in her eyes. "He won't dare interfere, and if he should try, I suggest you tell him that I made a few calls from this phone before you awoke. You won't be lying."

"What the . . . Ronnie?"

"Bad publicity is as much a tool as a weapon, Jim," she said soberly. "I suggest you quote me if the need arises for you to speak to father on my behalf. If anything happens to me, if I'm thwarted in leaving this house or reaching my destination, you may receive firsthand experience of how Jade Laquette lived for the past eighteen years of his life. That, too, you may tell our father . . ."

"I don't think I like the sounds of this, sis," he said soberly.

Regardless of how this situation turned out, she knew she wouldn't likely see her little brother again for a long time. If her father even suspected what she was willing to do to him, to her entire family, she'd be disowned. Reaching, she clasped James' head, scuffing his curls, and for an instant he looked as he had years ago, annoyed and ready to shove her hand away like any typical little brother. Something in her eyes halted him; something in his eyes enhanced a more worried, wary shine. "Take care, Jamison," she said and leaned, brushing a kiss on his forehead and smiling faintly at his more vivid concern.

His hand lashed out, catching her retreating hand, holding it, and looking into her eyes. "Don't pull this number on me, Ronnie," he said soberly. "This . . . it's a goodbye scene, and I really don't like it. I'm not a little kid anymore in case you haven't noticed. If you're in trouble, there's nothing I wouldn't do to help you, and you know it."

"I do know it, hon," she said sincerely. "But there's nothing you can do other than make sure father gets my message if you get any indication that he's interfered with my destination."

"You realize you're scaring the hell out of me, right? I mean it's not even what—ten a.m.? And you're scaring the shit out of me."

She smiled slightly, "Consider it a bad dream and go back to sleep, then. I have to go. If I get a chance, I'll call you this evening."

"Yea? Well, sis, you better get a chance . . . say around seven or eight? I don't hear from you by nine, I might just come looking for you. I'll be wide awake by then."

Seemed like such a long time since she'd shared a few comfortable moments with her little brother. Between him being away at college and the demands of her profession, they hadn't crossed paths since Christmas.

"You need a haircut," she mused if only to counter the emotions rising too close to the surface, then pushed off the bed. "See ya later."

In her room, she cursed and wiped at tears while tossing her clothes into her trusty bags. Seemed like packing and unpacking had become a daily routine, and it wasn't likely to change any time soon. Depending on what happened in the next few hours, she could be spending a lot of time on the road or in the air.

If not for Len Devinio, Jade knew he would be sitting in an 8' x 10' cell with a single barred window, but his thoughts offered no relief. Leaning on his forearms on the single wooden topped table which remained bolted to the floor, he gazed idly at the stout iron chain between his wrists. Time spent in a 10' x 10' room, with a large square of two-way mirror glass directly in front of him to break the monotony of pale gray paint, wasn't like ordinary time. The seconds seemed to drag into infinity even as the questions hammered into his skull.

Alone, perhaps for the first time since Jarvins had shoved him through the single door, Jade contemplated the absurdity of his situation. On the word of an accused and confessed killer, he rested, handcuffed to a table within a dull gray room. The woman of his dreams might hate him . . . and it struck him odd that he couldn't be positive of a thing in Veronica's regard. Not even a slight sense of her essence touched him as if she wrapped herself in her white light to blind him. An anomaly, this woman of his, and perhaps, that old wives' tale about opposites held a grain of truth. They were polar opposites, and she might have realized that by now. She was the light; he was the darkness, and he couldn't be more attracted if he were a miller and she the flame. But what did she feel for him?

And the epiphanies weren't improving his situation. With a little mind-bending, he might turn these tables—damn it! No.

He had the right to an attorney, according to the idiot who had begun this odyssey.

'. . . Sorry, Laquette, your attorney must have gotten lost . . .'

A reasonable assumption since Jarvins had allowed Jade to call his attorney, Al Kinkaid, from the county jail in Bender Falls, then promptly transported him. Presently, he rested inside a holding cell in the Federal Building in downtown Pittsburgh. With the oppressive weight of justice—or injustice—holding him, he remained in limbo. No official charges. No indictment. No hearing. Jarvins held the strings, and the maniac intended to tug them hard before letting loose.

To what end? Between Jarvins and several other interrogators from state and federal ranks, Jade had yet to determine just what end they sought. They hadn't asked many questions about the murders. They'd hammered him relentlessly about his trips to Europe and the missing years of his life between '74 and '89. They'd asked mundane questions about everything from his attraction to antiques to his shoe size, but no clear direction had he perceived.

The chain links rattled as Jade lifted his hand, nearly slapping himself in the nose as he slid his fingers through his hair and caught his head on his palm. The room was hot, over ninety degrees, but his interrogators remained cool and composed. None had lingered long enough to break a sweat, much less drench their armpits. Maybe he would bill Jarvins for his silk shirt and his suit. Tacked to the cost of the china, the fellow could cost the Bureau a bundle.

But even his attempt to divert his anger fell by the wayside as he recalled those moments when Jarvins had produced Veronica's notebook. Incontestably, Jarvins' tactics had hit nerves, only beginning with the reality that she'd spawned Jarvins' pursuit, and not ended by her instinctive, immediate distrust. She had, in fact, wondered if Isaac Bently was guilty of anything from smuggling drugs or arms to devil worship. *And wasn't she just the observant little witch? Damn it!*

As if scrolled indelibly neon across his mind, he read her flowing script of broken quips and question marks as Jarvins had continued.

'. . . Miss Bryson's investigative skills are beyond reproach, Mr. Bently-Laquette. ... Now, why don't you tell me about your religious beliefs? . . . Do you have religious icons in your shop? . . . What faith?'

'. . . About now, Mr. Laquette, I bet Miss Bryson's having a change of heart . . . I'd imagine she's realized you went to her room with the explicit intention to finish what your pal, Cal Farnsworth, started on Sunday night. . .

'. . . Isn't it true you arranged for Farnsworth to assault her, then stood back and bided your time to make it look good when you rescued her?

'. . . How long have you and Farnsworth been friends? . . . Was it his idea, or yours, to kill his father?'

Asinine, the questions regarding the murders were even more asinine than the mundane curiosities. This interrogation was a roller coaster of innuendoes and accusations designed for the single purpose of breaking him . . . but toward what end? What was Jarvins' ultimate agenda?

From creating doubts of Veronica to dredging the memories of Felicity Laquette—astrologer, psychic guru, a charlatan—Jarvins had volleyed the accusations like a pro, even producing ancient news articles accusing a ten-year-old of murder . . .

And Jade was tired, physically and mentally exhausted. He couldn't even recall when he'd last slept. His eyes stung; his head pounded with the throes of sleep deprivation. And he couldn't afford to nod off inside this small observation room. If he even dozed, the chances of escaping this room were slim to none.

Asleep, he couldn't control his insanity, and with his thought, Jade forced his hand down and dragged himself from his slump.

Leaning back on the stiff, metal-backed chair, he scanned his reflection on the two-way mirror, watching a cynical smirk creep into his mustache. He looked like a junky. Between red rims around his eyes and his anemic skin, he looked worse than most junkies . . . *a disco junky wearing handcuffs.*

But something was happening, now. He felt a change coming, could almost feel the heated exchange behind the mirror glass where at least two men had lingered for the past several hours. His gaze settling on his chained wrists, Jade refused to glance toward the door even as he sensed an approach, expected an arrival.

When the door cracked open, Jade watched Devinio enter. If the agent's faint smile was any indication, the farce was about to end.

"You look like shit, Amico," Devinio commented as he stepped around the table, not looking much better.

"Have you looked in a mirror, mon ami?"

The man twitched a smile, lifting a key between thumb and forefinger. "Look what I found."

"Do you know how to use it?"

"Stand up, and we'll find out," Devinio said simply.

Not needing told twice, Jade pushed from the chair and sidestepped, offering his wrists and watching with genuine relief as the key slid smoothly into the tiny slots.

"Hell, even the right key," Devinio said. "Guess that means I have to cart your rangy ass back to Bentwood."

For a long moment, Jade looked into the dark eyes, seeing the anger hidden there. Devinio was no part of this mess. "Who's driving you?"

"Actually, your buddy's waiting downstairs," Devinio said. "If there's anybody he hasn't chewed up and spit out over the past couple of hours, I have yet to come across one. So, you ready to get out of here?"

"Yesterday is too soon," Jade said dryly and accepted Len's signal to pass through the door. Rubbing his wrists, he avoided the glare of several familiar faces. In the first corridor, they stopped at a windowed cubicle and Jade signed a form to verify that no one had stolen or damaged his personal effects. Relieved by half, he followed Len through a few more doors to an ancient elevator. Was it an omen that he'd left his wallet in the Bentwood House Inn along with every other personal item? A portent that he'd left Isaac Bently's identification behind? As if the winds of time turned an about-face, Jade strode into the lobby and barely spotted Tim Spencer pushing smoothly off a chair against the wall. Halted as if slammed against a wall, he saw several heads spin and heard the rushed words.

"There he is! Jade! Jade Laquette!"

Heartbeat hammering, his ears pounding suddenly, he stood frozen, unable to move forward or backward. Through a tunnel, Spencer advanced, but time had slowed. Jade stood immobile as the bodies converged, the pressure slamming against him, compacting him, smashing him, suffocating him!

"Saaax . . ." The word droned inside his head.

"Jeeesssus, Bennntly . . ."

Bently was dead, he'd have told Devinio if he could. Not a word, not a sound, not a muscle twitched against the external pressure. As if the air pressurized, his skin pressed, mashed to his bones. Coiling, recoiling and sinking, and he couldn't move, couldn't breathe. Of its own accord, his head lowered, and his hands moved without a conscious direction, fisting and sinking into his pockets . . . recoiling, drawing inside . . .

Don't. . .! Don't. . .! Don't. . .!

His worst nightmare! His worst nightmare come to life! Outside his skull, words shouted, cringing him on the inside. ". . . Murder . . . Where've you been? . . . Are you helping in the homicide? . . . Are you a suspect? . . . Is there any connection? . . ."

Hands moved him, bruising him and pushing him, staggering him. Words echoed inside his pounding skull.

"Mmmy carrr . . . Gettt backkk! Givvve the mannn some aaair . . ."

"Isss it truuue youuu've been ouuut of the counnntry?"

"III haaave youuu, Issaaac . . ."

No Isaac . . . Isaac was dead . . . Jade. He was Jade.

Pushed and propelled, pushed, Jade passed through glass doors and stumbled onto a sidewalk, understanding only the panic inside of him as bodies pressed about him. Sounds of city traffic and voices railed against his mind. The safety of a car, a backseat, he understood and folded over, curling into himself. An engine droned from some distant place. He heard words. Strangers' voices . . . and he'd been here before.

"What the fuck'd you do to him, Devinio? What the fuck'd you and your people do?"

"He walked out of that goddamn elevator on his own power, Spencer. Whatever the fuck just happened here, it's nothing we did . . ."

"Yea? Well. Tell me why the hell a guy who can whip my ass at hand-to-hand is curled up like a fuckin' pretzel on my backseat staring like a goddamn zombie . . ."

"How the hell well do you know this guy, Spencer? And don't mess with me. How much do you know about him?"

"I know he didn't deserve to have a goddamn criminal charge filed against him, and he doesn't deserve the shit you and your pals just put him through."

"That's not what I asked you, Spencer . . . I want to know how much you know about Isaac Bently or Jade Laquette. How the hell much do you know about him?"

A long pause then, "I can tell you a whole lot about Isaac Bently, the antique dealer from Bentwood. The only thing I can tell you about Jade Laquette is what I've read in a few articles recently . . . and if you're getting this, Sax, don't get pissed. You hit me with a few off-the-wall comments. . .? I'm a cop, I get paid to look between the lines . . . ."

CHAPTER 27

Not sure when he'd faded out or faded in, Jade rested in the corner of the backseat. His focus and mind connected to recognize the passing scenery, to identify the car dealerships on the last long stretch of highway into Bentwood. He'd traveled the road a thousand if once, but he felt distant as if he might never have seen this place before. The sights were familiar, short stretches of fields and forests, blue skies stretching infinitely above mantels of emerald-capped hills, sunlight glistening on hoods of passing cars, stinging his irises. In the front seat, the two low voices continued to volley, and he understood the words, had even become accustomed to the voices, knowing the names. Distant. Something had happened inside of him, and this was nothing new. Sometimes he awoke like this, not certain of where he was, not connected to anything or anyone.

"You coming around yet, Sax?" the voice asked, and Jade knew if he looked, he would see the dark blue eyes reflected in the rearview mirror. His father looked at him in the mirror that way, too . . . watched him watch the scenery pass. The French countryside resembled this scenery with green fields and vines sagging under the weight of the grapes, like cow's udders bloated with milk . . .

"If you're pissed off, Sax, I don't blame you, but this silent treatment's getting to be a little much. Even a grunt would be better than nothing."

"You ever see him get like this before?"

"So, maybe he doesn't feel like talking. You bastard's probably been—"

"Look, Spencer, I'm goddamn sick of you accusing me of this shit . . . I didn't know a damn thing about that warrant. I was even more goddamn surprised when my partner busted in than your mute buddy back there."

"Your partner's a grade-A asshole, Devinio. How the fuck'd he get in the Bureau? Win the lotto? Buy a senator? Buy a senator a Caddie? What's his story?"

"He went through Quantico the same as everybody else and your opinion, notwithstanding, Spencer, he's a damned good agent."

"He's a loose-fucking-cannon, Devinio, and you know it even if you don't want to admit it. He's got one goal in mind and that's to lynch my buddy in the backseat. He's been working overtime on that goal and in the meantime, we have a timebomb ticking in Bentwood. Somebody's going to get hurt—if not killed—again because your prep-school flunky's got his nose out of joint. Granted, the lady might be worth it—"

"You can call it quits there, Amico—"

"You know, Devinio, we might look like a bunch of backwoods, shit-kicker hicks to you and your buddy, but if you think we can't see what's going on here, you better wise up and smell the cow dung, pal, 'cause you're standing in it knee-deep . . . And I'll tell you, just between you and me, if we didn't have a whole lot of extremely worried people, you'd be hearing the laughter all the way to D.C. . . .

"Nobody's laughing though, ace, except maybe our psycho. While your pal's trying to hang one of our favorite citizens for being a little on the mysterious side, we have farmers putting up cows a few hours early and locking doors that haven't even had locks on them, until now."

"For the record, Spencer, I'm the only reason this case is still getting any Federal attention at all," the low voice rebounded. "The minute one of your friends beat a confession out of Farnsworth, we were officially off the murder case. The only way I could even justify the Bureau spending man-hours is by convincing my department head that nothing jives here, and you'll find this ironic as hell, but it's my partner's profile that kept this case open . . ."

"What the hell . . . what now?"

His gaze vacant, Jade scanned the crowd of people gathered on the sidewalk ahead. Beneath a familiar, stylish dark gray awning, heads turned as the car rolled to a stop at the curb. Olden Time, his shop, his home. Funny how he could feel detached even knowing he belonged on the other side of the glass where the words were etched in Old English script. Automated, he slid a faint smile to his lips, not quite pulling it off. A sense of dread touched him as if he should be feeling that emotion, as well as curiosity. Forcing himself to feel emotions when he felt nothing at all could be an effort, and he felt nothing as he climbed from the backseat. He felt nothing as he glanced over a few of the tense familiar faces, reading their distress and dismay, reading hostility directed toward one of his escorts.

"Want you to know, Isaac, we all know you didn't deserve none of this here."

"If we could of stopped them, we would have."

"Sam tried, Isaac, but they came in like maggots waving a warrant and . . . well, we're just mighty sorry."

"What the hell . . . ?"

"Mister, unless you got official papers saying you have a right to be here, you better clear on out," a low angry voice ordered, and Jade recognized the broad-bellied Billy Skyles facing off with the dark-suited Devinio. "You boys done enough damage."

Wading through the bodies that cleared a path to his door, Jade glimpsed others, strangers, pressed back, and heard the shouted voices fall silent. His door glass was missing. He looked down to see tiny sparkles caught in the cracks of his steps, his threshold, his floorboards . . . and more people were inside, stopping, looking at him over the tops of shelves and from stooped poses in his rooms. His gaze landed idly on Wade Kreider standing a few steps away, his immense brown eyes shimmering with tears, his golden-brown hair flopped over his brow, and his face a mask of pure dread.

"I-I tried t-to stop them, Mr. Bently," the boy strained as his lips quivered.

His house, his castle . . . invaded. His vacant gaze trailed over the front room cubicles. Rearranged items cluttered every surface. Broken pieces of glass and ceramic were scattered under end tables and around table legs. A few people stooped with dustpans and brooms.

"God almighty," Spencer breathed in his wake.

Moving in automation, Jade walked forward and scuffed the familiar boy's head as he continued to scan the ruin. His attention dropped as the boy wrapped his arms around his waist. The golden head burrowed at his chest. "Not your fault, Wade," Jade managed as he rumpled the shaggy hair. A sob broke against him; the lean back lurched under his palm. Several paces away, Elaine Connelly stood, her face a ruined mask of blotchy red patches and tear streaks.

"The-ey were h-here whe-en I got here," she hiccupped and lifted a tissue to catch a flood of tears. "I'm s-*sorry.*"

"Not your fault, Elaine," he managed and looked around again, lifting his hand, and running his fingers through his hair as spiders crawled over his scalp. Easing the boy backward, Jade continued moving.

"You can sue 'em for this," someone muttered.

Still moving, Jade walked down the center aisle, his gaze panning the faces and the ruin. His fingers lifted to brush over the shiny surface of a breakfront . . . with a broken front where a chisel or pry-bar had broken open a door. *That drawer had stuck on occasion . . .*

Nothing, nothing at all had they left untouched. Jade continued, detached, looking at the broken glass case at the rear of his store, rounding the register, and still walking. His scalp crawled as he entered the devastation of his first office. His gaze drifted to the broken locks on his second door that hung open. A trail of papers leaked into the hallway.

For a long moment, he stood scanning the overturned drawers, papers, and receipts scattered and mounded on the floor. Books had been torn off the shelves; blown-glass figurines decorated the clutter. One undamaged piece rested on the mound of papers on his desk.

Absently, Jade lifted the unicorn, holding it in his palm and looking at the fine artwork. Flashing, he glimpsed the face of the man who had held it. Without a thought, Jade closed his fist with a quick, powerful grip and heard the crunch. Fire lanced his palm as he moved slowly around his desk. Leaning, he caught the arm of his chair and tugged it upright, sinking down into it, his gaze drawn to his fist resting on his thigh.

"Sax . . .? You uh . . . Christ, I dunno even what to say to you," Spencer said in a low strained voice. "This—"

"Sax is dead," he said absently as he watched the blood begin to squeeze from between his thumb and folded fingers. "Isaac's dead," he continued in a leaden voice and lifted his vacant gaze to find Spencer standing opposite the desk, his face a wooden mask of dread and sympathy. "Get everyone out of my house, then follow them."

"Listen, pal, like it or not, you have friends here and by now, you ought to know most people around here pull together to help friends. You don't have to handle this shit alone."

Clasping the arm of the chair, he pushed to his feet and walked through the second door, continuing through the narrow corridor. His other doors, the doors leading to his warehouse stood open. His heart tugged with the thought of his cars, but only for an instant. Nothing could hurt for long.

He paused in the doorway, looking through the dull light to see crates overturned, his Maserati doors gaping open, violated. Turning, he continued up the steps and through the shadows, aware of footsteps following him. His first two apartment doors stood open; books trailed into the hall. Without more than a glance, he continued through the last door, clasping the panel and slapping it shut, fast enough to twist the undamaged lock . . . he never locked his small apartment. Until now.

In the darkness, he moved to his office and eased down into his chair. No need even to close his eyes, the darkness inside his apartment offered the blackness of a crypt.

A few thumping sounds reached him, a muffled voice, but he felt no inclination to answer. He could sleep, now. The only place he could ever sleep was in a closet . . . or in a crypt.

Quaint, Ronnie remembered the word she'd used four days earlier as she sped over the last rise. In the early evening light, the small town still appeared 'quaint,' but how much more appealing that word seemed to her as she sailed down the exit ramp to the stop sign where she'd contemplating a square dance jingle over the road sign. Bentwood to the left . . . Hazelwood to the right. In appearance, nothing had changed. She made yet another mental note to stop into the greenhouse directly across from the exit ramp, but she had faces and names to attach to that opaque glass building, now. She knew the Tarkins, Betsy and Frank Tarkin. The elder couple had supplied gardening paraphernalia to Bentwood for the past twenty years.

No longer was the town a mere speck on a map, a place to pass over and leave behind. She'd left her heart in this screwy little town, left it in the hands of a man whose enthralling eyes had kept her awake even when her lids threatened to collapse. Until she saw him, until she knew without a doubt that he was alright, she wouldn't relax, wouldn't collapse.

He'd been released. That much she'd learned with the phone calls she'd placed before leaving the Pittsburgh airport. Little more than two hours ago, he'd gained his release without official charges, and her heart wrenched with the sidebar she'd heard to that event. Jarvins. Damn Mark Jarvins for what he was doing, for what he had done to the man she loved. If Jade hated her, now, she wouldn't blame him, but the thought brought new tears to her already stinging eyes.

The worst possible scenario had come to pass. Isaac Bently and Jade Laquette had made the news becoming synonymous, and once again, the media had resurrected the story with a vengeance. A few seconds of listening to the local radio station had convinced her to listen only to the wind blasting through her open window. After eighteen years . . . seventeen years of anonymity, Jade had surfaced and that was just the kind of story to improve circulation. Big bucks circulation. An eighteen-year-old unsolved murder, a child disappearing for eighteen years only to surface as a nonentity in a small town with two recent gruesome murders under investigation . . .

Her heart ached. Her head ached. Her teary eyes burned from staring at strips of gray asphalt with reflections of chrome and glass lancing her vision. If Jade didn't hate her, if he didn't blame her for all of this, she would be shocked . . . and where would they go from here? His life here, his serenity . . . destroyed. People would look at him differently, would question him, would hound him for either explanations or details. Some, like Spencer, would stick by him, but others . . .? How many others might be inclined to believe Mark Jarvins' theory?

Only on the surface, the town remained the same, but turning onto Maine, noting the increased traffic, the people meandering on the walks, Ronnie doubted even that revelation. In the park, she noted activity, her mind spying and rejecting the red, white, and blue streamers strung across the streets. The Fourth of July celebration, A fireman's fair . . . a street fair. Life moved on. Her world could collapse in the next few moments, but the town of Bentwood, like a million other towns, would celebrate the Fourth with picnics and fireworks, parades, and waving flags.

With only one block to go, she noted the unusual number of cars parked along either side of the street. Slowing, she passed the intersection in front of the Bentwood House. Behind dark sunglasses, which doubtfully offered her anonymity, she spotted activity in front of Olden Time. Several people milled under the awning. Her heart already pounded with a rise of instant fury as she recognized that obnoxious reporter, Grimes, hanging on the sidelines.

Pulling around the corner, Ronnie found a parking space just passed Andover's Hardware. Momentarily, her thoughts reeled with what she would say, what she would do when she saw Jade. If he hated her, if she saw hatred in his eyes . . .? It would kill her, but she wouldn't blame him. She could never blame him.

Climbing unsteadily from the car, firming her nerve, and calling on her last reserve of strength, she turned toward the corner. Knowing how word traveled in this town, she had little doubts about what kind of reception she should expect.

She would be blamed.

Whether the townspeople rallied for or against Isaac Bently, she was the newcomer, the outsider. She would be blamed, if not stoned like Mary Magdalene. What this town thought of her, what her associates thought of her or wrote about her, mattered not at all. What other people said or believed had never bothered her one way or another. Only one man could destroy her with his thoughts, only one man could collapse the world on her shoulders with a single glance. Him, she needed to see. Him, she needed to face.

Before she ever reached the corner, a few heads turned, steady eyes watching her approach. Holding herself together, Ronnie awaited a passing car and continued off the curb, her attention riveted. What were they doing? Why were so many people loitering outside that shop? Why were the doors open when she knew it was after six o'clock?

Dear God, had something happened to him? Her heartbeat quickening, she lengthened her stride. Her attention riveted to the entrance, she spotted the hammer in a brawny man's hand, the panel of plywood where glass should be. Scathing glances lanced her from every direction. Men and women alike leered at her. A few children lingered on the fringes, dangerously close to the street, peering at her from behind their parents and even their round faces appeared angry and accusing.

"Hey! Bryson!"

"Lady, ain't you caused enough trouble 'round here?" a low voice growled.

Ronnie pushed passed a young woman who stepped in front of her attempting to block her entry.

"Why don't you go back to the city where you belong?" another woman sneered.

Heart and head pounding in harmony, Ronnie shoved passed the stout man blocking the doorway and halted clumsily, seeing, not understanding, not grasping the full extent of what her stinging eyes perceived. Dazed, she continued forward, her gaze landing, fixing on the dark head of hair moving inside the open office doorway.

Tim Spencer holding a broom . . .? Everywhere she looked, people with brooms, a few with hammers, screwdrivers . . . the glass cases across the back of the store . . . glass missing, glass on the floors, in the carpets. The sound of vacuum sweepers whirled in a constant roar. What in God's name had happened here? Who . . . who had done this?

Why for God's sake? Why had someone done this?

Where was Jade? Where was he? Was he hurt?

The thought quickened her pace. Trotting, she swung around the counter, pushing past yet another stout-built woman who tried to grab her arm. Wheeling into the office doorway, her eyes darted in search of Jade. Hysteria and panic rising, she swallowed a scream as she pivoted her wide-eyed focus to Tim Spencer. Her heart skipped a beat as she looked into Spencer's chilly blue eyes. Barely able to catch a clear breath, she heaved, "Where is he?"

Anger crept slowly across Spencer's brow. His cheek muscles twitched with visible restraint. Coiled, he held her in a piercing gaze, as he would lance any unwanted stranger, his dark blue eyes cold and hostile. Knuckles white, he gripped the broom handle, keeping the bristles on the floor as if that were an effort.

With a long pause reflective of a few evenings past, Tim drew out the silence until she wanted to scream, lunge and yank the answers from his throat. Knees shaking, Ronnie clung to the doorframe, terrified of what Tim might tell her, terrified that Jade could have been hurt. Harmed. Physically lying in a hospital—

In a slow careful voice, Spencer vented his thoughts. "Think maybe you better go on back home to Arlington, Miss Bryson. There's not a whole hell of a lot more you can do around here to stir up trouble—"

"Tim! Where is he!" she demanded. "Is he hur—" She couldn't finish that word, that thought. Tears flashed over her eyes, blurring the hostility on Spencer's face.

"He's resting, Miss Bryson," Tim continued in a low tone. "The man's exhausted and I'll tell you, even if he was up to a visit, I don't think I'd let you get anywhere within ten yards of him."

"Tim . . ." *No, not you, too! Don't make me fight you, too!*

"Look, Miss Bryson," Spencer spoke with a formality reserved for strangers. "I don't know exactly what's on your agenda, but I do know, you don't belong in this shop or this town. Think you'd just best get back in your car and ride on out of here before anybody else ends up hurt."

"I need to see him!" she strained on the verge of a cry, a scream. "I'm not—"

"I don't particularly give a damn what you need, Miss Bryson," Tim cut her off coldly. His eyes cut like lasers through her tears. "What concerns me is what Isaac Bently needs, and the last thing he needs is any more hassle from some gal who's already cost him plenty. I'm damn sorry I ever let you get near him the first time. If I'd have had some hint of what you were really up to when I found you having dinner with my pal Saturday night, you can bet your sweet ass I wouldn't have invited you out to my place. But you're good, lady, you fooled the shit out of me with those big, concerned eyes and nice smile. Now, you turn yourself around, and you get your pretty little ass back in your car, and you get on down the highway. There are a couple dozen hotels over by the airport to accommodate you if you can't get a flight out."

"Think that's about enough, Spencer," the low voice came from behind and Ronnie jolted, her muscles gripping in a spasm as Len's hand came against her back. "The lady isn't responsible for any of the shit going down in this town—"

"If you got any brains, Devinio," Spencer said as he leveled his glare over Ronnie's head. "You'll get the little lady packed up and on her way. The last thing we need around here is one more reporter looking to make a name for herself, and I'd hate to see anybody else get hurt. The man's name doesn't make a shitting bit of difference to anybody in this town. He has friends here who won't likely take kindly to what she and your buddy did to him. Now, you take her and get out. The man's been cleared of suspicion for murder and by Christ, if I see either of you near him again, I'll personally file the goddamn harassment charges in his name. Both names—just so it's fucking legal."

In a daze, Ronnie moved, accepting Len's persuasion, her mind reeling in a horrible fog. Not Tim's words, not his hostility . . . she could handle that, could always handle verbal lashings. It was the thought of Tim's opinion, his observations, and insights that could reflect Jade's attitude toward her, to crush her. If this was how Tim felt, what he thought, how he saw all of this . . . Jade could feel the same, must feel the same. The two of them were a lot alike . . . like brothers. *If this was what Tim felt . . .*

Numb, in a numb daze, she walked alongside Len, positive the world had suddenly turned black. The man she loved, the only man she'd ever genuinely loved, she'd destroyed . . . and he hated her now.

"Ron," Len said as he settled into the driver's seat of her rental. "Much as I know you're not responsible for any of this shit, much as I know I'd like to slam that son of a bitch from here to Christmas for all the shit he said, I have to agree with him about one thing. You can't stay in Bentwood. This town's way too volatile and it wouldn't take much to light the fuse. Maybe once we get this homicide solved and things settle down, you could uh . . . you could come back and put things right with Laquette. No matter what that moron back there said, I think Laquette will want to see you. He's a smart guy. A bit on the screwy side, but he's alright . . .

"Right now, though . . . it's probably not a good time to try talking to him. Give it some time. Let things blow over a little bit . . . Hell, Ron, you look about out on your feet . . . How about I drive you back over to the airport and put you on a flight home . . .?"

She had no home, she could have told him; instead, finding sense to decide, "I can get myself to the airport, Len. Thanks . . ."

How she found her way out of town with the tears flooding and flowing, Ronnie would never know, any more than she knew how she managed to reach the airport. She had no idea what she'd said to Pete to snuff the story she'd intended to tell, had no idea how she bought a plane ticket or found the proper gate. In her apartment in Arlington, she was asleep before her head ever struck the pillow.

CHAPTER 28

The phone had been ringing nonstop for days. Two rings, then the infamous click of the answering machine, and her all-business voice suggesting the caller leave a message and expect a callback. Fat chance. Ronnie had no intention of calling anyone. She felt no inclination to speak to anyone about anything. The world would just have to turn without Veronica Bryson for a while.

For a long while, she confirmed, silently, as she gazed at a blank tablet page. Whatever she'd meant to write slipped from her mind in the wake of yet another phone message, this one from her younger brother, demanding she answer the phone if she was home. She was home. She was sitting in her favorite stuffed chair, feet tucked under her, a tablet open on her lap, prepared to write the next Pulitzer-Prize-winning article . . . but she couldn't think of a single subject. She'd managed to craft only one letter in the past three days, and that one had gone in the mail two days earlier.

If she never wrote another word, it would be too soon.

Absently, she continued doodling designs in the margins. What she needed was to find a new career, a respectable career . . . but none came to mind. She didn't feel like doing a thing with her life. She didn't feel like doing a damn thing at all. If she never faced another human—

The phone rang yet again. Two jarring rings, the click, then her hateful secretary's voice echoed from the speaker across the room. "Please, leave a message . . ." *Or go to hell.*

"Ronnie, this is your mother, dear," Fiona's voice breezed light and cheery into the room. "I know you're home, dear. I do wish you'd return my calls . . . Well, no matter, darling. Don't forget about Saturday. Your brother Linc and Vicky are coming in. Do come, darling . . . Speak to you soon. Love and kisses."

If she'd needed another reason to avoid the Fourth of July bash at her parents' house, the mention of her next older brother provided one, but then she hadn't intended to attend in the first place.

Tossing the notebook aside, she pushed from her chair, scanning her room and wondering if she should try cleaning. Why bother? The cleaning service kept up with the day-to-day dust and dirt . . . and she remembered all those people scattered throughout the shop with their brooms and dustpans . . .

No. She refused to think about all of that again. Seemed like she'd spent the last few days thinking of little else . . . and remembering.

If she tried—hard—maybe she could forget how his eyes could warm or chill, how his hands sent sparks flying through her system. Maybe, if a few centuries passed, she could even forget how that dimple emerged when he smiled, or how that deep sexy voice spoke her name . . . or how right it felt to lie in his arms . . .

Hopeless. The man had invaded her psyche, her life, her soul . . . and she brushed more tears as she flopped on her bed. For the first time in her life, she'd found a man she would like to spend the rest of her rotten life with, and in a matter of days, she'd destroyed him . . . destroyed his life, his love . . . even his livelihood.

As much as she hated Mark Jarvins, she couldn't even blame him. She'd known Mark's nature. She'd felt the sting of his jealousy as much as three years ago. Even now, Ronnie couldn't decide if Mark had shot the stalker out of duty or anger. Self-defense, Jarvins had claimed on his official reports. In self-defense, he'd shot and killed the stalker right in front of her . . . and even now, she couldn't be certain if Mark had truly believed the man was armed.

How . . . how could she have forgotten the extent of Jarvins' temper? How could she have ignored what she'd surely known . . .? That Jarvins might go to any lengths to keep any man from touching her. For God's sake, he'd even changed official records in the Bureau files to keep Len from getting any ideas. How could she have risked Jade's life, his safety? She should have backed away, should've stayed miles away from Jade Laquette if only to protect him. Knowing how much she'd hurt him by exposing him only to himself, how could she have allowed him to expose himself to Jarvins?

Yet, again, the phone rang, and she heard her clipped voice, then silence. Another hang-up call.

Ronnie sighed and rolled over, staring at the window where evening sun trickled through the lace curtains. She wished they would all hang up. She wished she could gather the courage to disconnect the phone altogether. Already, she'd unplugged the television, removed batteries from radios, canceled the daily paper . . . and told her editor mentor, Tom Fielding, as well as Pete Simons to forget her number. She wanted no contact with the world. If not for a hope, a single hope and desire to hear a smooth, deep voice issuing from that speaker, she would disconnect the phone.

She hadn't even spoken to Max or Karen Hagen, or Jesse, who'd left at least two messages on the machine. Only one voice she longed to hear. Only one face she longed to see. And in a paradox, she feared and anticipated having her prayers answered. He would hate her, and she couldn't even bear the thought of hearing the contempt in his voice or seeing the hatred in his emerald eyes.

If anyone had ever told her she could fall in love, much less be killed by a broken heart, she would've howled with laughter. Men were jerks. Egotistical. Tyrannical. Vane. Self-centered. Simpleminded and whimsical *jerks* led by hormonal imbalances of testosterone which sent them tripping over themselves to ogle a pair of long legs or a big bust. As if legs and busts didn't come attached to a mind which could likely slice them to shreds.

Jade Laquette wasn't a jerk . . . damn it! He had a right to be vain . . . and he cared about other people before himself. And she was hopelessly in love with the devil.

And he'd said he was in love with her, too. '. . . my final folly . . .'

"Oh God," she uttered into her pillow. "Why did he have to be psychic?"

She was driving herself crazy! Driving herself entirely, incontestably insane . . . and she just wished it would end soon. Wished she could slip completely off that slight edge into an abyss where it wouldn't hurt so badly to think, to remember, to love.

The doorbell blasted chimes through the apartment, jolting her. Her heart skipped a beat with hope and fell into a more leaden rhythm as she realized the impossibility. Jade wouldn't be at her door. Another reporter, a salesman, a Jehovah's Witness come to prophesy the end of the world . . . she could ignore the bell as easily as she ignored the ring of a telephone.

Staring at the lace curtains, she listened to several more gongs of the bell before a hand slammed the flimsy door, and an angry voice demanded, "Ronnie! I know you're in there! If you don't answer this damn door, I'm calling for the fire department to bust in!"

Jade would've busted in without any help.

Cursing, she pushed off the bed, not bothering even to look in her dresser mirror. She couldn't care less if her curls stood on end. If James took offense to her cutoffs and bare feet, her T-shirt from some obsolete rock group of the 60s, too bad. He was still pounding, demanding attention, when she unlatched the chain and deadbolt.

Luckily, he heard the locks tumble over his own din. He entered as she walked toward the kitchen.

"Ronnie?" he asked somewhat hesitantly. "Hey, aaa . . .?"

She passed into her compact kitchen, moving to the coffeepot and finding a half-full cup on the counter. Adding some of the rank-smelling black brew from the pot to the sludge in the cup, Ronnie considered the absurdity of her brother's cautious tone after he might have scared the hell out of her neighbors, none of whom were likely home. They had lives—

"Hey, sis? How's it going?"

Looking over at him, seeing the concern on his young face, in his pale blue eyes, she tried a smile. By his worry, she'd failed miserably. To hell with putting on a happy face. She settled into a chair at the table, pulled a heel onto the thin cushion, and began picking through the mail she'd collected earlier outside her door.

Life must go on. Utilities and rent needed to be paid. "If you have a reason for disturbing me, James, get to it, will you?"

"I've been calling," he said distractedly, dragging a chair from the opposite end of the table. "You're not too good at answering your messages. What've you been up to?"

"Getting old and fat," she said and looked over at him, seeing his troubled brow beneath a smooth walnut wave. "What were you calling about?"

He looked at her for a long lingering moment, thoughts and concerns weighing in his eyes. Of all her brothers, she suspected James was her favorite, but then, he was still young. Given time, he would follow in the male Bryson footsteps, finish school, move into one branch of the family trade or another, learn to control his finances, and run people's lives. If his visit were any sign, he was practicing for the future.

"Ronnie, you want to tell me what's going on?" he asked with a careful edge, his temper bridled with an effort. "You don't answer calls. You look like you haven't even combed your hair today. You look mad enough to chew me out, and you're not, so I know there's something wrong," he said with an effort to smile.

"Fuck you, James," she said dully. "Feel better?"

He stared at her, his expression caught between a start and alarm. "No . . . I can't say that I do, sis," he answered after a second. "You look and sound lousy, Ronnie," he said quietly, his worry winning over his indignation. "I told you a few days ago if there's something I can do, I will. Just tell me what's wrong, and I'll try to fix it."

"Go home, James," she said without effect. "It's a Friday night. I'm sure you have girls lined up around the block waiting for you. Go out and have a good time."

"Mom's worried too, sis," he said as if she hadn't spoken. "I know she stopped here yesterday . . . You didn't answer the door, huh?"

"Either, I wasn't here, or I was tied up."

"Don't lie, okay?" he said quietly, his gaze intent. "What did this guy . . . Jade? What did he do to you? What did he say to you when you went up there Tuesday?"

"Leave him out of this," she said, mildly annoyed. "He didn't do or say anything to me."

"So, that's it? He stiffed you?"

"God, you're an ass," she said absently, not truly feeling anything to convey affection. "No, he didn't stiff me. I didn't even see him or speak to him on Tuesday." Funny how even that admission could hurt. Looking over to her brother, she spoke simply, "The man's suffered enough aggravation, James. Don't even think about accusing him of anything. Just leave him alone. Leave me alone. If you really want to do something for me, that would be plenty."

"How do you expect me to do that when I know damn full well something's really wrong here? You're hurt or angry."

"Even if I were, what would it matter, James?" she asked dourly. "What makes me so special? For that matter, what makes me immune from feeling down on occasion? Maybe I'm a woman, after all," she said snidely. "Has it ever occurred to you, to any of you, that I just might be a woman, and I'm entitled to be moody?"

"You've always been moody, and I've never doubted your gender, sis," he said with a poor attempt at humor. His concern rolled back in force. "This isn't like you, though. You're one of the smartest women I know, as well as one of the toughest. I've never seen you let something get you down. God knows, I've seen you hot as hell, and I've seen you laugh over some pretty crude jokes, but this . . . you shutting out the world, refusing calls, refusing company? Ever think maybe I care about you? That maybe I worry about you even when you're off on one of your chosen assignments? Heck, more so when you're off tracking something I know could hurt you . . . or is that part of what's going on here?" he asked with enough doubt in his eyes to pursue the issue. "Getting hurt . . . is that maybe bothering you more than you want to admit?"

Farnsworth, she realized and shook her head. "He got lucky, and it could have gotten worse. . ." *If not for Jade.*

"Then it really is this other guy, this Laquette guy," James said absently and studied her with a sudden intensity. "You . . . you really are in love with this guy."

God! Then he wondered why she wanted no company? Shaking her head, lifting her coffee, she pushed off her chair and turned, ambling to the backdoor. If she'd ever trod on the postage-stamp-sized lawn off the patio, the occasion escaped her. "It's a no-win situation, James," she said in a moderate tone. "I'd appreciate it if you'd let the subject drop, and I'd appreciate it more if you'd not discuss my private life with anyone."

"Ronnie—"

"James, let it alone," she said quietly and turned, meeting his disheartened gaze as she leaned against the door. "Let me alone. I appreciate your concern, and your care, but right now, I just don't want to think about anything, and I'd rather not hear any lectures from anyone."

"If you didn't talk to this guy—"

"James," she said bluntly. "Drop it."

He hesitated, then nodded. "Alright, it's dropped. But there's another reason I came over," he said in mild dismay. "Mom won't be put off too much longer. If you don't answer her calls soon, she's liable to be over here picking your locks, and she's convinced that dad did something to alienate you. We're talking a lethal combination, sis. Her curiosity and her mad. If you truly don't want to be bugged, I suggest you plan on stopping over tomorrow."

"Out of the question," she said evenly.

"Then come tonight," he said smoothly. "Come with me, now, and let her know you're alive and well. Dad won't be home until late, and Bobby's been making himself scarce . . ."

Obligations . . . all her life she'd lived with obligations, forced to take responsibility and face issues contrary to her desire. Appeasing her mother's fear and concern had always fallen into that category. She and her mother might be strangers, but she had an obligation to appear before that stranger on occasion.

"Not tonight," Ronnie decided. "Maybe I'll stop by for a few minutes tomorrow."

In his first conscious act, Jade had crossed the street and braved Jen Andover's enthusiasm, rejecting her offer for a hasty trip to the stockroom long enough to buy a dozen sturdy locks and square iron brackets. Whether he'd bought groceries next, installed the locks, or scrolled the sign that now hung outside his boarded front door, Jade couldn't recall.

'Closed,' he'd printed without further explanation restraining an overwhelming urge to write either, 'Closed due to Illness' or '. . . due to a death in the family.' Either had seemed apropos; after all, Jade Laquette was sick, and Isaac Bently had died.

Unfortunately, had he hung either announcement, he would likely land on the six o'clock news. Safer, easier just to write 'closed' and leave the explanations to the imagination. As he knew only too well, anyone interested in reading his sign would likely invent an explanation anyway.

His castle fortified, Jade remained safely ensconced inside, the hatches battened down as tight as any seaworthy vessel on a raging ocean, and he should be content. He had plenty of work to do, thanks to the federal agents who had stormed through his realm via an official search warrant. More often than not, however, he found himself pacing restlessly from room to room, searching for God knows what.

Something he had lost. Something was missing inside him, and at odd moments he took stock to realize what he'd lost. The revelation only served to further his agitation and restlessness.

To complicate all things, several of his neighbors maintained a relentless pursuit to intrude on his solitude. One of whom suffered no qualms whatsoever about standing in the alley below the kitchen window and using a bullhorn to demand, "Open the goddamn door, or I'm coming back with a *bazooka!*"

Out of a sound sleep, Jade shot awake to that announcement, only further annoyed and stunned when he yanked open his side door to be blinded by brilliant morning sunlight. Blinking and dodging spots across his irises, Jade found Spencer leaning against his truck fender a few paces away. Ankles crossed, arms laced at his muscled chest, he stood in casual repose, a bemused kink in his lips. A megaphone dangled at his elbow like a Christmas ornament against the backdrop of an emerald hue. Not amused, Jade focused on Spencer's smirk.

"I'm not laughing, you should note," he commented dryly.

"Hell, you should consider yourself lucky," Spencer said idly. "You had about another thirty seconds before I intended to make good on that promise. A fella out the road, here, has at least two of those little gems, and I already arranged to borrow one. So, how you doing?"

"You wake me up at . . ." No watch. He'd lost his watch. "Whatever the fuck time it is to ask me—"

"It's about eight a.m.," Spencer offered smoothly. "Which makes it about seventy-two hours since anyone in town's seen hide or hair of you." Far more sober than his smile conveyed, he continued, "I'd have been within my legal-bound duty to blast my way in there and find your remains if you didn't show soon."

"I'm roaring, can you tell?"

"You look like shit," Spencer commented.

"I just woke up for Chrissake," he snapped and looked down himself, tempted to wonder, belatedly, if he'd gotten dressed. Apparently, he hadn't gotten *undressed*. He wore jeans and an open, wrinkled shirt. *Damn it. Pants unsnapped*. He corrected that mistake while looking at Spencer. "Now that you know I'm alive and well, I do hope you intend to go about your affairs more quietly. Some people are trying to sleep."

Spencer turned his gaze toward Maine, then down the block, wrinkling his brow as his gaze landed. "Old lady Handler's deaf, and I know Meg's awake. In fact, she has a couple cups of coffee and a heaping plate of eggs waiting for us."

Dropping his gaze to his feet, suffering a momentary discomfort to see his bare toes near the threshold, Jade backed a half-step as he shrugged. "I'll have to pass. One needs shoes to enter a public eatery."

"Sax," Spencer said as he pushed off his truck, unfolding his leaning length with the slow casual grace of a lion.

More uncomfortable than he cared to consider, Jade battled against an urge to back away as the man advanced. Superimposed, the image of a large, lean man with emerald eyes swam to the surface of his mind, spooking him as effectively as any apparition he'd ever witnessed. Swallowing a suddenly dry knot in his throat, he held Spencer's gaze with an effort.

"What's going on?" Tim asked in a low, careful voice. "What's bothering you so damn bad that you've turned into the town recluse rather than your usual hermity self?"

"I don't know that it's anyone's concern—"

"Come on, Sax, this is me. Your ole pal, Spence, remember?" he said with a faintly worried note. "You're not taking calls, not opening doors. Your mail's scattered all over the front of your shop, and I noticed you're not even leaving the security lights on at night anymore. I've seen you do some pretty wild shit over the past several years, but nothing quite this bazaar." He paused and took a step closer, notching Jade's tension another degree.

"If you're still worried about the Feds, you can forget it," Spencer continued. "Devinio's the only one still around, and I think he's thinking about putting down roots. If you're worried about reporters, those suckers packed up about two days ago when Cy Trascar brought out his 12-gauge and started wearing a coonskin cap." Spencer's eyes sparked with amusement. "Cy made the front page and ended up sleeping it off over in the station, but I'll tell you, you should have seen the rush for the registration desk over at the Inn. The way I hear it, those guys and gals couldn't get checked out fast enough . . . So, they're gone, is the point. It's just little old Bentwoodians and well . . . one psycho still on the loose, but you've never even planted birdseed that I know of, so you're safe in that department . . . So, what the hell's bothering you?"

"I'm agoraphobic," he snapped.

"Come again?"

"Forget it, just . . . just get out of my face," Jade snapped and started backing up. "I'm going back to—"

Spencer rammed the door with enough force to make his high school football coach proud, staggering Jade backward into the hallway and landing him on his tailbone . . . and his palms.

Fire spiraled up his arm and collapsed his elbow. Gasping a short breath, he folded and yanked his hand up, grabbing his wrist to stop the shooting pain. He probably still had enough slivers of ceramic in his hand to build half a unicorn, and the damned drawing salve had failed. Under the splash of light from the dull watt bulb overhead, Jade blinked against unemotional tears. Even without clear sight, he spotted the blood seeping into the strip of gauze wrapped about his palm. What annoyed him more? Spencer auditioning for Pro ball at his expense, the blood, or his own

"What the . . . I'll be damned," Spencer snapped. "That was your blood I wiped off your office chair," he said as he stooped, reaching toward Jade's wrist. "Let me see—"

"Do not even think about touching me," Jade said in slow, angry breaths.

"I hoped that blood belonged to one of those assholes, but I guess that was too much to hope for. So, how do you want to play this one, Sax? You want to get on your own two feet and walk out to my truck? Or do you want me to bust you in the jaw and carry your unconscious self over to Blackwell's office?"

Neither sounded appealing, but he needed to stand on his own two feet. With a speed Spencer matched, Jade rose and met the man at eye level. "It's a few cuts, which were healing just fine before you did the linebacker routine. Now, do step out and find another citizen to harass, will you?"

"If it's still leaking after four days, it's a little more serious than a few healing cuts, and you'd have a hard time lugging boxes around with one hand. You playing mole for a few days, that's fine. It's your business. I figure you have your reasons, and you'll come around when you're damn good and ready. But if you think I'm walking out of here when you could be messing with gangrene or some shit, you can forget it."

"Your confidence in my intelligence is overwhelming," Jade said in a dark tone. "I can't imagine how I survived without you for so long."

"Knock it off, Sax," Spencer said with slightly less severity. "You've been through a lot of shit this week, and it's no insult to your intelligence that I figure you'd ignore a couple cuts . . . What's it take to get through that thick skull of yours that maybe people really do give a shit about you? Maybe you got a whole lot of people worried about you? They sure's hell don't understand you, but they are concerned. So, you walking? Or am I decking you?"

With the thought of stepping out that door, Jade turned his gaze warily toward the brilliant light. He'd believed this phobia past, thought he'd beaten it long ago, but the crawling under his scalp contradicted that belief. What others considered so natural, just walking through a door, had always been a problem. Always. Then he'd found his mother lying in the foyer, and the world had tilted on its axis.

Unconsciously, Jade lifted his hand, raking his fingers through his hair as he shook his head. Still a problem. Still, after all these damned years. He was a grown man for Chrissake; he shouldn't fear passing through doorways, of entering the world, but things existed outside . . . and things could happen. One thing could lead to another, and if anything happened to her—

"Sax?"

Warily, soberly, Jade pivoted his gaze to the best friend he'd ever known, as close to a brother as he would likely ever acknowledge. In quiet desperation, he asked, "Have you ever been afraid, Tim? Have you ever, in your adult life, been so afraid of something that you—you can't see straight, and I mean that literally, ya know? I mean so fucking afraid that the world changes. The walls move and lose shape, and you feel as if you're standing in a fun house. But you're not having fun. You're too fucking shook to have fun. Your skin's crawling, your hands are shaking, and the world just keeps distorting. Have you ever felt like that?"

For a long moment, Tim just looked at him, weighing his words, reflecting. "Yea, I have," he said quietly, tensely. "One week ago last night, I walked into something that did that to me . . . and it still fucking scares the hell out of me. I come out of a sound sleep, and I can't breathe. I find myself about to scream, and the sweat pours out like I sprung a leak. And it's worse when I'm not even asleep and that shit flashes in my head . . .. Yea, I've been that scared, and there's no shame in it, ya know? Fear's healthy sometimes."

"But what if you . . . if you knew you had a reason to be scared?" Jade continued, searching Tim's intense gaze. "What if you knew something was waiting, maybe right outside a door, and if . . . if you pass through it, you're fucking had. There's no turning back. Whatever's waiting can get to you as soon as you step through the door."

Longer, Tim looked at him as enlightenment crept into his eyes. "Jesus," he uttered. "You're . . . you're not talking hypothetically. You really are psychic, and you're talking about something that you see happening . . ." His gaze turned toward the door and held for a moment before returning, only more alarmed. "What, Sax? What's out there?"

"Something bad," he said absently, his gaze not entirely focused. "Something . . . something maybe I can avoid if I stay inside."

"Does it work that way?" Tim asked carefully. "I mean if you hole up in here? If you don't go out, then it doesn't happen?"

"I don't know," Jade answered honestly, his fingers combing over his scalp. "I don't know."

"Do you see it not happening? Do you know when, where, how? Do you have some kind of time frame?"

He shook his head, his gaze listing. "Soon . . . soon is what I feel. I don't know."

"Does it happen to you? Do you see yourself getting hurt outside the door? Me? Anybody?"

He shook his head, desperation rising with a quick leaden beat in his chest. "I just know it's fucking coming . . . and I don't want her here. I don't want her near me . . . I don't want to risk her life."

"Who? Whose life, pal?"

"Veronica's," he heaved softly. "I had no right to fall in love with her. If something happened to her, I'd never survive. I wouldn't want to survive. It's better this way," he said and nodded, holding Tim's gaze where more enlightenment ignited. "It's better if I don't find her, better if I remain . . . here."

"She . . . she came back here," Tim said in a low, strained voice, his guilt not well masked. "She was here."

"I know," Jade said absently, his gaze listing. "I felt her . . . but I couldn't go to her. Can't. If . . . if I stay away, stay inside . . . something . . ."

"Something bad still happens," Tim finished in a low tone. "Something bad can always fucking happen, pal. That's a fact of life, or I'd be out of a job. You're not God, for Chrissake. You falling in love—that's not going to change the world. You staying holed up in this monstrosity you call home? That's not going to stop bad things from happening."

"If I lost her, it'd kill me," he said as he leveled his gaze on Tim, running into his intense blue eyes. "I couldn't handle it if I lost her."

"Hate to break it to you, but unless you find her, seems to me, you're already dead. This, you hanging out behind an arsenal of locked doors and drawn curtains . . .? It's not life, my friend. It's existence. And it's as good as dead. Now, why don't you go find your shoes? I'll run across the street, and grab us some coffee, then we'll see about finding Miss Veronica Bryson. Right after we see about getting your hand stitched up."

"You're like a dog with a bone," Jade said matter-of-factly.

Tim huffed a laugh. "Son, you've been living in this town too long. Now, hustle up. With all your bucks, if we can't get you on a shuttle flight, you can charter a plane to Dulles."

"I'm driving," Jade said as he started to turn, then halted with his words. In slow motion, he looked at Tim, who looked at him with a smug, amused smile. "Damn you."

"Son, if I had a nickel for every time somebody damned me, I'd be a wealthy son of a gun."

"If I had your money, I'd throw mine away," Jade said. "You better start attending church more regularly."

"What? Twice a year ain't good enough?"

Jade shook his head and started up the steps, wondering how he managed to engage in these asinine conversations. "Doesn't begin to cover it."

"Hell, by the sound of it, I'll have to make it three times this year anyway. What religion did you say you were?'

"Go to hell, Spence."

"Thought we just established that's a major possibility," Spencer said as he strode out, chuckling.

CHAPTER 29

If only in an attempt to lift her spirits which had ebbed after she'd decided to attend the Bryson bash, Ronnie had dressed carefully. Predominantly emerald, the shin-length flowy skirt boasted touches of crimson and enough jade hues to catch her eye. With a crimson blouse, dangling earrings, and several necklaces flashing gold sparks at her V-line, she could pass for a Gypsy, and she drew slight satisfaction at her mother's surprise and her sister-in-law's indignation.

Conservative proper picnic attire for one of the Bryson's annual celebrations generally leaned toward casual slacks or pullovers to designer shorts or skirts and sleeveless blouses. Harboring no desire to stay long had helped her choose an ensemble to qualify her opening statement— "Just stopped by for a few minutes, Mother."

Linc and Vicky, and their two-year-old son, Ryan, had indeed arrived for the bash, the latter of which accounted for Ronnie's decision to stop by. Regardless of how she felt about Robert, or Linc for that matter, after his first scathing glance, she hadn't seen her nephew in nearly a year. At two, the little fellow appeared as harmless as a puppy, but that would change. Faintly amused, Ronnie watched him scamper around the veranda, investigating everything from his grandmother's award-winning roses to an overflowing ceramic pot of geraniums. A shame he carried Bryson genes. Eventually, the poor beautiful boy with his black Irish ringlets would become just like his father, like his father before him.

Uncontrollably, Ronnie remembered Tee. Her mind miles away, she stood in the bright, rustic kitchen, watching the little dark-haired boy throw his arms around Jade's neck. That had happened after their first real kiss, a kiss to seal her fate. Her faint smile faded as she watched the toddler with her eyes, and in her mind's eye, watched Jade turning between two state police. He hated her. No doubt of that, now.

"Ronnie." Vicky Bryson, who generally feigned a sisterly familiarity, interrupted with a mocked pout as she continued. "You seem miles away, honey, and you've hardly said three words since you arrived. You really must tell me what exciting things you've been up to. Linc and I heard you just got back."

"Vic," Linc, lounging in one of the rattan chairs at the table across from his wife, interceded. "I'm sure Ronnie doesn't want to discuss work."

He might have more honestly admitted that he preferred not to hear about her work, but not even that subtle innuendo affected her. Ronnie truly had no intention of staying in this gathering for long. A few minutes. She'd promised her younger brother a few minutes to fulfill her obligation and maintain the illusion that the Brysons were one of the DC's most 'together' families.

"That's nonsense, dear," Vicky said like any good, ditzy wife. "I, for one, would love to hear all about it."

About Bentwood, Ronnie realized as she looked at her sister-in-law, wondering if Vicky was dumb like a fox. Perhaps, the ditz had finally realized there was no love lost between them and sensed a chance to use her claws.

"It seems to me," Vicky continued, her blue eyes shaded under ultra-thick lashes. "I heard something about you and Mark Jarvins getting back together—"

"Vic," Linc stated, his focus glued on his wife. Visibly, his knuckles tightened on a glass tumbler balanced on the arm of his chair.

"Wasn't he that gorgeous guy you brought to our wedding?" Vicky continued, smiling pleasantly, and drawing her tones in wistful innocence. "I thought, surely, we'd be attending your wedding next, with the way he fawned over you, and as I recall, you just adored him. You really must tell me if we'll need to start planning a wedding soon."

With a prickle sliding over flesh and lifting goosebumps, Ronnie wondered if Vicky had managed to kindle a few errant sparks of temper in her numb body . . . but anger wasn't quite what she felt. Canting her head, she looked toward the French doors. Anticipation? Both doors stood open, offering a clear view of the formal dining room. Sparks scattered off the Waterford chandelier above the table, oddly brilliant when so little natural light spilled into that room. She rested on a covered, screened veranda, her mother and brother across the table, the toddler investigating another flowerpot, on the verge of tipping it.

Vicky, more intent on her words than her son, her eyes emitting a musing satisfaction, continued, "Did you and Mark get a chance to talk about marriage, honey?"

What was that tingling at the nape of her neck? That sense of something . . . something very much like . . . *Jade's kisses?*

"Vicky, I think that's enough."

Impossible, she couldn't feel the man . . . Impossible! He couldn't be in Arlington. Wouldn't be coming here. She was setting herself up for disaster. Perhaps, she'd finally slipped off the edge. If she must lose her mind, at least she'd chosen the right place. Her father could arrange a quiet trip to the country, and she'd be spared the headlines. Another little scandal brushed under the carpet; another catastrophe thwarted.

"Ronnie, is something—" Linc started but stopped.

"Excuse me, Miss Veronica?" Albert, the Brysons' house manager, interrupted her daze. He halted as if startled by her expression. "There's a gentleman here to see you. He refused to give his name, however—"

Up and moving, Ronnie passed Albert without a glance and sailed through the dining room, her mind already racing ahead to the foyer. Three steps into the wide entry, her feet halted, her mind froze, her gaze locked on the jade green eyes. *Impossible.* He couldn't be standing so elegantly casual, sporting another black suit . . . and crimson shirt . . . couldn't possibly be here! In her father's house! A tiny smile haunted the corner of his mustache. His green eyes turned emerald as his gaze skimmed down her and up, heating her with a flash. *Impossible!*

"Ronnie, who's—" Her mother's voice ebbed behind her.

As Ronnie continued forward, she sensed someone coming down the stairway. A door opened somewhere out of sight. In front of her stood the only person who mattered.

As he drew a rose from behind his back, a long-stemmed red rose; a wondrous light danced in his emerald eyes. "Veronica," he said in a low silky voice to tingle her spine and flutter her stomach.

At the last second, she halted her impulse to throw her arms around his neck and strangle him in an embrace. Nothing would please her more, but all the reasons she'd feared to face him flew to the foreground of her mind. The pain, the trouble she'd caused him, the destruction and devastation . . .

His hands caught and clasped her fingers, sending sparks through her fingertips as he looked down into her. "What a fool I've been," he said in a soft, deep rhythm. "Will you forgive me for taking so long?"

Heart thumping in her throat, she couldn't find the words. She needed more than his hands. In a single motion, they abandoned the handhold and met in the middle. Her arms swept about his neck; his hands drew her hips against him, connecting them from heels to heaven. He was here! No impostor, this! No hallucination could send her mind away and wrap her within such an ethereal mist, lifting her from her body and enhancing the same.

"Who in heaven's name is that, Mother Bryson? Do you know?" a sharp, startled voice intruded.

"I have my suspicions," Fiona said lightly.

He broke the connection, lifting and looking into her eyes, appearing as bewildered and awed as a child. "You are even more beautiful than I remembered, m' love, and I have an excellent memory for certain details."

His love . . . he'd called her 'my love.' "H-how can you still lo—" *No!* She couldn't finish that question! He was here! Nothing else mattered.

Sober, he studied her. "How could you doubt, mon amour? How could you believe for an instant that I'd blame you for the faults of another?"

Tears moistened her eyes yet again. The pain of the past four days gripped her mind and squeezed her heart, but he simply drew her into his arms, enfolding her in comfort.

"No more tears, my darling. No more pain," he uttered against her ear, and his words spilled through her like a healing mantra to lift the sorrow from her mind.

Magic, he was magic, like some mythical creature who could chant away the evils of the world, wave a hand and bring light into darkness. The man was no devil. Her spirits rising, her heart racing with the excitement of his touch, Ronne lifted from the nook of his neck and looked at him, enthralled by the glittering shine lingering in his eyes.

Smiling, he lifted a hand and thumbed the tears from her cheeks without releasing her from his hold. His thumb sailed over her lips, his eyes devouring her. "Good God, woman, you are a wonder," he uttered.

A deep voice cleared close by.

Jade's lashes fluttered with the distraction, but he seemed in no hurry to break the physical connection. Instead, he cocked a smile, wondering, "Will you marry me?"

Startled, she blinked and stared into his entirely sober eyes, the spark of mischief as intense as his sincerity. "Yes," she said simply.

"Then, I suppose, I need to meet your family before I whisk you away from here."

Amused at the arrogance of his words, the lofty note in his deep voice, Ronnie smiled and accepted the mutual signal to part. He held her hand in a light touch, however, refusing to part entirely, until he'd delivered the rose into her hand. At the same time, she saw the gauze wrapped professionally about his palm. Her fingers clasped his as she started, "You're hurt . . ." God! How absurd! The man could turn her upside down with a smile, a look, a touch.

Amusement lifted more readily in his eyes. "Healing, m' love," he said smoothly and caught her fingers under his thumb. Lifting and brushing a kiss on her hand, he only appeared to disregard the crowd growing around them. His gaze fleeted passed her shoulder.

A half-second later, the front door opened, and James strode through, asking, "Okay, who owns the Jag?"

Another sparkle of amusement danced in his eyes as he sent his attention toward the newest arrival. "That would be me," he said simply. "Am I blocking your path by any chance?"

"You . . ." James darted a glance at Ronnie's quivering smile, and his warm blue eyes flashed as much relief as curiosity.

Breaking from his halt, James glanced over the more subdued ensemble as he came toward Ronnie, his full attention landing on Jade. "No, you're not blocking anyone," he said as he extended his palm. "James Bryson."

"Jade Laquette," he introduced himself with a hint of French accent to enhance the pronunciation of his surname.

"Nice car," James said absently and tilted his gaze to Ronnie with a coercive smile. "You failed to mention he drives a nice car. Had I known, I might have forgiven him sooner for that phone call."

"He owns three nice cars," Ronnie confided and caught Jade's amused eyes returning from her brother. "The county didn't need the loan, after all, hon?"

"My nemesis took pity on me," he said with a faint undercurrent of sobriety. "Someone mentioned I needed to fly to DC, and he was kind enough to return my wings."

"I don't think I want to know how long it took you to drive here," she decided.

"Hmm, better left a mystery, but I will admit, we'll not return in the same amount of time."

Glimpsing motion at the corner of her eye, Ronnie glanced at her father, remembering the last time she'd seen him. Presently, he wasn't happy with their unexpected guest, and returning her gaze to Jade, Ronnie sensed his mutual regard behind his smile. "Jade," Ronnie said quietly. "My father, Robert Bryson. Father, Jade Laquette."

And that was all the further she intended to extend an introduction. Her tension mounted as the two nearly equal-sized men shook hands.

"Mr. Bryson, an honor," Jade commented, sounding sincere.

"Mr. Laquette," her father said with similar courtesy, but his gaze conveyed a far deeper curiosity. Without so much as a glance at Ronnie, he commented, "As I've just overheard you ask for my daughter's hand and receive her acceptance, I do hope you'll accept my invitation to remain for the gathering this afternoon. It should allow us an opportunity to become acquainted, Mr. Laquette."

"Jade, sir. I'd be delighted to stay."

Fiona Bryson arrived next, her hand touching Ronnie's arm. Tears glistened in her eyes, barely restrained as she proffered her hand to Jade.

The man was a devil! No question about it. Favoring Fiona with one of his most winsome smiles, his dimple winking, his eyes sparkling, he pulled it off without a hitch. Lifting and kissing her hand as if meeting a queen without, for an instant, lowering himself to serf, he spoke with a distinctly European accent. "Madame, my pleasure," he said smoothly.

Not sure whether to be stunned or amused, Ronnie noted her mother's color rise, her eyes softening beneath her tears. "A pleasure to meet you, Jade, is it?"

"It is, ma'am," he said.

With Linc advancing into the family circle, Ronnie tensed, again offering the introduction with far more trepidation than Jade presented. Linc's curiosity and doubt on high, he needed only a moment before his brilliant mind flashed recognition. "I remember you. You attended St. Augustine's," he said, and by his tension, the past had left an impression on him. His gaze flashed to Ronnie; his sculpted cheek twitched.

"You were a year ahead of me, as I recall," Jade said and drew Linc's startled attention. "A fair-minded lad and gentleman, as I further recollect."

By God, that stopped Linc cold, halting whatever scene he might have created. "I'm afraid I don't remember you in quite that much detail," he admitted dryly

"Not well at improvising either, I see," Jade commented, his gaze as sober and intent as Linc. "But we all have our faults, and I tend to overlook those relating to ancient history."

Strike two, Ronnie calculated. Her brother would go down for the count unless he backed off. Her fiancé hadn't traipsed all over Europe to become intimidated by the Bryson clan regardless of the numbers stacking against him.

Vicky intruded in the nick of time to spare her husband, wheedling her way to the foreground and offering her hand. Her smile animated, a master production of charm and concerned familiar. "Mr. Laquette," she said. "I can't imagine why Ronnie didn't tell us you were coming. Victoria Bryson, I'm Lincoln's wife. Please, just Vicky, Jade."

He touched her hand, refraining from a kiss, tempering his charm. His gaze carried a subtle amusement. "Charmed, Vicky," he said, and Ronnie stifled a smile at his sour note on the diminutive name. The man certainly had a difficult time with nicknames. He flashed her a glance and insolent smile. "Hope I've not landed you in a fix arriving unannounced and uninvited, m' love."

"I don't mind if you don't, darling," she said as he dipped his head and brushed a kiss on her lips, waking yet another flash of sparks. How had this happened? How had she fallen so desperately in love with this man that a mere whisper of a kiss could taste like a cool drink against parched lips?

His head angled, a smile playing in his eyes and lips; he glanced down between them, then into her eyes. "This wasn't how I intended to propose to you, you know, mon amour? I've had wonderful fantasies of how I'd kneel before you like some love-smitten swain in the Middle Ages, but again, m'lady, you have me bungling like a court jester," he lamented and shook his head. "Nothing to be done about it now, I suppose." His fingers slipped under hers, turning more fully toward her as he lifted her hand between them. Locking his gaze to hold her, the world vanished around them.

Before Ronnie quite grasped his intentions, she watched his fingers slide an immense diamond-cut solitaire on her ring finger; the pale blue stone absorbed the light and shot a kaleidoscope of sparks from the intricate gold band. Stunned, she realized the nature of the gem as well as the reality of the instant. Her eyes lifting into his, she uttered, "This isn't a dream, is it, Jade? You are here, and it is happening, isn't it?"

"Without a doubt, Veronica," he said and lifted her hand, brushing a kiss on her fingertips. The promise of more to come lighted his eyes as he drew her against him with the mere force of will. As they sealed their oath with yet another kiss, Ronnie heard the door opening again, refusing to be interrupted.

"Dad, would you mind telling me what's happening here?" Robert asked with a restrained edge.

"You're in the process of gaining a brother-in-law as it would appear," her father said in a low tone.

Lifting, Jade flashed a dark shine. "Another brother?"

"Not one of importance," Ronnie said and held his lapel. The echo of her older brother's words sped through the foreground of her mind, kindling the hurt and anger in force. Her ire rising, she glimpsed at Robert's darting angry eyes, lancing him, and locking on him. "I have no intention of introducing you to the 'psychopath I had to sleep with,' quote, unquote," she snapped. "And if you intend to remain, my mad-lover and I will gladly depart—"

"Darlin," Jade interrupted, a bemused smile on his lips as he lifted his knuckles to her chin, drawing her lethal gaze. "As much as I love seeing that fire in your eyes, don't you think you're being rather hard on the man?"

"I won't forget what he said, and I can't forgive him for what he believed about me or you."

"I was in that room," Jade interrupted quietly, his gaze sober. "Had I been wearing his shoes, hearing what he heard, I'd have reached the same vile conclusions, Veronica. If he spoke words to hurt you or betrayed your trust and love for him, he did so out of love for you. And for that, I can't blame him. I'd have done the same were the situation reversed." He held her gaze. "We've had a wretched beginning, love, but I'm rather adept at starting over. Do you think we might try putting the past where it belongs?"

"How can you make everything sound so simple?" she asked sincerely, searching for the magic that had softened even her hostility toward her brother.

With a twitch of a smile and lofty shrug, he spoke with a lighthearted tone, not betraying his sincerity. "There's a prayer I've heard by an unknown author asking God for the courage to accept the things we cannot change, the strength to change what we can, and the wisdom to know the difference." He touched her nose with a spark of mischief in his eyes. "A motto to live by, eh?"

"You're a devil," she said with a smile, resigning with a sigh. "I was only beginning to accept the idea of having only two brothers, and one of those was close to extinction."

"I've never had a real family, love," he mused. "Even the illusion might be a welcome change until we begin our own."

They hadn't discussed children at all. They hadn't discussed a great deal of anything concerning the future, but he did love children, and his heart rested in his eyes. He wanted children, her children, and a family.

"Do you think you might reconsider dwindling their numbers? At least until I've officially met them all?"

Resigning, she smiled, sighing, starting, "It's extremely difficult to remain angry with—" His head tilted suddenly, alarmed. His eyes misted, startling her to silence.

In a flash, his eyes cleared, becoming tense. "Good God . . . a child? The child . . ." he uttered as his brow furrowed, puzzled. His head tilted more as if he heard an alarm; his focus listed over the faces, searching. In motion, his hand clasped Ronnie's fingers, tugging her with him as he snapped, "A child?"

Her nephew! Dear God, the veranda! Alone!

He broke from her grasp, ahead by four lengths as he passed through the open arches of the dining room. Heart already leaping with the panic in Jade's eyes, Ronnie flew after him with Linc catching on and flying in her wake, the others following.

Rushing through the French doors, she glimpsed Jade sailing through the screen door, leaping off the stone steps and vanishing behind the rose tresses.

Her heart lodged in her throat; she fell a step behind her brother as they passed through the door and launched onto the path. Barely, she heard the short cry, the snapping vines, and crackling wood. In stop time, she watched the stout little legs and arms flailing. Flashes of bright blue and yellow from his designer shirt and shorts mixed in the rainbow glow of a sunbeam slicing through the overhead leaves. Free-falling in a shower of breaking ivy vines and splintering white tresses, Ryan sailed from the high arches. In a single motion, Jade caught the slight body and swung Ryan smoothly away from the scattering debris.

The eye of a hurricane, Jade remained stopped and calm despite the whole of the Bryson clan racing toward him. Looking down at the startled bundle in his arms, he offered a musing smile. "Hello, there, little lad."

Ronnie skidded, nearly ramming her brother, who halted, hands outstretched.

In split seconds, the round flushed cheeks drained of fright. Quick blue eyes took the measure of the stranger who held him, and a broad smile spread across the toddler's lips. "Hewwl-low there!" Ryan said and burst into a giggle. "Me was f'ying!"

"You certainly were, lad," Jade said, stifling a laugh as he rearranged the plump little boy to deliver him into his father's hands. Meeting Linc's gaze with a peculiar indifference, he commented, "Quite a handful, I'd imagine."

"He's been in the terrible twos since he turned ten months," Linc heaved as much relief as grief. He drew his son into a more protective fold even as his wife and mother converged with breathless panic and manic hands. Over his wife's head, Linc looked again at Jade. Questions burned in his eyes as livid as his gratitude. "How in God's name did you know?"

"I've been accused of having exceptional hearing," Jade said smoothly and shrugged, his gaze darting fondly off the child. "Handsome lad."

"Thank you," Linc said firmly, perhaps, to counter any doubts about the explanation he'd just received. "And thank you for saving my son's life."

"You're most assuredly welcome," Jade said, and Ronnie clasped his hand, smiling with both joy and relief under his faintly amused gaze. "Apparently, the lad takes after his aunt," he said with the English pronunciation of the title. "Or is *daring* a hereditary trait in all of you?"

Before she could even begin to answer him, her mother turned on him, showering her praise and thanks in breathless notes. Vicky, with genuine tears in her eyes, her son cradled against her shoulder in a fierce hold, extended her gratitude enthusiastically.

In one fell swoop, the man endeared himself to her entire family, not excluding Robert, who clasped his hand, offering, "I owe you an apology, Mr. Laquette. R.J. Bryson."

"Jade," he said simply. If he harbored any grudge against her oldest brother, nothing showed, neither in his expression nor voice. "You received a rather biased version of the facts. I wouldn't expect you to have seen two sides. . ."

On the veranda, mixed drinks, snacks, and one restless child under close supervision, which annoyed the little fellow into fits of endeavors, the conversation rose and fell in various directions. Falling easily into the role of observer, Ronnie clasped Jade's hand, enjoying the sound of his voice, and musing over his evasive tactics to avoid either delicate subjects or his private affairs. The man was a master of deception and misdirection, not uttering a single lie while simultaneously skirting any serious issues.

"What business did you say you're in?" Linc asked at one point.

"I'm a collector and amateur antique dealer," Jade answered.

"Must be a lucrative business," James commented, undoubtedly thinking about the Jaguar. "What sort of things do you collect?"

"Unfortunately, nearly anything of intrinsic value."

"You can't possibly work exclusively out of your shop in Bentwood," Bobby commented.

"Actually, it's a fantastic geographical location. Easy access to interstate travel, two major cities within two hours . . ." He shrugged, "Between mail order and an earnest advertising campaign, it's become more lucrative than I'd anticipated."

At one point, her father excused himself from the gathering. Too soon, he returned and spoke the words Ronnie had expected with growing concern. ". . . Jade, if I could draw you away from my daughter for a few moments, I'd like to speak to you in my study. . .."

Rather than one of the chairs in front of the stately antique desk, Jade sat in a high-backed upholstered chair where Robert Bryson had motioned him. Accepting another brandy and lighting a cigarette when the man lighted a cigar in the catercorner chair, Jade took stock of Veronica's father. His senses keened as the man studied him over a spurting flame. Without a doubt, Bryson had a great deal on his mind, and Jade harbored more than a haunting impulse about where this conversation would lead.

"I'd imagine you know, I'm not entirely comfortable with the idea of you marrying my daughter," the man spoke directly.

"That, I do know, sir," he answered honestly.

"Over and above the fact that she's a headstrong, independent young woman, who might give any man a test, is the fact that I have certain reservations about you. Only beginning with your rather ambiguous past if you'll forgive my lack of finesse." He barely waited for Jade's slight nod. "Regardless of what Veronica may believe, I do love her, and I don't want to see her hurt. I'm sure you can understand my concern, Jade. You've only known my daughter for a week. Undoubtedly, you've swept her off her feet, but as a parent, I can't justify allowing her to become involved with a man I know very little about. As you well know, I'm a man of considerable means, both financial and influential, but you've covered your tracks well to conceal at least ten years of your life."

"You own considerable stock in Monterrey, Ltd, the shipping and transport company based in London," Jade said quietly and held the halted gaze. "As I recall, you were one of the first American entrepreneurs to buy into the company when stocks were opened to the American market. At the time, I owned the controlling interest. I've since sold a great deal of the company, but I maintain a nominal interest to cover expenses on other of my overseas investments."

For a moment, Robert Bryson gazed at him, searching for truth or lies.

"I'd imagine you've heard of Raphael Monterrey, sir," Jade continued smoothly. "If you haven't, I'll be happy to give you several references as well as his home address outside of London, where he visited recently."

"You're telling me that you are Raphael Monterrey?"

"Up until six years ago, yes," Jade answered succinctly. "I legally transferred all official documents into a trust to which Isaac Bently is still the sole benefactor in absentia through a solicitor in England. Unfortunately, quite a few people still know me as Raphael and, well," he shrugged. "I see no harm in maintaining the illusion on biannual vacations. As you know, f certain precautions weren't taken, I as well as my investors would lose a great deal of profit."

"Since you appear willing to discuss this, Mr. Laquette, would you mind telling me . . .? How exactly did you manage to transcend from Jade Laquette, a child who disappeared sixteen years ago, to an Englishman entrepreneur with considerable influence, to this Isaac Bently of Bentwood, PA.?"

Faintly, Jade smiled at the man's obvious annoyance. "It's been nearly seventeen years since I last wore the name Jade Laquette, sir. I was . . . shall we say, relieved of that cumbersome title by a Frenchmen with considerable affluence and a great sense of dark humor." Uncomfortable for the first time, he listed his gaze, wondering how much he should tell. With a fleeting thought of the woman he fully intended to marry, he sighed heavily, meeting the man's curious gaze. "Jean Pierre Jardonet, sir. The man's my father."

For a long moment, Bryson looked at him with enlightenment creeping slowly into his pale blue eyes. "Jardonet . . . the entrepreneur, who's said to . . ."

"Prognosticate his success," Jade finished for Bryson, nodding slightly. "When his wayward son displayed no similar talent, he was rather glad to be rid of him and more than willing to arrange yet another identity change."

His brow drawn, Bryson commented, "I'd imagine he regretted his decision."

"I haven't a clue, sir, nor do I care to dwell long on the subject," he said honestly. "I'm sure you've heard a great deal about Jardonet's other endeavors, which I'm not about to share with you or anyone else. Suffice it to say, I'm comfortable with the distance established between me and my biological father."

"I'd imagine you're referring to his affiliation with certain clandestine organizations."

"I'd imagine I am," Jade said evenly, wondering not for the first time how deeply Robert Bryson dabbled in similar interests as Jardonet. The ultimate power—to tap the universe of its final unlimited resource, the power of the mind. His mother had been a forerunner in that field, and perhaps, she'd possessed a few limited talents for prognostication. She'd known, if nothing else, how influential members of the government would romance such divine power . . . and she had, perhaps, with some foresight, set out to capitalize on that affordable commodity. Perhaps, as Jardonet had once professed, she'd sought a certain Frenchman to tap his inherent talent and had seduced him with the explicit purpose of procreation. Possible or not, Jade preferred not to delve too deeply. To consider himself something of a genetic defect was vexing enough; to wonder if his mother had deliberately cursed him at conception created altogether different distress.

"I should mention, Jade," Bryson interrupted, drawing his listless gaze. "All of this isn't exactly relieving my concern over your relationship with my daughter." His gaze intent, he continued, "I wouldn't want her involved in the type of endeavors we've just discussed. Frankly, I was willing to doubt you had any involvement with the trouble in Bentwood, and for my daughter's sake, I intervened on your behalf four days ago. If I was wrong—"

"You weren't wrong," Jade cut in, his gaze unwavering. "Yes, I possess an inherent talent for choosing successful ventures, but it's a talent I've neither perfected nor depended upon. Any more than I've followed in Jardonet's footsteps and developed any inclination toward alchemy and the like. I'll admit, I know about those things. I'd have needed to be blind, deaf, and dumb not to have become aware of them with the life I've lived. But I have no intention of pursuing any interest whatsoever in either the dark arts or any form of occultism."

"Your actions earlier this afternoon seem to indicate that you've developed more than your enterprising talents, wittingly or unwittingly, Jade. You do have your mother's talents and abilities."

"My mother was an astrologer," Jade said quietly. "And you know more about her demise than you'd be willing to tell me, don't you?"

Bryson hesitated only a heartbeat before speaking with a careful low tone, "If you're asking, do I know who had ordered her killed? The answer is, no, I do not. If you're asking if I know she was assassinated by someone who, I'm sure, felt threatened by what she knew or could learn, the answer's yes. And you're right again, I won't discuss this subject with you other than to admit, that I attempted to see justice done. What concerns me at this juncture is that you have your mother's talents, and frankly, that disturbs me more than I care to consider."

"Then you should know, sir, the talents were never my mother's," Jade admitted quietly. With his gaze locked on Bryson, he grasped the man's rising discomfort. "As I said, she was an astrologer. She could study star charts and prognosticate images with a degree of success, but she could never touch an object and feel sensations or foretell the future." And he suffered the pain of admission with the tension spiraling through him.

Dangerous.

This conversation was dangerous, and with a little mind-bending, he could divert the subject—

Damn it!

Resisting his dark thoughts, Jade pushed off the chair, pacing away. Too well, he recognized his inherent talents threatening to take over, and it wouldn't be the first time his subconscious ascended to protect him.

Consciously, he needed to remain in control if he had any hope of sharing a life with the woman of his dreams.

Haunted, still, Jade drew breath, recovering his thoughts and recalling where he'd halted. His mother's murder. Her death was on his conscience. He should have been able to save her. The prognostications and insights to target her were never hers.

"I've lived with that reality for eighteen years," Jade said and turned, finding Bryson's intent gaze. "The talent that eventually resulted in my mother's death was mine, and I swore to myself eighteen years ago, that I'd never intentionally use it again. I broke my vow for the first time Monday night in your daughter's company with the single desire to ensure her safety. I've never before consciously called upon the forces inside of me. Yes, I react spontaneously to sudden images, but no more than you would if you heard vines snapping and a child crying out in fear. That I saw your grandson about to fall, I won't deny. The image was crystal clear for a fleeting instant, and I won't apologize for that precognition if it spared the child's neck.

"I don't like it if that's any consolation. I wish to God I was as blind as every other man with only five senses to decide my fate; however, I have six, and I've learned to live a reasonably normal life with that curse."

Pausing, he returned to his chair, meeting the man's more critical gaze. "I am going to marry your daughter, Mr. Bryson. This conversation won't alter that decision. As a courtesy, I'm answering your questions as honestly as I can, and for Veronica's sake, I'd appreciate your blessing. Despite her feelings toward your negligence and apathy, she loves and admires you. I'd rather not be held accountable for any further distance between you. As I said earlier, I've never had a genuine family. I have a sense of what those connections entail if only through others. Those connections are without a doubt, the most powerful force on earth, and the consequence of subverting those ties can be devastating . . ."

"You're a very determined and persuasive young man," Bryson said in a reserved tone.

"I've never been in love before now," Jade said distractedly, an inkling of something he'd just said disturbing him, prickling. Subverted family ties . . . shaking his head, he met the man's gaze with a faint, troubled smile. "It's different."

Sober, intent, Robert Bryson relaxed his posture slightly as he commented, "I'd like my daughter married in the Catholic Church. As she is my only daughter, I'd prefer a rather elaborate affair."

Feeling sudden nervous anticipation with the simplicity of that announcement, the consent sinking in, Jade quivered a smile. "If . . . well, if that's what Veronica wants."

"She won't," Bryson said with the first inkling of a smile on his lips. "That's why you and I are discussing this, young man. I'd imagine you can use your powers of persuasion to convince her," he said evenly.

Good God, the man was serious. An elaborate wedding. A church?

"There is one more thing we should clear up before we return to the gathering," Bryson said evenly, sober again. "What last name do you intend to give her?"

Good God, he hadn't truly considered that dilemma. Asking Veronica to marry him had seemed like such a natural flow of events, such a simple endeavor . . . "Laquette," he decided with a thought of Veronica knowing him only by that name. "I'll begin taking care of the legalities on Monday."

CHAPTER 30

For three days, Ronnie felt as if she were sailing through a wondrous dream, propelled by a force of one, and what a force he was. From proper English gentry to an amorous Frenchman, the man switched hats with the speed of light.

Hands linked in a fold on the small console, Ronnie rested in the bucket seat, fascinated by the pure delight on his face as he maneuvered the Jag through traffic. Visibly, he restrained an urge to stomp the gas on every straight stretch. Convincing him that she trusted her life in his hands had taken nearly half of the five-hour drive.

The man did love to drive. He handled the car with the gentle touch of a lover, his single hand on the wheel barely skimming the leather-clad wheel to send the Jag zipping into bends or sweeping past semi-trailers on inclines. For long lingering moments, silence fell between them, and all the questions she thought she might like to ask passed through her mind, never touching her lips.

After three days, there was still so much she didn't know about him, so many things she'd like to understand, but they had a lifetime to learn about each other. She knew the most important details. She loved him, he loved her, and nothing else seemed important. A foolish notion, undoubtedly, an extremely foolish notion considering they were drawing closer to Bentwood with each passing mile. She need only recall his attempt to thwart her intention to return with him, had only to remember the glimmers of fear unmasked in his eyes, to know the danger ahead.

At every other moment, he'd appeared as lighthearted as a lark, whether he sat chatting about cars with James or accepting an unannounced visit from Max Hagen at the most inopportune moment. Only his eyes had betrayed the difficulty in seeing Max again, and Max had been likewise affected. Haunting memories had shaded both gazes through the first ten minutes of Max's visit. Very slowly, they'd accepted the past and put the memories away, and Max had departed laughing over one of Jade's more apparent nervous attacks at the mention of marriage.

Recalling Jade's look of astonishment when he'd caught himself lighting a second cigarette with one already burning in the ashtray, Ronnie smiled faintly. Clearly, his anxiety had amused and bewildered him, but he'd recovered in lofty arrogance, '. . . We need hurry to this marriage, love, or I'll need sedated just to find the altar . . .'

A devout bachelor. A week earlier, he'd lived as a devout bachelor, content with a frivolous lifestyle in conflict with whatever insights he possessed to the contrary. Falling in love had posed as another of his taboos. His thoughts about women were all too obvious in his ability to remain indifferent and oblivious to the attention he drew . . . and the man did draw attention. On one of the few occasions when they had ventured from her apartment, joining Linc and Vicky in a fine restaurant, they'd nearly created a scene.

Even now, Ronnie remained baffled by how easily Vicky had leaned over with shared conspiracy to comment, 'Is it my imagination, or is that young woman over there drooling over your fiancé?'

Under Jade's piercing gaze, Ronnie drew from her reflection, still smiling.

"Penny for your thoughts, mon amour," he commented.

"I'd go as high as a quarter to know how you managed to remain a bachelor," she countered.

He flashed her a wry grin. "Obviously, my evasive maneuvers aren't worth a wit when one lovely little witch can trip me up."

"I'll have you know, sir, I had no intention of becoming a house frau before you cast your spell on me," she said in mocked defense.

He stifled a laugh. "I have a difficult time picturing you as a *hausfrau*, love. A seductress whose distraction I'll welcome at every instant, yes. But a *hausfrau? No* way."

"Seen a lot of *hausfraus*, have you?"

"Tons," he said and drew her hand to brush a kiss on her fingers, his attention on the highway ahead. "And you simply don't qualify for the label."

The conversation slid toward sober as Ronnie voiced her decision to abandon her career, admitting for the first time that she had no idea in which direction she might like to travel as far as an occupation.

He fell silent, then, for a time, his gaze distracted as the wheels chewed up the miles beneath them. "You never turned to journalism to write about crime," he said after a while. "You never intended merely to document crimes, but to solve them, Veronica."

"Know that for a fact, do you?" she asked, watching his profile, and catching a glimpse of his haunted eyes.

"Yes."

By his quiet tone, the sobriety on his face, and a faint troubled line under the waves on his brow, Ronnie wondered at his insight and apprehension. How many times had they started to discuss Bentwood and stopped? How many times had the shadows fallen over his gaze, and she'd sensed his dread?

More times than she could count.

The man was a master at distracting her from serious contemplation and conversation. Whether he deliberately avoided subjects or suffered a subconscious knack for diversion, she couldn't decide, but his tactics were effective. They were already less than ten minutes from Bentwood, and they had yet to discuss what they both knew . . . that she'd accompanied him to finish what she'd begun, and he'd agreed by some insight or premonition inside of him. He'd attempted to convince her to remain behind, to wait in Arlington and allow him a few days to put his affairs in order. With fierce determination, Jade had strongly objected to her presence, but he'd battled only himself. And they both knew it.

"Will you help me?" she asked quietly and watched his lashes flutter, the only hint of his dread.

"I don't have a choice," he said quietly and glanced at her, his heart in his eyes. "I do love you, Veronica. What concerns you concerns me."

Remembering those moments in her room at the Inn, her heart wrenched with a sudden fear for him. "If I . . . If I ask you not to be involved, Jade. If I ask you not to become any more deeply involved than you already are . . . Damn it, if I ask you not to use your telepathy or psychic abilities, will you agree?"

"I can honestly admit, I would like nothing better than to agree, Veronica," he said without looking over. "What's inside of me . . . my mother called it a gift . . . when she wasn't afraid of me," he said, careful to conceal whatever he felt as he spoke. "She called my abilities my 'gift,' and forever, I've called them my curse." He was silent for a long moment. "I would like to have lived a normal life, to have lived as a normal child and never suffer a single neurosis. But I've grown old enough to know the futility of my desire. Yes, I would like to agree to your request. I would love to refuse the curse inside me, but that same curse tells me I wouldn't keep that promise. A feeling, a sensation, an innate knowledge tells me that I will be involved, that I'll use my curse . . .

"For all I know, I might have known a week ago when I tried so damned hard to keep my distance from you. An act in futility to deny my attraction to you the instant I saw you inside that rental."

He squeezed her hand, glancing over with a disheartened smile. "Therein lies the curse, Veronica, to ram my fool head against a wall to alter events while events propel me toward a certain end. It's forever scared the hell out of me and robbed me of more moments of my life than I can readily count, not excluding the four days I spent away from you. That time is lost to us, and my fear held me in limbo."

Sounding depressed, Jade glanced over, his gaze haunted. "Even knowing that your love for me is real, that what I feel for you is as solid as granite, I can wonder how you can truly be attracted to such an idiot as myself. You are a bright, beautiful woman who deserves to be with a man who suffers no curiosity over his own identity."

"I could say the same, you know, hon," Veronica said quietly, watching his profile. "You are an intelligent, handsome man with the world at your feet. You deserve a woman who won't make the kind of demands I've already made on you, who wouldn't have turned your whole life upside down in a matter of days."

"Fate's not been kind to either of us," he said with a softer note and sigh. "We're doomed to be together."

"Honey, I don't like to break this to you, but I haven't cursed fate for at least a few days, and I'm not about to start again now."

Amused, he glanced over. "I should admit, I haven't felt so good about being doomed in my entire life."

"Brat," she said simply with a sudden revelation that he'd done it again—had led her straight into a different subject. They'd progressed slightly further than any prior attempts, however. She decided to let him have his way, only amused when he glanced over in dumbfound.

"Brat. The lady called *moi* a *brat*," he uttered as if to himself and shook his head, lamenting. "How I've regressed since meeting you, mademoiselle. To be called a *brat* when I once engendered only pleasant endearments."

"Name one," she played. "Name one pleasant endearment your long line of women has called you."

"Hmm, my favorite to date seems in a word, my given name spoken off a certain pair of generous lips," he said smoothly. "Especially when I happen to be lying down very close to the source of that sound."

"God, you *are* a brat," Ronnie laughed.

"Again. *Again,* the lady's calling me names," he said in mocked disgust, but his words seemed suddenly abstracted, distracted.

A glance toward the stop sign approaching rapidly at the end of the exit ramp explained his sudden mood. Ronnie's heart skipped a beat though she was only vaguely aware of the car skidding down the ramp. All too readily, she recalled the last time she had navigated this slope and the hostility of Tim Spencer's words. She hadn't blamed Tim. She'd forgiven him even as he'd lashed out at her, and this time wouldn't be the same. Not with the hand squeezing her fingers in silent reassurance.

Still, a prickle slid down her spine. For a Sunday afternoon, far too many cars sped in either direction and an unnatural number of pedestrians meandered on the sidewalks.

"Shit," Jade said lightly. "The Firemen's Fair."

He sounded annoyed, but she felt a sudden relief. Not reporters. Not another vicious crime ahead. "It's not exactly a catastrophe, honey."

He glanced at her while braking, navigating a quick turn onto a secondary street before reaching the red light on Maine. "This may sound extremely foolish to be annoyed about, darling, but I just remembered I promised a few boxes of odds and ends for their flea market."

It didn't sound foolish. It sounded wonderfully mundane, wonderfully normal. After the chaotic past week, to hear his irritation over such a simple oversight seemed the most blessed of events. He was human! Not some mysterious creature of magical power. "Then I suggest as soon as we get our bags pried loose of the trunk, we deliver those boxes."

His smile quirked; he glanced over curiously.

"Well, if I'm about to become the wife of an antique dealer," she said simply. "Don't you think I should begin carrying my own weight?"

"We might work up to that scant amount, but we'll begin smaller," he said with perfect aplomb. "I do have a few shoeboxes full of costume jewelry I suppose you could carry without much strain."

"Oh, there's what I like, another of those underhanded compliments combined with a touch of chivalry. The man has a silver tongue. . ."

Not once had Ronnie stepped past his office into the inner sanctum of his store. Her attention riveted as he drove into the rear alley. With the ease of an eel, he slipped beneath an electronically rising garage door into a tremendous warehouse. Wide-open space, large enough for at least two cars, centered the tunnel of high shelves and stacked aisles. A pickup truck—apparently, four-wheel-drive but not of a style to compare with Spencer's monster—stood off in one corner like a dispirited child nearly lost in the shadows.

After shutting the garage door, Jade returned to the car and unpacked the compact trunk. "My little lady didn't handle too atrociously for having an extra ton on her axles," he commented as he feigned to struggle with Ronnie's suitcase.

"Oh, give me that, you wimp," she said and snatched the bag from his fist, enjoying the sound of his laughter. "Keep making fun of me, you'll be sleeping with your poor *taxed* little lady."

"Good God, you're a mean one," he mused and collected the remaining suitcases. "No, strike that! You're the most wondrous, bewitch-ugh . . . enchanting, devastatingly beautiful, charming—"

Nothing she said stifled his string of adulations, but he stood frozen a half step from the door, his head turning as if he followed something that only he could see in the shadows. Spine prickling, Ronnie watched his animated face and read the strain etched in every handsome line. "Jade?" she whispered.

He shuddered suddenly, jolted, and looked at her. His eyes lost the opaque film, but his brow remained troubled. "Nothing . . . it's nothing," he lied to her for the first time, but he appeared appalled enough with himself to prevent Ronnie from mentioning her talent in that regard.

As they passed through another door and started up a staircase, Ronnie noted the darkness, recalling the absence of windows in the warehouse and the minimal track lights strung from the high ceiling. This was his house, his realm, and she suddenly strained against a sting of tears with the pall of sadness haunting the ether of these gloomy, gray walls.

The shop . . . his showcase with every knickknack and item in perfect order, with lights arranged to land on displays, with his front windows letting daylight slip beneath the dark awning . . . His showcase was his fantasy home. His apartment reflected his nature. Tastefully decorated, his living quarters were a combination of massive, expensive furniture and regal trappings. Touches of brass, silver, and gold glittered under the colored light of a Tiffany lamp. Books stood on display between sculpted bookends on tiered stands and ledges.

For the first time, Jade appeared nervous as he combed his fingers through his hair, sweeping the waves off his brow. His mustache curved, quivering a smile as he glanced about. "I'm uh . . . it's . . ."

"Dark," Ronnie said with a glance toward the velvet drapes that covered a half dozen windows. Her gaze seeking his, she read his lingering discomfort as his eyes glimmered in the artificial light.

"I, well . . . I don't generally entertain visitors," he said with a resigning shrug. "Suppose it is dark but—"

"Honey," she said and strode to him, wrapping her arms around his waist and looking up at him. "It's dark, but it's beautiful, and you don't need to explain your tastes to me. Just promise me I can open a curtain occasionally, and we'll get along fine."

A smile slipped into his lips as he held her against him. "You're going to hate my bedroom," he mused.

"I think that will depend on where you are when I'm in it," she countered, wondering anew at this strange female power to play with words toward seduction.

Without a word, he scooped her off her feet and carried her through a stout door opposite the kitchen. Abruptly, they were cast in pitch black. With the prowess of a bat, he moved smoothly, landing her on soft, thick cushions. As she tried to blink spots, to gain even an impression of furniture, Ronnie heard a slide of iron rings. Seconds later, the mattress jostled, and she groped for him like a blind woman. With a single click of a switch, an electric candle within a brass coach light fixture above her head illuminated the curtained room.

"A bit Gothic," Ronnie critiqued with a straight face as she caught his emerald eyes watching her.

He glanced about the curtained cubicle and brought his gaze around with an impish smile. "Suppose that's better than a bit like a French bordello, right?"

"Sweetheart," she said with a soft smile, turning and cupping his cheek as if addressing a child. "How could I possibly see any resemblance to a French bordello?"

"I do believe the lady's insinuating something," he said haughtily.

"I wouldn't dream of it," she laughed and leaned into a kiss, wiping the smirk off his lips, and receiving ample return on her small investment.

The annual Firemen's Fair brought Bentwood's population out in force, only beginning in the municipal park. Concession stands, game booths, and carnival rides spread down Maine and into the side streets. The gazebo, Bentwood's pride and joy, built around the time of Eisenhower, formed a grandstand in the center of the park. Barbershop quartets and local bands exchanged places and belted out lively tunes while local politicians vied for microphone time. Carnival music echoed between the buildings. Children's shouts, adult laughter, and bursts of arguments created a constant crescendo of sound. The five-day blitz tended to bring out the best in everyone, whether manning a game or sales booth, entering a pie-eating contest, or sucking down snow cones.

This year, however, the atmosphere had changed. Whether the nervous tension in the air or something else triggered Jade's internal mechanisms, he sensed the difference as he strode alongside Veronica. Volleying between anxiety and genuine delight, he ignored the glances they received and appreciated the static hum of noise to create a word salad in his sixth sense.

The media had done its damage, compliments of Mark Jarvins. No longer was he merely Isaac Bently, the bungling businessman who had brought a little new life to Bentwood by diverting traffic off the interstate to visit his shop . . . Any more than Veronica Bryson was merely a reporter in their eyes. Where he was now a mystery with an obscure past concerning an ancient, unsolved murder, she was the trollop who had laid every good citizen in Bentwood for a story. Somehow, she'd also managed to land poor Cal Farnsworth in jail on a murder charge—a murder charge which everyone had begun to doubt since Jade Laquette had also nearly been charged. How soon would it be before everyone in town accused Veronica of using her influence to turn him—a possible psychopath—loose?

By the time they delivered his contribution to the flea-market booth, and he indulged Veronica's desire to meander through the festivities, Jade suffered a few second thoughts about staying in Bentwood. Some of the smiles and gazes were the same, some friendly and sympathetic, some even pleased after Veronica, with impressive dignity and courage, charmed them. With a few, she needn't even bother.

Relieved, Jade accepted Meg Price's warm embrace and watched her offer Veronica the same comfort.

The wisdom of her years sparkling in her eyes, Meg bounced a glance between them, commenting, "I knew when you two stopped shooting daggers, the fireworks would go off."

"Were we that bad?" Veronica asked with a fleeting rise of color that fascinated Jade to notice.

"Sweetie, I had to check my benches to see if I'd needed to make repairs when the two of you left my diner that first evening. Thought for sure my seats were singed with the heat between."

"Now, hold on, Meg," Jade interceded. "I'll have you know, I was perfectly calm when I left."

"Honey, I've seen roosters at a cockfight with fewer feathers ruffled," she countered with a laugh that Veronica echoed. Hugging his arm, Meg spied him, still smiling at his bewilderment. "I'm happy for you, sweetie. It's about time you proposed to the right woman."

"Hmm, and to think I'd worried how I'd break it to you that I'd lost my heart to another," Jade said with a sigh of remorse.

Meg smiled, patting his arm. "I'm heartbroken, but I'll survive. As long as you're both happy, that's what counts . . . and I'll expect to see both of you at breakfast tomorrow."

Meg was the first to offer Veronica a proper seal of approval, but she wasn't the last.

"About time you git hitched," Cy Trascar commented and shook Veronica's hand with an unnatural enthusiasm. "You keep a close eye on this boy, miss . . . He's a wily ole wolf . . ." And others, customers, stopped them and offered congratulations, slipping in a question to wonder if he would keep his shop in Bentwood. Even Sam Hayward flagged them over rather than leave his place in line where he stood awaiting his turn to buy a hot sausage. After sizing up the rock on Veronica's finger while shaking her hand, he managed to sound sincere when he professed, the town always welcomed newcomers . . .

Tim, Donna, and the kids showed up then, and to Jade's fascination, he noted both his fiancée and his best friend wearing similar expressions of guilt and apology.

"I'm sorry—"

"Don't, Tim," she said as she clasped his hand, affording him the same direct gaze that had impressed Jade at the onset. "It's not necessary. I understood."

"That doesn't make it right," Spencer said in a low voice. "I've never been more wrong about a situation in my life, and I sure's hell can't be proud of that mistake."

"Tim," Jade intruded and caught Spencer's startled gaze to hear his given name. "As much as Donna and I enjoy seeing you grovel, perhaps, I should remind you that it took you about ten seconds or less to kick some sense into me. I think you more than compensated for any mistake you made." His gaze slid to Veronica, seeing her smile. "What say you?"

"I agree wholeheartedly," she said and moved smoothly from under his arm into Tim's welcome embrace. "Thank you."

At his sleeve, Jade felt a tug and found Deedee looking up at him, morose. Without a thought, he hoisted her to his hip, touching her chin to lift her sad face. "What's the trouble, sweetheart?"

"You really gettin' married, Uncle Sax?" she asked with a desperate shine.

Considering how best to manage this, he decided, "Yes, I am, sweetheart, and perhaps, we can talk to your soon-to-be Aunt Veronica about you participating in the wedding. I do believe we'll need a flower girl."

Her eyes brightened. "Do you think she'll let me?"

Veronica timed her arrival perfectly to say, "I'd be disappointed if you declined, sweetie. I'd love to have you be my flower girl."

"Mommy!" Deedee cried happily. "Did you hear that? I get to be in Uncle Sax's wedding!"

Tee, who had climbed into his father's arms, wondered, "Me, too?"

Before Jade could speak, Veronica decided, "Of course, you too, honey. Your Uncle Sax will need a ring bearer, and I believe you're just the man for the job."

In the space of a single second, Jade chilled, his senses keening in time to glance over his shoulder and see Jen Andover advancing. In frayed cutoff shorts and a halter top which had looked better on her at twenty than twenty-six, her neon blond hair teased into a wild just-bedded style, she was in natural form. Beneath an expertly crafted layer of cosmetics to offer her a baby doll finish, her eyes sparked a blue shine to lend Jade pause.

"Really, Isaac, you're just too much," she said as she snaked her arm under his, startling and lurching Dee on his hip. Pivoting her bright smile toward the Spencers, Jen carried a laugh in her voice, offering, "Tim. Donna—it's been *ages*!" Toward Donna, she continued, "Can you believe the nerve of this guy? Of *both* these guys?" She glanced to include Tim then pivoted her gaze toward Veronica.

Having a sense of where this was headed, Jade signaled Deedee down, starting, "Jen—"

Keeping her claw in Jade's arm even as he slid Dee to her feet, Jen fixed on Veronica. "I can't believe you were dumb enough to fall for this scam, dear. I almost feel sorry for you—"

"Jen," Jade started again, clasping the fingers to release his caught arm as Jen cleaved her body against him.

"Isaac, baby, even for you, this is low," Jen said with a little laugh. Her eyes raised to him with a bright beguiling shine. "I mean to track the poor girl down and convince her you actually intend to marry her? Gees, baby, I knew you could be cruel, and you hated her for what her boyfriend did to you, but this is too much. Even if she is a tramp, I'm sure she has feelings."

Yanking her iron claw from his arm, he detached her with his hand on her wrist and his glare. "As much as I know what game you're playing, Jen—"

"Me, baby?" she asked innocently. Batting her lashes as if startled, she slashed her glance at Veronica, who remained at his side. "I know he can be charming, but you can't honestly tell me you truly believe this guy's going to walk down the aisle with you after the shit you pulled."

"I think that's enough," Jade said in a low chilly tone, his rage ascending with the woman in front of him.

"Ohhh, pleeease, babe," Jen drawled, glaring at him with a practiced wide-eyed innocence. "You don't really expect anyone from Bentwood to believe you'd actually marry this whore. You and Tim are such a riot."

Never had he wanted to strike a woman as he did at this moment.

"Jen," Tim intervened, sidestepping to shield Veronica and his wife. "That's enough."

Veronica slid between them, slipping her hand around Jade's arm, stifling his barely restrained tension. Looking down at her, Jade barely glimpsed her musing shine before she glanced at Tim. "Gentlemen, let her get this out of her system."

"I really hate to see anyone humiliated," Jen picked up smoothly, glaring at Veronica. "But in your case, I can make an exception. If you're dumb enough to think Isaac's serious about marrying some rich slut who tried to get him hung on a murder rap just because he wouldn't lay her, you deserve whatever you get, honey. He's got it in for—"

"As much as I can understand why you'd stage this little performance, dear," Veronica said in a suddenly chilled tone. "I'm inclined to mention, I'm not buying it. You're so transparent, it's ridiculous, and this feeble attempt to undermine my faith and trust in my fiancé is pathetic. As for considering me a whore, tramp, or whatever other insults are being bandied about . . . you, Miss Andover, should take stock." Veronica sent a scathing glance down her and up. "I've seen less obvious hookers on street corners than you, dear. Now I suggest you ply your trade and peddle your . . . lies elsewhere. I truly have no intention of listening to the town bimbo make some last-ditch effort to save her fantasy."

"You're going to pay for this, bitch!"

"Jen," Jade intervened, faintly dazed by the force of his little witch's calm, cutting fury. "I suggest you take my lady's advice and quit while you still have a shred of dignity. I'm hopelessly in love with the woman beside me, and I fully intend to marry her. No scam. No hoax."

"You bastard!" she hissed at him, her stricken eyes flaming higher. "If you think I'm going to sit by and watch you marry the first rich bitch who comes to town, you got another think coming! You can't treat people like this! You can't treat *me* like this! After all we meant to each other! After the plans we—"

"You can halt there," he said with his annoyance rising. Veronica was right. This was a pathetic performance, not even worthy of honest anger. "There was never a 'we,' nor any plans, nor any promises. I've made it clear just the opposite held true. So, don't annoy me further with this truly pitiful scene." A scene that quite a few people had paused on the perimeter to witness. "I'm the same man I've always been, and I don't appreciate the wicked scheming wiles of a woman, let alone one pretending to be scorned."

"You're gonna be sorry," she said in a soft vicious hiss. "I swear to the almighty, I'm gonna make you pay for this, Isaac. You and her, both!" Flashing a hot tear-shined glance between them, Jen pivoted and started away, pushing and cursing at the spectators who backed away quickly. Several, who hadn't stood near enough to hear the heated exchange, turned puzzled, bemused glances from Jen's retreating form to Jade and Veronica.

Shaking his head, he half turned and clasped Veronica's hand, drawing her troubled gaze to meet his. Why, when he possessed such wretched talents, couldn't he ever receive the warnings in time? Why had he failed to spare her this wicked scene on top of so many others? "Veronica, I'm . . ." Apologies never helped, and looking into her warm gaze, he understood she shared his thoughts, his distress, blaming herself for his hurt. Smiling slowly, he shook his head again, bewildered by how much he loved her. "You do get feisty, love," he said on a bemused note.

Slowly, her frown faded. Relief and soft humor lighted her eyes as she commented, "I have a feeling I'll need to be more than feisty to put up with your past indiscretions."

"I can't believe Jen just did that," Donna said as she touched Veronica's back, her eyes laced with concern. "Are you okay, Ronnie?"

"I'm fine," she said sincerely and managed a slight smile to relieve Donna's fear.

Relief and amusement crept over Donna's lovely face as she attempted to stifle a laugh. "You certainly put her in her place. I thought her eyes would pop out when you called her a bimbo."

"I was trying to be kind," Veronica said sincerely. "I can understand why she'd stoop so low, but for God's sake . . ." She shook her head, looking up at Jade and losing what remained of her concern. "Do you think we could forget Jen Andover for the moment? The smell of that hot sausage is driving me crazy."

Despite his lingering tension, Jade chuckled and drew her into a hug, dropping his lips to cover her laugh. "You're driving me crazy," he spoke against her lips.

Drawing back, she lifted her gaze. Pure and white, love twinkled in her eyes, enhanced tenfold by a tiny, wily smile curving her lips. "Hot sausage, French fries . . . a cup of coffee?" she cooed.

Looking over her head to Tim and Donna, he feigned helplessness. "The woman has a one-tracked mind."

"Yes, dear," she said while slipping away smoothly. "And at the moment, it leads directly to that cute little trailer over there."

"Woman, the things I wouldn't do for you," he muttered and glanced toward the long line. "Hot sausage, fries . . . and a coffee?" Normal as hell, and perhaps, her underlying reason for her request-cum demand.

"That does sound good, Tim," Donna commented with just the right touch of charm and eyed her twosome. "Bet you two are ready for a hot dog and fries, too, huh?"

"I'd like a sausage, Daddy," Deedee decided, exercising her female wiles with impressive skill.

Amused, Jade caught Veronica's expression of pure innocence as if she hadn't started a thing. Stifling a laugh, he spied his faintly scowling compadre. "Think we're had, Spence. Three hungry women are more than I can handle."

"I'm not touching that one," Tim decided tongue-in-cheek and resigned to gopher status. Recovering a fair amount of dignity, he suggested the ladies find a shady spot in the park.

Suffering a mild panic as Veronica left his side and cursing his foolishness, Jade walked to the end of the line, turning to watch the women ambling onto the grass. She was so unpretentiously attractive, very nearly glamorous despite wearing a pair of blue denim shorts and a plain yellow jersey. In perfect contrast, her dark, tumbling curls glittered in the sunlight, reflecting multi-colored sparks with the cant of her head and a wisp of wind. Good God, just watching that long-legged walk stirred him in a most unbecoming manner.

With a prickle at the nape of his neck, his attention shattered. His gaze darted to scan the scattered crowd, his senses keening to find anyone taking a casual interest in his black-haired goddess. Futility dawned quickly with the revelation that people automatically paused and glanced toward Veronica or him. Heads turned; eyes averted sharply. Most of the faces, if not all, Jade recognized, but very few had ever become more than casual acquaintances. Judging by voices and mannerisms, he read the nature behind each face, from casual gossips to the Cal Farnsworth variety. Paranoid. He was, without a doubt, paranoid to feel his panic rising in the light of day.

No more than twenty or thirty feet away, Veronica, Donna, and Deedee had settled onto the grass, shins tucked under them. Both women were intent upon Deedee, who rested a little closer to Veronica while sharing some splendid incite if her exaggerated hand gyrations were any indication. When he listened, Jade heard the soft lilting laugh spilling off Veronica's lips as she reached and touched Deedee's hand. Such a simple gesture, that physical contact, but it touched him, too, easing the misplaced panic in his mind. Hard to believe, of all the women he'd known, this spirited dark-haired beauty had captured his heart, but then, he might have only been waiting—

"Son, you do got it bad," Spencer interrupted in a low voice, a touch of amusement in his eyes as he glanced to the women and back.

Underlying Spencer's smile, however, Jade sensed a shared current of concern. If it were just Jen Andover's assault, he wouldn't worry. Hands down, Veronica could withstand a spiteful, jealous female, but an entire town of angry citizens? A maniac who'd already once contacted her? A shiver spilled down his spine as he remembered the words etched on the Inn stationery. Simple and direct, 'Get out of town, bitch.'

"I shouldn't have brought her here," he said absently. She appeared as natural and relaxed as any other woman in sight, but she wasn't oblivious to the world around her. Always in motion, those diamond-blue eyes sparkled. "I never should have brought her."

Tim had allowed a gap to widen ahead of them. His gaze intent and voice lowered, he commented, "I know you weren't planning on it. What changed your mind?"

Unconsciously combing his fingers through his hair, assuring himself that no one stood in direct earshot, Jade shrugged, "I don't know. Seemed like every time I tried convincing her to wait in Arlington . . ." He shrugged again. "It didn't work."

Nodding absently, his concern not well hidden, Tim divided his attention between glancing at Tee, who tugged his hand to move them forward, and glancing toward the two women. "Guess we'll just have to keep a close eye on her for the time being, but uh . . . what's your plan?"

Tim might just have asked if Jade planned to remain in Bentwood, and therein lay the paradox. Only tension filtered through his pulsing mind, knotting his muscles.

Why . . . why in God's name had he fallen in love with a woman who seemed bent on putting her life in danger? If he could have fallen in love with someone like Jen Andover or Lynn Kreider . . . His attention focus snagged on the slender, golden-haired woman walking with Wade toward the gazebo. If he could have fallen for someone whose goal in life would be making jam and winning first prize at the county fair . . . *and if wishes were horses, goddamn it, beggars would ride!*

He loved the little black-haired witch who tossed back a tumble of hair, brushing the back of her hand over her forehead to scatter the locks off her brow in a whimsical gesture to set his blood on fire. Somehow, he needed to protect her . . . and unwittingly, his gaze landed on the black-haired fellow strolling down the sidewalk near the corner.

Wearing his usual attire of dark slacks and white shirt with his sleeves rolled and collar unbuttoned in concession to the heat or the gaiety of the fair, Len Devinio idly scanned the crowd, no doubt searching for a particular face. When he spotted his target, he veered to cross the street, then darted his gaze in search of another. In a sudden pause, the dark focus locked on Jade's fixed gaze. A smile twitched on the agent's lips, and he nodded his acknowledgment across the distance.

With the start of wheels turning inside his busy mind, Jade watched Devinio reach the two women. Congenially, the fellow leaned as Veronica offered her hand, and he dipped lower to brush a kiss on her cheek. Apparently, Len offered a few sly words. Veronica glanced toward Jade, and her smile transcended the distance, enhanced by his smirk. With Len Devinio stooping to join the ensemble, Jade breathed his relief.

A presence of evil lingered like a dark cloud hanging over Bentwood. Oppressive, the weight pressed against him and threatened even his joy when he looked at Veronica. Something was here. Someone was here. Unconsciously, Jade searched the crowd. Somewhere in the cloak of normalcy, the maniac stood in plain sight. On point, poised, he sensed the wicked thoughts turning like a whisper at the edge of his mind. He recognized the tone, if not the face behind the voice. In a barn and in the quick of night, he'd heard that voice seething with hatred and contempt, hissing from the shadows . . .

'Ring around the rosy . . . pocket full of posies . . .'

As if he swallowed a wad of rotting meat, Jade's stomach churned in protest, his head filled with nausea. Somewhere in this crowd of innocent faces, a maniac hid, concealed behind surface sanity, as natural in appearance and nature as every other fairgoer.

Absently, Jade sidestepped forward, hearing the various conversations, aware of the offhanded comments and smiles sent to either Tim or Tee. Inside him, the conflicts continued, decisions weighing and balancing against consequences.

By the time Jade ordered, he felt no resolve. Only more troubled, he barely acknowledged Ed Hammond, who stood behind the high counter, doling out sausage and dogs, fries and colas, as dourly as he dispensed beer and shots over at Crowley's Bar and Grill.

"What's this I'm hearing, you getting hitched, Bently?"

"Sad but true," Jade said with a smirk to betray his bleak tone.

"Yea? Looks like you're just all broke up over it," Ed growled.

Hot sausages overflowing with onions, peppers, and sauce, with fries and coffees balanced in a cardboard box, Jade navigated the path into the park, unaware of buying the third meal until he handed a sandwich to Devinio. Shrugging, Jade handed over the extra coffee and fries, too, sensing Veronica's silent approval.

Devinio wasn't his partner's equal in jealousy. By tone and manner, the agent demonstrated his quiet respect and affection for Veronica . . . an acceptable admiration. A cheap dinner seemed the least Jade owed Devinio. If not for the agent's repeated intercession throughout that interrogation, those fifteen hours of incarceration could have been a hell of a lot worse.

Lost in a volley of thoughts, Jade rested close enough to Veronica on the grass for her to use his leg as a backrest. Repeatedly, his attention riveted to meet a glance, a smile, to revel in the sparkle of blue diamonds in her eyes.

Mischief dancing in her eyes, she skimmed a finger across his mustache, wiping a smear of sauce from his quivering lips, and just that tiny fissure of touch set his unruly self to twitching at the lower regions. As dumbfounded as he was anxious, he met her wild amusement when she grasped what that tiny sensation had done to his love-starved anatomy. God almighty, one would believe he'd lived a life of celibacy for as swiftly as he reacted to his little witch's every thought.

For her, he decided while finishing off the last of his fries.

Collecting soiled wrappers, Jade eyed Devinio, who appeared fully engaged in a conversation with Tee, talking hot dogs and baseball at a four-year-old's level. Catching the man's eye, Jade commented, "Could I drag you away for a minute or so?"

"Sure," Devinio said and winked at Tee. "Probably wants some pointers on his curve ball."

Veronica flashed a curious gaze, but Jade brushed a kiss on her lips, commenting, "Be back in a sec."

Walking to the nearest trashcan, Jade pitched the empty wrappers before turning and meeting Devinio's curious gaze. "Tell me, honestly, how close are you to finding Bentwood's psycho?"

"Honestly, I'm about tapped out. I should have been out of here Saturday, but I took a few vacation days to stick around a little longer."

"Don't guess you're sticking around for the tourist attractions," Jade said offhandedly, his gaze trailing. Even with the decision made, this was harder than he'd anticipated. Sighing, he leveled his gaze on Devinio. "What's the chance you and I could . . . could uh . . . damn it," he uttered and sent his tense gaze away, forcing a calm before reconnecting. "Can you get permission—do you need permission to get me into . . ."

Good God, he sounded like an idiot savant. Drawing a breath, Jade steadied his gaze. "The crime scenes, Devinio . . . can you take me there? Just you and me. I don't want Veronica to know about this. No fucking witnesses or uh . . . press."

For a long moment, Devinio studied him then his gaze wandered toward the gathering. The Quartet on the grandstand stage chose that moment to begin another round; their voice blared from speakers on the gazebo roof, but Len seemed not to notice. He looked over, speculating. "We have a problem, here," he spoke at a natural pitch. "First off, I'd like to jump at your offer because I'm about 99% sure you can hand me something I don't have. The problem is, I'd be taking a hell of a chance walking you into either of those barns."

"I won't do this on film, Devinio," Jade said soberly. "No documentation whatsoever. If I can't offer you something tangible to trace, if I can't point you in a direction to nail this maniac, then we haven't lost a damn thing . . . And I don't know why we're having this conversation. You're going to arrange it."

"You're one spooky bastard without half trying," Devinio stated uncomfortably. "What if I decline?"

"Then, I'll go alone," Jade said dryly. "One way or another, I have a sense of following through with this," and the sense wasn't comforting. Already, the knots formed in his stomach; a pulse and pressure registered at his temple. Flinching, he nodded, "No choice."

"When do you want to do this?"

"Soon. The sooner, the better. Tomorrow."

"One stipulation," Devinio said carefully, and Jade waited, watching Len glance again toward the gathering. His gaze returned firmly. "I want your buddy, Spencer, to be there."

"I don't—" Jade started, halted a split second before Devinio continued.

"That's my stipulation. The guy's on the level. He's won't run to the press or broadcast a damn thing. He comes, or it's a no-go."

Distracted, Jade flashed an image of Tim standing against a backdrop of a bright red barn aglow in the morning sunlight. "Alright."

"I'll call you this evening, and we'll work out the details."

Jade nodded absently. "Tim will pick me up around 8:30. We'll see you at Engler's at 9."

CHAPTER 31

Restless, for no clear reason, Ronnie meandered about the dismal apartment, taking affirmative action to wade through the thick velvet drapes and find a window. Throwing light into the room alleviated none of her tension.

Jade was up to something. After the past several days, of spending nearly every minute in his company, she'd learned to read the things she felt, to feel his thoughts and emotions, and she hadn't needed the frightening night past to realize his anxiety. Waking to his thrashing, hearing his moaning and growling . . .

At the memory, Ronnie shivered, clutching her hands to her upper arms as if to ward off the chill. For her benefit, an electric candle illuminated the bedroom; the drapes around the canopy bed had remained open. In the abstracted glow, she'd seen his contorted features, the sweat glistening on his face. His hands had felt like ice when she had finally restrained one of them. Almost at once, he'd calmed and drawn her against him, and she suffered his chilled dampness, his shivering. Against her ear, his face buried in her hair, he'd whispered calming words. In French, no less. A faint smile slid into her lips, but she hadn't been amused last evening. She'd been terrified by his physical condition and the certainty of horror and pain in his voice. Long after his breathing had returned to normal and his temperature had risen to warm her shivering body, she'd laid awake wondering and worrying.

Not a word of his nightmare had he spoken, but she had recognized the preoccupation behind his eyes. His smiles and lighthearted humor had offered a poor imitation of the man she'd come to know within her apartment. Even when they had crossed the street, accepting Meg's invitation for breakfast, he'd seemed distracted and anxious. His attempt to allay her concern by mentioning Tim picking him up to run an errand had failed miserably.

Foolish, for God's sake. The man was entitled to some privacy, to speed away with his buddy without her worrying or taking issue. She wasn't about to become one of those nagging, demanding women. If anything, she nearly uttered aloud, she should be grateful for some time to herself. Attempting to think in his presence had become almost impossible. The man had a way of dominating a room, dominating her mind, and her body fell willing prey to his endeavors.

If she had any hope of sustaining a career and her independence . . . well, possibly she could do without total independence, and that sudden revelation only disturbed her more. When had that happened? When had she voluntarily forfeited her independence and agreed to join her life to his? To let him share the responsibility of her existence? And why was she so blasted content? Why was she certain that he'd never demand her subservience? How could she be so blasted sure that they would keep only an illusion of independence between them? That they would be fully, happily entwined in dependency?

Her thoughts muddled, Ronnie stood at the window looking down on Maine and watching cars pass. The festivities would start again around ten this morning, and the thought brought a faint smile to her lips. Just holding his hand and meandering through the booths had been a joy. Nearly laughing aloud, she remembered him raking his hand through his hair, looking from her to the Ferris wheel and back. Feigning as much bewilderment as worry, he'd asked in near exasperation, 'You want me to risk both of our lives on that poor excuse for a safe thrill?'

He could have just asked if she was 'nuts.' He might have asked if she had bothered noticing the bearded, anemic carnie running the contraption. The carnie almost appeared as old as the Ferris wheel, which seemed to groan as it revolved slowly on spindles and pulleys, probably more aged than most of Jade's antiques. With a laugh, he'd dismissed his mocked horror and hugged her to him, then resigning to the ride, he'd fallen in line behind the Spencers.

'I should mention,' he'd whispered against her ear. 'There's wisdom to our companions' choice of partners, bearing in mind their weight distribution . . .'

The man was a devil, but she did laugh, recalling Tim and Deedee climbing into the first bucket, Donna and Tee climbing into the next. She'd clearly understood his implication, laughing then as she'd slapped his arm. 'If you're insinuating, we're too heavy . . .' And again, he'd laughed, low and deep in the voice to send tingles down her spine.

Last night had been fun and playful, but Ronnie had sensed his distraction as surely as her own when she'd caught herself glimpsing at faces. For herself, she could care less what these people believed, what they thought of her or felt about her. For him, she suffered annoyance as well as distress. Wherever he might have lived, whatever else he might have done with his life, Bentwood had become his home and these people, his friends. To see them turning against him, to feel the accusations against him over what Jarvins had started . . .

What she needed was to help Len Devinio solve these homicides. Once and for all, she needed to find the maniac and proof-positive to put this psycho behind bars. She needed to finish what she'd started nearly two weeks earlier. Only then would she and Jade be free to plan their future.

Her thoughts turning, she found a notepad and pen on the desk, curled on the chair in front of the window, and began jotting notes from memory.

Names, places, faces, dates . . . the entire collection of details she'd gathered before last Monday scrolled across her mind. Quickly, the page filled with disjointed words, initials, numbers, question marks, and doodled images. In record time, it looked like a child's drawing, something a psychiatrist might find fascinating, and a cryptographist might find frustrating.

Jade had asked her to stick around the store, although, by his haunted smile and troubled gaze, he'd known better than ask for a promise. For that, she could only be grateful. There was someone she needed to speak to, someone she needed to see . . . and that lonely little pickup in the warehouse could supply her transportation.

Arranging the meeting, however, wasn't quite so simple. Her third phone call found a mildly distressed Allen Spencer in the middle of a business meeting. Tapping into his ambition, she swiftly relayed the measure of her gratitude that could extend beyond her measly little body to the giant cog of government . . . if he would just do her this *one tiny little favor*.

That she would make good on her promise if or when Allen reached the Senate or House, relieved the guilt as she manipulated Spencer and thus, half the county and state officials in Bender Falls.

For two reasons, Jade hadn't informed Tim in advance of why he needed to be picked up at eight-thirty in the morning or why he needed the ride. First and foremost, he knew Spencer would attempt to talk him out of his intentions. Tim would take one look at him and decide it was a bad idea. The second was more practical. Giving Tim an entire night to consider his conscience, to think about the possible ramifications of taking a hokey civilian to a crime scene even with Devinio's authority, would take a toll on Spencer as a dedicated officer. At the same time, Jade knew Spencer wouldn't deny him.

"You want to tell me where we're going, now? Or do you just want me to drive you around the block a couple of times?" Tim asked.

Half sick with the tension spiraling through his system and his muscles already knotted, Jade glanced over to realize Tim had, indeed, driven around the block. They were stopped at a red light with opposing Maine St. traffic sailing past the intersection. Damn it, Maine was blocked off near the park. "Around the block . . . damn it." Several back streets were blocked off as well. "Head back to your place," Jade said as he watched a group of laughing adults and skipping children cross the street in front of them.

"I was afraid you were going to say something like that," Tim said as he sped across Maine, deciding on his route. "I was hoping you bought a shit load of furniture again and needed some extra muscle. But that's not the case either, huh? So, what exactly are we doing here?"

"Your suspicions are probably accurate," Jade said while listing his gaze through the side window.

"Just for the pure hell of it, tell me anyway," Tim said with a mocked musing tone. He was mad.

"Devinio's meeting us at the Engler homestead," Jade answered in a carefully restrained tone. Outside the open window, sun spiked through tree limbs overhead, jetting reflections off chrome bumpers parked at the curb; thin streams sprinkled through branches to create a mystical ambiance on front lawns. Conflicting with the sun and heat already beginning to rise, Jade shivered internally, needing every ounce of his concentration just to form words. "I've offered Devinio my assistance to . . ."

"I'm going out on a limb here, but I'm going to guess you're referring to psychic assistance, right?"

"Yes."

Tim was silent longer than usual. They were quite a distance past the cordoned-off area and creeping past the town border when he decided, "I don't know what exactly you intend to accomplish or how this is supposed to work other than the trumped-up shit I've either seen on TV or read, but I can tell you, I don't like the idea. You could be setting yourself up for a whole lot of bad publicity. Not to mention about thirty years to life. I think it's a bad—"

"Don't," Jade interrupted without bringing his gaze from the window. "If you're the friend I believe you are, don't try talking me out of this. Not for practical reasons or uh . . . or out of concern. Thirty minutes, thirty years, I wouldn't want to live either one without her."

Again, Spencer remained quiet for a time then, "You're that sure something's going to happen to her?"

"Something's going to happen."

"Okay," Spencer said in agitated resignation. "What do you want me to do?"

"Be there," Jade said absently. "And don't . . . don't interfere until you know it's time."

"How uh . . . how's this work? What exactly do you intend to do, or how do you go about it?"

"I don't have a clue," he admitted quietly. "I've never willingly walked into a . . . a crime scene. Not even my mother's," he said with his memory floating on the surface of his mind, his voice animating, reflecting. "I can remember sitting at my desk in school," he continued as his five senses ignited to the image of windows and a playground outside. He smelled chalk dust and heard the murmur of children stirring, pencils scribbling, iron brackets squealing as children's rumps shifted on foldout seats . . .

"Taking a test," Jade said absently, barely hearing his voice for as vividly as the memory erupted. He was ten . . . not quite ten. "It hurt," he said as he remembered. His body impacted, slamming backward into the wooden bench with enough force to jar the attached desk and startle a squeal from the little girl behind him. His hands had flown to cover his chest—searing pain. His breath halted; his lips parted on a silent cry.

"Oh, God, it hurt," he remembered. "I couldn't breathe . . . couldn't scream . . . and I knew . . . In those seconds . . . Christ, felt like an eternity . . . I knew it was my mother's pain. Her blood on my hands when I clasped my chest. Her terror and shock . . . Her death, I felt an instant before I blacked out."

In silence, Jade remembered. The reel of memory film shifted into high gear, but again it seemed like an eternity. "I woke up in the nurse's office . . . and I knew I had to get home . . . Couldn't remember why. Couldn't fucking remember what I'd seen or felt. I just knew I had to get home and . . . and I felt numb. The dreams . . . the dreams left me numb, too. Empty . . . like I was dead inside. I left school . . .ran out and raced home . . . and she was lying in the foyer . . . just lying there like in my dreams."

Black wings spread against white tile, arms and legs sprawled within the sheer black cloth. She'd been posed within a pentagram with the chandelier casting a circle of light around her.

"I begged her not to wear black," he uttered as his throat tightened. "I took all her black negligees . . . hid them. But she . . . she fucking bought another one just that morning. She fucking bought another one, Spence," he said while struggling to withdraw from the past. "I couldn't tell her why I was terrified of the black lace and sheer cloth she always loved . . . I didn't know why I begged her not to wear it, why I stole her clothes . . . but I told her. I did tell her once. I know I did . . . She was white as a ghost when I came out of the trance. I could feel her fright . . . but she was always afraid of me . . . Do you know what it's like to grow up with a mother who's afraid of you?"

"No," Tim said in a hollow tone. "I don't."

"She . . . she'd put me in trances," Jade admitted aloud for the first time in his life, remembering the feel of her hand on his wrist, remembering his hand hovering, splayed, and descending. "She'd make me touch personal things . . . She'd use my curse, but she was afraid to look at me, to look into my eyes, to . . . hold me. I . . . I knew I was a monster," he said in a hollow tone.

His mind swirled in a haze of distant memories, overlaid by the image of his mother's gypsy-black eyes staring up at him. In his mind, she stood, wings spread, black hair haloed about her beautiful oval face, her lips slightly parted. A crimson trail trickled down her cheek rather than her chin, spider-webbing from her forehead. "She never looked me in the eyes," he said absently. "Not until she was dead . . . and I've lived with the guilt," he said vacantly. "I . . . I killed her, Spence. What I could do . . . what I was . . . I got her killed, and that's the same as pulling the trigger myself. She'd still be alive if . . . if I wasn't a monster."

"I don't see it that way," Spencer said in quiet concern. "I don't see it that way at all, Sax. You were a little kid, and it sounds . . . it sounds like maybe you were the victim, maybe a victim of your mother's ambition. You didn't pull the trigger and you didn't get her killed. You said it yourself, Sax. She used you—"

"I could have saved her," he interrupted as he blew an exhale of smoke from a cigarette that he couldn't recall lighting. His gaze fixed on the highway ahead, on a tunnel of trees. Slowly, he woke to the absence of wind. Outside his window, the forest had frozen, drawing his gaze. Looking into the thick tangle of woods, breathing in the fresh scents, he uttered, "I could have saved her. What was inside of me . . . I could have warned her but . . . but by that time, I was already afraid. Afraid of what I could see. Afraid of the monstrous thing inside of me. I . . . I'd started modeling monsters out of clay . . . and watching horror movies, monster movies.

"I didn't have friends. We lived in one of the more elite sections of Arlington, surrounded by the upper echelon, the influential elite of our nation's capital . . . and none of them wanted to socialize with a charlatan or her bastard. A monster and a freak . . . and all I ever fucking wanted was to be normal. To spend one day knowing I was normal and not afraid of what my curse could show me.

"I think . . . I think by the time my mother was murdered, I was already nuts. Already afraid even to look at what was inside of me. I know I'd already started rebelling . . ." he remembered absently. "She'd grab my hand and force it down on whatever item she wanted me to read . . . and I'd be fucking helpless. The thing inside me would take over. There was nothing I could do . . . I'd be like a spectator, just along for the ride . . . and that's what will happen when you pull into that driveway ahead, Spence. I'll just be along for the ride. You . . . you and Devinio will need to make sense of what you see, what I tell you or show you. I'll . . . I'll try to hold on, that much I do know. I'll hold on for as long as I can but . . . but the evil there, the uh . . . the evil I've felt clouding Bentwood since this began . . . it'll be inside of me."

And with his revelation, Jade looked over slowly, focusing on Spencer's intent, intensely worried eyes. "If I can't get it out, Spence . . . If this is the 'something' I saw coming, and I can't get the evil out once I let it in, you . . . you have to promise me something." He hesitated only a heartbeat. "You have to promise me you'll tell Veronica I loved her."

"Buddy, you don't say something like that, then expect me to drive you the next eighth-mile," Spencer said in a low cautious voice. "If whatever the fuck you're about to do can be the end of you, then you're not doing it. It's that goddamn simple. We'll catch this maniac without your help, pal. The son of a bitch is gonna make a mistake."

"Already did," Jade interrupted as his gaze trailed toward the forest, his senses chilling, keening.

"What? What the hell's that mean?"

"Threatened the lady I love," he said listlessly. "Big mistake. Big fucking mistake."

The county jail stood on an entire city block of Bender Falls. Its towering black walls, built before the turn of the century, wore coils of barbed wire and electric cord that conflicted with the ancient style. Only the main red-brick entrance carried a modern slant.

As Allen Spencer had promised, Ronnie gained immediate access, escorted by a broad-shouldered warden who, by his carriage, could thwart even the most violent offenders. The majority of the offenders in the county lockup, however, were not serious criminals. The list ranged from petty crime, drug offenses, grand thefts, and DUIs to civil offenders caught up in marital disputes. Cal Farnsworth was presently the exception.

Standing in a closed, telephone-style booth, awaiting Cal to step into the opposing containment, Ronnie tried to decide just how best to approach Cal, to gain his cooperation, but her mind continued swaying toward Jade. Her heart tugged with the image of him led into this oppressive structure, to Warden Cahan standing over him, accusing him. Too clearly, she could picture the uniformed guards frisking and tormenting him. Not one word of that entire ordeal had he breathed to her; not one hint of either bitterness or contempt had he affected.

Through a thick pane of glass and mesh separating her from the adjoining cubicle, Ronnie's attention fixed. Stunned, she watched the familiar man, wearing orange fatigues, amble clumsily inside with a push from one of his two uniformed escorts.

Unexpectedly, her heart skipped a beat. Her sympathy leaped to Cal as she read the fear radiating in his blue eyes as he glimpsed at the larger guard. She'd expected to be bitter, to hate him, even to fear him a little. Only sick with dread, she studied his pathetic image. Stoop-shouldered, with his hands caught and locked at his wrists, chains rattled between his shuffling feet. He appeared on the verge of collapse. If he'd been gaunt and ragged a week earlier, he appeared a mere husk now. Only a week had passed, but his cheeks were already sunken, and a purpling-yellow streak slashed from his left cheekbone to his jaw. His focus found her and darted downward; his brown hair fell in ragged strings on his brow. Looking at him, willing away the tears threatening her eyes, she flashed a thought of a battered child in oversized prison garb, not the menace who had induced bruises or threatened her life. If she harbored any doubts about a forced confession, those doubts vanished. The signs of a physical beating remained, and doubtful, his tormentors had merely struck his flesh. Something inside of him had suffered the blows. His entire mind and body appeared broken.

Remembering his sadness when they'd stood in front of his pickup, remembering the effects of grief that had touched her then, she realized how swiftly he would have caved under a few wicked blows.

He leaned at the wall near the closed door, head hanging, body slumped like a derelict propped against a pub wall.

Swallowing the constriction in her throat, Ronnie forced her nerves steady, her voice calm. "Cal, I'd like to speak to you."

He shook his head, the effort shuddering through his once sturdy frame.

"I want to help you, Cal. I can't do that unless you speak to me."

"Mmm sorrry," he drawled in a voice barely loud enough to reach through the speaker. "Mmm sorry for h-how I done t-to you . . . mmm sorry."

"I know you are, Cal," she said in a low careful voice, refusing to offer him the full breadth of her sympathy. "What you tried to do to me was wrong. What you believed about me was wrong. I offered you my help and you abused my offer of friendship." She saw him shrink more before her eyes, knowing when to strike. "That's no reason to spend the rest of your life in prison for a crime you didn't commit," she said firmly. "Especially, not when I believe you can help to solve this case and bring the real killer to justice before someone else dies . . . and we both know that's going to happen unless we do something to stop it."

His head lifted only slightly, possibly only to rest more fully against the wall, but she could see something of the tension on his drawn, discolored features.

"Cal, I'd like to ask you a few questions, and I'd like you to think about them when you answer, alright?"

"Bently," he said heavily, his vocal cords strained and hollow. "S-said he—he's crazy. He d-did it. K-kill't m-my pa."

"Isaac Bently is no more guilty of that crime than you are, Cal," she said firmly.

His eyes lifted for the first time, doubt and confusion apparent. "That . . . that federal guy . . . he said Bently w-was using me . . . se-et me up."

Whether she interrupted to keep from hearing proof positive of Mark Jarvins' coercion which she couldn't ignore on a professional level. Or whether she meant only to remain in control of the interview, she spoke before he could continue. "Before you came to the Inn that night, Cal, who did you speak to? Where did you get the bottle of whiskey you had?"

His already muddled thoughts upset, he hesitated before grumbling like a stubborn child, "Already told 'em all that . . . Got ta bottle from home. Was out mowin' fields awl day . . . tried callin' you . . ." His voice fell away in remorse. His head hung lower.

She wouldn't have much time, not any time to waste on either his guilt or her own complicated emotions. She needed to know. "Who all did you speak to, Cal? From the moment you started drinking, who did you see? Who did you talk to?"

In broken hitches and catches, he named names beginning with his mother, Cora Farnsworth, his sister, Valerie who hadn't yet returned to college, and his younger brother, Victor. He'd stopped at the Club, the Elks in town where a man could ignore the Puritan laws of Sunday temperance and inhale a few drafts or shots. He'd intended to go to Crowley's, had stopped there first only to remember Crowley's closed on Sundays. In the Elks, he'd spoken to several people including two names from the selective list that Ronnie and Len had created. Talking Cal through that evening, Ronnie's attention riveted, her senses detecting off notes and glitches in Cal's voice.

"When you left the Elk's, Cal, did you see anyone? Speak to anyone?" she asked and again felt his hesitation, sensed something out of kilter. Cal had been sitting in a jail cell for over a week with time to think, to remember. "Cal, who did you see?"

He shook his head. His gaze lifted with a strange conflict of pain and anger, fear. "N-nobody. I we-ent the back way. Didn't see nobody."

God Almighty, he was lying . . . he was lying, and he knew the killer! "Cal, I can't help you if you won't be honest with me. Who did you see?"

"I didn' see nobody, okay? It w-was dark, and I-I had other things o-on my mind."

Ronnie Bryson. He had Ronnie Bryson on his mind.

"Cal, where did you stop on the Friday night of Fred Engler's murder?"

"Ain't none your business," he said bluntly.

"Where did you stop the night of your father's murder?" she asked with a sense of something happening between them. Cool and direct, she watched his eyes. She read his panic before anger and despair flowed over his entire face. As if a curtain dropped, he appeared as blank as an autistic child, shoulders and caught hands drooping.

"Lem-me go. Ju-ust lem-me alone, okay?"

"Cal, did you ever play hide n' seek when you were a child?" she asked.

His eyelashes twitched a hair wider before he nearly stammered, "Ever'body did."

CHAPTER 32

The pulse had begun throbbing at his temples like a monster trying to break from its cage, and Jade had a feeling that was exactly what it was. A primal thing. A beast of wicked construct which hovered inside of him, biting and feeding on him, driving him more than half insane with its lust . . . and the beast was hungry now. As if his years of denial had starved the thing, it throbbed and pounded on his skull, already catching the scent of whatever evil could feed it. Tense, anxious, he combed his chilling fingers into his hair, his elbow propped on the open window frame.

"Drive, Spence," he strained as he focused on the lane ahead, images overlapping, the beast screaming.

Too late to back out, too late to change his mind, but the fear remained, as bitter and overwhelming now as when he'd first begun to realize the thing inside his head wasn't natural, not a gift from a benevolent God. Putting it away, locking it up, denying it had been his only hope for a semi-normal existence. He would've gone mad, had gone mad for a while until the battle raging inside of him had reached a status quo.

Already shivering internally, his stomach fluttering, Jade knew the pressure, an external pressure as if the atmosphere had gained substance, the molecules of air cooling to form a natural depression. His breath weighted, becoming an effort to draw into his constricting chest. His eyes strained to remain focused, to see and grasp the glimpses of wooden gates and barbed-wire fence to mark the Englers' driveway. On one side, a hayfield spread out, past due for a first cut, rippling like water under the slight warm breeze and only further distorting his vision. On the other side, through his open window, Guernsey cattle milled on a hillside, brown and white hues running together like a watercolor painting. With an effort, he tried focusing on one cow, on just one single cow in the cluster but failed.

Closing his eyes, tipping his head to press his face against his arm, Jade drew a breath, willing himself calm, struggling for a clear, collective thought. Uncontrollably, the heel of his tennis shoe skidded onto the seat, and his elbow found purchase on his raised knee. His fisted hand remained pressed against his temple.

"I . . . Sax, I don't think we better go through with this," Spencer's voice echoed through a distant tunnel.

"Drive, Spence," he strained. "Thi-is'll pass . . . just the . . . the . . . oh, GGGod, it . . ." *Huuurts!* He nearly screamed as his system pressed and cramped, chilling. "H-hard t-to breathe," he heaved. "I-I don't know if it's wh-what's happened here," he drew a breath. "Or . . . or m-my own fear."

"Yea? Well, I can tell you, pal . . . you're messing up my head pretty good here. I've never wanted to turn this damned truck around and barrel out of a place as bad as I'd like to at this moment . . . feels like my fucking air conditioner's on the fritz!" Spencer leaned and slammed his hand on his dashboard.

The blast of sound finished what the words had started. Jade jolted internally, drawing a gasped breath, dislodging the constriction in his throat. His foot slid off the seat. He folded forward, catching his elbows on his knees, holding his head as shudders spilled through his system.

The truck had stopped; the engine vibration and sound stilled. At least two dogs brayed, and the sound of clucking chickens drifted over the crunch of gravel.

"If this was your idea, it fu—"

"It wasn't," Len Devinio interrupted. "You want to call it off? Suits me just f—"

"No," Jade heaved, shaking his pulsing head. "G-give me a-a minute . . ."

"Take your time," Devinio said in a low voice, attempting to sound helpful.

"Co-old," Jade heaved. Evil felt cold, like chilly arms pressing about him, enveloping him. Entrapping him. Shuddering, he pushed off his elbows, drew a breath, and pressed the heels of his palms into his eyes. "Jesus . . . it's c-cold. ."

"I'd have disagreed with you a few minutes ago," Devinio stated, and Jade grasped the warmth of Devinio's hand inside the window, pressing against the chill.

"Christ," he hissed and withdrew his hand. "Maybe you better drive him out of here—"

Shaking his head, dropping his hands, Jade clasped the door handle. "Have to . . . have to do . . ." He groped, shoving the door open, stepping and sliding off the seat.

Holding the door for balance, he scanned the collection of buildings. From the corncrib and silo to the house a short distance up the drive, the images were familiar though he'd never stood on this farm. He stood in front of a sprawling dairy barn, and at the edges of consciousness, the darkness threatened to engulf him. Shaking his head, restraining the monster, Jade glimpsed at Spencer rounding the front end of the truck, and in a heartbeat flash . . .

He wore his uniform, climbing hesitantly from the cab of his pickup, drawing his flashlight off the seat as he scanned the shadows around the barn. The dusk-to-dawn lights had ignited, illuminating the clearing, and a brilliant silver moon hung over the eastern ridge. He'd spotted that moon while coming down Shaler Rd., wondering how the hell many bar brawls he would need to break up over at Crowley's tonight. Fred's two hounds distracted him, braying at his arrival, still making a raucous. Only one of the two coon hounds had nearly taken a chunk out of the Hadley boy who'd come to buy a dozen eggs . . . Fred had started penning both mutts just to be safe. Where the hell is everybody? Disturbance call . . . "Fred . . .? Alice . . .?"

Panning his flashlight across the redwood from the corner of the barn, he lurched at the sight of Erin Engler, who stood statuesquely outside the open man door. Why the hell was she standing so still? She appeared frozen, locked in a trance, and even for Erin, who was well on her way to becoming a spinster, this was too strange. "Erin . . .?"

Casting his flashlight beam to cut into the darkness shadowing her narrow face, careful to keep the intense circle below her pointed chin, he barely glimpsed her ghostly white complexion, her wide staring eyes. Like a skeletal rendition of the grim reaper, she thrust her arm, her appendage tapering into a pointer toward the open barn door.

Short hairs lifting under his starched collar, he buckled to an unnatural urge and slipped his hand to his loaded holster. Unsnapping the safety strap, he prepared to draw like some damned cowboy out of a Louis L'Amour novel, and he wasn't laughing.

Something about Erin's odd frozen pose, something about the distant moan that he'd only now detected originating from the direction of the house . . .

"Erin?" *he asked again, moving forward cautiously. Glancing toward the porch, he caught only glimmers of light through tall hedges. In front of him, Erin just continued to point, ramrod straight in a pair of tight jeans and clinging blouse, which lent her a more crane-like countenance. He could make out a tremor in her arm and drew a sense of her straining to keep her rigid pose. His grip firm on his gun, not knowing what to expect, he took the steps toward the barn, flashlight beam cutting ahead of him, slicing into the dull lighted interior. Light overlapped from the dusk-to-dawn light overhead, his flashlight beam and the string of bulbs extending into the glow of single bulbs above the milking stalls.*

A dog? A wild dog? The Englers' bull? What? *And where the hell was Fred for Chrissake? Hurt? Jesus, was he dead?*

Hurrying with the thought of Fred in trouble, Tim managed only two long strides through the small door and stopped. Only for an instant, he believed someone had butchered a steer in the aisle directly ahead of him, only for a second before his mind sprinted past the shock to horror. Human . . . oh Jesus . . . human! *He registered the shape of boots, legs twisted. Not flesh, not skinned raw meat of a steer! The saturated dark cloth shined crimson under the flashlight beam quivering in his grip. The smell of blood and bile wafted into his nostrils. His focus riveted on the shaft protruding from the red mass of a chest. A pitchfork, a short-handled pitchfork . . . trails of blood spilled, puddling and rolling over the scattered hay. Stomach acids twisted in his gut; his senses reeled with his revelation . . .*

Just like Vic! Just like Vic Farnsworth!

"Oh Jesus . . . Fred . . . oh Jesus . . ."

Bile rising, his head spinning, Jade twisted and staggered, stumbling out of the barn where his vision had led him. Ramming past the bodies, he landed on his hands and knees. Choking, gagging, his entire body convulsed with the effects of what Tim Spencer had nearly done two weeks earlier. Under the handclasps on his shoulders, Jade shuddered. Through a tunnel, he heard Tim's voice, the same voice echoing inside his mind, but he understood nothing of the words as he collapsed to his hip. Still heaving, gagging, his mind spun with the vision of Fred Engler. In vivid detail, the grizzly image continued to blaze inside his mind. The red spider webs spewed from ugly black-red wells. The puncture wounds were evenly spaced, spread in a crisscross pattern over the exposed chest, penetrating the cloth . . .

Oh, GGGod . . . he heard a rhythmic young voice tweeting a nursery rhyme . . . a lulling, lilting voice singing.

"Ring . . . a-round . . . the rosy . . . Pocket full a po-osies," Jade whispered in heaved breaths. "W-we al-all falll down . . ." His body spasmed. Hell's fire sliced through his system, snatching his breath, lurching him.

"Jesus! Isaac! Sax . . . Fuck, Jade!" Spencer demanded. His hand clasped, tugging Jade's arm. "Quit! You hear me! We're done . . . You're done! Wake up!"

Jade's hanging head shook. Cold sweat lifted, crawling through the roots of his hair like spiders. "Ohhh . . . shit . . . shit . . ."

"Nursery rhyme," the lower voice spoke at close range. "What's that mean, Amico? Last week, a child's game . . . now you're singing a nursery rhyme. What the fuck are you telling me? We have a kid doing this?"

"What the hell do you mean, last week?" Spencer snapped. "You had him out here last week?"

"Not out here," Devinio said in a low voice. "Come on, Amico, talk to me . . . You talked last week. Tell me what you're seeing, feeling . . ."

"You don't need to ask him, Devinio," Spencer said in a low volatile tone. "He just walked through the motions of what I did over a week ago . . . I know what the fuck he saw and what he feels . . . I damned near tossed my fucking dinner in this very spot."

"You're sure?"

"Yeah, I'm sure," Spencer said in a low strain. "I just watched him play out the entire scene—right down to the words I spoke and the pause I took to look at Erin Engler standing like a fucking scarecrow against the wall over there. Yeah, I'm sure, and I've got the chills down my goddamn spine to prove it."

"If you did that to prove you're legit, Amico, you wasted your energy," Devinio growled.

"What the hell's that supposed to mean?"

"It means, I have confirmation that he was across town about the same time you were walking into that barn. He wasn't out here hiding in the eaves to see you or hear you . . . So, what the hell does a nursery rhyme have to do with this?"

"R-regressing . . . games . . . children's games . . . child's pain," Jade heaved and lifted a hand to wipe his drenched face, to clear the sting of salt off his lips, out of his eyes. Blinking, he eased into a more natural pose. Drawing a knee to catch his elbow, he combed his fingers through his sweat-soaked hair and caught his head. He'd forgotten the weariness, the long moments of exhaustion where he'd needed to lie on his bed or a couch before he could even lift his hands or move his toes. Long horrible moments of weighted limbs and heavy head. He was still shivering, still cold . . . and he could still hear the lyrical, lilting voice at the edges of his mind, knowing at this moment. "Your psycho's a f-female, Devinio . . . Sh-she's s-so sick."

"Female . . .? You're sure?"

He nodded heavily. "Female . . . regressing."

"Do you know who, Amico? Do you see her?"

Jade shook his head. "H-hear her . . . s-still hear her . . . voice . . . familiar." He'd heard that voice, older. He knew he had. "She's s-singing wh-while—" His system lurched. His eyes snapped with the shock of seeing those prongs descending. His mind recoiled, and his breath hitched.

"Sax!" Spencer snapped, clasping his shoulder, jolting him, and shattering through the slice of pain suspending him.

"God, help me," he breathed softly. "I-I don't w-ant to step inside . . ."

"Yea, well and good! Fine!" Spencer snapped. "When you're ready, I'll haul your ass over to my truck, and we're out of here. No problem."

"I ca-an't leave yet," he said, knowing his accuracy, feeling the certainty. "Can't leave—"

"Bullshit," Spencer hissed. You've given us something to go on. With some footwork, we oughta be able to nail this bitch—"

"Spence," Jade interrupted and lifted his desperate gaze. "I'll see her. I'll know her . . . before we leave here." His gaze turned slowly toward the open barn door. A scent of cow manure crinkled his nostrils. His mind reeled as he drew the breath of hay and grain, fresh evening air.

"Damn dogs," he spoke in a voice already changing. Like a beast unleashed, his mind lashed out, finding and devouring the incorporeal essence of Fred Engler ambling toward the small door. ". . . Damn dogs barking again . . . barking every damn night. Gonna have to let 'em loose again . . . damn coons gonna be raidin' my corn sure's hell . . ."

"No! Goddamn it, Jade! No," Spencer demanded and jolted Jade from the started trance. "No."

Barely, he lifted his gaze to Spencer and started a protest. The words were lost. A shiver spiraled through him, and the flashes erupted, quick, and fierce. Pinpricks spiked over his nerve endings, with the cold chill slithering inside him. "Ohhh, Christ . . . inside," he uttered. Already his head turned, his gaze shifting toward the open door . . . and he found her crouched, waiting, watching. "Sh-she came in wi-ith the cows . . . followed the cows . . . inside. Waiting . . . watching . . ."

And he heard her soft voice, counting, counting . . . "One, one hundred . . . two, one hundred . . . three, one hundred . . ." And the flashes swirled in the darkness, memory flashes. An image of a man leaning against— "A wooden bin," he uttered. "Holding s-something in his hand . . . counting . . . voices joining . . . hiding . . ." She was hiding, tucked in shadows, a scent of hay wrapped around her, comforting. Someone had helped her hide . . . had hidden her to protect her. "Hiding . . . she has to hide . . . help her to hide . . . hide her." His brow knitted. Sweat lifted on his forehead as he strained to clear the image, to see who had helped her. "Feels s-safe with them . . . they help her . . . hide her."

"Who . . . who do you see, Jade?" a distant voice asked.

"N-not Fred . . . not Fred. Boys," he uttered, nodding, but another image overlapped. The black wings flew in front of him, a hand wrapped chilly about his wrist, pressing his smaller hand downward. "N-no, Mom`ma," he whined and strained, struggling to pull his hand away. "Nooo please," he pleaded as tears lifted. "Donnn't maaake meee . . . Pleeease don't . . ."

'Once, more ba'be, joost once more.'

"Liiies . . . nnnever once . . . Mom`ma, nooo . . . h-hurts! Ha-hurts mmmeee . . . Gonna diiie, Mom`mma."

"Devinio, that's it," a distant voice whispered. "We have to get him out of here."

"Back off, Spencer," a far deeper voice whispered. "We let him play this out. Don't touch him . . . Talk to me, Jade. Look around you . . . Where are you? Do you know where you are?"

Heaving shallow breaths, feeling a sob threatening his voice, he fisted his hand, knuckling the tears from his eyes and looking at the man speaking. Brows furrowed, he stared at the dark-eyed stranger, nodding slowly. "I know you. You're in the evil place," he said with a nod, remembering the evil place in his dreams. Always in dreams, frightening dreams . . . the girl. "You know the girl . . ."

"What girl, Jade?" the man asked.

He smiled slowly, his mystic green eyes lighting a shine of mischief. "My girl . . . she's gonna be mine."

"How old are you, pal?" the man asked with an intent gaze, a strained smile.

Troubled, his brow notched. His gaze listed to scan the farmyard. His smile faded as he pondered the question. "I-I don't know . . .? Something . . . oh, gggod, the bad place. The man's dead in the barn . . . The girl's dead inside." He nodded. "She's dead inside. Her daddy . . . he did bad things," he said with a troubled frown and pushed slowly, steadily to his feet.

His gaze panned the strange familiar, unfamiliar world around him. He'd been here before, often. Deja vu . . . precognition. He understood those things; his mother explained them to him. His talent. His curse.

Still listless, raking his fingers through his hair to swipe it off his brow, he lifted his gaze and landed on the man standing beside him. The blue eyes locked on him, intent and troubled. "I know you, too," he said matter-of-factly and smiled hesitantly as the warm flood of emotions swam into him. Awed, he studied the man, feeling a connection, feeling the fellow's concern for him. "Don't be afraid for me," he said earnestly. "But don't leave me, either . . . Don't leave me here in this place. I don't want to be here forever, alright?"

"I won't leave you, pal. Honest," the man strained.

Jade studied him a moment, then nodded, knowing the sincerity. "The girl's inside," he said and listed his gaze toward the barn. "I have to go inside."

"Maybe not, S . . . kid," the man said carefully. "Maybe you can just look inside? Can you do that?"

He shook his head slowly. "Touch . . . have to touch something . . . I'm a sensitive . . . That's what my mom`ma says. I'm sensitive. I think . . . never mind what I think," he decided as he continued to look at the barn, its gaping door and forbidding entrance. He could see the hazy outline of wood and stone walls and drew a scent of hay and manure. A sweet fragrance of fresh oats touched his nostrils.

"I've never been inside a barn before," he said quietly. "I don't think I want to go inside that one . . . There's a smell . . . evil has a smell. Sometimes I just pass someone in a crowd, and I can tell they've got evil inside them . . . death smells, too," he said candidly and shivered. "And both smells are in this place. Think it's making me sick," he said thoughtfully. "Feel like I have to vomit . . . ohhh God," he heaved and staggered, clutching his head, waking with a searing pain through his skull. His knees buckled, and he hit the ground on his shins—his fall cushioned by the hands grabbing his arms, setting him down.

Buckling, he rested his head between his knees, his breath heaving and lurching.

"Take it easy, kid. Just catch your breath . . ."

Kid? Len Devinio called him 'kid?' Shaking his head, Jade heard Spencer talking down to him, and felt the sturdy hand massaging his shoulder.

"It's okay, kid . . . just take deep breaths, then we'll call it quits, okay? I'll get you out of here . . ."

"Dammm-it," Jade heaved softly. "Time warp."

"Sax?"

"Jade?"

"Shit," he heaved and eased onto his shins and haunches. Raking his frigid fingers through his sweated hair, he dropped his hands to dry his palms on his thighs. "Shit."

"Sax?" Spencer asked more hesitantly.

"Ye-ea . . . Sax, Isaac, Jade . . . back," he said as he watched his hands turning, and looked down at his slick trembling palms. "In the trances," he said heavily. "Sometimes in the trances, I'd see things . . . people . . . people I'd meet . . . Places

I'd be . . . I-I never talked to them . . . except once. Here . . . in this place. I spoke to you . . . both of you long ago," he said as he lifted his gaze to find Spencer.

"Veronica's my catalyst," Jade said as an eerie calm spilled over him. "I-I think I knew that before she ever came, felt her coming. She's my catalyst . . . My link between what I was and whatever I am now . . . my link to the past . . . and maybe my fucking sanity. Years . . . years ago. Before my mother's death, before I had to shut down inside or go mad, I saw her. Just a few moments, a few seconds of eye contact. I never even knew her name, but it was a communion of minds, a combining of spirits . . . and I don't know why I'm trying to explain this. Why I'm telling you any of this." His gaze drifted over his surroundings, suffering déjà vu in its purest form while orienting himself more firmly in the natural realm and time.

"Yes . . . yes, maybe I do," he realized and tipped his gaze to Spencer. "I'm not crazy. I didn't just snap and regress to my childhood no matter how it probably appeared or how it sounded. I've been to this place. God knows, I've blocked the memories for more than eighteen years, but . . . but I was here as a child. Perhaps, I knew the significance of this place then. Knew it would affect my life one way or another as much as eighteen or twenty years ago. Maybe I just blocked it out the way I blocked other things that scared the hell out of me. It doesn't matter, though. Not now. I am here, now. The past and future are at an impasse. Either I enter that barn again and handle this . . . or I lose my mind trying. Either way, Spence, you can't attempt to stop me again. Veronica's life . . . my life . . . depends on what I do in the next few minutes. Nothing . . . of nothing have I ever been more certain. She is my catalyst, the place where my past and my future merge. Either I save her life, or we're both lost."

CHAPTER 33

Palms sweaty, Ronnie gripped the steering wheel, her mind reeling with the discoveries and connections. She could have questioned Cal further and pushed him toward the admission that she'd seen in his eyes, but as he'd stared at her with such blatant desperation, she'd known the precarious state of his sanity. Nothing could be gained by breaking Cal Farnsworth, and nothing had been lost by leaving him alone. Only one other question had she asked as he'd pushed hurriedly to his feet, wanting to retreat and escape the revelation he'd read in her eyes.

'Your pa carried a stopwatch, didn't he?'

Forever or an instant, his eyes flooded with emotions from anger, pain, and horror to confusion and desperation.

Fred Engler had carried a pocket watch . . . Victor Farnsworth, a stopwatch. By no coincidence, not one of Victor Farnsworth's children had admitted to that missing item, and Ronnie wondered if Cora, Victor's wife, even knew of its existence. People, even people living in the same house, could lead vastly different and private lives, and perfect harmony existed only on the surface.

She need only think of her life, her parents, and her brothers. To their large circle of acquaintances, her family was considered the epitome of close relationships and a model unit to be emulated. On the surface, Robert and Fiona were the most nurturing and loving couple in the whole of their social circuit. Not many people outside the home knew that Robert and Fiona adhered to an age-old custom, each occupying a separate bedroom. Modeled in Victorian style, one room connected to the other through an immense dressing-room closet; their wardrobes hung on detached racks, a visible reminder of their separate lives. Ronnie supposed they slept together often, but she recalled her and her brothers' quandary over their parents' estranged arrangements. Separate bedrooms, separate lives. Her father's life revolved around political and financial affairs; her mother's life revolved around keeping an image of dignity and charity, the perfect political wife. Ronnie wouldn't be surprised if her father had indulged in an affair or two over the years and even less surprised if her mother had remained oblivious.

Shaking her head and concentrating on the road ahead, she thought again about Cal Farnsworth and the signs she hadn't even considered until now. Anger and aggression, the combination had manifested in him at least fifteen years ago. He would have been no more than ten or eleven . . . and Ronnie remembered sitting on the front porch of Green's house, listening, hearing how Cal had ridden into town with his father and hooked up with the slightly older crowd. And Victor Farnsworth had let him. The fellow had driven him into town and let him run amuck despite his alleged firm religious convictions. If she'd stopped at the church and visited Rev. Phearson, would she have learned anything of significance and caught on sooner?

Cal had rebelled outwardly and early, becoming aggressive, avoiding his home and family, and undoubtedly, suffering internal conflicts. Almost two weeks ago, he'd admitted, 'I'm the oldest . . . I should of been there . . . Should of been able to do something . . .' The oldest and the one most likely to suffer the conflicting guilt, the helplessness, and despair.

Who had Cal spoken to? That question had burned in her mind as she'd driven the twenty minutes to Bender Falls.

Who had Cal spoken to? Who could have fueled his drunken obsession? Who could have known where to find him or when to follow him? Who could have known that he might have an alibi, one he refused to admit to the authorities on the night of a full moon? Who had known that Cal's wicked fraternity met on the eve of the full moon to conduct whatever ceremonies dictated?

Granted, there were eleven other names on that list, and they'd supplied alibis for each other. But that pattern had only confirmed Ronnie's suspicion of an arcane ritual escalating into murder. Cal had found his father, and he'd neither time nor presence of mind to contact the others and secure his alibi. Like an obstinate child, he'd refused to change his story to explain the missing period between stopping at Crowley's after work and finding his father. Someone had known where he was, though. Someone had known he wouldn't return home early to assist his father with barn chores on the eve of a full moon. Someone who might just harbor a subconscious rage toward Cal and enough insight into his nature to want him punished as surely as Victor Farnsworth.

Victor had been the first, and in the mind of this psychopath, an obsession. The satisfaction, the release of pain and anger, hadn't been enough, or perhaps, too much. Perhaps, the release after years of pent-up rage and hostility had offered too great of thrill, the euphoria too overwhelming to be denied . . .

The image of Victor Farnsworth Jr. flashed in her mind, a gangly youth standing at the edge of a sophomore class photo. Nothing of his features could she distinctly recall. The man was two full years younger than Cal, two years younger than the age she and Jarvins had profiled. But it made perfectly good sense . . . perfectly logical sense when the animal slaughters were not the progression of a serial killer, but rather the advent of a cult.

All too easily, Ronnie recalled Victor Jr's alibi on an official police report. Allegedly, he'd been at his frat house in Pittsburgh, holed up in his room, studying for his finals. The chaos at the crime scene hadn't settled until after midnight, which was probably when Victor and his sister had received the panicky call and raced home to Bentwood. Two hours . . . two hours was plenty of time to return to his dorm after the deed was done. And Vic Jr was the bright one as Ronnie had heard. He'd applied for his own scholarships and financial aid, worked part-time near the campus, and maintained an impressive GPA to graduate from Pitt University with a BA in Science, eleventh in his class. He was currently taking undergraduate courses, working toward his goal to become a psychiatrist . . . and even that should have tipped her off.

If everything hadn't gone so blasted topsy-turvy from the moment she'd met Jade, she might have remained focused long enough to solve this crime a week ago, but Ronnie wasn't foolish enough to regret the circumstances. As she pulled Jade's pickup into the alley behind the warehouse, she held only one clear desire, to hold him in her arms and announce her findings. With his help, she'd decide how best to approach Len and lay a foundation for seeking concrete evidence to support her claim. Knowing and proving the acts of a killer, who'd left no physical trace of his presence, were two vastly different things, and God knows, before she could accuse another Farnsworth, she'd need a great deal of evidence. Doubtful, even Len would move too quickly on this accusation. After Mark Jarvins' damage to this case, after all of the publicity, they couldn't afford to take any chances and let this psycho walk away free.

Preoccupied, Ronnie stepped from the truck cab, intending to open the garage doors to the warehouse.

"You! Miss! You just stop right there!"

Startled, Ronnie froze and looked toward the scratchy, high-pitched voice. She found the frail little woman leaning on a cane at the entrance of a vine-shrouded porch. White puffy hair and hunched shoulders denoted latent signs of osteoporosis. The elder woman glared at Ronnie beneath thinning gray brows, a scowl on her lined lips. Offhandedly, Jade had mentioned something about Mrs. Handler. His eyes had sparked his amusement, contradicting the dry disgust in his tone when speaking of their running feud over the hedges that cramped his warehouse entrance.

Glancing backward along the black fenders of the pickup, Ronnie verified that she hadn't scraped the paint or snapped even one of the lovely pink roses blooming abundantly throughout the thick hedges. The rose of Sharon truly made a splendid hedge, but these could use pruning, a detail she might keep to herself.

Spying the feisty little woman who appeared poised and prepared to accuse her of violating her bushes, Ronnie stifled a smile against the image of Jade standing off against this frail octogenarian. No wonder he'd been amused. He'd probably never even bent a twig in passing.

Deciding on the instant, Ronnie veered through the jungle of wild hedges.

On the porch, the woman stiffened, apparently preparing to engage in battle, hitching her knitted shoulders as best she could. She wore a dress of paisley-blue print, the hem sagging nearly to her thick ankles where blue socks puddled against what appeared to be black-leather orthopedic shoes. Her hands, one clutching the cane, the other gripping a thin white knit sweater, bore all the traces of age, from gnarled-enlarged knuckles to brown liver spots sprinkled liberally over paper-thin skin. Only her eyes, clear and direct, lent credence to the quick wit behind her wrinkled face.

Rather than intimidate her, Ronnie halted two strides from the rickety, gray steps and looked up at the woman who visibly took her measure. How many rumors had this elder heard or believed? What was she thinking behind her steely glare? "Hello, Mrs. Handler. I know we haven't had the pleasure of an introduction, but I'd hoped to visit you sooner. I'm—"

"I know who the blazes you are," she snapped. "I might look like death warmed over, but I'm not senile yet, gal, and there's not likely a soul in Bentwood don't know you. Don't much make no never mind to me who you want to shack up with, I just mean to tell you, if you intend to be driving in and outa that garage over there, you watch my hedges! I won't have nobody coming here thinking they can bust up my place—"

"I assure you, Mrs. Handler, I wouldn't dream of harming your roses. Rose of Sharon, aren't they?"

The woman halted, eyeing Ronnie suspiciously even as her head bobbed slightly. "Yes, they are and—"

"My mother's always been partial to roses," Ronnie interrupted smoothly, letting her gaze meander fondly over the shroud of climbing vine on the porch. "Your garden rather reminds me of my mother's," she continued with a faint smile. "Try as I might, I've never been able to emulate my mother's talent. I do envy people with a green thumb. Your garden truly is lovely, and I assure you, I'll take every precaution to see that it remains tip-top on the alley side."

Wizened gray eyes studied her with suspicion; the white head bobbed. "You see you do, gal."

"I wondered if you might spare a moment?" Ronnie asked before the woman could chasten her further or turn toward her screened door. "As I'm sure you know, I came to town to investigate the trouble here in Bentwood. Before the media circus the Sunday before last, several critical points had come to my attention, and try as I might, I haven't been able to get those out of my mind. I'd intended to speak to you then; however, at the time, I was attempting to avoid your neighbor in hopes of sparing him any undue publicity. Futile, as it turned out, with my colleagues churning out atrocities about him and me faster than you could shake a stick." Letting a hint of her genuine disgust and dismay rise, Ronnie continued, sighing, "Anyway, I would like the opportunity to ask you a few questions. It concerns an incident that happened about fifteen years ago—"

"If you're looking for gossip to slander our town, missy, you can just—"

"I assure you, gossip's not what I'm seeking, but rather a greater truth and understanding of certain events which may have led to the present horror. In a very short time, Mrs. Handler, I've come to appreciate Bentwood, and I'm appalled that anyone would attempt to destroy its tranquility. That I've also fallen in love with a man, who's claimed Bentwood as his home, only strengthens my conviction. I'd very much like to help apprehend the monster behind these heinous crimes. If you could spare me a few moments, I believe you might provide the insight I need."

"Seems to me, missy," the woman started, eyeing Ronnie more suspiciously. "You already helped nab the mangy culprit."

"I'm not so sure that I have," Ronnie said honestly. "I won't take up much of your time, Mrs. Handler."

Either out of curiosity or resignation, Mrs. Handler grumbled some inaudible comment and began sidling onto her porch. "No use you standing down there. You may's well come on up here."

Over a week ago, Ronnie had meant to speak to this woman about her dognapping. As she strode up the steps, that was the furthest thing from her mind. Still, it was a springboard, and settling onto a metal chaise lounge with worn, hand-sewn pillows to cushion the iron slats, Ronnie wasted no time. As she'd intuitively surmised, this old woman appreciated the direct approach. "The incident I've been questioning happened about fifteen years ago," she began simply. "I understand you had a miniature Schnauzer . . ."

Over the next ten minutes, Ronnie confirmed her belief that the woman had a mind like a steel trap. The details of that incident and her anger were as sharp now as fifteen years earlier. With no children of their own, she and her husband, John, had pampered their pair of Schnauzers.

"Hansel and Greta," she'd said with sad reminiscence. Hans had met his fate at the hands of what she'd come to think of as the "Heathen Band," and somehow, Ronnie wasn't surprised to hear Mrs. Hazel Handler, former head teller of the bank branch in town, recite at least ten names on Ronnie's blacklist.

"Heathens, the lot of them," the elder woman said with a bitter note. "You'd see them on Sunday morning, standing out back of the church, sucking on cigarettes and whatever else they could get their hands on . . . If you saw one, you'd see two or three others, and that's sure's shoot not changed. Didn't surprise me none in the least to hear that devil Farnsworth got up to no good . . ."

Hazel hadn't been born in Bentwood, but rather over in Bender Falls. She'd met John back 'about the time boys were signing up for the draft for WW II.' Just barely out of high school, she'd volunteered her services to the war effort . . . John had gone off to war. For the two years of his absence, they'd corresponded by mail. When he returned home, they were married at once, and she'd moved into this very house where John had been born and raised . . .

The conversation took a natural turn, and Ronnie needed little talent for the woman to reveal a great deal about the Farnsworths. Ole Vic, 'God rest his soul,' was always 'kinda shy and backward.' Even with poor Cora, who fell for him back in high school. Hazel had already been a bank teller by the time Vic Farnsworth had attended high school. His folks, being good Christians, had seen to it that he and his sister, 'God rest her soul,' attended the high school and made it to church every Sunday . . . *And it was a shame about his little sister, Rose.*

"Vic was never the same after Rose's accident . . . if hanging her own self could be considered that. Most times, ole Vic kept to himself," Hazel remembered, *but then that Cora* . . . "She was a shy little thing, but she started gravitating toward Vic. Not much of a life that young Cora had. Her daddy and the Spencers—the elder ones—had a row about fifty years back, and her pa set to drinking hard . . ." Hazel figured the gal turned to Vic because he was about the quietest, gentlest boy in town. Never ran amuck with any other boys that Hazel knew of . . . but she had her curiosities about him and Fred Engler dying the same way . . . About whether there was more to that connection than maybe any folks wanted to admit.

"Fred was a good six—maybe eight years older," Hazel said in a casual momentum, and Ronnie wondered just who had intended to speak to whom as she listened. "Wasn't nothing I could put a finger on, mind you, but there was talk . . . There's always some talk in small towns. . . and there's no accounting for why some youngsters are drawn to each other. Now, Fred, he was always a bullying sort. His pa was the same way, John used to say . . . Could be the nicest guy you'd ever want to meet one minute, want to give you the shirt off his back. The next, my lord, he could be mean as a snake, wanting to light into you sure as look at you . . . Hear his oldest boy's just like him. I don't get around town as good as I used to . . ."

For a woman who didn't get around, not much further than Meg's Diner or the Superette two blocks down Maine, Hazel Handler possessed more of an inside track than anyone Ronnie had encountered in Bentwood to date. In casual notes, the elderly woman talked about Fred and Alice Engler's whirlwind courtship, about Allister Engler-Hall, the Englers' younger daughter, being a 'loose woman' and only marrying Ken Hall, the grocer, for his money. "That gal still gets around a good bit the way I hear it, but Ken, he's a good bit older than her . . . guess he just puts up with her carrying on . . . Wasn't more than a year or so ago, I noticed her sniffing around over next door after that blasted beau you're planning to marry . . ."

Noting the woman's feigned agitation at the mention of Jade, Ronnie nearly smiled, sensing Hazel took as much pleasure in harassing Jade as he took in firing back his waves and smiles.

"Now, I ain't saying that boy's all bad, you understand? The good Lord knows, he's a handsome devil. Reminds me of my John . . . and I don't figure the boy's as bad as some . . . but blast him for tearing in and outa that garage."

Without any coercing, Hazel veered back to the Farnsworths and Englers, and again Ronnie wondered just who controlled this interview. She was beginning to think this old woman had more than a few suspicions that she'd just been waiting to share . . . and the longer Ronnie sat, taking careful note of words and inflects, the more convinced she became.

". . . I've been retired now, just about fifteen years," Hazel said at one point. "Right up until then, I worked daily from nine a.m. to five p.m. every weekday," she rasped in her age-worn voice. "You see and hear a lot of goings-on when you work with the same public every day, and you look out the same windows . . .

"Ole Vic, he used to come in with one of his youngsters in tow about every two weeks . . . That li'l gal of his sure was a pretty li'l thing but shy, just like her pa. The middle boy, too, was always afraid to look me in the eyes. Used to keep a bowl of lollipops under my counter, but those two, they never took a one unless Vic handed it to them. That gal of Fred's, the one that's still living out there, just going to seed . . . Now, she was one gal I never much cared for . . . had a temper like Fred's, and the coldest pair of eyes I ever saw on a young girl . . . Guess she'd be in about her mid-thirties or so now . . . Fred's youngsters are all a good bit older."

"You were saying earlier, Cal Farnsworth used to hang about town. Did you ever see his little brother or sister with him?"

"That middle boy, I heard he was something of a bookworm," she said smoothly. "I can remember Mrs. Emory, she used to teach over at the elementary, saying how he was one of the smartest youngsters in her class. Course, the gal wasn't no dummy either, according to Carol. It's no wonder the two of them are off to college trying to make something of themselves . . . I just never quite figured out why it was that Cal went sour when those other two seemed to adore their daddy . . ."

Ronnie decided she wasn't about to enlighten this old woman.

"There's something I been meaning to tell that fella of yours," Hazel said abruptly, her gray-aged eyes looking steadily at Ronnie. "He and I have never seen eye-to-eye since he called my roses 'scrub brush'—him with that dandy foreign accent—calling my roses 'shroob broosh' the first time he laid eyes on them," she scoffed. "But all the same, he's my neighbor, so maybe you could just pass this on to him," she hesitated thoughtfully. "I didn't think much of it at the time. My eyes ain't all they used to be, but I thought I spotted somebody back there in my bushes . . . the same night all that hullabaloo went on over at the Inn, but it was later. I don't sleep so well at night. Sometimes I come down here and have a cup of tea . . . wouldn't have even noticed at all if I hadn't seen him sneaking in his own backdoor earlier. That boy has some funny ways I never quite figured out."

She shook her white head as if bewildered but pressed on without touching whatever opinion she held of the subsequent name changes and accusations. "Anyway, I thought I saw somebody sneaking about back there, and it seems to me like maybe I've spotted somebody back there a few times since. I don't know if he's got the police watching him like that same Sunday when they lit out after him in the afternoon or if he's got somebody thinking to burglar him, but I thought he best know before I go and call Sam Hayward about this."

"Hazel," Ronnie said carefully. "Did you happen to notice anyone out there . . .? Say, last night?"

She appeared uncomfortable for the first time, her gaze shifting toward the thick growth of her back lawn before nodding. "Seems like maybe almost every night he's been over there, including when he holed up for those few days. That's why I thought I'd talk to him first. If he has those damned Federal agents still watching him, didn't figure it would do any good to call Sam or Sheriff Grant."

"Hon, did you by any chance, get a look at whoever was back there? Could you describe maybe their size or anything?"

"Sure wish I could," Hazel said worriedly. "The fact is, I wasn't even sure it was a person till I went and poked around down by the end of my hedges this morning. Found a couple places where it looked like somebody's been sitting or stooping, crouched down. We haven't had no rain to speak of in near on a month. The ground's about as soft as powder back there."

Tense, Ronnie cast her gaze toward the hedges. Spotting only flecks of black paint between the heavy leaf and flower cover, she understood how the woman might not be able to judge an intruder's shape or size.

"Missy, I didn't tell you that to worry you," Hazel said. "Could be nothing. Wouldn't be the first time that boy's had somebody spying on him from my hedges. Why it was just . . ." She halted, her gray eyes misting. Thin gray brows crinkled, forming a pensive frown as she looked toward the hedges.

"What is it, Hazel?"

"Just come to think of it," she said speculatively. "I think the last time he had to chase someone off, it was that little Val Farnsworth," she said and looked at Ronnie directly. "That boy sure does stir up the ladies, and that li'l gal sure pined over him a good two or three years back. I had to give him credit there. I heard him with my own ears tell her in no uncertain terms to go on home when he finally caught wise to her spying. They stood right back there in plain sight, and I think he made certain he stayed right where I could see him. He's had himself some trouble with the gals in this town . . . Now, don't you go telling him this, missy, but I'm glad to see he's finally thinking of settling down with a proper lady. That Andover gal, she's a pretty thing and all, and I've known her daddy since I first helped arrange a loan for him at my bank to start that store of his. His gal, though, she's a little floozy if I ever saw one. Her and those heathens she runs with . . ."

Sharing Hazel's sentiment, Ronnie smiled faintly, but thinking about Val Farnsworth and a possible psycho stalker, her grin faded. "Just to be on the safe side, Hazel, I'm going to phone Chief Hayward and have him poke around your hedges. Maybe he could get a footprint or something and find out who's been spying on the warehouse. Jade — Isaac does have a great deal of expensive merchandise in his shop, and with all the publicity, I'd rather be safe than sorry. I know he'll want to thank you for keeping an eye on things for him." *Which was probably an understatement.* "At the moment, I better get over there. He should be getting back soon. But I do hope you won't mind if I stop back sometime. I've truly enjoyed speaking with you."

"You stop over any time, Veronica," the woman said with a relaxed smile as she reached a gnarled hand to shake. "Meg, she's a pistol, but she's a pretty fair judge of character, too. I'll look forward to talking with you again."

Thanking Hazel again, Ronnie walked off the porch, her mind reeling with the details, with the worry. Could it be so simple as a woman stalking Jade? Or was Hazel right in her first assumption? Could Jarvins have kept surveillance . . .? No. Any competent surveillance team would set up a base camp in a van or apartment . . . And to believe that possibility even for a second could be only wishful thinking.

Bypassing the pickup's front end, Ronnie walked to the garage doors, digging the keys from her purse and unlocking the state-of-the-art locks. Only last evening, Jade had handed her the keys to his castle and walked her through the process of breaching his security. He'd spent a great deal of time and spared no expense to secure his building. Unfortunately, his precautions hadn't safeguarded his life from an official federal search warrant.

Even knowing the proper procedure, Ronnie suffered a momentary anxiety while disabling the alarm. In no particular order, the keys were numbered to open various doors throughout his building, and the security codes were likewise random. At the control panel inside the door, she punched the proper numbers and held her breath until the signal light turned green.

Opening the door on well-oiled hinges, Ronnie returned to the pickup and climbed aboard. Navigating the wide swing into the warehouse, she stopped when the back bumper cleared the opening. Leaving the engine running, she returned to the electronic panel and hit the button to lower the garage door, which automatically engaged the alarm.

Her fiancé certainly had his quirks, and until speaking with Hazel Handler, Ronnie had wondered if he might be just a wee bit paranoid. With the thought of someone standing outside those doors a week ago, perhaps, plotting more than a midnight rendezvous, Ronnie shivered as she returned to the truck. If not for the alarm system, the farmyard slayer could have slid into the warehouse and lay in wait . . . but that wasn't likely. Sunday night. Jade had returned to his apartment alone to pack an overnight bag after seeing her safely ensconced in Tim Spencer's pickup . . . and the maniac had lingered outside the Inn, probably already planning to frame Cal for the murders. Rings, watches . . . this psycho had come prepared, but he couldn't have anticipated Jade's intervention. Was it possible this psycho had meant to intercede instead? Intended to play the hero after inciting Cal . . .? And fixated on Jade for thwarting his plan and leaving Cal in the gravel, sprawled like a Christmas gift?

Had Victor Jr decided that night to frame his brother for the murder of his father?

As she maneuvered the pickup into its lonely corner, Ronnie considered her next move. First, she needed to contact Sam Hayward and apprise him of the situation. Until she uncovered something more substantial than theory and supposition, she wouldn't risk involving Len. The Bureau already looked like an outfit of bungling amateurs, compliments of Mark Jarvins.

Next, there was one more person she needed to see, who just might shed more light on the Farnsworths.

With Devinio and Spencer following, Jade walked alongside the barn, passing between a weathered hay wagon and red walls. Without pause, he climbed through the weathered plank fences of paddocks that separated calves from the Englers' bull. He passed around the tall metal bins, his nostrils recoiling from the scent of compost, which Fred spread as fertilizer in the spring. Only the larger dairies had implemented the more modern stacks for processing manure without quite the stench. In effect, Jade's senses reeled with the overpowering odor until he rounded the furthest end of the barn. Passing through the main corral, he drew images of cows milling in the evening light with bladders filled, and he heard them bawling as if over a great distance.

Halted in the patch of stomped earth rutted and mulched with hundreds of hooves, Jade stood staring at the wide Dutch door. The top panel stood open, latched with a long, rusted eyehook to the outer wall; the bottom door remained closed and locked with a simple rusted iron bar. Swaying slightly against the overlapping image of the door cast in morning and evening light, Jade shivered and started backing away. Like a vision from hell, a red-orange stream lighted the interior.

Shaking his head against the pulse, he turned, scanning the hillside, watching the brilliant morning light transitioning to an ominous orange glow. The blue sky darkened. Vivid shades of salmon and yellow, deep pink and purple highlights swirled and smeared against a cloud on the horizon. Reeling, Jade scanned the panoramic sundown, and his focus trailed toward the adjoining hillside where the herd of Guernsey ambled lazily into a procession. Defined paths led off the steeper hills. One trail cut a clear trench from a dense patch of woods to the ravine below.

He felt her rather than saw her, knew from which way she'd come. Within the ether, he suffered the sway as the first arriving cows brushed against him, touching him, passing through him. Weightless, he lingered in a vapor, grasping a need to speak with the urgency prickling the nape of his neck until the words formed.

"Through the woods . . . she came through those woods," he announced in a hollow tone. His gaze followed her abstracted path, feeling her advance as certainly as he recognized the cows against his physical essence. "C-came in with the cows," he said and shivered with her presence passing near him. "She—she was already inside . . . inside when Fred came . . ." He turned slowly, seeing a superimposed image of a human form within the swaying frame of the door. In broken flashes, he watched a calloused hand diving over the weathered boards, lifting the latch. Nearly transparent, another delicately-boned hand lifted the same latch. Something . . . he felt something wrong, saw something wrong. His brow furrowing, he reeled in the image of her hand reaching toward the latch . . .

"She let herself inside," he said absently, his gaze fixed. "Hands . . . ivory . . . something. Plastic. Latex . . . surgical gloves? . . . Heavy latex on her slender fingers," he said with a breath of relief. Nodding his verification, he continued forward, his footsteps leaden. "Inside. She's already inside . . . waiting. Counting," he said as he heard the silent chant in the back of his mind. *One-one hundred, two-one hundred* . . . "She's counting to herself . . . silent . . ."

But he suffered movement throughout his body. An incorporeal motion. "D-doing something," he strained as he watched his fingers lifting the bar, tugging the door. Shuddering, with as much dread as chill, Jade hesitated, clinging to the wood, holding himself afoot against the tidal wave of twisted emotions. Unconsciously, he lifted his hand and combed his chilled fingers through his hair as if he could scrape the crawlies from his roots. A nervous gesture . . . even in trance, his nerves rattled.

He felt it coming, sensed her moving, preparing with the anxious delight of a dancer preparing for her debut. "She's . . . she's planning . . . preparing . . .

"Excited," he said absently and forced himself to step into the shadowy barn. Minced hay and dirt coated the solid pad underfoot: the cement trenches overflowed with manure, discharging an overpowering scent. Swaying between light and darkness, Jade recognized the iron bars of headstalls and half fences spaced to accommodate three or four cows in a section. Only the heifers dwelt in this long span of cement. The sound of pigs routing drew his attention to another doorway. Dark. All was dark, but she'd come prepared. A thin stream of light slid across the cobwebbed walls, illuminating milk canisters, feed bins, bales of hay . . .

"She found it . . . found the pitchfork . . . been in here before . . .

damn," he heaved and reeled with the force of cold air against him. Stumbling a step, he groped blind and found purchase on warm cloth, a sturdy form. "God . . . the hatred pouring off—"

In lightning-quick flashes, images assailed him, halting his thoughts, and his breath. "Small," he heaved as visions raced into his mind. A child's panic raged through him. Thin-spiked prongs pierced the hay mounded around him. Quaking, he gasped a breath, covering his head and ducking, cowering from the jabs in the loose hay to hide him. At the slice of fire on his ankle, he swallowed a cry and froze as the pain seared his flesh and warm blood trickled over his foot, filling his thin canvas shoe.

"Nnnooo, Paaa," his voice released, changed, soft, whispered in terror.

Only at the edges of his mind, Jade knew himself cowering and clinging to a solid form, hearing his breath and the voice of a child issuing off his mustached lips. "Nooo," he cried softly and heaved a breath, stiffening.

His body manifesting yet again, firming, he chided, "Pappa found his little girl . . . Come out, come out, wherever you are—"

His body broke from the grip of terror. One hand clasped a shiny object; one massive hand gripped the handle of a short-bladed fork. "Time's up—" Jade said and slashed the invisible prongs into the hay.

Experiencing the man's anticipation and the little girl's terror, Jade trembled in a paradox.

"Time's up, lamb . . . papa played your game . . . now it's time . . . Oh God," Jade heaved. His hands flew, pressing the heels of his palms into his eyes as if he could mash the wicked flashes from his mind's eye. "Good God," he heaved in his natural voice, strained and aching. "What he's done to her. . . What he did . . ." Heart aching, mind reeling, he suffered the atrocities unfolding before him. A groan trailed off his lips. "Them . . . all of them . . . the boys . . . the girls." Inside, outside, he suffered the children's pain and terror, their humiliation and despair.

"Jade, who . . . who do you see?" a low voice intruded, drifting.

As if a wheel turned inside his skull, he heard the gentle rhythm, the humming. He recognized the notes of a lullaby, recalling the song though he'd never heard it sung, not to him. *Mom'ma had never sung to him, never promised him a mockingbird or a diamond ring* . . . but that was the song. The melody sent a shiver through him. No lyrics. Not yet. But he would hear the soft fluting sounds, the words, and on another plane, he moaned in protest. He wanted not to hear this song, wanted not to be in this place . . . but he was here, now. A spectator.

A noxious blend of smells assaulted his nostrils, waking him more to the world around him. Bitter, tangy odors of cow manure mixed with sweeter tastes of hay and wheat, corn and molasses . . . he was here now. The Englers' barn.

"Nnnooo," he moaned, but the sound was lost, filtering away from him, flowing into a tunnel where all sound became distant. Distant . . . another voice called from far away, calling to him, talking to him . . . Jade. The monster . . . the child.

Far more clearly, the soft rolling syllables and gentle rhythm flowed. In a paradox, the dread and black rage built inside of him, and he felt dirty. Small and dirty. A rancid scent of human sweat crept beneath the sweet odors of hay and molasses. Child's sweat and fear . . . fear carried a scent.

At the sight of a hulking figure moving deliberately through the shadows, Jade's muscles gripped. Himself, and not himself, he caught a glint of light reflecting from the intruder's hand, something in the calloused hand. The shadowed image glanced toward that shiny object . . . a pocket watch. The face glowed. Hatred and fear battled inside of him. His muscles coiling, tensing, he was distracted by an unnatural shift of cloth or a footfall and peered through shadows, searching. Not alone here. Another spectator huddled in the shadows not far away . . .

'*A game* . . . papa wants to play the game,' the odd words twittered in his mind. A near giggle slipped off his lips, worrying and frightening him. Paradox.

"Goddamn it, quit your singing and come help me milk these damn cows," a deep angry voice called from a distance away.

No! He wanted out of here! Away from here! This was the wicked place! The place he'd been before, although no clear memory surfaced . . . and the soft humming notes of yet another lullaby slipped off his lips. His senses swam with a weird delight; images of children's faces swirled around and around on a carousel, and one of those faces lingered nearby . . . one cast in shadows, worried and waiting. Watching.

"Git your ass out here and help with the chores!" the raspy, angry voice demanded.

His hand gripped around a stout, age-worn spindle, its shape reflective of the top of an hourglass. An hourglass. Time. Almost time. A gnarled smile crept over his lips. Cold and clammy, his hand gripped the crossbar handle. His focus slid down the shaft to the four flat prongs jabbing the filthy cement. Hazy white, his bare feet poised to propel him from the shadows.

Grumbling, the farmer stepped from the final stall, cursing, and mumbling as if to override the soft fluting melody of yet another song. Lugging the last two canisters, dirty coveralls sagging off drooping shoulders, Fred Engler ambled through the dull light. Relieved of their burden, content, the cows munched and clattered their iron stanchions. Tails swished, swatting away gnats swarming from the trench at their hind legs.

Skin crawling, insides trembling, Jade listened to the clatter inside the milk house in its separate barn. Clearly, he recalled those silver cuffs dangling from chords attached to the heavy canister, but the memories ignited, blazing from the fires of hell. Twisted memories flashed of those industrial-sized suction cups affixed and tugging on delicate skin, and the melody seethed louder off his lips. The whisper-hiss haunted the very edges of the barn and stirred the hounds to bray outside in their pens.

Silence.

As Fred ambled from the milk house, the melody silenced but he'd heard that wicked serenade.

"I don't like the damned game you're playing, gal," the man growled as he strode down the aisle toward the small man door, toward the moonlight. To himself, he grumbled, "Still playing damned kids' games. Ain't no wonder you can't land no husband . . . damn fool—"

Sprung from a catapult, he lunged from the shadows as if propelled. Four wicked prongs cut a deadly path in front of him. With the speed and precision of an arrow shot from a bow, he directed the prongs ahead, advancing on the ambling figure with a mere whisper of sound. A raging thrust sank the prongs through the worn denim cloth at the base of the stiffening spine. A short, gasped cry . . .

Confusion and pain blasted through his mind as his knees buckled; his arms flailed as something tugged at his back. He lost his balance and flung himself back to regain his footing. His legs! His back! Something struck his back! Toppling backward, he landed. His breath expelled on a short cry; his head thudded, slamming the cement with vicious pain.

Blinking, heaving, his arms flailed for purchase to pull himself over, but his attention caught and froze. His mind rejected the sight of the naked form standing directly above him. Squinting, flinching, he saw a mound of light-colored fur and small perky breasts. His mind swirling with confusion and shock, he found the thin sliver of a smile on a smooth, moon face floating above him. Narrow shiny eyes crinkled in laughter. "Jesus . . . Jesus . . . what—"

His focus froze on the descending prongs; his vision magnified the glistening bloody tips. Riveted, he stared, started a denial, meant to fling his arms over his face . . . too late. The prongs drove under his chin, sinking into the larynx with surgical precision. Only a gurgle of sound escaped with his horror as he groped to cover his throat . . .

"Ring around the rosy . . . pocket full of posies . . . ashes, ashes, we all fall down . . ."

CHAPTER 34

After the third or fourth glance at her watch and at least that many glimpses at the Regulator on the wall in Jade's apartment, Ronnie reached only one conclusion. She couldn't afford to sit around and wait for Jade and Tim to return, not when every time she thought of Jade, she suffered an unnatural tension as if she needed to fear for his life. Irrational, she knew, but she couldn't shake the feeling, conceivably, a latent paranoia brought on by Jarvins' attempt to frame him for murder.

She still needed to decide how to address that situation. Regardless of Mark's motives, his conviction, he'd coerced a false statement from Farnsworth and secured a federal search warrant based on that premise. Inevitably, Jarvins had covered his tail, and in the end, any official action would come down to his word against the word of a man who'd confessed to murder. Whether Farnsworth was eventually proven innocent or whether he went to trial for murder, his word would be suspect, and his credibility destroyed.

Her thoughts muddled, bouncing between a paranoid concern for Jade and details which careened from the dark corners of her mind, Ronnie placed the first call to the Bentwood precinct only to learn that Chief Hayward wasn't in his office. The dispatcher in Bender Falls offered to patch her through to his radio, but Ronnie declined, opting to leave a message and Jade's number. With her second call, she learned that Rev. Phearson could be found officiating over a youth group booth at the fair.

Her decision made, Ronnie jotted a note to Jade, leaving it on the edge of his desk, collected her purse, and navigated the murky hall.

Stepping from the side entrance, Ronnie heard the funneled sounds of carnival music and words echoing from loudspeakers across town. Recalling the evening past, the simple pleasure of sharing a snow cone and listening to another fine barbershop quartet while enveloped in Jade's arms, she felt a smile quivering on her lips. Despite the tension in the atmosphere, the estranged glances, and the indiscreet whispers, she'd felt safe within his embrace.

Ted Grimes had never shared a byline in his life, not even when he'd written his first article for Bender Falls Extra, his junior high school paper. This wouldn't be the exception no matter what he'd promised Emily Landslow. This was his story. The story he'd been born to write, the one big story that would put his name up there in bold print with all the other greats. As much as a month ago, he'd known this was his shot at the big time . . . then that bitch had showed up.

He'd known the moment she'd horned in on his interview with the Farnsworth kid, she wasn't some highfalutin bitch from social services. At first glance, he'd believed she was another Fed, or some other official broad brought in by the county or state, someone new from the DA's office or affiliated with the coroner's office. The bitch had that look about her, the look of a professional, aloof and confident. The kind of all-business broad who'd put career before family and probably snip a guy off at the balls for suggesting a roll in the sack. Frigid. That had been Ted's first take, and he hated broads like that. Reminded him of his first wife, ole Eileen Timbel-Grimes. The bitch had walked out on him nearly ten years ago, taking damn near every last cent along with his kids.

A career woman, now, he seethed. The bitch had left him to go back to school, of all the half-assed things. His salary with the paper wasn't enough for her while she was living with him, but she sure got along alright on his salary when she packed up and took off.

This bitch, Veronica Bryson, reminded him of the last time he'd seen Eileen, her with her tailored suit and high heels clipping along the sidewalk outside Gateway Center in downtown Pittsburgh. The bitch worked for some big law firm, a legal-friggin-secretary taking night courses toward a friggin law degree.

The same friggin law firm that Isaac Bently had used to pull off his scam in Bentwood. Ted needed only to think of Eileen's soft sniggering laugh when he'd asked her to heist details from Bently's files, to consider the pleasure he'd take in adding the final lines of his Pulitzer Prize-winning article.

First the article, then the book. Eileen would rue the day she walked out on ole Ted Grimes. No doubt about it. By the time this was done, he'd be rolling in dough, and his face would be plastered over every worthy magazine and TV station in America . . . maybe even Europe.

When this was all said and done, a whole lot of people would rue the day they messed with Ted Grimes, not the least of whom would be that bitch with her expensive friggin lawyers who'd made the whole thing possible. Maybe he'd send her a thank you *note—anonymous naturally—when this was all over. Of course, if all went well, he'd be addressing her correspondence to a penal facility. He wasn't sure what the max number of years was for aiding and abetting a murderer, but he doubted the bitch would get off too easy even with her connections in DC.*

The hand radio squawked on the car seat beside him, drawing Ted from his pleasant reverie. Lifting the radio as the whispery, whiny voice squeaked, "Scoop One. You read me? Scoop Two, over."

Christ, she sounded stupid! He sneered as he spoke into the radio, "Yea, go ahead."

"She's coming out the side door. Want me to approach? Over?"

"Lock the microphone on and keep it with you."

"Roger, Scoop One."

He hated even pretending he'd share his byline with this half-wit, but the circumstances called for extreme measures. If Bryson's friggin attorneys found out he was even this close to her, he could end up behind friggin bars. Better safe than sorry. Lifting the radio to his ear, he propped his elbow on the open window.

Tucked behind hedges, parked far enough to the rear of the empty house that carried a for-sale *sign on the overgrown front lawn, Ted listened to the mechanical sounds.*

He'd offered Emily just enough inside scoop to start her frigid heart pumping, and considering her preordained disposition toward Bryson, the one he'd fostered, winning Emily over to his cause had been a breeze. Considering the biological and social differences between the two women, Ted couldn't help but smile again. He almost felt sorry for his newfound ally. Bryson was everything ole Emily could never be, from young, beautiful, and talented to intelligent.

If nothing else, this encounter should be entertaining.

Barely, Ronnie started up the sidewalk toward Maine when she spotted the woman stepping from the car across the street. In an instant, she recognized the coppery hair, the jutting chin and noted the dark glasses that failed to mask her identity. In a conservative beige skirt, short-heeled pumps, and a dull-colored blouse, she'd again dressed to appear secretarial. Without more than a heartbeat pause, Ronnie continued toward the corner, already dreading when she heard the woman call.

"Miss Bryson!"

Weighing her rudeness, Ronnie paused and turned to watch the woman advance briskly. Undoubtedly, Landslow carried her recorder inside the purse cleaved to her hip, but she had enough good sense not to hold a notebook in plain sight.

"I'd like a word with you," Emily huffed as if the need to hurry offended her tremendously. "If you could just spare a few moments."

"I'm rather pressed at the moment," Ronnie said simply. "If you'll excuse me."

"I know we got off on the wrong foot," Emily said crisply. "I'd like an opportunity to make amends. From one reporter to another . . . I won't take up much of your time."

"From one reporter to another, Miss Landslow, I have absolutely nothing to discuss with you," Ronnie said with an equally crisp note. "And you may quote me, dear," she added with a slight smile. "Now, if you'll excuse me?" She spoke while turning and glimpsed the face at the corner, the mop of golden hair, and a spot of chrome on a bicycle wheel. In the next instant, the claw-like fingers clasped her arm, and Ronnie pivoted by reflex, leveling a cool direct glare on the black glasses in time to see the thin lips part in a start. "I don't know who exactly you believe you are, Miss Landslow, but I suggest you keep your hands to yourself."

"I need to ask you a few questions!" the woman said sharply.

"I'll give you some advice instead," Ronnie said without raising her tone. "Learn how to approach a prospective interviewee with an open mind and genuine empathy, Miss Landslow, and failing that, get a personality transplant. Your tactics are crude, rude, and insufferably annoying. Now, excuse me," she finished and saw the cheeks tighten beneath the black rims before she turned and continued toward the corner. Wade . . . the boy's name was Wade, and at the moment, he rested straddling his bike, glancing between her and the woman in her wake.

"You won't get away with this, bitch!" the woman hissed softly. "Sooner or later, this whole town's going to know you set up Cal Farnsworth. They're going to know you're only using Bently to get a story! He's the killer isn't he, Bryson? And you know it! You and that agent lover of yours, you know he's guilty so you're undercover! I know all about you!" She spoke while dogging Ronnie's heels. "I know you're working for the Federal Bureau! I know all about you and Agent Mark Jarvins! I know you worked with him before on a *stalker* case in Chicago! If you don't stop and talk to me, I'll blow your cover! I'll tell this town all about you! I'll tell them how you and the Agency have been after Laquette for years! You know he's a killer! He killed his own mother when he was *ten* years old! You've probably been tracking him for years! You know he's insane!"

Recognizing the fury growing in the light brown eyes leveled past her, Ronnie recovered her ebbing control and turned slowly, meeting the black-masked eyes. "I've warned you once about fabricating details to support your outlandish accusations, Miss Landslow. I will not tell you again. Should you even try to print this defamation of my fiancé's character, I will see that you and, whatever unscrupulous editor considers printing that garbage, both face a personal civil suit. Not to mention a suit against the publishers—"

"If you think you can scare me off with a threat—"

"This is no threat, I assure you, miss. This is a promise. I will have my attorney contact you." Not awaiting another comment, Ronnie turned and continued to the corner, tempted to smile at the boy studying the woman with a scowl. "Hello, Wade."

"Hi ya," he said offhandedly, still watching the woman in her wake, his brown eyes narrow with anger.

"I don't frighten easily, Miss Bryson—"

"Why doncha get lost, ya lyin' old bitch," the boy sneered.

Startled, Ronnie stifled a smile and glanced over her shoulder to see the black glasses level on the boy.

"You need your mouth washed out with soap, young man!"

"You need a facelift, ya ole bag," Wade snapped.

"Wade," Ronnie said as she reached him, winking to defuse his temper. "That's not very polite or in good taste. People—elder-adult-women in particular—do detest having their faults pointed out to them." She reached and scuffed his tousled golden hair, barely glancing at the flow of pedestrian and vehicle traffic on Maine.

"Well, she shouldn't be telling lies about Mr. Bently," the boy said defensively, scowling at Landslow as he continued, "And if you keep it up, lady, I'm gonna go find Mr. Cyrus Trascar. Remember him, ya ole bag? He made the front page for taking a shotgun after you and your kind. We don't mess 'round with reporters in Bentwood! We just shoot 'em and be done with it. Saves us a lot of lawyer fees."

"What is your *name,* young man!" the woman snapped.

Smiling, Wade started to answer.

Ronnie cut him off, pivoting on the woman. "That's none of your business, Miss Landslow—"

"Grant," Wade sniped. "Wade Grant, lady. You be sure and spell it right, too, so my uncle, Sheriff Grant, knows 'xactly who you're writing about."

God, this youngster must've been taking lessons from his apparent hero. Stifling her smile, Ronnie glimpsed the woman's flushed cheeks before she spun away, snorting an unladylike sound. Shaking her head, Ronnie eyed the boy, who grinned up at her with a glint of laughter in his eyes.

Only when Landslow was far enough away, Wade leaned and whispered discreetly. "That lady's a viper."

"A viper with a pen, dear," Ronnie mused. "That's the worst kind."

"Boy, that's the truth," he said with a humph of disgust in his wizened young voice.

Appreciating the boy's resilience as well as his emulation of the man she loved, Ronnie smiled. "I believe I owe you one, honey," she said and started to thank him only until she noted the troubled line across his brow. "What's wrong, hon?"

He looked over his shoulder toward the shop windows, then lifted his gaze to her. The laughter had vanished from his eyes; his face sobered as he asked, "Is Mr. Bently really closing up his shop for good?"

With the desperate hope in the boy's eyes, she decided to be entirely honest. "I'm not sure, hon."

He nodded distractedly, his gaze listing down the walk past the diner, returning, disheartened. "I don' even know what ta call him, now, Miss Bryson," he said glumly. "Everybody's saying how his name ain't even Bently. How he'd his name changed and stuff. How he's probably gonna move away, now. I mean since he's uh . . . getting married."

"I don't think he'd mind if you continue to call him Mr. Bently, Wade. Legally, that is his name."

Wade studied her with a suddenly more critical gaze. "What that lady said, it ain't true, is it? You're not just saying you're gonna marry him to get him in trouble, are you?"

"No, Wade, that I can assure you, is not true," she said with a soft smile. "I happen to be very much in love with him, and I have no intention of ever hurting him."

With the intense perception that only a child can manage, he judged her words, then smiled slowly. "I'm glad," he said then. "Yesterday, when I saw yous at the fair . . . I saw him look so happy before, ya know? I was gonna come say 'hey,' but," he shrugged. "Just seemed like you and him was getting along fine, and I didn't wanna seem like a pest. My mom says I ain't supposed to bug him, 'n stuff. 'Specially since, now, he's getting married . . . I just come by to see if maybe he was gonna open today, but I guess he ain't, huh?"

Ronnie stood in a position to scan the images of fine glass and furniture haunting the shadows behind the glass. Maybe the best way to squelch a lot of the rumors and ill-will in town might be staring her in the face. Glancing down the sidewalk, again noting the increase of pedestrian and car traffic, sizing up the crowds which would eventually pass his shop en route to the fair, she looked down at Wade. "You've helped Mr. Bently in his shop before, haven't you?"

"Yes, ma'am," he said gravely. "I never wrote up any sales tickets or took anybody's money, but I helped folks out and stuff behind the counters. Mrs. Connelly was even showing me the ropes."

Her discussion with the Rev. Phearson could wait, and she might as well wait for Chief Hayward to return her call. "I don't know a great deal about running an antique shop. Do you think we might give Mrs. Connelly a call and have her come to show us both the ropes?"

His eyes brightened with excitement. "Bet she'd be happy to!"

Jade might never leave her alone again with his keys, Ronnie mused as she began fishing the wad from her purse while moving toward the door. Clattering his bike against the brick, Wade hurried to her side.

Studying the lock as well as the alarm system to which she held the separate key, Ronnie suffered a second thought. Blast it anyhow, the man had a life in this town, an image to uphold at least until they decided on a definite direction. If opening his shop could restore a little goodwill and faith, then by God, she'd open his shop. If he pitched a fit, which seemed highly unlikely, she'd just face the music

Holding her breath, counting, she turned the locks and pushed the door inward. Her hands trembling, she fumbled the alarm key into the panel to defuse the system before the allotted fifteen seconds passed. In the nick of time, she keyed in the code and breathed a sigh of relief as the red light turned green.

Flashing Wade a smile, she commented, "Appears we're in, hon." Moving aside, she spotted a few scraps of mail scattered on the floor inside the door and stooped, collecting those as Wade joined her. Impulsively, she decided, "I think we better keep the door locked until we find all the lights, and we call Mrs. Connelly for direction. What do you think?"

"Think mebbe that's a good idea," Wade said gravely, clearly suffering second thoughts. "Think Mr. Bently's gonna mind we're opening?"

A little nervously, she smiled and flipped the deadbolt. "I certainly hope not."

"Think we better call Mrs. Connelly," Wade decided with more conviction.

Finding the light switches on the inside wall, Ronnie ignited those before heading toward the back of the store, glancing over the mail she'd lifted. A few pieces hadn't been delivered via US Post. In fact, one was no more than a sheet of folded notebook paper with 'Jade Laquette' scrolled on the front.

Flashing a thought of how he'd invaded her privacy and read her messages a week earlier, she unfolded the tablet paper and halted in her tracks. A photograph? Riveted, she studied the photo of her and Jade sitting beneath the oaks in the park with the Fireman's booth in the background. In bright red magic marker, a circle ringed Jade's walnut waves, and in equally bright red marker, a bold X crisscrossed her face. A shiver skittered down her spine; Ronnie held the paper against a tremor. An instant camera. The shot had been taken from a distance by a Polaroid camera, and recalling their position, she calculated the angle to pinpoint the area near the gazebo where Jade's admirer had stood.

"Miss Bryson?" Wade asked while sidling next to her. His brown eyes flashed curiously off her to the jittery paper.

Jolted from her thought, she took care to avoid either dropping the photo from the fold or adding any more fingerprints to the paper. The need to contact Chief Hayward, and Len, had just increased tenfold. Whether this was a prank or a serious threat, she couldn't afford to take it lightly.

Continuing to the back of the store, suddenly chilly beneath the cloying heat in the shop, she laid the folded paper and photo on the counter and fumbled with the keys to unlock the office door. Over her shoulder, she told Wade, "Don't touch anything yet, hon. I need to make a phone call, then we'll call Mrs. Connelly."

The office had been straightened but by no means organized. Stacks of papers and folders cluttered every available space, including the chair. Carefully, Ronnie waded through the mess and found the telephone. After attempting Devinio's base number, which should lead directly to the precinct, as well as the Inn, she dialed the direct line to the police dispatcher. Without hesitation, she accepted the offer to patch her through to Hayward.

In moments, the familiar voice commented, "Hayward, here. Go ahead."

"Chief Hayward, Veronica Bryson," she said simply. "Would it be possible for you to come to Olden Time? I need to speak to you at your earliest convenience."

Hayward was quick, needing only a second to decide. "I can be there in a few minutes."

"Thank you," she said and glimpsed Wade watching her from the doorway as she replaced the receiver. "We may need to postpone opening for a few minutes, hon," she said quietly.

Not slow by any means, the boy glanced toward the counter. "You okay?"

"Fine, hon," she said smoothly. "How about waiting up front for Chief Hayward? Don't let anyone else in other than him, all right?"

"Sure thing," the boy said and turned, hurrying just a little.

Finding a Rolodex in the clutter, Ronnie flipped only as far as the C's and found an Elaine Connelly listed. As she dialed the number, she contemplated how best to word this call, not entirely positive who this woman was or what help she could hope to be. At the hesitant voice offering a formal leery "hello," Ronnie plunged, "Elaine Connelly?"

"Yes? Who's 'is?"

"We've not formally met, Elaine—" And introducing herself as Ronnie Bryson might not be such a good idea. "This is Jade's . . . Isaac's fiancée, Veronica Bryson," she said smoothly. "Would it be possible for you to come to work this morning? We're opening the shop, and I'm afraid I haven't the foggiest idea what I'm doing. Wade suggested you might be willing to lend us a hand."

"Mr. Bently's opening the store?" she asked, dubiously

"Technically, no," Ronnie said honestly. "Wade and I are trying to open. Mr. . . . Bently's running an errand this morning. He left me the keys."

She hesitated long enough for Ronnie to believe she'd hung up, then almost worriedly, Connelly decided, "I can be there in about ten minutes."

"That would be wonderful," Ronnie said with genuine relief. "Thank you immensely."

Between hanging up and awaiting Chief Hayward's arrival, Ronnie returned to the counter, using a pen to flip through the remaining mail. Uncomfortably, she noted nearly half the correspondence was addressed to "Jade Laquette" . . . one of which caught her eye if only by the red and blue striped border and the number of stamps and postmarks designating France as the country of origin. Without fully considering her actions, she slipped the letter into her purse and continued her perusal, finding two other unmarked messages.

One carried a simple, 'Congratulations and Good Luck;' however, the other wasn't so kind. 'You can't reelly be dum nuff to merry that slut.'

Certainly calling the kettle black, Ronnie mused as she read the misspelled words and judged the sloppy handwriting. If not for the connotation, she might consider this note from a child.

Returning her attention to the photo, she nudged the folded paper open with the tip of her pen and glimpsed the red marking on the page. Sliding the photo aside, she stared at the words written in poetic verse:

Roses are red.

Violets are blue.

Get rid of this bitch!

Or we'll do it for you.

"Here comes the chief!" Wade called from the front of the store, successfully breaking her trance.

Chief Hayward wore his full regalia from his hat pulled regulation-low in military precision to the .38 Glock holstered on his hip. He sidestepped through the door, his gaze darting past Wade and honing in on Ronnie. Passing the boy a few words, he set a brisk pace down the center aisle. Glimpsing at Wade trailing Hayward, Ronnie raised her voice to tell him, "Miss Connelly should be coming soon, hon. Could you watch for her and let her in?"

"Sure thing," Wade said and reversed course.

Already scanning the clutter on the counter, Hayward commented, "You sounded a bit anxious, miss."

"I am a little anxious, chief," she admitted smoothly and lifted the pen, turning and flipping the ominous page, drawing his attention. "Someone was kind enough to leave this in the door with the mail. I made the mistake of opening it without taking precautions, so you'll find my prints on the corners, but I didn't touch the photo."

Hayward studied the photo, then used his pen to slide it aside and looked at the printed message. Nothing showed in his firm jaw or steady eyes. Enlisting her method, he turned the other notes and read those as well.

"There's something else," she started and enlightened him of Mrs. Handler's observation. By no surprise, Hayward tried to alleviate her concern by the same method Hazel had implemented, mentioning Jade's past encounters.

"Hazel first noted this person back there the Sunday before last, chief," Ronnie said directly, dismissing a need for solace. "I'd imagine there's a connection, and to be perfectly honest, whether Jade and I have become a fixation to a jealous female, or we have somehow become the obsession of a psychopath, I'd feel much safer if you'd speak to Mrs. Handler. She said the ground's as soft as powder back there. Perhaps, you could take photos or lift footprints."

"I didn't mean to imply I wouldn't take this seriously, miss," Hayward said quietly, his gaze conveying his sobriety. "You can be sure, I intend to call over our lab boys from the county and these," Hayward said as he skimmed his glance over the messages. "I'll send it off to the lab for analysis. In the meantime," he said as he caught her eye. "I think it'd be a good idea if you stick around close to home here, and I wouldn't advise going off by yourself." He paused a moment before asking, "Where'd you say Isaac is this morning?"

"He didn't say where he and Tim were going," she said. "I'd imagine they'll be back soon though."

Locked into the madness of a psychopath, Jade clung to the fringes of his sanity, a silent witness to a macabre play. Torn between the sensations of terror flowing off the man writhing in the dirt and the twisted euphoria of a child living out a wicked fantasy of revenge, he heaved and sobbed. Song lyrics and nursery rhymes spilled off his mustached lips in fits and starts; his breath broke into giggles and childish taunts as the bloodied figure twisted, trying to crawl away. No escape, not for the dying man, or Jade, as wicked scenes played in vivid detail, seconds and minutes becoming hours as the naked form danced and skipped around its prey.

"Round and—round the—mulberry bush—the monkey chased the—weasel . . . Pop!!!" The prongs descended with unmerciful speed and strength, convulsing him to kick and spasm in the dirt. "—goes the—weasel . . ."

Only at the edges of his mind, Jade heard the deep anxious voices calling to him, felt the hands trying to hold him, shake him. With the precision of an adult, the methodical rhythm of a surgeon, the maniac doled out her torture. Periodically, she paused to spy the watch that she'd lifted off Engler at the onset.

The last moment, he sensed the last moment coming, suffered Engler's last gurgling breaths and spasms. The maniac paused and leaned on the short-bladed fork, watching with ghoulish pleasure, laughing low and soft. Only now, only as the man lay breathing his last, this maniac's blood pumped with euphoria and triumph. Knowing, seeing what she'd done, she was elated in the victory of destroying this thing she considered a monster. Believing in her twisted mind, she'd wrought justice upon a fiend . . .

"All better now, Fred," she said. "You're better off dead."

Laying the pocket watch, open-faced, in the gore, she drove a single prong into the glass sphere, shattering the face as easily as she'd shattered Engler. Stooping, she collected the watch, ignoring the blood as she snapped the gold case shut and rose. Looking once more at the jittery carcass, she spoke as she drove the pitchfork down, "Tiiime's uppp!"

In a convulsive heave and spasm, a gurgled cry strangled in Jade's throat; bile and blood wedged momentarily, choking him before blasting from his own depths. Coughing, gagging, he struggled blindly against the hands. Panic echoed in the low voices around him. Anxious hands tried to hold him . . . but he felt her, still.

Pure madness poured through her mind as she stood naked, reveling in the gruesome image, breathing the death smells mixed with biting scents of cow dung. Madness, pure madness rose in triumph and pleasure, issuing off her lips in a laugh as she turned from the corpse and strolled leisurely along the runway.

"Game's over, girls," *she consoled the nervous heifers as she passed*. "He won't ever put his filthy hands on your teats again . . ."

In the milkhouse, she stripped off the gloves, wadding them inside out. Meticulously, she collected her clothes and dressed. Her rage festered, ascending as she lifted one of the milking nozzles from a ledge, tucking it into her jeans pocket. Methodically, she donned another pair of surgical gloves, then let herself out the same way she'd entered.

In mind and body, Jade followed her through the Dutch doors. His footsteps faltered, and he staggered a dozen paces. Darkness and brilliant light swirled inside his mind; tastes of blood and scents of bile wrenched his system. On hands and knees, he landed heaving and lurching. Senses reeling, he collapsed sideways, caught and steadied on his hip. Anxious words filtered in broken quips within his spinning mind.

Absently, Jade dragged a hand to wipe his mouth, wanting the bitter taste gone.

Swaying, he glimpsed at the bleary red streaks on his flesh, his system suffering a shudder within shudders, his breath catching.

"That's it, Devinio . . . a few more seconds and I'm taking him out of here . . . Christ a'mighty, he needs a hospital!"

Shaking his hanging head, blinking tears and spots from his eyes, Jade focused on his hand dropping heavily to dangle off his shin, his numb fingers brushing the blackened dirt. Sounds . . . natural sounds began to filter over the nocturnal sounds of restless cows and yapping dogs. Sunlight squeezed out the shade lingering in his mind and vision. Night chills clung to him; night air and silver moonlight lingered inside of him, shivering him.

"Sax . . .? Come on, pal, say something. Tell me you know me . . . you know you. Christ, say *something*!"

"Some . . . thing," he strained softly.

"Terrific . . . you fucking take ten years off my life, and now you want to be a smartass," Spencer growled.

"So-sor-ry," he heaved and leaned more heavily against the solid form. His head sank against the muscled chest. His muscle control waned. "Ha-ave to rest a-a minute . . . few minutes."

"Ahh, shit! He's passing out!"

Jade tried shaking his head, tried lifting from the slouch, but the exhaustion poured more leaden through his veins. "Ressst," he struggled weakly. "Few . . . minutes. Shoul-ld ha-ave re-membered . . . sooo tired, now."

"Would it help if we get you out of here?" Devinio asked. "You want us to carry you out of here?"

With the sunlight pouring over him, the heat only beginning to penetrate the night chill, he managed to shake his head a notch. "Here . . . rest here . . . warm."

"I have a blanket up in my truck, Len. If you wanted to—"

"No blanket," Jade said and struggled with his lagging muscles to try sitting up. "Shiiit," he heaved softly with the futility. "Minutes . . . few minutes."

"Think you could talk to me, Amico?" Devinio asked carefully. "Maybe tell me what—"

"Christ, man, you can see he's wiped out—"

"She . . . she's sooo sick," Jade heaved with a shiver, closing his stinging eyes against the sunlight. "Games . . . child's games . . . H-her father a-abused h-her . . . them . . . all of them . . . others . . . another . . . there's another . . . A-always in the b-barn . . . her . . . her brothers . . . hide 'n go seek . . . He . . . he always f-found them . . . they . . . Farnsworth . . . Engler . . . always . . ." His mind reeled in confusion, faces swaying back and forth, images flashing, confusing. *Two . . . two faces . . . two entities . . . two girls . . .?*

"Who, Jade?" Devinio asked. "Who is she?"

Fleeting, fleeting and flashing, the images assailed his mind's eye. Heartbeat quickening, his muscles tensed within seconds. "Ohhh Chriiist," he hissed as he struggled, clasping anxiously at Spencer's shirt. "Help. Me. Up!" he demanded.

"Who, damn it! Who is she?" Devinio asked even as he lent his hands to help.

"Far-r-r-nsworth!" Jade heaved. "Valllerie!"

CHAPTER 35

Only moments after Chief Hayward departed, Elaine Connelly arrived, and after a few uncomfortable moments, Ronnie convinced her they could open the shop without repercussions from the hierarchy. Without a doubt, Elaine neither trusted her, nor appreciated her presence, but with a little help from Wade, Ronnie gained at least a tentative détente.

Almost amused, Ronnie paid close attention as the woman adopted an attitude of authority, talking to her like a misfit child. Elaine had missed her calling. She should have been an elementary school teacher. Carefully, she'd demonstrated the salient details of writing sales slips, stapling adding-machine tape to the corners, and operating the antique cash register, which amounted to pressing the 'cash-tender' button and catching the drawer before it sprung out and bruised her hip.

Already quite a few customers had meandered into the store, probably more out of either curiosity or loyalty than a genuine interest in antiques. That possibility thwarted neither Elaine nor Wade, both of whom meandered into the showroom aisles to offer their first patrons a sales pitch. As Elaine had instructed, Ronnie dallied at the counter, listening to the various sales techniques and pleasantries exchanged in the store. With a modern symphony playing a tune with vague undertones of medieval instruments and melodies, she drew strange comfort in the atmosphere. For the first time, she understood why Jade had created this haven, why he'd become entirely comfortable in Bentwood.

With the first ring of the telephone blasting her from her reverie, she sidestepped and lifted the receiver. Adhering to Elaine's instruction, Ronnie adopted a pleasant voice to announce, "Olden Time Antiques and Collectables. Can I help you?"

Hesitation then, "Miss . . . Miss Bryson?"

Unconsciously, her fingers clenched. With an effort, Ronnie relaxed, relieved by the soft voice. "Yes?"

"I . . . I have to speak to you," the lyrical voice whispered anxiously. "It's really important . . . It's a-about my brother, Cal Farnsworth. Please, could you . . . could you meet me somewhere? Not in town. I don't want anybody to know

I'm talking to you, Miss Bryson, but if . . . if they find out I'm talking to you. You can't tell anybody, okay? Please, you have to help me. Cal . . . he didn't kill nobody . . . but I-I think I know wh-who did. Please, Miss Bryson. I don't know who else to talk to. You have to help me. I'm scared."

If this was Valerie Farnsworth, Ronnie could understand the girl's fear. "Where uh . . . where are you, hon?"

"I'm at home but . . . but I don't want you to come here. I don't want m-my Ma or — or Vic ta know I'm talking to you. They . . . they don't want me talking to nobody. But I got to. I-I can't just let Cal hang."

More likely he would get the electric chair, but Ronnie decided against correcting her. The young woman truly sounded frightened and desperate. "Alright, hon. Where would you like me to meet you?"

"There's . . . there's something I want to show you," she said hesitantly. "If you could . . . Do you have a car or something? Could you meet me out on Shaker Hollow Rd.?"

For lack of a notebook, Ronnie flipped over a sales receipt and found a pen. "I'll need directions, hon. Go ahead."

In anxious breaths, Valerie whispered the directions that led out of town, promising to meet Ronnie in ten minutes. "Please—please don't tell anybody where you're going, Miss Bryson. If they find out . . ."

'They' . . . the Heathen Band, Ronnie knew, sensing what Valerie Farnsworth meant to show her and tell her. "I won't tell anyone, hon—"

"Not even Mr. Bently, please. I'll explain everything, I promise . . . but you can't tell even him."

The young woman was paranoid with good reason. "I won't tell anyone," Ronnie promised and folded the sales receipt as she spotted Wade ambling toward the counter. Replacing the receiver, she glanced over the shop to spot Elaine's gray-streaked head between a highboy and brass hall tree, apparently engaged in a sale.

Looking at Wade, Ronnie decided, "I have to go out for a little while, honey. Do you think you and Elaine can hold down the fort, and when Mr. Bently comes, tell him, I shouldn't be long?"

"Think he's gonna be mad we opened?"

With a thought, she tore off the top layer of the receipt and jotted a quick note to release Elaine and Wade from responsibility, finishing, 'See you soon, brat. Love you, Veronica.' Folding and handing the paper to Wade, she smiled. "That should appease him until I get back." As an afterthought, she withdrew the note and added, 'PS: I borrowed your pickup. Love you.'

The man would never leave her alone again with his keys. Musing, she let herself out through the office, cutting across the hall and into the warehouse. Shifting her thoughts to more immediate concerns, namely, what she might learn from Valerie Farnsworth to release one brother and possibly incriminate the other, Ronnie breached Jade's security again and rescued the pickup from the corner.

Careful not to sideswipe Hazel’s bushes, Ronnie backed the pickup from the warehouse. Maybe they could open a street-side entrance to the warehouse if, on the outside chance, they decided to settle in Bentwood.

The sleepy little town had grown on her in a short time. A smile slipped onto her lips as she waved a greeting to Hazel while pulling out. She truly wouldn’t mind living here, although she might be more inclined toward one of the old stately homes with yards for gardens and children to grow.

First things first, she considered, pulling her thoughts together and again concentrating on the moments at hand. If anyone could help find the concrete evidence against Victor Jr, Valerie was that person. Whether or not the young woman would offer the evidence was yet to be determined.

“Ted!” *the voice screamed at him, jolting him from a doze. His head snapping and eyes darting, Ted collected his bearings. He’d been having such a wonderful dream. One of those snatches of dreams where he stood behind a raised podium, like a priest’s pulpit, and how fitting to see himself on an altar, an orator of old.* ‘I owe it all to Veronica Bryson, ’ *he’d been saying, and laughter had broken out, the crowd understanding his joke.*

“Ted! Scoop One! Are you there?!” *the anxious voice intruded again.*

Scowling, he suffered the reality of sweat gathered under his armpits. The sun had shifted; the car no longer remained in the shade of an overhanging oak. With the sunlight pouring through the windshield, he was going to cook while waiting for this dumb bitch to gain some headway. Grabbing the radio, and fumbling the button to send his voice, he growled, "I’m here. Go ‘head.”

“She’s leaving! She’s in that pickup! The one I saw—”

“Where’s she—” *Damn it, the problem with using these stupid two-ways was that he couldn’t press the button and talk over this half-wit until she released her button. He released his and caught the tail end of her sentence.*

“. . . coming your way.”

Almost at that moment, the shiny black pickup rolled past the mouth of the driveway, and a charge of adrenaline started him. He dropped the radio aside as Emily continued squawking like a windup parrot.

“Are you there? Are you there . . .?”

Grimes fumbled with his keys, coaxing the borrowed Dodge to life. His beat-up Fairlane wasn’t much more reliable than this one, which was just one more reason to despise the bitch and her murderous boyfriend. Bryson had waltzed into town in a spanking new rental, and him . . . Laquette had the friggin audacity to race around in his foreign sports cars as if he owned the friggin world.

Grant . . . good ole Sheriff Taylor Grant might get a sidebar in the article, especially after the crap that scruffy boy fed ole Emily. Nephew . . . yea, Grant would get a sidebar, and to hell with getting a confirmation from any reliable friggin source. It's a damn joke, Grant borrowing that sports car for his personal pleasure instead of impounding it the way he should. Once Ted finished with Grant, he wouldn't get elected as a head trash collector.

Keeping the nifty black pickup in sight, Grimes dropped back far enough to be inconspicuous, staying two blocks behind. He knew how to tail a prospective mark. He'd perfected the talent a few years back when digging up dirt on that black lawyer running for DA. So what if the black chick in the photos had turned out to be the guy's niece? She'd looked enough like a high-priced hooker to fit the bill, and by the time Ted had finished with him, that boy had needed to make himself pretty scarce around the courthouse.

'Unconfirmed sources.' *That was Ted's favorite line, and if, on occasion, the word was misprinted to read* 'confirmed' *what did it matter? Any reporter worth his salt knew he needed to climb out on a limb every once in a while and take a few liberties. Getting the story out—that was the name of the game. The public had a right to know.*

Taking a chance, Ted advanced an extra block, driving on a parallel street, coaxing the Dodge to race to the next block. He reached the stop sign in time to see the sleek black fenders cruise through the collateral intersection. Stomping the gas pedal, he sped to the next block, mentally calculating the road on which Bryson traveled. His instincts kicked into high gear, and excitement raced in his veins. She was meeting someone.

Probably, Laquette.

That name still struck a sore spot. Ted had known Bently was off. He had known a story existed behind that SOB. As much as five years ago, Ted had tried digging up dirt on that arrogant bastard. Nobody with the kind of cash he threw around would settle in a shit-hole town like Bentwood, not unless he had something to hide. The trail had dead-ended in New York, and before Ted had even written a word, Eileen had sicced her friggin bosses on him. She'd threatened everything but his life if he printed anything more than an advertisement for that friggin antique shop. Then her bastard bosses had jumped over his head and squelched his story with Jack Hague, his editor, and Dalcourt, the friggin owners of the paper. Not one blasted word had reached print to taint young Bently's pearly white image.

If not for that hotshot Pittsburgh reporter stealing his thunder, Ted might feel vindicated to have Hague and Dalcourt missing out on the glory. A damned TV reporter, no less. Another broad who probably used her body to cultivate her snitch in the friggin Federal Building. To hell with Hague and Dalcourt, too.

Not again, he wasn't taking any chances on having this story stolen by some lame-ass editor or that chicken-shit owner of the Bender Falls Trib. He wouldn't even mention that paper when he blew this story wide open. Laquette . . . matricide, political conspiracies, scams reaching into some of the most sensitive issues of recent history? *Christ, if he tried, maybe he could hit on Watergate and wind a few questions into that old can of worms. He could tie in Bryson and a few Federal Agents and a conspiracy angle to throw the whole friggin Federal Bureau into question.*

He needed just the right title for this story, something catchy, he considered while navigating turns to land on Shaker Hollow Rd. Ahead, rounding an S-curve, the truck's bumper reflected a flicker of sunlight.

'Sex, Murder and Government Conspiracy' . . . *Naaa, he needed something really jazzy.* 'Feds Conspire to Set Slayer Free' . . . 'Farmyard Slayer Stalks While Feds Twiddle Thumbs' . . . *Naaa, he needed something really* really *catchy, maybe something on the psychic shit angle and matricide.* 'Scam Artist or Matricide?' 'Psychic Slayer Kills Mother First . . .'

Shit, something would come to him.

Breaking from the hands that attempted to help and managed only to hinder, Jade staggered a few steps and lurched into a trot across the cow pen. Nearly blind with the throbbing pain at his temples, he groped and clamored clumsily through the wooden fence, tumbling and scrambling through the slots. Veronica! He needed to reach her! No other thought held more firmly in his reeling mind.

Spencer grabbed him, breaking him from another fall, propelling him afoot while demanding, "Valerie? Christ, Sax, are you sure?"

Not sure of anything, Jade tugged and staggered past the compost pile, his breath catching and choking as he heaved, "Have to *hurry*! Hurry!"

"What! Damn it! Slow down! What do you see?" Devinio snapped while clasping his arm, yanking him about and staggering all three of them. "What do you *see?*"

"Veronica!" he demanded as he tried shoving the hands away. "Have to—get to her!" Breaking the hold and pivoting toward the rails, his focus landed on the spindly image standing outside the fence. White-hot pain flashed through his skull; his hands flew to his head as he staggered backward.

"Good God!" Jade heaved as the hands caught and halted him again. Stopped, he struggled to keep his knees under him. His entire body vibrated with the force of pain lashing through his skull. Heaving breaths, he knew himself slipping away, heard the songs, children's voices inside his head . . .

"Sax!" Spencer demanded. "Ronnie! What about her!"

Veronica! As if the word carried magic to break through the whirlwind in his skull, Jade withdrew from the tunnel, firming. Control! For Veronica! To save her! To reach her! He needed to cling to his sanity! He needed to control what was inside of him! Had to take control! Use it! *Control it!* "Veronica!"

"That's it, pal, catch your breath," Spencer coached in a barely restrained tempo. "Veronica . . . what about Veronica? What do you see?"

"Ha-ave to reach her," he heaved softly, combing his tingling fingers through his hair. With an effort, he firmed his balance between the fierce grips.

"Where?" Devinio said. "Where is she?"

To the question, he drew a sudden blank, his mind wiped as clean as washed slate, black. "N-no," he uttered swinging his head, lifting his stricken gaze. Blackness. Inside his skull, he saw only blackness; in his watery vision, he identified mounded manure, fences, and fading sunlight. The anomaly held his focus. In dumfound, he watched the light withdrawing from the ground around him as if sucked into the clouds receding rapidly across the sky.

"No." *No*. This couldn't be happening. He couldn't be drawing only blackness, an unnatural blackness as if someone had drawn a curtain inside his head . . . or the lid had slammed shut even tighter than before. Unnatural. Something unnatural. He could feel it . . . could feel the invasion of something unnatural playing against him, intruding. "N-no."

"What, damn it! What *no*?" Devinio demanded.

Swaying mentally, if not physically, Jade shook his head; his nearly blind gaze landed on the tense face at his side. "I-I can't s-see her."

"What the hell does that mean?"

"Bla-ack . . . oh, God," he uttered as the revelation spilled through his reeling mind. "Black . . . magic . . . I can feel it." He could feel it as surely now as he'd felt it a dozen years ago within his father's villa. Even with the forces locked inside of him, he'd sensed the cold black power emanating from his father. He'd feared that chilly ambiance almost as fiercely as he'd feared the giant himself. A monster . . . he had seen Jardonet as a monster . . . a wicked monster who could cloak himself in darkness. A mystical monster who'd wielded power to throw a terrified child into eternal blackness. Even without his conscious grasp on his abilities, Jade had been forced into blackness by his father . . . a warlock.

'You have inside of you, the power to move mountains,' the man had hissed at him, outraged by his refusal to open his mind to the practices. *'But you—you wre'shed boy—you would rather be blind!'*

One, only one of many arguments which had filled those wicked years, but the echo of his father's angry hiss, the piercing glare of his emerald eyes . . . the blackness. With a word and a wave, his father had thrown Jade's mind into blackness, stealing even his natural sight for days and weeks at a time.

Even now, Jade couldn't be certain if his own power had battled those curses or if his father had granted him the slow advance of his natural sight only to torment him anew.

"Jardonet," he uttered, unconsciously continuing in French rather than English.

"Amico! English!" Devinio snapped. "I haven't taken French since high school! Speak English!"

Jolted by the words and the bruising grips wrenching his arms on either side, Jade shuddered from head to toe before fully firming on his feet. Still, he felt it, the forces of darkness pressing against his mind, shivering him from the inside out. And he suffered the pulse throbbing behind the black veil. "*Monnn Dieu* . . . I'm fucked," he uttered again as tears lifted over his eyes.

"Great, switch back to English and say something I really don't want to hear," Devinio snapped.

"You said, 'black magic,'" Spencer said in a calm, careful tone. "What's that mean exactly?"

"M-means I-I ha-ave enemies," he said with an effort to regain his balance, to collect a clear thought. "M-means I could end u-up losing m-my soul to s-save her."

"Maybe you better try that once more from the top," Spencer said more carefully. "What t'hell are you saying?"

Breaking one arm free, Jade dragged his arm over his bleary eyes and drew a calming breath. Finding Spencer's tense eyes, Jade realized, "My father found me again. I-I can't even explain this. I don't know how to explain it. But he's . . . he's here. His presence . . . I can feel it. His power's here . . . and I've never been able to break one of his fucking spells. He's blinded me again."

Even without his sixth sense, he read the doubt and concern in Spencer's shaded blue eyes. On his opposite side, Len Devinio studied him with equal speculation and skepticism.

Shaking his head, Jade cast a desperate gaze toward the fence, and again his attention landed on the spindly image of Erin Engler standing at the fence, watching them. Hawk-nosed and rail-thin, the woman could disappear if she turned sideways, but she rested, arms crossed on the top board, her eyes frosted with a black shine, her lips drawn in a straight tight line. The mind of a child . . . she possessed the mind of a child . . . and he knew abruptly, he'd heard her voice. He'd recognized her voice and sensed her whimpering inside the barn . . .

With the echoes of her presence, he knew Alice Engler hadn't found her husband.

Against the black curtain in his mind, he began walking toward Erin, his voice animating, "Ring around the rosy . . . pocket full of posies . . ."

She began backing away from the fence, her arms falling at her sides, eyes widening, head shaking.

"Ashes . . . ashes . . . we all . . . fall . . ." He reached the fence and climbed through, rising to her level as he snapped, "Down!"

She dropped, landing on her rump less than two steps away. Her mouth dropped open and her black eyes widened with shock.

Glaring down at her, pinning her with his gaze even as he heard the advance of footsteps from the side and others behind, Jade forced his voice calm and smooth, not betraying the turbulence in his mind. "You saw her, Erin. You saw what she did to your father. You watched her."

She shook her head in ragged jerks, her mouth gaping open.

"You and Valerie were friends," he continued in a low melody. "You played together . . . She was so much smaller than you, but she was your friend, and she listened to you . . . She always listened to you . . . and you wanted to hurt them, Erin, you wanted them hurt for what they did to her . . . and to you—"

"What the hell are you doing here!" the deep angry voice cut in sharply. "I want you people out of here—"

Jade lifted his gaze to Frank Engler. "You're next, Frank. You're next on their list."

"You're insane, Bently or Laquette, or whoever the hell you are. You're nuts, and I want you off my property. I want all of you—"

"Frank," Spencer stated. "I suggest you keep your mouth shut and listen to the man."

"Unless you'd like to be held for obstruction of justice," Devinio added smoothly.

"Erin," Jade stated and drew her stricken eyes from her older brother. "You have to tell the truth now, sweetheart," he said gently. "You saw Valerie inside the barn. You saw what she did to your pa. You always told her they were evil . . . evil men . . . fiends. You told Valerie years ago about how you got that scar on your leg. How your pa used the pitchfork to find you hiding in the hay. You told her how he hurt you when you were small like her. And you knew she was responsible for her father's death a month ago, just as you knew she'd come for your father on the night of the full moon. You watched her, Erin . . ."

"I dint . . . dint thin' she'd dooo it," Erin whined. "We jussst talllked 'bout it—"

"You saw her, Erin," Jade stated smoothly and watched the stringy brown hair bob slowly. "You watched her play the game you taught her to play. The game your pa played."

"Stop it!" Frank Engler demanded as he closed the distance, reaching to clasp Jade, to shove him. "I want you—"

The fingers barely touched him when Jade's hand shot out. His eyes flashed pure green fire as he jettisoned Frank backward, lifting and propelling him off his feet. Time slowed inside his mind. Frank's eyes widened as he sailed and descended, skidding on his haunches several feet away. Jade's hand tingled with a thousand needles dancing on the nerve endings from his fingertips to his wrist. Even as time sped up, his mind rejected the flow of energy racing in his veins.

Engler scrambled off the ground as Devinio rounded on him, blocking his second assault, warning, "Don't even think about it."

"If you people think you're going to accuse my sister of this—"

"Erin," Spencer said as he stooped down in front of the ashen-faced woman. "Did you see Valerie Farnsworth murder your father?"

Her wide eyes darting fearfully to Jade, she looked at Tim as she nodded, uttering, "Yessir."

Spencer looked at Devinio while pushing to his feet. "That's good enough for me, Len. I'm calling the station."

"You put this over your radio, Spencer, we'll have every nut in the county pulling out shotguns. Let's get these two on ice and in the car before we call it in," Devinio stated and pulled his gun from the holster under his jacket lapel, leveling the weapon at Engler. "On the ground, face down, hands behind your head."

"You can't arrest—"

Devinio cocked his gun. "You have three seconds," he stated, and Engler needed only two to decide against an argument. Cursing, Frank dropped and complied, sputtering something to the effect that he would sue for false arrest. Only after he clamped the cuffs at Engler's spine, Len remarked, "Consider yourself detained for questioning."

"Too long. No time for this," Jade said absently and caught Spencer's gaze as Tim lifted Erin Engler off the ground by her upper arm. "Too fucking *late!* We have to go . . . have to go. Now!"

CHAPTER 36

Following Valerie's directions, Ronnie navigated the back roads out of town while contemplating possible scenarios and her approach to this interview. First and foremost, she wouldn't make the same mistake with Valerie as she'd made with Cal. She'd let Valerie talk, but even if she were tempted to sympathize, she vowed to keep a cool detachment between herself and this young woman. After all, if Ronnie was right about the killer, Valerie could be as insecure and impressionable as her oldest brother.

Shaker Hollow Rd. was little more than a one-lane gravel lane tunneled into an overhang of tree bows and vines. The foliage clung close enough to the edge of the road for an occasional vine to scrape the pickup's flanks. Very little sunlight sprinkled through the branches eliminating the need for sunglasses. As Ronnie shoved her glasses headband-style into her hair, she glimpsed at the swatches of sky overhead, verifying that the sun had vanished behind clouds. Through her open driver's door window, a cool, fresh forest scent drew her attention, distracting her.

Perhaps, she and Jade should build a home like the Spencers' chateau. A log cabin lodge, free of neighbors and spectators. She could always buy a Doberman as she'd suggested to Donna.

A smile slipped onto her lips as she recalled the Spencer children's excitement over their new Irish Setter puppy. With the memory of Tim's mocked growl, Ronnie nearly laughed aloud.

'Damn dog's about as useless as tits on a bull for anything other than chewing shoes or eating furniture . . .'

Spotting the car bumper just ahead, Ronnie focused her attention in quick order and pulled into the dirt clearing alongside the battered old car. One way or another, she needed to gain this young woman's trust and assistance.

Like Cal's truck, Valerie's car carried battle scars from rusted patches on the fender to a layer of dust on oxidized blue paint, and its driver wasn't much better. Despite her mirror sunglasses, Valerie wore the haggard signs of grief and mourning, visible the instant her head popped above the roof. Thin and pale, her slender face dwarfed behind the natural adult-sized glasses lending her the appearance of a child playing dress-up.

Even with the shades, Ronnie recognized her and wracked her brain to remember if she'd seen a photo or if she merely recognized the girl's features through her brother. "Valerie?"

"Yes, ma'am," she said over the roof. Her soft voice barely carried the short distance. "We . . . we have to go the rest of the way in my car," she managed while turning her head in quick jerks, glancing about nervously as if she anticipated someone hiding in the woods, spying on them. "Please," she said and again leveled her gaze across the hood. "Hurry. It's not too far from here."

A prickle of doubt touched Ronnie's senses, but considering the risks she'd already taken, considering the possible benefits if this interview produced results, she threw caution to the wind. Collecting her purse, rolling up the window, and locking the truck, she stepped out, moving to the passenger door as the girl slid behind the wheel.

As Ronnie expected, the inside was as bad as the outside. A smell of burnt oil and baked vinyl trapped inside the heated car. The window crank was missing; a mere stub of stripped gears jutted from the hole in the door panel. Ditto on the door handle, Ronnie noted, before turning her attention to the gaunt young woman behind the wheel.

In a thin long-sleeve blouse and faded jeans frayed at the knees, her arms and legs remained hidden, nearly lost within the cloth. Anywhere else in the world, the style might be part of a teenage fashion statement. Ronnie doubted that could be the case here. In profile, Valerie bore an even more striking resemblance to her older brother with a straight, nearly pointed nose and thin cheeks. Strings of dull brown hair, cut in a stylish bob, barely touched her drawn shoulders. At one time, possibly before a month ago, Valerie might have been a very pretty young woman.

As the gears clanked from reverse to drive and the engine emitted an unusual clatter, Ronnie reviewed what she knew of Valerie Farnsworth, age 20. The yin to Victor's yang, she was allegedly a very bright young woman though an underachiever. She'd barely maintained the GPA to attend a secretarial school in Pittsburgh. Rather than commute, she lived in an apartment near the school, not too far from Victor, who'd probably helped her attain financial aid and been instrumental in her decision to attend college. If Ronnie was right, coaxing the young woman to incriminate her brother could be extremely difficult. Siblings of abusive parents could become either close or distant, and Ronnie sensed that both extremes could be found in the Farnsworth clan. That Valerie might prefer to save her older brother remained Ronnie's only optimistic thought, but she knew better than to believe the girl would implicate Victor as a suspected psychopath.

In the lapsed silence, Ronnie studied the young woman's slender fingers gripped, knuckle-white on the steering wheel and noted the clenched jaw, the thin lips pressed firmly together. Not a hint of makeup hid the hollows of her cheeks or enhanced her pale skin.

"Valerie," Ronnie said lightly. "Why don't you tell me where we're headed and what you intend to show me?"

"The turn's right up here," she said hesitantly, her attention glued to the lane ahead. "Not too far. You'll understand when we get there. It's easier that way."

"Understand what, hon?"

"Frank . . . Frank Engler's the leader," she said in a hesitant voice. "They don't think I know but I do. I know all about them. Was Frank who got my brother Cal caught up in it. My pa and his daddy, they been friends forever. Grew up together and all. We used to . . . to go over there a lot. Erin was like my big sister and stuff for a long time. I never liked Frank though. He was a lot like his pa, sorta mean and stuff. Always yelling at Erin and me . . . Erin's never been too . . . well . . . she's slow, ya know?"

Ronnie had heard something to that effect in passing.

"I think it's 'cause her pa hurt her when she was little or something, but nobody wants to admit to that. People in Bentwood—they don't want to talk about bad things. They like to pretend everything's just fine and dandy."

Catching a faintly bitter note in the soft lyrical voice, Ronnie remained silent, watching the tension twitch the young woman's slightly jutting chin, glimpsing the tree-shrouded lane ahead as the car slowed.

"It's all a big joke. A big lie," Valerie continued in a hollow tone. "There's nothing ever been fine and dandy in Bentwood. It's a cesspool of evil people and wicked deeds."

The bitter venom whispered in the soft voice lifted short hairs at the nape of Ronnie's neck.

Valerie slowed the car, glancing over behind her sunglasses as she said, "You'll see what I mean in a couple minutes."

Barely glimpsing the opening between the trees, Ronnie recognized the rutted signs of a tractor path as the front end dipped into a wall of high weeds and grass. Almost glad she hadn't managed to lower the window, she cringed as the vines scraped the dirty glass at her shoulder. Her attention remained on the path ahead.

"They don't think nobody knows how they come back here once a month. They think it's all their big secret, but a lot of us know about this place. Me . . . me and some others, we followed them out sometimes and saw how they do . . . and it's enough to make ya puke," she said with a soft pause. "I hate even thinking about how Cal got caught up in something like this but . . . but I guess I can understand it, too."

Sensing where she was headed, Ronnie remained silent as the girl navigated the car through high weeds and tree trunks. On a winding path, they descended a hillside. Just ahead, Ronnie registered an outcrop of black wet rock narrowing on the increasing grade. Somehow, she wasn't surprised when the road dead-ended on a bed of packed leaves and thin vines below a ceiling of wild cherry trees.

"We have to walk from here," Valerie said as she turned off the clattering engine which expired with a hiss, a rumble, and a puff of blue smoke. Reaching down in front of the seat, she collected a faded denim purse that appeared as overstuffed as Ronnie's. "I'll have to let you out. That door's broke," Valerie said and slipped from the driver's seat.

The soft voice had changed subtly, firming. Uncomfortably, Ronnie gathered her purse, stringing the strap over her shoulder, watching the girl stalk toward the back of the car. Something was definitely out of sync, and Ronnie wasn't entirely relieved by the fleeting thought of the small handgun that Len had shoved into her hand last week.

Something had changed. Whether the absence of fear that Valerie had expressed on the telephone or the present undertones of anger, Ronnie couldn't decide but something . . . something truly didn't ring true about Valerie Farnsworth. Unbidden, Ronnie recalled the mention of the girl being admitted briefly to a hospital after her father's murder. A mental breakdown, Ronnie remembered.

When Valerie opened the door, the hinges squealed protest like fingernails on a chalkboard, but Ronnie doubted the sound created the prickle down her spine.

Something amiss.

"It's a good thing you wear sensible shoes," Valerie commented as she motioned and started them toward an outcrop of rocks. "This whole place used to be a rock quarry," she said on a softer note. "Maybe back a hundred years ago," she continued. "Lots of the older houses in Bentwood are made of stone. You probably noticed that though, huh, since you're a reporter an' all."

Was there a note of contempt in that observation? Distracted, Ronnie admitted, "I hadn't noticed."

"It's down here," Valerie said and strode confidently onto the narrow path.

With black stone stacked to form a sheer cliff on one side and jutting boulders on the other, Ronnie watched her step, noting the wet shine on the stone and dead leaves. Ahead and in every direction, the forest spread in endless shadow. The natural sounds of birds chirruping and branches clicking echoed on a shallow breeze. Mentally, Ronnie calculated where she might be standing in relation to the town, but even if she dug the map from her purse, she doubted she would find this spot.

"Are you and Isaac really engaged?" the girl asked over her shoulder.

Recalling Hazel's mention of Valerie's early infatuation, Ronnie considered lying before realizing the futility with the diamond glinting on her finger. "Yes, we are," she answered evenly.

"You tricked him into it, huh?" the girl said with a hint of humor not well masking an undertow of contempt. "I mean, not that it's any of my business, but it just seems pretty funny. You only been around a week or so, and already you got him trapped. Lotsa other girls have tried hooking him, but he's a lot like that old carp over in Rigby's Pond, hits on the bait but never bites."

"How much further, Valerie?" Ronnie asked if only to change the subject and counter the strained note in the soft voice.

The girl barely glanced over her shoulder, a thin smile on her lips as she commented, "Funny you should ask. We're here."

Rounding a sharp rock, Ronnie understood only the tunnel-like entrance into which she walked in Valerie's wake. On three sides, stone rose nearly twenty feet overhead before a shag of weeds and trees rose on the incline to become a forest. A stone basin and dead leaves formed the canyon floor; an open spring spilled a steady stream onto the bedrock and flowed steadily toward the continuing descent of vines and trees. They stood on a plateau within a circle of strategically placed slabs of bench-high rock. A manmade ring of blackened stone stood to one side, ashes and bits of soot-covered logs stacked within the circle.

Almost skipping, Valerie strode to one long stone dais and sat down, a wry smile curling her lips. "Bet you can guess what this is, huh?"

On closer scrutiny, Ronnie noted the symbols, recognizing at least the pentagram carved into the stone beyond the perch—or alter—on which Valerie rested. Suffering a chill, Ronnie needed nothing more to confirm her suspicions. "I'd imagine I can," she said slowly and found Valerie smiling.

Too late. Far too late. In slow motion, Valerie dipped her hand into her purse and emerged with her fingers wrapped around the butt of a rather large handgun.

"You shouldna come back here, ya know? I mean to Bentwood," she said almost softly. "I dint want to have to kill you, but you dint leave me no choice, Miss Bryson. I mean, it's nothing personal, but, well, maybe it is, too. Isaac . . . see? He's mine. He's always been mine."

Heartbeat quickening, Ronnie studied the face with its oversized mirror glasses and gaunt cheeks. In contrast to the softspoken voice, a thin bitter smile twisted the pale lips. And too late, Ronnie knew she was looking at the 'Farmyard Slayer.'

"It . . . it's happening again . . . it's happening," Jade uttered as he stood against the truck. H braced at the fender to stay afoot with the vibrations raging through his system.

Overlaid against the blackness in his mind, he saw the black wings and his mother's face. Her body splayed on the brilliant white tile, arms, legs, and head positioned to fill the five points of a pentagram. Whether her killer had meant to thwart psychic intervention, Jade had never discovered, but he knew the effectiveness of that ploy. If not much else about her murder, he knew that the careful placement of the body had blocked his insight and prevented him from clearly seeing that tragedy. "Happening again," he uttered, his head clasped between his hands, elbows on the truck hood.

And this time was worse. This time, he couldn't even glimpse his future beyond the black curtain behind which Veronica remained cloaked. Her life and his own had become entwined. If he lost her, he would lose himself. No future. Without her, he had no continuation of life . . . and the black forces had, once again, conspired against him.

"Len's making his call. We can take off, Sax," Spencer interrupted, coming alongside him. "You alright?"

Shuddering under the hand clasping his back, Jade pushed off his elbows suffering the leaden weight through his muscles, seeing the world through a watery blur. "I never should have left her alone," he uttered to the bleary outline in front of him, dragging a hand over his eyes.

"Listen, she's fine," Spencer stated in a low firm tone. "While I had Sam on the line, I asked him to send someone over to check on Ronnie. He said he just saw her about a half hour ago over at your shop. She's fine."

Grasping the words as if clinging to a life preserver, he tried to read Spencer's crooked smile. "She's alright? You're sure?"

"She's probably a lot more alright than you at the moment, pal. You look beat. How 'bout I help you into the truck and I get you home?"

Neither the urgency nor tension had abandoned him. His head thumped and pulsed with the intensity of a migraine distorting his vision even with the tears clear. Nodding, he moved a little clumsily, needing Spencer's help more than he cared to admit. Inside the truck, Jade leaned, catching his throbbing skull in his hands, his elbows on his knees.

Something still felt wrong . . . all wrong, but then nothing had ever felt entirely right in his life. He'd always been more of a fatalist than an optimist. Veronica was alright. Spencer said she was fine. Hayward had seen her a half hour ago. She was fine.

Jade needed to believe that, but he could still feel the pulsing and thudding, the warning signal. Not for a second had the pulse ebbed, not for a single second, and the blackness remained immovable inside his mind as if an entire vault had sealed inside his skull. Only the tension remained fixed, vibrating through him and crawling under his scalp.

Pushing off his knees, he slumped back, dropping an elbow to the window, looking at the bleary world ahead of the emerald hood, a world tilted on its axis, not in focus. "Hurry, Spence," Jade uttered barely above the wind cutting through the open window. "She's in trouble . . . feel it. Faster. Drive faster, alright?"

"Things uh . . . things got pretty hairy back there," Spencer said in a pensive tone. "Even the Suit looked pretty shook and uh . . . I know my blood pressure skyrocketed for a while. So, I guess what I'm saying is, maybe that uh . . . maybe that was the thing you were worried about happening, Sax. I mean, I don't know how much you know, how much you remember about what you just did, but there were a few times . . . Christ," he said in a shaky tone. "I saw the blood. I fucking saw it and I know Devinio saw it, too. He'll probably never admit to it, and if anybody ever asks, I didn't see a thing, but . . . but what I'm saying is this, I'm about 99 percent sure you nearly died back there, and that rates right up there on the 'real bad' list. So, maybe that was the 'something' you've been worried about happening. You told me yourself, you couldn't see what was coming, and if what I just saw is any indication, I don't blame you one damn bit for trying to avoid it—"

"Drive faster, Spence," Jade interrupted, his awry gaze watching the road, his skull thumping against his palm. "Faster, alright? She's . . . something. Feel something."

If only to appease him, Spencer applied his boot more effectively to the pedal and the engine sang delight, harmonizing with the monster wheels whining against the asphalt. "She's fine, Sax," Spencer stated again but something in his voice rang off-key, his conviction wavering with a shaky new belief in psychic phenomenon. "Sam mentioned she was in the process of opening your store for business when he saw her—"

"Faster. Drive *faster,*" Jade stated with his voice firming, his need rising. "Hurry . . . We have to hurry. She's in trouble . . . feel it. Know it."

"This isn't your goddamn Ferrari, pal," Spencer stated with mild irritation. "If I go much faster, we'll be topside in a fricken ditch."

"Don't own a goddamn Ferrari," Jade stated as he tried firming the world in front of him, welcoming the blast of wind in his face. "Drive . . . Faster."

"Calm down, Sax," Spencer said with a tight rein on his desire to panic. "If the chief says he just saw her a little while ago, then she's fine and I did ask him to send someone over to your place. By now, she's probably fuming with both of us, and we probably ought to be figuring out how to explain why we both look like we've been ridden hard and put away wet—"

"She's in trouble, Spence," Jade said as he glimpsed the main highway just ahead. "Hurry, goddamn it."

"Grant's gonna be knocking on my fucking door next," Spencer growled and downshifted, hammering the gears, barely slowing to satisfy the stop sign before sliding all four oversized tires onto the highway.

Driving a fine line between safe speed and insanity, Spencer cut across the back streets, swung onto Maine at the intersection in front of the diner, and nearly jammed his push bar into the low-hanging rails of an eighteen-wheeler's rear end.

Without a thought, Jade swung out of the truck and slammed the door, needing to sidle between the bars and barely glimpsing the oncoming traffic before bolting across the lane. His shop was, indeed, open. Even with his vision distorted, he saw two elder women passing through the door, disappearing inside. Not slowing until he passed through the same door, he skidded to a sudden stop, his senses swimming against the disorienting normalcy of his shop. Symphony music, the soft track lights and spotlights cascading over sparkling china, murmured voices and familiar faces . . . several of which turned toward him and froze, undeniably, judging him at least half mad with the filth and grime clinging to him. Swiping his hand through his hair as if that would help, he swayed his focus, searching for a single face, instead landing on the boy who started hesitantly toward him. "Veronica," he said hesitantly, not sure if he meant to demand or question.

Worried, the youngster advanced. His hand dipped into his pocket, producing what looked like the top copy of a sales receipt. "Uh . . . Mr. Bently, she said to give you this."

Hand trembling uncontrollably, Jade accepted the note . . . feeling absolutely nothing of Veronica's essence as he unfolded the page, hearing nothing of her voice as he read the words scrolled in her lovely script.

CHAPTER 37

Looking into the black hole of the handgun in Valerie's hand, a hole into which the entire barrel of her own little gun might fit smoothly, Ronnie suffered an almost uncontrollable urge to laugh. Hysteria wasn't a condition she could afford to embrace if she intended to spend a lifetime with the man she loved. Before the quiver could take hold of her lips, she forced her gaze to the mirror glasses. Insanity blazed behind those mirrors, but Ronnie saw only her dual reflection on the oversized disks. If she fully intended to survive, she needed to buy time. She needed to think. What in God's name does one say to a psychopath who happens to be holding a cannon . . .?

"Does—" *Not Jade.* "Isaac know how you feel about him, Valerie?" she asked, surprising herself with the calm in her voice.

The girl shrugged one shoulder, and neither shoulder remained slumped now. She sat as ramrod straight and posture-perfect as a student in a finishing school and looked as if she might cross her tattered blue-jean-covered knee at any moment in reflection of her secretarial school training. Offhanded, Valerie commented, "Maybe not right now, but he will eventually." With a slight tip of her head, she donned a thin smile. "I figure this way," she spoke in a conversational tone, no longer whispering. "Once I get you out of the picture . . . along with a few others, he'll need a shoulder to cry on. Guys . . . they're like that, ya know? They can be real crybabies sometimes."

"I'd imagine you're referring to your brothers," Ronnie said and glanced sideways to another raised slab, her thoughts turning. "Would you mind if I sit down, Valerie?"

"Sure, go 'head," she said amiably, apparently in no hurry to pull the trigger. "Just don't do nothing stupid, ya know? I'm pretty good with a gun, and this one's loaded."

"I don't doubt it in the least," Ronnie said as she sidled carefully to the slab. Her attention gliding around the enclosure as if sightseeing, she wondered how fast she could find the .22 inside her purse, if, on the outside chance, she could avoid being shot while backflipping to safety behind the stone slab. Not fast enough. Not nearly fast enough. There had to be another option. Her thoughts raced for a haven from the fear threatening to engulf her. Jade. For

Jade, she must keep this maniac from pulling that trigger. She needed to believe he would find her, and, in the meantime, she needed to keep Valerie talking. "You started to tell me . . . I'd imagine they carry on some sort of rituals here. Black masses?"

"More like just orgies and shit," Valerie said in offhanded contempt, shrugging. She crossed her knee then, her legs thin enough that one ragged tennis shoe dangled alongside the other, idly kicking. She appeared only more childlike with the pose.

Perhaps, a skirt and high heels would make a difference, but Ronnie doubted it, then cursed her insanity to consider fashion at a time like this. *God, help!* Falling in love, learning what it felt like to be a woman, to feel like a woman, had dulled her damned senses and turned her into a flipping airhead! "Cal . . . Cal was involved," she struggled to pull her scattered thoughts in order.

"Frank dragged him into it," she said with a defensive tone.

Good, now upset her. Jerk! "I met Frank briefly," Ronnie said absently, remembering. "I didn't particularly care for him. I'd have to agree with you. He strikes me as a man who could be extremely cruel."

"Like his pa," the girl said with a terse note, near childish in her contempt. "They were all mean, the Englers. I mean, except for Erin. Allie—she's such a slut. Everybody knows she only married old man Hall for his money. He's a real asshole if you ask me. He could get just as much pussy a lot cheaper if he went to Liberty Avenue in Pittsburgh, and it'd probably be better, too. Allister's a real dog," she said with a smile. "Did you meet her, too?"

"No, I'm afraid I haven't."

"I'm surprised," Valerie said obtusely. "Me, I'd want to know all the bitches who tried getting my guy, but then, I guess I don't gotta tell you that," she said as she waved the gun as an indication. "What I want to know, Miss Bryson, is how you trapped him into getting engaged," she said with a far more sober note. "Did you really use that blond Fed guy, the cute one, to set Isaac up?"

She wasn't asking out of mere curiosity. She fully believed the rumor and apparently contemplated how to implement a similar strategy. *God*. "I'm not sure I understand, hon," Ronnie said as she tried to decide how to use this insight. "What exactly have you heard?"

"Well, like how you had that agent bust him and then maybe threatened to charge him unless he married you."

*God. Did someone—*anyone*—actually believe that? Were the women in this town that incredibly devious to even consider that possibility? Did it matter?* This particular woman seemed to believe it, and she was holding the gun. Ronnie decided not to point out the stupidity. "That's a very clever scenario," she said instead. "Unfortunately, it's not very accurate."

"Look, everybody knows Isaac only uses women," she said in mild irritation. "So, how'd you trip him up? If not blackmail, what?"

"I played hard to get," Ronnie said with sudden inspiration even as she considered the absurdity of her situation. She was about to offer lessons in capturing a man, to a psychopath holding a gun, *and not just any man*, for Chrissake, *her man*, providing she wasn't around to claim him. "A man like Isaac, he's so accustomed to having women throwing themselves at him . . . Well, let's face it, on a scale of one to ten, he's a fifteen or twenty. A girl would be crazy not to want him."

"Boy, that's the truth," Valerie said wistfully. "I knew when I first saw him . . . I was only about fourteen when he came to town. Gees, he was like a movie star . . . and that accent. He had the coolest accent. Like from a foreign country. France or England or something." She smiled, and even in the gloomy atmosphere, a flush rose in her gaunt cheeks as she admitted, "I took French in high school. It's the only subject I got straight A's in. Ain't that wild? I mean, me just knowing he was French. Laquette . . . God, even his name is dreamy. Jade David Laquette."

God help, Jade! This girl intends to kill me because she's in love with you! "It does have a nice ring to it."

The sound of a sole skidding on stone interrupted, and Ronnie glanced toward the sound, praying it would be Jade in one instant, praying *not* in the next. God knows what the girl would do if Jade strode around that corner and saw her holding a gun. *Insane! The child was insane!* And no matter who advanced, they needed warning! Ronnie barely parted her lips when the mirror glasses leveled on her, and the gun clicked into the cocked position.

Very slowly, the girl shook her bobbed head, lifting her hand to hold her index finger over her pursed, thin lips. Even puckered, the lips smiled like some demented librarian.

Heartbeat slamming a quickened beat, Ronnie darted her gaze at the opening, to the girl, back to the crag in the wall. *A warning! God! She needed to do something! Say something!* Whoever neared the entrance to this black pit could be *killed!* "Jade!" she said sharply and bought an instant . . . but only an instant before the overweight man bumbled around the corner of the stone. Like Ronnie, Valerie needed only a glance to recognize the intruder.

"Don't even think about trying to turn around, Mr. Grimes," Valerie said in a calm, deadly tone. "Come on in and join the party."

The ass! The sneaky rotten ass! Ronnie nearly screamed until she witnessed his deeply lined face draining of color and his eyes widening with revelation. "Grimes," Ronnie snapped and drew his stricken eyes. "Do as the young lady says. Come and sit down."

"Two reporters," Valerie said while kicking her tennis shoe idly, wavering the gun between them as Grimes stumbled toward Veronica. "Wonder if I'll get an award or something," she said with a smile and lifted her hand, lifting her mirror glasses, darting her gaze heavenward for a half second as if she questioned the clouds rolling over the sun. Again, she eyed Ronnie. "Lot of people don't like your kind in Bentwood," she said as she leveled her gaze on Grimes, who bungled clumsily to plop on the stone. "That asshole there is the reason," she said evenly. "He's been making up lies about folks for as long as I can remember."

"Ugh I-I-I—"

"Can-it, asshole," Valerie said evenly, the gun level on him. "Somebody shoulda shot you a long time ago."

Ronnie eyed the slack-jawed man who stared, wide-eyed, at the young woman ten paces away. As much as she'd despised this sleaze, Ronnie suddenly felt bad for him.

His pale face had broken into a sheen of sweat, and his brown eyes remained transfixed. Within seconds, his thinning hair lay matted to his scalp.

"Guess it's better late than never, huh, Grimes?" Valerie taunted. "I just wish I had a pitchfork to stick in you. You're fat enough to bleed like a stuck pig," she said in childish chiding.

Oh God, the insanity! As if it were a living thing rising inside of this young woman, the manic shine rose in the pale eyes, and on an even keel, Ronnie's tension mounted. Something about Grimes, something about this mid-aged potbellied man, had just loosened the girl's rein, and abruptly, Ronnie knew . . . mid-aged . . . fifty to sixty . . . Both Farnsworth and Engler were over two hundred twenty pounds . . . her father . . . thinning hair. *Grimes was reminding her of her father!*

Echoing between the rocks, the sound carried startling Ronnie from her revelations even as she recognized the voice calling. "Hey, Valerie, don't panic. It's just us . . ."

Dumbfounded, Ronnie looked at the wraithlike young woman who barely darted her feral eyes toward the crag as a smile crept slowly, wickedly onto her lips.

"Don't worry, Miss Bryson. I invited them," Valerie said in a sweet soft tone.

Lifting his stricken gaze from the piece of paper that felt like a lead weight in his hand, Jade focused on the boy in front of him, seeing the worry creasing the brow. "H-how long ago did she leave, Wade?"

"Just uh . . . just maybe fifteen minutes ago er so," the boy answered.

"She didn't say where she was going?"

He shook his head, his soft brown eyes darting worriedly over Jade's tense face. "Are you okay?"

No! Not okay! When he needed his damned curse—when he truly needed it . . . gone. *Useless!* He was cursed! Damn it, not the time to panic! He had to think! There had to be another way to find her! A rational—natural way to find her! Hayward. Sam Hayward had said . . . why had Sam been here? "Wade, were you here when Chief Hayward was here?" he asked with a soft strain.

The boy nodded.

"Did you . . . do you know why he was here? Did you hear them talking at all?" *Please, say you heard!*

"I wasn't supposed to," Wade said worriedly. "I was upfront by the door . . . but I sorta did hear some."

"Think, lad. What did you see? Hear?" Jade said while reaching, touching the boy's shoulder. In an instant, he knew what the boy had seen, what he'd heard. A message, a photograph. The boy had understood Veronica's anxiety when she'd seen the photo. He'd understood her attempt to shield it from him, but Wade had caught a glimpse of it. Big red X and O on an instant print . . . something written on the paper. Hayward had taken it with him in a plastic bag.

Before the boy even parted his lips to answer, Jade released his grip, uttering, "Thank you, lad."

Already turning, he nearly ran into Spencer, who halted a hair's breadth from ramming into him. "She's gone," Jade stated and started around Spencer, who pivoted with him. "Come on! I need your help!"

"Where are we going?" Spencer asked as they passed through the door.

"The station," Jade snapped and broke into a trot toward the corner, his thoughts turning over the details that continued to filter through his mind. She'd received a phone call . . . Wade had seen her replacing the receiver, and noticed the pensive expression as she'd hung up.

"She's at the station?" Spencer asked, catching up at the opposite corner in front of Meg's.

"She's not—" Jade stated as he started off the curb, but he drew back, already pivoting when Meg came through the door. Spencer turned clumsily in his wake. "Meg?"

"Honey, there's a whole lot of screwy things going on here this morning," Meg stated with an edge, her soft blue eyes darting off Spencer, fanning as if to check anyone standing in earshot as she strode across the walk. "First off," she started. "Did you know that other agent . . . the one who caused you all the trouble? You know he's back in town?"

He knew it now. "Where is he?"

"Rae Ann spotted him back yonder a couple blocks. He was hanging around a van that's been sitting in the same spot since she came to work yesterday afternoon. It ain't sitting there now, though. On a hunch, I called on over to my cousin Gina's, and sure enough, it pulled out about fifteen, maybe twenty minutes ago . . . right about the time I saw your pickup scooting down the back road, here . . .

"Now, that's just one of the things mighty screwy," Meg continued. "Right around the corner, here, we had a gal I've served a few times, calls herself Emily Landslow. She was just talking up a blue streak into a little radio that looked like a child's walkie-talkie. Now, she got really excited about twenty minutes ago, yelling loud enough to startle ole Brigs, who was coming in for his noon cup. One of the things Brigs heard real clear was a shout for 'Ted,' who I'm betting is Ted Grimes . . . seeing as how somebody spotted that little weasel hiding out a few blocks down the lane behind the old Buryl house that's been empty since old Hank passed on . . .

"And I'll tell you, sweetie, I'm *still* not done with all the wackiness," she said with a disgusted humph and glance across the street toward Andover Hardware. "Appears li'l Jen and her sidekick, Trish Freshcorn, both got a sudden urge to fly on out of here in Trish's little convertible—"

"Let me guess," Spence snapped. "About twenty minutes ago."

"Honey, wherever all these folks are headed, there's liable to be more fireworks than Mayor Lawson planned for tomorrow night," Meg said with a bewildered gaze.

"Where—where are they all headed?" Jade asked.

"I can't say for positive," Meg said carefully. "But I spent a few minutes on the phone a bit ago, and I hear Shaker Hollow Rd.'s starting to look like a freeway, and if you boys intend to catch up, you better get your asses in gear." She stood close enough to Jade that not even Tim could have seen her hand slip from behind her apron and press the small handgun into his palm. "Better safe than sorry, honey."

Leaning, he brushed a kiss on her cheek as he sidled past, dipping the gun under his belt. "Thank you."

"You just be careful, sweetie," she threw after him and landed a glance at Spencer. "That goes for you, too, Timothy Spencer!"

"Scout's Honor, Meg!" Spencer snapped as he caught up. "You know, Sax," he said as they rounded the corner. "If those boys in the van are Feds, there's a helluva good chance Ronnie's fine even if that asshole Jarvins is with them—"

"She's not fine," Jade stated, positive of little else. "She's in trouble . . . I never should've left her out of my sight. Never! If anything—" *No!* He wouldn't even think about it! He would find her! Nothing else could he allow himself to believe. He would find her!

At the back of the truck, they parted. Tim raced to the driver's side as Jade scrambled into the passenger seat. By habit alone, Tim turned on his police band under the dash after twisting the ignition key. They were already wheeling away from the curb before the first cryptic words erupted through the speaker.

"Devinio must have had the papers ready and waiting for a name," Spencer said offhandedly. "Sounds like they've already got the warrant to move on the Farnsworth homestead."

"They . . . they won't find her there," Jade said as he stared absently at the passing lawns. "She's not there."

"Bet you never had a fucking surprise party in your life, huh?" Spencer growled.

Uncomfortably, Jade drew from his daze with the edge in Spencer's tone and glimpsed the agitated eyes. "No," he answered quietly. "I never did."

An apology washed over Tim's tense features, his eyes fleeting sorrow. "So, I'm sorry . . . It's been one helluva morning, Sax . . . and you're sure about that, huh? You know Valerie's not at the farm?"

Did he? "If I said so, I guess I do," he said as he turned his awry gaze through the side window. Not for an instant had the pulse let up, nor had the curtain lifted.

"Where's Ronnie?" Spencer asked abruptly.

"Behind the curtain," he answered.

"Come again?"

Looking at Spencer, Jade replayed the words he'd heard and spoken, understanding what Spencer had just attempted to do. "I can't see her, Spence."

"You uh . . . you said something back at the Englers'. Something about enemies, your father, and uh . . . black magic. You started talking in French. What were you saying? What did all that mean?"

Turning his gaze through the window, he was vaguely aware of houses passing, of oversized tires skidding into turns. Reflexively, his hand dropped to the seat to hold him upright. "My uh . . . my father. I suppose you'd call him a sorcerer or uhm . . . a warlock," he said absently. "Alchemy . . . Necromancy . . . You name it; he engaged in it . . . but his true love was the black arts. He uh . . . he wanted me to apprentice under him, to uh . . . to become his prodigy. I almost believe he loved having a son . . . one with his . . . his own weird talents . . . He had other sons. Has. Three of them, in fact. None of them appreciated having a bastard in their midst. I-I've never been certain which was worse, having a father who despised me or having siblings who refused to acknowledge me. Even without . . . without my telepathy, I could feel their contempt for me, could sense them avoiding the rooms where I stayed. I lived in that manse for six fucking years, and I still think of it as hell on earth," he said absently. "Darkness. That's what I remember the most about that realm. Always darkness."

"You uh . . . you said something about your father finding you . . . him being here. Is that possible? Is this guy here?"

"Something . . . something of his presence is here," he said absently. "I uh . . . I've seen things, Spence. Seen him do things that defy natural law . . . and I've uh . . . I've lived with the effects of his damned magic. You . . . you can consider me insane. God knows, I've spent most of my life convinced I should be in a padded cell . . . but what Jean Pierre Jardonet is capable of doing is real . . . and if what I'm feeling is truly his presence, he's learned some new tricks. He's here and he's . . . oh, Christ, Spence, *hurry!*"

"There's your truck—"

"Fuck that truck!" Jade snapped, his gaze riveted on the lane ahead. Unconsciously, he scanned the thick branches overhead, realizing the absence of sunlight. Platinum gray clouds roiled angrily over the blue sky like a herd of dark gray horses overtaking the white cumulous clouds. "Ohhh, shit . . . shit . . . shit, Spence! A storm . . . storm's coming."

"You're not making me happy, pal," Spencer stated and jammed the gas with enough force to lift the front end. If the beast had hooves, it would be rearing.

CHAPTER 38

"Look what we found wandering around," Jen Andover said as she propelled a pale-faced Emily Landslow through the opening. Dressed in black, from a pair of sensible black flats and tight jeans to a tank top that clung to her tiny waist and enlarged boobs, Jen sashayed down the slope with a slightly less anxious young woman on her heels. As always, Jen wore her electric blond hair in a fluff of glamorous curls, her cosmetics as heavily applied as a plastic mask. Her thick black eyeliner, stretched at the temples and lent her a cynical leer.

Her companion, who Ronnie recognized with a fleeting thought of a yearbook entry, couldn't compare with the dramatic effect, though she tried admirably. Black slacks, a silver halter-top, and a shoulder-length wave of copper hair, she, too, wore enough cosmetics to enhance her small narrow-spaced eyes. Unfortunately, with her long thin nose, Patricia Hawthorne-Freshcorn resembled a poorly made-up witch for a Halloween masquerade.

In seconds Ronnie judged this strange ensemble, noting Emily drawing up short. Landslow's posture stiffened as she focused, round-eyed on the young woman, who rested almost idly on the black stone, foot kicking, gun barrel swaying, smiling. As Landslow's face drained of color and her wide eyes magnified behind glasses to appear frog-like, Ronnie looked at the two members of the Heathen Band.

Jen's focus darted; her crimson lips twisted into a smile as she eyed Ted. "This probably belongs to you, huh, Teddy?" Jen said as she tossed a two-way radio to bounce off the stone near his knees.

Grimes jolted with the impact, although the walkie-talkie never touched him. His brow furrowed, his fleshy face reanimating as if he suddenly believed this was a hoax.

Trish shoved at Landslow, staggering her toward Ronnie and Grimes. "May's well join your pals, cutie."

"What the hell's going on here?" Grimes demanded.

Hips swinging, Jen started toward Valerie, smirking. "I can't believe you did this, Val. This is wild. We should have brought you in—"

"You should stop there, Jen," Valerie said as she leveled the gun and her gaze on the blond.

Without wasting an instant, Ronnie slipped her hand into her purse, clutched possessively on her lap. *Not a hoax. Not a game.* If nothing else about this ensemble made sense, that alone blazed crystal clear in her mind.

"Maybe one a you better tell me what the hell's going on here," Grimes stated as Emily groped and collapsed onto the stone, nearly landing on his lap when he shoved her aside. "If this is some kind of goddamn game—"

"No!" Ronnie snapped, reaching sideways to halt Grimes from his started rise. Her mind snagged on the words Jade had spoken over a week ago. 'Game. A child's game.' By whatever means her mind ejected that thought and knew the potential danger, she couldn't begin to fathom . . . but she knew. Knew without a doubt, that word tipped the precarious balance of the young woman sitting almost sedately on the stone. A little princess holding court . . . she simply turned her gaze and the barrel.

As the blast ricocheted within the stone, Ted lifted off his soles and sailed backward. Arms flailing, knees and heels catching on the stone slab, his dull brown oxfords rose in slow motion to follow him out from between Ronnie and Landslow. Up and over, Ted vaulted; his lips parted, and eyes bulged as he followed a spray of blood to slam the stone floor and jagged wall, toppling in a heap.

Ears ringing, Ronnie dropped her palm to halt her momentum. Her heart pounded a leaden beat in the stopped time; her other hand remained buried inside her purse. Twisted, she suffered a clear view of the crumpled body. The crimson stain spread as if a floodgate had opened over the thin cotton shirt at the man's girth; red smears glistened on the blackened stone.

At the squeaked sound, the glimpse of motion at the corner of her eye, Ronnie believed she'd missed the sound of another shot. Her thoughts speeding up, she realized Landslow starting to collapse and reached a hand by instinct to clasp the fainting woman's shoulder. At the same time, Trish and Jen staggered in a half turn; wide-eyed, they stared toward her, toward Grimes. Further away, Valerie Farnsworth remained seated, gripping the .38 that swayed almost idly toward Jen. Landslow crumbled on the slab where Ted had been sitting; her limbs scattered with the tensile strength of a scarecrow.

"Y-you sh-shot him," Jen stammered as she swung her face toward Valerie, apparently, not grasping the import of her words. "Val-er-ieee, youuu—"

"I always knew you weren't dumb as you look," Valerie said with a chiding tone, like the voice of a child who had just bested another. A ghastly smile turned the corners of her lips as if she strained not to laugh aloud. Waving the gun barrel, she said, "Back up, Jenny. I got plenty of bullets in this peashooter. Plenty to go around."

Moving only one hand off the gun lowered to rest on her raised knee, her finger still locked inside the trigger guard, Valerie reached to the oversized bag on the stone and dipped her hand inside. "And ain't it lucky, I brought an extra one?" she said as she drew a smaller handgun from her bag, one more befitting a woman but just as lethal as the first. Gunslinger style, she held both weapons, one directed toward Ronnie, the other toward Jen, with Trish frozen in the center position.

"W-we were j-just gonna scare her," Jen spoke as she began backing away clumsily. "N-Nobody w-was sup-posed to get hurt, Val—"

"Mebbe you are dumb as you look," Valerie decided as her feral eyes darted over each of them, favoring Ronnie with a long look. "These dumb bitches really think they could scare you off a Jade . . . talk about dumb, huh?"

No remorse, no fear, no thought of consequence. Ronnie nodded her shallow agreement, retracting her hand slowly from the unconscious woman at her side. Struggling to grasp a clear thought and maintain her calm against the racing hammer in her chest, she drew a breath and held Valerie's feral blue eyes, which appeared nearly black with the distended pupils and manic glaze. "Yes, I'd say that's very foolish of them."

"Guess I knew you'd come back, knew I was gonna have to kill you. He thinks he's in love with you. Them—" she said and tossed a scathing glance to the two women, a thin smile on her lips. "He don't care about them, none. I mean, look at them. They dress up like hookers and bounce their boobs around in his face. I almost knew he'd fall for you soon's I saw you. You got class like him."

"Thank you, hon," Ronnie said politely. Her thoughts ricocheted in double time as she sought a way out of this. Somehow, she needed to find a means to spare any more bloodshed, her own included. Inside her purse, her fingers twitched, touching ever so slightly through the debris in search of that stupid little gun. How effective a .22 Midnight Special could be against a .38 Browning, she dare not ponder too long or hard.

"Real slow, Miss Bryson, get up and come over here," Valerie ordered as she uncrossed her knee, dropping her ragged tennis shoe to the stone.

As Ronnie willed her jellied limbs into motion and started to rise, she realized the wind was intensifying inside the small canyon.

The sky had clouded, casting them in a twilight shade. Overhead, angry clouds seemed to roil and roll, and a low idling sound announced the distemper within that gray miasma. Unnatural. Warm and cool air colliding, the wind seemed to be dropping the temperature within the walls at a speed to defy natural law.

Even before Ronnie collected her balance afoot, the tempo of the wind had increased. Leaves and twigs sailed from the ledge overhead and swept inward from the forest at the wide mouth of the canyon. Fleeting, Ronnie glimpsed at the two stricken women darting their fearful glances at Valerie's manic eyes pinwheeling in mild confusion.

In a fleeting instant, Ronnie knew when those mad eyes turned to her, knew she was being held to account for this sudden madness in the air. By reflex alone, she started lifting her purse as if it were a shield to deflect bullets; her senses slowed to hear the words droning in stereo as if echoing through a tunnel.

"Youuu! Youuu're doooing thiiisss! Yoouuu'rrre aaa wiiitch!"

"Throoow dooown youuur wwweapons!"

Mark Jarvins?

"Where the fuck's this *storm* coming from!" Spencer yelled over the rage of the wind and the roar of the 429 engine racing under the hood. Tree branches and vines whipped against the windshield and open windows as the truck plowed through the tangle, bouncing and leaping ruts with the four oversized wheels mulching saplings in their path.

They'd passed the white van tucked discreetly in the brush where the Federal agents had abandoned it to proceed on foot. Spencer barely lifted his foot off the gas pedal before Jade snapped, "Drive!"

Likewise, they sailed past a small beige economy car wedged into a tangle of vine and a battered brown Dodge nearly camouflaged in weeds with the grime on the hood. For neither car had Spencer braked; instead, he jammed the gas pedal, pitching the truck forward like a destrier of old charging into battle.

"Brakes!" Jade demanded as he sensed rather than saw the final cars in the procession. Even as the truck began a sideways slide, he grabbed at the door handle, yanking it open. Time! Time was running out! If nothing else, he knew that much by the impact of the pulse slamming his temples. Launching from the cab, his foot skimmed on deadfall leaves, touching down. The wind lashed against him as chilled as a December breeze. Twilight shade swept through the forest, closing in faster than his tennis shoes striking the earth as he raced past the battered Fairlane and Milt's little blue Datsun. As if he'd become one with the descending darkness, he located the bodies traversing the forest, one finding a position above the jutting rocks, another picking a cautious quick path to round the outcropping on the lower side of the granite ledges. Ahead, Jade identified the third body, sensing Jarvins' presence as he raced downward over the slippery terrain.

With the wind covering his advance, Jade rounded the final bend in time to hear the outraged cry echoing inside the canyon, to see Jarvins lunge forward into the opening, his voice carrying ahead of his weapon.

Even as the explosions erupted, one after another, he grasped Jarvins' jacket, yanking the man behind the rocks. He heard the startled breath and gasp of pain and saw the blood spray splattered on the stone. A flash of fiery pain slashed through his own arm as he glimpsed the stricken blue eyes and the federal issue Glock dropped from the limp hand. Throwing Jarvins to the path at his back, Jade pivoted, the 9 mm Walther already in his grip as he rounded the jagged stone. As if he were entering a battlefield, the screams and resounding blasts hammered his skull, but time had stopped inside his mind.

The pulse and throbbing ceased. In slow motion, he saw Veronica lifted, sailing toward the wall, her oversized purse raised like a shield, compacted against her slight frame. Stricken, her pale blue eyes touched him even as she struck the wall. Rage and terror flowed through his mind as he rounded on the others in time to see the neon blond hair trailing after the flying black form with yet another blast of sound. Clutching her mop of copper hair, Trish Freshcorn stood frozen, her mouth gaping and a scream issuing a siren wail to match the explosive blast. With his focus turning in slow motion, Jade found the source of madness. Wraith-like, the lone woman stood gunslinger style, feet spaced, guns thrust in either direction slowly coming together, both barrels lining up toward his chest.

As if windows to the gates of hell, her eyes glowed with fiery madness; her slender face twisted into a fiendish gnarl of smile and snarl. Wind whipping her short-bobbed hair to slash at her gaunt cheeks in snakelike tendrils, she stood frozen, both triggers semi-engaged, her fingers crooked within the guards.

Time stood still, halted entirely as his mind took in the flashing images, the evil locked within these stone walls, the years of chanting wicked incantations. As if he truly stood in the pits of hell, Jade saw them cavorting like the devil's own minions. Men and women, men and men, women and women, their minds afire with unholy concoctions of henbane and witch hazel. The smells of those potions woke memories of his past, his father's lower chambers. These fools had no idea what powers they had unleashed in their bungling worship of dark forces, the madness they had incited to hang like a loaded gun over the whole of Bentwood . . . but the evil had found a worthy vessel in this tormented young woman. In her, the sins of the fathers, brothers, and sisters had festered and blossomed into a pure black rage.

With the wind buffeting around them, black dust swirled, lifting into funnel clouds of soot from the pit where years of unholy fires had burned. Frozen, Jade looked into the manic eyes, seeing something of himself within those twin gates. He was damned. He'd been damned since conception no differently than this child, and once again, the black forces had won, waging against him and stealing his only chance for salvation. He would go mad. Perhaps, he'd already gone mad. As if a black hole had formed inside his mind, he felt the darkness spiraling and expanding in the place Veronica had occupied, a vortex rising to overtake him and suck him down. Without her, he had no future.

"It's over, Valerie," Jade said as he began lowering his extended hand, his weapon. "Finish it."

"We're m-meant t-to be to-gether," the girl heaved, her words nearly lost in the wind.

"Only in hell," the deep hollow voice resounded, resonant even within a rumble of thunder. "Only in hell."

"I-I had t-to do it . . . I had to . . . you . . . me . . . I had to kill her . . . she was gonna take you away from me . . ."

Dazed, Ronnie struggled for a clear breath, a clear thought, hearing the words, blinking against tears. Through an unnatural haze, she saw him, saw his gun lowered to his side while the girl held both weapons aimed at his chest. *Nooo!*

"You're mine!" the girl demanded on the verge of a scream.

"God help me if that were true," he said in a low leaden rhythm. "Finish it, Valerie. Set me free to be with her."

Through her swaying vision, Veronica saw the tears begin spilling down the girl's cheeks and the guns wavering unsteadily. Gun! She clutched a gun!

"Youuu lllove herrr!" the girl cried.

"Heart and soul."

"Youuu bassstard!" Valerie screamed. "Youuu're jussst like the ressst of themmm! Plaaaying gammmes!"

"Jaaaddde!" Veronica heaved as she struggled to rise, gripping the gun. "Nooo!" Her hand rising, she pushed onto her knee. The blazing black eyes swung toward her along with the guns. Hatred ignited like a flame to engulf the girl.

Only at the fringe of her mind, Ronnie watched as Jade's arm thrust forward, and in that instant, she glimpsed something akin to blue flames arc off his gun-laden hand. In stop time, the blue fire touched, lifting the waif-like figure and propelling her to sail over the unholy altar. As an afterthought, it seemed, a bullet ejected to follow the young woman as several explosions ricocheted, blasting and blowing away in the wicked wind.

With a blast of thunder and crack of lightning, the clouds burst overhead, releasing the first heavy drops of icy rain as Jade pivoted. *She was alive!* Wet blue eyes shining a near ethereal light, she lanced him in her stricken gaze as her hand collapsed with the weight of the small gun and her body began to crumble. *Alive! She was alive!*

As if he'd become a magnet, her arms shot about his neck, and her slender body leaped into his arms. The emptiness, the blackness that had begun inside him, filled as if lightning had struck in illumination.

Alive! She was alive! Her heartbeat merged with his; her breath heaved at his neck, warming him as swiftly as the icy drops attempted to chill him.

Only now waking to the world around him, Jade heard the siren-wail scream breaking, moaning, short cries of pain, and shouts from outside the canyon. A battleground, he stood on a battleground with bloodied bodies strewn about. One collapsed before his eyes as he pivoted. *Hell!* He stood in *hell!* A smell of sulfur and blood threatened to engulf him, held off, perhaps, only by the woman vibrating in his arms. *Blood. Good God, the blood!* Even with the rain quickening, trails of blood smeared against the stone wall and pointed to the crumbled body of Ted Grimes, around whom Jade passed at a hastening stride.

He had to get Veronica out of here! *Out of this wicked black pit!* No other thought held more firmly as he broke into a run, barely glimpsing Mark Jarvins at the opening, standing, leaning against the stone entrance. Pale, his face gritting against pain, Jarvins held his bloodied arm and gun with the same hand.

Halfway up the path, Jade nearly rammed into Spencer, who skidded, halting, clasping his arm.

His face gripped with panic; his blue eyes darted off the black hair at Jade's collar to his eyes. Only an instant passed before Tim's instincts kicked in, and he snapped, "Emergency vehicles and backup are on the way! How—"

"Battle's over. Two wounded. Two . . . Get to them," Jade stated and broke from Spencer's hold, wanting, needing to carry Veronica away from the madness. Already, they were drenched. The unnaturally cold rain chilled him as he ran, slipping and sliding up the path, propelled upward as if the fires of hell raced at his heels.

Sideways in the slight clearing, Spencer's truck waited; the passenger door hung open, offering refuge. He needed to see her, to see with his eyes what his senses told him. Swinging into the cab, he tried unfolding her on his lap, tried unlocking her arms for a clear view. Fiercely, she clung to him, heaving soft strained breaths against his collar. "Pleeease, Veronica. I need to know—"

"H-hold me," she heaved at his neck. Her words carried on a mere wisp of breath beneath the slashing wind and staccato beat of the rain pelting the hood and bed of the truck. "J-Just ho-old me."

Not bleeding . . . not shot. Her body trembled against him; her breath strained, no doubt from the impact against the stone. She wasn't shot. She wasn't bleeding. Burying his face against the wet strands, feeling his tears mixing with the flood of water off his head, Jade drew the scent of her hair and her essence. Relief spilling through him as surely as the warmth, he held her, breaking only one hand free to stroke the wet curls, uttering the only words he dared to believe. "It's alright, sweetheart. You're alright."

Her face buried against him, her soft silent sobs broke, venting as much relief as sorrow, the images of horror and fear flowing through her mind into his. No words need to be uttered; he understood, sharing the panic she'd felt, sharing her fear . . . sharing her strength.

Outside the truck, vehicles began to arrive, chaos erupting within the torrential downpour as bright orange and yellow slickers raced past the truck windows. Shouts and shrill cries merged with the wind and rain. Safe and warm within the cab, Jade continued to stroke the black hair, but on another plane, he watched the mayhem as if he stood at the entrance of that unholy black pit.

Valerie Farnsworth lay in a twisted heap against the rear wall. Blood spilled over her thin blouse and washed away in a flood of ringlets toward the small creek. One or another of Bentwood's officers laid his raincoat over her as one of the county deputies afforded Grimes the same respect. Emily Landslow huddled in a raincoat on the stone bench, an officer steadying her from collapse.

Revived from her faint, Trish sat on the alter rocking and staring blindly toward the covered body beyond the stone; she appeared oblivious to the officers who stooped about her attempting to speak to her. When the paramedics tried lifting her, she screamed and began kicking and flailing. Mindlessly, she rained blows against them until Sheriff Taylor Grant intervened. Almost gently, despite his size, he wrapped his arms about her and lifted her off her feet. He held her long enough for two of his deputies to grab her legs and lay her on the stretcher, where she was swiftly belted into place.

Jen Andover was likewise lifted and strapped, moaning, to a stretcher as paramedics worked furiously to squelch the flow of blood spilling with the flood of rain off her blond hair. Whether the excessive blood flow or the tendrils of black tears spider-webbing at her temples worried those men more, Jade couldn't decide. A monstrous image, she presented with her long red strands flared medusa-style over the black vinyl and her gnarled face a collage of black veins.

Spencer was the first to arrive at the door, breaking the trance. Someone had given Tim a slicker, and he wore the hood dripping a shower on the running boards as he flashed his blue eyes off Jade to the black hair. "You're alright? You're both alright? You don't need the medics?"

"We're alright," Jade said as he looked through the rain into Tim's tense eyes. "We weren't hit," he said though even as he spoke the words, he remembered seeing Veronica lifted and propelled, her blue eyes wide with shock, lips parted on a scream of pain and terror. Not hit. She wasn't hit, not bleeding . . . but she had been shot. The impact of a .38 had lifted and slammed her against the stone at her back. Her purse . . .

Mark Jarvins came next, yanking the door open with his uninjured arm, the other arm wearing a tourniquet wrap and sling barely visible under the black flap of an official FBI slicker. Echoes of pain touched his squinted blue eyes to dart off Ronnie and lock on Jade. "She's alright?"

"She's fine," Jade said and watched Jarvins look at her, the pain not all physical and his concern genuine. "Are you?" Jade asked.

Nodding, Jarvins flashed a single glance to Jade, unspoken gratitude in his eyes before he backed and closed the door with a civil thump.

Whether Jarvins' visit or an internal strength started Veronica's recovery, Jade didn't bother to wonder; instead, he welcomed her animation, loosening his encompassing hold to let her lift her head, and wipe her eyes. She was still pale, her delicate face taut with the strain, her soft blue eyes misted with the horrors too fresh in her mind, but he could almost feel her shaking off the initial trauma, could see her struggling for clear thought. God, she was beautiful, so beautiful even in distress. Fingering the wet curls off her lined brow as she wiped her eyes, Jade broke the silence between them, stating the obvious, "Coming around, sweetheart?"

Blinking long wet lashes, she looked up with a strained quiver on her lips, "We . . . I . . . we should be doing something."

"We are doing something," he said quietly. "You're recovering, and I'm holding you."

"Hurt . . . Grimes . . . the others—"

"We're surrounded by paramedics and ambulances, police, deputies, and Federal agents, darling. There's nothing we need to do but wait for our chauffeur."

"We . . . I have to tell them," she said with a collective breath. Her eyes searched him with a near desperate need. "A statement . . . We have to give—"

"When you're ready, Veronica," he agreed as he massaged the tension at her shoulder.

"Jade, it was . . . Valerie is . . . she's *sick,* Jade. She's the . . ."

"I know," he said simply, looking into her misty blue eyes.

Her brow furrowed as she lifted her gaze through the watered panes of glass. In slow degrees, she was awakening to the continued chaos outside.

He'd almost lost her, almost lost her to the black forces. Even now, he recognized those forces moving around them. His father's cold, oppressive presence lingered within the unnatural downpour and within the cab.

He'd almost lost her to those evil forces, and it would've been his own fault. His fear had immobilized him, his wretched cowardice to reject the weird talents that had plagued him since conception. Good God, the price he'd nearly paid. Shivering uncontrollably, Jade drew her to rest more fully against his chest, looking into her still opaque gaze. "I do love you, Veronica."

"I . . . oh, God," she heaved softly, finding and clasping his hand. Her eyes lifted a shine of tears. "I love you, too . . . heart and soul," she said smoothly.

Dipping his head, he tasted her lips; relief and comfort spilled through his mind. With a sense of Len Devinio's presence outside the door, Jade stifled his need and lifted from the kiss, squeezing her hand gently and forcing a slight smile. "We have more company."

Devinio assured himself they were both unharmed before asking a few brief questions, one of which concerned a 9 mm Walther found lying in the center of the cove.

"I'd imagine it's licensed to Megan Price, but you'll find my prints on it," Jade answered evenly.

"I'm cutting Spencer loose to take you back to town," Len stated. "I'll be around in a bit to take your official statements."

The ride to town was quiet. The rain continued to pound the hood and windshield; the wind continued throwing leaves and branches into their path, following them to the shop. Drenched again by the time they passed through the side door, they trudged up the steps single file, leaving water trails in their wake. Only after he convinced Veronica to soak in a warm tub and delivered a brandy into her hands, Jade collected towels and dry clothes for himself and Spencer. Tim was just hanging up from talking to Donna when Jade flopped the collection on the desk in his office.

"Donna's dropping the kids off at my folks and coming in," he commented. "How's Ronnie?"

"Soaking," Jade said and returned to his room to dry off and change, checking on her again before returning and pouring himself a brandy. Taking a swallow, he settled into the chair behind his desk.

"The rain's letting up," Spencer commented from his idle pose near the open curtains. His gaze returned and a peculiar half-smile haunted his troubled expression. "First time I've ever been in this room and not needed a lamp to keep from ramming my shins and knees. Makes a difference."

Funny, Jade hadn't even noticed the absence of lamplight. Belatedly, he recalled bypassing the light switches when entering his apartment. Glancing off the open window, he scanned the gray luminescence in his office and living room, realizing the natural light truly did make a difference. Name changes and different dwellings hadn't lifted the past from his mind. He'd brought the darkness with him, had lived under the pall of his mother's death, of his father's dark practice. He'd existed so long without light.

The door buzzer resounded on the wall, and Tim offered to answer it.

Offhanded, Jade commented, "It's Meg. She's in my shop office." Along with several others taking shelter from the rain and satisfying their curiosity, undoubtedly, alerted by the grapevine. "Let Meg up and have Elaine send uh . . . Devinio up when he arrives."

Spencer halted partway past the desk and looked at him with a more peculiar expression, his gaze intent. "The light in here's not the only thing different," he commented offhandedly. "Are you alright?"

"Time will tell," Jade answered absently as his gaze listed with his revelation. The lid had blown sky-high. The seal he'd clamped over his talents had shattered entirely, and he suffered the strangeness inside of him . . . almost as if he were uniting with an old friend, his only friend for the first ten years of his life. If he tried now, he could trace the heritage of the brandy snifter in his grip, could feel the essence of those who'd held the glass throughout history to the very first hands to create it. His talents, his abilities had never truly foretold the future. He'd been a sensitive, more in tune with the past with the ability to touch the past through objects and people. Only glimpses of the future had he ever prognosticated . . . and his mother had used those glimpses, building entire futures for those who'd willingly fallen under her power.

Glimpses, only glimpses of the future had he suffered as a child, and those had been enough to scare the hell out of him. Only glimpses, most in dream-state or trance. But he'd sealed off his talent. He'd locked out the entire world around him and divested himself of emotional contact with the human race if only to protect himself from the fear and pain in empathy with others. The world had scared him. Whether he lived in shadows behind locked doors or wandered crowded streets, the abstracts had terrified him. His mentalism and the illusions created by that weird talent had intimidated him.

With a sense of Veronica moving about the bedroom, Jade rose absently and sought the source of strange light and warmth, which seemed now like a lifeline for him to follow. In the bedroom doorway, he paused, leaning against the frame with a sense of his weariness. She stood at the massive vanity, running a brush through her wet black strands, catching his eyes in the mirror and pausing. As if he'd seen her here a thousand times, standing as she was now, a sleek, beautiful woman looking at him through the reflection of a mirror image, Jade felt the last of his doubts and fears draining. "We'll be alright," he said quietly if only to hear himself speak those words.

She nodded, understanding him, her pale blue eyes penetrating him with her innate weird talents. "I'm not cursing fate, Jade," she said quietly, the tension still in her eyes. "And nor should you," she continued as she turned toward him, coming to him. Her hand lighting on his side, tingling and warming, she looked into him. "Don't blame yourself for what's happened today . . . no matter what happened or happens tomorrow, don't blame yourself. Some things, honey . . . maybe they're just meant to happen."

In those few words, she verified her understanding and confirmed her acceptance of the weird talents inside of him. Talents that had failed to protect them entirely, failed him when he needed them the most. She might just as easily have said, 'You're psychic, yes. But you're not God.' And with those words, she released him from the guilt gnawing at the edges of his weary mind.

"I a-almost lost you," he uttered. "I thought I had lost you."

"I know," she said with haunting fear in her eyes. "Don't . . . don't you ever scare me like that again," she said with a soft, firm tone. "No matter what, promise me this minute, you'll never—*ever*—scare me like that again."

She had seen him lower the gun, had heard him ask for a bullet to end his own wretched life in the wake of losing her. Lifting his hand to her cheek, caressing her quivering lips with his thumb, Jade looked into her eyes. "I don't ever want to feel what I felt today, Veronica. Not ever again. Don't ever let me think you gone, and I'll cling to life with all that's inside of me."

She studied him, searching him like an ancient with the wisdom of the universe tucked behind her hazy blue orbs. "I can live with that," she decided and slipped her arms about him.

Wrapping his arms about her, feeling as if the weight of the world had just lifted off his shoulders, he decided, "That makes two of us."

For a few moments, they stood, held up by the wall, clinging to each other and drawing strength before the sound of new voices intruded.

Meg hadn't arrived empty-handed. She distributed coffees and set aside a bag full of pastries, including the cinnamon variety Ronnie had raved about hours earlier. She fussed over Veronica, gifted with her own sixth sense not to press for details.

Not much time passed before Donna arrived, and after strangling Tim in an embrace, she calmed down enough to hug Jade and Veronica with equal intensity, joining Meg in her effort to lift the gloom from Veronica's eyes. How exactly the mention of his "French bordello" came to pass, Jade couldn't decide, but all three women migrated to his bedroom, chatting and giggling like schoolgirls. Wearing a vaguely puzzled smirk, Jade trailed after them. One of them, probably Meg, had paused long enough to open the curtains in his kitchen and natural light spilled into his bedroom.

Somewhat like opening a door to a candlelit crypt, Jade considered as he leaned again at the entrance, sipping brandy and fascinating in this strangeness to watch Veronica demonstrating the curtains around his seventeenth-century bed. Privacy was a thing of the past. Vaguely amused, he watched Meg cross her arms, brow lifting as she looked at him.

Almost relieved, he heard Devinio arrive and caught Veronica's gaze across the room. Both Meg and Donna, as if by prearrangement, excused themselves from the apartment with a promise to be right downstairs.

"If you don't mind, I'll tape your statements and have them transcribed for you to read and sign," Len stated as he settled on the edge of the desk, a tape recorder already stationed at his side. "Emily Landslow's already given us enough to figure out part of what happened out there, but there's a lot of gaps. You know the ropes, Ronnie," he said lightly. "Start with how you first made contact with Miss Farnsworth and tell it at your own pace."

Settled on the couch, his arm about Veronica's shoulder and his hand gripped in her fingers that felt like a vice as she spoke, Jade listened in silence. Heartbeat quickening, he relived the episode through her mind, feeling her panic rising as she reached conclusions and discoveries. Sick with dread, Jade realized how deeply obsessed with him that child had been and how dearly, he'd nearly paid for her jealousy. If he'd opened his mind sooner . . .

Distracted, he gazed at the oversized leather purse resting on the desk where Veronica had dropped it when entering the apartment. In his mind, he heard the shots resounding, and saw the .38 swinging toward him even as he'd seen Veronica lifted and propelled by the impact.

As she neared the end of her account, reaching the moment when she'd known the gun would swing in her direction, Jade eased away from her and stood, sidling the few paces to his desk. Lifting, and turning the leather satchel, he barely noticed the silence dropping within the room. Finding, fingering the round gaping hole in the leather, his attention fixed while opening her knapsack-sized purse.

He felt it. The cold chill enhanced within the bag as he reached inside. His fingers jolted and tingled as the source of the chill touched his fingertips. Flinching, he lifted the envelope from the debris. His focus locked on the strange sight he held.

Perfectly round, the nipple of the .38 slug protruded from one side of the envelope; the flat end protruded from the other side. Turning the envelope as if he feared being bitten, his attention landed on the scrolled black script. Without a need to read the return address, or even glimpse at the multiple postmarks, Jade knew who had penned his name on this envelope. As in all else, Jean Pierre Jardonet's script was bold and nearly artistic in design. Between Jade's first and last name, his middle initial had been removed by the bullet presently held within the paper.

Shivering, Jade looked at Devinio, who stared at the trembling anomaly.

Slowly, Devinio lifted his hand, snapping off the recorder before reaching and slipping the envelope away. Spencer had stepped closer for a better look, and Ronnie rose, closing the circle to gaze at the letter.

Turning the envelope, Len studied the tip of the bullet, then ignited the desk lamp and further inspected it under the light. His silent scrutiny continued for several moments before he met Jade's troubled gaze. "Any chance you know who sent this?"

"Every chance," Jade admitted absently.

Spencer began inspecting the bag, looking at Ronnie as he asked, "Think you could go through the contents, Ronnie? See if there's anything in there to stop a bullet?"

She accepted the challenge as well as the bag. Systematically, she extracted the odd assortment of paraphernalia from lipstick tubes to full and small-sized notebooks to a small handheld unscathed recorder and a stack of other notes, papers, and envelopes, to a wallet and change purse. If only to salve her curiosity, she dumped the entire contents on the desk and welcomed Tim and Len's assistance to paw through coins, pens, compacts, and other odds and ends.

If not for the tension created by the envelope, Jade might find the situation almost amusing, considering the mound of whatnots inside the bag. The little witch even carried a few empty candy wrappers, a mashed snack pack of crackers, and soda-can tabs in the debris, but it wasn't amusing. Not another item in her purse had either been scored or damaged by the bullet protruding through the envelope. Aside from the black powder flash at the flat end of the slug, the deadly projectile remained as clean as if it had never been fired.

"Where was the .22 when that bullet hit?" Len asked after a reasonable time.

"In my hand . . . inside my purse," Ronnie said as she looked over to him, then glanced at the envelope again.

Not one of them needed to voice the thought aloud. Without a word, Len picked up the envelope and needed to tug to remove the slug. He handed the letter to Jade, refusing even to acknowledge the tremor in Jade's hand as he accepted the delivery. Motioning Ronnie to sit down again, Len suggested, "Why don't we continue with your statement? About the time Miss Farnsworth started shooting, you saw her turning the gun toward you . . ."

Starting and stopping the recorder, they finished taping Ronnie's statement, concluding she blacked out when she stumbled backward against the wall, gaining consciousness in time to see Valerie holding her weapons on Jade. At that point, Len paused the recorder and turned to Jade. "I spoke to Mark Jarvins. According to his account, you pulled him to safety, then caught Farnsworth's attention as she drew a bead on Ronnie. You distracted her long enough for him to squeeze off two shots as she was about to fire on you and Veronica. Anything you want to add for the record?"

"I'd imagine that covers it," Jade decided.

Devinio hesitated, then glanced between them. "I don't guess I have to tell either of you not to speak to anyone about this until we work out the details and record your statements." He looked to Spencer. "If I can borrow you for an hour or so, we can have a chat with your chief and clear up a few things in the meantime."

"Len . . .?" Ronnie halted him, her tension apparent as she caught and held his gaze. "The others . . . Grimes . . . Jen Andover . . . Trish?"

"How about letting me get this sorted out, Ron," he said smoothly. "We'll talk again this evening."

"Valerie . . . she killed them . . . her father . . . Engler—"

"We know," Len said and barely glanced off Jade before he commented. "We found Farnsworth's watch, along with the suction device she snipped off the equipment in Engler's milkhouse." With a glance toward Jade, he added, "And we have an eyewitness to that murder. It's just a matter of tying up a few loose ends to close the case."

CHAPTER 39

More than two weeks had passed since Jade had carried Veronica from that unholy pit, and nothing had settled in her mind or his if his present state of distraction were any indication. Almost as quiet and preoccupied as the first time they had sat together in the Spencers' backyard, Jade gazed toward the forest. His mustache curved at an angle to appear curious, if not bewildered, by something beyond his grasp. The clouds lingered in his eyes, shaded by a thick fan of lashes that could drop like a cloak to shield his thoughts at whim or whimsy.

Comfortably, they'd lived within the same rooms, shared meals, and engaged in heated debates over the decision to keep the store open. On the surface, Jade wanted to sell the shop and move, but on a separate plane, Ronnie sensed his conflicts. He loved his shop and this town, his friends who had become family. Inevitably, they had settled their differences long before ducking through those thick curtains to share the finer pleasures where they met on equal ground. She loved him, and incontestably he loved her, but that wicked morning lingered like a cloud over them.

Valerie Farnsworth hadn't survived. The autopsy had revealed the slugs from a 9 mm Walther and a .22 Midnight Special mashed together in a freakish position inside the most cherished of all organs. That detail still baffled Roberta Lincroft, Forensic Pathologist, and Len had personally driven Roberta to the scene on two separate occasions. Meticulously, she'd recreated the scene, attempting to gauge the trajectory and calculate the exact angles from which those two bullets could have been fired to land at the same instant, dead center, in Valerie's heart. On the official death certificate, Valerie had been killed by a .38 Browning Automatic. Roberta had concluded that Mark's bullet had pierced Valerie's cranium and lodged inside the black mass of her tortured brain.

Ted Grimes hadn't survived. Only two days earlier, a large envelope had arrived anonymously, carrying typed drafts of a half dozen articles bearing his writing style. Allegations, which would've wreaked havoc on several lives and disparaged some of the most revered names in Washington, were randomly scattered throughout the factual collection of abused details. One line was repeated several times, with the first two letters crossed off editorially. 'Unconfirmed sources told this reporter . . .'

According to Meg's latest gossip, Emily Landslow was still making her rounds, attempting to gather details about Valerie Farnsworth. Allegedly, she'd approached both Victor and Cal Farnsworth for book rights. In no uncertain terms, Victor Jr. had declined; a decision Cal, who had needed to be transferred from the county jail to the state hospital after hearing of his sister's demise, had found the sense to reiterate with equal intensity.

Jen Andover, after being treated for a bullet wound that had grazed her skull and resulted in a wide strip of bald scalp, was facing criminal conspiracy charges. Her fingerprints had been found on the message, and the photograph meant for Jade's eyes only.

Trish had been likewise charged with several counts of conspiracy and criminal mischief, although those charges might be dropped. The last Ronnie had heard, Trish was still talking up a blue streak about the nefarious members of her coven, not the least of whom was Frank Engler, the founder, and master of ceremonies. Doubtful Trish's diatribe could be used in court, however. According to the latest gossip, Trish could be heard ranting and accusing little green men of abducting her and her pal. Allegedly, the entire coven had been carried away in a flying saucer which, according to Marge Henderson, the head nurse on the psychiatric ward of Bender Falls Memorial, resembled an oatmeal bowl resting upside down on a breakfast tray.

Erin Engler, in a smaller, more contained room down the hall from Trish, could be heard singing lullabies at all hours.

All things considered, not the least of which was the number of bullets flying within that canyon, Ronnie and Jade had been lucky.

Why then, this cloud hung between them, over them, Ronnie couldn't decide, and every attempt to discuss it had met with the usual subterfuge. The man had more ways to change a subject than a crooked politician.

Listlessly, Ronnie watched Tim dousing the chicken parts in his crimson sauce. Spencer, according to Jade, harbored an unnatural obsession with barbecue sauce, an excuse Jade had attempted to use to decline dinner. 'I don't need to feed my ulcer.' Calling him a 'wimp' had stiffened his jaw, but he'd persevered, claiming an overabundance of work in the warehouse. After all, the latest shipment from Europe was expected to arrive any day, '. . . I truly don't have time to go traipsing off to a barbecue.'

If she didn't know better, Ronnie might believe he was currently sulking over her threat to leave him to his tasks and visit the Spencers alone. He wasn't sulking any more than he'd been sulking a few weeks earlier. In every stopped moment, the shadows slid over his eyes, and preoccupation took hold.

"You two have a spat on the way out here?" Spencer asked as he sidled to the table, collecting his beer bottle. If only to bait his pal, Tim had directed his words to Ronnie, and she welcomed the intrusion.

"If we did, I missed my half of it," Ronnie commented and fleeted a glimpse at the jade green eyes and raised brow. Her attention lifted to Tim., "I think we still need to work on his communication skills," she continued lightly. "Most of our conversations tend to run along these silent veins."

"Whachu sulking about, Sax?" Tim asked with an offhanded smile.

"I don't sulk," he stated without effect.

"Wanna bet?" Ronnie asked and caught his more intent gaze, noting a flicker of his dimple. "I saw you sulking just yesterday when that New York couple walked out with that Tiffany lamp." She lifted her gaze to Tim, appreciating the avid interest and spark of amusement. "I've never seen a grown man look so devastated. You'd have sworn they stole his favorite teddy bear."

"I've seen it time and time again," Tim said with a mocked sigh.

"If either of you truly believes I intend to defend myself against these ludicrous allegations, you're wrong."

"Face it, pal, you're a sulker," Tim professed.

"The world's chock-full of comedians," Jade said and reached for his beer, resigning to the torment in good sport, but the bottle never reached his lips. It thumped on the table, still gripped in his fist. His focus remained fixed on the amber glass for three seconds before he trapped Ronnie in his gaze. A troubled line flashed across his brow; his smile wavered into a conflict of dismay. "Len's coming?"

"I invited him," Tim intervened and drew Jade's curiosity. With a twinkle in his eyes and a smirk on his mustache, Tim added, "Rae Ann Anderson should be coming shortly, too."

"Good God," Jade huffed softly, looking at him with a conflict of bewilderment and amusement. "You don't think . . .?"

With a fleeting thought of Rae Ann, the lovely brunette who spent time slinging hash over Meg's counter and attended night school toward a nursing career, Ronnie felt a slow smile slipping onto her lips.

Spencer rumbled a laugh, looking at Jade with an enhanced spark of amusement in his deep blue eyes. "Pal, you just confirmed my suspicions without half trying. You're better than a God Blessed barometer."

"I didn't . . . I'm not . . . shit," Jade stated and idled a laugh. "If I had a moral bone in my body, I'd race down the drive and warn Devinio."

"Like hell, you would," Spencer mused. "When you're not sulking, you're too happy to spare the man a similar fate."

"I don't *sulk*, for Chrissake," Jade stated.

The screen door slid open, and Rae Ann gladly commented, "You most certainly do. I've seen it a hundred times."

Jade's feigned expression of both surprise and dumbfound was priceless. The devil should have been on the silver screen, Ronnie considered before the memory of Valerie's like consensus stifled her laugh. *Time.* It would take time to heal those wounds, to put those wretched memories away, and forget the madness issued in that soft tormented voice.

As he had a million times in the past few weeks, Jade reacted to her sudden distress, slipping his arm about her shoulder, touching her chin to lift her eyes to his. Oh, the power of those warm green orbs, a healing power to comfort and soothe . . . as skillfully as he could scorch. That his kiss could halt every blasted thought in her head came only as an afterthought. "You're a devil," she uttered and watched the spark of humor in his lifting eyes.

"That's a wretched thing to say to your future husband, my own little witch."

'Witch,' she considered, again recalling those horrible seconds in that unholy pit and Valerie's mad pronouncement assailing her as the gun had turned on her. Even now, Ronnie couldn't decide why Valerie had held her accountable for that unnatural wind . . . any more than she could grasp how that bullet had stopped dead less than inches from her breast.

What she remembered was Jade finding the hole in the outer layer of her purse and reaching inside . . . and finding the bullet wedged in the letter that she'd lifted off the floor of Olden Time. Len had handed the letter back to Jade, and she hadn't seen it again since. Not for the first time, however, she wondered about its contents, wondered why Jade had appeared as shaken when accepting that letter from Len as when pulling it from her purse. Even now, she suffered a mild internal tremor thinking about that blasted letter.

Saved from further contemplation by a delightful four-year-old and proper young lady of six, who decided to share her Uncle Sax by plopping down at his opposite side, Ronnie dismissed her worries. Amused, she heard his low silky voice taunting the little girl to side with him.

"Your Uncle Sax doesn't sulk, does he, sweetheart?"

"That's silly," Deedee professed. "Everybody knows *all* men *sulk*. Right, Aunt Ronnie?"

"Absolutely," Ronnie agreed soberly, then lost rein on a laugh when Rae Ann burst into laughter.

Somewhat hesitantly, Len arrived amid the banter, and Ronnie laughed all the harder with a mere glimpse at Jade's bemused emerald eyes. When Len handed Jade a brown-wrapped package, they both sobered.

"This came for you today, Amico."

In a position to read the label and the return address, Ronnie's attention halted. She knew what Mark Jarvins could be sending in a 12" x 8" parcel. Meeting Jade's faintly amused eyes, she verified the revelation without a single word.

In the package atop the carefully wrapped plates, Mark had provided a brief note that Jade handed to Ronnie. She nearly laughed aloud at the words which could have been spoken off the twitching lips within her reach. 'I'm not very good at apologizing for my mistakes, but I owe you one. Take care of her. She's a special lady.'

"The man may be an ass, but I certainly can't fault his taste," Jade commented with a bemused shine, concentrating on the Haviland plate he'd unveiled as if he referred to the fine china.

"Brat," Ronnie stated.

"Good God, the abuse I need endure," he said dryly and ducked, laughing when she swung at him.

More leaden than the sales receipt which he'd held that wretched morning two weeks past, the envelope weighted in his hands. Paper, just plain paper, Jade attempted to convince himself even as he saw the spike of moonlight lancing through the circular hole. Just the feel of the paper sent tiny prickles through his fingertips and lent him flashing visions of that wretched canyon with its consortium of evil. Almost oily to the touch, the envelope merely appeared normal.

Shivering, listening to the soft even breaths of Veronica in the next room, Jade stood at the kitchen window, staring at the envelope that glowed nearly silver in the streak of white moonlight.

Was it any surprise that the damned thing had called to him under a full moon and dragged him from a sound sleep to bring it from his safe in the next room? He stood within a stream of moonlight, the full silver orb smiling down at him through the kitchen window that he hadn't the heart to cover despite the lunar strip sliding through his bedroom door. He needed to open the damned thing, needed to get it out of his system once and for all. He needed to read whatever the hell his father had written. Unless he read the words now, his curiosity would drive him half crazy . . . which could leave him entirely mad.

Uttering a curse and breath, Jade turned the slippery envelope and lifted the sterling letter opener from the countertop. Foolish, perhaps, but he'd deliberately chosen a tool laced with the purest metal, suffering his own madness to hope the silver could protect him from whatever evil might be unleashed when he broke the seal. Nervously, he slipped the dagger under the flap and ran it through smoothly, trembling more as he slipped the folded lanced page from the envelope. No doubt at all, Jean Pierre Jardonet had sent this letter. Jade's skin crawled as he unfolded the page; his hands trembled with the sheer force of whatever incantation had accompanied this script.

In the brilliant moonlight, Jade saw clearly, the black outline of a circle . . . within the circle, a five-pointed star . . . within the star, the gaping hole into which the bullet had scored a bullseye. Trembling more fiercely, his focus slid down the quivering page to the smooth handwritten words, hearing the low silky voice as if the man stood next to him inside the kitchen.

"If you are reading this, your white witch has survived, and thus, my own, you owe me. Congratulations on the upcoming nuptials. P.S. Take care of my grandson. J.P.J."

EPILOGUE

AUGUST

If ever a more diverse collection of people had gathered on the lawns of Spencer Manor, a sprawling two-story mansion nestled near the bluff of a hill overlooking Bentwood, no one in the living realm had ever seen it. From several of Capitol Hill's most reverent personages to Cy Trascar, who took off his coonskin cap only in church, the personalities and attire clashed and mingled as diplomatically as a meeting of the United Nations. From champagne and caviar to beer and hickory smoked ribs, the abundance of cuisine could be matched only by the appetites which demanded a troop of uniformed caterers to bustle between canopied tables and an immense pavilion.

As Jade had assured her time and again, the weather remained picture perfect, with blue skies and soft white clouds to drift over the sun and a gentle breeze to offset the smoldering August heat. Children of all sizes and ages raced between the tables and chairs, not the least of whom was little Ryan Bryson. Deedee, self-appointed nanny, chased after him, not pausing long enough to collect the satin ribbons that slipped from her auburn hair. Catching Jade's bemused eyes as he leaned and caught one of the wayward strands before it touched the canvas floor, Ronnie stifled a laugh.

Time had healed the wounds. The bustle of planning a wedding, the details, which saw them racing back and forth between Bentwood and Arlington, had kept them from dwelling too long or hard on that dreadful morning. Ronnie needed only to pan the sea of faces to realize the healing process had begun for the town of Bentwood as well.

Nearly half of its citizenry meandered on the sprawling lawn. Engaging more than a few of the town's leading citizens in planning the wedding had been a decision neither she nor Jade had made. Between Meg, Donna, Rae Ann, and Hazel Handler, with an abundance of assistance from Fiona Bryson, who'd nearly lived in the Bentwood House Inn over the past two months, whatever animosity the town had harbored for one Veronica Bryson and Jade Laquette had evaporated rather swiftly.

Not unnaturally, Jade sensed her thoughts and leaned, whispering against her ear, "Have I told you, you're as enchanting as a fairy princess lately?"

'My fairy princess,' he'd whispered and winked when he'd taken her hand from her father in the church. Looking into his mysterious eyes, she whispered, "Not in nearly ten minutes. I was beginning to doubt it."

He flashed a glimpse of his dimple, but a shadow fleeted over his eyes. His smile faded, and his brow troubled before the laughter ever reached the surface. In slow animation, he turned his gaze and eased back in his chair as he scanned the crowd spread before them.

If ever she'd seen him appear more intense, more haunted, she couldn't recall the occasion, and her tension rose in rapid degrees as his eyes locked and flashed emerald on something—*someone*—at the widest opening of the pavilion.

The instant she saw the man, she knew him, knew by his walk, by the cant of his head, the curve in his mustache, the color of his eyes . . . emerald. Dressed in black from his silk suit to his shoes, gold chains rather than a tie glinting at his chest, the fellow advanced with the smooth gate of a tiger. Two other men, attired in ostensible suits and ties, flanked him. Heads turned, conversations stifled, expressions wavered from curiosity to serious concern. Several security guards, who'd stood unobtrusively about the pavilion watching over a few prestigious attendees, perked up. One man slipped a hand under his jacket, instinctively alarmed, and Ronnie chilled as the emerald eyes landed on her.

God! The power of those eyes! Like a deer caught in a headlight beam, she suffered an instant of terror without a clear thought to the cause . . . and cold, as if the temperature under the canopy had dropped twenty degrees in ten seconds.

This was Jade Laquette's father. *Her father-in-law?*

Stopped, in stark, dark contrast to the white tresses and immense centerpiece between them, the man stood with a smile tilting his thin black mustache. His emerald eyes warmed; a spark of dark humor flared. Canting his wavy hair where the merest trace of gray touched his temples, he spoke in French, the flowing tone like Jade's, yet different, almost threatening. Transitioning to heavily accented English, he barely continued. "A plea-shore to make la acquaintanz ov soosh a beautiful yooung woomon—"

No invitation had been sent. In French, Jade interrupted while reaching, clasping Veronica's chilled fingers under the table. "*Je ne me souviens pas t'avoir envoyé une invitation—*"

The emerald eyes flashed fire, silencing him without uttering a word.

Only on the surface, Jardonet maintained his smile, leaning, offering his palm across the table, his eyes conveying his intensity and issuing the command even as he spoke, "*Félicitations, mon fils.*"

His hand locked in the chilled vice, Jade stiffened with the shock of the grip, too late, remembering how that hand could clasp him and hold him enthralled. *Not a child!* He wasn't a child! And Jardonet had no more arrived for a token gesture of familial ties than he was capable of offering a blessing. In a heartbeat pause which could have been an eternity, Jade realized the ulterior motive, understood the mentalism probing and testing him by the simple physical contact. The strangeness washed over him, coursing through his system like quicksilver . . .

His mother and Jardonet. In his mind's eye, Jade saw them together, walking the streets of Paris hand-in-hand . . . tumbling together in joint throes of passion . . . his mother taking flight . . . escaping to America to avoid the scandal . . . his mother's funeral. Jardonet had stood in the crowd . . .

Through the emerald eyes, a reflection of his own, Jade saw himself. A small stone-faced boy cloaked in a shroud of grief staring endlessly at the mound of flowers draping the golden casket. In flashing, fleeting instants, he saw strangers' faces twisted in agony, writhing against pain. Faces he surely knew . . . faces belonging to men who'd died in questionable circumstances within a year after his mother's death. And on the heels of revelation, yet another epiphany assailed his mind in a lightning flash. His mother hadn't relied exclusively on things he'd told her. She'd engaged other more natural means to spy on some of the most prominent families in the Capital.

Had she been killed over something she'd overheard while lying in a senator's bed . . .?

Whether his talents had wrenched the truth from Jardonet or the man had parted willingly with his secrets, Jade had no idea. By the time their palms parted, Jade had reached yet another weird and wary revelation. His father had just confirmed his belief that his son had inherited his innate talents, and those talents were restored.

"I should nev'air hov let you shange your name again," Jardonet said as his gaze slid to Veronica. "Ahh, but whoo knows whot le fushure holds, eh, mon fils?"

"Not that, I assure you," Jade said with an abstracted thought, but he couldn't help a sudden revelation. He and his father wouldn't remain strangers or adversaries. Opposing forces and separate identities, Jade had no doubts, but if not for that spell cast upon that envelope . . .?

Looking at Veronica, seeing her warm, curious gaze turning from Jardonet to him, Jade knew how much he owed this haunting figure. "Veronica, I'd like you to meet Jean Pierre Jardonet . . . my uhm . . ."

She smiled faintly and tilted her gaze to Jardonet, extending her white-laced-covered arm. Boldly, her slender fingers clasped the ring-laden hand like a white witch of old touching the sorcerer himself. "My pleasure, Monsieur Jardonet . . . Please, will you join us?"

She knew what they both owed this man, Jade realized, recalling the blackness into which his talents had failed to trespass. That wretched pit had been

Jardonet's territory. And if a master of dark forces truly existed, sparing Veronica, a white witch, couldn't have won Jardonet any favor in his realm. Come a day, that debt would come due.

Catching a fleeting glimpse of the fire sparking within the emerald eyes, Jade chilled. Vaguely, he heard the silky, deep voice accepting the invitation in a natural cadence.

To dwell too deeply in the darkness couldn't fare well on either his future or his sanity. If only for his own sake, Jade refused to acknowledge the green glitter and bemused smirk. Instead, he tilted his gaze to Veronica, meeting her warm blue eyes. From those blue-diamond orbs, the promise of light and laughter shined as brilliantly as the sun streams spilling through the tresses behind them. Blue diamonds, rare and wondrous, and his.

Leaning, touching her cheek to draw her lips to his, he blocked the tinkle of silverware striking crystal and drew a calming breath as he whispered, "White witch."

"Green-eyed devil . . . 's son," she uttered in return.

The woman did have her talents.

ACKNOWLEDGMENTS

My thanks to a few of my favorite critics, Suellen Brady, Mary Trunick, Anne Graff, Andrew Grueber, and William Grueber for keeping me honest to my craft, adding insight to my characters, and letting me know when I'm getting it right (or wrong!) Thank you!

JKGRUEBER.COM

www.ingramcontent.com/pod-product-compliance
Lightning Source LLC
Chambersburg PA
CBHW030350310726
48979CB00001B/247

* 9 7 8 1 9 6 5 7 9 6 0 5 4 *